Marcia Gruver

TEXAS FORTUNES

TRILOGY

BARBOUR
PUBLISHING

ISBN 978-1-61626-217-4

All scripture quotations are taken from the King James Version of the Bible.

This book is a work of fiction. Names, characters, places, and incidents are either products of the author's imagination or used fictitiously as explained in the athor's note. Any similarity to actual people, organizations, and/or events is purely coincidental.

For more information about Marcia Gruver, please access the author's Web site at the following Internet address: http://www.marciagruver.com

Published by Barbour Publishing, Inc., P.O. Box 719, Uhrichsville, OH 44683, www.barbourbooks.com

Our mission is to publish and distribute inspirational products offering exceptional value and biblical encouragement to the masses.

Member of the Evangelical Christian Publishers Association

Printed in the United States of America.

Texas Fortunes *Book No. 1*

DIAMOND DUO

Marcia Gruver

Dedication

To Lee, my gift from God.
You taught me the impossible is "no step for a stepper."

To Diana Dinky-Do, my mother and biggest fan.

To my children, grandchildren, and Rae Rea.
See, you really can do all things through Christ.

Acknowledgments

My thanks to Janice Thompson—without you there'd be no book. To ACFW Crit3—you're brilliant. You make me look good. To Seared Hearts—my beloved cheering section. To Fred McKenzie, historian and owner of Bayou Books in Jefferson, Texas, for your tireless love of anything Jefferson. To Karl Frederickson, manager of Excelsior House Hotel, for going out of your way to help. And to Era E. Johnson of the Marion Central Appraisal District in Jefferson, Texas, for your kind assistance.

CHAPTER 1

Jefferson, Texas
Friday, January 19, 1877

With the tip of a satin shoe, the graceful turn of an ankle, the woman poured herself like cream from the northbound train out of Marshall and let the tomcats lap her up. In the beginning, an upraised parasol blocked her visage, but no lingering look at her features could erase the impression already established by her pleasing carriage, lavish blue gown, and slender fingers covered in diamonds.

Bertha Biddie waited with stilted breath for the moment when the umbrella might tip and give up its secret. All about her, most of Jefferson had come to a halt, as if the whole town waited with her.

Without warning, the woman lowered and closed the sunshade.

Enchanted, Bertha followed the graceful lines of her form to her striking and memorable face. At first sight of her, Bertha thought she was the devil's daughter. She bore no obvious mark of evil. Just smoldering eyes and a knowing glance that said life held mysteries young Bertha had yet to glimpse.

Her hair sparkled like sun rays dancing on Big Cypress Creek. Her lashes were as black as the bottom of a hole, and her lids seemed smudged with coal. Delicate features perched below a dark halo of hair, and a pink flush lit her fair cheeks. Her expression teemed with mischief, and her full ruby lips curled up at the corners as if recalling a bawdy yarn. She turned slightly, evidently aware of the gathering horde for the first time. With a tilt of her chin and barely perceptible sway, she cast a wide net over the men in the crowd and dragged them to shore.

Bertha watched them respond to her and realized Mama had been less than forthcoming about the real and true nature of things. Forgetting themselves and the women at their sides, they gaped with open mouths, some in spite of jealous claws that gripped their arms. Even the ladies stared, the looks on their faces ranging from admiration to envy.

The reaction of the men only slightly altered when the lady's escort stepped out of the Texas & Pacific passenger car behind her. Though his clothes were just as spiffy and he carried himself well, the man who accompanied that gilded bird lacked her allure, bore none of her charm. Yet despite her confident display of tail feathers, the bluebird at his side clearly deferred to him as though he'd found a way to clip her wings.

With great care, the porter handed down the couple's baggage, the matched set a rare sight in those parts, then held out his hand. Her companion tipped the man, gathered the bags, and walked away from the platform without offering a single word in the bluebird's direction. She cast a quick glance after him but stood her ground, her demeanor unruffled in the face of his rebuke.

As was the custom, the Commercial Hotel, Haywood House, and Brooks House, three reputable hotels in town, each had transport standing by to haul incoming passengers from the station. Dr. J. H. Turner, landlord of Brooks House, waited on hand in the conveyance he called an omnibus.

The woman's friend secured passage with Dr. Turner and helped him load their belongings and then turned and crooked a finger in her direction. She pretended not to notice.

"Bessie!" he barked. "For pity's sake."

She lifted her head, reopened the parasol, and strolled his way without saying a word—giving in but taking all the time she pleased to do so. He handed her up into the carriage, climbed in beside her, and settled back to rest a possessive arm around her shoulders.

Dr. Turner eased onto Alley Street and trundled away from the station, breaking the spell cast over the denizens of Jefferson. In slow motion they awoke from their stupor and returned to their lives.

Bertha released the breath she'd held and gripped her best friend's arm. "What was she, Magda? I've never seen anything like her."

When Magda shook her head, her curls danced the fandango. "Me neither. And we never will again. Not around here, anyway."

Bertha leaned past Magda trying to catch another glimpse. "She's no earthbound creature, that's for sure. But devil or angel? I couldn't tell."

Magda laughed. "She's human, all right, just not ordinary folk." She pressed her finger to her lips. "Could be one of those actresses from a New York burletta."

Bertha gasped. "From the Broadway stage? You really think so?"

"She's certainly stylish enough."

Bertha squinted down Alley Street at the back of the tall carriage. "That man called her Bessie. She doesn't look like a Bessie to me."

"Further proof that beneath all her fluff, she's a vessel of clay like the rest of us."

"How so?"

"Who ever heard of an angel named Bessie?"

Grinning, Bertha leaned and tweaked Magda's nose. "Oh, go on with you."

Of all the souls wandering the earth—in Jefferson, Texas, at least—Bertha Maye Biddie's heart had knit with Magdalena Hayes's from the start. They were a year apart, Magda being the older, but age wasn't the only difference between them. Magda easily reached the top shelves in the kitchen, where Bertha required a stool. And while big-boned Magda took up one and a half spaces on a church pew, Bertha barely filled the remaining half. Magda's russet mop coiled as tightly as tumbleweed. Bertha's black hair fell to her waist in silken waves and gave her fits trying to keep it pinned up. Nothing fazed self-possessed Magda. Bertha greeted life with her heart.

Magda nudged Bertha with her elbow. "Earthbound or not, I can tell you one thing about her. . . ."

"What's that?"

The look in Magda's big brown eyes said whatever the one thing was, it was bound to be naughty. She leaned in to whisper. "She knows a thing or two about the fellas."

Bertha raised her brows. "You can tell that just by looking at her, can you?"

"Not looking at her, smart britches. I can tell by the way she looks at them." She fussed with her curls, her eyes pious slants. "No decent woman goes eye to eye with strange men in the street, and you know it."

"I guess some decent woman told you that?"

"Bertha Maye Biddie! Don't get fresh with me."

Bertha tucked in her chin and busied herself straightening her gloves. "Maybe she's fed up with their scandalous fawning. Ever think of that?"

"Any hound will track his supper."

The words made Bertha mad enough to spit, but she didn't know why. "A pie set out on a windowsill may be a fine display of good cooking, but not necessarily an invitation."

Magda narrowed her eyes. "What on earth are you talking about?" Before Bertha could answer, she stiffened and settled back for a pout. "Why are you siding up with that woman anyway? You don't even know her."

The truth was, Bertha's head still reeled from the first sight of Bessie. The way men reacted to her flooded Bertha's young heart with hope and provided an opportunity, if the beautiful stranger would cooperate, to fix a private matter that sorely needed fixing.

Bertha knew a few things by instinct, like how to toss her long hair or tilt her chin just so. Enough to mop the grin off Thaddeus Bloom's handsome face and light a fire in those dark eyes. But she was done with turning to mush in his presence and watching him revel in it. If Bertha could learn a few of the bluebird's tricks, she'd have that rascal wagging his tail. Then the shoe would be laced to the proper foot, and Thad could wear it up her front stoop when he came to ask for her hand.

One thing was certain. Whatever Bessie knew, Bertha needed to know it.

She tugged on Magda's arm. "Come on."

"Come on where?"

Already a wagon-length ahead, Bertha called back over her shoulder. "To the hotel. We're going to find her."

"What? Why?"

"Save your questions for later. Now hurry!"

Bertha dashed to the steps at the end of the boardwalk and scurried into the lane.

"You planning to run clear to Vale Street?" Magda huffed, rushing to catch up. "Slow down. It ain't ladylike."

"Oh, pooh. Neither am I. Look, there's Mose. He'll take us."

Just ahead, Moses Pharr's rig, piled high with knobby cypress, turned onto Alley Street headed the opposite way. The rickety wagon, pulled by one broken-down horse, bore such a burden of wood it looked set to pop like a bloated tick. When Bertha whistled, the boy's drowsy head jerked up. He turned around and saw her, and a grin lit his freckled face.

"Bertha!" Magda hustled up beside her. "If your pa gets word of you whistling in town, he'll take a strap to your legs."

"Papa doesn't own a strap. Come on, Mose is waiting."

She ran up even with the wagon and saw that the mountain of wood had blocked her view of Mose's sister sitting beside him on the seat. They both grinned down at her, Rhodie's long red hair the only visible difference between the two.

"Hey, Rhodie."

"Hey, Bert. Where you going?"

"To Brooks House. I was hoping to hitch a ride."

Mose leaned over, still grinning. "We always got room for you, Bertha. Hop on."

Magda closed the distance between them and came to stand beside Bertha, breathing hard. When Bertha pulled herself onto the seat beside Rhodie, Magda started to follow. Mose raised his hand to stop her.

"Hold up there." He looked over at Bertha. "Her, too?"

Bertha nodded.

Mose cut his eyes back at the wood and then shrugged. "Guess one more can't hurt. But she'll have to sit atop that stump. Ain't no more room on the seat."

Magda adjusted her shawl around her shoulders and sniffed. "I refuse to straddle a cypress stump all the way to Vale."

"Suit yourself," Bertha said. "But it's a long walk. Let's go, Mose."

Mose lifted the reins and clucked at the horse. Magda grabbed the wooden handgrip and pulled herself onto the wagon just as it started to move. Arranging her skirts about her, she perched on the tall stump like Miss Muffet. "Well, what are you waiting for?" she asked. "Let's go."

Laughing, they rolled through Jefferson listing and creaking, ignoring the stares and whispers. When the rig pulled up across from Brooks House, even the spectacle they made couldn't compete with Bessie and her traveling companion.

The couple stood on the street beside their luggage, the carriage nowhere in sight. They seemed at the end of a heated discussion, given his mottled face and her missing smile.

When Bertha noticed the same sick-cow expression on the faces of the gathered men and the same threatened look on the women's, she became more determined than ever to learn Bessie's secret.

The man with Bessie growled one more angry word then hefted their bags and set off up the path. Not until Bessie followed him and disappeared through the shadowy door did the town resume its pace.

Mose gulped and found his voice. "She looked as soft as a goose-hair pillow. Who is she?"

Bertha scooted to the edge of her seat and climbed down. She dusted her hands and smoothed her skirt. "I don't know, but I intend to find out."

"Roll up your tongue, Moses Pharr," Magda said from the back, "and get me off this stump."

Mose hopped to the ground and hurried around to help Magda.

Rhodie, twirling her copper braid, grinned down at Bertha. "What are you going to do, Bert?"

Magda answered for her. "She's going to get us into trouble, that's what."

Bertha took her by the hand. "Stop flapping your jaws and come on."

They waved good-bye to Mose and Rhodie then hurried across the street, dodging horses, wagons, and men—though their town wasn't nearly as crowded as it had once been.

Jefferson, Queen City of the Cypress, lost its former glory in 1873, when the United States Corps of Engineers blew the natural dam to kingdom come, rerouting the water from Big Cypress Bayou down the Red River to Shreveport. Once a thriving port alive with steamboat traffic, when the water level fell, activity in Jefferson dwindled. To that very day, in fits of Irish temper, Bertha's papa cursed the politicians who were responsible.

But through it all, Jefferson had lost none of its charm. Brooks House was a prime example of the best the town had to offer, so it seemed only right that someone like Bessie might wind up staying there.

Bertha and Magda positioned themselves outside the hotel and hunkered down to wait—the former on a mission, the latter under duress. It didn't take long for the girls to learn a good bit about the captivating woman and her cohort. Talk swirled out the door of the hotel soon after the couple sashayed to the front desk to register under the name of A. Monroe and wife, out of Cincinnati, Ohio.

The gentleman, if he could be counted as such, addressed the woman as Annie or Bessie, when he didn't call her something worse. The two quarreled openly, scratching and spitting like cats, and didn't care who might be listening. By the time the story drifted outside, the locals had dubbed her Diamond Bessie due to her jewel-encrusted hands, and it seemed the name would stick.

Bertha shaded her eyes with her hands and pressed her face close to the window. "I don't see her anymore, Magda. I guess they took a room."

"Of course they took a room. Why else would they come to a hotel?"

Bertha ignored her sarcasm and continued to search the lobby for Bessie. Still catching no sight of her, she turned around. "Isn't she the most glorious thing? And even prettier close up."

"That she is."

"Did you see the way men look at her? I never saw that many roosters on the prowl at one time."

"And all for squat," Magda said. "That chicken's been plucked. The little banty she strutted into town with has already staked a claim." She grinned. "He wasn't all that hard on the eyes himself."

Bertha frowned. "That strutting peacock? Besides his flashy clothes, she was the only thing special about him. Don't see how he managed to snare a woman like that. He must be rich."

Magda arched one tapered brow. "Did you see the rings on her fingers?"

"I reckon so. I'm not blind."

Magda stretched her back and heaved a sigh. "I guess that's it, then. Let's go."

Bertha grabbed her arm. "Wait. Where are you going?"

"Home. This show's over. They've settled upstairs by now."

Lacing her fingers under her chin, Bertha planted herself in Magda's path. "Won't you wait with me just a mite longer?"

"She's not coming out here, Bertha. Besides, you've seen enough for today."

"I don't want to see her. I need to talk to her."

Magda drew herself back and stared. "Are you teched? We can't just walk up and talk to someone like her. Why would she fool with the likes of us?"

"I don't know. I'll think of a way. I've got to." She bit her bottom lip—three words too late.

Looking wary now, Magda crossed her arms. "Got to? Why?"

"Just do." Bertha met her look head-on. She wouldn't be bullied out of it. Not even by Magda.

Resting chubby fists on rounded hips, Magda sized her up. "All right, what does this have to do with Thad?"

No one knew her like Magda. Still, the chance she might stumble onto Bertha's motives was as likely as hatching a three-headed guinea hen. Struggling to hold her jaw off the ground, she lifted one shoulder. "Who said it did?"

Magda had the gall to laugh. "Because, dearie"—she leaned to tap Bertha's forehead—"everything inside there lately has something to do with Thad."

"Humph! Think what you like. I am going to talk to her."

Magda glared. "Go ahead, then. I can see there's no changing your mind. But I don't fancy being humiliated by another of your rattlebrained schemes, thank you."

Bertha caught hold of her skirt. "Don't you dare go. I can't do this on my own."

"Let go of me. I said I'm going home."

"Please, Magdalena! I need you."

Magda pulled her skirt free and took another backward step. "No, ma'am. You just count me out this time."

She turned to go, and Bertha lunged, catching her in front of the hotel door. They grappled, tugging sleeves and pulling hair, both red-faced and close to tears. Just when Bertha got set to squeal like a pestered pig, from what seemed only a handbreadth away, a woman cleared her throat. Bertha froze, hands still locked in Magda's hair, and turned to find the bluebird beaming from the threshold—though *canary* seemed more fitting now that she'd traded her blue frock for a pale yellow dress.

"What fun!" Bessie cried, clasping her hands. "I feared this town might be as dull as dirt, but it seems I was mistaken."

CHAPTER 2

There wasn't much Thaddeus Bloom liked better than fishing, and he looked for any excuse to wet a hook. An uncommon passion for the sport took young Thad at an early age and plagued him till now. It started when he was barely old enough to sink a line in the muddy waters of Baton Rouge, and he'd trolled the lakes and bayous ever since. So it was no surprise that shortly after Papa moved the family to Jefferson, Thad discovered Big Cypress Bayou.

He decided early on that a man could solve most of the world's problems while dangling a cork from a cane pole. As it happened, he came to be standing at bayou's edge while in search of just such a remedy and a rest for his troubled soul.

As if life weren't burdened with complication and abundant challenge for a man his age, Thad found his forward motion of late impeded by a most fetching obstacle—in the person of Bertha Maye Biddie. In the whole of his nineteen years, he'd never beheld so lovely a girl. Many a young lady seemed determined to tempt him from his goals, but no matter how much they swished and swayed or how fast they batted their eyes, Thad remained focused. Now one comely Irish elf had turned his head with just the tilt of her dainty chin.

It would be a stretch to call Thad's college plans his dream.

DIAMOND DUO

As long as he could remember, his papa had spoken of places like Harvard, Boston College, and Yale in reverent tones. From the moment Papa heard they opened Texas Agricultural and Mechanical College in Brazos County, his ambition became obsession, and Thad's fate was sealed. Oblivious to the fact that it was his younger son, Cy, who loved the books, Papa worked tirelessly, saving toward the day when Thad would leave for the military college, vowing to let nothing stand in his way.

Nothing had until Bertha Biddie sashayed onto the scene, so small she could sit on the edge of a rug and her feet would still dangle, with dimples so deep he could swim in them and a smile so bright she didn't need candles. With every move, she had wriggled deeper into Thad's head and etched out a spot in his heart.

But he couldn't drag a bride along to military school, and he wouldn't ask a girl like Bertha to wait. Besides, he knew her father would never agree to such a lengthy engagement. Consequently, Thad's need to lose himself in fishing had increased tenfold of late.

He heard a splash and turned to look. Water rings played out in wide bands from the base of a big bald cypress. He searched the area just shy of the bank for clues. Too big for a bass. Probably not a gator. Could be a paddlefish, and if so, he wasn't interested. From the sound of the splash, it was a big one. Folks had reported seeing paddlefish as long as a man, weighing close to seventy pounds. Thad didn't much care for spear fishing and wasn't carrying a hook big enough to snag him.

The ripples stilled and with it Thad's interest. He shifted his attention to the gentle lapping of water against the tree. Submerged cypress trunks always reminded him of an overgrown foot, not unlike a giant elephant's or dinosaur's. He almost expected to follow the trunk up and find a brontosaurus lurking above. It wouldn't surprise him one whit to find such a curiosity in these waters. More than once he'd hooked and pulled to shore things he'd never laid eyes on before. Not just fish. There were creatures in those murky depths that had no name and defied description.

Thad picked up the bucket of worms, hoisted the rest of the

gear to his shoulder, and edged along the grassy bank, pushing aside streams of Spanish moss and a potbellied spider on a dew-beaded web. He lined up even with a dilapidated boat shack, just down shore from where he'd spotted the water rings. He leaned his cane pole against a tree then propped the net and his daddy's pole, which he'd taken without permission, against the side of the old building and sat down to wait.

The crunch of a broken twig behind him gave Thad a start, more so than it would have if his mind weren't crawling with monsters and bugaboos. He turned and gave a low whistle as he watched Charles Gouldy step into the clearing with a fishing pole in his hand. Charles picked his way over the ruts and cypress knees and joined Thad on the bank.

"Hey, Charlie. You came."

"Said I would."

"That don't always hold salt."

Charles sidled up beside him and baited his hook. Thad set to work threading a worm on his, hurrying despite himself. For some reason, they had an unspoken challenge to see who would be first to get a line in the water. Charlie bested him this time and started to whistle as soon as his cork settled onto the muddy surface. In no time his whistling became a quiet song.

" 'Had a fine reputation until he sold it. Liked corn liquor, but he couldn't hold it.' "

Thad laughed, his eyes still trained on his cork. "What's that you're singing?"

" 'Old Dan Tucker.' Don't tell me you never heard it?"

Thad looked at him. "Those ain't the words to 'Old Dan Tucker.' "

"Are, too."

"I'm telling you they ain't."

Charlie glanced up. "My papaw sings it thata way."

"He made it up, then."

Charlie shrugged and nodded. "Probably did."

"Well, try not to sing anymore, how 'bout it. You're here to catch fish, not torture them. And I know I can do without it."

"You wouldn't know a good singer if he sat on you."

"I know I'd rather you sat on me than sing."

Charlie grinned and gave him a light shove.

A quick flash of movement across the water caught Thad's attention. He studied the tree-lined bank until he caught another glimpse between the cypress trunks, just enough to identify two windblown shocks of red hair. The Taylor boys, sitting tall in their old beat-up skiff, skimmed along effortlessly, pulled by the flow, using only the occasional furtive dip of a paddle to steer.

When the faded blue boat pulled past a clearing, Thad nudged Charlie. "Looky there."

"Where?"

"That dinghy slipping up on us."

Charlie tensed. "Who is it?"

"T-Bone Taylor and that rogue little brother of his."

Beau and T-Bone, each barely out of knee britches, lived upstream a short row from town. They were known around Jefferson as the biggest thieves this side of the Red River. T-Bone had been asked, and not so politely, to forgo any further notions of an education at Samuel Ward's Paradise Academy due to unruly and downright naughty behavior. Beau, two years his junior, seemed destined to follow in his brother's footsteps.

Charlie craned his neck to see better. "What're they up to this far downriver?"

"No good, I'd wager. Look how much pain they're taking to be quiet."

Charlie leaned forward, ready to shout, but Thad stayed him with a hand on his arm. "Wait, let's watch what they do."

Thad pulled his line to shore, and Charlie followed suit. They ducked for cover under a yaupon bush and spied between its branches. The Taylor boys skimmed past and pulled stealthily beneath the shack, Beau lifting one hand overhead to drag the skiff well under. Thad watched them scurry around in the boat, both scrawny bodies bent under the suspended floor.

"What them rascals doing?"

"Hush, Charlie! Wait and see."

Before long, a skinny, freckled arm appeared from under the pilings to where the net was propped. Grimy fingers lifted it and disappeared. The arm was soon followed by a hand reaching for the bait.

When a smaller, more freckled version snaked out to grab Papa's pole, Thad sprang to life. "Hey, hold up there! That's right, Beau Taylor, I'm talking to you. Don't think I don't see you two scoundrels."

Thad hurried to the shack and ducked to look under, just in time to see Beau lower his hand, Papa's cane pole and all, beneath the water. "Nice try, Beau. Pull up my daddy's fishing pole and place it where you found it." He moved closer, trying to look fierce. "T-Bone, that there's my net and bait. Put them back or suffer the consequences."

"Didn't see you there," T-Bone mumbled. "Just reckoned somebody left it."

"If they had, it wouldn't make it yours, now would it? Save your excuses. Ain't no right reason to do a wrong thing."

Beau raised his ill-gotten bounty from under the water and eased it back onto the bank. Reluctantly, his older brother followed suit, propping the net against the piling then tossing the bait on the bank.

Charlie stormed up behind Thad, puffed like an adder, and chimed in: "What's the matter? You boys ain't familiar with the eighth commandment?" He clenched his fists and took one more menacing step. "What are we waiting for, Thad? Let's drag 'em out and teach 'em 'thou shalt not steal.' "

Thad grabbed Charlie's arm. "Didn't you just hear what I said about doing a wrong thing? They put the stuff back. It's over now." He turned to the boys. "You two get on home. You keep looking for trouble, it's bound to find you."

The brothers danced past each other, holding on to keep from falling in the drink. They found their seats and paddles then backpedaled from under the shack. When they cleared it, they turned the nose of the boat in the same direction they'd been traveling and left without another word.

Charlie shot an arm in their direction. "You see that, Thad? You just wasted your breath. Those two ain't headed for home. Their minds are well set on some thieving raid." He rested his hands on his hips and shook his head. "We should've beat them and sent them running home to Mama. Now they'll get their hides filled with buckshot."

Thad watched the boys catch the current, maneuver around a curve, and disappear. "I hope not, Charlie." He sighed. "I truly hope not."

"Why? Lord knows them two deserve it."

Thad gave him a long look. "Now you're an authority on what the Lord knows?"

Charlie glared and then feigned an elaborate bow. "I beg your pardon, sir. I get ahead of myself sometimes." He flashed a devilish grin. "We all know Saint Thaddeus is the authority on God. Too bad the Sisters of Charity sold Saint Mary's to them Jew boys and let 'em turn it into a synagogue. You could've joined the convent." He pulled his shirt up and fashioned a makeshift habit then pranced in a pious circle. "Sister Thad. Has a nice ring to it, don't it?" He stopped pacing and fell to the ground, howling and slapping his knee. "*Lord knows* you'd make a fine nun."

Thad felt rage boil up inside. "I'll excuse your ignorance concerning the good brothers of Sinai Hebrew and chalk up your lack of decorum to the one who raised you."

The last comment lifted Charlie's hackles, as Thad expected it might.

Charlie pushed off the ground. "What do you mean by that, Bloom?"

"Come on, Charlie, you know your sister's morals are questionable at best and her profession the talk of the town."

Charlie balled his fist. "Take it back! Isabella don't do those things no more. Not since Mama died. And who are you to talk?

Some folks think skinning every sucker dumb enough to sit across a hand of poker from you ain't exactly the Lord's work."

Thad shrugged and slung the two poles over one shoulder, picked up the bucket of bait, and turned to go.

"Where are you going?"

"It's not a good day for fishing, after all. I've got too much on my mind to wrangle with all this besides."

Thad started up the incline, careful to dodge the jutting roots on his way to the top. He heard rustling behind him and then running, stumbling feet.

"I take back what I said about you and the rabbis," Charlie panted, falling into step behind him. "I didn't mean no harm."

Thad stopped and turned to face him. "I had no right to bring up your sister's past. It ain't no concern of mine. And you're right. My life ain't been perfect." He held out his hand. "Truce?"

Charlie grinned and clasped his outstretched palm. "Truce. And here. You left your net."

Thad put his hand on the net, but Charlie held it. "Can I ask you a question?"

"Shoot."

"Why *did* you quit playing cards just when you got so good at it?"

Thad thought a minute then decided to tell the truth. "You ever have a coonhound latch onto the back of your shirt and go to tugging?"

Charlie chuckled. "A time or two, I reckon."

He nodded. "That's how gambling started to feel. Figured I'd better quit before it brought me down." He grinned. "Besides that, Mama found out. Needless to say, she wasn't very happy about it."

On the water behind Charlie's head, the blue dinghy shot from behind a stand of trees with Beau and T-Bone leaning into their paddles. Loud laughter and excited chatter sounded up the hill to where Thad and Charlie stood. Charlie whirled and watched with Thad as the boys skimmed past. Twin streams of smoke trailed behind them from the rolled-up tobacco that dangled from each boy's mouth. A large, misshapen bundle rested between them in the bottom of the boat, covered in stolen hides.

"There they go," Thad said. "Looks like some poor fool lost his tobacco tin."

Charlie chuckled. "Lord knows what they have stashed beneath those pilfered skins."

"And therein lies their fate," muttered Thad, flashing Charlie a somber smile. "The Lord knows."

CHAPTER 3

Sarah dipped two dark fingers in the murky bayou and sighed. Cold. Like the wind that whipped the bare tops of the sweet gum trees on the far bank before it skipped across the water and found its way up her dress. One thing for sure, it was too miserable cold to kneel in the mud pounding the stink out of Henry's britches. But no matter. Hands be numb, bones be chilled, her man needed clean drawers, and she'd see he got them.

Not that he appreciated it any. She could freeze stock-still and he'd just shrug and hang his hat on her, bothered not a whit until suppertime. He'd moan then but wouldn't lift a finger to change it. Henry King would sit down and starve plumb to death while waiting for her to thaw. Sarah was of the opinion that her husband set far too much stock in his family name.

She held the heavy denim overalls up to the sun to inspect her progress. The grass stains were still there. She could beat until the stones in her hands wore smooth, but the dirt ground into those old britches was there to stay. She dare not scrub the worn-out legs for too long. Already the only thing standing between Henry's knees and the world were a few crisscrossed patches of white thread. And the world wasn't ready for Henry's knees.

She lifted the soggy mess of cloth, heavily weighted by water, into her pail with a grunt. She'd draw a bucket of water to pour over them and let them sit till later. A good soaking could do them no harm.

"Woman! Where you be?"

Sarah gritted her teeth, wondering when in life's unfolding she'd find herself in a place where men didn't holler and order her about. She turned, shading her eyes from the sun. A shadowy outline of Henry stood atop the grassy knoll above the creek, his hands on his hips. Even with irritation crowding her throat, she couldn't help but mark the fact that her man cut a fine figure in silhouette.

She stood up and assumed his same stance. "What you doing bellowing at me like that? You ain't my daddy. 'Sides that, you know where I am. I'm down here washing your drawers, just like I washed his."

"Well, leave all that. I need you to ride into town with me."

Sarah bent and hoisted the heavy pail onto her hip then took her time walking up the hill. "What you be needing from town? We hauled in staples and dry goods on Wednesday, and this ain't but Friday. We still got potatoes and onions in the larder, and I made plenty of soap."

She stopped in front of him and tilted her head to study his face. He shifted his eyes at first but then gave her a bug-eyed stare. "Why you got to understand everything? Maybe I'd like the pleasure of your company. That's all you need to know." He reached around to swat her hard on the behind and then took the pail, laughing and dodging when she tried to hit him back.

"Go on, now. Quit acting up. And no more questions. Jus' get yourself inside and dress for town." He flashed a toothy grin with his audacious white teeth. "And hurry up, you hear? Don't hole up in that house and leave me here till my hair turns gray."

"I need water poured over them raggedy britches, Henry King. Make sure you see to that." She continued up the rise, tossing the last word over her shoulder like a pinch of salt. At the top she paused and turned her head. Not enough to see his face, but she knew she had his attention. "And I'll be ready when I'm ready. You look for me then."

Deep laughter rumbled behind her, causing warmth to spread through her core. Even being the exasperating man that he was, her husband could stoke a fire in her heart with very little effort.

The natural slope to the creek leveled out to a wide expanse of tilled ground running from where she stood to the edge of the backyard. To her left at the end of a long furrow, Henry's plow sat right where he'd left it, the blade still burrowed deep in East Texas soil. Just ahead, a line of young hickory trees marked the boundary of their yard.

A big oak with knobby, exposed roots shaded the house against the summer heat and provided a fine napping spot for old Dickens, Henry's hound. On a warmer day she'd find the dog sprawled on the cool, hard-packed dirt beneath the tree, growling and twitching in his sleep. But on such a blustery morning, he was more likely in the barn curled up in a nest of hay.

As she neared the porch, the hens left their pecking and pranced away, squabbling and complaining among themselves. They were meant to be inside the weather-beaten old coop, but Henry had given up on keeping them in, so they wandered the grounds at will.

On the top step, Sarah paused and glanced at the corner yard, wrinkling her nose at the odor wafting from the pigsty behind the picket fence. She and Henry had argued about bringing hogs on the place. She never wanted the smelly beasts, though she had to admit the occasional rack of bacon alongside her buttermilk biscuits was a mighty tasty addition to breakfast.

Once inside, Sarah didn't take long to get ready. She washed off the stench of bayou mud in the basin of water atop the dressing table handed down by her mama. Then she lifted her blue gingham day dress from a hook on the wall and pulled it over her head. Back at the dressing table, she smoothed her black hair into a tight braid, grateful again that she'd inherited Papa's manageable curls instead of Mama's wiry cap.

Henry waited outside near the rig. He glanced up and then

turned away smiling when she stepped out the door, but not before Sarah saw him trying to hide his grin. She joined him without a word and let him help her onto the seat. Whistling all the while, he gave Dandy's harness one more check before climbing aboard the wagon.

No doubt under heaven, her man was up to something, but she couldn't imagine what it might be. There was no special significance about the nineteenth day of January. No birthday or anniversary. No particular reason to mark a Friday morning, because one day on a farm was like the next, except for the Sabbath.

She wouldn't ask and ruin his pleasure. Whatever frog had Henry hopping, she'd know it soon enough. Because sure as sure was, it would croak when they reached town.

"So tell me, girls. . .is this a private game, or can anybody play?"

Bertha's surprise at Bessie's bawdy laughter rivaled the shock of finding her watching from the doorway of the Brooks House hotel. Breaking free from Magda, she whirled to face her. "Yes, ma'am. I mean, no, ma'am. I mean—"

Magda pushed Bertha to one side. "Pardon my stuttering friend. We couldn't help but notice you've just arrived in town. We've come to say hello and to extend a sincere Jefferson welcome to you and your companion."

Surprise flickered in Bessie's bright eyes before she offered her hand. "Well, thank you."

Magda seemed to settle fast into her welcoming committee role. "My name is Magdalena Hayes, and this here's Bertha. Bertha Maye Biddie." Magda nudged Bertha hard with her elbow. "Say hello to the lady, sugar."

So amazed by the manner in which Bessie's broad smile enhanced her face, Bertha couldn't muster indignation that her name had inspired it. She took the proffered hand in her own and felt a current pass between them. "Hello," she managed. "I'm. . .so pleased to meet you."

"But you haven't really met me yet, now, have you, Bertha Biddie? I'm Annie. Annie Moore from Cincinnati."

Bertha blinked. "Annie? But I thought—" She started the question before she had time to think better of it. And the minute she asked, she remembered the man with Bessie had called her Annie, as well.

Annie arched one feathered brow. "I see you have the advantage over me. You know I go by more than one name, yet I don't know a thing about you." She smiled, but this time it never reached her eyes. "Your confusion is justified, so allow me to clear things up. You see, I've been called many names in the course of my life, and believe me, I prefer Annie to all the rest."

She took a few seconds to look around while tugging satin gloves onto her long, slender fingers. Up close, the diamonds were more impressive, in particular one very large gem surrounded by smaller stones. Annie turned back to Magda, her mood light again. "I must say this is a curious town. Do they always send brawling girls to welcome visitors?"

She laughed, and Bertha winced. She'd never heard a woman laugh so loudly in public. Not even Magda.

"Quite the mismatched scrap, too." She regarded them each in turn, the mischievous glint back in place. "One so tiny she can't block the wind, and the other descended from hardier stock. You two are friends, you say?"

Magda took Bertha's arm. "Of course we're friends," she said a bit defensively. "What's so peculiar about that?"

"Well, darling, I must say I'd never have guessed."

Bertha nudged Magda with her elbow. "She means because we were quarreling."

"Quarreling? It was a round of fisticuffs. And a very entertaining bout, I must say. You might've sold tickets."

Bertha knew Magda's sheepish grin likely matched her own.

Magda waved a dismissive hand in the air. "Oh, that was nothing, really. It's how we often settle things."

Annie laughed. "May I point out that it's an unlikely form of communication? When Abe communicates with me like that, I end up with beefsteak on my eye."

Magda frowned at Bertha, and Bertha returned the expression. In the silence that followed, Annie seemed entertained by their discomfort.

"Say," she said, breaking the spell, "can you girls point me in the direction of the general store? I've got a hankering for something sweet."

Magda looked relieved to change the subject. "Sure we can, considering we spend a good deal of our time there. I have a right demanding sweet tooth myself on occasion."

Annie leaned closer to Bertha and dropped her voice to a whisper. "The truth is, I could use a stiff drink"—she cast a nervous glance over her shoulder—"but Abe wouldn't like it. He don't like me drinking alone." She straightened and gave Bertha a wink. "So a sweet will have to do for now."

Bertha swallowed hard and nodded then squared around and pointed down the street. "Stilley's is just over there a ways, on Dallas Street. We can take you, if you like."

Annie tucked her velvet reticule inside her yellow sash and linked arms with them. "If I like? Well, I certainly do like, ladies. Lead the way."

"Whoa, mule," Henry called, pulling back on Dandy's reins.

Sarah looked up to find herself in front of the last possible place she'd reckoned on going. She glanced over at Henry, but his purposeful blank expression offered not a clue. After securing the wagon, he hopped to the ground and came around to lift her down.

"Stilley's?" she asked, ignoring his outstretched arms.

He nodded.

The general store wasn't a likely setting for the caliber of surprise Sarah expected. She'd spent a fair amount of time inside those walls engaged in commonplace things such as sorting through flour sacks to find one without weevils or picking over packets of seed. To the best of her knowing, there wasn't a blessed thing behind those doors that would set a woman's tender heart to pounding. This made Henry's behavior quite a poser.

"Why can't you tell me what it is you might be needing in there?" Without waiting for an answer, she stood up on the seat and leaned into her husband's outstretched arms.

He swung her up and out of the wagon, set her down on the boardwalk, and reached to straighten her hat. "Girl, I guess you must be the nosiest woman in Marion County." He tweaked her nose and then tapped the end of it with his index finger. "It's a wonder this thing is still cute as a button and not stretched all out like a corncob."

Sarah slapped away his hand. "Curiosity ain't the same as nosy. Considering how hard you've worked to stir mine up, you have only yourself to blame."

Henry enjoyed a hearty laugh at her expense. "Funny, though, how it's always my business you get curious about, ain't it?"

She crossed her arms over her chest. "You reckon you're funny, don't you?"

He pulled her close for a hug. "Don't fret, now, Mrs. King. You gon' find out everything directly—that is, if I can get you to hush long enough to go inside."

She allowed him to nudge her across the boardwalk to the door. They passed beneath the sign reading W. F. STILLEY & CO. and stepped inside. Sarah stood blinking while her eyes grew accustomed to the dim light and her nose to the acrid odor of animal skins and cut tobacco, not a pleasant mix. She held her breath as they passed the racks hung with stiffened fox and coon-shaped furs and a shelf laden with bags and tins of chaw, the source of the cloying smell.

Barrels littered the floor, some filled with corn, some with wheat. Large sacks of flour and sugar were stacked on one side of the room, bags of beans on the other. On the counter, tall jars filled with licorice, peppermint sticks, and assorted penny candies were arranged in a lively display.

Sarah's inventory of the familiar room uncovered something new. Against the back wall, a row of bright colors caught her eye. Two steps closer revealed the only thing in the store she might be itching to get her hands on.

"Mr. Stilley! Why, looky here. You done got in a shipment since I was here last, ain't you?"

Behind the counter, the clerk smiled and nodded.

Sarah crossed the room and ran her fingers over the new bolts of fabric while a shiver of pleasure ran down her spine. They were pretty. Every single one. She'd take the plainest of the lot and still be as pleased as a suckling pup.

"These just come in from New Orleans?" she asked without looking up.

"Nope," Mr. Stilley called. "Brought 'em back from New York. Got a good buy that I can pass on to you folks."

She looked over her shoulder at him. "That so?"

Mr. Stilley nodded again. "Pick you out a nice color, Sarah." He winked over at Henry. "I'm sure me and Henry can strike a fair bargain."

Henry traded with Stilley on occasion, hauling in hides on consignment and corn to sell outright. But the money they got always went toward the bare necessities.

Sarah glanced at her husband. Might this be Henry's surprise? It wasn't the sort of thing he would think of. And she reckoned he knew nothing about her fondness for piece goods or her longing to have a new dress.

Henry stood shifting his weight back and forth, his cheeks nigh to splitting from the grin on his face. One thing was sure. Whatever they had come here for was about to take place.

Oh, please, please, Lord.

"I ain't come here for no trifling cloth," Henry announced, still grinning like a dolt. "I got something sweeter in mind."

Sarah's heart plunged to the muddy depths. She barely heard his next words.

"I come here to buy Sarah a slab of that chocolate."

Stilley beamed. "The new milk chocolate? I see word gets around." He reached under the counter, beneath the jars of candy, and pulled out a wooden box brimming with dark brown blocks in irregular shapes and sizes.

Henry beckoned. "Get on over here, sugar, and pick you out a nice piece. I got enough corn in the back of the rig to cover whatever you want."

Whatever I want? Sarah sighed. *If only you knew.* She forced a smile to her lips as fake as George Washington's teeth.

"Special occasion, Henry?"

Because Mr. Stilley had asked the question she'd wondered all day, Sarah looked up. The pleasure on Henry's face made his dark cheeks glow. "No, sir. No special occasion to speak of." His voice grew soft with embarrassment. "Jus' wanted to show my wife a little appreciation for how hard she been working. Heard about your chocolate and figured she might like some."

"A fine choice, Henry. I understand you can mix it in milk to make a sweet drink or eat it right out of your hand. It's all the rage up north." He winked at Sarah, and Henry turned to face her.

"Sarah?" Henry King had the look of Christmas morning on his face. "Ain't you coming, girl?"

She pulled her shoulders back, gave the bright bolts one last glance, and headed for her husband's side. " 'Course I'm coming. Mr. Stilley, scoot that box a little closer if you please, so's I can reach it better. I got to pick me out a piece of chocolate."

"Did you say chocolate?" someone bawled behind them. "That sounds like just the thing I need."

The bold, strident voice seemed better suited to a man, but when Sarah turned, she found a powerfully beautiful woman standing on the threshold, flanked by two girls. When they stepped into the store behind the woman, Sarah realized she knew them both.

It took one look to know their companion wouldn't be welcome to Sunday supper. But daring as day and big as you please,

Bertha Maye Biddie and Magdalena Hayes congregated with her like long-lost friends. If their mamas were anything like Sarah's had been, those two would feel the sting of a hickory switch before nightfall.

CHAPTER 4

Sarah watched the fancy white woman stroll to the counter, plant the tip of her parasol on the floor, and cross her delicate hands atop the handle. She aimed an unexpected smile and nod at Sarah then fixed Mr. Stilley with an amused expression.

"Am I to understand that there's chocolate for sale in this establishment?"

Mr. Stilley's face lit like sunshine. "Step back, folks." He waved a dismissive hand in Sarah's direction. "Make way for these good people."

Henry jumped as if poked with a hatpin. "Yessuh, Mr. Stilley," he mumbled then shuffled aside, pushing Sarah along with him, his eyes shifted to the floor.

Sarah gritted her teeth and turned away, too late to hide her disgust from Henry.

He winced as if he'd been struck and ducked his head again.

Mr. Stilley took hold of the wooden crate, pulled it from Sarah's side of the counter, and presented it to the three breathless women with a flourish. "You heard right, ma'am, but only half the story. It's not just chocolate I have here. There's genuine imported Swiss in this box, and at a reasonable price." He pushed the container a bit closer to the lively one. "Go on, then. Help yourself."

"Imported Swiss?" the swanky lady squealed, in a manner not fit for civilized company. "Perfect!" She rummaged, looking for the biggest of the lot, took a sizable wedge in each hand, and turned to the girls behind her. "Would you look at this? Have you ever seen as much pure pleasure?" She handed a chunk to Magdalena then tossed one to little Bertha, who juggled to keep from dropping it. "I do love this delightful concoction," she cooed at Bertha. "Don't you, honey?"

Bertha stared with big eyes at the wrapped brown block. "I've never tried it." She brought the confection closer for a sniff. "But it smells divine."

Sarah could smell it just fine from where she stood. All the stirring of the box had raised a rich, pungent cloud that hovered in the room, setting Sarah's mouth to watering. She tasted sweetness at the back of her throat.

The woman gasped. "You say you've never tried it?"

Magda leaned forward and stared at Bertha. "Come now, dear. Of course you have." She let go an uneasy laugh. "You'll have Annie thinking we're tight-fisted hicks."

Bertha gave a determined shake of her head. "I've had it mixed in milk before and once in cake. But never like this." She turned it over in her hands, leaving smeared spots beneath the clear wrapper where her fingers gripped. "What's it like, Annie?"

At first the woman named Annie looked at Bertha as though she didn't believe her. Then she spun around to the wooden box and set to scooping up sweet-smelling hunks with both hands. "There's a remedy for this cruel injustice, my dear. Never fear. You're about to be enlightened."

She unloaded the bundle of candy onto the counter in front of a beaming Mr. Stilley before reaching for one more piece. "There. That should just about do it. Now what do I owe for this child's education?"

Sarah had never seen Stilley with such a big smile. He reached behind him, producing a tablet and a fat leaded pencil. "Very good, madam. Will that be all?"

Annie nodded. "Yes, I believe it will."

The eager man bent over the pad, ciphering figures so fast Sarah waited for smoke to rise from his fingers; then he pushed the paper forward.

Without flinching, Annie reached for the reticule stashed at her side and pulled out more money than Sarah would see in two years' time. After counting out what she owed, Annie pulled the wrapped pieces toward her and asked Mr. Stilley for something to tote them in.

He smiled and shook out a flour sack. "Here we are. Allow me to wrap them for you." He opened the mouth of the sack and started to load her purchase, but she reached to stay his hand.

"Just a minute, if you please." She waved her finger over the mound until she decided which one she wanted. "Ah, yes! This one will have no use for your bag, good sir." She turned and flashed a smile with teeth as white as Henry's. "Will it, girls?"

The three of them laughed together, acting so silly over a fool piece of candy that it set Sarah's teeth on edge.

Annie took her bundle from Mr. Stilley and turned with a flourish. "Shall we go, ladies? We need to find a discreet spot and indulge ourselves to the full."

Bertha held one finger aloft, a glint in her eyes. "I know just the place."

Worry settled over Magda's face. "Bertha. . .you're not thinking what I think you're thinking."

Bertha dismissed her with a swish of her skirts. "Hush your fussing. You sound just like my mama. It won't hurt a single thing for us to go there for a spell. Besides, who'll know?" She shot a warning look over her shoulder. "Unless you tell."

No one need bother telling Sarah. She knew right where they were going. The fifty-foot bluff overhanging the Big Cypress Bayou drew all the youngsters around Jefferson, no matter how much their parents fussed. It was the only place that would arouse the cornered-fox look in Magda's eyes.

"Don't be silly." Offense straightened Magda's spine, and her nose went in the air. "I'd be daft to tell."

Despite her raised chin and put out tone, she seemed less than convincing.

Annie clutched both their arms. "Let's go, then. What are we waiting for?"

When they turned from the counter, Bertha's face paled, and Sarah realized the girl had forgotten she and Henry were there. Sarah watched her weigh the chance she'd been overheard. Then good nature overcame Bertha's fear, and she grinned in their direction. "Hey, you two."

Henry answered for them both. "How you today, Miss Bertha?"

"Just fine, and you?"

"Oh, we doing all right."

Bertha's kind eyes settled on Sarah. "And your papa?"

Her daddy's warm smile and merry eyes crowded Sarah's mind, and she grinned. "Much the same, Miss Bertha. Thank you kindly for asking. He still gets the crimps in his knees of a chilly morn. Slows him down some, but mostly he's all right."

Bertha gave a sympathetic nod. "My papa suffers something fierce with that old rheumatism. Makes him dread the winter."

"Tell him to carry a potato in his pocket," Sarah said eagerly. "Draws the misery right out of your bones."

Bertha's brows met in the middle. "A potato?"

"Daddy swears by it."

"Well, thank you kindly, Sarah." Bertha reached to pat her arm. "I'll pass that along to Papa." She lifted her chin toward the smiling stranger. "This here's my friend Miss Annie Moore from Cincinnati. Annie, meet Sarah and Henry King."

Annie's face lit with a sweet smile.

Sarah gave a brief nod of her head. Ill at ease in the company of the lady, she hurriedly changed the subject. "Been meaning to come by and tell you folks we got plenty of those turnips your mama be so partial to. Had a bumper crop this year. Come on around and pull some before they get stringy. You can take all you like. Henry just gon' plow them under soon." She glanced back at her husband.

"Ain't that so, Henry?"

"It sho' is." Obviously pleased with her gesture, he flashed all his teeth. "That goes for you, too, Miss Magda." His gaze lit briefly on the older woman before he squirmed and looked away. "Well, for all of you."

Sarah tried to picture this Annie person kneeling in a turnip patch, but her imagination failed her. She doubted the woman knew what to do with a turnip.

"We'll ride out and get some, then," Bertha said. "It's a generous offer." She winked up at Henry. "I see Sarah got wind of Mr. Stilley's new shipment. Bet your arm's fairly sore."

"My arm?" Henry rubbed his right shoulder. "Why you say that?"

Bertha grinned all over. "From the twisting Sarah gave it to get you in here."

Sarah watched the meaning of the girl's words fly over Henry's head like southbound geese.

Bertha didn't seem to notice. "Have you picked out something nice, Sarah? Something bright like you been pining for?"

Sarah shook her head. "We come for something else today. You see, Henry—"

"Don't hold these ladies up, Sarah," Mr. Stilley boomed behind them. "They want to be about their business."

The woman called Annie took a tighter grip on Bertha's arm. "You ready, sugar? It's time to go. My man won't sleep all day."

Bertha turned and stared up at her companion as though hexed. "Yes, Annie. I'm ready."

"Well, come on. Show me this mysterious place of yours so we can commence with your edification."

Arm in arm, the three turned and made their way to the door, and Sarah wondered how they'd pass through linked up like a chain. Forgetting herself in her concern for Bertha, she called after them. "You girls be careful, now, you hear?" When they left the store, she spun around and made big eyes at Henry.

He smiled.

Mr. Stilley turned from watching the door and swiveled the box in their direction. "All right, now, Sarah. I believe you were just about to have some of this for yourself."

Henry cleared his throat, anxious eyes on Sarah while he spoke. "Mr. Stilley, we've had a minute to ponder, and I believe we've changed our minds."

Sarah smiled and nodded her approval. Her broad-shouldered, straight-backed husband became a giant in her eyes.

His gaze locked on hers, Henry crossed the room and rested his arm around Sarah's shoulders. "We decided Sarah might better have some nice ice cream or a soda drink instead."

Mr. Stilley looked about, as if trying to figure how to produce the items Henry had named, his brows a puzzled line on his forehead. He nodded at the chocolate. "A minute ago, you had your mouth set for one of these." He pushed the box toward Sarah, as if a closer look might change her mind. "Don't you want to be the first of your kind in town to try it?"

Henry cleared his throat and pulled Sarah tighter against his side. "No, sir, she don't. I think we'll run on over to Mr. Nighthart's and buy her something from the fountain." He looked down at Sarah. "Ain't that right, sugar lamb?"

She nodded.

Stilley glanced between them. "You folks sure?"

Sarah beamed up at Henry, feeling proud enough to pop. "Oh yes, we right sure. Never been more sure of a thing."

Outside, Sarah stood on tiptoe and gave Henry a big kiss on the cheek.

He pushed her back and glanced around but had a wide grin on his face. "You ready for that soda drink now? Or maybe some ice cream?"

She cupped his strong chin in her hand, caressing the dimple with her thumb. "Reckon I already had myself a treat for the day. If I had my druthers, I'd sooner go back out to the house."

"Home?" Henry frowned at her and scratched his head. "But I ain't fetched you nothing yet."

Every ounce of her love for him pushed to the surface and spilled over into her voice. "What you gave me in there tasted better'n a whole box of chocolates with ice cream on top and a soda to wash it down." She lowered her lashes and dropped her voice to a whisper. "How about we go on home now and let me treat you?" She'd never said a thing so bold, and it brought a flash of heat to her cheeks.

Instead of the smile she expected, Henry tightened his jaw and brushed her aside. "I ain't did nothing that special."

"But you did. You—"

He put his hand on the small of her back and guided her, none too gently, toward the rig. "Go on, woman. You want to go home, let's get there. I got work waiting on me."

She stumbled along, hastened by the pressure of his hand, so taken aback she hardly felt her feet touching the ground. "Henry," she demanded over her shoulder, "what's wrong?"

"Ain't nothing wrong. I got work to do, that's all."

Sarah ground to a stop and dug in her heels. If he pushed on her back till day's end, she wouldn't mount the wagon without knowing what had turned his mood. She faced him, letting the set of her jaw and flash of her eyes tell him she'd brook no more. "Henry King, if you're swelled up because of what I said, then unswell. I shouldn't have talked so loose, but—"

"It wasn't that."

"It's just that I'm so proud of you."

"I said it wasn't that!"

She took hold of his hands and peered up into guarded eyes. "Well, what, then?"

Henry jerked free and swept past, crossing to the rig and climbing aboard, leaving her to clamber up by herself. When he snapped the leads and Dandy pulled away from the boardwalk, Sarah sat so close to the far edge of the seat that she feared bouncing onto the ground at the first deep rut. But she preferred sprawling in the dirt to sitting next to her vexing man.

Not a word passed between them on the way. Sarah used the time to replay in her mind every detail of the day, desperate to pin down what she'd done to anger him. It had never set well with Sarah to have a body displeased with her. Especially Henry. But given her quick temper and saucy ways, life had proved a peculiar dance up to that point.

She spent an unreasonable amount of time waltzing on people's toes and then two-stepping her way out of trouble. Henry once said he considered her sassy mouth to be part of her charm and the very trait that first attracted him. But with the passage of time, he'd grown less enamored by her rowdy tongue.

When they turned down their lane, Sarah made a last cautious attempt to talk to him, but Henry offered a cold shoulder in return. By the time they reached the yard, hot rage had crowded out all desire to make up. She made her way down from her perch before Henry could offer his hand and swept out of the barn, leaving him to tend the rig and settle Dandy.

She stormed into the house and into their room, slamming the door behind her. Her shoes flew off one at a time with kicks that sent them crashing into the wall. Next came her dress, pulled overhead in angry jerks with the sound of ripping seams. She yanked her nightshirt from the hook and stomped into it, tossing the torn dress into a heap by the bed. By the time she locked the door and slid beneath the quilt, she heard Henry's heavy steps inside the house.

She listened while he walked from room to room. First the kitchen, then the parlor, and back again. He paused then crossed to the double windows that faced the side yard and outhouse. When next he moved, his determined stride led him just where she knew it would.

Least he could do is take off them muddy boots. I know he never wiped his feet.

Henry stopped outside the door and tried the knob. "Sarah?"

She turned away, hurling a string of insults in her mind.

He rattled harder. "Open up. What you doing in there?"

She knew if she didn't answer, he'd stand there asking addlepated questions all night. "I'm resting, Henry."

"Resting?" he called in a low voice. "It's midday. You ain't ailing, are you?"

How like him to act like nothing was wrong. "I'm just tired, that's all."

The long pause from the other side of the door said things she knew Henry couldn't find the words for. When he finally spoke, he said just the wrong thing. "What about dinner?"

She sat up and threw her pillow. "There's chickens running over the yard because you can't mend a fence. Pluck one and eat it. Frying pan's on the hook."

She'd have some apologies to make later, but for now Sarah hunkered down, swaddled in spiteful indignation, and tried to sleep. No more sound came from inside the house. In the silence, she listened to the racing pulse in her temple beat a rhythm against her pillow. She couldn't quiet it any more than she could silence the gentle voice in her head. Frustrated, she flopped on her back and kicked the covers to the floor.

Why should I, Lord? I don't care to feed that stubborn-hearted, perplexing man. Why would You ask me to? She had searched her heart and couldn't find a single excuse for Henry's bad behavior. If he couldn't offer her one, let him starve.

Sarah turned on her side again and huddled against the cold until it became more work to resist than to obey. Miserable, she spun around and sat up. Very well, she'd give him food, but that was all. There'd be no need to speak to him. She slipped a shawl around her shoulders and opened the door.

In the kitchen, Henry sat slumped at the table, but his head jerked up when she entered the room. He had already fetched the kettle of beans and ham she'd cooked the day before from the springhouse he'd built down by the bayou. He'd been right proud of himself for building the small house over the water to keep her vittles cool, but the thing had become a source of irritation for Sarah, considering Jefferson boasted an ice plant. The folks in town sat in their parlors and waited for the iceman to put blocks of ice in special wooden boxes sitting right in their kitchens. A pot of beans would last for days in a contraption like that.

Without a word, she took down the iron skillet and scooped in bacon grease from the jar near the blacktop stove. The solid grease turned to liquid as soon as it hit the pan, so she know the fire was hot. She hurried to mix the cornbread, poured the batter, and set the skillet on the stove with more force than was called for.

Behind her, Henry cleared his throat. "Did you see all the chocolate that woman had, Sarah? She done bought herself a whole mess of chocolate."

Sarah planted her knuckles on her waist and twisted to look over her shoulder. "I saw it all right, and some other things, too. I saw you looking mighty hard at that fancied-up white woman."

Henry drew back, and pain flickered in his eyes. "What you going on about?"

Sarah knew when she said it the accusation was unjust. In all the years she'd been Henry King's wife, she'd never once caught his eyes on another woman. She reached for the beans, slamming the pot on the stove. "You know just what I'm talking about."

It would be nice if she knew it herself.

"How could I be looking at a woman? You're all these eyes have wanted since they landed on you four years ago at Lawetta Draper's backyard social. You still in braids and looking so sweet in that pretty white frock we had to fight off the bees. From that day until now, I can't see past you to look at anyone else."

"The bees swarmed because Markas Scott sloshed cider on my dress." She kept a hard edge in her voice, but still Henry chuckled.

"Markas Scott was jus' trying to sit close to you. The man knows a good thing when he sees it."

Sarah longed to turn but kept right on stirring the beans. The scrape of Henry's chair on the pinewood floor told her he was coming to stand behind her. She steeled herself until his hands on her shoulders melted her resolve as fast as the skillet had melted the grease. When he pulled her close, she leaned into him despite herself.

"Girl, what's wrong with you?" he whispered. "Your man takes you into town to fetch you a surprise, and this is how you act?"

She picked up the dishcloth to wipe her hands and turned. "You the one acting up today. What happened to you down at Stilley's?"

The glow in his eyes faded, and waves of pain rolled in to take its place. He squirmed like he didn't want to answer her question, and his expression changed so many times she gave up trying to read him.

"Tell me, Henry."

"I don't care to start it up again, Sarah."

"Well, I need to know."

He shook his head. "You know I can't sort the words in my head good enough to say 'em aloud."

"Try."

Henry stared at the floor without speaking until Sarah pulled his attention back to her.

"Just say it."

He rubbed circles on his thick brows with his thumb and forefinger then looked up with anguished eyes. "All right, then. If that's what you want." His big chest moved up and down, and he opened his mouth twice before the words came out. "Sarah, today was the first time you ever said you was proud of me. Did you know that?"

She could only stare.

"And for what?" he continued. "For showing spite to Mr. Stilley? Never mind that I took you there in the first place to buy you something nice."

Sarah back-stepped and slung the dishcloth across the room. "I can't help it! I can't abide all that bowing and scraping! If you want to surprise me, Henry King, then live up to your name." She knew she'd gone too far but couldn't stop. "Looks like, you being a farmer and all, you could grow yourself a nice backbone."

She pushed him aside and moved about the room with gyrating hips, batting her eyes and spouting hateful words. " 'Yes, suh, Mr. Stilley, suh. Let old Henry move his big black bottom out the way for these fine white folk.' "

When she dared a glance his way, she saw his face was red, his fists clenched.

"That's enough, Sarah. You wrong, and you know it. I don't show out like that. And Mr. Stilley treats us good as anybody."

"Good as anybody?" She sneered and nodded. "Why, sure he do. When nobody's looking."

His fierce glare cut straight through her bones. "What you want from me, Sarah? This ain't St. Louis. I told you it would be different here."

When she didn't answer, he shook his head. "Small as you are, you got a sizable ornery streak. I love you, but your pride's gon' see me hanged."

Sarah returned to the stove, her back as rigid as her mind-set.

The door opened then closed behind Henry, and only then did the enormity of her words overwhelm her. She stood as if poured out and forged to the spot by the heat of her anger, until the acrid smell of burning beans and deep regret assailed her nostrils. She pushed the pot off the fire, untied her apron, and sank into Henry's chair. On a shelf above the sideboard, the ragged spine of Mama's Bible leapt out at her. A single verse from Proverbs seemed to sprout wings and fly out from the dog-eared pages.

"Death and life are in the power of the tongue: and they that love it shall eat the fruit thereof."

She sat for a bit, gingerly chewing the fruit of her words, finding it less than tasty. If she'd ever doubted that particular scripture, she didn't now. The pall that settled about her, heavy in the room, felt like the death of her husband's love.

What has my big mouth done?

She turned and stared at the place where he'd gone out, her pride, more than the solid oak door, an impenetrable wall between herself and Henry. A simple apology wouldn't do for this one, no matter how fast she danced.

Dear Lord, what have I gone and done now?

CHAPTER 5

Avoiding the main road was the smartest plan. One of the nosy old hens Bertha saw scratching about town might ask too many questions and then go squawking to Mama. If Mama caught her at Lover's Leap, it'd be the woodshed for certain. The fact that no one ever forbade her to go to the bluff was but a trifle, though one she'd use to her advantage should she be caught. Mama's unreasonable views on the subject were clear, voiced or not. But it was the only interesting place left in the whole of Marion County.

If they timed it right, they could catch Mose and Rhodie in an empty wagon, headed back to the bayou for more wood. Bertha squinted at Annie's fine yellow dress. "We have to run. Can you keep up?"

Grinning, Annie tucked her parasol under one arm and extended her hand. "Just try me."

Bertha returned the smile with an equal measure of glee and clasped Annie's hand. "Come on, Magda. Follow us," she cried and then darted between two shops with Magda's plaintive cry to wait echoing in her ears.

Bertha clung to her new friend and led her down the cluttered lane past discarded barrels, stacked crates, and piles of odorous trash. At the end, they cut to the left and ran behind staggered rows of shops along the back alleys of Jefferson with Magda panting far behind.

Bertha longed for her soft, low-slung boots instead of the bronze leather heels fastened by little buttoned straps that Mama insisted she wear that morning. They were far too tight with ridiculous pointed toes that pinched her feet. Bertha detested shoes and always had, much preferring the comfort of worn-in boots or bare feet. She wondered if the day would ever come when she might learn to tolerate fashionable shoes.

They passed behind Mr. Steinlein's clothing store on Walnut Street and cut across an open field before bursting onto the road in time to see Mose's rig approaching in the distance. Bertha and Annie doubled over in laughter, clutching their sides.

Magda, still hobbling across the field, gripped her waist in apparent pain and scowled her displeasure. When she reached them, her complaint was an accusation aimed at Bertha. "You didn't wait."

Guilt tickled the edges of Bertha's conscience. "I clearly said we had to run," she panted. "You heard me say it."

"But I asked you to wait."

"I don't have the wind to argue, Magda. Besides, here come Mose and Rhodie."

The boy spotted Annie from forty feet away. His wide eyes were fixed on her, and the freckles on his pale face stuck out like stars in a cloudless sky. The ever-unflappable Rhodie sat quietly beside him, hands folded in her lap. They drew alongside, and Mose reined in the horse. "Why, looky here, Sissy. If this ain't our lucky day."

His openmouthed smile reminded Bertha of a happy jack-o'-lantern. She moved closer, pulling Annie along for bait. "Hey, Mose."

He pulled his gaze from Annie long enough to address Bertha. "Well now, it ain't often I get to see the prettiest flowers in Jefferson, much less stumble upon them twice in one day." His eyes swiveled back to Annie. "And I see there's a mighty fair rose been added to the bunch."

"Hello." Annie stuck out her hand and clasped his palm as if it weren't calloused and covered in filth. "I'm Annie. Bertha's friend."

It wouldn't seem two simple words held the power to induce such joy, but they swept over Bertha in waves, leaving a rush of contentment behind. Her elation lasted as long as it took to catch the wounded expression on Magda's face.

Mose tipped his hat with his free hand. "Moses Pharr. Pleasure to meet you, ma'am. This here's Rhodie, my little sister."

Annie released his hand and beamed past him at the girl. "Oh, but this darling girl isn't so little. She's a young woman, and a pretty one, too. I always did envy girls with red hair."

Whether the compliment was genuine or a simple courtesy, it pleased Rhodie to no end. She returned a smile as sweet as hot cross buns, and a flush rose to her cheeks. "Thank you kindly, ma'am."

With a furtive glance behind her, Bertha decided they could exchange pleasantries later. "Mose, are you two headed back toward the bayou?"

A light flickered in Mose's eyes. "Why? You gals needing a lift?"

Bertha grinned back at him. "We sure are."

"Hop aboard, then. We got an empty wagon this time, so take all the room you need." He looked past them to Magda and spoke to her for the first time. "You can come, too, if you like."

Magda's frown darkened. "Really? Well, ain't I blessed?"

Bertha let go of Annie and caught Magda's hand. "Come, my beloved. Your carriage awaits."

The struggle not to smile played over Magda's face, but the effort proved too great, and she allowed Bertha to pull her toward the rig. "Save your sweet talk for those who don't know you so well, Bertha Biddie."

Bertha grinned and squeezed her fingers. "Just get in, you sour old crabapple."

Mose ordered Rhodie to the rear so Annie could join him on

the seat. Though Rhodie complied swiftly and without complaint, Annie refused to take her place even after Bertha tried to convince her. Instead, Annie hiked up her skirts and climbed into the wagon bed, seemingly oblivious to the cypress twigs and wood chips. When all was said and done, Annie, Bertha, and Rhodie sat cross-legged in back, and Magda wound up on the seat beside a scowling Mose.

Bertha leaned against the rail, watching the residents dwindle and the shops thin out as they pulled away from town headed west.

They'd gone less than a half mile before Magda leaned to whisper something to Mose, and he pulled up on the reins. When they came to a full stop, Magda gathered her things and stood up.

"What are you doing, sugar?" Bertha called.

"I decided not to go. It's time for the noon meal. Mama will be looking for me."

"You can tell her you ate with me. It won't be completely untrue." She winked and pointed at Annie's bag. "We'll be eating candy."

"Mama won't like it. She got mad the last time I did that. And she'll mention it to your mama. I know she will."

Bertha narrowed her eyes, causing Magda to lower hers. "You're scared, that's all."

Magda looked ready to make more excuses but then traded her wilted demeanor for a stamp of the foot. "All right, then. Yes, I'm scared. There, I've said it and feel no worse for it. You would be, too, if you had any sense at all."

Showing interest in the conversation for the first time, Rhodie leaned forward. "What you afraid of, Magda?"

Magda pointed an accusing finger at Bertha. "She's taking Annie to the bluff."

Rhodie came alive. "To Lover's Leap? I want to come!" Rhodie whirled to plead with her brother's back. "Oh, Mose, can we go?"

He shook his head. "Can't, Sissy. We got three more loads to get done before nightfall." He tilted to the left to gaze up at Magda.

"But there ain't nothing on the bluff to be scared of."

Magda regarded the top of his head with disdain. "What do you know, Moses Pharr? You're dumb as a box of rocks. The main thing I'm frightened of is Papa finding out. Bertha should fear the same."

Bertha sighed. "I told you they won't find out. If you don't come along, you'll miss all the fun." She plied the bait that always worked with Magda. Food. "And don't forget about the chocolate. You won't get any."

Magda reached inside her drawstring bag and produced the piece Annie had given her in the store. "Oh yes, I will."

Bertha shrugged and looked away. "Go on home, then. I can't stop you." She angled forward, propelled by a sudden troubling thought. "But you'd better not tell."

The words seemed to rock Magda as if a cannon had gone off inside. She flailed a hand in Bertha's direction while she struggled to find her words.

In a true act of fearlessness, considering she still towered above him, Mose smiled and nodded up at Magda. "Yep, she's bound to tell. Ain't you, Magda?"

Magda froze and fixed him with a disbelieving stare. Then she climbed down off the rig, muttering under her breath. When she reached the ground, she didn't say a word to Bertha or anyone else before she flounced away in a huff. They watched her cut across the field and duck into the dense woods that lay east of her house.

Annie's low voice broke the silence. "Will she be all right?"

Bertha glanced her way. "Magda? Of course she will."

"But she went off into the woods all alone."

Bertha laughed. "Ain't nothing in that grove of pine with the boldness to stand up to Magdalena Hayes."

Annie shifted her eyes toward Bertha. "You just did."

She nodded. "Why do you think she's so mad?"

Annie smiled. Bertha looked toward the spot where she'd last seen Magda's blue shawl bobbing through the trees, but all trace of her had disappeared.

"What's there to be so scared of?"

She squinted up at Annie. "At Lover's Leap, you mean?"

Annie nodded.

"Nothing, really. It's a dark and moody place, a sheer bluff fifty feet high that plunges straight down to the water's edge. The trees grow thick before it opens to the bayou, so not much light gets in. A lot has taken place there over the years. Even more things people talk about that never really happened."

Rhodie chimed in, her low voice laden with dread. "Rumor has it folks have taken their own lives by jumping off the bluff. And there was a murder happened there once." She peeked at Bertha. "Or so they say."

Annie's eyes widened. "A murder?"

"And a suicide," Mose said over his shoulder. "Some poor muggins caught his wife on the ridge with his own brother. Rolled them off the edge and then sailed in after them." He chuckled, raising his hand to the sky before dipping it low again. "Took him a leap, he did. I heard it wasn't the trip down he minded so much. Just the sudden stop."

Bertha raised her brows at Annie and shook her head. "That story's not true."

Mose turned around to look at her. "Sure is, too."

"Then why doesn't anyone know their names? If there was any truth to it, someone around here could say who it was. It's a legend, Mose. You shouldn't spread it about."

Mose looked from Bertha to Annie while a slow flush colored his cheeks. Without a word, he faced the front and flicked the reins, and the old horse eased into motion.

Rhodie reached to pat Annie's hand. "Don't worry your pretty self, ma'am. Even if it's true, nothing as bad as murder happens around Jefferson anymore."

"Why, thank you, darlin'. I'm comforted by that thought." The radiant smile Annie turned on Rhodie caused her to blush brighter than Mose and duck her head.

Bertha stewed about Magda for the rest of the trip. The others seemed lost in thoughts of their own, until Mose pulled to the side of the road at a spot where a small muddy clearing narrowed into an overgrown trail. He wrapped the reins around the post and jumped off to open the rear end and help Annie climb down. She thanked him then straightened her skirt and reached for her bag and parasol.

Bertha held up her hand. "Wait, Annie." She reached for Mose's outstretched arm and scooted to the ground. "Why don't you leave your things right here? Mose can pick us up when he's done. Can't you, Mose?"

"Sure, but I won't be back for an hour or so. And I'll be packing wood when I come."

Bertha looked at Annie. "I don't mind if she doesn't."

Annie shook her head. "It's better than walking."

Mose raised the tailgate. "Meet you right here, then. If you ain't standing on the road when I come, I'll send Sissy in after you."

Rhodie gasped and slapped her brother's arm. "Nuh-uh! I ain't traipsing through those woods alone."

Bertha chuckled. "Don't worry. We'll be here. And, Rhodie, mind Annie's nice things, won't you? Don't let Mose pile cypress on them."

Rhodie rose up on her knees and peered at the matching yellow parasol and reticule with anxious eyes. "I won't. But they're sure to get filthy in the bottom of this raggedy old crate. Give them to me, Mose. I'll hold them up front."

Bertha tried to pass the items to Mose, but he threw up his hands and backed away. "I ain't touching them girlie things."

Annie laughed aloud. "Go on. Take them. They won't bite."

He retreated farther and shook his head, staring as if facing down a copperhead.

"I swear," Bertha cried. "The more I learn about men, the more outlandish they seem." She shook her head and walked around to give the things to Rhodie. "Don't let any of this yellow silk touch your brother. We wouldn't want him to perish."

Rhodie grinned. "I won't."

Bertha turned to face Annie. "Ready now?"

"Ready as I'll ever be."

They were halfway across the clearing when Bertha remembered. She pivoted on the ball of her foot and ran toward the road.

"Mose, wait!"

He pulled the horse to a stop and turned on the seat. "Yeah?"

Bertha hurried to Rhodie's side of the rig and reached for Annie's reticule then held the bag aloft. "We forgot the chocolate."

Annie waved her hand. "Go ahead and get it, Bertha. I don't mind. And give them each a piece while you're at it."

Bertha rummaged inside, pulled out four pieces of wrapped candy, and handed one each to Mose and Rhodie. "This is for you."

Rhodie took it and turned it over in her hand. "What is it?"

"It's a block of candy. You're supposed to eat it. But you'd better hurry; it's starting to melt."

She tossed the bag to a still skeptical Rhodie and rejoined Annie. "*Now* we're ready." She grinned. "Let's go."

They dodged muddy ruts and boggy holes until they reached the end of the clearing and stepped into the mouth of the trail. Loblolly pine had succeeded in crowding out most of the sweet gum and oak along the edges, and underbrush threatened to overtake the sandy path. Bertha led the way, stopping occasionally to hold back a droopy pine bough or step on a vine laced with stickers so Annie could pass.

The summer sun in Jefferson blazed high and white-hot, but in the shorter, overcast days of winter, old Sol hovered in the sky like a dollop of fresh-churned butter. They made their way deeper into thick vegetation where the meager light began to lose its battle with the thick cover of trees and a cloudy sky.

As the forest dimmed, Annie hustled a few steps closer and took Bertha's hand.

Bertha grinned and peered at her. "Are you scared?"

She nodded and licked her lips. "A bit. All that talk of murder has me skittish. I keep waiting for some poor muggins to jump out with an ax."

They both laughed.

"Want to go back?"

A determined look replaced the worried expression. "After coming this far? Not on your life, dearie. Let's go eat some chocolate."

When the track opened onto the bluff, they linked arms and crossed to the edge. Once they stretched out Bertha's shawl and settled on the ground under a spreading oak, Annie seemed to relax and enjoy the view. They broke out the soft, squishy candy and divided a piece, laughing at the gooey mess it left on their fingers.

Bertha felt deliciously naughty reclining under wide-open sky in a forbidden place, nipping delicate bites from a decadent treat.

Annie seemed to have an endless supply of funny stories and epic tales. She told of her travels to faraway places and her house in Cincinnati. And about growing up in New York, though a shadow passed over her eyes when she mentioned her parents, as well as each time she mentioned Abraham Roth.

She described Edward R. Rice's production of *Evangeline* on Broadway so well Bertha could almost see the spouting whale, the dancing cow, and James S. Maffit's performance as the Lone Fisherman.

Annie paused to take a breath and glanced across at Bertha. "Have you ever been to the theater, sugar?"

She shook her head. "The closest I ever came was a poster on Mama's wall. It's a billboard from *The Magic Deer*, and it reads 'A Serio Comico Tragico Operatical Historical Extravaganzical Burletical Tale of Enchantment.' "

Annie laughed so hard she nearly choked on her candy. When she composed herself, she put the uneaten piece down and wiped her fingers on the grass. "Sounds like they covered all the bases."

Bertha grinned. "They didn't miss a one."

Annie scooted closer to the oak and leaned her head against the wide trunk. "Now then, darlin', how about telling me the real reason you brought me here."

Bertha stopped midbite and jerked her head around to meet

Annie's gaze. "What do you mean?"

Grinning, Annie studied the toes of her shoes. "Come on, now. Don't try to bamboozle me. I'm onto you."

"I beg your pardon?"

"Honey, you can't fool me. We're too much alike."

A surge of pleasure stole over Bertha's heart. "You think we're alike?"

Annie slid closer, took Bertha's candy, and laid it aside. "Allow me to demonstrate how much." She squared around to face Bertha and took hold of her hands. "Tell me you don't have a fire that burns inside all the time, pressing you to speak out when you don't agree with the general consensus, urging you to throw off antiquated conventions, the dictates of ceremony and social structure, and just be yourself."

Though she'd never have found such elegant words to describe her feelings, it seemed as though Annie had peeled back a layer of her skin and peered right down into her soul. She nodded dumbly.

"And tell me, little Bertha Maye, that you don't long to skip just because you feel like it, to dance a jig when no one's looking, and to run barefoot through the town square, sans bonnet, corset, or shawl."

Bertha felt undressed before Annie's wisdom and insight. "However did you know?"

Annie tapped her chest. "Because I recognize you. We're kindred spirits. And now that we have it all settled, answer my question, please. What's this all about? Why did you bring me here?"

Bertha ducked her head. "Well, you see, there's this boy. . . ." She looked up to find a knowing smile on Annie's face.

"I might've guessed. It's always a boy." She patted Bertha's hand. "Honey, you don't need my help on that subject. Why, look at you. You're lovely. Any man who can't see how wonderful you are, inside and out, doesn't deserve you."

Bertha shook her head. "I don't know what Thad sees, and that's the trouble. I go all trembly inside at the sound of his voice or the touch of his hand. But I can't tell how he feels about me."

Annie settled back and regarded her with soft gray eyes. "Well, if he's not mad about you, he's a fool."

Bertha shook her head again. "He's anything but a fool, but I don't think he wants me. I'd give anything to be like you, Annie. To have your enticing effect on men."

Annie released Bertha's hands and turned away. "Don't ever say that."

"But why? It's true. You're a splendid creature. Just looking at you makes people feel special."

Annie's laugh sounded harsh and hollow. "Is that a fact, little chicken? Well, not men. Looking at me makes men feel something else."

Warmth spread to Bertha's toes. "I know what you mean. Desire."

The lines of Annie's beautiful face turned to carved stone. "No, more than that. They feel the need to possess. To control."

It pained Bertha's heart to imagine what misdeeds had caused Annie to say such a thing. "Not all men. My papa would never treat a woman like that."

Annie smiled, but it didn't erase the hard lines. "Then I need to meet your papa. If it's true, he'd be the first of his kind I've run into."

"There are a lot of good men in the world. Thad's one of them."

Annie chuckled and held up her hand. "Don't be so hasty. He's too green to determine that yet. Let's give him a few years. Now tell me about your Thad."

They dwelled at length on Bertha's favorite topic. She described Thad in glowing terms–tall, with shoulders so broad she couldn't see around him, dark brown eyes, and sandy hair. A quick smile and rumbling laugh. She told Annie she'd been in love with Thad since the day Abel and Leona Bloom moved him into Jefferson. She shared that she longed to be his wife, said she knew in her heart he felt the same but something held him back.

"And I'm running out of time. He's leaving town."

"Leaving? Why?"

Bertha broke eye contact and stared at the ground. "College. He's going away to school."

"Oh, Bertha. When?"

Her voice broke when she answered. "I don't know for sure. Soon."

Annie picked up her hands and squeezed them. "I have no quick answers for you, honey." Annie's sincere gaze pierced Bertha's heart. "But I promise you this. I'll do my best to come up with a plan."

CHAPTER 6

A strong breeze kicked up, howling through the cut below and sweeping over the face of the water in a fury. Bertha watched it sway the oak and tangle the tops of the pine overhead while the branches complained aloud with ghostly groans and creaks. The brisk wind was the sort that ushered in a hard rain, so it seemed likely the gathering dark clouds on the far horizon were the cause of all the fuss.

Annie had stretched out on the shawl on her back and closed her eyes. She remained quiet for so long, Bertha thought she'd fallen asleep, until she spoke.

"Are you afraid to die?"

Bertha rolled toward her. "Mercy! What sort of question is that?"

Annie peeked at her from under her long lashes. "The nosy sort, I'm sure. But, well. . .are you?"

"Um, a little, I guess."

"Come on. You have to be more than a little. Isn't everyone?"

Bertha giggled. "Not everyone. My mama says she's scared of the process, but not what comes after."

Annie turned to her side and leaned up on her elbow. "But who's to say what that is?"

Bertha blinked. "You're joking, right?"

When Annie shook her head, Bertha knew she should proceed with caution. Raised by a Christian family in a Christian community, it seemed impossible to her that a person might not know and believe the Bible.

Before she could respond, Annie pressed her again. "So you're not absolutely terrified of death?"

Bertha swallowed hard and weighed her words. "I guess I feel the same as Mama. I don't want to suffer in death, but once it's over, I'll suffer no more."

Annie leaned back and rested her arm over her eyes. "Oh, I see. You're religious." The tone of her voice told Bertha that Annie considered "religious" as distasteful as warts.

"If by that you mean someone who believes the Bible, then yes, I am. Very much so."

Annie sat up and stared at the far bank while her tortured eyes revealed a struggle inside. Without warning, she shot to her feet and began to wrestle with something behind her. When she wiggled all over and then stepped out of her bustle, Bertha recoiled in shock.

"What on earth?"

Annie held the bustle up before Bertha's disbelieving eyes. "I can't abide this thing another second," she cried and then hurled it over the edge of the bluff.

Bertha stared in stunned surprise before she stood up and unfastened hers, as well. With an Indian whoop, she spun it overhead before letting it fly. They raced to the edge and watched the current carry the offending garments out of sight.

"Oh, Annie, I've always wanted to do that."

Annie beamed. "Well, darlin', now you have. Will you be in trouble when you go home without it?"

"From whom? Mama won't even notice. She still wears pantalets." Bertha had a sudden inspiration. "Now these infernal things." She leaned against the oak, unbuttoned her shoes, and slipped them off. Then she reared back as if about to fling them over.

Annie covered her face and squealed. "You wouldn't dare!"

Bertha sagged and tossed the pumps on the ground behind her. "You're right. I don't dare. As much as I'd love to see them floating downstream."

They giggled their way back to the shawl and slumped to the ground.

Annie sprawled on her back and sighed. "Now isn't this better? I have to say, though the bustle's a nuisance, the Basque bodice is worse. It wasn't enough to make the contraption so tight a girl can't breathe, they had to go and sew in rigid bones. I'd swear it was invented by a man." She laughed and rolled her eyes at Bertha. "Or spawned by the devil himself."

Bertha dropped her gaze and sat upright.

Behind her, Annie grew silent. Then she sat up, too, and touched Bertha's shoulder. "Did I say something to offend you?"

Bertha turned. "I'm not offended. Just surprised. We don't jest about the devil in our house."

Annie gave an uneasy laugh. "But that's silly, isn't it?"

"It's not silly at all. The devil is nothing to make fun about. We aren't frightened of him or anything, but we're sure not on speaking terms."

Annie laughed again, this time in earnest. "You think he's real?"

"Sure he's real."

Still in a frivolous mood, Annie held up one finger. "Oh, wait. Of course he's real. In fact, I've met him in person. I found him aimlessly roaming the lobby of Niblo's Garden during a revival production of *Seven Sisters*. I guess he was awaiting the last curtain call before taking the demon sisters back home to hell."

The loud Annie, the abrasive, boisterous Annie, was back, and Bertha didn't like it. She turned away and covered her ears. "Stop it. Don't make jokes. It's not funny."

She waited until Annie hushed laughing before raising her head to look. Annie sat and quietly stared at her, a puzzled look on her face. "It's absurd, Bertha. There's no such thing."

"Yes, there is. And it's serious business. Such matters aren't to be dallied with outside God's protection. Scripture says it like this. . . ." She leaned closer and lowered her voice the way Rhodie had earlier. 'Be sober, be vigilant; because your adversary the devil, as a roaring lion, walketh about, seeking whom he may devour.' "

Annie shuddered. "It says that?" She looked over Bertha's shoulder and then behind her. "That gives me gooseflesh."

Bertha felt guilty about scaring her. "Don't worry, Annie. There's a terrible end in store for him and all the workers of iniquity."

Annie stared back at Bertha with blank, hollow eyes. "Let's not talk about it anymore, please."

"Sure, if that's what you want. You brought it up, remember?"

"And I regret it." She glanced around anxiously. "Bertha, how long have we been here?"

"I can't say. Why?"

"I don't know. It suddenly seems as if a long time has passed."

Bertha gazed through the trees at the sun. "Oh my, it sure does."

"How much time, do you think?"

"An hour, at least."

Annie gathered her skirts about her and stood up. "Oh, Bertha. I think it's been more than an hour. Much more." She walked to the edge of the thicket and peered down the trail. "Where's Mose? He said he'd send Rhodie. We need to get back to town. Abe's sure to be awake by now, and he'll be wondering where I am." She clutched the sides of her head and moaned. "Why did I come out here? Whatever was I thinking?"

Bertha got the impression it wasn't the first time Annie had asked herself that question, or the first time her reckless nature had caused her grief. The way her face paled and panic crowded her eyes, she also gathered Annie feared Abraham Roth more than any threat of the devil.

"Bertha, I'm going. I can't wait for Mose."

Bertha stood and brushed off her backside. "It's too far. Let's wait a bit longer."

"No, I can't." She paced from the woods to the edge of the bluff. "You don't understand."

As if on cue, the sun dropped behind a cloud and the wind stilled. The trees and shrubs surrounding them seemed to lean close with Bertha to hear Annie's explanation, but the only sound was the whisper of the water below. The once-cheery spot had become the gloomy site of Mose's murderous story.

Annie swept past her and started up the trail. "That's it. I'm going right now."

Bertha hurriedly fastened her shoes and snatched up the shawl. "Wait, I'll go with you."

They struggled through the brush, this time with Annie in the lead. Bertha dodged swinging limbs and hurdled stickers in Annie's wake. They came onto a group of vultures huddled over a hapless meal. As the two approached, the birds abandoned their feast and took flight with a flutter of wings that startled Bertha but didn't even slow Annie's gait. She stumbled just ahead, muttering frantic words to herself, which Bertha heard in bits and pieces.

Bertha wished they could go back under the tree and recapture the merry mood. She knew she should ask what had Annie so upset, but she feared the answer, because somehow she already knew. So she plodded along behind her and said nothing.

When they broke into the clearing, Mose's rig lumbered toward them in the distance. Annie charged toward it, and Bertha followed.

"Where were you?" Annie demanded when they came within shouting distance.

"Sorry, ma'am," he called. "We got stuck."

He pulled alongside and tipped his hat, the only piece of cloth on his body not covered in muck. "Thought we'd be spending the night out in the woods until Julius Ney happened along in his oxcart." He wiped his sweat-beaded face with a handkerchief, smearing all the spots on his face, except for the freckles, into a pale muddy mask. He jerked his finger toward the back. "Nothing less than a team of oxen could've hauled us out with a load like that weighing us down."

The wood was stacked so high, Bertha didn't know whether to laugh or console the poor horse.

Mose saw the look on her face and hurried to defend himself. "You heard me say I still had three loads to get. We're running short on daylight. I was trying to make up for lost time."

Rhodie sat pouting on the seat. Muddy water had recolored her blue overalls and bright auburn hair to a dull grayish brown. "I told you not to cross that ditch, Mose. I knew we were bound to bog down." She raised her head long enough to scorch him with her eyes. "You don't never listen to me."

As if to prove her point, Mose ignored his sister. "I should be headed into town with this cypress, Bertha, but I figured we'd best come and fetch you."

Annie brought her hand down on the side rail so hard it had to hurt. "Let's go, then. Stop all this messing about."

"Sure thing, Miss Annie. Only. . ."

"Only nothing. Turn this thing around and let me get on."

Mose flicked the reins and spun around so tightly that Bertha held her breath until he straightened out again. She could just see Rhodie, Mose, and the wood becoming an oversized game of jackstraws in the center of the narrow road. When he pulled alongside them again, Annie headed straight for the tailgate.

Mose's eyes widened, and he stood up. "Wait, Miss Annie. Don't."

She stopped with her hand on the latch. "Why not?"

He shook his head. "If you open that, you'll be high-jumping logs. Besides, there ain't no room for a passenger now. Not in the bed, at least. Ain't safe." He inclined his head toward the buckboard seat. "And only room for one more up here."

Bertha watched while Annie figured it out.

When the truth dawned, she gasped and covered her mouth. "Oh no. Oh, Bertha."

Bertha placed an arm around her shoulders and walked her to the front of the rig. "You go on ahead. I'll come later."

"No, I couldn't."

"Yes, you can. You have to."

"But it's going to rain."

Bertha patted Annie's back. "Don't worry. I'll be fine. Mose will come right back, and when he does, he'll find me even closer because I'll be walking."

Mose scrambled down to help her, but Annie didn't wait. She lifted her skirts and clambered aboard before Mose could offer his arm. He jerked his gaze from her exposed legs and then leaned to check the load's balance.

Annie turned to wave her hand at him. "Leave that, Mose. Just get me back to town. And hurry!"

CHAPTER 7

Lightning, visible between the trees on the high bank of the bayou, prowled across the lowering sky. Standing on the bank, Thad did a slow count to five before thunder echoed over the tops of the tall cypress.

In the distance, T-Bone Taylor stopped paddling long enough to sit up straight on his seat and gaze toward the gathering clouds. Then he dipped his oar with renewed vigor while shouting to his little brother seated at the opposite end of the boat. Thad couldn't make out the words, but it became obvious what he said when Beau bent his shoulders to the paddle and dug in.

Thad nudged Charlie. "That storm is about a mile away. Looks like they're bound to get wet."

Charlie chuckled. "And all their loot, too. I hope that pilfered 'backy's in a tin, or tomorrow they'll be spreading it in the sun."

Thad joined in the laughter. "I heard there ain't nothing worse than soggy tobacco. Too smoky–if you can keep it lit."

Charlie peered up at him. "You ever smoke, Thad?"

Thad shook his head. "Never had a use for it." He looked back at the water.

The boys had rowed almost out of sight but still had a long way to go to reach their own dock. And the dark, paunchy clouds inched closer. Several fat droplets pelted the layer of pine needles at Charlie's feet with a muted *thwack*. Time to go.

Thad gathered the fishing poles then jerked his head at Charlie. "It'd be downright foolish to stand laughing at the Taylor boys while the same fate swirls our way. Let's get going before we're struck by lightning."

Charlie nodded and fell in behind him. They reached the top of the incline and hustled toward the spot where they'd tied their horses. On the way, Charlie kept up a panting discourse, and his topic made Thad weak in the knees. "So what did Bertha say when you told her you're leaving?"

Thad batted branches out of his way as he weaved through the slim, meandering trunks of a sapling grove. He dreaded answering, so he took his time.

Charlie took hold of his arm and hauled him around. "You haven't told her."

The flat statement held the same disbelieving tone Thad had endured from his conscience all week. He leaned his head down and massaged his brow. "There's nothing you can say to me that I haven't already shouted at myself."

Charlie took off his hat and dashed it against his leg. "Except maybe this—Sunday's the day after tomorrow, and then you'll be gone. Bertha will be looking for you, but she won't find you, will she? I hate to state the obvious, my friend, but you're out of time."

Thad turned pleading eyes to Charlie. "Tell me what to do." He paced the clearing, his booted feet causing a riot of sound in the blanket of dry leaves. "Charlie, I'm convinced I haven't told her yet because telling would make it real. And I just don't see how I'm going to leave that girl behind."

Charlie ducked the swinging poles slung over Thad's shoulder then grabbed them out of his hand on the next pass. "Why don't you ask her to wait for you?"

Thad shook his head. "Don't think I haven't considered it. But it wouldn't be fair. To Bertha."

"Don't Bertha deserve the chance to decide for herself?"

"There's more to consider. Her papa would never agree to such a long engagement."

"Marry her, then. Before you leave."

Thad stopped pacing and faced him. "I can't take a new bride with me to military school. And as hard as it will be to leave her now, it would be impossible if we were hitched." He turned on his heels and set off again in the direction of the horses. "I've thought this thing through, and I don't see any other way. I have to leave Bertha, and it's twisting my mind. I think about her every second of the day. I hear her voice in my head. I see her face around every corner."

"Hmm. Is that right? Say, Thad—"

"I tell you, the whole thing is driving me mad."

"Um, Thad?"

Irritation spiked through him. Clearly Charlie had no inkling of how Thad felt or he would allow no diversion from the topic at hand. "Heavens, man! Don't you see I'm in pain here? What is it?"

Charlie cleared his throat. "I'm thinking I must be a little smitten with Bertha myself."

Thad stopped so fast that Charlie ran into him. He turned on his friend, his back as stiff as a picket, and took him by the front of his shirt. "Why would you say such a fool thing?"

Charlie pointed past his shoulder. "Because I'm starting to see her, too."

Thad whirled and followed the direction Charlie pointed. The fleeting figure of a young woman came up the road in the distance, her image flickering as she passed in and out of sight between the trees and high brush. He might've discounted it as a vision, except Charlie saw her, too.

Thad stared hard at the woman's face. "You're right. It is Bertha. What the devil's she doing way out here, and on foot?"

Charlie nudged him. "There's only one way to find out. Come on."

Charlie walked fast toward the road, and Thad followed. They reached it just as the clouds started to make good on their threat and the occasional plump raindrop became a scattered shower.

Bertha, facing down with her hands up to shield her hair, picked up speed. She hurried their way, very distressed by the look of her, and didn't seem to see them yet. Thad cupped his hands around his mouth to call out to her when she raised her head and looked about, likely searching for shelter. Her gaze fell on Thad and Charlie, and she halted, staring as if unable to believe her eyes.

"Stay there, Bertha," Thad called. "We're coming."

He rushed to his horse and mounted in one fluid leap then whirled and rode hard in Bertha's direction. Drawing even with her, he slowed and reached for her hand. She latched on and allowed him to swing her up behind him. Thad felt her arms go around his waist and her cheek rest against his back, and he tasted bliss.

It seemed the space of a heartbeat from the time Bertha saw Thad until he pulled her onto his horse. She sat sidesaddle on the back of the galloping filly, clinging to Thad for all she was worth. The rain came down in sheets now, and she fought the improper urge to crawl up under his shirt. Instead, she cuddled close against the heat of his back and closed her eyes.

The rumbling thunder overhead, pounding hooves beneath her, and the rapid beat of Thad's heart against her face made her feel giddy and reckless. She had no notion where he might be taking her, or why. Such earthly details held no merit. She wanted only to cry out for Saint Peter to open wide the Pearly Gates, because surely the mare would carry them straight into heaven.

Too soon the road to Beulah Land became the trail to Crawford Street when Thad reined firmly to the right and into Julius Ney's pasture. The horse roared up the path to Mr. Ney's barn.

Bertha clung so tightly to Thad she feared for his ribs, but any less of a grip and she'd spring off into mud and certain disaster. No matter how marshy the surface, the harsh summer sun had baked a brick-hard crust on Jefferson's soil. Bertha doubted she'd bounce if she went down.

With Charlie fast on their heels, Thad galloped the horse past the barricaded front of the structure and around back where the wide doors faced the open fields between the barn and the main house.

In the distance, Bertha saw Mr. Ney running from the outhouse, suspenders down off his shoulders and shirttail flapping. He waved a permissive hand in their direction just as they ducked beneath the threshold and dove inside.

Thad eased Bertha to the ground and dismounted. Charlie led his horse to a post in the corner and tied him up. Thad did the same with the mare. When Charlie turned, Bertha couldn't help but laugh. Mud spattered him from head to toe in big gray blotches like the markings on a dappled hound.

Thad followed Bertha's gaze to Charlie then halted and stared. "Followed a mite close to my heels, didn't you, old friend?"

Charlie looked down at himself and grinned. "Never intended to follow. I was trying to gain the lead." He brushed at his clothes. "I'll think better of it next time."

Thad took the handkerchief from around his neck and began blotting raindrops from Bertha's head and shoulders. She watched him while he worked, his face close and intent on the task. When he dried her to his satisfaction, he took a rolled-up blanket from behind his saddle, shook it out, and spread it on the hay. Then he took her arm and led her to it. "Sit on this side. It's still mostly dry." After he saw her well settled, he sat beside her on the blanket, a shy smile on his lips.

He loves me.

The truth of it washed over Bertha, making her feel weak and warm, as if her bones were melted butter. There'd be no more wondering, hoping, praying. Thad loved her, all right, and now she knew.

His actions hadn't confirmed her belief that he cared–any gentleman would do the same for a lady in distress–it was more the manner in which he went about his ministrations. The way he touched her, led her, succored her, with the tenderness a mother might show toward a beloved child. These things gave Thad away, no matter how distant he kept his feelings or how hard he tried to deny them.

Thank You, God.

"Bertha?"

She averted her gaze. She'd been staring. "Yes?"

"Are you cold? I can close the doors."

She shook her head and met his eyes again. A water droplet found its way past his hairline and started a slow trek down his face, pulling her attention to his tanned cheek. Her finger twitched with the urge to touch it. "I'm fine. No need to fret."

He grew suddenly stern. "What in the dickens are you doing out in the woods by yourself? You might've been lost or shot by a hunter." He stopped and raised his brows. "Say, how did you get here anyway?"

"Mose brought me."

His face iced over. "Moses Pharr left you standing in the woods in a thunderstorm? I'll need to say a few words to that bump-headed boy."

She held up her hand. "There's no need, Thad. He's coming right back for me. He promised."

Thad looked skeptical, so she tried to soften him with a smile. "He should be here any minute, in fact."

Charlie loped over to join them, a welcome distraction. He dropped onto the blanket beside Thad and reclined his lanky body, placing both arms behind his head for a pillow. "Sure is cozy in here." He stretched and closed his eyes. "Wouldn't take me a minute to fall asleep."

Thad nudged him. "Wouldn't take you a minute to fall asleep if you were balanced on a broom handle." He winked over at Bertha. "I hear tell Charlie slept his way through the last two years of school."

Charlie poked him back. "Don't believe everything you hear, pilgrim. More like the last three." They laughed together, and then Charlie turned on his side as if ready to demonstrate the virtue of his statement.

Bertha watched him turn and shared a smirk with Thad. But the smile that began as shared amusement blossomed into an intimate meeting of eyes and soul. The encounter caused Bertha's breath to catch. Flustered, she turned away to exhale.

When her breathing settled, she tried to ease the strain between them with small talk. "Mr. Ney did a right fine job on this barn, didn't he?" She let her gaze follow the neat row of new planks along the wall to the sturdy overhead beams. Above their heads, a wide hayloft seemed bursting at the seams with bales, and matching tied bundles lined the walls on the floor.

The smell of fresh-milled pine and cut hay filled the room, mixed with the odor of wet clothes, damp earth, and the headiest scent of all, Thad's hair balm. It smelled of nameless spice and pomade. Mingled with the odor of soap on his cheeks from his shaving mug, it wove an intoxicating halo about him. She grew hesitant to turn his way, because when their eyes met, she felt herself sway toward him against her will.

She stole a sly glance and discovered Thad seemed rattled, too. He focused on his hands, which wouldn't stay still in his lap. She expected at any minute he might sit on them.

Instead, he reached for her hand, pulling her shy fingers with his determined ones, gently tugging until her hand was close enough to gather up and squeeze. The simple gesture made her stomach lurch. The warmth and pressure of his strong hand around hers thrilled her and related how he felt without his saying a word.

"Bertha, there's something I—"

Sloshing footsteps outside cut him off. Mr. Ney appeared in the door of the barn with a feed sack held over his head.

"You kids all right in here?"

Thad struggled to his feet. "Mr. Ney, sir. Yes, we're fine. We just ducked in to wait out the storm." He jabbed a finger toward the slumbering Charlie. "The three of us, I mean. Sure hope you don't mind."

Mr. Ney stepped inside and shook the water from his sack.

"The missus sent me out here to fetch you." He glanced behind him at the pouring rain. "Says you're welcome to sit in the kitchen until this thing blows over."

For some reason, Thad had become as edgy as a cat the moment Mr. Ney appeared. He smoothed one hand through his wet hair and shook his head. "No disrespect intended, sir, but we'll stay put until it slacks off, if it's all right with you. We'd just repay her kindness by tracking half of Texas onto her floors."

Mr. Ney shot a look toward Charlie, who hadn't moved. Then his eyes swept to Bertha. "That all right with you, child?"

Bertha gave him a wide-eyed stare. "Why, yes, sir."

Mr. Ney cleared his throat. "All right, then. I guess that'll be acceptable. But leave this door open, Thad." His attention returned to Bertha, and he pointed behind him at the house. "We'll be just inside. . .if you need us for anything."

Bertha wondered why Mr. Ney acted so stern about such a trifling thing as sitting outside in the barn. She guessed she might never understand the ways of men. She offered Mr. Ney her brightest smile. "Give my best to the missus, won't you?"

He said he would, then with one more weighted look toward Thad, covered his head with the sack and darted for the house. Bertha giggled at the nervous look on Thad's face as he watched him leave.

"I can't imagine how difficult it is to be a man." She had his attention. Likely more by the way she squinted up at him than by her words.

"What do you mean by that?"

"Oh, just that men spend so much time guarding the virtue of women that they forget to safeguard their own."

His mouth drooped in shock. "Bertha Biddie. What a forward thing to say."

"Oh, pooh. It's only the truth. Annie would agree if she were here."

When Thad looked blank, she remembered he didn't know about her new friend. She scurried up and dashed to his side.

"I didn't tell you, did I? I've met the most wonderful person. Her name's Annie Moore, and she's lovely. And elegant. And mysterious. And ever so wise. I've never seen anything like her. I'll wager you haven't, either."

She paused to gulp air then continued. "In a very short time we've become fast friends. Annie's offered to help me with–" She felt her cheeks heat up, so she lowered her lids. "With a most vexing dilemma." Her voice dropped to a whisper. "Annie's just the one to help me, too. I know she is."

She found his eyes again. "I do want you to meet her. Oh, promise you will."

Thad took her by the shoulders and laughed down at her. "Whoa there, sugar. Dig in your spurs. I'll meet Annie twice if it means that much to you."

A cloud fell over Bertha's excitement, heavier than the one over Julius Ney's barn. "The only thing is, I don't know when I'll see her again. The last time I saw her, she was very upset."

Thad's brows puckered in the middle. "What about?"

She gazed up at him, trying to decide if she should speak the whole truth. After all, it was Annie's affair and none of her own. So despite the concern in his big brown eyes, Bertha made up her mind not to tell. "I believe Annie's in terrible trouble. That's all I'm at liberty to say. And I don't know how to help her."

Thad lifted her chin. "I can't imagine what sort of trouble might put such a worrisome look on your face, but there's no trouble in the world bigger than God."

His words struck Bertha's heart like a thunderbolt and kindled fire in her muddled mind. "Oh, Thad, that's it! Annie needs God's help, not mine." She pulled him low and kissed him on the cheek, surprising him by the look on his face. "It's so clear to me now. I know just what to do."

They heard the sound of an approaching wagon at the same time and moved to the door. Voices shouted Bertha's name from the road at the end of Mr. Ney's lane.

"Bertha!" The deep bass bawl had to be Mose.

"Bertha Biddie, where are you?" The high, tinny mewl belonged to Rhodie.

"See! I told you they'd come back for me."

She started out the door, but Thad clutched her arm and pulled her back. "Bertha, wait. I'll take you home."

"I'm not going home. I need to see Annie first."

"Then I'll take you to see Annie."

"It's out of your way."

He held up one hand. "I don't mind. Honest."

It sounded tempting but made no sense. Thad's clothes were soaked through. He needed to get straight home before he came down with a fever. She shook her head. "There's no reason to put you out. Those two are here for me, and they're headed straight into town."

The rain had stopped, but heavy drips fell from the eaves over the barn door. She waited, timing her exit to avoid getting splashed on the head.

Thad moved up behind her, his voice unsettled. "Bertha, there's something I haven't told you."

"We'll talk later. I promise. Don't forget you still have to meet Annie." She turned and patted his arm. "Good-bye, Thad. And thank you ever so much for your advice." Darting out the door, she ran around the barn just as Mose and Rhodie rolled past.

"Wait! I'm here!"

Rhodie whirled on the seat. "Stop, Mose. There she is. Bertha, where were you? We've looked everywhere."

Bertha pointed back at Julius Ney's barn. "I took shelter in there. It started to rain."

Mose gave her a disgusted look. "I guess we know that." He and Rhodie sat atop the unprotected buckboard as wet as two bedbugs on wash day.

Bertha pressed a hand to her mouth to hide her smile. "Let's get going, then. Before it starts up again."

Rhodie moved aside to let Bertha board then elbowed her brother. "Don't get stuck this time."

Mose clucked at the horse and pulled away.

Bertha looked back to find Thad standing outside the barn with a curious look on his face—part longing, part desperation, with a touch of sadness around the edges. She leaned to peer closer, but the jostling wagon had put too much distance between them. She raised her hand in a last merry wave, but Thad didn't wave back.

As she watched, Charlie came around the side of the barn and joined him. He patted Thad on the back with what could only be described as sympathy. Charlie's gesture was the last thing she saw before the two men fell out of sight around the bend of a tree-lined curve.

CHAPTER 8

Sarah leaned closer to the window, so near her breath fogged the glass. She stretched to her tiptoes to peer over the misty spot and checked the road again. No sign of Henry. When he first slipped out, without angry words or slammed doors, her shame and pride had pronounced him weak. With the passage of time, his meekness turned to strength against the memory of her railing fit.

She traded her nightdress and shawl for the torn dress and boots and set out to find him. She soon learned he didn't ride away, because Dandy stood in his stall munching hay. The indisputable sight of the big gray mule meant the wagon would be in its place. Though Henry's rage may have given him the strength to pull it, he'd lack the inclination.

He wasn't in the fields. She roamed the yard and peered in every direction, at first sashaying in a casual way, stealing furtive glances in case he lurked somewhere and watched. The longer she searched, the more scared she became, fear turning her easy sway into determined strides.

Though it made no sense, he had vanished. Unless the Lord had come for his children and left her to stew in her sins, Henry had departed the place on foot—walked when he had a perfectly fine means of transportation lollygagging in the barn.

After one more rambling search of the place, Sarah stumbled back inside to begin her vigil. A glance at the stove reminded her she had placed a towel over the corn bread and set the beans off the fire a good two hours ago. She lifted the lid and stared into the pot. The mingled odor of pintos and ham hock wafted up. Her favorite food. Another day she'd give in to the grumble in her stomach and dish up a bowl, but dread had taken her appetite. She needed to put them away before they spoiled—*Lord knows we have no food to waste*—but she couldn't muster the strength to care. Henry was all that mattered. She had to find him, confess her sorrow over how she had treated him. Again.

Her mind settled, Sarah pulled off the blue gingham dress just long enough to sew up the seam she'd ripped under the arm in angry impatience. Another casualty of her unbridled temper. If she hadn't stripped down and hopped into bed in the middle of the day to pout, she'd never have torn her dress. She held it up, surprised to see a neat row of stitches despite her haste. Slipping it overhead, with more care this time, she ran out the door, without stopping to return the sewing kit to the drawer in the console table or to store the corn bread and beans.

Dandy stood in the same place she'd found him earlier, pulling lazy bites of hay from a handcart in the corner. She slid the bridle onto his head then jerked him away from the hay and over to the saddle rack hanging on the wall. Sarah's size and Dandy's interest in the hay made the task hard, but she got him saddled and led him from the barn, where Henry kept a stool near the fence just for her. She stepped on it and slipped her foot in the stirrup then swung up on Dandy's back and gave him a swat. "Let's go, mule."

Dandy heaved a rebellious sigh against the straps on his belly and listed to the side. Sarah knew what came next. The ornery cuss would side-step to the fence and try his best to rake her off, a trick he knew not to play on Henry. She outsmarted him by lifting her leg just in time, but it was a close call.

"Blast you, Dandy! We got no time for your shenanigans today. You best smarten up and recall who feeds you. If you don't help me find Henry, I'll let you starve, I swear it."

As if he understood every word, the mule took off down the lane, lit out for the road, and gave her no more trouble on the way into town.

The distance to Jefferson was walkable for sure but an easier ride, and Henry had no reason to go there. They only rode in earlier in the day on account of his notion to buy her a treat, the foolish idea that started the whole dreary mess. Common sense said he would be down by the bayou, skipping stones across the water or lying sprawled under a tree to pout. No matter how unreasonable, something led her straight to Jefferson as fast as Dandy could plod.

Once there, Sarah had no idea where to look. She relaxed the reins and let Dandy follow his nose. She hardly expected him to snuffle the ground for his master's scent like old Dickens would've done before he led her straight to Henry. But she reckoned Dandy could put forth more effort than it took to follow the same route he trod every trip into town. She couldn't rightly blame him. It did seem like just another trip to Stilley's to trade skins. She closed her eyes and allowed herself the luxury of pretending it was.

Her eyes flew open when a high-pitched squeal from nearby startled her. Dandy, too, by the way he flinched. She looked toward the grating sound and found it came from Charles Gouldy's sister, Isabella, her face puffy and red, her hair a wild nest of tangles. A strange man, somebody's husband no doubt, had Belle pressed against the wall in a nearby alley. Sarah wondered how much he had paid for a bit of time with her.

Belle turned her painted face toward Sarah as she passed. Her eyes were glazed and her mouth a big red smear. She offered a brazen smile. "Afternoon, Sarah."

Embarrassed, Sarah turned away. Dandy passed up the alley just as the man pulled Belle deeper into the shadows. Sarah shuddered. For all her problems, she wouldn't trade places with Isabella Gouldy if they threw in fame and fortune to sweeten the deal.

Up ahead, Jennie Simpson stepped off Lafayette Street onto

Polk, looking none too spry. She wore a stiff black dress and white apron, but the woman inside the dress had lost her starch. Doc Turner insisted all his help wear the same sort of clothes, except the men, who pranced around in black bow ties and knickers. Most likely Jennie had spent the morning changing beds and cleaning floors behind Doc Turner's paying guests over at Brooks House.

The thought of it caused guilt to twang in Sarah's heart like a chord from a busted fiddle. She knew if not for Henry, she'd be a chambermaid at Brooks House, too. Or maybe the Commercial Hotel. She worked as hard as anyone, but when she smoothed fresh sheets on a bed, she and Henry slid between them that night. And when she wiped a table and served food, she got to sit right down and eat. For all of her trouble, Jennie Simpson got a bent back, calloused hands, and a pitiful, pinchpenny wage. Jennie was another poor soul with whom Sarah wouldn't agree to trade fortunes.

Since her man had given her so much in life, Sarah wondered why she seemed driven to throw it all away. And why she continued to hurt him. She sighed. All roads in her mind led right back to Henry. She wished the one Dandy trudged down now would do the same.

Sarah rode up even with her friend just as she started to cross the street. "Afternoon, Jennie."

Jennie looked up at her with tired eyes. "Why, Sarah King, don't I see you in town most every day of late? Ain't you got enough at home for to keep you busy?"

She waved her hand. "Pissh! Got me more'n enough, thank you kindly. Say, you ain't seen Henry around anywhere, have you?"

Jennie gazed all about as if she expected to see him then shook her head. "Naw," she said, drawing the word out the length of Dandy's ears. "Not since yesterday." She scrunched her chubby face. "Don't see how you managed to lose a man that size. Didn't he ride in with you?"

Sarah cleared her throat. "Not this time."

"Then how'd he get here?"

Sarah avoided the question by standing up in the stirrups and making a show of searching the street. She'd be careful not to say anything more to set off Jennie's curiosity. "Don't fret yourself. I'll find him."

Jennie opened her mouth to speak, but Sarah cut her off. "Girl, you look plumb tuckered. Are you finished for the day?"

Jennie shook her head in exaggerated fashion. "Uh-uh, honey. Don't I wish? I jus' come to fetch a jar of molasses for Doc Turner's tea. He swear by it as a restorative for the blood." She rested the back of her hand on her hip. "S'pose I need some myself to get me through this day. When I get back, I still got me a mess of laundry and two more rooms to clean."

Sarah's heart went out to her. "Sound like you gon' be there most all night."

Jennie reached to stroke Dandy's neck. The old mule's coat trembled in pleasure at her touch. "Don't know why I bother to drag myself to my room some nights, when I got to be back in the main house before sunrise to start all over again."

"Forget about molasses. What you need is a good tonic. Ride out to the house, and I'll give you one made from blessed thistle. It's the best thing there is for the droops."

Jennie's eyes bulged. "You never said you practiced healing arts, Sarah."

"I know how to steep herbs and make remedies. Mama taught me. I have a store of them in fruit jars sealed with wax. Come by when you can, and I'll give you some for what ails you."

Jennie smiled as brightly as if Sarah had offered to dole out redemption. "I'll walk out in the morning a'fore I starts my day at Brooks."

Sarah nodded. "That'll be just fine. I'll look for you."

She glanced around again for Henry but caught no sign of him, so she turned her attention back to Jennie. "Doc Turner have a full house this week?"

"Jus' mostly the usual. The judge and a few more."

"Judge Armistead?"

"Tha's right. He staying a few days." Her eyes grew wide. She pressed against Dandy's side and motioned Sarah closer. "Honey, you ain't seen nothing in your whole life like what done checked into number four upstairs."

Sarah leaned farther down. "Is that right?"

Jennie rolled her eyes "Well, I ain't never seen the like. Them two be a special breed of folk."

"Which two?"

"Some highfalutin couple out of Boston, New York."

"Boston, New York?"

"That's what the gentleman say. I asked him where they come from, and he say, 'We's from Boston, New York.' "

"I thought Boston was in Massachusetts State."

"I don't know nothing 'cept what he tell me. The woman, she ain't said much. Jus' sat there and looked sorrowful. Saddest, most prettiest woman I ever laid eyes on. All done up in floozy clothes like a high-dollar coquette."

"I reckon I know just who you mean. She come into Stilley's today with Magdalena Hayes and little Bertha."

"What you mean, 'with' them?"

"I mean walking in just as big as you please, laughing and talking like long-lost friends. They left together, too."

Jennie clucked her tongue. "What they doing gallivanting about with the likes of her?"

"I can't say, but when they mamas get wind of it—and they will 'cause the whole town's talking—mercy, the fur gon' fly."

Jennie smiled. "The place I'm thinking of ain't got no fur. Missy Hayes and Missy Biddie won't sit to supper for a spell." Jennie's gaze left Sarah and fixed on something across the way. She raised her finger to point. "Looky there. I believe I found something what belongs to you."

Sarah's heart lurched. She peered back over her shoulder to find Henry standing outside of Stilley's. He gazed back at her, but she couldn't read his mood. At the sight of his dear, familiar face, shame washed over her. She lowered her eyes.

"Sarah King."

At the sound of her name, she jerked up and fixed her gaze on him.

He motioned with his head. "Come on over here."

She nodded without saying a word and turned back to Jennie. "All right, then. We'll see you in the morning. You take care, now, you hear?"

"Tha's right, you run on quick when yo' man call. I don't blame you none a'tall. I wish I had me a man to take care of me the way Henry do you." She gave a hearty laugh that jiggled her broad bodice.

Her words pricked Sarah's conscience, but she hid her shame with a bright smile. "Get you some rest, Jennie. Lord knows you need it."

"No, ma'am, not till Sunday." She had already turned to make her way up the street, so Sarah barely heard her last words. "I'll get me some rest on the Sabbath, but not a minute before. Bye, now."

Sarah turned Dandy, which wasn't hard to do now that he'd caught her husband's scent, or maybe the smell of what Henry had stashed in the wrapped package tucked under his arm. When they pulled up beside Henry, his eyes swept her face, as if searching for traces of her spiteful anger. The realization cut Sarah through the middle, especially when his shoulders eased.

They both knew what came next, and it embarrassed her. She would plead for his forgiveness. He would say she'd done nothing to forgive. She hated Henry's tolerance the most. If he'd fuss, hurl accusations, even admit how badly she'd hurt him, and then forgive, she'd feel forgiven. . .instead of unworthy.

Henry peered at the sky. "You shouldn't be here. Get on home. It's clouding up to rain."

"Ain't you coming?"

"I'll be along directly."

She knew she should just go, obey him for once like she'd vowed on their wedding day. "I don't want to go without you. I was so worried, Henry. You ain't never just took off like that." She pleaded with her eyes. "Can't you go with me now?"

He dipped his head and raised a finger toward the horizon. "Woman, them clouds are ripe. They ain't gon' hold off much longer."

"All the more reason for you to come now."

"Dandy's back can't hold us both, and you know it. Somebody be heading our way soon, and I'll hitch a ride."

"We can take turns on Dandy. Better still, I'll walk the whole way if you like. Since you already walked it once."

Henry sighed. The first sign of his dwindling patience. "Fine, Sarah. I guess I'd best go if I want any sleep tonight."

She cringed at the familiar sound of cross resignation in Henry's voice. But it didn't outweigh her relief. She needed her husband at home.

Henry opened Dandy's saddlebag and pushed the package he held deep inside. Then he took the reins from her and set off down the street leading the mule.

Sarah watched his back with a mixture of pleasure and pain. Pain because of the wide sweaty blotch on his shirt, already dry at the edges, which meant he'd walked hard and fast into town despite the sultry heat. Pleasure because he'd agreed to return home with her.

She glanced again at the white-rimmed stain. "Henry, come get up on Dandy. You've walked enough today. Your bunion must be throbbing."

He trudged ahead at a slow, steady pace. "That's all right. I'm fine."

Sarah studied his feet but saw no sign of a limp. Still. . . "I don't mind walking. Honest. I want to."

"I said no."

She bit her lip and focused her anxious energy elsewhere. "It's coming up a mighty blow sure enough. From the north, too. There'll be cold weather in behind it. I figured this heat couldn't last."

Henry raised his head to the darkening sky and mumbled a reply, but she couldn't make out his words.

She tried again. "Guess I never will get used to the mixed-up weather in Texas. In St. Louis, you don't see folks breaking a sweat in the middle of January. Most unreasonable thing I ever saw."

When Henry failed to respond, Sarah decided to hush. They made it a quarter mile in silence until curiosity won out over caution. "Say, what is it you got in this package back here?"

"It'll keep."

The tone of his voice said he'd abide no more questions on the subject, so she held her tongue. But whatever Henry had wrapped in paper and tied up with twine seemed to heat up inside the saddlebag and spread enough warmth through the bag to scorch Dandy's fur, singe the leather saddle, and light a fire in her gut.

She imagined every possibility, from the part Henry ordered for the plow to a new pair of trousers to replace his worn-out pair. He may have bought a bullwhip to keep his ornery wife in line. But knowing Henry, she doubted it.

"Sarah?"

She startled at Henry's sudden, strident voice and all but toppled from Dandy's back.

Before she could answer, he continued without turning around. "I know you'll want to talk things out like always. So if it's all the same to you, I'd rather hash it out before we get home. I need myself some peace at the house." He cleared his throat. "I mean, if it's all right with you."

She winced at Henry's guarded tone. It cast a shadow of condemnation squarely on her head. She'd heard Mama and her aunties whisper about a coarse, abusive wife who kept her husband on a short lead, carrying his dignity chained about her neck. Other husbands ridiculed such men and called them names behind their backs. The thought of herself as one of those women, of Henry as one of those men, made her blood run cold.

"We don't need to talk at all if you'd rather we didn't." Shame rendered her voice so low she wondered if Henry heard her at all.

"No, Sarah, I'd rather get it over and done with. Go on and start."

She tried to comply but found she couldn't speak. She knew her silence might anger him but found it hard to muster the will for a conversation her husband wanted over and done.

Henry glanced over his shoulder. “Fine. If the cat got your tongue, I’ll start.”

The words stunned Sarah. Henry King mostly kept his emotions dammed up tight. Getting him talking about his feelings generally took a three-day pout followed by two days of nagging. She guessed he must need peace at the house in the worst possible way.

Henry cleared his throat. “When I left the house, I had no place in mind to go. Jus’ walked without thinking. When I come to myself, I seen I’d walked all the way to town, but I wasn’t even tired. Felt like I’d done sprouted wings and flew.”

Henry put a hand back on Dandy’s nose to bring him to a stop and came around to stand at Sarah’s knee. He stared up at her without speaking at first then reached for her hands where they were clasped together over the saddle horn. “I looked up and saw I done walked a beeline to Stilley’s. Then I knew why I came to town.”

In one quick move, Henry lifted Sarah down from the mule and stood her in front of him. He clung to her hands, and his eyes bored into hers with fierce emotion. “Today I set out to give you something special to show how I feel about you, and I intend to finish the task.” He let go of her hands and reached behind her into the saddlebag.

When he came up with the package and handed it to her, Sarah frowned at him and then at the tied bundle. “What is this?”

He stifled a grin. “If you open it, you might see.”

She held his eyes for three heartbeats then got to work on the twine. Impatient with her slow and careful fingers, Henry reached to tear a hole in the paper. When Sarah lifted the other end, white fabric poured out and settled in his hands like woven snow. She jerked her eyes to her husband’s face. “What you got here, Henry King?”

His familiar smile warmed her heart. “I ain’t completely daft. . .or blind neither. I seen the way you fingered those bolts at Stilley’s.”

She wiped her palms on her skirt then held them up to receive the soft folds. Struggling to believe she really held it in her hands, she lifted the shimmering cloth in his direction. "Why would you buy me a gift after the way I treated you?"

He wrinkled his brow and gave his head a little shake. "I ain't stopped loving you, woman. I never will. No matter how you treat me."

She cringed and lowered her head. "Why'd you choose white?"

Henry moved closer and cupped her face in his nimble hand. "I know you like all them bright colors. But I sure like to see you dressed in white." He traced the line of her jaw with his finger then lifted her head with one knuckle. "It looks so nice against your skin."

His words reminded her of their conversation that morning, when he'd spoken of the first day they'd met at Lawetta Draper's backyard social and the white dress she wore. From the yearning in his eyes, he remembered, too. He nodded at the cloth. "Hope you don't mind."

She reached up on tiptoe and pressed a soft kiss to his cheek. "Not one bit." She opened the paper to tuck his gift inside but paused and rattled the package. "There's something else down in here." She tucked the fabric under her arm and then reached in and brought out a smaller parcel. She held it up. "Now what's this?"

Henry took it from her hand. "Almost forgot about that." He tore it open to reveal a small chocolate block.

Sarah squealed. "Candy, too?" She reached to grab it, but he held it just out of reach.

"Uh, uh, uh. This one I bought for me." He peeled back the clear wrapper and took a huge bite. Then he closed his eyes and threw his head back while he chewed and swallowed, his face a mask of pleasure. "Ooo-wheee! If that ain't the best thing since pure sweet honey."

Sarah lunged and tugged at his upraised arm. "Stop, now. Give it here!"

He laughed and backed away. She followed until she'd chased him in a wide circle around the mule. He finally stopped and turned.

Still holding the candy far overhead, he pinched off the tiniest bite and pressed it into her mouth. "There," he teased. "Now you know what you're missing."

The small piece delivered a strong, delightful taste, reminiscent of the potent smell and taste in the back of her throat at Stilley's. She wondered at what a full-sized bite would be like.

"Don't tease, Henry. It's mean."

A strong gust of wind bore straight down on them from out of the treetops, followed by a distant clap of thunder. Dandy laid back his ears and shuffled his feet. Sarah felt a raindrop hit the top of her head.

Henry looked to the sky then crossed to Dandy and held up the stirrup. "Climb up, Sarah. Let me get you home before your pretty cloth gets wet."

She rolled the paper around the fabric and hurried to his side. "Put it back in the saddlebag, quick."

He took the package from her and fastened it inside the leather bag then hoisted her into the saddle. He took up Dandy's reins and they started up the path.

"Good thing we almost home." Henry looked back at her with raised brows, winked, and patted his pocket where he'd stashed the candy. "A good rain might ruin my toothsome chocolate."

She waited until he glanced back again, a huge grin on his face.

"Your chocolate, is it? We'll just see about that, Henry King."

CHAPTER 9

Bertha held her shawl above her head, but it proved pointless. She surveyed the mess that made up Mose, Rhodie, and herself and stifled a laugh. Mose's battered hat hung like a woman's bonnet, channeling sheets of water past his chin. Rhodie, so drenched her eyelashes drooped in streaming tangles, sat upright next to Bertha. She had no shawl, given she wore her usual tattered overalls, no longer spattered with mud because the rain had washed them clean. Rhodie accepted the downpour, pelting her head and running off her braids in twin rivulets, the way she accepted most things—with quiet dignity.

The sky had opened up a quarter mile back, just when Bertha figured she'd make it to town high and dry. And no matter how hard Mose flicked the reins or how loudly he bellowed, the overburdened horse had given his all. A slow, lanky pace proved the most the poor creature could muster, hardly enough to save them from a good soaking, though the weather did seem to perk him up. The way his head had lifted and swung from side to side, Bertha reckoned his refusal to hurry might be on purpose, as if he were bent on taking revenge.

Mose raised his voice to be heard over the roar of the pounding rain. "We have to turn here, Bertha. Can't take you clear to town.

Our pa will be watching for us in this weather."

Rhodie picked up Bertha's hand. "Come, go home with us. You can dry off and change into something warm. Our baby sister's garb should fit you fine."

Bertha shook her head. "Just drop me by Magda's place. I need to see her anyway."

Rhodie scrunched up her face. "Are you sure?"

Bertha smiled at the wringing-wet girl. "Yes, but thanks."

They lumbered to the lane up ahead, hardly more than a rut that had been cut through the trees on each side. Overgrown branches crowded the entry, causing recent travelers to veer to the right, if the circle of tracks in the high grass were any sign. Past that point, what had been the long byway to Magda's house now appeared to be a wide, shallow lake.

Bertha placed a hand on Mose's arm. "Stop here. You'll just get stuck if you turn down there. I can walk across the pasture where the ground's higher."

Mose pulled back on the reins, and she climbed down and sloshed around to where he leaned over waiting to speak to her. "You gonna be all right? I sure don't like leaving you out here."

Bertha looked to the sky where the cloudburst had dwindled to a hard shower. The murky clouds that once swirled over their heads had slid off to the southern horizon and piled up over the town of Marshall like a billowing swarm. "It's slacked off now. Looks like it's blowing to the south."

Mose stared down at her, chubby bottom lip laced behind his top row of teeth. "Ain't you cold?" he asked, releasing it. "Feels like a norther's done snuck in behind that front."

As if to underscore his statement, a strong gust howled through, shaking the wagon and raising the hair on Bertha's neck. She wrapped her arms around herself and shivered.

Mose shook his head then turned around to dig under the seat. "Ain't we got a blanket under here somewhere, Rhodie?"

Rhodie nudged him with her shoulder. "It's wet, Mose."

Bertha pointed up the path to the tumbledown shack where

Magda lived. "Don't fret yourself, Mose. Look. I'm nearly there."

Rhodie leaned behind Mose's back to point at Bertha's shoes. "Don't see how you plan to make it in them infernal things."

Bertha looked down at her feet. The low leather pumps were soaked and filled with muck where they gaped at the ankles. Wet grass plastered the pointed toes, and rust-colored pine needles threaded the delicate buttoned straps in a scattered crisscross.

She smiled up at Rhodie. "Better than bare feet, but just barely."

Rhodie giggled. "Sounds like a limerick."

Mose nodded toward the field. "Be watchful of snakes out there." Then he faced forward and released the brake. "We'd best get going. Pa will be in a stew."

He jerked the reins, and the wheels started to roll. Without thinking, Bertha stepped back to avoid being splashed with muddy water then smiled at the futile notion.

Rhodie turned on the seat and raised her hand to the sky. "Bye, Bertha."

Bertha waved back. "Much obliged for the ride."

She waited until they'd gone a respectable distance then lifted her soggy skirt and pulled plastered petticoats away from her legs. Holding the whole sodden mess in her hands, she jumped the ditch, nearly landing on her bottom on the other side. She fought for balance then picked her way to higher ground, came close to losing her shoe in a soft spot, and shuddered when more thick mud spilled over the instep.

Halfway across the pasture, dodging crawdad mounds and roving clusters of homeless ants, she wished she'd been less stubborn and taken Rhodie up on the offer of shelter and dry clothes. Or Thad's offer to take her home, for that matter. He'd have seen her straight to her doorstep, dry as gunpowder. And it might've given him the chance to say what seemed to be gnawing at him.

The last few yards to Magda's house put her in floodwater up to her ankles. She thought of her new bronze heels and tried not to imagine the look on Mama's face when she saw them, but at least the water sifted the sludge from between her toes. Thankfully, there was no sign of snakes.

The door opened before she reached it, and Magda's mama appeared on the stoop with a blanket. She rushed to Bertha the second she stepped up on the porch, enveloped her in scratchy wool, and hauled her inside as if pulling her to safety.

"Ach, Bert'a! Your *mutter* knows you're out in *das schmuddelwetter*?"

Bertha drew the cover closer and stamped her feet before she entered the house. "Foul weather, indeed, Mrs. Hayes. Bless you for taking in a poor drowned wretch."

Mrs. Hayes scurried to the hearth, scooted a low stool in front then waved Bertha closer. "*Bitte kommen.* Sit by the fire, *kleine*. Ve roast dem feets lest you're taken vit fever."

Bertha smiled. *Kleine* meant "little one," yet Magda's mama stood no taller than Bertha, her body as slight as a hummingbird. And the braided blond ropes that crowned her head made up a fair portion of any weight she carried.

Tiny Gerta Fricks had traded the home country and her German culture for big Jacob Hayes of Nacogdoches before coming to settle in Marion County. Magda took after her big-boned papa's side of the family and could easily lift her mama straight off the ground. Magda's papa came from mixed culture himself, his father a Texan, his mother a Sicilian immigrant.

For the first time, Bertha noticed Magda at the stove. She stood with her back to them and seemed in no hurry to turn around. Bertha knew she would still be miffed because they called her a talebearer. But Magda's mishandling of a confidence reminded Bertha of a quote she'd read by C. C. Colton: "*None are so fond of secrets as those who do not mean to keep them.*" Only Magda never betrayed a trust on purpose. It seemed the weight of the secret pressed the words right out of her mouth.

Still, Magda was Bertha's dearest friend, and she felt bound to make amends. She sidled up behind her. "Hey there."

No answer. Magda lowered her left hip and shifted her body away.

Bertha tried again. "Say, what's in the pot? Sure smells tasty."

Magda paused her stirring and raised her face to the ceiling. "It's sauerkraut, Bertha. You hate sauerkraut."

"Sauerkraut? Why, fancy that. I'd never have guessed." She moved a bit closer. "You must've done something clever to make it smell so nice."

Magda didn't speak. Just went back to pushing the pungent shreds of cabbage around a skillet with a broad wooden spoon.

"Come, Bert'a. Sit and take off dem shoes, *liebchen.* Dey are soaked clean through."

Bertha waved toward Mrs. Hayes, her attention still on Magda's back. "Yes, ma'am. One second, please." She took a step closer to the stove. "I came to talk to you, Magda. It's real important. Come sit by the hearth for a spell, won't you?"

Mrs. Hayes scurried to her daughter and took the spoon from her hand. "Dis kraut is done, Magdalena. You von't make it any more so by vorrying de life out of it." She set the spoon on a saucer and shoved the heavy pan to the back of the stove. "Go now, *Tochter.* Stoke the fire for your friend and sit vit her." The tiny woman nudged Magda aside with her hip. "Dat's right, go on. Go help Bert'a vit dem shoes. And fetch hot vahter for her feet."

Magda scooted to the side at her mama's urging but stood like a headstrong statue, as rigid as the cast iron stove.

Bertha gathered the blanket tighter under her chin and closed the space between them. "Very well. If you won't come sit with me, I'll stand with you. Of course, there's a draft through here, and it's caused me quite a chill. My teeth are starting to chatter." She edged closer. "It's likely you can hear them if you listen. I'm sure to come down with lung fever."

She leaned around to look. Magda still scowled, so she tried again. "My feet are so cold I can't feel my pinkie toes or their nearest neighbors. I imagine they're as blue and shriveled as dead toads." When this brought the hint of a grudging smile to Magda's face, Bertha went on. "If I find them loose inside my shoes, I'll save them for Thad. They'll make good catfish bait."

The words melted Magda's resolve like honey in hot tea. Her

stingy smile became a generous toothy grin that brightened her eyes and lifted the apples of her cheeks. "Hush your crazy talk and go over by the fire before your silly words come to pass." The power of her smile dimmed a bit when she turned to stare into Bertha's eyes. "I'll fetch water for your dirty feet, just like our Savior did for His betrayer." She flipped the hand towel from the counter over her shoulder and lifted a washtub from the corner. Then she glanced back at Bertha, her smile completely gone. "But you owe me an apology, Bertha Maye Biddie. I intend to get it if you'd like me to ever speak to you again."

Thad turned his horse. He couldn't just ride home and let another day pass without telling Bertha he was leaving. He never should've let her get away from him again. But she'd been so upset about whatever bee buzzed inside her bonnet, the weight of her excitement pushed aside his important news. But the time had come to fess up. He had handed off the fishing gear to Charlie along with a promise to tell Bertha before the sun went down. He pressed the edges of his heels to the horse's side. If he hurried, he could catch up to them.

He thought of Bertha unprotected in such heavy rain and winced. If she became ill, he'd blame himself. He never should've let her go off with that scatter-thought Moses Pharr. The boy only paid attention to cypress wood and a well-turned ankle and had trouble juggling between the two. He lacked the common sense required to find shelter for Bertha and Rhodie.

As if to confirm his thoughts, the fresh wagon tracks never veered from the road, where they might've sought relief at a farmhouse or under a thick grove of trees, but carried on straight through the mud.

He glanced up the road and sighed then felt his jaw tighten.

Wait'll I get my hands on that careless boy.

CHAPTER 10

Bertha's gaze followed the row of bundled herbs that hung drying over the mantelpiece from a length of twine like laundry pinned to a clothesline. She recognized some, like the puccoon Mrs. Hayes used for red dye and the root of Dutchman's-pipe, a remedy for snakebite. Most of the fragrant bunches she'd never seen before but guessed they played a big part in the wonderful German meals Magda's mama stirred up.

The chimney corner in Magda's house had become the hub of the family wheel. The fireplace took up most of one wall in the tiny two-room dwelling and served the household well. The women used it to roast meat and vegetables, boil water, even make coffee when they had the stove tied up with other chores. Along with the wood-burning stove, it provided a source of heat when the weather turned cold. Magda, an only child with no warm siblings to curl up with, slept near it for warmth in the wintertime.

To the left of the fire pit, in back of the low, sturdy stool where Bertha perched, stood a box filled with split oak, fuel to feed the benevolent fire. On the right, behind where Magda stood, barrels of dried corn were pushed into the corner, the drums so full a few ears spilled out onto the floor. Staggered in front of the corn was a collection of baskets overflowing with plump new pecans, some in husks, others shucked down to their mottled shells.

Bertha loved the room. The sights and smells that dwelled in the Hayes kitchen always set her stomach to rumbling even if she'd just had a respectable meal.

"Watch out, now. It's hot."

Bertha snapped to attention and lifted her feet so Magda could set the pan of water on the smooth stones of the hearth. But she barely got her toes wet before she jerked them back. "Too hot!" She held the sides of the stool to maintain her balance while her feet dangled precariously over the steaming water. "Did you do it on purpose?"

Magda slid the pan to the side so Bertha could lower her legs, sloshing at least a quart of the scalding water onto the floor. It ran along the mortared lines and deep cracks, spilling over into the flames with a snap and sizzle. "Don't talk foolish. I'm not mad enough to disfigure you. Though I may have the right to be."

"Aus einer Mücke einen Elefanten machen," Magda's mama called over her shoulder. She leaned against the sideboard across the way, cutting venison into lean red chunks.

Magda rose up and frowned at her. "You're supposed to take my side, Mama. I'm your daughter, remember?" She pointed at Bertha. "This here's a neighbor child." She crossed to the table and returned with a pitcher of cold water to pour into the metal pan on the floor. Still pouting, she cast a sullen look at her mama. "Honestly, sometimes you act like it's the other way around."

Bertha peeked up at Magda. "What did she say?"

Magda laid the back of her hand on her hip. "She said I'm making an elephant out of a mosquito. Her way of saying I'm blowing things out of proportion." She took a poker from the corner and bent over to stir up the fire but twisted around to look at her mama while she worked. "Another German proverb. Just what we need around this house. Thank you, Mama."

"Yer velcome."

Magda tossed the poker aside and flapped her hands in frustration. "Mama! Why do you always defend Bertha? You don't even know what our quarrel is about." She gave Bertha a meaningful stare then leaned down next to her ear. "That's right," she hissed in a forced whisper. "She doesn't know a thing about it. Just like I promised."

Bertha considered it most prudent not to respond. She busied herself with checking the heat of the water then eased her feet down into the pan.

Mrs. Hayes scraped the diced meat into a wide stew pot and replaced the lid. "I go now and give you girls a little privacy. Only keep one eye on dis Rehragout, vill you, Magda? Don't allow your little spat to ruin your papa's meal." A satisfied smile softened her face. "You know how Papa likes my venison stew." She took off her apron, wiped her hands with it, and left it in a heap on the table. "Look, dere's no more rain. I tink I go help Papa vit chores."

She lifted her coat from a peg by the door then turned for one last word before she went out. "Have yourselves a nice little talk, girls." She squinted one eye and leveled it on Magda. "But have dis ting over and done before I come back vit Papa. Ja?"

The obstinate look on Magda's face told Bertha she felt no pressing need to settle the *ting* between them. But she lowered her head and regarded her mama with raised brows.

"Yes, ma'am."

As soon as the latch clicked behind Mrs. Hayes, Magda stalked into her parents' tiny bedroom and came out with another stool. She dropped it in front of Bertha so hard the three legs did a clattering dance, until Magda's weight settled them onto the floor. Seated directly across from the pan, she stripped off shoes and stockings, pulled back her dress, and crowded her sizable feet in alongside Bertha's.

Bertha watched her until she looked up. "What are you doing?"

"Soaking my feet. I never meant this water for you. Not in my heart. I only let Mama think I fetched it for you."

Her smile reminded Bertha of an overindulged child.

She flicked her first finger in the direction of Bertha's feet. "So kindly withdraw yourself from my foot soak."

"Magda. . ."

Magda wriggled her feet around Bertha's until she had forced her ankles to the sides. "Fine. Keep them there, but you'll have to take whatever room is left and be happy with it. I drew this water for me."

Bertha eased her toes from under Magda's. "For corn's sake. This is silly."

"Oh? Silly, is it? But I thought you liked silly. After all, you like silly city women well enough. You like their silly laughs, their silly clothes, and their silly candy. Seems to me silly would set just fine with you." Magda spouted her tirade in a low, even voice, but the pain laced through it struck Bertha's heart like a piercing shout.

"I came here to apologize."

Magda crossed her arms. "Did you bring a list? Because you'll need it."

Bertha hung her head. "Where do I start?"

"With not trusting me, maybe? Or forgetting who happens to be your best friend?"

Bertha rose up and gasped. "I'd never forget that."

Magda's feet stopped warring for position in the pan, and her whole body stilled. She turned her face to the fire and seemed to study the dancing yellow flames while tears on her cheeks glimmered in the reflected light. "You made me feel like a bother, like unwelcome company." She took a ragged breath and shook her head. "I've never felt so bad in your presence, Bertha." She looked up and sought Bertha's eyes. "I don't ever want to again." Magda's tears flowed freely now that the dam had burst, and she wiped her nose on her apron.

Bertha stood up in the pan and leaned to wrap her arms around Magda's neck. The awkward angle of her feet, still curled on each side of Magda's, rendered her bent and bowlegged, but she didn't care. "I'm sorry, sugar. I never meant to hurt you. Can you ever forgive me? I'll do whatever it takes to make it up to you. I swear."

"Don't swear. You know you're not supposed to."

"Promise, then. I promise on my life."

"You don't have to go that far. I'll just take your word that you'll never do it again. A mite less costly than your life, don't you think?"

Bertha laughed and nodded. "Just a mite."

"But you have to mean it, Bertha. If I know you mean it, I'll forget it completely and not hold it to your account."

Bertha drew back to look her in the eye. "I mean it. On my honor, I mean it."

Magda gave a solemn nod. "All right, then."

Bertha leaned to kiss her ruddy cheek. On impulse she kissed her cheek again then twice more on the other side.

Magda squealed and pushed her away. "You don't have to get me all soggy. And speaking of soggy, kindly sit down before you land bottoms-up in this bucket."

The words had barely left her mouth when Bertha lost her footing, and her toe slid hard against Magda's side of the pan. She squealed in pain and thrashed wildly to regain her balance. Magda caught both her hands and held on while she lowered her backside onto the stool.

She picked up her foot and scowled down at the throbbing big toe. "Look what you made me do. If this thing puffs, it won't fit into my shoe." She looked up at Magda and found her smiling. "Stop it, now." She held her toe higher. "This hurts to beat all."

Magda's grin turned to a belly laugh. "I imagine it smarts, all right, but I'm not laughing at your toe. I'm laughing at your ruckled-up face." She pointed at Bertha's shoes drying in front of the fire. "It's about as puckered as those poor things, which, by the way, will never fit you again, swollen toe or not."

Bertha followed Magda's gaze to the crumpled brown shoes on the hearth. "And that will be a bother to everyone but me. Those things were fashioned in the pit of perdition."

"But what will your mama say?"

"Oh, she'll be scandalized. She'll pester and fuss for days and make me work off their cost with chores." Bertha winked at Magda. "And it will be a small price to pay to never have them on my feet again."

He had found her.

Thad knew the deeper ruts meant Mose had stopped long

enough for the weight of the wagon to sink the wheels a bit in the soft mud, and there were marks on the ground from restless hooves. They'd stopped, all right, and the lone set of footprints that led to the swollen ditch in front of Magdalena Hayes's house meant Bertha would be inside.

Runoff rain poured into the trench, causing it to crest. Bertha had jumped it before it filled; otherwise she'd never have made it across the rushing surge. And the lane was completely gone, swallowed up by standing water. She may have walked up to the house, but she'd never make it out on foot.

He turned his horse, jumped the ditch, and rode across the pasture to the house. Magda's parents came out of the barn and picked their way across the higher ground in back of the property. Thad waved and they waved back; then he rode up to where they waited on the porch.

Tall, potbellied Mr. Hayes wore the same wide grin on his face he had plastered there the first time Thad ever saw him. According to local legend, he was born with it and couldn't change expressions if he tried. The man pushed back his hat with two fingers and beamed in Thad's direction.

Thad worked hard not to look straight at him, because the infectious nature of the jolly gentleman's smile made it impossible to keep a straight face. He returned the wife's nod instead. "Good day, folks."

"Thad," Mr. Hayes said, as if apprising Thad of his name, "what you doing way out here on a day like today?" His brows, raised in twin peaks over laughing eyes, told Thad he already knew.

Thad squirmed in his saddle and pointed back over his shoulder. "Me and Charlie–Charles Gouldy, that is–were over yon way, fishing."

"Catch anything?"

"Not this time. Seems we were the ones caught. Out in the storm, I mean."

"Where's Charlie now?"

"Well, sir, he rode on home." In his nervous state, Thad allowed his gaze to linger too long on the older man's face and right away felt his mouth begin to twitch.

"And you didn't?" Mr. Hayes found so much humor in Thad's discomfort, the tops of his cheeks reddened from the strain of overtaxed muscles.

Thad lowered his head. "No, sir, I didn't. I came out here to see about—"

Mr. Hayes held up his hand. "Don't tell me, now. Let me guess. You started out this day a-fishing, and now you've come a-hunting." He pointed back toward the house. "A mighty fine tracker you are, too, since your prey sits cornered inside that door. Get on in there, boy, and flush her out."

Thad looked to Mrs. Hayes for help but found no comfort in her toothy smile.

"Ja, go inside, Thad. A bowl of venison stew should sit vell on such a day."

Thad tipped his hat. "I won't likely turn down such a fine offer on a good day, ma'am, much less on this dreary afternoon. If you're sure there's enough. . ."

"There's more than plenty, son," Mr. Hayes boomed. "And I can smell it from here. Get down from there and come on in."

Thad dismounted and tied his horse to the porch rail. By the time he made it to the top step, Mr. Hayes had opened the door. From somewhere past the entrance came shrill laughter and a spate of uproarious giggles.

Mr. and Mrs. Hayes exchanged a look.

"What them gals up to, Gerta?"

She gave him a vacant stare. "I couldn't say, Yacob."

Grinning, Mr. Hayes led the way past the entry with his wife on his heels. Thad, burning with curiosity now that he'd recognized Bertha's laugh in all the glee, brought up the rear. When Jacob and Gerta Hayes parted before him like the Red Sea, Thad smiled every bit as widely as Mr. Hayes.

CHAPTER 11

It started to rain in earnest as Sarah and Henry pulled past the gate. They barely got Dandy inside the barn before the sky opened all the way up. Behind the rain came a chill, blustery wind that rattled the wide doors and raised the hair on Sarah's neck.

She left Dandy in Henry's care and hightailed it to the house to kindle a fire. When the flames blazed high and hot, she put the kettle on and ran shivering to their room, pulling the gift from Henry out of the saddlebag as she went. Dropping the wet leather bag on the floor outside the bedroom door, she stepped inside and carefully placed the wrapped parcel in the middle of the bed.

She peeled out of her blue gingham dress and threw it over the door to dry, certain she'd never changed in and out of the same garment so many times in one day. The square of linen cloth she pulled from the bar on the washstand to blot her wet hair reminded her of her new fabric, so she crossed to the bed where the package lay. Wiping her hands on the linen rag, she laid it aside to open the end of the wrapper and shake the material out onto the quilt.

She wondered at Henry's choice. Not that the sight of it didn't set her heart racing and make her limp with joy. But she couldn't imagine where in their dusty country house she might store it, much less where in their dusty Texas town she might wear it. If they were still in St. Louis, it would be different.

Sarah smoothed one finger over the glistening white weave. The cloth was truly the most beautiful thing she'd ever seen, much less owned. What a lovely dress it would make.

And I know exactly which one it should be.

She dropped to her knees and reached under the bed, using the feel of the boxes against her fingers to find the right one. When she had hold of it, she pulled it out into the light. The wooden crate held every favorite gown that ever belonged to her or her mama. Of course they weren't really garments anymore, just the cut-out parts. The tied-up bundles resembled stacks of puzzle pieces more than clothes—an arm here, skirt there, a bodice and back. Whenever Sarah got ready to make a new frock, she'd choose from one of the old fabric puzzles and cut out a pattern. Sometimes she mixed and matched just for fun.

Near the bottom of the box she found the right one and slid it from under the rest. The dingy pieces were wrinkled and smelled of camphor, but no matter. She'd wash and press them before she started. The pattern would fit her too small now, but she would adjust for that when she traced.

A tender smile stole over her face when she held up the stack of cloth pieces that had once been a sassy white dress, the same one she wore to Lawetta Draper's house the day she first laid eyes on Henry. It might need a touch here and there to make it more stylish, but she'd chosen the perfect pattern.

When the kettle on the stove began to whine, she shoved the crate back under the bed away from Henry's prying eyes and tucked the new fabric in the bottom dresser drawer. Then she shimmied into her housedress and scurried into the kitchen.

In the darkest corner of the pantry sat a small red tin where she kept the last of the tea leaves given to her by Miss Susan Blow, her former mistress and teacher. Miss Susan gave the tea to Sarah during her last visit home to see Papa. The kettle came from Miss Susan, too. Sarah brought it with her when she first left the French settlement in St. Louis and moved to Jefferson.

The most precious gift her teacher gave her was an education, a prize with no value in her new hometown. It seemed the longer she stayed where people considered her ignorant, the more ignorant she became. Some days she wished Miss Susan hadn't bothered.

Sarah picked up the tin, pried off the lid, and drew in a deep whiff of the pungent plant. The familiar smell built a bridge in her mind from Texas to Missouri. It carried her along the river, past St. Louis to the wide streets of Carondelet. There it wound through the rooms of Miss Susan's fine house then straight to the Des Peres School, Miss Susan's kindergarten where Sarah used to cook for the children.

She sighed and pulled a small wad of dried leaves from the can. Before closing it, she peered inside and mourned the fact there was barely enough left for one more pot. Relaxing her fingers, she allowed a few leaves to fall back into the can and dropped the rest into the steaming kettle. Closing the lid, she set it aside to steep.

Henry stepped up onto the porch, whistling and stamping the mud off his feet the way he always did when he came in from the barn. The screen door squealed behind her.

"Get yourself out of those damp clothes," she said without looking back. "And don't bother hanging them up. After the way you sweated today, they'll be stinking without a wash."

Sarah waited for him to grumble. The trousers he wore were his favorite pair, the only britches he owned without holes in the knees. When he didn't say a word, she turned to see why. Henry stood by the door unbuttoning his shirt with one hand and gnawing on her chocolate with the other.

"Put that away now. You're bound to ruin your supper."

"Can't hep it. This ain't ordinary candy. It's black magic." He used the back of his hand to slide a stray piece from his bottom lip into his mouth. "Once you start in on it, you lose the power to stop."

"Let me help you with that." She hustled over and swiped the sweet treat out of his hand, wound the wrapper around it, and took it to the pantry—picking up the red tea can on the way. When she came out, Henry's gaze latched on and followed her around the room. Sarah grew fidgety under his meddlesome stare and spun around to face him. "What is it now?"

"What's what?"

"Why are your peepers glued to me? Has my face turned blue?"

His big brown eyes, still so intent, narrowed and crinkled. "Naw, your face still dark and sweet like that chocolate but stronger magic than any old candy."

A warm flush crept up her neck, but she kept her guard up. "Fine. Now answer my first question. Why you looking at me in such a way?"

Henry lifted one broad shoulder. "Jus' noticed you making tea, I guess."

She stiffened. "And what of it?"

"Means you homesick again, that's all."

"What you going on about, Henry?"

"Woman, I didn't meet you yesterday. You go to making that tea, it means you thinking 'bout St. Louis and Miss Susan's house."

Sarah turned back to the sink. "What a fool thing to say. When I make tea, it means I have a hankering for a cup, that's all. Don't go readin' things where there ain't no writin'. Go wash for supper, now. I'll have food on the table before you're done."

Henry laughed and raised his hands in surrender. "Yes'm, Missy King. I'll do like I's told."

He pulled off his shirt and wadded it into a ball then started toward the hallway door. When he stopped just short of it, Sarah cringed. It would be nice if he'd just leave it be, but she knew he wasn't about to.

"I reckon I know why you act how you do 'bout folks 'round here."

She snorted. "I know, too. They're cruel, narrow-minded bigots, every last one of them."

He turned from the door, big hands busy rolling his shirt. "You seem right fond of little Bertha."

"Miss Bertha's different, her and Magda both. They speak to

me no matter who's watching. They don't wipe their hands on their skirts if our fingers touch. Least not where I can see them."

"You act like Bertha and Magda the only good folks in this town. They's jus' as many good apples in the barrel as bad."

Sarah feigned shock. "Where they hiding the good crop, then? All I come across are sour and wormy."

Henry's face puckered like sun-dried corn. "Like I said, I know why you act how you do. I reckon you're jus' mad all the time. But it ain't the people 'round Jefferson you're mad at."

She dropped her dishrag on the sideboard and propped one hand on her hip. "It ain't, huh?"

"No, ma'am, it ain't."

"Well, who am I mad at?"

"Me."

He might've said Dickens and made more sense. Sarah waited to see if he meant the witless words. He stood not moving a muscle, his face a blank wall. She cocked her head. "Why would you say so foolish a thing?"

He uncoiled the shirt ball and slung it across the kitchen. "Weren't it me what took you away from St. Louis? From your papa, Miss Susan, and the schoolhouse?"

"Henry, St. Louis is over and done. Jefferson's my home now."

He challenged her with a look. "You can't tell me you don't miss it every day."

Now he'd sashayed too close to the truth, his prying words plundering near that place in her heart she kept all to herself. She picked up the rag again and went to work cleaning the stove. "Quit spewing nonsense. If you don't let me get supper done, you won't eat tonight."

He closed the gap between them and grabbed her arm. "You told me I'm reading what ain't wrote. Well, now you wiping up what ain't spilt." He took the rag from her hand and tossed it in the corner along with his shirt. "Stop all this dancing around the truth. You wish you'd never left St. Louis. I know you do."

The pigheaded man had stumbled right onto it—the only place

in her heart he didn't belong–and his blunder made her mad enough to tell him.

She jerked her arm free. "You want to know so bad? Well, here it is. Miss Blow treated me like a person. Like I mattered in this world. She taught me to read and write, cipher numbers, to talk like a lady, not the child of a slave." Sarah glared up at him. "I don't miss St. Louis. Or Carondelet, or my house, or the school. Not even Miss Blow, though I love her with all my might." Pushing his hands away, she backed into a tight wad. "I miss feeling good about myself, Henry King. I miss walking proud along the street instead of slinking like a hang-tailed dog."

Henry pressed her to the stove and pulled her struggling body close. "Hush, baby girl," he cooed against her hair. "I'm so sorry. I didn't know you hurt this bad. God, help me, I jus' didn't know." Shame masked his face. "You was happy in St. Louis, and here I come along and take you away from there. You followed me to Jefferson without a peep or a mutter, and look at what a sorrowful trade you done made. A broken-down farm and two sorry old mules for your trouble."

Sarah sniffed. "Two?"

He nodded toward the barn. "One out yonder with his face in a feed bag and the other right in front of you."

Her stomach lurched. She unfurled from the wretched place she'd allowed herself to go and took hold of his face with both hands. "Don't you say that, you hear? I could do without Dandy, but my life would be a wearisome mess without you."

Henry tried to pull away, but she held him fast. "Look at me, now. Don't you know I can survive any sorrow as long as you're by my side?"

He looked down at her, the challenge back in his eyes. "Anything?"

She stilled. "I thought we agreed not to talk about that."

"I reckon it's a good day for airing things out."

Sarah pressed her forehead to his bare chest and ran the palm of her hand down the back of his head. Stopping at his neck, her fingers lingered there and caressed the smooth, warm skin. "There's no way of knowing why we haven't had children, Henry. It could just as likely be down to me."

She raised her head and sought his eyes. "Mama always said these things are best left to the wisdom of the good Lord, and I agree. It's only been four years. We could still—"

His finger on her lips stifled the rest. "Don't say no more. Four years is enough time to give it. I ain't wasting no more hope. But I can't help thinking you'd have settled in better if we'd had a child."

Seeing his tears flooded her eyes. She pushed away and wiped her cheeks with her palms. "How'd we get back on this same old tired subject?"

Henry shrugged. "Don't we always?"

"I guess we do." Lifting on her toes, she kissed him on the cheek. "Will you kindly go wash for supper now? You've stirred enough trouble for one day, even for you."

He swatted her behind, the old Henry once again. "If I clear my plate, can I have me some more of that chocolate?"

Sarah went back to her stove. "I believe you've had quite enough. Besides, I might like one more little taste before it's all gone."

"I reckon Dandy would, too."

She glanced back at his too-innocent face. "What did you say?"

"I said Dandy might want him one more bite. That old mule sure liked it."

She swiped at him. "You ain't fed my candy to that no-'count critter!"

Henry laughed and dodged. "Jus' a taste. But he sure was hankering for more."

"Well, I hope he enjoyed it, because neither one of you sorry mules will see another morsel of it." His words from moments before came back to her, and she wanted to whack off her tongue. But he still grinned like he didn't notice, so she hit him with the towel.

"Git on, now. And don't come back until you're fit for the table."

Smiling, Sarah watched him leave the room. Their talk had lifted some of the weight from around her heart. They should try it more often.

She turned back to the stove and gasped. *The tea!*

Lifting the pot, she raised the lid to peer inside at the oily dark brown liquid.

Ruined.

It had been left to steep far too long, and the result would be a bitter, distasteful brew. Given the way the day had gone so far, it seemed a fitting addition to scorched beans and crumbly, dried-up corn bread.

CHAPTER 12

Thad had tried hard to turn away. His mama would expect no less of him. But it wasn't every day he saw two grown women—though the scene before his eyes made him question that estimation—standing in a bucket of water. There they were, Magda and his own little Bertha, up to their calves in a washtub. They clung to each other, inching their way in a tight circle and laughing like addlepated loons.

Gerta Hayes reacted as if miles of skin were showing, instead of the two inches of bare leg above the line of the pan. "Girls! Vot on earth? Cover yourselves!"

The two froze and looked her way, but the hilarity didn't leave their tear-streaked faces until they spotted Thad. Then the jostling in the pail increased tenfold as they worked their way around to their stools and sat down hard. The visible skin disappeared to the point where Thad knew their hems had gone under.

Mr. Hayes, evidently content to let his wife fend for their modesty, never flinched. But his curiosity proved less restrained. "What y'all doing, Magda? Ain't never seen that jig danced before. Least not in a tub of water."

The red-faced girls, still feet-first in water like a pair of wading ducks, watched owl-eyed as their audience drew near.

"Answer your papa, Magdalena, and be quick about it."

Magda averted her eyes and lowered her head. Bertha, cute as a newborn calf even with her mouth agape, gawked at Thad.

When Mr. Hayes cleared his throat, Magda dared to raise her eyes. "Sorry, Papa. We were turning, see?" She twirled her finger in the space between them. "To opposite sides."

Bertha awoke from her daze and pointed behind her. "The fire. It got too hot on the one side."

Magda nodded. "So we turned."

"Yes, to the cooler side."

Thad groaned at the manner in which they had stumbled into Mr. Hayes's web. Innocent lambs to the slaughter.

The older gentleman stepped forward, nodding his head. "Oh yes, I see it now." He glanced behind him, his expression sincere. "Don't you see it, Thad?"

Thad could only grin and wait.

"So, girls. . .what you're saying is you were done on the one side, so you flipped over to roast the other'n." He fell forward, clutching his knees to stay upright, and laughed at his own joke. He pointed at the pan and all but shouted as he delivered the kicker. "I see you saved some time by sitting in your own basting sauce."

Mr. Hayes's laughter turned out to be more contagious than his smile, and Thad felt his good breeding start to slip. His own grin turned to a chortle then a full-blown howl. He leaned into Magda's papa to stay upright, and the two braced each other while they laughed. The girls pouted at first, but a quick glance at each other's faces set them off, too. The only sane person in the house stood scowling from the stove.

"You two best be glad this stew's not ruined. Now hush, all of you, and come to supper."

Thad followed Mr. Hayes to the table, still wiping his eyes. He tried to avert his attention from the circus ring near the fireplace but found the performance too engaging. His headstrong gaze wandered there against his will.

Magda pulled her skirt free from where she had wadded it under her sash and stood up. Bertha, the most fetching clown in the show, freed her dress, too, but remained seated. Magda stepped out on a towel, dried her feet, and slid her shoes on.

Bertha broke eye contact with Thad and tugged on Magda's skirt. "What about me?"

"What about you?"

"I don't have shoes to wear."

Magda handed her the towel. "Dry your feet before they prune up. I'll see if your shoes are dry."

Bertha swung her feet to the floor and stared down at them. "Too late. They've been wet so long they're pickled."

Thad covered his mouth to hide his grin.

Magda bent over a pair of button-strap shoes and lifted one from the hearth. "Still soaked clean through. They might be dry by Christmas."

Magda's mama glanced at her from the stove. "Ve just had Christmas."

"I know."

After Mrs. Hayes laid another place at the table, she crossed to her bedroom door. "Vait, dumpling," she called to Bertha. "I think my shoes might fit you, ja?"

Bertha discreetly turned and wrung out her drenched hem over the towel. Then she leaned toward the fire pit and held the damp fabric closer to the flames.

Thad found something else to look at until Mrs. Hayes returned with a pair of worn black boots.

"Not so pretty, but varm and dry at least."

Bertha took uncommon pleasure in the sight of the boots. Smiling as though she'd been granted a wish, she looked them over. "Oh, these will do fine, Mrs. Hayes. Much obliged."

Mr. Hayes slapped both beefy palms on the table. "Enough about shoes, womenfolk. That venison tastes good from here. Serve it up, Gertie, before my lint-catcher caves."

As if her husband hadn't spoken, Mrs. Hayes stood over Bertha while she tried the boots. "Dey fit you nice. *Das gut*. You may keep dem, Bert'a. Too big for me."

Bertha gaped up at her. "Oh, I couldn't possibly." Thad watched the idea flit around in her pixie eyes. "But suppose we trade?" She pointed at the bronze shoes, her voice high-pitched with excitement. "Those will never fit me again, I'm sure of it."

Mrs. Hayes stared toward the hearth. "You give me dose nice shoes?"

"With pleasure."

Mrs. Hayes gave a quick nod and held out her hand. "Ve have us a deal."

"Gert, you'll have more than a deal if you and your daughter don't start shaking those pots. I'll give you a knot on the head."

"Hush, Yacob. We're coming." She waved him off as she passed but hustled to the stove with Magda on her heels.

Bertha finished lacing her new boots and stood. Patting her stringy hair and smoothing her mud-caked skirt, she eased toward the table.

Thad leaped to his feet to pull out her chair, and she sat down with a shy smile.

Mrs. Hayes ladled the stew with a flourish. She passed between them nodding and winking, grinning down at each bowl as though she'd birthed rather than cooked the pleasant-smelling dish. Magda brought a basket of hot, crusty bread and a saucer of soft, churned butter and then returned to the stove for a large bowl of sauerkraut and sausage. She placed it in front of Mr. Hayes and surveyed the spread with a practiced eye.

"Need anything else, Papa?"

"Just space for my elbows and a little time, sugar."

When they settled around the big oak table, Mr. Hayes bowed for prayer, and Thad followed suit. The amen was barely said before clanking spoons and spirited conversation commenced.

Mr. Hayes lifted his face from his bowl long enough to nod at his wife across the bread basket. "Fine vittles, woman. Mighty fine vittles."

Thad winked at Bertha and smiled at the older woman. "Your husband's right, ma'am. This here's good eating."

Mrs. Hayes beamed so brightly she lit up the room. "You really tink so?"

"Oh yes, ma'am. You could serve this with pride to Ulysses S. Grant."

Mr. Hayes stopped eating and glowered at Thad. "Watch your tongue, boy. Don't go putting crazy ideas in the poor woman's head. There ain't no way she could serve this stew to President Grant."

Thad's gaze jumped back to Mrs. Hayes. She had lowered her head and folded her hands in her lap. All trace of her pleasure had vanished.

Magda, red-faced and scowling, rose to her mama's defense. "And just why not, Papa?"

"I don't intend to leave him any, that's why!"

Mrs. Hayes, who Thad reckoned should know her husband better by now, tittered with relief and picked up her spoon. "Aw, go on, Yacob Hayes. Eat your stew and behave."

The tension eased around the table and a spell of quiet, companionable eating followed. The venison stew really was hands-down the best Thad had ever tasted. Especially when he dipped the soft middle of the fresh bread in the thick, dark broth and followed it with a bite of chewy, buttered crust. Never one for eating cabbage, the savory kraut and sausage surprised him. He sat contemplating seconds when Gerta Hayes broke the silence.

"Your mama vill be vorried about you, Bert'a?"

Bertha swallowed a bite and wiped her mouth on her napkin. "Yes, ma'am. I expect she'll be on the porch craning her neck when I get home."

Thad took his chance. "Bertha, I'll be glad to take you straight home after supper."

Mr. Hayes shook his head and spoke with bread-stuffed cheeks. "No sense in you young people riding horseback in the rain, not when we got Gert's two-seater in the barn. I'll see her home, Thad. But you kin tie your horse to the back and ride with us."

Thad raised a finger to protest, but Mr. Hayes cut him off. "Won't be no trouble a'tall."

"I'm coming with you, Papa."

"No, daughter. You stay put and help your mama. I won't be long."

Magda settled back in a pout while Bertha leaned forward to help Thad. "Won't we bog down in the surrey, sir?"

Mr. Hayes shoved another broth-soaked piece of bread in his mouth and proceeded to talk around it. "Never been stuck a day in my life. A body just has to recognize when it ain't smart to push your luck." He slapped the table near Thad with his free hand. "Get it, son? You ain't got to know where to go, just where not to."

He ducked his head to peer under the tasseled shade on the window. "Most the water's run off anyway, now that the rain's dwindled. The ground under that lane is packed solid, little Bertha. Take a bigger cloudburst than we had today to soften it up." He dismissed any more discussion with a wave of his hand. "Eat up, now. Let's get this young lady home before they round up a search party."

Thad went back to his bowl, but his heart found no more pleasure in venison stew. He comforted himself with thoughts of sitting next to Bertha in the surrey on the way to town. If Mr. Hayes cooperated by focusing his attention on the road ahead, the trip presented the chance to cuddle close to her on the rear seat, maybe even hold her hand. The prospect caused a chill down his back that had nothing to do with the steadily plummeting temperature outside.

The rain had ushered in a cold snap no one had prepared for, especially Bertha. She wore a lightweight dress with short sleeves and no stockings inside her boots. After they finished the meal and cleared the table, Mr. Hayes went around back to hitch up the horse while his wife found Bertha a suitable wrap. When the wagon pulled to the front door, Thad thanked Mrs. Hayes for dinner and helped Bertha into her borrowed coat. Bertha kissed the still-pouting Magda on the cheek, and they ran outside.

Mr. Hayes had arranged purchase of the ten-year-old surrey and the horse to pull it at the same time. Thad reckoned the seller knew he'd never unload the poor creature otherwise. The gelding looked white some days, gray on others, depending on the quality of the light. The grayish cast of his skin extended to the rims of his smallish eyes, his overlarge mouth, and the insides of his droopy ears in such a way that he always appeared slightly dirty. His overlarge teeth, which he displayed with amusing regularity, were stained brown as if he smoked a pipe.

Despite being hard on the eyes, the aging horse was a favorite with the locals. More than sixteen hands tall with the disposition of a kitten, he made up in size and character what he lacked in good looks. Mrs. Hayes had rigged a straw hat for him to wear, cutting two large holes in the sides for his ears, and insisted on braiding his tail. To his credit, the old gentleman never seemed to mind.

When Mr. Hayes jumped down from the surrey and lifted Bertha onto the leather seat beside him, Thad's mood bottomed out. A ruinous trick of fate, somehow stronger than his love for Bertha, was determined to keep them apart. He exchanged a grim look with her as he climbed into the backseat alone. Her mournful eyes told him she must be thinking along the same lines.

True to his word, Mr. Hayes expertly guided them down the long drive and onto the street without mishap, and they set off toward town. Bertha lived on the other side of Jefferson, near the bridge on the road that led to Marshall, so Mr. Hayes turned off Broadway and headed south on Polk.

Bertha started to fidget, and Thad leaned to touch her arm. "What is it, Bertha?"

She stared west toward Vale Street, her eyes narrowed, brows drawn. Instead of answering Thad's question, she squared around to face Mr. Hayes. "Excuse me, sir. Would it be too much trouble to cut over and drive past Brooks House? There's someone there I need to see."

Mr. Hayes reached a finger to scratch a spot up under his hat. "Well, I don't know, darling. Didn't you say your mama would be watching for you? We don't want to fret her none, do we?"

Up ahead and one street over, the back side of the hotel

appeared through the trees. Bertha swiveled on her seat as they passed it by, squirming as though she might jump off and run if the surrey didn't stop. She latched onto Mr. Hayes's arm so tightly her fingers turned white. "Please, sir. It will only take a minute. I have an urgent errand to attend."

Thad scooted to the edge of his seat and cleared his throat. "I'll gladly go along to see that she returns in a timely fashion."

Mr. Hayes pulled up on the reins, and the horse eased to a stop. He looked back at Thad, still not convinced. "I don't know, boy."

"I assure you it will be quick, right, Bertha?"

Her head bobbed up and down. "Oh yes. Very quick."

Before Mr. Hayes could say anything more, Thad hopped to the ground and turned to help Bertha down. He untied his horse from the back and climbed into the saddle, pulling Bertha up behind him. The next idea came to him before he had time to feel guilty. "As a matter of fact, there's no reason for you to wait. I'll help Bertha with her errand and see her straight home. You have my word."

Mr. Hayes spun around on the seat. "Now wait a second, Thad."

Thad tipped his hat. "You can count on me, sir. I won't let you down." He tapped the horse with his heel and reeled into the street with Bertha clinging to his middle.

They rode the short distance to Austin Street and turned back up toward Vale before Bertha started to laugh. "Shouldn't you be ashamed of yourself? You left him with his mouth gaped so wide he'll be catching flies."

Thad chuckled. "As fond of the man as I may be, it's worth him eating the odd fly to have a moment alone with you. It's right hard to steer you away from prying eyes, you know." He patted her hand. "Besides, I got you a chance to go see your friend."

She tightened her grip around his waist, and he could hear a smile in her voice. "You most certainly did. And for that, Mr. Bloom, I thank you."

Within a few feet of the next crossroad, he felt Bertha tense behind him. "Speaking of Annie, there she is now."

Thad's head swung around. "You see her? Where?"

She pointed past the horse's nose. "There. Coming out of the Rosebud."

At the corner of Austin and Vale crouched a saloon of dubious reputation. Said to be "the rendezvous of judges, lawyers, and men with notched guns," the Rosebud was a lively watering hole, and it nagged Thad a bit that someone Bertha cared so much for would find the gin mill worthy of her time.

The woman Bertha indicated was in the company of a tall, dark-haired man. Unaware of Thad's approaching horse, they clung together and lurched toward Vale Street. When Thad and Bertha drew alongside them, it took the couple a moment to realize they were there. But by the time Thad dismounted and helped Bertha down, the two stood swaying and staring their way.

Without waiting for Thad, Bertha hurried toward them. "Annie!"

The woman glanced at the man with panicked eyes. Then she shoved him aside and started to walk away, but he clutched her arm and held her.

"Whoa, now! Where you going in such an all-fired hurry?" He dragged her around to face him, but she wouldn't meet his pointed glare.

"Where do you think I'm going, silly? Back to the hotel."

Her companion gave her a little shake. "S'matter, you deaf? This little lady's speaking to you."

Annie flung her head from side to side. "No, Abe. You're mistaken. She isn't."

He shook harder. "You know right well she is."

Thad sensed trouble and crossed to stand beside Bertha. Annie pulled free, and Bertha closed the gap between them and touched her arm. "Wait, Annie. Don't go. It's me."

The "Abe" character tilted his chin toward Bertha. "Who is this? How does she know you?"

"I tell you, I don't know! I never seen her before in my life."

Abe grasped both of Annie's shoulders and leaned close to her ear, hissing every syllable through gritted teeth. "I asked you a question, Bessie. Who is this girl?"

Annie winced under his cruel hands. "I swear I don't know."

"Don't give me that. That's twice now she's called you Annie."

"I don't know what her game is," Annie shouted. Her voice lowered to an ominous tone. "I bet she heard you call me that." She leaned close and attempted to focus bleary eyes on Bertha. "Go away, little girl. I don't know you. Why are you trying to make trouble for me?"

With that she pulled away from Abe's grip and reeled down the street. "Come on, baby. I thought you were in a hurry to get back to the room. We ain't getting no closer standing around here."

The man watched her go with narrow, flashing eyes. He gave Bertha another suspicious scowl then followed Annie up the road.

Bertha stood on the grass where she had backed away from Annie's angry words.

Thad joined her there and slid one arm around her shoulders just as Annie's voice floated back to them on the night air. "Don't be silly, sugar. Why would I waste my time on that foolish child?"

Bertha turned and burrowed her face against Thad's shirt. "Oh, Thad. That's exactly what I am. A foolish child."

He tightened his hold around her. "Don't take it to heart, Bertha. Your friend's so pie-faced she could enter her profile in the county fair. She'll remember you tomorrow, when she sobers up."

Bertha looked up at him, her lips trembling. "That's what you don't understand. She remembered me, all right, but for whatever reason, she doesn't want him to know. I think I just got her in terrible trouble. Lord knows what he'll do to her now."

She shuddered and pressed close to him again. "Did you see his eyes?"

Across the top of Bertha's head, Thad watched the man named Abe wrestle the woman named Annie up the steps of Brooks House. He breathed a prayer of thanksgiving that Bertha didn't see it. In the distance, the struggling couple disappeared through the door, and Thad tacked on one more prayer.

He asked the Lord to send an angel for Annie.

CHAPTER 13

Saturday, January 20

Sarah stepped out the back door with every intention of feeding the chickens. The second her feet touched the cold, damp boards of the porch, she scampered back inside for her shoes and a wrap to lay over her shoulders.

Most days the weather stayed so warm and dry she wandered the place barefoot, especially the hard-packed trails leading to the barn and the chicken yard. Sarah loved feeling the smooth dirt under her feet. Some mornings the earth would be cool against her skin. On others the heat from the day before lay just below the topsoil.

Walking barefoot outdoors was a new experience. Folks in St. Louis wore shoes all the time, from field workers to scullery maids, and it disgraced the household to be caught without them. Things in Jefferson were different, and Sarah had to admit she liked going without her shoes.

But not today. Yesterday's storm had chugged through like a steam engine pulling a chilly caboose. And from the looks of the dark swirling sky, the tail end of the rain-train was in no hurry to leave the station.

There would be no sunrise setting for her clothesline daydreams, no bright rays dancing through her garden rows. She would slap the clothes on the line willy-nilly then ply the hoe in haste. She prayed that the rain held off till her laundry dried and that the cold would spare her greens.

But first came those chickens. The wayward, self-centered fowl were confused about the sort of bird God made them, considering they skulked near the back porch each morning like vultures. Squawking and sparring, they followed her to the chicken house where they belonged to start with and pranced around with jutting necks and impatient mutters while she dished out a bowlful of feed.

"Wait your turn, sisters." She swatted a speckled red pair away from her legs. "First one to peck me winds up on the table."

She had a good mind to leave them to scratch out a breakfast of crickets and worms the way the good Lord intended. Except she feared finding the lazy critters on their backs, drumsticks aimed at the sky, stone dead of starvation. And there would go Henry's eggs.

At the thought of her husband and his eggs, she stood up and scoured the surrounding fields. He'd been up since daybreak hoeing trenches to drain standing water and trying to plow the grassy rise, so she knew he'd be mighty hungry by now.

She covered the feed and slipped out of the chicken yard, fastening the gate behind her. As she neared the porch, she spotted Dandy in the distance, plodding on the east side of the farm. Henry couldn't be far behind.

Sure enough, he passed into her line of sight from behind the house, shoulders bent, head down, and far from a point where he might stop anytime soon. She still had plenty of time.

Sarah hoisted the metal tub full of washing off the porch and struck out for the bayou. Her thoughts flew to the day before when she'd complained about cool water and a breeze up her skirt and realized folks never knew when they had it easy. She reckoned she'd trade the nip she felt that day for the teeth-chattering chill she suffered now. When she reached the water's edge, she dumped the laundry on the ground and kneeled down to let cold, clear water run into the pail.

Henry had shown her how to dip just the rim of the pan so she wouldn't take up sludge or the muddy bottom water, but she still had to watch what streamed in at the top, or she'd fill it with floating debris.

She smiled. Her first time to try she'd dipped so low she caught a perch. The poor fish didn't know what to think about swimming with dirty overalls, but it pleased Henry to no end. He'd held it aloft and declared it "eating size" then set out to prove it by laying his chores aside and catching a stringer full to fry alongside hers for supper.

Sarah pushed the memory back and dragged the sloshing washtub to shore. She decided it wouldn't hurt the bundle of clothes a bit to soak until after breakfast. The day should be warmer by dinnertime.

She crested the rise and sighted Henry again. Looked like she still had time to hoe, but pure laziness crept in, so she decided against it.

Dickens had moseyed out to find her. When the old hound saw her top the hill, he lowered his lanky body to the ground and wriggled up to meet her.

"Morning, boy. What you doing way out here?" She scratched behind his ears, and he thanked her by curling his long tongue around her wrist. When he tasted bayou water on her arm, he sat upright and got busy drying her off. He had to be starved, or he'd never have moved from the porch. She drew her shawl around her shoulders and set out for the house to feed him.

Despite his hunger, Sarah beat old Dickens to the yard. She ducked into the kitchen and poured bacon grease over stale bread, threw on the scraps of beans and corn bread left from supper, then spooned the slop into the rusty metal dish beside the steps.

She stood up, her mind on starting Henry's breakfast, and heard a low whistle. Jennie Simpson lumbered up the road in the distance. She waved, and Jennie waved back.

The tonic. Jennie's energy tonic had entirely slipped Sarah's mind. Thankfully, she had a batch made up in the pantry.

Dickens lifted his droopy snout from the dish and rolled onto his side with a groan. Sarah shook her finger at him. "You might try chewing, Dickens. Make it last longer."

He didn't respond and appeared half asleep, his nose just inches from the plate. The old hound could do with a shot of restorative himself.

Jennie made it to the far corner of the yard and cut across to the back of the house.

When she got within shouting distance, Sarah shaded her eyes against the cloudy-day glare and smiled in her direction. "Morning, stranger."

"Morning, Sarah," she called, breathing hard. "It sho' nuff cold out here."

"You poor soul. I can't believe you walked all this way in such grievous weather."

Jennie laughed her good-natured laugh. "Honey, don't you worry. I's bundled up real good." She patted her ample thighs. "And got all this extra paddin' to keep me warm. 'Sides, I ain't had no choice. I needs that tonic to keep me going." She made a wrinkled face and shook her head. "Gots a tiresome workday ahead at Doc Turner's."

Sarah couldn't help thinking the get-up-and-go Jennie used to walk from town would've taken her through two days' labor, but she kept such thoughts to herself. "Well, I'm sure glad to see you, at any rate. You're just in time for breakfast."

"Breakfast?" Jennie stopped at the bottom step, panting and clutching her side. "Well, I already took me some biscuit and gravy right 'fore I left home, but I wouldn't want to offen' you none."

Sarah stifled a grin and turned to open the screen. "Come on in and let a body cook for you for a change. You can just sit back and watch."

Laughter rumbled in the big woman's chest. "I ain't that shiftless, chile. I might be able to crack an egg or two." She stopped and winked. "But I'll let you fry 'em."

Once inside the kitchen, Jennie seemed to forget even the promise to help. She perched her behind in a cane-bottomed chair and caught Sarah up on all the doings at Brooks House while Sarah did all the cracking, frying, and serving of eggs—alongside bacon, biscuits, and grits.

Henry trudged through the door and hung up his coat and hat just as Sarah slid a sheet of golden-topped biscuits from the oven. He took one look and hustled to wash up, with a grin and a nod toward Jennie as he passed.

Having just arrived at the scandalous part of her tale, Jennie offered him only a scanty tilt of the head. She was still talking when Henry came back in and settled across from her. Not just with her mouth—thrusting shoulders, waving hands, and rolling eyes stressed the finer points of Jennie's stories, not to mention the constant bob of her head. And she prattled with nary a break throughout the meal.

Sarah smiled across the table at Henry as Jennie wound up her latest yarn with a slap to her knee and a laugh to rival Dandy's bray.

"I'm tellin' you," she crowed, "I ain't never seen a body run so fast. And his wife right behind him with a broom. Funniest sight I ever seen."

Henry nodded in agreement, his cheeks too full of egg to laugh, but his manner laughed along with her. He swallowed and beamed at Jennie. "And the funniest thing I ever heard."

It rested Sarah's heart to see Henry appear so carefree. Far too soon, he sopped the last bit of running yolk with his last bite of biscuit, stood up, and reached for his coat.

"Pains me to leave good company, but I got a few acres standing between me and quitting time."

Jennie gazed up at him with big eyes. "How you working that soggy ground, Henry?"

He shrugged. "Ain't no way to plow the dirt. Too wet. Thought I'd try to turn over the grassy hill on the east field. Hard work, though. Too much rain, I guess." He tugged his hat down on his head. "Old Dandy don't much cotton to it."

Jennie cackled. "Cain't say as I blame him. You take care, Henry. It sho' was good talking to you."

Talking at you, more like.

The spiteful thought came to Sarah's wayward mind in the time it took to blink. She felt ashamed for thinking it, but it was nothing short of the plain truth. Jennie Simpson could talk a soup bone from a dog's mouth.

The door shut behind Henry, and Sarah's heart gave a tug. Her husband worked too hard. That was the plain truth, too.

"Wish he'd stayed a mite longer," Jennie said, echoing Sarah's own thoughts. "He won't get to hear me tell 'bout Miss Bessie."

"Who?"

Jennie leaned closer and raised her voice, as if shouting would give Sarah better recall. "Miss Bessie Monroe, over to Brooks. Number four?"

Sarah gave her a blank stare.

"We talked about her yesterday. That highfalutin couple what come in on the northbound train."

"Don't you mean Miss Annie Moore?"

"Who Miss Annie?"

"The woman in Mr. Stilley's store. Don't you remember? I told you I saw her in Stilley's with those two reckless girls?"

Jennie shook her head. "I don't know nothing 'bout no Annie. The gal what's staying in number four's named Bessie."

Sarah's brows knit together. "I'm certain they called her Annie Moore in the store. We must be talking about two different folks."

"Can't see how. Ain't but one woman staying at Doc Turner's."

Sarah shrugged. "Never mind. Go on with the story you're busting to tell."

Jennie's eyes opened up and her voice dropped to a whisper. "It's about Miss Bessie and her man. Sarah, them two spar like wet cats."

"They have a squabble?"

"Honey, squabble don't tell it all. You could hear them all over the house. I heard her crying from the third floor."

"What was it all about?"

"Something 'bout he woke up from a drunk and she ain't wearing her bustle, and so where is it. And then he find her fancy parasol in the closet, soaking wet and covered in mud, and her jus' finished swearing she ain't never left the room."

"My, my."

"When I went up to clean, she still be crying. And when she cry, he jus' sit hisself in a chair and read. The louder she bawl, the more he read. Beat all I ever seen."

Sarah shook her head. "He sounds hard."

"Cold as ice. Shame, too, 'cause she's a pretty little thing. I asked her how long they been married"—she gave a wide-eyed nod—"you know, to take her mind off it. Only she don't say a word. He up and say they been married two years. So I asked him how long they been traveling, and she say three weeks. But when I asked where her folks be from, she started crying again."

Sarah clucked her tongue.

Jennie leaned back and stared at the ceiling. "So I asked the gentleman if they be traveling for her health." Her gaze jumped back to Sarah. "You know, 'cause she acting so poorly like. He say yes they is, 'cause she has a spleen in her side."

"A spleen?"

"Tha's right." Jennie placed two fingers beneath her ribs. "It's right here, next to your gizzard."

Sarah nodded.

Jennie continued, "After that, I don't know nothing else they said, 'cause my eyes done lit on her hands. Sarah, that woman be sporting diamond rings so big she can't hardly lift her hands."

Sarah leaned forward. "Diamond rings?"

"Big ones. That's why folks around here call her 'Diamond Bessie,' on account of all her diamonds."

"So it is the same woman I saw in Stilley's."

"You reckon?"

"It has to be. Fancy parasol? Diamond rings? Pretty? Ain't

two strangers wandering Jefferson at the same time to fit that description."

Jennie touched a finger to her chin. "Wonder why she go by two names at once?"

"Jennie, they ain't no telling why white folk do like they do. You know that same as me."

"Hmm. I suppose so."

Sarah snorted. "Sounds like Diamond Bessie brought her problems on herself, what with lying lips and missing bustles."

Jennie shook her head. "Don't know what she trying to hide from that man, but they ain't nothing that woman done to deserve how he treat her. She jus' kindhearted as they come, Sarah. I can see it in her eyes. Around the hotel she treat everyone the same, black or white. Don't seem like she see color at all."

The words hit Sarah hard. Had she misjudged the dark-eyed stranger?

Jennie pushed her plate away and leaned back, eyes wide and blinking as though she just woke up. "Say, what's the hour getting on to be? Doc Turner say he gon' shut the door in my face if I be late one more time." She turned to look out the window, and panic gripped her face. "How long you reckon I've been here flapping my jaws? Can't rightly tell with those clouds hiding the sun. If it's too late, I'll be high-stepping clear to town."

Sarah laughed and got up from the table. "If that's your plan, you will need a tonic." She crossed to the dimly lit pantry and rummaged around the bottom shelf until her fingers closed around one of the last two bottles in the batch.

She handed the brown glass container to Jennie. "Take one teaspoon in water every morning. Not boiling water, but it can be hot. Sip it like tea until it's all gone." She tapped the cork with her finger. "You'll feel spry as a girl before you can say Pete's pig."

Jennie raised the bottle and peered at the dark brew. She gave it a shake, but the thick potion just oozed like cold molasses. "You sure I can't jus' take a swig right now? It's an awful long walk back."

Sarah scowled. "No, you can't take a swig. It's too potent. You liable to take off and fly from here to Brooks House."

Grinning, Jennie started toward the door. "That be all right by me. My feet hurt."

Sarah walked outside with her and gazed in Henry's direction. "I could whistle for Henry and have him harness the rig."

Jennie waved her off. "Let that man work. If I'm late, I'll tell Old Doc I came out here after an energy tonic. He'll be so busy trying to get some of it for hisself, he won't notice the time." Chuckling, she stashed the bottle in her pocket and made her way off the porch, lowering one leg at a time and settling her weight before taking the next step. With both feet firmly on the ground, her gaze went to Dickens, still sprawled in the dirt beside his pan.

"Mercy me! Them's the biggest ears I ever seen on a hound."

Sarah looked over her shoulder at the dog and laughed. "Ain't they, though? Henry says if we propped up Dickens's ears with sticks and pushed him off the house, he'd soar from here to Longview."

Jennie's shrill laughter cut the morning stillness, sending the chickens scrambling. "Girl, he'd pass right by Longview and sail clear to Dallas." After a giggling fit, she turned with a warm smile, wiping her eyes on her sleeve. "Sarah, thank you kindly for the tonic. And for breakfast. That was some fine eatin'." She took a couple of lumbering steps. "If you ever need work, I can vouch for you in the Brooks House kitchen."

Sarah stared across the field where Henry struggled behind the mule. "I hope I never need take you up on that offer, considering my husband swore to care for me as long as he's able."

Jennie followed her gaze. "Can't see as you have anything to fret over in that case. Henry's a fine figure of a man." She turned to go with a backward wave. "I better git if I'm gon' beat that storm back to town. Take care, now, child. And thank you again."

"You're welcome anytime," Sarah called. "To breakfast and my tonics."

When Jennie crossed the yard and passed from sight, Sarah gazed toward Henry and pondered the woman's last words. She allowed herself to consider, just for a moment, how life would be without him. Startled, she pushed away the image of St. Louis that fluttered to her mind. She loved her husband too much to entertain such wicked thoughts.

Didn't she?

A cold, wet nose against her ankle gave her a start. "Dickens! You old rascal—I thought you was sleeping." Sarah nudged him with her foot. "You might warn a body before you slip up behind them." She looked down at his droopy, pleading eyes and shook her head. "You don't need no more to eat, but I reckon I can scare you up some breakfast scraps."

Feeling guilty, she glanced toward Henry and wondered if she'd have jumped so high if she had a clear conscience. Luckily, there was no time to dwell on it. A dish-cluttered table and greasy stove awaited her inside. She pulled open the screen door and stepped into the kitchen. The smell of bacon and biscuits hung heavy in the air, less enticing on a full belly.

Life on a farm revolved around food. Sarah no sooner got breakfast cleared than it was time to start dinner. Most days she planned supper while they ate the noon meal. Hard work honed Henry's appetite as sharp as his plow. Thankfully, she worked just as hard, or she'd be as wide as the barn door.

She pulled on her apron and set to work on the dishes, scraping bits of bacon, egg, and biscuit in a pan for Dickens. Then she heated water and washed dried yolk and grits from the plates, milk and coffee from the tin cups. Lifting the heavy cast-iron skillet with a grunt, she poured bacon grease into a ceramic jar on the stove. Dickens would be hankering after the fresh drippings, but she had to save them for dinnertime biscuits.

The screen door squealed and slammed behind her.

Sarah jerked around. "Henry. You scared me out of ten days' growth. What you doing back at the house two hours before the noonday meal?"

He chuckled and held out his hand. "I come to get me some salve."

She left off cleaning the skillet and joined him by the door. "What happened?"

"Jus' a little cut. Me and Dandy got crossways 'bout which way to go."

Sarah reached for his big hand and with her apron wiped away the blood flowing from a spot between his thumb and forefinger. She held it up to the sparse light struggling through the kitchen window. "It's a poke, not a cut, but it ain't reached the bone." She rubbed her thumb over his knuckles. "At least he left your fingers."

Henry grunted. "Only 'cause I got out of his way. When that old mule reckons it's time to quit, it's a hard sell to turn him."

She ruffled his hair. "Maybe he's smarter than you. Sit at the table. I'll get my poultice powder."

She opened the pantry door and lit the lamp. She needed light to find the powder because she wasn't sure where she'd left it. It could be on the top shelf near the cough syrup she boiled up for croup and the grippe or behind the pokeweed tonic she kept for putrid sore throat. Maybe on the lower shelf next to the last two bottles of energy tonic. She reached to move them aside and froze.

Two bottles? She'd given one to Jennie not one hour ago.

Her eyes shifted to the identical brown containers next to the tonic, and her heart reared up in her chest. She dashed out of the pantry and stood staring at Henry, one twin vessel in each hand.

"We got to get ourselves to town right this minute."

Henry looked up, and his eyes bulged. "What happened, Sarah? You look like you seen a spirit in there."

Dazed, she shook her head. "Not yet, but I might get the chance. I've done killed Jennie Simpson."

CHAPTER 14

Bertha opened her eyes to a darkened room. She thought she'd awakened early until distant thunder pealed, and she realized stormy weather still lingered over Jefferson.

She reached with her big toe to push aside the tasseled shade. The roiling black sky promised rain, but the threat had yet to come through. No new raindrops sprinkled the windowpane, no fresh puddles dotted the path, and Papa puttered with his roses near the trellis, though he wore a heavy coat.

The chill in her room made her loath to give up her quilt, and in her head were memories of Thad she wanted to linger with a bit. He'd been so tender on the ride home, so mindful of her feelings. He even tried to explain away Annie's rebuke in an effort to lift Bertha's spirits. When they arrived on her porch, she knew he itched to tell her his important news. Instead, he pressed his lips to her forehead and insisted she get some rest.

But rest hadn't come easy. After tossing all night on her cotton mattress, she wound up encased in a blanket cocoon. In the early morning hours, she finally surrendered to drowsy lids and fell into a fitful sleep where she and Annie skipped arm in arm through town dressed in nightshirts and corsets, chased by a menacing Abe.

"Bertha Maye!"

She cringed. The tone of Mama's voice meant she'd found Gerta Hayes's boots—Bertha's boots, now—and would require an explanation.

Last night Mama had been so busy scolding her for coming home late, she never noticed her feet. Though Bertha preferred getting all the fussing done at once, she hadn't the heart to rekindle Mama's ire once she finally settled down. So she left the boots on the porch and hustled to her room without mentioning her trade with Mrs. Hayes.

She would pay for it now.

The door swung open and slammed against the wall. Mama stood on the threshold holding the boots away from her with two fingers, as if afraid they might bite.

Bertha took her stature from Papa's pocket-sized family. Emeline Biddie, a foot taller and pounds heavier than Bertha, struck an imposing figure hovering in the doorway.

"Bertha Maye Biddie, did you hear me call?"

She swung her feet to the floor. "Yes, ma'am."

"Why didn't you come?"

"I was about to."

It would do no good to explain that between Mama's call and her appearance, there hadn't been enough time to come. If Bertha had tried, she'd be crumpled in a heap between the door and Mama's prized William Morris wallpaper in the Daisy pattern. Such logic generally escaped the woman's notice.

Mama held the scruffy black boots higher. "Would you care to explain?"

Bertha pointed. "Those are boots." Not a wise response.

Indignation swelled Mama to twice her size. "I know what they are, Bertha Biddie. What I don't know is how they came to be in your possession." She widened her eyes as a warning. "Don't try to deny them. Not even your papa's feet are this small. You're the only one here who could wear them."

She hadn't planned to deny them but decided not to mention it.

"I've tolerated your old lace-ups because Papa said you need them for chores. But I won't abide a second pair." She took a closer look at the footwear dangling from her hands. "And these are even more horrid. Where on earth did you get them?"

"They were a gift."

Disbelief shaped Mama's posture from tilted head to jutting hip. She took advantage of the protruding hip and rested her free hand on it. "Do you intend to sit there and break three of God's commandments at once?"

Bertha drew back in shock. "How have I managed that?"

Mama ticked them off on her fingers. One finger. "Your answer is clearly not the whole truth, which makes it a lie by default." Two fingers. "I believe your attitude toward me in this matter is far less than honorable." She shook the boots at Bertha and held up the third digit. "Your evasive answer about these monstrosities gives me cause to believe you stole them."

Bertha grinned and nodded. "That's three, all right."

"Don't be fresh, Bertha Maye." She tossed the boots in a corner and lifted a rigid shoulder. "I never imagined a daughter of mine would have such an aversion to shoes."

It seemed a cruel twist of fate on both their parts. The fashionable shoes Mama loved to the point of obsession, Bertha considered instruments of torture. In the past she'd tried to conform but had never found comfortable footwear that pleased her finicky mama.

"I'm sorry." Bertha stood up and walked around the end of the bed. "I didn't lie or steal, and I never intend to dishonor you. It just happens."

Mama jabbed her finger toward the corner. "No more nonsense, then. Tell me where those came from."

Bertha steeled herself and plowed ahead. "Magda's mama gave them to me in exchange for my shoes."

It took a full three seconds for the news to sink in before Mama turned around and stared in disbelief. "Your beautiful bronze pumps?"

She held up both hands. "Before you bust a gut, just listen. They weren't beautiful when I gave them."

Mama sagged against the door frame. "What do you mean? They were brand new."

"Yes, they were, but not anymore. I got caught out in the storm and wound up tramping through muddy floodwater." She nodded at the boots on the floor. "Those look better than the shoes did when I finally made it to high ground."

Mama cringed but didn't speak, so Bertha went on.

"The boots don't fit Mrs. Hayes, so she offered them to me. And they're ever so comfortable, as if made for my feet." Mama scowled, so she ducked her head. "Mrs. Hayes took a liking to my shoes, though I can't imagine why."

Mama crossed her arms and raised one dubious brow.

"They were puckered and ruined, I promise. When she offered the boots, I suggested an even trade. It seemed only fair."

This brought Mama ramrod straight. "So the lovely pumps I saved weeks of egg money to purchase—shoes in the latest fashion, I might add—were an acceptable exchange for. . .for. . ."

Papa, who had come to stand behind Mama without her knowing, started to mimic her stiff posture and wild gestures. When he broke into a jaunty Irish jig, Bertha plastered both hands over her mouth. Laughing would be the ruin of them both.

Still oblivious to Papa, Mama stopped waving her arms and glared. "What are you doing, Bertha?"

Papa tugged his twisted vest into place and stepped forward with a poker-straight face. "The girl's speechless with remorse, my dear Emeline."

Mama whirled. "And well she should be. I'm glad you're here, Francis. You need to deal with this girl. I've reached the end of my tether."

"Ah, me lady, surely there's an inch or two left. What dastardly thing has the wee snippet done?"

"Ask her yourself. I'm taking leave of the situation before I lose my temper."

If Mama hadn't already lost her temper, Bertha would just as soon see her go.

Papa put on his pious face. "It can't be that bad. Can't we afford her a bit of Christian charity?"

Mama waved off his suggestion. "Francis, I fear your daughter has depleted my ration of Christian charity for the day and with the sun barely over the horizon." She shoved past him and started down the hall then turned for one last remark. "This time see to it you're not overly lenient, Francis, or you'll answer to me." She left in a huff, still muttering.

Papa raised his hands to his throat and mimicked strangling himself, causing Bertha to erupt in stifled laughter. He waited until the angry clack of heels faded toward the kitchen before he winked and grinned at Bertha. "Stretch out on the bed so I can beat you, daughter. I'm getting too old for the chase."

She clutched her head and moaned. "Can't you do anything with her?"

His cheeks reddened. "Been trying for years. Haven't made much headway. It's my penance for marrying a city girl." He sighed. "Let's get your punishment over and done."

"Do we have to?"

"If you want to save me hide, we do." He touched the end of his chin. "Let me see, now. Can you live with adding Mama's chores to your own until the Sabbath?"

"Tomorrow?"

"Not so easy, me girl. Sabbath next."

She winked. "Can't fault me for trying."

"You would, you rascal. Do we have a bargain?"

She nodded. "We do."

He raised both shaggy brows. "You're sure? It's not too late for a beating."

Bertha laid her cheek on his shoulder, one of the few shoulders she could reach. "The extra chores will do nicely, thank you."

He patted her back and gave her a tight squeeze. "Fine, fine. Now squeal a bit or work up some tears—else you'll land me in trouble, too."

She giggled and pulled away. "Stop it, now. And kindly take leave of my room. I have to dress and get started on all those chores."

He held up his hands. "I'm going, lass. I have to get dressed meself."

She looked him over. "You are dressed."

"Aye, for the barn, not for town."

She widened her eyes. "You're going into town?"

"Right after breakfast."

She clutched his hand. "Oh, Papa, I need to go with you."

He screwed up his face. "I don't know, lass. What about your work?"

"I'll do all I can before we leave and the rest when we get back. I promise." She grabbed both of his arms and pleaded with her eyes. "I need to see about a friend of mine."

Concern creased his forehead. "Is your friend ill?"

She looked away. "She needs my help with a problem."

"I see."

She put both arms around his neck. "Oh, please. It's very important or I wouldn't ask."

His staunch resolve crumbled before her eyes. "This will get us both a lashing, but very well. We'll slip away after we eat."

She kissed his ruddy cheeks. "You're a wonderful papa."

His rosy face turned crimson. "So it's flattery you're up to, is it? Save yourself the trouble, lass. No bit of trickery or slip of the silver tongue can sway Francis Biddie." At the door, he spun on the ball of his foot. "Ah yes, and those extra chores can wait. You may start them Monday morn."

She tried to hide her grin. "Thank you, Papa."

He winked and turned to go.

"Papa?"

"Yes, wee girl?"

"Why are shoes and such so all-fired important?"

He cocked his head and squinted both eyes. "Ah, Bertha, me love. One barefoot day spent dealing with the trials of those too poor to buy shoes and you'd be begging to wear them. Trust your old papa on this one. Now ready yourself for breakfast and be quick about it."

Quick she was, with chores and with breakfast, and in no time they were ready to leave. Mama scowled when Papa announced Bertha would join him on his trip to town, but she held her tongue. Bertha slipped out of the house fast when he pulled the horse and buggy to the door, before Mama decided to make her stay home.

In the two hours since daybreak, Jefferson had come to life. Nearly all of the locals shopped and ran errands on Saturday in preparation for Sunday rest. Lone riders on horseback and families on outings swarmed the streets, and the boardwalks teemed with farmers, merchants, laborers, and backwoodsmen. Gentlemen planters stood in clusters bemoaning the price of cotton and lamenting the decline of trade brought on by the dwindling steamboat traffic.

The ladies, unmindful of their husbands' woes, pranced about in high-dollar duds. Not the elaborate gowns reserved for balls and garden parties or the chaste and unassuming frocks set aside for church—these colorful dresses were their town clothes, topped off by matching parasols and feathered hats.

The carriage from the Commercial Hotel rumbled past, and the toothy driver tipped his hat at Bertha. Papa frowned at the young man then shook his head and winked when Bertha grinned. He reined in the wagon in front of Rink Livery Stable and set the brake. "Won't be a minute, sugar. When I come back, we'll head over to Sedberry's Drugstore." He patted her hand. "I'll let you pick out some nice penny candy."

Bertha pulled her hand free and placed it over his. "I hate to tell you this, Papa, but I'm not ten years old anymore."

He leaned nose to nose with her and scrunched up his face. "Is that a fact? When did it happen?"

She swatted his arm. "A good while ago. A detail you'd notice if you paid better attention."

He pulled her close and chuckled. "Daughter of mine, a man can't see what he ain't looking for." He leaned back and regarded her from a distance. "So that's why the young upstart driver's eyeballs popped?" He stretched his arms out in front of his face. "Out to here, they were."

Her face flushed with heat, and she lowered her head. Papa chuckled and lifted her chin. "You turned into a right bonny lass while me head was turned."

His words flooded Bertha's soul with warmth. "Thank you, Papa."

He kissed her cheek and climbed down then peered up from the ground, scratching his head. "So you're not ten years old, you say? Funny how you never grew."

"Oh, go on with you," she sputtered.

His laughter rang out in the morning air. "Sit tight, then. I'll be back directly. I just need to check on Sol."

"Is Mr. Spellings ill?"

He pushed out his bottom lip. "Nothing any doctor can fix. He's having a hard time dealing with Carrie's loss, is all. If he didn't have the livery to keep him busy, I expect he'd go clean out of his mind." He furrowed his brow and stared toward the livery door.

"Papa?"

Lost in his own thoughts, he regarded her with dazed eyes. "Yes, love?"

"I still have the errand of my own to attend." She pointed. "It's just over on Vale Street. Is it all right if I walk?"

He tilted his head and stared across the distant treetops. "I suppose, since you're not ten anymore, I won't ask what your errand might be." He shook his finger at her. "Go on, then. Just don't cause me any more trouble with your ma."

"I won't. I promise."

He finished securing the reins and helped her to the ground. "I'll pick you up at the corner of Lafayette and Polk in one hour. See that you're there."

"Yes, Papa." Bertha smoothed her bodice and straightened her skirts around her. She looked back, but he had already disappeared through the wide doors of Mr. Spellings's livery.

It took all of her strength to walk in a dignified manner to Brooks House. She longed to break into a mad dash and run, the way Annie described on the bluff—sans bonnet, corset, and shawl.

After last night, the need to ensure her new friend's safety swelled in her heart, pushing reason aside. She didn't know how she would go about it, but she had to speak to Annie away from her frightening companion.

Bertha drew near Brooks House, a grand yet inviting place where the white picket railing and four columns on the ground floor perfectly matched the wide balcony and four columns up top. Inside its walls, weary travelers who could afford it found comfort and rest under the vigilant eye of the hotel's owner, Dr. J. H. Turner.

She had no idea how to find Annie inside or how to get her away from Abe when she did. She just knew she would do it if it took all day and night, although squeezing so much time into the hour Papa had given her might pose a challenge.

Dr. Turner's omnibus approached from the opposite end of the street and pulled to a stop near the steps. Judge Armistead and another man, engaged in quiet conversation, stepped down from the big carriage and strolled to a spot by the front steps. The door of the hotel opened, and Bertha's heart ricocheted in her chest when Abe stepped out on the porch and lit a fat cigar.

Ever so slowly, so as not to attract his attention, Bertha pulled her shawl up over her head and faced the other way. As naturally as she could manage, she took three steps to put a shrub between her and the porch. From the cover it provided, she watched Abe while he watched the judge and his crony. When the two older men sauntered into Brooks House, Abe tossed his cigar over the rail and took the two steps down to the street.

For one heartrending moment, Bertha thought he would head her direction, but he turned right instead and strode down the street whistling, his hands shoved deep in his pockets. Sending a prayer of thanksgiving toward heaven, she made a beeline for the hotel but kept her gaze fixed on Abe's back until she reached the entrance and ducked inside.

Brooks House seemed quiet for a Saturday morning. Bertha expected to find staff buzzing about the dim lobby and guests lounging in the well-appointed parlor. But the judge and his friend must have retired to a room, and there were no porters or maids in sight. Surprisingly, Dr. Turner himself manned the front desk.

Bertha pulled back her shoulders, licked her lips, and sauntered toward him as fast as she dared. "Good morning, Dr. Turner."

He looked up from the copy of the *Jefferson Jimplecute* he had spread open across the desk. "Bertha Biddie. How nice to see you, child. How's your father? We've missed him at the lodge."

"He's well, Doc. Mama's been a mite under the weather, but she's fine now."

He closed the newspaper and crossed his arms on it. "Good, good. Now what can we do for you?"

Bertha cleared her throat. "I need to see a friend of mine. She's one of your guests, but I don't know what room she's in."

Doc pulled the hotel register around so he could see it. "Well, of course, dear. Which guest?"

"Her name is Annie Moore."

When he frowned and flipped the page, Bertha waved her hand at the book. "Forgive me. I guess you know her around here as Bessie Monroe."

Drumming on the desk until Bertha wanted to scream, Doc stared at her as though trying to cipher a disturbing puzzle.

"I'm sorry, Dr. Turner, but I'm in a bit of a hurry."

Frowning, he awoke from his ponderings. "I have a couple of guests registered as A. Monroe and wife. I believe the wife might be the person you seek, considering she has a trunk labeled 'A. Moore.' "

Bertha nodded. "Yes, that's her. Please tell me what room she's in."

He cocked his head. Bertha could almost read in his eyes the questions he wanted to ask. She supposed he thought Annie Moore wasn't exactly the sort of friend she should have.

"I guess it'll be all right," he finally said then pointed behind him. "Go right down the hall to number four. I think you'll find your friend inside."

She pushed away from the desk but stopped and turned back

after only a few steps. "Can we keep this between us, please? I don't want anyone to know I was here."

He pulled on his mustache. "Somehow I can believe that, Bertha. You be careful, now, you hear?"

She nodded then rushed down the ornate hall. She found number four with no trouble and knocked. No one answered, so she knocked again, this time louder. Though she saw Abe leave with her own eyes, her flesh crawled as she pictured him standing behind the door.

"What now?" Annie blustered from inside. "You have the key." She opened in a rush, and all the blood washed from her face. With wide, darting eyes, she looked down the hall before yanking Bertha inside. "What are you doing here? You can't be here."

Bertha's legs threatened to give out, so without an invitation she hurried to sit on the end of the bed. "I'll only stay a minute. I had to see for myself that you're all right."

Annie pointed at the door. "Abe–"

"He's gone. I saw him leave."

She pulled Bertha off the bed by her wrist and herded her toward the exit. "Trust me, he won't be gone long. You have to get out of here before you get us both killed."

The warning sent terror spiking through Bertha's heart. "Killed? Oh, Annie. . ."

Annie seemed surprised by her own choice of words. She waved her hand back and forth, as if the gesture could erase what she'd said. "A figure of speech, silly girl. People say it all the time. It doesn't mean. . . Abe would never. . ."

Bertha wasn't convinced. Annie's lips were smiling, but her eyes were afraid. "Let me take you out of here. You can hide out at my house until he leaves town. Please, Annie."

Annie's put-on confidence crumpled, and she gathered Bertha in her arms. "Oh, sweetie, I'm so glad to see you. I really am. I've wracked my brain for an excuse to leave this room and come find you." She leaned back and peered into Bertha's eyes. "Can you ever forgive me for the way I treated you last night? I felt so bad about it, but I had to pretend I didn't know you. I did a foolish, impulsive thing by running off to the bluff. And then I lied to Abe about it. Only he caught on that I left while he was sleeping. He thinks I'm holding out on him."

"Holding out?"

"Money. He thinks I–"

She bit back the words and turned her face aside. "Well, it doesn't matter what he thinks. I should've told him the truth from the beginning. Now I have to hold my ground, no matter what. Abe hates it more than anything when I lie."

Bertha took hold of her hands. "You can tell me, Annie. He hits you, doesn't he?"

Annie swiped a tear from her cheek with her finger. "Hits me? Don't be silly." Sudden panic crowded her eyes. "Bertha, you have to go now. Please."

She hurried to the door, opened it a crack, and peered out. "Come on. The hallway's empty."

Bertha crossed to her and touched her trembling arm. "I'll go. But there's something we need to discuss. Can you get away from him? Just for a little while?"

She nodded. "Tonight. I'll wait till he's soused and sneak out."

"Is it safe?"

"I've done it before, and I'm still here, ain't I? I'll be fine as long as I don't stay too long, all right?"

"All right."

"We can't go far, though. I need to stay near the hotel. Somewhere out of sight."

"Remember where we met up with Mose to hitch a ride to the bluff? The spot at the end of the alley?"

Annie nodded.

"Meet me there. I'll look for you at sunset, but I'll wait no matter how long it takes."

"I'll be there." Annie peeked out again and pulled Bertha to the door. "It's now or never, sugar. Please go."

Bertha paused long enough to give her a tight hug then slipped out the door. Annie had no sooner closed it than Bertha heard approaching footsteps. She dashed across the hall and stood in front of another room, her hand on the doorknob as if she'd just come out. She feared he'd be suspicious if she lingered, so she headed toward the lobby, though he came right toward her.

They passed in the corridor. Bertha kept her face turned away, her shawl pulled tight against it. Abe mumbled a greeting, and she managed to nod and return it in a low voice. When Annie's door opened and closed behind her, relief flooded her bones.

As she passed the front desk, Doc Turner cleared his throat. "Everything all right?"

She swallowed her tears and nodded.

He picked up his paper and gave it a shake to straighten the pages. "Then good day to you, Bertha."

She smiled at him. "Thank you, Doc."

He winked at her across the *Jimplecute* as she backed toward the door and stepped outside.

CHAPTER 15

Dense clouds had managed to hold the light over Jefferson at bay for the better part of two days. Sarah thought it fitting when the overhead sky parted and the sun fired an accusing ray through her kitchen window, as if God had aimed the light of judgment full in her face. She sagged against the pantry door in tears. "What have I done to that poor woman?"

Henry got up from his chair and took her trembling body in his arms. "Slow down, baby. Jus' tell me what happened."

Sarah pointed in the direction of town. "The tonic I sent home with Jennie Simpson. It ain't no energy tonic at all."

Now Henry looked scared, which scared her more. "What'd you give her, Sarah?"

She held up one of the vials. "Aloe and sacred bark. With some other cleansing herbs."

Thunder sounded, and somewhere overhead a cloud doused the sun ray, drenching the kitchen in shadows again. When the light left, a cold draft rushed in to take its place.

Henry stared at the tonic and swallowed. "Poison?"

"Maybe. If she takes too much. . ." She shook her head. "I don't know for sure."

"What's it gon' do to her?"

She blinked up at him. "Remember those stewed prunes you liked so much at Miss Blow's house last Christmas?"

He tilted his head and answered real slow. "I do."

"Remember what it done to your insides?"

He made a face. "I sho' do."

"Henry, if Jennie mixes the tonic in water like I told her, she might as well done ate ten pots of those prunes all by herself. She left here ready to drink it straight from the bottle."

This time he blinked. Then came the slightest twitch at the corners of his mouth.

Sarah gave him the eye. "Don't you dare laugh."

And that was all it took. Henry laughed so hard the plates rattled. He laughed until tears rolled down his cheeks. He laughed until he doubled over, holding his sides.

Sarah longed to join in, but she couldn't because she still held the terrible mistake in her hands.

He finally rose up and looked at her, likely to see how mad she would be.

She stifled a grin. "I never knew you to be a cruel man, Henry King."

He wiped his eyes with his shirttail. "I'm sorry, Sarah. I jus' keep seeing Miss Jennie running along Polk Street, trying to make it home in time." Saying it must've brought the picture back, because he fell into another howling fit.

Sarah pushed him toward the door. "Go bray it to Dandy whilst you hitch him to the wagon. We should've been halfway to town already."

Henry turned at the door when he heard her gasp. "What now?"

"Jennie said Doc Turner would be itching to try her tonic, too. Said she'd bribe him with it if he saw her coming in late."

He wiped his forehead with his sleeve, no trace of laughter left on his face. "Then you best pray she ran the whole way."

On the porch, Bertha took her first easy breath since she'd entered

Brooks House. After a glance back at the door, she scurried down Vale with plenty of time to spare before she had to meet up with Papa. She reached Lafayette and headed for Polk Street, where Papa said he'd be waiting. A loud whistle sounded behind her, and she turned to find Magda coming up the road in her mama's red surrey.

The two-seater pulled next to her, and she grinned up at Magda. "Remember, ladies don't whistle in the streets like common pitchmen. Your pa will take a strap to your legs."

Magda snorted. "Fine. He can borrow your papa's strap. The one he doesn't have. What are you doing alone in town this early on a Saturday morning?"

Bertha climbed up on the seat beside her. "I reckon I could ask you the very same."

"I ain't alone. Papa's at the barber. Mama's at Stilley's." She dug in the pocket of her dress and produced a sheet of paper. "Meanwhile, I'm to hustle on over to the drugstore and fetch everything on this list."

"Sedberry's? I'm headed there to meet Papa."

"Where've you been this morning?"

Bertha glanced around them before she answered. "Can you keep a secret?"

Magda drew back and glared. "Did you just ask if I could keep a secret?"

Bertha laughed. "Don't get your bustle in a bunch. Long-standing habits are hard to break."

Magda waved a dismissive hand. "Just get on with it."

"I've been to see Annie over at Brooks House."

Magda stiffened. "Oh?" she asked with an air of indifference. "How is she?"

"Truth is, she's in terrible trouble. I can't go into it now, but I'm awfully worried about her."

Magda gave her a look. "It's that man she's with, isn't it?"

Startled, Bertha looked into her knowing eyes. "Goodness, how'd you guess?"

Magda sniffed. "I know trouble when I see him."

Bertha gripped her friend's hands. "Oh, Magda, I believe he's dangerous. Annie's scared witless of him. There has to be a reason."

A wagon veered close, driven by an agitated woman and loaded down with rowdy youngsters. Six stair-step boys, all with runny noses and unruly shocks of brown hair, stared up from the wagon bed.

Bertha nodded at the poor mother then watched them rattle off down the road.

Magda tugged on her fingers. "What are you going to do?"

"There's nothing I *can* do. I'm smart enough to know that much. But God can do plenty, and I intend to tell Annie so."

"Think she'll listen?"

"Her life may depend on it. Her eternal life, at least."

Magda sat back against the seat and crossed her arms. "At least it's given you something to worry about besides what's happening to your own life. You seem in awfully good spirits, considering."

The baffling statement didn't bode well. Magda knew something Bertha didn't. Something bad. "Good spirits considering what?"

"Papa was ever so mad when he got home last night. Ready to skin Thad and hang him in the square for running off with you. But today Charles Gouldy explained why. Now Papa understands completely."

Bertha gripped the sides of her head. "Understands what? What are you going on about?"

Magda heaved an irritated sigh. "You know. About him leaving tomorrow."

"Who's leaving tomorrow?"

"Thad, of course."

The three words rushed at Bertha in a fuzzy white fog, and her ears started to ring. The noisy, bustling town around her faded to the far distance. She tried to shake the haze enough to understand. "What did you say?"

"Thad." Magda's tone sounded less sure. "He's leaving for school first thing tomorrow morning." She covered her face with both hands until only wide-open eyes were visible above her fingertips. "Oh, sugar, you didn't know."

Bertha struggled for her voice. "Who told you that outlandish story?"

"Charlie." She pointed behind them. "I just left off talking to him and his sister in front of the barber shop. He said Thad swore to tell you last night."

A seething cauldron of rage tipped over inside her chest. She writhed with shame at how she'd lingered in bed nursing fanciful notions about Thad's motives. He hadn't put her feelings above a desire to share his news. He'd simply run out on her. She'd mistaken cowardice for consideration and careless disregard for concern.

"Turn this thing around," she demanded, pointing back over her shoulder.

Magda, pressed into the corner of the surrey waiting for her reaction, seemed taken aback. "Why?"

"I'm going to see Thad. I need you to take me."

Magda looked more thunderstruck than when she'd first let the news slip. "That's the most improper suggestion I'll ever hear. You won't do any such thing. You can't."

Bertha met her scandalized gape with gritty determination. "I can, and I will."

Magda's head rocked back and forth. "I won't be a party to it. It's too reckless bold, even for you."

Bertha waved her finger in the direction of Thad's house. "Thaddeus Bloom can show you a thing or two about reckless bold. The deceitful scoundrel held my hand in Julius Ney's barn. Kissed my forehead on my own front porch. He's dangled me like a lovestruck marionette for the sake of his ego, all the while knowing he'd be riding away tomorrow. Nothing I do at this point can stack up to the shameless thing he's done."

Magda tilted her head, compassion clouding her dark eyes. "Oh, Bertha. . ." Steeling herself, she held up her paper and waved it. "What about my list? I'll be in trouble with my folks."

Bertha patted her hand. "Don't fret, then. I understand. I'll find my own way." She started climbing down, but Magda latched onto her skirt and pulled her back.

"No, you won't, blast you." She released the brake and whipped the surrey around in the middle of the street. "I must be teched in the head, but we're on our way. We have to hurry, so sit tight and hang on to your corset."

As they raced through town, Bertha's thoughts went to Papa, waiting for her in front of the drugstore, and her promise not to get him into any more trouble. Then her jilted heart took over again, crowding guilt aside. She took the reins from Magda's hands and urged the horse to go faster.

Henry pulled to the servants' entrance behind Brooks House, and Sarah scrambled to the ground without waiting for his help. She left him to tether Dandy and, with no thought to who might be watching, lifted the hem of her dress and ran. After a series of undignified knocks, she lost all patience and reserve and pounded the door with clenched fists. The door jerked opened at the same time Henry bounded up to join her.

Thomas Jolly, Doc Turner's head porter, scowled at them from the threshold. "Well, if you two ain't the last folks I expected to see making a ruckus behind this door. Why you be trying to beat it down, Henry?"

Traitor Henry pointed her way. "Ain't none of me. It was Sarah."

Thomas shifted his lazy gaze. "You, Sarah?"

"Yes, me. Now stand aside. I need to see Jennie Simpson right away."

Still blocking the door, he gave her a puzzled look. "You heard already? Can't see how. It jus' happened."

Sarah and Henry shared a look.

"Poor old Jennie," Thomas went on. "I's loath to see harm come to such a fine, hardworking woman, but the good Lord done decided it be her time to rest."

Sarah clutched Henry's hand so tightly her fingers ached.

Thomas stepped aside. "I guess you come for to see her. Step right this way. We laid her out on the kitchen table."

Sarah's world spun. Sweat popped out on her lip, and all the sap drained from her legs. Henry's hand on her back was the only thing holding her in place. If only he'd just remove it, she could ease out of there and find the strength to run.

Thomas's voice echoed in her head. "Well? Is you coming in or not? I got to shut this door before Miss Jennie draw flies."

Sarah's stomach lurched. She turned and buried her face in Henry's shirt, but he gently guided her to the door, whispering in her ear all the while.

"Stop it, now. Straighten up and act natural. Don't attract no attention to yourself."

Trying to say yes and no at the same time, her head bobbled like a fishing cork. "I can't go in there, Henry."

"Yes, you can," he hissed. "We come to see, and we gon' see. If we leave now, it won't look right. You got to carry through."

It felt like Henry had ten arms at work behind her, pushing, prodding, and lifting, until she made it down the long, dim corridor outside the kitchen. Thomas, who led them the whole way, opened the door and went inside.

Sarah dug in her heels. "I can't, Henry. I won't stand looking down at her, knowing it's all my fault."

He gripped her arm hard. "Shush your mouth, Sarah. It was an accident." He let go of her arm and cradled her face in his hands. "Whatever happens, we face it head-on. I ain't gon' let nothing bad happen to you. But you got to hush saying it's your fault, or I can't protect you."

He ran his fingers through her hair. "Straighten your back, now. Raise your chin. That's right. Now follow me."

He took her wrist, his hold so tight she couldn't break free if she tried. When he opened the door and pulled her inside, she closed her eyes, dread squeezing her chest. She heard milling footsteps and low murmurs in the room, and a woman's clear, steady voice rising above the others.

When Henry gave a low chuckle beside her, Sarah thought she must be hearing things. She opened one eye and peeked at him. A mixture of glee and sheer relief warmed his face, and his firm grip on her waist became a caress. The next sound was the loud bray she'd last heard at breakfast.

"Dat's de funniest story I ever heard, Miss Bessie. Go on, tell another."

Sarah opened both eyes and spun toward the sound. Jennie sprawled on the sturdy oak table, her jolly face aglow. All activity in the usually bustling kitchen had ceased, and the staff stood in a quiet circle around her. Everything that once graced the table—assorted utensils, a lantern, several baskets, and a set of nested bowls—they had placed beneath the table or pushed to the floor. One of Doc Turner's maids had a rag and a pan of water and was washing Jennie's legs, while the woman she called Miss Bessie, but Sarah knew as Annie Moore, sat at Jennie's feet prodding her bruised and swollen ankle.

Before Miss Annie could speak, Jennie caught sight of Henry towering above the others and sent her roaming gaze in search of Sarah. "Why, looky who come to see about me. Ain't that nice. You two heard about my fall, then?"

Henry cleared his throat. "We heard a little, but not the whole story. Why don't you tell us what happened?"

The woman needed no stronger bidding. "All right, den. You see, I was hurrying to get to work on time, only I know'd for sure I's gon' be late. So I crawled under a fence and struck out over a pasture, thinking to save time travelin' as the crow flies. I got clear to the other side of the field when I stepped in a hole, and down I come, right on a fresh cow patty." She rolled her head on the table and laughed, her cheeks so round they hid her eyes. "I was a funny sight, I'm tellin' you. Busted my ankle up real good, though."

Jenny rose up and motioned for Sarah. When Sarah came close, she understood why the young maid who scrubbed Jennie's legs held her nose and why Thomas had fretted over flies. Jennie had brought most of the cow pie back with her.

"I'd be laid there still, wallowing in my mess, if Mr. Ney and his boys hadn't come along. They helped me up and loaded me on their big old wagon then brung me all the way here."

Jennie waved toward Miss Annie with the handkerchief she held in her hand. Pale blue embroidered silk. Sarah knew it didn't belong to her.

"This sweet soul got wind of my troubles and come all the way downstairs, fussing over me and wiping my brow with this nice little hankie." She held it up for Sarah to see. "Then insisted on tendin' my broke ankle herself."

The well-dressed woman glanced up from her work, a smile in her bright eyes. "Jennie, my dear, you have a sprain, not a break. You'll be fit as a fiddle in a few days. But you need to stay off of it until then."

Jennie leaned up on her elbows with alarm in her eyes. "What you mean stay off it? I cain't stay off it. How am I supposed to work standing on one foot?"

Miss Annie flashed Sarah a wink and a smile. "A sprain is good news. Have you forgotten you believed your ankle to be broken just a moment ago?" She finished winding long strips of white cloth around Jennie's injury then patted her leg above the wrap. "I'd say this means you're not supposed to work, for a while at least."

Thomas stepped closer, nodding his head. "I jus' said the same to Henry by the door. The good Lord must done decided you been working too hard, Miss Jennie. The scripture do say, 'He maketh me to lie down. . . .' The good Lord means for you to rest a spell."

Henry surprised Sarah by speaking up from his place by the door. "God ain't struck this woman in the leg, Thomas. He don't do such things."

Jennie fell back and commenced to thrashing and wailing. "I cain't rest for a spell, Thomas. I'll find myself wanting a job if I do." She covered her face and started to cry. "What am I gon' do? Doc Turner gon' fire me now for sho'."

Miss Annie stood, her lacy blue gown out of place in the greasy, cluttered kitchen. "Now, now, dear lady. Dr. Turner seems a reasonable man and a kindly sort. I doubt he'd be inclined to fire you for getting hurt."

Sarah eased out of the way as Miss Annie moved to Jennie's side. When Jennie uncovered her face and stopped her tossing, Miss Annie smiled down at her. "If you think it'll help, I'll be happy to say a word to him on your behalf."

Jennie blinked away her tears. "You'd do such a kindness? For me?"

Annie leaned down and patted her wet face. "And why not? I'll go tend to it right away." She picked up Jennie's hand. "Will you be all right now?"

Jennie gazed up at Miss Annie as though she'd sprouted a halo and wings. "Oh, yes'm. I will, now you done fix me up." Smiling, she held up Miss Annie's handkerchief. "Here's your pretty hankie back."

Miss Annie patted the hand holding the delicate scrap of cloth. "Would you like to keep it?"

Jennie's eyes bulged. "Oh yes, ma'am. If you really don't mind."

"I don't mind one bit."

It amazed Sarah how comfortable Miss Annie seemed, how at home in a messy hotel kitchen filled with Sarah's people. She marveled at how Annie listened to them with interest, how she touched Jennie with genuine affection. Sarah had never seen such behavior from a white woman before, not even in St. Louis.

The fancy woman. . .no, the special lady met Sarah's eyes. "Don't I know you? Sarah, from the dry goods store, isn't it?"

Sarah tried to lower her gaze, but the soft gray eyes held hers. "Yes'm. That's right."

Miss Annie held out her hand. "It's good to see you again."

Astonished, Sarah reached a timid hand and let the lady take it in her own.

"May I leave our Jennie in your care? You'll see she gets up to her room, won't you?" She raised her brows at Henry. "You'll help her?"

Henry nodded. "Yes, ma'am. We'll see to it."

"Thank you both," Miss Annie said and gave Sarah's fingers a gentle squeeze.

When she started for the door, Sarah watched her closely, because she needed to know. Miss Annie crossed the whole length of the kitchen, pausing once to give last-minute instructions to Thomas, then left the room, without once wiping her hand on her skirt.

Jennie tugged at her sleeve. "You want to hear the worst part, Sarah?"

Fighting tears, she pulled her attention from the door. "What's that?"

Jennie patted a wide stain around her skirt pocket. "I done broke my bottle of tonic. Now what am I gon' do?"

Sarah smiled down at her childlike pout. "Sounds to me like you ain't about to need no energy tonic. But if it makes you feel better"—she reached into her own pocket, pulled out a brown bottle, peered closely at the contents, and then slipped it into Jennie's waiting hand—"just so happens I got another one right here."

At the door, Henry started to laugh. "Miss Jennie, take some advice from old Henry. No matter how much you like the first helping, don't go for seconds. Some things is better in small doses."

CHAPTER 16

Halfway to Thad's house, Bertha pulled the surrey to a stop along the dense wall of pine by the side of the road. She met Magda's gaze and answered her unspoken question. "Go back, Magda. I've changed my mind."

When she handed over the reins, Magda's confused look changed to bewilderment. "After all this? Why?"

"I shouldn't have asked this of you. It's bad enough I've brought down calamity on my own head. Poor Papa's, too, more than likely. I have no right to pile it on yours, as well. Go on back and see to your errands. I can walk to Thad's from here."

Magda sighed. "I've come this far. It's no more trouble to take you the rest of the way." She flicked the reins and whistled, goading the horse back onto the street. They rode in silence until Magda cut her eyes at Bertha. "I am still wondering if this is a good idea. I mean, it is sort of. . ."

Bertha twisted on her seat. "Sort of what?"

Magda swallowed and faced forward, taking her time to answer. "You know."

"Please quit studying that horse's behind and say what you're itching to say."

Magda glowered at her. "Brazen. It's downright brazen."

The words caused anger to rise in Bertha's throat. She whipped around and slapped the wooden seat so hard it rattled her bones. "You just don't know when to hush, do you?" She pointed at the ground. "Let me off this thing right now."

Magda hauled back on the reins. The surrey rolled to a stop and the two sat facing each other in angry silence. Magda crossed her arms. "Well, go ahead. Get down and run off. It's why you stopped, ain't it?"

Bertha managed a nod.

"Well then, why don't you?"

Grief crowded Bertha's throat, blocking her answer. The weight of her predicament pinned her to the seat, so heavy she could barely lift her shoulders in a helpless shrug. Tears stung her eyes, tears she couldn't stop if she tried. When Magda's startled face dissolved into a reflection of her pain, she released the pent-up flood.

Magda scooted beside her and gathered her close. "Don't cry, sweetie. Please don't." She smoothed Bertha's hair and rocked her on the seat while she fished a hankie from her bodice. "Here you go." She tucked the cloth in Bertha's hand. "You're right. I should learn when to keep my mouth shut." She leaned back and tilted Bertha's chin. "Dry your face, now. I'll take you straight to Thad's and won't say another word about it."

Bertha wiped her eyes and tried to swallow the hedge-apple-sized lump in her throat. "No, you were right to speak up. Running after him is the wrong thing to do. If Thad cared about my feelings, he'd have told me himself. Not let me hear it on the street."

"Honey, I think he tried."

Bertha banged her fist on one knee. "No, he didn't. He had plenty of chances to tell me."

Magda raised her hands in surrender. "All right, then. Thad's a scoundrel of the first order."

Bertha whirled on her. "Don't say such a thing. He wanted to tell me all along. Isn't that what Charlie said?"

Magda patted Bertha's clenched fists. "Whoa there. Remember, I'm on your side—whatever side it is. But you have to make up your mind." She lifted her chin toward the road. "And you have to decide if we're going to Thad's house. Otherwise I'm turning this contraption and heading back to town."

The easy stride of Thad's horse didn't match the determination in his soul, yet dread had gathered and settled in the pit of his stomach, preventing him from urging the mare on. The task ahead weighed heavily, pulling him so tight his bones ached.

His thoughts turned to the words King David cried while in distress. *"Have mercy upon me, O LORD, for I am in trouble: mine eye is consumed with grief, yea, my soul and my belly. . . . My strength faileth because of mine iniquity, and my bones are consumed."*

The ancient words twanged a familiar chord with Thad. His joints hurt as much as his empty, knotted stomach.

He should've told Bertha days ago. Putting it off had spared him seeing her upset, but waiting only stacked up the pain and gave him so little time to say good-bye.

Well, no more. Though long overdue, today was the day. He swore to himself he'd not return home until he spoke with her.

He came to the cutoff that led to a shortcut into town, a path the mare always took without his bidding. When she plodded right past and kept with the road, he wondered briefly why she chose the long route but didn't bother to rein her back. Then he wondered at his willingness to let her go the long way and hoped his cowardice hadn't returned.

He didn't have far to go before he understood why the mare didn't turn. Around a bend in the road, Magda's surrey came into sight, pulled to the side with Magda and Bertha aboard. His mare must've smelled the old gray horse and decided a visit was in order. Or maybe God Himself desired a swift end to Thad's procrastination.

Heart pounding, he approached the carriage. The two girls sat with their heads together, Bertha leaning toward her friend. When Thad saw her wipe her eyes, his heart stopped pounding and crawled up his throat.

She knew. Somehow Bertha knew. It was the reason they were on the road to his house and the reason she cried. He shoved down the yellow-bellied urge to flee and rode their way.

Magda saw him first. She watched him come with a mixture of sorrow and anger on her face. Then she sat up, nudged Bertha, and pointed over her shoulder. He came alongside and Bertha stared into his eyes with a look he couldn't describe.

He gave her a curt nod. "I was on my way to see you." It sounded weak, even to him.

She blinked a few times, as if to convince herself she really saw him there. "I was, too. Until I came to my senses."

He hated himself for her tears, her red-rimmed eyes, the pain so evident on her face. "I should've told you myself, Bertha. I tried."

She looked away, and the rebuff twisted his stomach in knots. He glanced at Magda for help, but she shook her head and put her arms around Bertha.

"Magda, can you leave us alone? I need to talk to her."

The balance of sorrow and anger shifted, and Magda glared at him over Bertha's head. "I won't leave unless she tells me to."

The wind picked up, whipping and bending the overhead trees, chilling Thad's poor scattered bones. His insides danced and tossed in time with the treetops while he waited for Bertha to speak, and for the first time that morning, he felt glad he'd had no stomach for breakfast. When her silence stretched on, he thought to turn the mare and ride away, but his heart insisted he stay.

"I'll beg if I have to, Bertha, but you can spare me muddy knees if you'll climb down and come here."

"Why should I spare you anything?" she asked without looking up. "The sight of you on your knees might be just what I need to feel better."

Thad swung his leg over the horse and dismounted. "Then it's a small price to pay."

By the time he reached the surrey, Bertha had turned. "What do you think you're doing?"

He knelt in the cold, miry clay beside the road. "Making you feel better."

"No, don't!" She scurried to the edge of the seat and dropped her legs to the step. "Thad, you stop it right now." She came even with him and took his arm, trying with little success to pull him to his feet.

Down on his knees, his face wasn't much lower than hers. "Do you feel better yet? This ground is mighty cold."

"All right. I feel better."

"Will you stay awhile with me and let me explain?"

"Whatever you say. Just get up from there."

The look she returned as he gazed up at her gave him courage. He got to his feet and pulled her in front of him. "I have so much I need to say to you. I just don't know where to start."

Magda cleared her throat. "While you're trying to sort it out, kindly get out of the way so I can turn this thing around."

Thad eased Bertha off the road, and Magda urged the horse around. She stopped beside them and leaned down. "I suppose you'll get her safely home, then?"

Thad nodded, and she flicked the reins. He tucked Bertha under his arm, and they stood together while the surrey moved along Line Street toward town. He watched Bertha's face as she stood staring after Magda. He had powerful feelings for the girl beside him, feelings that had gone unspoken for too long. So many nights he'd wrestled with his thoughts and his sheets, wondering if she felt the same. But he knew then what he knew now. He had no right to ask her.

"Bertha?"

She lifted teary eyes to his. "Yes?"

"Can you ever forgive me?"

"It's true, then. You're leaving Jefferson."

"You knew one day I would."

"Yes, one day. Just not tomorrow." She blushed. "I thought we had more time."

He reached to touch the soft spot under her chin. "I have no choice. My fate was decided a long time ago."

Her brow furrowed. "Your fate? You make it sound like a trip to the gallows." She whirled away from him with a swish of petticoats. "Surely a man can decide for himself if he's ready for hanging?"

He took her by the shoulders. "You don't understand, sugar. It's Papa's dream that I attend a good school and be the first college graduate in our family. I can't let him down."

Her frown deepened. "So it's your Papa's dream, not yours?"

"The man's talked of little else since I can remember, planned and saved for years. I've watched Mama and Cyrus do without while he stashed away money for school." Desperate for her understanding, he gripped her arms. "When Papa got wind of Texas AMC opening right there in Brazos County, it was all it took to send him over the edge."

Thad let go of Bertha and began to plod back and forth. "You should see him when he talks about it. I tell you, his face lights up, and he looks ten years younger. The last few days. . .well, you'd think he was the one leaving for school in the morning."

Bertha grabbed his arm to stop his pacing. "Do you hear yourself?" She tightened her grip on his arm. "Has any of this ever been about you?"

Her simple words leapt to life, striking hard and boring to the center of his gut, to the secret place where he'd buried the same ungrateful, disloyal question. Bertha, by voicing it aloud in her sweet, sincere voice, had rooted straight through and exposed it and somehow shed a different light on his betrayal.

"What are your dreams?" she persisted.

"My what?"

"Every man has dreams, Thad. What do you want out of life?"

He sighed. "Not much, really. All it would take to make me happy is some farmland, a pond for fishing, and a place to raise dogs." He blushed and grinned. "And a good woman to share such bounty."

"Dogs?" She laughed, but not at him, and he loved the throaty sound.

"Hunting dogs. Men pay top dollar for good hunting dogs.

With proper breeding and training, there's money to be made." Just talking about it stoked a fire deep in his heart. "Like Henry King's bloodhound, for instance. Old Dickens is one fine-looking animal. Did you ever get a good look at him, Bertha?" He cupped his hands beside his head. "Ears on him like an elephant's."

She laughed louder. "Thaddeus Bloom, you're glowing. You sure don't shine like this when you talk about going to school."

Thad looked away. He'd never clear his head by staring into her bewitching eyes. "Bertha, I should've told you I had to go before now. I have no excuse for such ill treatment, and I hope you'll forgive me. But no matter how much I love you, only one thing really matters. I'm leaving tomorrow, and I don't know when I'll be back. Nothing can change it."

A hurt looked erased her glowing smile. She crossed her arms over her chest and presented him with her back.

He reached to touch her shoulder. "Bertha?"

She jerked her shoulder from under his hand and walked a few steps away. "You really think your leaving is all that matters, Thad? Well, you're wrong." She spun and ran at him, burrowing into his shirt. "I think loving each other should be what matters most."

He didn't trust himself to hold her the way he wanted, so he patted the top of her head as if she were a sister and then felt silly for having done it. Bertha loved him, too. She'd just said so. And he had nothing to offer for her trouble.

Thad moaned at the sky. "I don't want to leave you, Bertha. Especially now. But I have to go, and I can't take you with me."

She nodded in his arms. "I know you have to go, and I understand. I really do. Though I can hardly bear the thought."

"Will you write me? Your letters will make the time go by faster." He mentally kicked himself. He had no right to expect that sort of commitment.

"I'll write to you every day. I promise."

"No, sugar. No promises. I can't ask you to keep them. I can't even ask you to wait for me. It wouldn't be fair."

She opened her mouth to speak, but he pressed his finger to

her lips. "Bertha, let's not think about what comes later. If your Papa will let me come see you tonight, I'll stay with you as long as I can."

"Oh, Thad. That sounds so nice. I'm sure Papa will let you stay late if I tell him you're leaving tomorrow. And Mama will want you to come in time for supper."

He grinned. "You sure know how to sweeten the pot."

She laughed, and the lighthearted sound of it lifted the anchor from his heart.

"I wish I'd known sooner I could lure you with food. How about if I ply you with cobbler for dessert?"

"I'd say it sounds like I'd better rush home and pack. I won't have time later." He pulled her to him for a chaste hug, as chaste as he could manage, at least. "Bertha, I want us to be together every minute until I leave."

She leaned back and focused on his eyes. "We will be. If I have to move heaven and earth to be with you tonight, I'll make sure it happens."

CHAPTER 17

No two ways about it, Miss Annie had the gift. Wonder of wonders, she convinced Doc Turner to put Jennie in a room upstairs at Brooks House while she mended. Thomas, who witnessed the whole thing, said Miss Annie insisted he would be doing her a great kindness, considering she wouldn't need to walk clear back to the servants' quarters to tend Jennie's ankle. Thomas claimed that Doc Turner, who didn't stand a chance against Miss Annie's beguiling ways, just lifted his hat and nodded while grinning like a love-struck boy.

When the shock from the unlikely arrangement wore off, Sarah had Henry and Thomas brace the jabbering Jennie between them and help her to the foot of the stairs. Then Henry took over, winding her arm about his neck while she hopped on one leg up the steps. A wide-eyed Thomas followed, holding his fidgety arms out front as if ready to catch Jennie's tumbling body. Sarah figured he might as well save himself the trouble. If Jennie fell, she'd take them all to the bottom with her.

Sarah brought up the rear, one hand laden with a bowl of Cook's hot broth, the other with fresh linens. At the top landing, Jennie nodded to the right, too busy talking to stop and give directions. Henry guided his cumbrous burden around the polished banister post then along the hall to the first door. Thomas bobbed in front to turn a key that dangled from the lock.

Henry glanced back at Sarah and shook his head. By the look on his face, she knew what he had on his mind. He often pondered white folks' uncommon fixation with bars and bolts, considering his people had fought so hard to be free of them, so a key stored on the outside of a locked door would be just the thing to vex his mind. But Sarah knew the reason. Jennie once mentioned it let the maids know which rooms were empty and needed cleaning.

Thomas swung the door open onto the prettiest room Sarah had ever seen, even counting Miss Blow's house back home. The walls, so high you could stack two and a half men against them head to toe, were covered in wallpaper the color of a sunset, like pink stirred up with orange peels. Rows of tiny flowers, the shade of eggshells, dotted the pink. Tall mahogany posts of equal height jutted to the ceiling from the four corners of the high bed. The same molasses-colored wood as on the posts, rubbed with carnauba wax to a high shine, made up every stick of furniture in the room.

Jennie pointed at a spindly-legged bench that looked too fragile to hold her. "Jus' drop me on the settee, Henry, while Sarah makes the bed. Thomas, pull up the stool yonder for my poor old foot. Sarah, you can put my broth on the side table to cool, but lay a napkin over it so no dust settles on top. And by the by, hold the pillow out the window and beat it good a'fore you covers it. Nothing I hates worse'n a dusty pillow." She chuckled. "Less'n it be dusty soup." She frowned at Thomas, who had done her bidding but now edged toward the door. "Come back over here and pull in this stool so I can reach it better. My leg ain't made of rubber."

Sarah stifled a grin but couldn't help raising one eyebrow at Henry, who seemed to have a harder time hiding his amusement. He busied himself by taking hold of the other corners of the sheet Sarah held, raising his side high overhead and flapping so hard she nearly lost her grip. As the sheet settled to the bed between them, he gave her a playful wink. She turned away and bit her lip to hold in the laughter.

Henry rescued her by drawing Jennie's attention over to him. "Mighty nice of Doc Turner to open up this room for you, Miss Jennie."

Jennie sat on the edge of the settee turning her ankle back and forth, studying it from every angle with puckered lips. At Henry's words, her fretful look turned to joy, and she beamed up at him. "You got that right, Henry."

She gazed around the room as if she'd never seen it before. "All the times I swept and dusted in here, I never once imagined I'd be sleeping in that bed." She turned a squinty eye on Henry. "But it weren't really Doc's idea, you know. He didn't have the starch to stand up to Miss Bessie, that's all."

They all nodded and mumbled their agreement.

Jennie drew her shoulders back and raised her chin. "Not to say Doc don't hold me in the highest regard." She lowered her voice and peered at the three of them in turn. "But we all know things don't happen this way 'round these parts. If Doc hadn't been plum bothered and befuddled by Miss Bessie, none of us would be sitting here in this nice room."

Sarah cast a quick look at Henry. Sure enough, Jennie's talk about the way things were around Jefferson had him squirming.

He grabbed a feather pillow and blustered over to throw open a window. Leaning on the bustle bench under the sash, he pounded the pillow until soft tufts of down formed a cloud around him and drifted like snow to the street. "Hard to believe it's jus' past noon," he called over his shoulder. "This storm got it dark as gloom out here. Cold, too."

Jennie pulled the afghan from the back of the small sofa and wrapped it around her shoulders. "Hurry up and close off that draft, Henry. All I need is the croup to go along with this ankle."

Henry shut the window and tossed the pillow to Sarah. "There now, Miss Jennie. Your bedding's dusted, and all danger of the croup is past."

Sarah slid on the crocheted pillow slip and patted out the lumps then turned to give the room a careful look. "I guess that about does it, Jennie. Unless you can think of anything else you might need."

Jennie took a look around and smiled up at Sarah. "Seem like you done thought of everything."

Sarah placed an extra blanket at the foot of the bed. "You sure I can't stay and sit with you tonight?"

Jennie waved her hand. "My sister's girl gon' be here directly. Should've been here by now, in fact. Don't worry—I got Thomas to care for me till she come." She peered past Henry to where the startled man still lurked by the door. "Ain't that right, Thomas?"

He spewed and sputtered, backing toward the door and shaking his head.

Jennie shook her finger and fixed him with a warning look. "Hush, now. Bring yourself over here and sit down. You ain't gon' no place till my niece show up."

Sarah picked up the broth and handed it to Thomas, who reacted as if she'd handed him a skunk. "This is cool enough to sip now. See she drinks it down."

Laughing, Jennie took it from the stricken man. "It's my ankle what's ailing, Sarah. Not my hands. You two git on home to your chores. You've wasted enough of this day foolin' 'round with me. Not to say I ain't grateful."

Sarah leaned down to hug her. "I'm just glad you're all right, that's all." *Powerful glad.*

Behind her, Henry cleared his throat. Sarah guessed he must be thinking along the same lines, remembering what they feared had happened to Jennie. She decided if he laughed, she'd skin him.

Outside, Sarah drew in fresh air laden with sweet relief. It felt good to be headed home instead of to the jailhouse. She sat tall and proper in town, but when the wagon rolled past the Polk Street Bridge, giddy laughter bubbled to the surface. Henry stole a look behind them then pulled back on the reins, climbed down, and ran around to her side. She stood up, fit to bust, and soared into his arms. He swung her around in circles, both laughing so hard their tears mingled each time he kissed her.

"I never been so relieved of a thing in my life!" Henry yelled.

"I thought sure I'd be watching you hang."

Still clinging to his neck, she jerked her gaze to his face. "But you said–"

"Never mind what I said. I'd done give you up to the noose. Figured nothing on earth could save you. 'Specially if you'd done killed Doc Turner, too."

If not for his rascally grin, she'd have throttled him. "I've never been so scared in all my born days."

His arms around her waist tightened, and his grin disappeared. "Neither have I, Sarah. I always figured I could protect you from any harm that came your way. I learned today they's some things only the Lord can shield you from. Don't think I didn't call on Him."

Sarah leaned her head against Henry's broad chest and let him hold her. She couldn't tell which of them trembled the worst, but she felt his heart pounding against her cheek.

Henry kissed the top of her head. "I'm jus' grateful the Almighty took care of you."

She rose on her tiptoes and kissed his chin. "Me, too."

He pulled back, a glint in his teasing eyes. "You reckon it's the first time the good Lord used cow manure to save one of His own?"

Sarah laughed again, and he pulled her close for a tender kiss, but they sprang apart at the sound of approaching hooves. Henry tightened his arm around her waist at the sight of three men on horseback headed their way. One of them, a pale-skinned man with long, stringy hair the color of jerked beef, rode out in front. Henry took her arm and gave her a gentle shove toward the rig. "Get aboard, Sarah. Those men are strangers."

The edge in his voice set her feet in motion. Without waiting for him to lift her, she grabbed the side rail and clambered onto the seat. In his haste, Henry made it around Dandy and into his place before she ever sat down.

"How do you know they're strangers?"

The men were close enough now to hear, so Henry whispered his answer. "The horses they're riding came from Rink Livery." As he spoke, a winsome smile slid over his face, and he raised his hat in greeting. "How ya'll doing?"

The men had started reining in their mounts before Henry said a word. Sarah sensed it didn't bode well. Her legs tensed under her, ready for flight.

Up close, the first man wasn't much taller than the others. He only seemed so from a distance because he held himself high in the saddle and wore a proud smirk on his face. He turned cold eyes on Henry and called back to his men in a sassy tone, "What we got here, boys? This uppity whelp thinks he can address us without permission, like he thinks we're one of his kind." He turned to a portly man with thinning hair. "Do I have anything black smeared on my face, Edward?"

Edward laughed. Sarah figured he spent a lot of time laughing just to please the haughty man. She seethed inside, but Henry's leg pressed hard against hers sent a clear warning to behave.

As for Henry, he kept right on grinning. "You folks lost? 'Cause if you was lost, you ain't no mo'." He pointed over his shoulder. "Not a mile back sits Jefferson, right there where you left it."

The scrawny man on the right, actually more of a boy so thin Sarah thought he could use a pot of beans, attempted a smile that became more of a grimace. She reckoned he needed more practice.

The tall leader pulled a gold watch from his breast pocket. Not to tell the time but to twiddle it between his fingers while he seemed to mull over something in his head. His next words shot fire through Sarah's heart. "You two stole that rig, didn't you?"

Henry's senseless grin faded. His Adam's apple rose then fell. "Excuse me, suh? What did you say?"

Pocket Watch Man swept Sarah's body with a downright meddlesome gaze, so slowly her skin crawled, and then fixed soulless eyes on Henry. "You ain't deaf, boy. I said you stole the rig. The mule, too, because that there's my mule. Been looking for my animal all day, ain't I, boys?"

The grinning dullards alongside him nodded.

"And here you come, riding up with my mule hitched to my wagon, sitting there pretty as you please on a stolen rig."

Terror melted Sarah's bones. Her dress was all that held her useless sack of skin on the seat. Henry's face looked the way it had the time Dandy kicked him in the stomach and laid him out on the ground gasping like a trout.

"No, suh! Ya'll mistaken. We ain't no more stole this rig than fly." He jabbed his finger at Dandy. "I've had this here same mule going on three years now."

The fearsome stranger waited while the stillness behind Henry's words settled around them like pitched hay. Then he rose up in his stirrups and eased back with a grunt. His squirming seemed to set off the other two riders, because they leaned over their saddles, watching his face and waiting. Sweat pooled at the base of Sarah's spine.

The man cocked his head at Henry. "Know what I say to that, charcoal boy?"

Henry trembled beside her. His face shifted from fear to terrible rage then relaxed to show no emotion at all. . .until he smiled. Sarah stared up at his even row of shiny white teeth and decided he'd lost his mind.

"Naw, suh, I don't know what you might say. I sho' don't." Henry leaned back against the buckboard seat and adjusted the raggedy brim of his hat to cover his eyes, which made his broad grin stand out like a polecat at a party. "But I know you sho' 'nuff 'bout to tell me."

The man's eyes narrowed, and his face flushed red. "I say you're a low-down liar and a thief!" Flecks of spit spewed from his mouth into the air.

All three horses lurched toward them at the same time. The skinny, pock-faced boy, who hadn't yet said a word, reached for the pistol strapped to his side.

Sarah stood up and screamed then lunged forward to cover Henry with her body. A shot rang out, the exploding boom loud in Sarah's ears. She'd heard that gunshot wounds burned like melted lead poured in an open sore, so she stiffened and waited to feel hot pain.

When her body spun, she opened her eyes to see if Henry or Jesus held her. Through the haze of fear muddling her mind, she realized Henry had turned his back on the men. Puzzled, she followed his gaze to the edge of the woods.

T. M. Bagby, the sheriff of Marion County, sat astride his horse in a clearing not ten yards off the road. Sheriff John Vines, who held the office just before Bagby, stood next to him, the reins of his dun pony in one hand, a rifle pointed to the sky in the other. Wisps of smoke still streamed from its barrel.

"What's going on here?" Sheriff Bagby growled.

Sarah's shaky legs failed her, and she slid down Henry's body to the seat. Sheriff Vines mounted his horse, and the two men rode their way. Never in her life had Sarah been so glad to see two white lawmen.

Sheriff Bagby came alongside the wagon, his angry glare aimed at the strange men, a fact that greatly eased Sarah's mind. "I asked you men a question. What the devil's going on?"

Edward, the fleshy one, lowered his head like a hang-tail dog and backed up behind the others. The hungry-looking boy pulled his hand away from his holster, but by the snarl on his face, it pained him.

The prideful man in front lost no trace of his swagger. He took his time answering while he circled the face of his timepiece with the thumb of his smooth white hand. For the first time, Sarah noticed his slender fingers looked more like a woman's than a man's. He pointed at Henry. "This business is between this man and myself. No one else. How about you two ride on off and let us get it settled?"

Sheriff Vines tightened the grip on his rifle and eased closer. "I'd sure like to oblige you, mister, but"—he pointed over his shoulder at the clearing—"from over there it appeared your business had gotten a little out of hand."

Sheriff Bagby looked even madder than before. "What say

you let us in on the details? We'll decide whether or not it's our business."

Sarah nudged Henry hard. He gave her a look like nobody was home but came around in time to speak up in a jumble of words. "Sheriff, this stranger say I done stole my own wagon. Old Dandy, too." He straightened his shoulders and scowled at the man. "Ain't stole nothing. He knows it same as I do."

The sheriff glanced back at Henry. "Why, that's foolish talk. Henry here is no thief."

Pocket Watch Man regarded Sheriff Bagby with one raised brow then spat on the ground between them. "Suppose I want to contest? It's the word of three white men against one colored boy."

Sheriff Bagby frowned at each accuser in turn. "Gentlemen, I know this man well enough to say he's the owner of this rig and the animal pulling it. I can vouch for him myself."

Sheriff Vines snorted. "So can I, which means you need to refigure your math. Looks like it's the word of three white men against one colored man and two officers of the law. By my ciphering, our sum's higher."

Pocket Watch Man's jaw worked in circles. "What if I said I bought the rig from him fair and square, paid good money for it, and he slipped around and took off with it again?" He sneered over at Henry. "I know he don't look smart enough, but he's got himself quite a racket going down by the docks." He sat back with a haughty smirk, clearly proud of his lying story. "Now then. What avenues for justice does this town afford?"

The two lawmen shared a grin. Then Sheriff Vines's amused look turned hard. "Sir, one of the avenues for justice around here is the truth. So I'm sure you won't mind giving me a truthful answer to a direct question."

"Not at all. Ask what you will."

Sheriff Vines tipped his hat. "Let's start simple. You got a name?"

"Indeed I do. Frank Griswald, from the Boston Griswalds, at your service."

The sheriff raked him with doubtful eyes. "If you don't mind, I have a few more questions, Mr."—he paused and raised one brow—"*Griswald*."

Sarah and Henry shared a knowing glance.

Sheriff Vines edged closer on his horse. "You boys staying here in town?"

The lead man nodded. "We are. We're paying guests over at the Commercial Hotel."

The sheriff nodded then leaned forward on his saddle horn. "The Commercial Hotel, you say? Well, tell me this, didn't I see you three get off the *Maria Louise* when she put into port not an hour ago?"

Griswald opened his mouth to answer but closed it again when Sheriff Vines held up his hand. "Since I know right well I did see you crawl off the *Louise*, I'm wondering how you found time to negotiate purchase of a rig, manage to lose it again, book a room, find the livery, and hire these horses, then track down this man to accuse him. That's a busy hour, my friend. It just don't sound reasonable."

Sheriff Bagby interrupted before the black-hearted scoundrel had a chance to answer. "If you don't mind, John, I have a couple questions of my own. First, your name isn't Griswald at all, now, is it? Fact is, you're Jack Thibeau, a two-bit gambler out of New Orleans. You stole the Griswald name just like you were about to steal from this man. . .after murdering him and his wife in cold blood."

Sarah tensed as the three scoundrels started to fidget, but they stilled when Sheriff Vines lowered his rifle. Sheriff Bagby unsheathed his own gun and lifted the business end in their direction. "Before you boys start lying and denying, what say I escort you into town and lock you up for attempted murder?"

CHAPTER 18

Bertha slid a satin ribbon around her neck and pulled it up into her hair then wove it through the tied-up curls and fashioned a pretty bow in front. The dusky green fabric against her black hair set off her eyes to perfection. Leaning closer to the looking glass above her dressing table, she ran her finger back and forth over her two front teeth. The resulting squeal sounded loud inside her head. Twice since dinner she had scrubbed her teeth with tooth powder until they gleamed.

She picked up the container of Sozodont and read the label. *"For relief of impure breath caused by catarrh, bad teeth, or use of liqueur or tobacco."*

Catarrh? Bertha glanced at her reflection and sniffed. No runny nose.

Bad teeth? She drew back her lips to check. Not yet, thank the Lord.

Liquor? No, thank you.

Tobacco? Never!

Still, the powder promised sweet breath and pearl-like teeth. With Thad coming soon, she wanted her breath as sweet as possible. She ran her finger across her mouth again and listened, grinning at the satisfying squeak.

She crossed the room to her wardrobe and threw open the doors. As she thumbed past her everyday frocks to find her favorite green dress, the lyrics to the song she hummed came to her mind.

Oh! why am I so happy,
Why these feelings of delight?
And why does gladness cheer me?
Why everything so bright?

To say things were bright would be false. The very gloomy fact of Thad's leaving hung around her neck like a millstone. But she couldn't mourn today, not when Papa had given permission for Thad to come for supper and stay as long as he liked. A dangerous offer, considering the two of them had so much time to make up.

Bertha sang aloud as she slipped into the lacy dress.

"Why am I so happy,
Why these feelings of delight?"

Why? Because at long last Thad admitted his love for her. After the many times she had thought of it, prayed for it, daydreamed about it, Thaddeus Bloom would stand on her doorstep, come to court. She wouldn't allow herself to think beyond tonight.

Bertha checked herself in the looking glass. Though she had taken extra care getting ready, the image staring back surprised her. Her hair never looked so glossy or her eyes so bright, as though the joy churning in her heart had oozed its way to the surface.

Only one thing missing—jewelry to accentuate the plain, high bodice of the gown. She reached inside her collar and found the chain around her neck. A few years past, Moses Pharr had found the beautiful silver necklace by the docks and given it to Bertha, an act of generosity Rhodie had never forgiven. With two fingers, Bertha pulled the necklace free, kissed the filigreed cross, and centered it on her chest. Perfect.

Perfect necklace, perfect dress, perfect night.

"Perhaps I should change me mind. If Thad sees you like this, he's bound to carry you off, and I'll never see you again."

Bertha smiled at Papa's reflection in the glass then turned to where he stood in the doorway. "Oh, Papa, thank you for letting Thad come."

"Allowing such a fine boy to court you is easy. Telling your mother he'll be staying past respectable was the hard part. Well, that and sitting up half the night playing chaperone. I admit I don't look forward to it."

"You, Papa? You'll be my chaperone?"

Papa lowered his head. "Aye. 'Tis a woman's place, I know. I might as well don a skirt and corset." He lifted pleading eyes to Bertha's. "But what can I do? Your mama refuses. Will you be very ashamed of me?"

Bertha put her arms around his neck and kissed his cheek. "Ashamed? I'm glad. You'll make a much better chaperone than Mama."

When he made a face, she laughed. "Comfort yourself with knowing tonight is the first and last time I'll be courted."

He pushed her to arm's length. "What folly is this?"

She squeezed his shoulders. "I mean it, Papa. If Thad leaves tomorrow without proposing first, I'll live out my days a spinster."

He flashed a roguish grin. "Then I'll keep you to meself forever? So much the better." He cupped her chin in his hand. "But I fear it's too much to ask for with a daughter as lovely as you."

Warmth crept up her cheeks. "I only want Thad, Papa."

"Aye, and from what you told me this morning, I suspect he wants only you."

"Then why is he so stubborn? We've wasted too much time already, and he refuses to ask me to wait."

Papa pulled her down on the bed beside him. "We men are complicated creatures, me love. Matters you can't understand consume our hearts, but these things nurture traits you will someday find of great value. Traits like honor, self-sacrifice, and commitment. Thad loves you, and you love him back. This is the foundation of a good relationship. The rest are minor details. Can you trust God with the details, Bertha?"

He wrapped his arms around her, and she leaned her head against his shoulder. "Your words encourage me, Papa. Until now, I've been afraid to hope."

He patted her head. "Never fear hope, me girl. Not with the Great Hope in your life. He's well able to work out the details of a surrendered life." He took hold of her shoulders and raised her up to face him. "The cantankerous man in question will arrive any minute. Are you ready?"

Bertha grinned. "Oh, Papa, I've been ready for months." Then she held up her finger. "Except for one last thing." She picked up the Sozodont powder from the dressing table and held it up for him to see. "I need to clean my teeth."

He covered her hand with his and pushed the bottle down. "Your teeth are fine, Bertha. Too much of this stuff will eat away at them."

Groaning, she set the can aside. "I just want everything to be perfect tonight."

"*You* are perfect, dearie, and the only thing old Thaddy Boy will notice."

Mama leaned inside the door. "Francis? Here you are, for heaven's sake. I've been calling until my ears rattled."

"If you'd rattled the windows instead, I might've heard you. I take it you're ready to go?"

Bertha sought Papa's eyes. "Go? You can't go. Thad will be here any minute."

Mama unfolded and pulled on her gloves. "Don't fret, Bertha. We'll be back before he arrives. I promised Dr. Eason I would look in on Mrs. McKenzie and her new baby. Supper is ready to serve, and we'll return before Thad comes. Set the table while we're gone, would you?"

"Yes, ma'am, I will."

"And remember. . .should Thad happen to get here before we get back, serve him hot tea on the veranda."

Bertha pointed toward the window. "But it's cold out there."

"Just do like I say. Don't dare take him inside the house. Understand?"

"No, ma'am, I won't."

Papa grinned past Mama at her. "Heaven forbid I should have to shoot the poor lad the first time he comes calling."

Bertha herded them toward the door. "If you're going, then go. I won't leave Thad to languish on the porch until he dies from exposure."

When they left, she turned back to the mirror for one last check of her appearance. Satisfied with how she looked, she ran her tongue over the roof of her mouth and glanced at the tooth powder.

Papa's reflection appeared in the glass, peering around the doorpost behind her. "Ah, ah, ah! Leave it alone, now."

She burst into giggles and tossed the Sozodont container. He dodged it then disappeared, but she heard his hearty laughter until the back door slammed.

On the road to Bertha's house, Thad made up his mind. Considering the situation in which he found himself, maybe, just maybe, the trait his mama often cautioned him about had waylaid him again. She claimed Thad had a habit of deciding too soon about the expected outcome of a situation and, once he decided it would turn out one way or the other, lacked the flexibility to consider a different end.

Might self-imposed blinders have blocked his sight? If he could wait however long it took to be with Bertha, why shouldn't he believe the same applied to her? And Francis Biddie's willingness to receive him tonight, knowing full well he'd be leaving tomorrow, cast new light on whether the man would be agreeable to a long engagement for his daughter.

Thad allowed the decision to settle around his heart. He would ask Mr. Biddie for Bertha's hand in marriage. He wouldn't leave their place tonight without the man's blessing and a promise from Bertha to wait.

The murky clouds had folded back in the last couple of hours, allowing sunshine on Jefferson soil for the first time in several days—not that it warmed things up any. Thad approached the turnoff to Bertha's just as the sun settled onto the horizon and began its slow ride down. An orange haze spread over the western sky, and Thad entertained the pleasing notion that it was the last sunset he would see before he and Bertha were betrothed.

He turned down the lane, leaving the painted sky at his back. Up ahead, the Biddie place sat back about a quarter mile off the road. In the fading light, the house and tall trees surrounding it stood out in sharp relief, like black cutouts on a gray background. Excited and impatient, he gave the mare a light tap with his heel to speed her along. As he neared the yard, he noticed the Biddie wagon approaching from another direction.

"Hail, Thad!" Mr. Biddie called.

Thad raised his hand in greeting. "Evening, sir." He nodded toward Bertha's mama, who sat straight and proper on the seat. "Mrs. Biddie."

The woman nodded back but waited until her husband helped her down and Thad joined them on the front walk before she spoke. "Good evening, Thad. We're ever so glad to have you tonight. I hope you're hungry."

Thad took off his hat. "Yes, ma'am. And thank you for the invitation."

Mr. Biddie shook Thad's hand then motioned toward the gate. "Come inside out of the cold. Bertha's waiting for you."

Mrs. Biddie nudged him and frowned. Mr. Biddie lifted his shoulders at Thad and grinned. She turned and offered her arm to Thad then nodded toward the horizon as they made their way up the walk. "How pleasant to see a sunset, no matter how unexpected and brief. I do detest wet weather. I like the snow, mind you, but not the rain. Have you ever witnessed the sunset on a snow-covered hill, Thad?"

The Louisiana boy ducked his head and grinned. "Can't say that I have, ma'am."

"Well, it's a sight to behold."

"Yes, ma'am, I imagine it would be."

Mr. Biddie ducked around them to open the door. Thad allowed Bertha's mama to pass through; then he followed her inside. His stomach jumped as he entered the hall, and he couldn't corral his searching eyes.

Mrs. Biddie touched his arm. "Show our guest to the parlor, Francis; then summon Bertha from her room. I'll bring in hot tea. We'll relax a bit and get acquainted before we eat." She fixed a bright smile on her face. "If it's all right with you, Thad."

"Oh yes, ma'am. That'll be fine." As long as they hurried to the "summon Bertha" part, everything about the evening held promise.

Mr. Biddie left Thad perched expectantly on the edge of a high-backed chair. He sat alternately drumming on the arm then gripping it, crossing and uncrossing his legs, and biting his lower lip until it hurt. The door finally opened and he jumped to his feet.

Instead of Bertha, Mrs. Biddie came in alone and set a tea service on the low, claw-foot table. She glanced around, surprised. "They haven't returned?"

He shook his head. "No, ma'am. Not yet."

"Well, goodness." Pulling her anxious gaze from the door, she smiled at Thad. "We'll just have to start without them. I'm sure they'll be along directly."

When Mrs. Biddie served him, he wished she hadn't. His hands shook so much, the delicate cup clattered against the saucer until he braced it on his knee. Thankfully, she pretended not to notice. But he caught her casting worried glances at her china when she wasn't staring nervously at the door.

Bertha's mama gave him a shaky smile. "I can't imagine what's keeping those two."

She'd no sooner spoken than Mr. Biddie entered the room. His wife glared up at him, and Thad stood, so nervous he nearly tossed the lady's china in her lap. Mr. Biddie remained just inside the doorway, frowning and gnawing on his lip.

Mrs. Biddie leaned forward. "Francis? What on earth? Where's Bertha?"

"I can't say."

For the first time, Thad noticed that all color had drained from the man's face, and at his words, Mrs. Biddie's paled to match it, her bright smile long gone.

"What do you mean?"

"I mean I can't say, because I don't know. Your daughter's not here, Emeline. Not in her room, inside the house, or anywhere on the grounds. I've search the whole place. Bertha's gone. Just plain gone."

CHAPTER 19

Bertha rode hard toward town, her attention drawn to the setting sun. She'd already lost too much time by circling around the usual route, but she had to avoid the road to miss Thad.

Her spirits sank lower at the thought of him. What would he do when he arrived to find her gone? She'd bungled things before, but never with such heartrending consequences.

As she stood staring at the cross around her neck in the looking glass, her heart had seized in her chest and she'd stumbled back to sit on the bed before she fell. To her shame she considered forgetting her promise to meet Annie just as fast as she'd recalled it, and after a few deep breaths to settle her nerves, she'd gone right on preparing for Thad's visit.

Until the reminder came that the time she planned to spend with Thad didn't belong to her. The evening belonged to God in sacrifice for Annie. But when she'd offered it, she'd had no way of knowing how dear the cost.

The last bit of daylight faded to the point where Bertha could hardly see, which made it necessary for her to pick her way with caution through the woods. She would be late. What calamity if, after all of this, Annie gave up on her and went back to her room.

Suppose Annie didn't show? Bertha had to admit she'd be glad.

She already hoped the meeting went fast enough to get her home early, though she'd have some explaining to do when she got there. If she didn't see Annie standing in the alley, she'd hightail it back and enjoy her evening with Thad, her conscience clear.

"I'll look for you at sunset, but I'll wait no matter how long it takes."

They were her words, spoken with conviction just hours before. At this latest reminder, anger welled up along with sudden hot tears. "Very well, God!" she cried aloud. "But I don't understand why You're doing this to me."

Thad would be hurt at losing so much of their time, especially after her promise to move heaven and earth to spend the evening together. When she got back, she'd have to make him understand. Her determination may have succeeded with moving the earth, but she found her stubborn streak no match for God's heaven.

At the last turn into town, Bertha slowed her horse so she wouldn't attract attention but rose up in the saddle and peered toward the alley. "Where is she?" she whispered to the horse. She leaned over the saddle and strained her eyes. *Where is she?*

There!

Annie stood in the shadows near the corner building, huddled against the cold. She faced away from the road and the streetlamp, and away from Bertha. To keep from scaring her, Bertha got off the horse, tied him to a post, and walked the rest of the way. "Annie?"

Startled, Annie's shoulders jerked, but she didn't turn around.

"It's me. Are you all right?"

Annie turned, and Bertha saw why she hadn't at first. Tangled hair fell around her head and shoulders in a stringy mess. Powder and paint ran in streaks, and her face appeared swollen and wet with tears. She wore a coat over what appeared to be her nightdress. In the dim glow from the nearby gaslight, Bertha noticed the nightgown had been ripped off one shoulder.

Her steps faltered. "Oh, Annie. What has he done to you? "

Annie stumbled close and fell against her. "He hurt me. He always hurts me. I hate him so much."

"Did he hit you?"

She rocked her head from side to side. "Not with his fists. Not this time. He can't afford to mar the merchandise."

"Merchandise? What do you mean?"

Annie tugged her coat around her and looked away. "Nothing. Never mind." She cleared her throat and licked her smeared red lips. "Abe pushed me around a little, that's all. Pinned me to the bed and screamed insults in my face. When he let me up, I ran." She fingered the tattered fabric on her arm. "He made a grab at me but missed and ripped my gown." She rubbed her shoulder. "Twisted my arm a bit, too."

Bertha groaned. "Is this my fault? Did he catch you trying to leave?"

She shook her head. "Oh no. His anger's been building for hours. He started guzzling right after you left today, and Abe just gets meaner with every drink he pours down. I took his abuse for as long as I could before I made a run for it."

Bertha crossed her arms over her chest. "Well, you can't go back."

Annie gave a nervous little laugh. "Sure I can. I just have to wait until he passes out. If I'm lucky, he won't remember a thing by morning." She snorted. "You think it's the first time this has happened?"

Then she leaned to peer into Bertha's eyes. "I'll be fine, I promise. But thank you for caring, huh? And thank you for being here for me. You're the best friend I have." Her laugh sounded bitter. "What am I saying? You're the only friend I have. Abe won't allow anyone to get close to me."

Bertha felt a tug in her heart. This was her chance to say what she'd come for. She took a deep breath and forged ahead. "Annie, I'll always be your friend, for as long as you'll have me. But I know Someone who'll make a better friend to you than I ever could." She reached to smooth tangled hair from Annie's face then plucked at the torn fabric of her gown. "He can help you out of this mess, too, if you'll let Him. What do you say, Annie? Would you be willing to meet Him?"

A hard look crossed Annie's face and her hand came up. "Stop right there. I've had my share of those kinds of friends. Got me one now, in fact. And, honey, I don't need another. You can tell him so, too, whoever he is." She tilted her head slightly and narrowed her eyes. "Is that why you're here? Some two-penny hustler put you up to conning me?"

"Of course not! Oh goodness, you don't understand."

Annie turned her back. "And I don't care to, thank you."

Bertha gripped her shoulder. "You've got it all wrong. Or rather, I didn't say it right. Let me try again." She swallowed hard and said a silent prayer for courage. "You know yesterday at the bluff, when we talked about the devil and dying?"

Annie's eyes changed, as if a curtain dropped inside her head. "What about it?"

"I believe God can protect you from both of those threats."

"Whoa, there. Abe's pretty bad, I'll admit, but he's not the devil." She smirked. "At least, I don't think so." She took a few steps away. "Look, I know where you're going with this. I've heard it all before. I'm not interested."

Bertha cringed. "But why? God just wants to care for you. Why would you reject such a loving offer?"

Annie stared off into the dark alley behind them. "Sugar, your God doesn't want someone like me."

"Yes, He does."

Annie's tense shoulders slumped in an attitude of defeat. "Then He doesn't know what all I've done."

Bertha cocked her head to the side. "I wouldn't count on it. God knows things you can't even remember and those you wish you could forget."

Fear paled Annie's face. "Bertha, I don't want to talk about this anymore. I mean it."

"But–"

"I mean it."

Bertha felt heartsick. Begging Annie to accept God's grace seemed like force-feeding a starving man. But if she didn't want to hear it, Bertha could only do as she asked.

When the idea came, Bertha knew it wasn't hers any more than standing in the dark streets of Jefferson while Thad stood on her porch was her idea. Without trying to reason it out, she reached behind her neck to undo the clasp of her cross necklace and held it up to Annie. "Very well, I won't say another word. But take this as a reminder of what I did say."

Annie's startled eyes followed the motion of the swinging necklace. "I can't take that."

"I want you to have it. Turn around and let me fasten it for you."

Annie backed away as though the chain would burn if it touched her flesh. "I could never wear it."

Embarrassment burned Bertha's cheeks. Maybe she hadn't heard from God, after all. Why would someone who owned diamonds wear her secondhand silver? "I'm sorry, Annie. You don't like it."

Annie's mouth gaped. "What? Don't be silly. Of course I like it."

"What, then?"

Tears clouded her tortured gray eyes. "It's a cross, Bertha. I'm not worthy."

Bertha's own eyes blurred. "Stop it. Why would you say that?"

Annie started to cry in earnest. Great splashing teardrops hit the front of her coat and rolled down her cheeks, making watery tracks through already-smudged makeup. "Because I do things with men. Shameful things. Things that make me feel sick."

Bertha's insides recoiled in shock, but for Annie's sake she held her ground. "Why would you. . .with those men. . .I mean, if you don't want to?"

"He beats me, all right? Abe beats me if I say no. He slaps me and drags me by my hair. He pushes me down and hits me with his fists until my eyes swell and I can't see."

Bertha covered her ears with her arms. "No, Annie. I can't bear to hear this."

Too wound up to stop, Annie paced the alley and sobbed. "After he's finished with me, he gets even madder when he realizes what he's done."

"Because he's sorry?"

"Oh, he's sorry enough. Sorry he won't get as much money now that I don't look so nice."

Annie cried so hard by then, Bertha feared they'd hear her clear to Dallas. She took three steps back to peer up and down the dark street but saw nothing. "Annie, why do you stay with him? How can you even think of going back there tonight?"

Annie sniffed and swiped her arm under her nose. She spoke, and her voice held a mournful tremor. "I have nowhere else to go. No one to take care of me."

Bertha frowned. "Why can't you go home?"

Annie shuddered. "That's impossible."

"Why?"

She crossed her arms and paced back and forth again, this time in a calmer stride. "I left home when I turned fifteen. Ran off with an older man I thought I loved. He claimed to love me, too. Even said he wanted to marry me." Shame flashed in her eyes. "But he left me high and dry. My parents were so angry, and I couldn't go back after disgracing them."

"What did you do?"

She looked at the ground. "The only thing I knew how to do at fifteen. I turned to strange men for money and love." She looked up, and her eyes had welled again. "I'm not the least bit proud of it, but I was alone and so scared. When Abe came along, I took him to be my ticket out, and in some ways he was. He treated me good at first. Still does when he's not drunk or broke." Annie leaned against the building and continued to pour out the dreadful story of her ill-fated life, complete with all the desperate, wretched things she'd ever done.

Bertha longed to stop her ears, to run away from the vulgar tale, but she sensed Annie needed to confess her past in order to cleanse herself from its hold. So love held Bertha fast.

Annie's halting words drained her so that by the time she finished talking, her body slumped against the wall and her voice sounded strained. When it seemed nothing else festered inside,

Annie raised her head. Water droplets glistened on the hood of her coat. Whether beads of rain or dew from the heavy night air, Bertha couldn't tell, but they sparkled like Annie's tears in the glow from the gaslight.

She breathed a hopeless sigh. "Now do you understand why I'm not worthy to wear that cross?"

Anger stiffened Bertha's spine. Not anger toward Annie, but toward the man who abandoned her so long ago, toward her parents for doing the same, toward the cruel-hearted Abe, and toward every other beastly circumstance of Annie's life that had robbed her of hope.

Bertha dangled the necklace in front of her eyes. "Annie Moore, you listen to me. The gift this cross represents is more powerful than any laundry list of sins you may be guilty of, no matter how heinous. The cross covered them all." Annie turned her face away, but Bertha cupped her chin and pulled her back. "All, Annie. You just have to accept it for yourself in order to be free."

Annie wrung her hands and searched Bertha's face with anxious eyes. "I just don't know how to believe that."

"Don't take my word for it, then. Ask God yourself if He's able to forgive the things you've done." Bertha opened Annie's hand, pressed the necklace into her palm, and closed her fingers around it. "Hang on to this for now, while you think about what I've said. Will you do that much?"

Annie nodded. "I'll hang on to it. Thank you, Bertha." She held up her closed fist and looked at her rings. She wore two on that hand, lovely pieces with big diamonds that sparkled even in the sparse light. "How I wish I could repay you in kind. I'd love for you to have one of these."

Bertha gasped. "For heaven's sake, Annie, those are far too costly. I could never accept."

Annie met her eyes. "Sadly, I could never offer, or Abe would kill me for sure. He's tried every trick in the book to get his hands on my diamonds." Her jaw tightened. "Not that I care two hoots about any of my jewelry, but it's the only thing left he hasn't taken."

She gave a twisted smile, her gaze on the rings. "Besides, if he ever walks out on me, I'll have these to fall back on. I could at least trade them for a meal."

"They're worth a sight more than a meal, Annie."

Annie closed her eyes and shook her head, as if coming out of a trance. "I think it's getting late. How long have we been here?"

Bertha stepped to the end of the building to look at the empty street. The chill wind whipping around the corner almost took her breath, and a light drizzle had started. "Way too long." She ducked in the alley and took Annie's arm. "Come. Let me take you home with me. You can have my bed, and I'll take the chaise. Don't worry—I can fall asleep anywhere, even sitting upright in a chair."

Annie gave her a sidelong glance. "What are you thinking, Bertha? Your folks won't allow you to drag someone like me in off the streets, and you know it." She waved at her clothes. "Especially in a getup like this."

"They will if I explain."

"Oh, sugar, can't you just hear that? 'Mama, I've brought this beaten, half-dressed trollop home to sleep in my bed. I just know you won't mind.' "

Bertha imagined explaining Annie to Mama. She couldn't conceive of it. Still. . .

Annie must've read the struggle in her eyes. "Don't give it another thought. I know it's out of the question. Besides, if I don't go back, it'll just make matters worse."

Bertha clutched at her hands. "Annie—"

"He's asleep by now. Passed out, I should say. He won't hurt me any more tonight."

"What about tomorrow night? And the next?"

"Stop worrying about me, little Bertha. I've been taking care of myself for a long time. Let me get back to the room before Abe wakes up. With any luck, he'll be sick in the morning after all he drank and stay in bed all day. That'll be fine with me, because there's nothing better to do in this horrid rain. You get up on that horse and go home before your parents send a search party."

Bertha hugged her and for some reason hated to turn her loose. "Let me walk you back to the hotel, at least."

"No, sweetie. I can't be seen with you."

The words made Bertha's stomach ache. "If you say so, but please be careful."

"I thought we decided you'd stop fretting over me."

Bertha shook her head. "I decided no such thing." She squeezed the hand where Annie held the cross. "Do you promise to think about what I said?"

"I promise. We'll talk some more tomorrow. All right?"

Bertha tried to hide her pleasure but couldn't. She smiled so widely her cheeks hurt. "I'll hold you to that. Good night, Annie."

"Good night, little Bertha. Now go!"

Back in the saddle, Bertha mouthed a silent prayer when Annie waved and then slipped into the darkness. She whirled her horse into the street and headed for home at a full gallop, unsure of the hour or how much time had passed while they huddled in the alley. She only knew she had fulfilled her duty to God and Annie, so whatever remained of the night belonged to Thad. She'd find a way to make it up to him, and they'd spend every possible hour together until he left.

Nearing her lane, she jumped the narrow ditch to cut the corner and thundered toward the house. At the gate, she leaped to the ground and led her horse to the porch. She expected Thad would have tied his horse out front, but it wasn't there. She told herself it had to be in the barn, had to be somewhere.

"Bertha?"

Her hand froze on the hitching post. "Papa, I didn't see you. What are you doing out in this weather?"

"You took the words right out of me mouth. I hope you have a reasonable explanation for turning our hair gray this night. Mama is beside herself, Bertha. She's taken to her bed."

Bertha rushed to join him on the porch. "Where's Thad?"

"And that's what frets you, daughter? No spare word of concern for your dear mother, after what I've just told you?"

Bertha ducked her head. "I'm sorry. I didn't mean to worry her."

He didn't answer, so Bertha sneaked a peek at his face then recoiled in shock. "Oh, mercy. You're not crying–?"

He swiped angrily at his eyes. "Mama wasn't the only one worried, you know." He took her by the shoulders and gave a gentle shake. "Where were you, girl? With you all a-flutter over young Thad's visit, it made no sense that you'd leave."

"Where is he, Papa?"

Papa looked grim. "Where is he, you wonder? Well, that makes two of us."

Her stomach lurched. "What do you mean? Didn't he show up?"

"He came, all right, and found you gone." He tucked in his chin and furrowed his brow. "Are you saying Thad never found you? That you haven't been with him this night?"

"Of course not. You're making no sense at all."

"Bertha, Thad rode off to search for you but never returned. For his dear mama's sake, I pray he's at home warming his backside at the hearth."

Bertha's head reeled. She tried hard to grasp what he had said, to lay all the facts in a neat row and sort them out, but they wouldn't line up. Each time she tried, the only important detail rose to the top and consumed her. She had to find Thad.

"I'll explain everything. I will. The minute I return. But I have to go bring him back." She brushed a hasty kiss across Papa's cheek and rushed down the steps, making it clear to the hitching post before he bellowed from the porch.

"Bertha Maye Biddie! Kindly march yourself right back. You won't be going anywhere else tonight."

Unwilling to believe her ears, she turned. "You can't mean it."

"Oh, I mean it."

She shook her head. "But I must."

"No, miss. Not without good reason. And I've heard not a reason, explanation, or apology from you tonight."

An apology would be easy. She hadn't meant to hurt them. If

he wanted an explanation, she had one of those, too. Could she find fit words to give it?

She hustled back to the porch and blurted out a short account of her story with the promise to fill in the gaps later. Papa's hurt, angry expression changed to sympathy and understanding as she spoke of her mission to save Annie.

When she finished with another plea to go after Thad, Papa set his stubborn jaw and shook his head. "Mama will have my gizzard on a spit."

"Papa, please. This is the most important night of my life. Can't you at least ask?"

Releasing his breath in a rush, he nodded. "All right, then. I'll speak to her. I suppose I need to tell her you're home before she frets herself sick."

Bertha wanted to mention he'd bawled her name loudly enough to alert Mama and half of Jefferson of her whereabouts. One look at his face, and she decided against it.

Papa opened the door then turned and wagged his finger. "Don't expect miracles."

She raised her brows. "Too late. I need a miracle with all that's at stake."

He disappeared inside but returned right away, his heavy footsteps echoing through the house. It didn't bode well for her cause. It meant Mama wasn't in the market for Francis Biddie's blarney.

The screen opened and Papa joined her on the porch. "Her mind is made up. She absolutely forbids it."

Bertha's head expected the answer, but her heart clung to hope. "No. Please go try again."

"She's in no mood for it, daughter."

Bertha stamped her foot in anger, and frustration loosened her lips. "Who wears the trousers in this family anyway?"

Silence. Papa held her gaze, but shame veiled his eyes. Bertha bit her bottom lip and wished she'd bitten her tongue. When she uttered the unimaginable words, she'd leaped a forbidden line and didn't quite know her way back across.

She touched his arm. "Oh, Papa, I'm so sorry."

He patted her shoulder. "No, sprite. It's a fair question. And here's your answer, since you asked. Your mama herself wears the trousers and holds me on a short tether. I allow it because otherwise it's impossible to live with her."

Considering the amount of time Bertha spent dancing around Mama's ire, his words plucked a familiar chord. She'd never considered her papa a fellow survivor of Emeline Biddie, the whirlwind. Seeing him as such forged a kinship that had little to do with blood ties.

"I did try, Bertha. I even asked if I could fetch Thad for you. She said it's unseemly to disturb the family at this hour."

Bertha crumpled onto the porch swing. "Blast unseemly! When I'm mistress of a house, I'll make my own rules. I'll talk as I wish, dress as I wish, go where I want, when I want, and never, ever wear shoes. If my daughter asks for something important to her, I'll care more about her feelings than the opinions of others." She lifted wet, sorrowful eyes to his. "I will, Papa. I swear it."

He laid a heavy hand on her shoulder. "Don't stay out much longer, darlin'. There's a cold wind a-blowin'." Then he stepped quietly to the door and went inside.

Bertha sat on the damp, drafty porch remembering how glad she'd been such a short time ago. The song she'd warbled to her empty room while dressing for Thad rose up to mock her.

Why does gladness cheer me?
Why everything so bright?

With a heavy heart, she crowded the song from her mind with more fitting lyrics.

Wilt thou be gone, love, wilt thou be gone from me?
Gone, I must be gone, love, I must be gone from thee.

She stood up and walked into the house, furious with her parents, Annie, and God.

CHAPTER 20

Sunday, January 21

Bertha opened her eyes and grimaced. Her tongue was stuck to the roof of her mouth and covered with a thick, unpleasant coat—one part mint and three parts glue. The Sozodont. The peppermint-stick flavor of the tooth powder never hinted at the hideous aftertaste. She groaned and struggled to free her arm from the quilt pulled up to her shoulders and saw the green cotton sleeve of her favorite dress. Why was she in bed fully dressed?

A strong sense of urgency fairly lifted her from the mattress, but she couldn't imagine why. She threw back the cover she'd fumbled for sometime in the night and swung her feet to the floor, shaking the fog from her head so she could think.

"Papa!" she shrieked, scrambling across the cold floor for her shoes. "Papa, come quick!"

Her parents' startled faces appeared at the door. Papa, still barefoot and dressed in his nightshirt, rushed to her side. "What is it, child? Are you ailing?"

"I need you to take me to Thad's house right away."

Mama, her robe pulled hastily over her gown and her hair tied up in curls with strips of cloth, slumped against the door frame. "Bertha, for heaven's sake."

"I got the idea last night. If we get there before he leaves for the station, we can go with the Blooms to see him off. Mama, I knew you wouldn't allow me to go alone, but Papa can drive me."

Papa rubbed the stubble on his chin. "It's a mite early, darlin'. What time does Thad's train leave?"

"I don't know. That's the trouble."

Mama squinted down at her. "Don't tell me you slept in your clothes."

Embarrassed, Bertha looked away. "With time so precious, I didn't want to waste it getting dressed." She finished fastening her shoes, a pair she'd picked to gain her mama's favor. "I must see Thad before he goes—to explain about last night and ask him to forgive me."

She stood up and reached for her shawl. "Hurry and dress, Papa. I'll go hitch the wagon."

Mama clamped a hand on her arm as she passed. "Just a minute, young lady. No daughter of mine will go calling on a young man uninvited, and so early on a Sunday morning."

Papa, who had watched from the door without comment, cleared his throat and leveled a warning look at Mama.

Mama watched his face for a second then nodded and gave Bertha a weak smile. "I meant to say, no daughter of mine will go calling on a young man at this hour—without first washing her face and combing her hair."

Bertha cried out and jumped up to hug her. "Thank you, Mama."

Mama pulled back and made a face. "You might want to use some of your minty tooth powder while you're at it, dear."

Bertha covered her mouth. "I'm afraid the powder might be part of the problem. I'll rinse with water and chew a sprig of parsley on the way." She gave her papa a gentle push toward the door. "Go dress, please. My entire future hangs on how quickly you can slip into your trousers."

He grinned and rocked on his heels, his thumbs hooked in imaginary suspenders. "I'll go, but did you happen to notice who's back in rightful possession of his trousers?"

Mama frowned, so he gave her a playful swat on the bottom. "No sass out of you, Mrs. Biddie. And by the by, I'll expect breakfast on the table when I return. Eggs, fried bread, and black pudding will do nicely." He planted a kiss on her check and sauntered to the door.

Horrified, Bertha froze, waiting for the anger, the shock and outrage, the whirlwind to spin off and consume him. To her amazement, Mama's face softened, and she smiled like a smitten girl. When she saw Bertha watching, she ducked her head and followed Papa out the door, as tame as an autumn breeze.

Somehow Bertha managed to close her gaping mouth. She returned to the basin to splash water on her face and arrange her hair, determined to find an explanation for the miracle she'd just witnessed. She'd start by asking Papa about his astonishing conquest on the way to Thad's house. Perhaps he could offer a few tips on how she might approach Thad. After last night, she'd need them.

Papa rushed past her door in a whoosh. "Let's go if we're going. I'll fetch the rig."

"Yes, sir. I'm coming."

With no time to get warm water, she picked up the ceramic pitcher left there from the night before and poured a cold stream into the basin on her dressing table. She dipped a rag and wiped her face, tucked back a stray curl and pinned it then hurried to the kitchen.

Mama stood at the stove warming milk for black pudding. Still wary, Bertha pushed past her and pulled a few sprigs of parsley from the cold box. Unsure what to make of the strange woman in the kitchen, she tucked the parsley into her mouth and opened the door. "We're going now. Please say a prayer we reach Thad in time."

The stranger pointed at Bertha with her ladle. "Speaking of prayer, try to be home in time for church. And don't forget your wrap. It's still cold out."

"Yes, ma'am," she called then grabbed her hat and coat from a hook by the door and scurried out to the wagon.

Papa stood waiting. She rushed over and hoisted herself up before he had time to offer a hand. He gave her a mock frown then hustled around to board on his side.

They were quiet on the ride to the Bloom house. Planning what she would say to Thad distracted Bertha from asking Papa how he'd reclaimed his trousers. By the time she remembered, they were nearly to Thad's and Papa seemed lost in his own thoughts. Sitting tall on the seat, he wore a silly grin on his face, and Bertha wondered if he sat basking in his recent victory. More in keeping with his character, he likely sat basking in expectation of fried bread and black pudding.

A lump rose in Bertha's throat as they neared the big white house northwest of town. She twisted on the seat and latched onto Papa's arm. "What will I say to him?"

He patted her hand then loosened her fingers. "Don't fret, darlin'. The words will come."

She rubbed the red marks on his forearm. "Sorry, Papa. I'm just so afraid."

He tilted her face up to his. "Remember the thing I asked you? About trusting God with the details?"

She nodded.

"Well, if you have a mind to ever trust Him, this is your chance."

Bertha nodded again and leaned against his arm, her heart too full to speak. Her breath caught when they pulled up and stopped in front of the low picket fence surrounding Thad's yard. She sat up and stared past the tall magnolia, past the smaller Eve's necklace, and down the cobbled path to the two-story house, wondering which window stood between her and Thad.

Papa set the brake and shook his finger under her nose. "You sit tight till I come 'round. We'll have no more hurtling into wagons, young miss. You'll wait for help like a proper lady."

"Yes, Papa. But hurry, please."

He grumbled but climbed down and hastened around to her side. Together they rushed up the walk to the white double doors. Papa questioned her with his eyes and she nodded, so he lifted the heavy brass knocker and let it fall. As the door swung open, Bertha thought her heart would burst. She held her breath and readied the words she needed to say.

"Mr. Biddie. Little Bertha. What a nice surprise to find you on our doorstep."

Bertha's body wilted. She couldn't answer Mrs. Bloom because Thad's words still pressed her tongue. Papa cleared his throat then slipped past Bertha and lifted his hat.

"Mornin' to ye, me lady. Apologies for disturbing your fine household so early on the Sabbath morn. But we fancy a short chat with your boy, if you don't mind."

Leona Bloom lifted her brows. "Of course. One moment, please." She left the door open and slipped away. Bertha stared at the entry, waiting for Thad's broad shoulders to fill the empty space.

"You all right, love?"

"Yes, Papa."

After a wait that lasted forever, Thad's lanky little brother appeared with his mama on his heels. Cyrus looked nervous and clearly couldn't imagine what Papa might have to do with him. He squinted out the door, pushing his wire-rimmed glasses higher on his nose. "Yes, sir, Mr. Biddie?"

Disappointment and impatience warred in Bertha's gut like cats in a bag. Papa gave a nervous little laugh and addressed Mrs. Bloom. "While we're double-blessed by young Cy's handsome face, I fear it's Thad we mean to see."

Cy stepped back, his cheeks going crimson. Mrs. Bloom tented her fingertips over her lips and shook her head. "Of course you do. How silly of me. It's not as if I didn't think of Thad first, but since. . . Well, you see. . ."

The door swung wider, and Thad's papa appeared behind his wife.

"Why, Francis, how nice to see you." He leaned past his family to clasp Papa's hand then frowned at Mrs. Bloom. "Leona, where are your manners, dear? Don't leave our guests on the stoop."

She flushed a bright pink and moved away from the entrance. "Oh my. Forgive me, Abel. I'm not myself with all that's gone on around here."

Mr. Bloom motioned them inside. "Come in, come in, before you ice over." He held out his hand. "This way to the parlor, folks. Leona, brew some tea to warm their bones." He glanced at Papa. "Unless you prefer coffee, Francis."

Papa waved off the coffee and the parlor. "Don't go troubling your good wife, sir. The warmth of your foyer is sufficient. We can't stay long."

They stood discussing foul weather and trading good-natured remarks until Bertha feared her pounding head might explode. At long last Papa pulled her forward, and Mr. Bloom turned his attention her way.

"Look who this is." He accepted the hand she offered and kissed it. "Bertha, you're lovelier each time I see you."

"You're too kind, sir. I wonder if I might be allowed to see Thad now?"

Papa cleared his throat again, louder than before, and laid a restraining hand on her shoulder. "What my wee daughter means to say—"

"Hold up. You came to see Thad?"

Mr. Bloom wore a puzzled look. Behind him, Mrs. Bloom pressed a hankie to her lips and spun away from the door, leaving Cyrus staring after her with startled eyes. Mr. Bloom lowered his head and frowned then took hold of Bertha's hands. "I thought if anyone knew, it would be you, dear. Thad's gone."

Bertha peered into eyes so like Thad's and tried to make sense of his words. "Gone? You mean he left for the station without you?" She looked from Mr. Bloom to Papa to Cyrus, trying to work it out. She couldn't imagine Thad's family not seeing him off to school. Well, no matter. She would. A renewed sense of urgency pulsed through her heart. "It's so early I doubt the train has arrived. There's still plenty of time to catch him before he leaves, and we can all ride to the station together. Won't Thad be surprised?"

Mr. Bloom came toward her with his mouth open, about to speak.

Done with talking, Bertha rushed for the door and opened it. "Forgive me, Mr. Bloom. We have to be quick or we won't make it." Outside she made a mad dash for the rig.

"Better stop her, Francis." Mr. Bloom's voice behind her sounded strained.

"Bertha, wait right there," Papa ordered.

She stopped and turned.

Papa, Cyrus, and Mr. Bloom gaped at her from the porch.

"Wait? For what? We're going to miss him if we don't hurry."

Compassion softened Mr. Bloom's eyes. "You won't find my boy at the station, Bertha."

Papa asked the question for her. "Why's that, Abel?"

"Thad left last night. Seemed in a powerful hurry to go, so I let him take one of our horses. He planned to ride to Longview, sell the horse for spending money, and take the first train out to Bryan."

Bertha knew she stared openmouthedly but didn't care. "What did you say?" she asked, her voice a feeble croak.

"I said he's gone, Bertha. Thad's already gone."

Something had Henry's long johns in a knot. Sarah knew it for a fact after he shoveled food around his dish at supper then left the breakfast table without cleaning his plate. Anything that interfered with her man's vittles would be no light matter, but Henry wasn't talking—and it scared her.

Worse still, he'd left early that morning without her. Said he had business in town. Said he wouldn't be back in time to fetch her for Sunday service, but he'd stop along the way and ask a neighbor to bring her. On his way out the door, Henry promised to finish his dealings in plenty of time to join her at the meetinghouse.

The reason these things troubled Sarah?

Henry never did business on the Sabbath. When Sarah asked him outright what he planned to do, he mumbled and shuffled then dashed out the door.

By the time Thomas Jolly pulled into the yard, the bed of his wagon overflowing with laughing children, worry had curdled Sarah's stomach. After giving him a wave out the door, she went to her room for a wrap. Sarah wore a dress made of heavy fabric but didn't own a proper coat, so she grabbed the warmer of her two good shawls and dashed outside, braced for a cold morning ride.

Thomas raised his hat. "Miss Sarah."

Sarah nodded. "Thomas." She stepped to the back of the wagon and grinned at the turned-up faces. "Children! How spry you look, all washed and polished."

"Morning, Miss Sarah," rang out from eight different voices.

Sarah tried hard never to question God, but as her hungry eyes roamed the tiny faces, she wondered about His ways. Why bless some folks with more babies than they could feed yet withhold one tiny suckling mouth from her barren breasts?

Thomas leaned to wipe off the seat while one of the older boys handed Sarah up beside him. She thanked him and settled the skirt of her Sunday dress around her. "Where's Arabella this morning?"

"Sent her on ahead with Thomas Jr."—he jerked his thumb behind him—"so you wouldn't have to ride in back with those ruffians."

She laughed. "I wouldn't have minded that a bit. I hope I'm not putting you out."

He winked and grinned. "Not a whit. We more'n happy to help."

"Well, the Lord gon' bless you. I know I sure do appreciate it. I bet you're glad Doc Turner lets you off on Sunday mornings to go to worship."

Thomas snorted. "He know I'll quit before I work on the Lawd's day." He gave her a sidelong glance. "Say, what's old Henry up to this morning? He come by my house in a right big hurry. Didn't say where he had to get to so quick."

Sarah's clabbered stomach lurched. She wasn't about to admit she didn't know what business her own husband was about. She squirmed and glanced away. "You know Henry King. Probably found him a good trade or some such. I don't pay no mind to that man's mischief."

Just as she hoped, Thomas laughed and asked no more questions. They didn't talk much after that because the teasing, giggling children made it impossible. Sarah settled back and tried to forget Henry's strange doings. She set her mind instead on thoughts more suited to the day.

Thomas began to hum a gospel hymn in a deep baritone. The clamor behind them ceased, and several small voices rose with the lyrics of the song. The tension in Sarah's body melted. She turned on the seat and joined her high soprano to the swaying angel choir clustered in back.

Just as her heart rose up and soared to the throne of grace, the thundering hooves of an approaching rider reached her ears. A boy on horseback galloped toward them, shouting and waving his arms.

She looked at Thomas. "What's that about, you reckon?"

Thomas stared at the rider and shrugged, but worry drew lines over his brow.

When the frenzied rider reined up so fast he almost landed in her lap, Sarah's back stiffened, and her stomach forced bile to her throat. One glance at the boy's frightened eyes—his gaze locked straight on her face—and she knew. Something bad had happened to Henry.

"Best come quick over to the Commercial Hotel, Miss Sarah. There's trouble out back." Without another word, the boy, who turned out to be Cook's son, dug his heels in the horse's flank and sped away.

"Is it Henry?" she called after him, but he raced away as if the weight of the disaster rested on his young shoulders.

She stood up in the wagon. "Wait! You come back here!"

The wind picked up her useless cry and blew it behind her as the rider disappeared in a cloud of dust.

"That foolish boy. I could've taken his horse or rode with him at least. Oh, Thomas!"

Thomas gripped her hand and pulled. "Sit down, Miss Sarah. We'll get you there." He slapped the reins hard and roared, and the horse took off as though he'd been stung.

Holding on to the seat, Sarah twisted to look behind at their precious cargo. Fear had the children as wide-eyed as a basket of owls, especially the little ones. She gave them a steady smile while she lifted up a prayer.

I know I deserve it, but don't take Henry from me. And please don't let harm come to these babies on my account.

CHAPTER 21

Thad rode into Longview in the wee hours, cold, hungry, and heartsick. The only accommodations available at that time of night happened to be a shabby little room above the saloon—a fact he'd forget to mention to his mama. He paid the bartender in advance then slipped past a drowsy dance-hall girl and a cluster of men engaged in an all-night poker game.

The so-called room consisted of little more than a cot hidden behind a curtain in an alcove off the hall. The plain cotton mattress smelled of a hundred unwashed bodies, and the fetid pillow turned out to be a drool-stained sack stuffed with hay. Thad feared bedbugs and lice, but rather than sit up all night or risk a crick in his neck, he pulled a clean shirt from his travel bag to cover the pillow and slept on top of the quilt. He was cold, but better cold than share a warm bed with crawling critters.

The woolen curtain across the cubbyhole smelled so musty he couldn't breathe. He pushed it aside, which allowed the gaslight on the wall to burn a path past his eyelids straight through to the back of his head. He turned his face to the wall and buried his nose in the shirt-wrapped pillow that now smelled mostly of the lilac water mama sprinkled on her wash. The familiar scent made him want to cry like a boy in knee pants.

He finally fell into a troubled sleep that didn't last. He drifted in and out between brawls among the gamblers and fits of shrill, tinny laughter from the saloon girl, who must've found her second wind. He spent the wide-awake parts of the long night wondering why Bertha had let him down.

As soon as Mr. Biddie had discovered her missing, he headed off one way to search while Thad went another. Bertha's mama stayed behind in case she came back. Thad deliberately chose the road toward town. Despite her papa's insistence that Bertha would never go there alone at night, something told Thad that Annie Moore had everything to do with her disappearance.

He rode straight for Vale Street and Brooks House but found Bertha standing on a street corner with Annie before he ever got that far. He held back and waited to talk to her until watching from the shadows made him feel like an intruder. Feeling miffed and more than a little hurt, he had eased his mare around and headed for home.

Not many deeds in Thad's life had caused him shame, but the disgrace of running away from Jefferson without seeing Bertha safely home or easing her parents' minds made him cringe. He'd focused on his own hurt feelings, disappointment, and jealousy until his bruised heart had swept him away. All the way out of town, in fact. Now regret over not asking Bertha to marry him or even telling her good-bye gnawed holes in his soul.

The remorse tumbling in his gut mixed with the racket from below made his jerky attempts at sleep more of a chore than actual rest. He gave up trying and spent the last hours before dawn praying for forgiveness and direction. When the sun rose high enough to light the dim hallway, Thad rose, too, and set about finding a buyer for the Appaloosa.

He stepped out of the livery a few minutes later, one horse lighter and a few dollars richer. He gave the silver coins another quick tally then tied them up in a red bandanna and tucked it deep inside his pocket. Now to find breakfast and locate the depot.

"Good morning, my good man. A bright and beautiful day, is it not?"

The loud, cheerful voice and curious remark set Thad on his heels. He frowned up at the overcast sky then turned to see who would say such a thing. A tall, smartly dressed man in a bowler hat stood not three feet away.

The gentleman winked and tipped his hat. "All a matter of perspective, my boy." He pointed toward the sky. "Up there it's dim and gloomy. But in here"—he tapped his temple with a long, slender finger—"it's sunny all day long."

Thad returned the tipped hat gesture, nodded, and turned his back on the unfamiliar person. Couldn't be too careful.

Undeterred, the man sidled closer. "Hope you won't mind my saying, but I couldn't help noticing you've come into a bit of good fortune there." He jabbed a finger toward Thad's pocket. "Monetarily speaking, that is."

Thad's body tensed. *Dolt!* Who but a dolt would flash his money on the streets? He decided it best to ignore the inappropriate comment. "I hope you'll forgive my rudeness, sir, but I have a train to catch." He hitched his bag higher on his shoulder and stepped down off the boardwalk.

"You'll not catch one in that direction."

Thad turned, feeling foolish.

The fancy man grinned and pointed his index finger. "That way."

Thad nodded his thanks and set off again.

"I'm afraid you won't find a train to board for hours yet," the man called out behind him. "Looks like you're stuck here for a spell."

"That's all right. I'll wait at the depot."

The inquisitive stranger hurried along the boardwalk to draw even with Thad. "So where you headed?"

Thad frowned to show he resented the question. "South, to Bryan."

"Bryan, eh? Signed up at the new school there, unless I miss my guess." The dandy held on to a post and vaulted off the boardwalk directly into Thad's path. "What's your handle, son?"

"My what?"

"Your handle. Your name."

"Name's Thad," he answered, not sure why he had. "Thaddeus Bloom."

The stranger stuck out his hand. "Darius Q. Thedford at your service, Thad. Now I ask you, good son, why would a young man full of spit and vinegar choose to spend his morning in a dusty old train station? Especially when I can point the way to more"—he raised his brows and winked—"*stimulating* activities."

On a different day—a day his heart didn't throb in his chest, a day he hadn't just left behind everything he cared about, a day he wasn't mad as spit at his papa, even a day he hadn't been up all night—Thad would've been smart enough to turn and walk away. Instead, he peered at the smiling face across from him, and though he recognized the look of a man who'd just hooked a fish, he took a step closer.

"Did you say stimulating?"

The fisherman's dark eyes twinkled. "Downright exhilarating." He looped his arm around Thad's neck and led him up the boardwalk steps in quick little hops. "Ever try your hand at cards, lad?"

The words set his heart racing and tickled a memory to the surface. Thad knew where he'd seen the man before. The same mustachioed face had smiled up at him from the circle of poker-playing men in the saloon.

The taste of bait in his mouth, Thad dug in his heels and held up his hand. "Stop right there. I want nothing to do with gambling."

Darius removed his arm from around Thad's neck and backed away, looking him over. "So that's the way it is, eh? Very well, boy. I understand where you're coming from. Don't give it another thought." He pulled a pouch from his breast pocket and commenced to pouring tobacco in a line along the edge of a thin sheet of paper. With a practiced hand, he rolled it into a cigarette and licked it to seal the end. "Sorry I asked."

Confused, Thad stared at the man. He hadn't expected him to give in so easily.

Darius leaned against a pole and tucked away his tobacco. "When you're ready, I'll direct you to the train. Wouldn't want to worry your mama none."

The stress Darius placed on the word "mama" raised Thad's hackles, especially since he'd hit the nail right on its head of silver curls. At the mention of cards, Mama's face had drifted into Thad's mind, her voice warning him of the perils of flirting with Lady Luck and dabbling in games of chance.

He pushed her image away and swaggered closer to Darius. "What do you mean to imply, sir?"

Darius shrugged. "Only that a fine, strapping boy with a pocketful of money and a lot of extra time should be ripe for a little action. Of the competitive sort, I should say." He lit his hand-rolled smoke and shook out the match then gave Thad a sideways glance. "I figured the only thing holding you back from our little game must be a pressing need to mind your mama."

Thad saw himself standing on the bayou playing out the line on his Kentucky reel, teasing a fat catfish to shore. He had enough sense to know that Mr. Darius Thedford, still fishing, had just used the same maneuver. Enough sense to know it, but not enough to care.

The hook had set. Nobody called Thaddeus Bloom a mama's boy.

Thomas's bucking, skidding rig clattered across the Polk Street Bridge so fast Sarah feared soaring off into the bayou. They cut across on Dallas Street to Vale then took the turn over to Austin on two rumbling wheels. Sarah abandoned her place beside Thomas and crawled in back to help shield and comfort the babies. When they bounded up to the rear entrance of the Commercial Hotel, she did a quick head count for fear one of the children had bounced right over the side.

Satisfied they were shaken but all right, she gathered her skirts and clambered out of the wagon. It didn't take long to locate the trouble. A crowd of men stood out back of the building, their waving arms and raised voices pointing the way Sarah needed to run. She slowed to keep from mowing down onlookers at the rim of the circle then started elbowing her way through.

"Make way, now," she cried, realizing how deep her anguish flowed by the sound of her own voice. "Oh, please. Move out my way."

On the other side, a worse sight than Sarah could imagine met her eyes. She took it all in then slapped a hand over her mouth to keep from crying out. Henry slumped in the saddle, hands tied behind his back and a noose around his neck. Bruises covered his face, and blood flowed from a busted nose. The only thing standing between Henry's legs and empty space, between life and certain death, was the most cantankerous mule in the good Lord's creation.

Dandy, don't you move.

The three dreadful men from the day before, laughing like drunken hyenas, hovered around her man. Skinny Boy held a handgun on the crowd. The one called Edward waved a scattergun with shaking hands. The man claiming to be Frank Griswald stood on the bed of a wagon tightening the noose around Henry's neck.

"This ain't right," a voice called out behind her. Sarah looked back to see who spoke, but it could've been any one of ten frowning white men standing among the other locals and shopkeepers who had gathered, most of them red-faced with anger.

"We don't do things this way in Jefferson," a distant voice cried.

"No problem, then," the thin one growled in a stone-cold voice. "We ain't from around here."

"What crime did this man commit?"

Sarah glanced to her left. This time she recognized the scowling owner of Sedberry's Drugstore. Frank Griswald leaned away from Henry and pinched the butt of a drooping cigar from his mouth. He answered without looking at Mr. Sedberry, squinting through his smoke at Henry instead. "This boy's a thief." He pointed at the rope. "Where I come from, this here is a thief deterrent."

"You fellows won't get away with this," Mr. Sedberry shouted. "That man deserves a fair trial."

Thomas and his two older boys pushed in behind Sarah. Thomas gasped and laid a hand on her arm. "Did anyone go for the sheriff?"

Sarah clutched his hand. "It don't matter. By the time he gets here, Henry will be dead."

She weighed her options. Despite the guns, despite the cold look in the men's eyes, she longed to rush headlong in Henry's direction. But if she did and lived through it, what would it accomplish? Dandy would bolt for sure, leaving Henry to dangle.

Desperate, she turned around to search the crowd for help. A cluster of her people stood off to the side, the men puffed up and spewing, the women wringing their hands. A closer look at their faces told Sarah fear had them by the throat. She'd find no help among them.

Too scared to cry, Sarah clung to Thomas and hid her face in his stiff woolen shirt. "We have to do something quick, Thomas. Henry's gon' die if we don't."

Please help us, Lord! Please spare my good-hearted man.

Sarah raised her head when the babble around her died. Certain it meant the dreadful men were about to finish their grizzly task, she jerked her head in Henry's direction, but he still sat slumped on Dandy. Her gaze darted, searching for the reason the crowd had stilled.

Drunken singing swelled from the alley, lifted on the morning breeze, and carried into the hotel's backyard. A man's voice, loud and getting louder, neared the back corner of the building. Even Henry's tormentors paused and stared.

Thomas craned his neck. "What's going on? What is that?"

Sarah stood up on her toes. "I don't know. I can't see."

The source of the racket shot bobbing and weaving from the shadows, singing an Irish chantey in a rowdy bawl. Behind Sarah, a woman gasped and a youngster giggled. Muttering voices uttered shocked surprise.

"Is that Mr. Stilley?"

"Sure is!"

"Can't even walk a straight line."

"Drunk as a skunk."

"Can't be. The man's a deacon."

"And a teetotaler."

Mr. Stilley wore his hat shoved down so far it covered his eyes. The buttons of his coat were fastened into all the wrong holes so that the lapel flapped under his chin on one side and the tail hung to the ground on the other. He carried a big bottle of scotch in his left hand and a broken umbrella in his right. He plodded with a lurching, halting gait, still singing the sailor's song at the top of his lungs.

Sarah prayed for God Himself to steady Dandy.

Oblivious to the meaning of the scene he had stumbled upon, the stodgy owner of the dry goods store meandered straight toward the thin, pock-faced young man and his pistol.

Skinny Boy raised his free hand. "Hold up there, grandpa. Where you think you're going?"

Mr. Stilley tipped his head back and peered from under the brim of his hat. "Heard a party," he slurred in a loud voice.

By the way they snickered and shot each other looks, this tickled the men's funny bones to no end. Their evil leader stooped down on the wagon and jumped to the ground. "Don't think you want an invite to this party, old man." He nodded at the nervous Edward, who waved Mr. Stilley away with the barrel of his gun.

"Move along, now, pop," Edward ordered in an important voice. "Go somewhere and sleep it off."

Sarah bit her lip and tasted blood when Mr. Stilley lumbered past the mule, headed straight for Edward. "Now see here, young man," he slurred. "I won't be spoken to like that. Don't you know who I am?"

With the quickness of a striking snake and the boldness of a senseless man, Mr. Stilley clutched Edward's shotgun and raised the business end toward the sky. In the same instant, he grabbed Dandy's halter and held him fast.

Her eyes busy with this spectacle, Sarah missed how Doc Turner and Sheriff Vines got the jump on the other two. By the time she thought to look, both bad men had dropped their weapons and raised their hands out of respect for the guns buried in their backs.

Mr. Stilley, cold sober and looking right proud of his acting skills, glared at the crowd. "Don't stand there gawking like fools. Someone go fetch Sheriff Bagby."

Cook's boy, who had remained on his horse the whole time, most likely to see better, whirled his poor horse and sped away in the direction of the jailhouse.

Sarah felt the knot in her stomach unwind like a child's whirligig and feared she might lose control of her bowels. She rushed toward Henry, fully expecting one of the white men to order her back. They didn't, and she made it to the wagon bed, scrambled on, and stretched up to remove the loathsome rope from around Henry's neck. When she couldn't quite reach it, she began to cry for the first time since laying eyes on her husband's plight.

Thomas leaped up beside her and gently pulled her hands away. "Here, let me, Miss Sarah."

She hadn't been able to look at Henry's battered face since that first horrid glimpse but dared a peek while Thomas lifted off the noose. What she saw stabbed grief to the center of her heart.

Henry stared straight ahead, as he had since she first saw him. His busted face wore shame forged there like a mask. His lips, chin, cheeks, all trembled, and silent tears welled in waves that spilled over and tracked down his face.

Unable to look any longer, Sarah pressed her belly against Dandy's back and tore at the ropes on his hands. "Don't you fret, Henry King. You hear me, now? Don't you fret no more." She heard her own babbling voice, teetering on the edge of hysteria, but couldn't stop. The need to comfort raged too strong. "Don't let them whip you down. Don't you dare let them win. Those men gon' be at someone's mercy now. They'll be bound in cuffs and shackles, but you'll be free."

She got his hands loose and cringed when his arms fell to his sides like wilted celery stalks. Thomas jumped down and wrapped Henry around the waist to pull him off Dandy's back. Several other men, black and white, rushed to help lower him to the ground. Not until Henry's knees buckled did Sarah realize he had injuries she couldn't see. She leapt to the ground and rushed to his side to help Thomas hold him up.

Cook's son rode up with Sheriff Bagby. The sheriff sprang from his horse and joined Sheriff Vines where he held Griswald at gunpoint. "Thought sure you fellows would take fair warning and clear out of town." He glanced around at each of them. "Ain't too bright, are you?"

After all she had suffered at the hands of the haughty gang leader, Sarah deemed him above the law and impossible to break. She held her breath and waited for him to spin like a whirling dervish, guns blazing. Instead, he ducked his head and gave in without a peep. Sarah's jaw went slack.

The two lawmen shared a guilty look; then Sheriff Bagby stepped closer to Henry. "I'm real sorry this happened, son. But like I told you this morning, we had nothing solid to hold them on. Had no idea they were capable of something like this."

Sheriff Vines took the handcuffs from the other lawman. "We know now, and we have enough to hold them for a very long time."

Sarah stared up at a stone-faced Henry. So that's where he'd gone that morning. But why? And how did he wind up on Dandy's back with a noose around his neck?

Thomas left the job of holding Henry to Sarah and the others and moved out front to clear the way. "Let us pass, folks, so's we can get him over to my wagon."

Dr. J. G. Eason, in his long black coat and stovepipe hat, pushed through the crowd waving both hands in the air. "Hold up there, Thomas. Where are you taking this man?"

Thomas looked baffled. "We 'bout to take him home." He sought out Sarah behind him. "Ain't that right, Sarah?"

The doctor shook his head. "He needs medical attention." He glanced at the owner of the Commercial Hotel. When the man nodded, Dr. Eason pointed toward the rear entrance. "All right, you men take him inside so I can examine him."

The gang of helpers shifted directions and carried Henry toward the door. As they passed where Mr. Stilley stood holding the spineless Edward captive with his own gun, Sarah gazed over her shoulder and met her hero's eyes. "Thank you," she whispered.

Mr. Stilley winked and gave her a warm smile then returned his attention to Edward.

Sarah surrendered her place at Henry's side to a man for the hard trek up the steps. The last thing she saw before ducking inside was a parade of men—Mr. Stilley, the lawmen, and some others—marching the prisoners off to jail.

Sarah expected the men who carried Henry to go straight to the kitchen and put him in a chair near the servants' pantry, but they trudged on through to the parlor. Henry shook his head when they steered him toward the pretty settee, nodding instead at a straight-backed wooden chair. It angered Sarah that even in his busted-up state, he felt unworthy to sit on the beautiful couch. When they settled him on the chair, he found a spot in the corner and fixed his eyes there, refusing to face them.

Besides the two who bore Henry's weight, a group of curious and concerned folks had followed them inside. Sarah stepped around them to tend to her husband, and Henry tilted his head toward hers, muttering something she didn't quite make out.

She leaned closer. "What's that?"

He shifted his eyes to hers then right back to the corner. She bent down and put her ear against his lips. "What is it, Henry? Tell me."

She felt him shudder. "Take me home."

Before she could decide how to answer, Dr. Eason swept through the parlor door with his medical bag under his arm. He stopped short and looked at Henry sitting upright. "What's going on here, gentlemen? I can't examine a man in a chair. Let's get him stretched out on this couch."

Henry didn't protest this time, and Sarah wondered if the pain he felt had anything to do with it. She sent up a quick prayer that nothing serious might be going on inside him.

Thankfully, Dr. Eason ordered all but Sarah to wait outside. When the last of them shuffled through the door, the doctor pulled up a chair, raised Henry's shirt, and commenced to poking and prodding his chest. Henry winced and rolled away from his hands, and the doctor nodded. "Thought so."

Sarah moved closer. "What, Doctor?"

"It's a fractured rib, Sarah. Maybe two."

"Is he gon' be all right?"

He mashed Henry's stomach for a long time before he answered. "No sign of injury to the internal organs." He asked a few questions, and Sarah felt relieved when Henry answered every one.

Finally, the doctor stood up and smiled. "He'll be all right. Just sore for a spell. We'll wrap him up tight and send him home to bed. You make him rest for a few days, you hear? Don't let him get out there chasing behind that mule tomorrow. It'll be a month or so before he's fit for hard work."

Henry frowned.

The doctor pulled a roll from his bag and wound yards of white cloth around Henry's chest then offered a hand so his patient could sit up. He grimaced before moving gentle fingers over Henry's nose. "Nothing much we can do for this sort of thing, I'm afraid. Just clean it up when you get home and pray it heals without causing you any problems."

Sarah searched his eyes. "Problems?"

The doctor shrugged. "Trouble breathing, excessive snoring." He glanced back at Henry. "You won't be as pretty as you were before if it heals crooked or bumpy."

Sarah cringed at the thought. She liked her husband's nose just the way it was.

Dr. Eason lowered his voice to a whisper. "I'll be happy to bring out a bottle of wine to cut the pain, Henry. I make it myself on my own winepress. The grapes come from a vineyard I set up near the old Welch Bridge."

Henry struggled for something to say. Sarah said it for him. "No, thank you, sir. We're abstainers."

He gave her a thoughtful nod. "Well, it's there if you need it."

Henry raised his pain-filled eyes to the doctor. "Can't I go now?"

Dr. Eason nodded. "I'll get someone to help you to your wagon. Go home and rest, now. You hear?"

Henry nodded.

The doctor picked up his bag. Sarah couldn't imagine what other instruments lay in the depths of the shiny black satchel and didn't care to know. Not if it came to using them on Henry.

Wincing, Henry scooted to the edge of the settee so Sarah and the doctor could help him to his feet. She couldn't help wondering why he seemed so weak if his injuries weren't that serious.

Dr. Eason seemed to read her mind. He gripped her husband's arm and gave him a gentle shake. "Henry, the human body wasn't designed to suffer what happened to you. In episodes of great pain, fear, or humiliation, the mind shuts off, like when your old mule decides he won't take another step."

He waited for Henry to speak. When he didn't, the doctor carried on. "Just like that mule, as soon as you get a little food and plenty of rest, you'll be good as new again. Do you understand what I'm trying to say?"

Henry nodded and even tried to smile. The sight of it lifted Sarah's heart.

Dr. Eason left after giving her a few more instructions but kept his promise to send someone to help Henry out to the wagon.

Thomas and his usually rowdy sons slipped into the room, the boys so hushed at the sight of the fancy parlor that Sarah didn't recognize them. The oldest, though only sixteen, stood as tall as Thomas and likely weighed more. Plenty big enough to help support Henry's weight. Thomas's eyes lit up to see Henry acting more like himself. He hustled over, ready to brace him.

Henry held up his hand. "I'm obliged, Thomas, but I can make it on my own now."

Sarah clutched his arm as he passed. "Wait, Henry. Let them help you."

He turned–slowly, deliberately, with eyes so scary her scalp tingled. "Don't touch me, woman. I said I can make it." He limped around the settee and stumbled for the door, leaving Sarah unable to breathe.

CHAPTER 22

Thad picked up his bag and strutted closer to Darius Thedford. "On second thought, mister, I reckon I got some time to kill. Where's this poker game of yours?"

Darius tried in vain to hide a satisfied smirk. "That's my boy. Follow me."

Something told Thad he'd regret heeding those words. He fell in line with Darius and retraced his steps to the same place where he'd spent the night. No surprise when Darius slowed his stride and pushed past the swinging doors into the saloon.

A collection of men still huddled around the card table. Likely the same bunch, considering their bloodshot eyes and stubbly chins. Gone the boisterous laughter and loud arguments of the night before—fatigue had reduced them to nods and grunts. When Darius approached, the gamblers squinted up at him through a haze of cigar smoke and nodded.

"What you got there, Thedford?" growled a man in a wide-brimmed black hat. "Did your cur throw her pups?"

None of them spared the energy to laugh, but they all grinned and nodded their approval. Darius clutched Thad by the shoulders and guided him closer to the table. "Make room for two more players, gents."

A scruffy man, tobacco-stained teeth visible behind a bushy gray mustache, tilted his head up at Darius. "What you doing back here? Thought you was all tapped out." His voice ground out like iron on gravel, probably hoarse from smoking, if not from shouting all night.

Darius poked a sleeping man in the ribs then moved in to take his seat when he stumbled away. He motioned for Thad to take the empty chair next to him.

Thad complied, tucking his travel bag securely between his feet.

Darius picked up a deck of cards, shuffling so fast his hands blurred, and nodded at Thad. "My good friend here has enough to guarantee my stake."

Thad's head whipped around. "What?"

Darius leaned close to whisper. "Just a few dollars until I'm back in the chips. Don't worry, old boy. I'm good for it. Now ante up."

Before Thad could protest, the other players had their money down. The raspy-voiced man tapped the end of his cigar on the leg of the table and scowled. "Well, pup? You in or out?"

Thad glared at Darius.

Still shuffling, he winked and smiled. "Go ahead, boy. We'll be all right."

Feeling snookered, Thad turned his back on the players and dug out his kerchief-wrapped bundle. He counted out double the required amount and slid it into the pot. He'd scarcely drawn back his hand before cards were flying and the first bets were placed.

Just as fast, Thad found himself down to his last silver dollar.

He never expected the excitement of the game to snare him, never expected the same old flutter in his stomach or the familiar surge of heat through his body each time he held a fair hand of cards. As a boy, he'd read of Homer's Sirens, beautiful women who perched on the shore and lured sailors onto the rocks to shipwreck and enslave them. Sitting at a card table in a gaudy, smoke-filled saloon, Thad could hear the Sirens' song. And it scared him.

More than that, it stripped him of every last coin in his

possession, save the one in his hand. Hardly enough for a train ticket south.

Mama's scowling face rose up in his mind, but her pointing finger and well-earned "I told you so" paled in comparison to Papa's angry eyes.

He opened his mouth to tell the men he'd made a dreadful mistake, that he hadn't meant to play, and could he please have his money back. But the ruthless gamblers seated around him weren't kids playing Lanterloo for buttons. His money would pad their pockets, and he wouldn't be seeing it again. The realization struck that he'd simmered other men in the same stew he found himself in, and it shamed him.

Thad felt the weight of the dollar he held, enough to see and call the last wager. Should he fold and leave the table with enough for a much-needed bath and a plate of food or throw all his lot toward recouping some of his losses? He stared at the pair of kings in his hand and decided they weren't good enough.

When he moved to lay down his cards, he felt a bump against the side of his boot. Convinced it was an accident, he moved his foot. A pointed toe followed and nudged him again, so he stole a glance at Darius's unreadable face. Without looking at Thad, he gave a barely perceptible nod.

Since Thad couldn't exactly lean over and ask what Darius meant for him to do, he had to assume he should stay in the game. He grimaced and laid down his dollar. "I see your bet, and I call."

"That's it, then," Darius announced and threw out a pair of jacks. "Beat those or fork it over, friends."

With grumbles and rude remarks, the others folded their cards and threw them facedown on the table.

Thad stared at the cards in his hand until the spots ran together. Then his gaze moved to the mounded pot. He'd won. All his money back and then some. Grinning like a youngster at a birthday party, he slapped down the two kings with a satisfied shout and reached to draw in his loot.

A hand shot out and latched onto his wrist so hard he winced.

"Hold up there, partner. I think there's been a mistake."

His arms still stretched around his winnings, Thad blinked at the man's scowling face. "What mistake? You all folded, and two kings beats two jacks last time I checked."

Fingers still locked on Thad's arm, the cigar smoker glared at Darius. "Well, I reckon there's some sort of a mix-up. Right, Thedford?"

Darius went on shuffling with his quicksilver hands then slid the deck toward Thad. "Son, I believe it's your deal."

The angry man stood to his feet. "I asked you a question, Thedford."

Darius shrugged and leaned back. "I suppose everyone's luck runs out after a while, Billy." He scooted to the edge of his chair and calmly scooped up the money. No one made a sound while he counted and stacked the coins. Then he reached for Thad's neckerchief and tied the money into a wad. "Let the kid take his winnings, Billy. He won them fair and square."

Billy's brows met in the middle. "Oh, I follow now. You and the tadpole struck a bargain of your own." He leaned over the table, shifty eyes bouncing from Thad to Darius. "But I got news. Nobody cuts Billy Eddy out of a deal." With a furious roar, he shoved over the table, sending cards and money flying. Thad and Darius leaped out of their chairs, and Darius backed away from the swarming men, one hand held up as a shield.

"Now, Billy, you know I'd sooner kiss a rattler than cross you boys."

Thad spun and shot Darius a fierce look. It all made sense. Thad hadn't been an angler's fish. He'd been a swindler's pigeon. Darius Thedford was a crook. A crook burdened with a sore conscience, but a crook nonetheless. He'd brought Thad to this saloon to double-cross him.

Thad wasn't about to risk his neck for the no-'count cheat. He snatched up his travel bag and inched toward the exit.

The gamblers, intent on a pound of Darius's flesh, didn't notice.

When Thad's groping hand connected with the swinging doors, he eased out and quick-stepped to the corner then ducked down the alley. He picked up speed as he neared the back of the building, but his mind lingered inside on the bandanna filled with lost money.

Why hadn't he listened to his mama?

Why? Because insufferable arrogance had tripped him up, and temptation had brought him on down. Darius's challenge had pinned Thad to the wall by his own weakness. He'd really thought he could use his skill at cards to fleece those men but found himself stripped of wool instead.

"Pride goeth before destruction, and an haughty spirit before a fall. Better it is to be of an humble spirit with the lowly, than to divide the spoil with the proud."

The words from the Bible rocked inside his mind. In his case, pride had brought such a great fall that there would be no spoil to divide. He lowered his head before the eternal truth of God's Word.

Forgive me for the sin of pride. And for gambling when I know it's wrong. I'll try and do better next time.

If not for the need to hurry, he'd slip to his knees and say a proper prayer. Under the circumstances, his whispered plea would have to do. He'd be sure to thank his mama for her wise counsel when he got home—and apologize for not heeding it.

The burden inside him lifted as the wall beside him exploded. He jerked around in time to see Darius soar from a boarded-up window. His body landed and rolled with the grace of a dancer, and he wound up on his feet next to Thad.

"Let's see how fast you can run, boy. Follow me."

The same two words had gotten him in this fix to start with, but Thad had little time to consider the wisdom of following. The band of gamblers fired two shots from the window behind him then scrambled through the opening shouting curses. Thad burst out of the alley on Darius's heels.

They thundered down the narrow passageway behind the row

of buildings, turned into the back door of a livery stable, and came out the front. Then up the boardwalk a ways, weaving between disgruntled pedestrians, before turning down a side street just past the mercantile.

By then, Thad couldn't tell where he was going or where he'd been. The rest of their escape passed in a blur of shops and startled faces–until they ran to the end of a block, cut across a field, and wound up in front of the train depot. Darius wheeled to a stop near the ticket window and bent over, panting to catch his breath. Thad dropped his bag and leaned against the wall, breathing hard.

Darius recovered enough to speak and rose up grinning, his lips pulling the edges of his handlebar mustache into twin peaks. "A close one, my boy. We gave them the slip, though, didn't we?"

Thad glowered. "I get the feeling you've had plenty of practice."

Darius reddened and glanced away. Still, Thad had little pity to offer the man. He'd left his compassion in a dingy saloon tied up in a worn bandanna.

Still clutching his side, Thad straightened and looked around. A big Texas & Pacific passenger train loomed on the tracks beside them, boarding travelers of every description. Thad frowned at Darius. "What are we doing here? I don't expect they're giving away tickets today."

His wide grin back in place, Darius held up the knotted kerchief. "You didn't think I'd leave without this, did you? Go on. Take it."

Thad shook his head. "It's not mine."

Darius dangled it closer. "Why, sure it is."

Thad pushed his hand away. "I didn't win that money. You cheated those men out of it."

Darius raised his brows. "I just cheated enough to get back your investment. Since I took it by cheating to start with, I figure that makes it all right."

Thad gritted his teeth. He didn't want any part of the stolen money, especially Billy Eddy's or the other men's tainted loot. He reckoned he deserved to lose his portion for going against his parents' advice. "I'm telling you, I don't want it."

Darius shook his arm. "Come now, Thad. How else will you get to school?"

When Thad didn't answer, Darius grunted and pushed him out of the way. He stepped up to the ticket window, spoke to the smiling man behind the bars then slid a few dollars under the window. Before he walked away, he paused and asked the agent for a pen. Using the protruding ledge as a desk, he pulled a piece of paper from his pocket, scribbled on it, then stashed it again. He returned to Thad, picked up his hand, and slapped the ticket into his palm. "Take this, at least. It's your passage to Bryan."

When Thad didn't close his hand, Darius folded his fingers for him. "Thad, even a mule knows when to quit being stubborn."

Thad lifted his gaze to the man's earnest face and grinned. "Thank you."

The conductor for the noon train headed their way shouting the last chance to board. Darius placed his hand on Thad's shoulder. "You're a fine young man. I envy the direction you've chosen for your life and regret any action on my part to hinder you. I pray you'll forgive me."

Thad searched his eyes and found true sorrow there. He gave a little nod.

"And, son," Darius whispered, "my mama tried to sway me from gambling, too. I only wish I'd listened."

Thad laughed aloud, and Darius pounded him on the back. "Time to get on that train, unless you plan to chase it."

Wiping the dust off on his trousers first, Thad held out his hand.

Darius winked and gave it a hearty shake. "Wait right here. I'll get your things." He took two sliding steps to the wall, returned with the travel bag, and laced the strap over Thad's arm.

Thad shifted the weight of it and tucked his arm around the middle. "Thank you, sir."

Darius gave the bag a thoughtful pat. "It's the least I could do, son. Good luck to you."

"I appreciate it, Darius, but I rely on a Power more dependable than luck." He ducked his head then lifted a sheepish grin. "Well, most days, at least. I'm sorry my actions didn't bear witness of Him." He gripped Darius's shoulder and held his gaze, wanting to say more, to tell him the Power he depended on was a better way.

The last whistle blew beside them, the haunting blast so loud they both jumped. Darius beamed, lifting the edges of his mustache again. "Better go, son."

Thad returned his smile then ran for the open door of the passenger car. Handing over his ticket, he hopped aboard just as the wheels began to turn. He lumbered down the aisle, found an empty seat, and eased into it.

Darius shouted his name, and Thad leaned out to find him trotting alongside the train waving a folded piece of paper. When he saw Thad, he picked up his pace and ran up next to the window. "Here! Take this before I change my mind."

"What is it?"

Darius tucked the document into Thad's outstretched hand. "Maybe a worthless waste of ink, but maybe enough to soothe my sore conscience and settle our score."

"There's nothing left to settle."

He grinned and stopped running, cupping his hands to shout, "Let's just say I have a lot to atone for."

Thad thrust it at him, but Darius had fallen too far behind and didn't seem inclined to take it back. He lifted his hand in a mock salute and turned away. Thad stared after him until the track curved and he could no longer see the platform.

Puzzled, he settled against the seat, unfolded the paper, and tried to make sense of what he had. At the bottom, a name had been crossed out and Darius's penciled above it. Then Darius's name was struck through and Thad's printed on top. His eyes lit on the word "property" then the word "deed," and his breath caught in his throat. He leaned out the window, as if Darius might still be there to explain.

Why would Darius give it to him? He said it might be worthless, so he'd never seen the property, which meant he'd likely won it playing cards.

Thad held it in a shaft of light to read the small print. The official sounding words described a parcel of Texas land in a place called Humble, somewhere north of Houston. Was it really his? From the look of it, after a trip to the courthouse to record the deed, it would belong to him, worthless or not.

Could he accept such a valuable gift? A gift Darius won at poker, no less? A better question, how would he go about giving it back?

Didn't the Bible say the wealth of the sinner was laid up for the just? Well, he hadn't behaved very justly by disobeying his parents and risking Papa's money in a game of chance. But God also promised to forgive a man's transgressions when he asked.

He hauled his bag from under the seat and undid the loop from the button holding it shut. Pulling aside a stack of trousers and his long johns, he tucked the deed beneath them. When the pile of clothes fell back, a flash of color in the opposite corner caught his eye. Heart racing, he pulled the red bandanna from its hiding place, untied it, and counted out the coins. They totaled every dollar of the money he'd lost playing cards, less the price of his ticket south.

Darius.

Another scripture, this one from the book of Romans, drifted through Thad's mind.

"Be not forgetful to entertain strangers: for thereby some have entertained angels unawares."

Did he really believe Darius Thedford, a cigar-smoking, card-cheating dandy was an angel? Hardly. But God had used the man to teach Thad a valuable lesson and even turned to good what had been a very bad offense on his part. He lifted a prayer of thanksgiving then tacked on a plea on Darius's behalf. Thad wondered if he'd ever see the man again.

Lost in thought, he jumped like a frog when the train whistle blew at a crossing. Grinning, he patted the bag still clutched in his hands and thought about the deed inside. In His mercy and grace, the Lord had chosen not only to forgive Thad but to bless him right out of his socks.

CHAPTER 23

Monday, January 22

Bertha laid her needlework aside. A good thing, really, considering the mess she'd made of it. Tiny stitches were hard to see with tears in her eyes.

She sat with her mama in the parlor, a basket of sewing between them—Bertha huddled in a corner of the settee, Mama perched in a straight-backed Windsor chair. The fireplace crackled beside them but did nothing to warm Bertha's heart.

She raised her head and met Mama's sorrowful gaze. "Stop watching me, please. I'm all right."

Her mama flushed. "How did you know with your chin on your knees?"

"I feel your eyes on me like twin brands. They've seared holes in my head."

Mama poked her needle into her pincushion. "Well, you don't seem all right to me, dear. You hardly touched your dinner, even after sleeping straight through breakfast."

Bertha grimaced. "I wasn't sleeping. Hardly slept all night." She rubbed her midriff, fighting tears. "And food makes the ache worse."

Mama winced and ducked her head. She'd tiptoed around the house since yesterday morning, shamefaced and apologetic. "Try to drink something, then. Let me steep you a cup of chamomile tea. It'll ease your stomach and relax you."

Bertha stood, her bleary eyes going to the window again. She couldn't stop searching the lane for Thad, though she knew he was long gone.

"*Gone, I must be gone. . . .*" The words sounded so final.

She moved behind Mama's chair and patted her shoulders. "I know you mean well, but tea won't help. Nothing short of Thad's return will make me feel better."

Reaching back, Mama squeezed her hand. "I'm responsible for all of this. Can you ever forgive me?"

A catch rose in Bertha's throat. "There's nothing to forgive. I know you didn't realize how much it meant. I would've told you, but–"

She paused so long that Mama twisted around to look. "But what?"

"You'll think me fresh."

Mama waved her hand. "You go right ahead and speak your mind."

"It's just that you're so different now. I don't remember you ever apologizing to me before." She gave a nervous laugh. "Or allowing me to speak my mind, for that matter. If you'd been like this that night. . ." She couldn't finish. The boldness of her words sealed her tongue to the roof of her mouth.

Mama sighed. "You're free to say it. It's only right that I hear what I've done to you."

Bertha pressed the backs of her fingers to her mouth. "I can't," she whispered when she could speak.

Mama took her wrist and guided her around in front of the chair. "Let me say it for you. If I'd been approachable, as I am now, you'd have come to me, told me about Annie and Thad, and together we'd have worked things out. But I was rigid and inconsiderate instead, and I failed you." Her voice broke on the last three words.

Bertha knelt and pressed her forehead to Mama's calico-covered knee. "It doesn't matter. Please don't cry."

With a trembling finger, Mama lifted Bertha's chin. "It matters. So I ask you again. Will you forgive me?"

Despite the fact they belonged to her mama, Bertha stared into warm, caring eyes she'd never seen before. "Of course I will."

Bertha rose up and fell into the first real hug she could remember them sharing.

When they parted, both smiling and wiping their eyes, she stole a long look at her mama's serene face while Mama fished a hankie from her waist pocket. Drying her cheeks, she shifted her gaze to Bertha. "Now you're staring."

Bertha giggled. "I've been wondering what Papa did to, well. . ."

"To change me?"

Speechless, she nodded.

"Simple. He threw the Bible at me."

Bertha clutched her lace collar. Throwing the Holy Book seemed extreme, even for her feisty papa. Mama tittered and waved her hankie. "Not literally, dear. He merely pointed out the scriptures directing a wife to submit to her husband and a husband to love his wife." Her eyes lost focus. "Funny how a verse can be right under your nose, or in this case right before your eyes, yet you can't see it. I must've read those passages a dozen times and never recognized it as the formula for happiness I'd been seeking."

Mama shook herself from her daze and motioned for Bertha to sit across from her. "So we struck a bargain." She stared at the ceiling and smiled, as if reliving the moment. "Francis promised abundant affection from here on out if I promised to honor his place in our home." Her slender white throat worked with emotion. "That silly man's devotion is all I've ever wanted. I just never knew how to get it."

Bertha leaned forward, confused. "I don't understand. Papa's such a loving man."

Mama nodded and delicately blew her nose. "Of course you'd perceive him that way. Besides the fact he adores you, when I built a wall to shut him out, he still had you to lavish attention on. Your father confessed that he's longed to show me the same love, but my rigid insecurity and lack of respect held him back."

She glanced at Bertha with grief-stricken eyes. "I shut you out, too. I don't know how I allowed it to happen. Now we've lost so much time."

Bertha rushed to embrace her. "Just think. We'll have a fresh start. It's never too late for love, you know."

Mama caressed her cheek. "Bless you, daughter." She kissed her then held her at arm's length. "And that's what you must remember about your Thad. It's never too late for love."

Bertha straightened and peered at the window again. "I do hope you're right. But we have a long wait to prove it. Thad won't be home for months."

"You'll see him soon. He'll come back to Jefferson on breaks and holidays. The time will pass quickly—you'll see."

Bertha stood, hoisting her basket and the frock she'd been hemming to her hip. "May I be excused? I can't sit in this house moping for another second." She walked around and rested her hand on Mama's shoulder. "If you don't mind, I'm going to ride into town to try to see Annie. I left her in such a terrible state."

Mama took Bertha's basket from her hands and placed it on a side table. "I hate to see you go into town alone. Wait and let Papa take you."

"I don't need to trouble him."

A stirring at the door caught their attention. "When in time have you caused me a mite of trouble, me girl?" Papa boomed. "I've a matter or three to see to in town meself. Let me fetch an overcoat, and we'll be off."

He disappeared, returning to peek around the corner at Mama. "Be ready to warm me supper then warm me bed, Mrs. Biddie. I'll be back in a trice."

Mama blushed like a girl. "Francis! Not in front of Bertha."

He winked and went away chuckling.

Mama busied herself with a sock and darning egg, her red face almost in her lap.

Bertha tried hard not to laugh. She turned away and covered her mouth with both hands.

Behind her, Mama let loose a small titter. They both giggled softly until Mama stood and gathered her sewing. "The man is scandalous," she announced.

"That he is."

"I can't do a thing with him."

Bertha grinned. "He may be a lost cause."

Mama beamed back and pinched Bertha's cheeks. "Yes, but in the most charming fashion." She cupped Bertha's chin in her palm. "Don't forget your wrap, dear. It's cold out."

Her papa, small in stature with a giant's presence, filled the doorway again. "Ready, me girl?"

Bertha pushed past him, planting a kiss above his scruffy beard on the way. "As soon as I fetch my shawl."

Papa stood by the wagon when Bertha came out, ready to lift her aboard. "Where to, young'un?"

"Brooks House. I need to see that Annie's all right."

He nodded. "I'll take you right to her doorstep. Just let me swing by the livery on the way."

"Isn't Mr. Spellings coping any better with losing Miss Carrie?"

Papa looked grim. "He'll be fine if loneliness and grief don't kill him. We just need to rally 'round him and keep him in our prayers."

Bertha sat silent for a moment then cleared her throat and sought his eyes. "I don't mean to show disrespect, but it's been awhile since Miss Carrie passed. Shouldn't he be getting on with it by now?"

Papa studied her with a somber look. "I'm afraid husbands don't fare well after losing a wife." He nudged her with his elbow. "If you ever tell I said this, I'll deny it. Understand?"

"Yes, sir."

"Womenfolk are far and away stronger creatures than men. It's how the good Lord fashioned you because of all you're required to endure."

"Like what? You seem stout enough to endure anything."

He drew back and made a face. "Can you see me birthing a babe?"

She blushed and grinned. "So you reckon we're stronger, do you?"

He gave a solemn nod. "Without doubt. You're the glue that binds us together. Thankfully, Sol's not yet forty, so youth is on his side. We older men don't last long after our wives pass. I think over time we forget how to care for ourselves."

She sat back and pondered his words. She had to admit she knew of many elderly widows but hardly any widowers. She stole a look at Papa, chewing on his mustache while deep in thought, and tried to imagine him alone, fending for himself. They rode the rest of the way in silence, Papa distracted and Bertha fighting tears.

When Mr. Spellings limped out of the livery to greet them, Bertha saw him with new, more compassionate eyes. He waved and lumbered their way, dodging mud holes and scattered piles of manure. Just before he reached them, he took off his battered Stetson and beat it against his leg, sending hay straws flying. "Francis Biddie and little Bertha. To what do I owe such a pleasure?"

Papa raised his derby and let it settle back onto his head. "The pleasure's ours, Sol. Stopped by to see if we can do anything for you today."

Mr. Spellings's cheeks rose in a warm smile. "Can't think of a thing. I take most of my meals over at Kate Woods's restaurant, and I hired a girl to see to my wash. Much obliged, though."

Bertha leaned past Papa. "Are you certain, Mr. Spellings? What about sewing? Do you have any clothing in need of repair?"

He scratched his head. "Now that you mention it, I do have a bag of tattered duds at the house. Some things Carrie never got around to." Tears clouding his soft brown eyes, he peered up at Bertha. "I'll bring them by the house, then. If you really don't mind."

She swallowed the lump in her throat so she could speak. "I'll be proud to do it."

He swiped his eyes with his sleeve and tucked his hat on his head. "Thank you kindly, Bertha."

Papa propped his boot on the side rail. "How's business, Sol? This weather must be pinching your purse."

A look of disgust came over Mr. Spellings's face. "Nothing to brag on, that's for sure. Folks don't much care to ride around in the rain." He raised one finger. "Except I did rent out a few horses on Saturday to some fellows just off the boat. And a man came in that day inquiring about a rig for Sunday. But when he came back for it yesterday, I decided not to let him have it."

Papa frowned. "Didn't like the color of his money?"

"Never saw his money. Didn't want no part of it, whatever the shade. Something about him I didn't trust."

Papa propped his arm on his knee and leaned closer. "Local fellow?"

Mr. Spellings shook his head. "Out of Boston, I think. Staying a few days over to Brooks House."

A sensation of dread wriggled fingers in Bertha's belly. "Excuse me, sir. I don't mean to interrupt, but what did he look like?"

Mr. Spellings took off his hat again, as if he couldn't think with it on. "What'd he look like? Well, let me see." He rubbed the top of his head as though he was trying to coax the memory back. "Sort of a fancy dresser, with a high-blown manner. Tall but not too thin. Had an overlarge mouth, if I remember right. A surly mouth, at that."

Her stomach lurched. *Abe Monroe.* "Did he say why he needed the rig?"

"Claimed he wanted to take a lady around town." He widened his eyes and curled his top lip. "In this weather, if you can believe it. I asked him to put up collateral, and he offered very little. Didn't like it a whit when I insisted he'd have to do better."

Papa smiled. "What'd he say to that?"

Mr. Spellings mimicked a haughty voice. "He said, 'I guess, then, that we can walk,' and took off down Polk Street."

She scooted forward on the seat. "Was the woman with him, sir?"

"No, darlin', she weren't. I asked who his lady was, thinking she might vouch for him. He told me I wouldn't know her, and anyway he left her over at Kate Woods's place."

For some reason the news unsettled her. If Abe knew Saturday evening that he planned to take Annie around town on Sunday, why didn't Annie know about it on Saturday night?

What was it she'd said? She hoped Abe would be sick from drinking and rest in bed all day. Obviously, Annie had no idea Abe planned to take her anywhere on Sunday. Why hadn't he mentioned it?

Bertha scarcely heard the rest of Papa and Mr. Spellings's discussion. She squirmed like a netted fish until Papa finished his business. When they finally said good-bye and pulled out of the muddy yard in front of the livery, a mixture of relief and worry weakened her knees.

"Can't we go faster, Papa?"

"What's the hurry, love?"

"Nothing really. Just anxious, I guess." She bit her lower lip. "There is one thing I haven't yet mentioned."

He swiveled to face her. "Well, mention it."

"I won't be able to see Annie if her companion is there."

Papa scowled. "What are you saying?"

"Just that we'll have to make sure he's nowhere around the hotel."

His eyes popped. "And why is that?"

She bit her knuckle and searched for the right words. "Abe won't allow Annie to see me. He doesn't let her have friends."

He swung his head back and forth. "You can forget it, then. Sneaking behind a man's back was never my style, and I won't start now. We'll walk up and knock on the door like proper guests or not at all."

Fear crawled up her spine. "You don't understand, Papa. We can't. Abe Monroe is mean to the core."

His hand shot up. "Stop right there. What sort of person speaks ill of a friend's spouse? It's not how we raised you, Bertha." A crop of blotches sprouted on his cheeks. "What were you thinking, coming between a man and his wife?"

Bertha looked away, her face on fire. "Annie's not his wife."

Papa cleared his throat. When she glanced at him, he appeared as red as she felt. "I don't like it, Bertha Maye."

She swallowed hard and peered into his face. "I don't either, Papa. But I told you some of Annie's story. Can't you see? She needs my help."

He looked straight ahead again, his face grim. His mustache twitched as he chewed one side of his bottom lip then the other. "You know it's a mighty heavy burden you've shouldered. Are you certain it's your load to bear?"

Her heartbeat quickened. "It's cost me dearly. I need to see it through."

He released a heavy breath, gave a curt nod, and spurred on the horse. They rode up Vale Street in silence, Papa's Irish temper still seething beside her.

When they pulled up to Brooks House, Bertha started to climb down. "Wait here. I won't be long."

Papa latched onto her arm. "There'll be none of that."

Frustrated, she plopped back. "Sorry, I forgot. Hurry, please."

"I ain't referring to helping you down." He pointed at the door, his face crimson and mottled like a ripe red plum. "I mean there'll be none of you going inside there alone."

She heaved a sigh. "Papa, listen. I'll inquire at the desk first. I promise not to go near her room until I'm sure he's gone out."

"I'm going with you, Bertha. To the lobby, at least, until I'm satisfied you'll be safe."

"Papa—"

"Else we leave here right now!"

Bertha winced and drew back. Papa never raised his voice to her. Defeated, she nodded. "Very well, then. Let's go. But please. . . let me do the talking."

After looking around the grounds in front, they passed through the doors of Brooks House and checked the lobby and parlor and then the dining room out back. Feeling like a player in one of Annie's Broadway shows for all their skulking about, Bertha gingerly approached the desk.

Thomas, Dr. Turner's porter, leaned over the registry, his lanky elbows planted on each side. He glanced up as they drew near, his face lighting up at the sight of Bertha's papa.

"Well, well, well. Mr. Biddie, suh. How you? You catched any mo' dem big old catfish?"

At the mention of his favorite subject, Papa's bright face matched Thomas's glow. "I ain't been fishing any more since that day. Too much work around the house."

"What? Too busy to fish? Mr. Biddie, that's way too busy." He chuckled then pursed his lips, the picture of innocence. "Well, dat's a shame, ain't it? I reckon since you ain't using yo' secret catfish bait, ain't no reason you cain't tell me what goes in it."

Papa jabbed his finger in Thomas's face. "A worthy attempt, laddie. You'll not be gettin' it out of me that easy."

They laughed together; then Papa leaned in toward the desk. "Doc Turner around?"

"Naw, suh. Went home fer a spell. He be back over here directly." He pointed at the well-appointed parlor. "You folks mighty welcome to wait."

Bertha stepped closer and lowered her voice. "Maybe you can help us. Do you happen to know if the gentleman staying in number four is in his room?"

Thomas started around the edge of the desk. "No, ma'am, Miss Bertha, but I'll be glad to find out."

Papa clutched his arm. "Let's not do that, son. We don't necessarily want to see him, just wanted to know if he's home."

Thomas gave Papa a blank stare. "Yes, suh, Mr. Biddie. But it won't trouble me none to go see if he's in there."

Footsteps in the hallway sent Bertha's heart rumbling like loose boulders. She jerked around to find Jennie Simpson limping into the foyer. Jennie stopped to stare, probably because none of the Biddies ever came inside the hotel.

"Well, I swear, if it ain't little Miss Bertha. Afternoon to you, as well, Mr. Biddie, suh."

Bertha hurried to her. "Afternoon, Jennie. Tell me, have you been cleaning the rooms?"

Her long lashes fluttered, and she pointed at her ankle. "No, ma'am, I ain't s'posed to."

For the first time, Bertha saw it was swathed in white cloth.

Smiling, Jennie turned her foot back and forth so Bertha could get a better look.

"Mercy, what happened?"

"Twisted it. Near to broke. Wouldn't be standing here now 'cepting I be about to starve to death upstairs." She glared at Thomas. "A body could lay up and die for all they care around here."

Thomas made a tent with his brows. "How you gon' starve when you find your way down those stairs in time for every meal served in this place? If you ask me, you're fit enough to work if you're fit enough to trot around huntin' up food all the time." He nodded at her feet, his lips curled in a smirk. " 'Sides, I just seen you limp out here on the wrong foot. Better not let old Doc see you do that."

She planted her knuckles on her hips. "Shush your mouth. Why you gon' lie on me like that?"

Bertha ducked in front of her scowling face and pointed down the hall. "Do you know if Miss Annie Monroe's, um, husband is in the room with her?"

It seemed a dreadful struggle, but Jennie pulled her attention from Thomas to Bertha's question. "Who?" Then her frown became a slow grin. "Oh, I know. You mean Miss Bessie's man."

"Miss Bessie. Yes, that's right."

"He ain't here. And she ain't neither."

Disappointment swelled. Bertha hadn't considered that possibility. "She's not here?"

"No, miss. Ain't seen her since they went off together yesterday morning. The mister, he come back all by hisself that afternoon."

"By himself?"

"Yes'm. When I went to fetch them for dinner"—she shot a

vengeful look at a grinning Thomas—"Mr. Abe say he already ate over to Miss Woods's place. So I asked him, 'What about Miss Bessie?' He say he left her at the restaurant, and she gon' be home that night." She stopped to draw a breath. "Only this morning at breakfast"—a glare at Thomas—"she weren't there."

"Not there?" Bertha felt like a parrot but couldn't stop repeating.

"No, miss. Mr. Abe be sitting at the table by hisself wearing those two big rings of hers." She touched a finger to her lips. "Or did I see that on Saturday night? Can't recollect which time, but I seen it."

The front door opened behind them, and Bertha whirled. Dr. Turner stood in the foyer hanging his coat. Relieved, she clutched at her collar and drew a ragged breath.

Doc turned with a playful frown. "Does anybody work around here when I'm gone? Francis, don't give these two any more reason to lollygag, if you don't mind. They manage quite nicely on their own." He widened his eyes at his two employees. "I'm back now, so get to work."

Panic gripped Jennie's face. "Dr. Turner, what about my leg?"

"I reckon you've nursed that excuse plumb to death." He studied her mournful face then slumped his shoulders. "Very well, get upstairs and rest your leg. But I expect you for light duty tomorrow morning."

Jennie backed away with a sullen look on her face. "Yes, suh. I'll make it. . .somehow."

When Jennie turned to follow Thomas from the room, Bertha was almost positive she favored the wrong foot.

Dr. Turner frowned. "Where you going? I said to get upstairs."

She whipped around. "I's hongry. Thomas ain't tended me no way like he should."

Before Thomas could protest, Doc nodded at the stairs. "Get on up there. I'll have him fetch your supper in a bit."

She cut sulky eyes at Thomas and smiled. "Yes, suh, Doc."

Laughing, Doc shook Papa's hand. "What can I do for you, Francis?"

Papa nodded toward Bertha. "Nothing for me. It's my girl here. She's worried about her friend. Thought maybe you could tell her where she is."

He turned. "Your friend Annie?"

Close to tears, she only managed a nod.

"Sorry to say she's not here. We haven't seen her since early Sunday morning."

Papa spoke up in Bertha's stead. "That's what Jennie said. Do you have an idea where she might've gone?"

"I saw her gentleman friend around two or three o'clock yesterday. The lady wasn't with him. After dinner I asked if she had returned from wherever she'd been, but she hadn't. So I asked from where he expected her return. He said he left her across the bayou visiting friends."

Bertha's head reeled with the information. Annie had friends across the bayou? She'd never once mentioned it. She found her voice. "When she comes back, will you tell her I'm looking for her?"

"I will." He tilted his head toward the row of rooms down the hall. "For now, you'd best not let him see you here. It'll just make more trouble for that poor girl."

Bertha clutched her papa's arm. "He's here? Jennie said he wasn't."

"Oh, he's here all right. Not answering the door is all. Paced his room all through the night, according to the other guests. Came down for breakfast this morning but didn't eat a bite. Said he was sick last night. Stinking drunk, more like it." He hooked his thumb toward number four. "Been moping in there all afternoon." He grinned and winked at Papa. "Just between us, I think she finally wised up and left him."

Bertha couldn't get outside of Brooks House fast enough. Even with Papa beside her, the thought of coming face-to-face with Abe Monroe raised the hairs on her neck. In her nearly eighteen years, she'd never had to fear a living soul, but something about Annie's companion stuck pure terror in her heart.

She thought of the day on the bluff when she first saw Annie's fear of Abe reflected in those lovely gray eyes. Annie had dreaded Abe's wrath more than an encounter with the devil himself. Then the night outside the Rosebud, even with Annie's senses deadened by drink, Bertha had witnessed the depths of her terror.

Maybe Dr. Turner was right. Maybe Annie had found a way to escape.

Bertha jumped when Papa touched her arm.

"I'm talking to you, Bertha. Haven't you heard a word of it?"

She gave him a tight smile. "Sorry, Papa."

"I asked if you knew of a place Annie might be hiding."

She shook her head. "She never mentioned knowing anyone in Jefferson. Of course, we weren't friends before she came. Annie's so kindhearted and outgoing, I can't assume I'm the only person in town who was drawn to her, now, can I?" Bertha had to admit the thought brought a peculiar sensation to the pit of her stomach. A sensation a little too close to jealousy. Jealously blended and stirred with anger and a generous dose of hurt feelings.

How could Annie turn to someone else after Bertha's offer of help? How could she up and leave town without even saying good-bye? Especially after Bertha's considerable sacrifice.

Then again, while grieving for Thad, she'd let a whole day pass without finding out what happened to Annie after she left her standing on a street corner in her nightdress.

God, forgive me. I've made a real mess of things.

"Bertha, what's ailing you, lass? I might as well be talking to a picket."

"Please forgive me. What did you say?"

"I asked you what's next, then."

His question ricocheted through the empty chambers of Bertha's heart, once so filled with fond affection from a friend and abiding love from a man. The same question applied to both Annie's fate and Bertha's future with Thad.

She drew a shaky breath. "What's next? Papa, if only I knew."

CHAPTER 24

Henry hadn't spoken to Sarah since the ugly words he spat at her in the hotel parlor. All the way home he sat silently in the back of Thomas's wagon, pale and gritting his teeth. When they pulled into the yard, he managed to thank Thomas and the boys, even greeted Dickens on the porch. But then he walked straight to their room and climbed into bed with nary a spare word left for Sarah.

Desperate to be near him, she followed him inside. "Henry?" she whispered. "Don't you want to eat something?"

He turned his face to the wall and drew up his shoulders. She knew he wanted her to leave, but she couldn't. Instead, she pulled the shade without making a sound, eased her way to the corner rocker, and sat so quietly in the dim room that he didn't seem to know she was there.

She watched while he tossed and turned, cried and groaned, twitched and moaned. When his breathing deepened and his face relaxed in sleep, Sarah finally dared to move. Easing her body from the chair, she crept out of the room. To keep the old hinges from squeaking, she left the door open and tiptoed down the hall.

In the kitchen, she sought the comfort of her red tea can. She took it down from the shelf and shook it, and only then remembered she had enough left for one last cup. While the water heated, Sarah wracked her mind. What had happened to make Henry so angry? What had she done to cause his hateful glare? To lace his voice with spite?

Dr. Eason said Henry's mind had shut down like a stubborn mule's. Well, she didn't believe it. She knew what a stubborn Henry looked like. The sullen man in the bedroom was a stranger she'd never laid eyes on.

Sarah lifted the kettle just as it started to whistle and sprinkled the last bit of her tea leaves over steaming water. Before closing the lid, she watched as swirling color leeched from the dried leaves. Some nameless disaster swirled about her in much the same way, threatening to stain her marriage and darken her happy life.

She found no consolation in the tea and let more than half the cup go wasted while she sat at the kitchen table lost in thought. She knew she should fix something to eat. They hadn't had a bite since breakfast, and Henry barely touched his plate then.

Leaning over the table, she folded her arms and rested her forehead there. The day had been the hardest of any she could remember. Of course, it would've been unthinkably worse if Dandy had bolted from under Henry. Still, she felt like those men had strung her up and beaten her right alongside her husband. She wondered if Henry's beating hurt worse than the heartache she felt.

Beneath the table, her stomach growled. She sucked it in as hard as she could, but it rumbled again in protest. They had pork chops left from supper last night, with baked beans and stewed apples to go with them. She could stir up a batch of biscuits fast, though skillet corn cakes would taste better.

Startled, she realized how quickly she'd gone from pure misery to thoughts of feasting. How odd the workings of the mind.

"I need a poultice for my nose."

Henry's voice brought Sarah to her feet as though she'd been bucked from the chair. "You're awake?"

He ignored her foolish question. "I can't abide this pain another minute."

She longed to reach for him. Comfort him. Instead, she scurried for the pantry and brought out jars of salves and herbs. "Your nose, you say? What about your ribs? You'd think your ribs would be giving you fits instead of your nose. 'Course, I ain't never had a broken rib, or a busted nose for that matter, but it just seems a rib would be bound to hurt worse."

Why was she babbling like Jennie Simpson? A better question—why was she talking to Henry as if he hadn't ripped the heart clean out of her chest?

He settled at the table and sat quietly while she tended his nose. When she finished, she got up without saying a word to pull out the pork chops and beans. After she warmed them and they ate, Henry pushed his empty plate aside. "I reckon I owe you some answers."

She put down the bite of apple between her fingers and met his eyes. "I only need one."

He looked away. "I'm sorry I treated you so poorly, Sarah. I had no right, and I hope you'll forgive me."

She felt her heart start to mend. "Can you tell me why?"

He wrinkled his face. "I think so. I'll try."

"Good enough."

He shifted in the chair and cleared his throat. "Yesterday, on the road when those men harassed us jus' for sport, I got real mad. When that little one pointed his gun straight at me and you jumped between us, I had so many thoughts swimming in my head I couldn't keep 'em straight." He scooted to the edge of his chair. "First thing, I ain't never had no gun in my face before. I wasn't ready for how it made me feel. Second thing, I realized if he had shot that gun, you'd be dead. Maybe both of us. That's when I passed up mad and went to crazy. Stayed crazy all the rest of the day."

She gave him a look. "You didn't seem mad."

He nodded. "I kept it pent up, like I always do. But I tossed in bed half the night thinking. When I woke up this morning, I had it figured you'd been right all along. White folks jus' plain mean and no 'count. Ain't a one of 'em care a whit for any of us, and I was wrong not to defend you better in this town."

"Oh, Henry."

"So I decided I wasn't about to let them men get by with what they done. I'd go see the sheriff and make sure he doled out proper punishment on those mongrels." He snorted. "Come to find out, the sheriff done turned 'em loose." He leaned over the table, looking at her with bulging eyes. "Turned 'em loose, Sarah. Like they ain't done one thing wrong." He slapped his hand down so hard he rattled the dishes. "There ain't no justice in that."

Remembering, his eyes glazed. "I didn't know what I was about to do next. I was in such a state by then I couldn't think. Wouldn't you know it, about that time I happened up onto them dogs. Instead of going the other way, like a man with any sense, I pranced past 'em glaring like I owned Austin Street." He flexed his jaw. "That's all it took to set those devils off. Next thing I knew, I was trussed up like a butchering hog on Dandy's back."

Sarah shuddered at the memory. "But that still don't explain—"

"Sittin' up there on Dandy, I think I went insane for a spell." He chewed his bottom lip. "All sorts of crazy thoughts took over my mind."

"What sort?"

He gave her a sheepish glance. "For one thing, I thought I was about to die, and I decided it was your fault."

She swallowed. "My fault? How'd you come up with that?"

He puffed his cheeks then released his breath in a whoosh. "Before you come to Jefferson, I didn't have no problems with these folks. I minded my business and stayed out of their way. Shucks, I even cared about most of them and believed they cared about me."

"Henry, I—"

He held up his hand. "Let me finish. Sarah. You put all these uppity thoughts in my head. You the one had me looking at white folks different. That's why I wound up talking back yesterday on the road. If I'd handled those men the way I know to, they would've gone on and left us alone. Jus' like today when I passed them on the street. If I'd ducked out of their way, I never would've wound up with a rope around my neck."

"So you think doin' things the way you always have makes it right?"

He slammed his hand on the table again, harder this time. "I don't know what's right anymore, Sarah. That's what I think. I jus' learned how to make it, that's all. I've been ducking and dodging for so long, I don't know any other way."

She knew she shouldn't lose her temper, too. Not now. Not with Henry hurt and already in such a state. But she did anyway. "If I'm the cause of all the problems in Jefferson, why'd you ever bring me here in the first place?"

He lifted cold, hard eyes. "I've been asking myself that same question lately."

They stared, neither giving an inch until Henry propped his elbows on the table and gripped the sides of his head. "All my life I've tried to believe what I read in the Good Book, where it says we supposed to love our neighbor like ourselves. That they ain't no race or color in Christ.

"When I was a boy, I remember thinking the white folks' Bible must have different words than mine, because the men coming out of the meetinghouses holding Bibles were the same ones buying and selling our people, cursing and whipping 'em. The Good Book say we all free in Christ, but the last thing they wanted was to see us free. None of it made sense to me then, and it still don't now."

"Henry, slavery didn't start here, with these people. Papa said slave trade has existed in Africa for thousands of years. He said our own brothers brought us down to the ships, bound and gagged."

Henry's eyes bugged. "Your papa's been yanking your leg."

"No, it's true." She patted his hand. "And not only white folks have owned slaves. He told me many colors and races of people are guilty. You want to know what I think? I think slavery's not a white or black problem, or even a people problem. It's a sin problem."

He snorted. "Well, it sure is a Jefferson problem. They jus' won't let us be free."

Sarah reached across the table and held his hands. "We don't need them to *let* us be free. Or haven't you heard about emancipation?"

He shifted his gaze to her. "That's an awful big word around these parts, Sarah."

"Maybe, but now I feel like there's hope for a life in Jefferson. I didn't feel that before today." She stood up and walked around the table, kneeling at his side. "Didn't you see who came to your rescue?"

"No. I mean, I don't know." His forehead wrinkled. "I don't remember much about it."

"Well, I do. They were our white friends and neighbors."

He drew back and stared. "When did you ever have a white friend or neighbor in this town?"

"Since today, and from here on out." She gripped his arm. "I'm trying to say I've been wrong. Well, partly, anyway. Like you said before, it's wrong to lump everybody into the same barrel. It's still true that some are wormy, but most of the apples in this town, though they be lumpy and blemished on the outside, are sweet at the core."

He made a face, and she stood. "This is so peculiar, Henry. About the time I change my mind, you go and change yours?"

He gazed up at her with doubtful eyes. "What has you talking like this, Sarah?"

She didn't have to think about her answer. "Miss Annie."

"Miss Annie?"

"The pretty lady we first saw in Stilley's, the one tendin' Jennie yesterday."

"I know who she is. She'd be right hard to forget. What about her?"

Sarah stared past the kitchen window. "I learned something from her. I ain't never seen a kinder soul in anyone, black or white. And that's what I'm starting to understand. It's the heart that matters, not the color of our skin. Miss Annie taught me that."

"So about the time I get you figured out, it's time to start all over?" He pushed away from the table. "I don't want to talk about this no more. My whole body hurts. I feel like I done been—" His startled eyes flashed, and he bit off the rest. Sarah knew what he'd almost said, a phrase he used all the time, especially after a long day in the field.

"I feel like I done been whipped."

His jaw worked, and he swallowed, hollow eyes focusing just over her head. "Move out my way, Sarah. I'm going to bed."

CHAPTER 25

Tuesday, January 23

Bertha awoke the next morning with Dr. Turner's words ringing in her ears. She scooted higher in the bed and propped herself on her pillows. After weighing the facts half the night, she decided it would take a lot more to convince her that Annie ran off without saying a word. In fact, she refused to believe it until she had proof. Something definitely wasn't right, and in the light of a new day, another visit to Brooks House seemed the only option.

More than likely she'd find Annie shut up in number four, Abe's prisoner again. If not, she'd talk to every person there, even knock on Abe's door if need be and question him on Annie's whereabouts. And she'd stand right behind Papa while he did the knocking and the asking.

Her punishment for losing the horrible bronze shoes had started the day before. While pining for Thad, she forgot and barely got done with her regular work. Mulling over Annie's plight made her aware of how God had blessed her, so she made up her mind to honor her parents with a more obedient daughter. Maybe the extra work and the mystery surrounding Annie's disappearance would take her mind off Thad for a bit and provide a welcome distraction from her wounded heart.

She kicked off her quilt and sat up. The odor of fried bacon hit her nose as soon as her feet hit the floor, eliciting a deep groan from the pit of her stomach. Surprisingly, her appetite had come back. She dressed as fast as she could and hustled to the kitchen. "Morning, Mama."

Flipping hotcakes, by the warm, buttered-wheat smell in the room, Mama stood by the stove. She looked over her shoulder and smiled. "Good morning, dear. Sit down and I'll pour your milk."

"Don't trouble yourself. I'll do it. I wouldn't want to hinder your efforts. It smells like you're doing a fine job."

Laying her spatula aside, Mama turned. "Why, look at you. If I didn't know better, I'd say you're a different girl."

Bertha grinned. "No, it's me. I saw myself in the mirror."

Mama's stunned look turned to alarm. "Are you all right, Bertha? After the state you were in yesterday, your mood is unnaturally light. You're not feverish, are you?"

"I'm fine, Mama. In fact, I'm starving, so don't let my hotcake burn."

Mama crossed to the table and flipped the golden circle onto Bertha's plate. "I must say, I'm finding this nothing short of miraculous, dear."

Bertha served herself two strips of bacon. "It's no miracle. I didn't touch a bite all day yesterday."

"Not your hunger. Your upbeat mood."

Bertha swallowed a big bite then smiled. "Oh, that. Well, I've had some time to think and pray, so I have a whole new outlook. Papa counseled me to trust God with the details. After pondering some of those, I've come to a few conclusions."

She counted them off. "As you mentioned yesterday, Thad does live in Jefferson. He has to come home sometime, doesn't he? Meanwhile, there's less chance of a girl stealing his heart at a military school. Despite his anger, if he misses me a fraction of how I miss him, he's still miserable. And last but really first, if God wants us together, we will be. I have to believe that."

Mama laughed and forked another steaming flapjack onto her plate from a stack on the stove. "I knew we raised a sensible daughter, but I had no idea of the depths of your wisdom." She squeezed Bertha's shoulder. "I'm very proud of you. Papa will be, as well."

She grinned. "Oh, pooh. You'll embarrass me saying such things." She reached for the ceramic pitcher and poured a glass of milk. "Speaking of Papa, where is the old rascal?"

At the stove again, Mama poured more batter into the skillet, lowered the empty bowl into a dishpan, and leaned against the counter. "You just missed him. He ate enough breakfast to stagger a horse then rushed out."

Bertha craned her neck and looked out the window. "Is he out in the barn?"

"No, dear. He's gone off on an errand."

Her heart sank. "Without me?"

"Had you planned another trip into town? Lately you spend more time there than at home. I don't think you should go today." Standing with her hand on her hip and a disapproving look on her face, Mama resembled her old stormy self.

Fearing the damaging winds of the past, Bertha dared to protest. "I plan to do all my chores first, including the extras. I won't be long, and you can pick which shoes I wear." Mama's slight grin gave her courage. "Please?"

Understanding dawned on Mama's face. "You're going to look for Annie again, aren't you?"

When she nodded, Mama stiffened. "You can't go alone. Wait for Papa."

"That won't work. There's no telling when he'll be home."

"Magda, then."

Bertha wiped her mouth and stood. "We have a bargain. Thank you, Mama. Now move aside and let me at those dishes. The morning's getting away from me."

By the time Bertha completed every task, her hands were sore and her back ached. She longed to slip into the parlor and put her feet by the fire, especially since the temperature had steadily dropped all morning. Instead, she fetched her hat and warmest wrap, saddled her horse, and struck out for Magda's house northwest of town. She ran into her coming out of the end of her lane.

Magda reined in the big gelding and stared at Bertha as if she had spots. "Well, fancy that. I was just coming to your place."

Bertha nodded at the surrey. "Do you live in that thing? You're sitting up there every time I see you."

"It beats walking. What are you doing here? Are you all right? I mean, about. . ."

"I need a favor."

Magda nodded. "Sure, if I can."

"I need to go into town. Will you take me?"

She shrugged. "I was headed there after I left you. Ride your horse back to the house. I'll turn around and get you."

The surrey sat waiting when Bertha closed the barn door. She pulled herself up opposite Magda and smiled. "I'm grateful. Mama wouldn't let me go alone."

The morning chill had Magda's lips a deep cherry red and her cheeks a bright pink. The striking color against her pale skin and brown hair made her resemble a china-head doll. As soon as Bertha settled on the seat, Magda gathered her up for a hug. "I'm so sorry about Thad, sugar."

Bertha leaned against her shoulder. "Why haven't you been around to see me, then? Before now, I mean. I could've used a friend."

Magda pulled away and looked at her. "I did, Bertha. I came around on Monday. Didn't your mama tell you? She said you were in town seeing about a"—she raised her brows—"friend." Twisting around straight, she gathered the reins and signaled the horse to go.

They rode a ways before Bertha could think what to say. "I was worried about her. You don't know what Annie's been through."

Magda quirked the corner of her mouth. "And how could I? Since I'm not counted worthy to keep company with the two of you. Why hasn't Annie worried about what you've been through? I know I have."

Bertha cut her eyes at Magda then made up her mind. "Pull this thing over in those trees there. We have to talk."

It surprised Bertha when Magda did as she asked without argument. When the surrey came to a stop in the shaded grove, Bertha reached under the seat for a blanket to cover them then settled back on the seat and began to talk. She told Magda about believing God may have arranged for her to meet Annie in the first place and the reason why. She confessed how hard it had been to put Annie before Thad and about meeting with Annie and giving her the necklace that she felt unworthy to wear. She described Abe's cruelty and some, but not all, of Annie's past. When she came to the end of her story, Magda had tears in her eyes.

"Bertha, we have to do something. We have to help her."

She scooted close and kissed Magda's cheek. "I knew you'd feel that way. Will you help me find her?"

Magda wiped her eyes and picked up the reins. "Where do we start?"

"Brooks House. Let's go see if she came back last night."

Magda nodded and circled the wagon out of the wooded confessional. The two chatted easily on the way into town, laughing and teasing like they always had. It felt nice, and Bertha breathed easier.

They pulled up to the hotel just as Jennie Simpson reached the front walk. She flashed her chubby-cheeked smile their way and waved. "Looky who's here again. And you brung Miss Magda with you. How ya'll doing this mornin', little misses?"

"Morning, Jennie. Goodness, but you're bright and chipper today."

Jennie wagged her head. "Oh yes'm, I am indeed." She looked over her shoulder then moved closer and dropped her voice to a loud whisper. "Got me some energy tonic." She straightened. "Best thing I ever found for the droops." Then she winked. "A sip or two even warms a body on a blustery day like this."

Bertha laughed. "Sounds like something I need."

She clutched the pocket of her dress. "Ordinarily I'd offer up a taste." Her worried look turned to a pout. "But after ol' Doc done found out I had it, I ain't hardly got a drop left."

Bertha reached for the post to climb down, but Jennie raised a hand to stop her. "I reckon I know why you're here, and you just be wasting time coming off there." She flashed a grin. "You come to see if Miss Bessie come back, but she ain't. She ain't even coming back to the hotel on account of Mr. Abe say she gon' meet him at the station this morning, and they gon' catch a train to Cincinnata. Mercy, don't I wish I could'a told that sweet chile good-bye."

Bertha reached behind her and gripped Magda's hand. "So they've gone?"

"Don't know if the train come yet, but Mr. Abe done checked out and lef' awhile ago."

Magda squeezed Bertha's fingers. "Let's go. Maybe we can get there in time for you to say good-bye."

"I doubt I'll be able to get that close, but at least I'll get to see for myself she's all right."

Jennie beamed. "All right? Sure she all right. God gon' take care of a good-hearted soul like Miss Bessie."

Bertha called her thanks as Magda maneuvered the wagon into the crowded street. The ride up Vale to Alley Street north of town took forever at the busy morning hour. Bertha thought for sure they'd arrive too late. When they finally drew close to the bustling station, Magda pulled onto a side road and set the brake.

"What are you doing?"

She secured the reins and scrambled down. "It'll be quicker to walk from here. Come on."

Bertha caught up to her, and together they hustled the rest of the way to the station. Bertha saw Abe Monroe right away and tugged on the back of Magda's skirt. "Stay in front of me. There he is."

"Where?"

Bertha pointed. "Right there. Seated behind the driver of that hired two-seater." She scanned the area near the hack. "Where's Annie?"

The frightening man didn't sit as tall as he did the day Bertha saw him leaving the station with his arm around the bluebird. He sat hunched over, both arms resting on his knees, studying something at his feet. Despite the weather, he didn't look cold, but one knee rose and jiggled every so often, as if he couldn't hold it still.

Bertha hid behind a shivering Magda and studied him. It was the closest look she'd ever had.

He parted his thick, curly hair a touch off center, and his eyes were too small—or just looked that way centered over the wide bridge of his nose. He was far from balding, but a high forehead made it look as if his curls had receded. He had big, pouting lips and smallish ears set too high on his head.

She had to admit that somehow this odd assortment fit together in a pleasing manner but felt it must be due to his youth. As he matured, he wouldn't be the least bit attractive. The coldness of his hollow eyes caused her to wonder what Annie ever saw in him in the first place.

Though Abe kept his attention focused on his feet, Bertha still hung back, scanning the milling crowd for Annie. "Where is she?"

Magda sighed. "Nowhere."

"Are you sure?"

"Bertha, someone like Annie is hard to hide."

Bertha shaded her eyes and stared at a glint of steel in the distance. "Well, she'd better hurry. Here comes the train."

Abe became jumpier as the big engine approached. When the whistle sounded, he stood up in the wagon and squinted, taking long draws on a cigarette and blowing billows of smoke from a puckered bottom lip. When he wasn't staring down the track, he patted his breast pockets, looked at his ticket, or glanced back at his luggage. He continued his anxious dance until the Texas & Pacific belched into the station. Then he pressed a bill into the driver's hand, gathered his bags, and ran for the open car.

Her gaze locked on Abe, Magda tilted her face toward Bertha.

"What's he doing? Isn't he going to wait for her?"

"He must plan to wait inside."

Magda nodded. "Maybe."

Bertha looked up and down the platform, behind them on the street, at the ticket window, then back to the train, until the big engine roared to life and started pulling away. She watched with an open mouth as the car Abe Monroe had boarded passed out of sight. Without Annie.

Magda jabbed her in the side. "He left her."

She felt weak in the knees. "Yes, he did." She turned a bewildered look on Magda. "But he didn't leave her luggage."

Magda stared after the caboose. "He had her luggage? Are you sure?"

"Completely."

"Why would he take it?"

Bertha pinched her bottom lip together with two fingers and stared at the ground. "I can't imagine. Unless she's planning to meet him later." Her heart surged at the thought of Annie still in town without Abe watching her every move.

She pushed the thought away. "He'd never allow it. The only time she escaped his grasp is when he drank so much he passed out. Then she took chances she shouldn't."

"Out of desperation. I'd do the same in her shoes." Magda tapped both temples with her fists. "What am I saying? I'd never be in her shoes, because I'd never allow a man to treat me like that." She swiveled toward Bertha. "Would you?"

Bertha gritted her teeth until her jaw popped. "Never."

"Why do you reckon she puts up with it?"

Bertha pulled her wrap tighter and stared across the treetops in the direction of the bluff. "Annie said her beauty makes men feel the need to possess and control her. For some reason she thinks that includes all men." She shrugged. "Maybe she feels that's all she deserves."

Magda made a tsk-tsk sound. "Such a pity."

"I know." Standing on tiptoes, Bertha did one more thorough

search. Beside her, Magda squeezed her hand.

"Give it up, sugar. She's not here."

Bertha released an uneven breath. "I know that, too."

They waited a few more minutes, until the chill wind forced them to hustle back to the surrey. As they rode through town, Bertha found herself watching the crowded boardwalk for a bright yellow dress or a crop of high black curls. The surrey reached Magda's yard with hardly more than three words passed between them.

When Bertha slid to the ground by the barn, Magda called her name. Bertha paused and looked up. "Yes?"

"I'm sorry I didn't understand about Annie."

Bertha smiled. "Just be sorry for thinking we won't always be best friends."

Magda smiled back. "I'm the most sorry for that. I'll try not to forget it again."

"See that you don't." She winked and turned to go.

"Bertha?"

She spun, laughing. "What now?"

"Don't worry about Annie. She'll turn up somewhere. I'll be praying hard in the meantime."

"Thank you for that. Oh, and for taking me to the station, too."

Magda waved a dismissive hand. "Anytime. You know I'll always be—" Her eyes widened. "Great-Grandpa's knees! I forgot my errands."

Bertha covered her mouth. "Looks like I'm the one who's sorry this time. Oh, Magda. Do you want to go back? I'll go with you."

"Heavens, no. I'd rather go in and take my medicine. It's getting too cold to be out." She pulled back the rim of her bonnet and peered at the sky. "Look at that. You don't think it's going to snow, do you?"

Bertha followed her gaze. "Wouldn't that be fun?"

Not much snow fell on the piney woods of Texas, but Bertha had to admit the clouds looked different. Mama spoke often of her memories of the onset of a "snow sky" in the town in Maine where she grew up. Bertha wondered if the odd gathering of clouds overhead was what she meant.

She led her horse from the barn and held the door while Magda pulled inside. They hugged; then Bertha mounted and started up the lane.

"Be careful, and be safe," Magda called. "Don't get caught in a blizzard."

Bertha laughed and took off at a trot. She hadn't gone far when the laughter died, replaced by thoughts of Thad. She wondered where he was at that very second, who might be with him, what he might be doing. She wondered what he ate, where he slept, if the weather in Bryan was cold. Most of all, she wondered if he wondered about her.

She reached their road and saw Papa riding in from the opposite direction. She reined up and waited. He waved when he saw her and took off at a gallop. When he reached her, he tipped his derby and smiled. "What's a lovely lass like you doing on these perilous roads without an escort?"

Bertha bowed from the waist. "Waiting for my Prince Charming, and lo, he has arrived."

He wagged a finger. "No fair turning a fellow's own blarney back on him. You've been spending far too much time with me, I see. Besides that, me poor farsighted princess, it's a frog you've stumbled upon, not a prince."

He sidled up beside her and they turned down the lane. "No sign of Annie, I suppose."

She wrinkled her brow. "Abe Monroe left town this morning. . . without her. He boarded an eastbound train with her luggage. I saw him."

"You don't say, now?" He watched her, chewing on his mustache. "What do you suppose it means?"

"I've tried to figure it out. I just don't know."

Papa reached for her reins and pulled both horses to a stop. He cleared his throat and met her eyes, his expression grave.

"What is it, Papa? What's wrong?"

He shifted his weight. "Darlin', I did some checking myself

today. Asked a few questions, talked to some folks."

"And?"

He squinted at something over her shoulder, the corners of his eyes worried crinkles. "I learned some things. Frank Malloy saw Annie and Abe at Kate Woods's place on Sunday. It wasn't even the noon hour, but Abe was plying her with drinks. Frank said she seemed pretty well into her cups by the time they left. He seen them head down Austin Street to Gill's Corner then turn and cross over the Polk Street Bridge. Said they both carried bottles of beer."

"Was he sure it was Annie?"

"Said she was real pretty and wearing two big diamond rings."

Bertha nodded.

"Two or three hours later, Frank saw Abe come back alone."

Bertha thought for a minute. "So he did leave her across the bridge. I wouldn't have believed it. It's so unlike him, from all Annie said."

"You think she spoke the truth?"

Bertha's head reeled. "I don't know what I think anymore."

Papa lifted his gaze. His leather saddle creaked as he leaned to peer closely at her eyes. "Bertha, I think this is over now. Abe's gone. Annie's gone. You did the best you could for her. It's time to lay it down."

Bertha caught a glimpse of the sun between a break in the low-lying clouds. One thing was certain. That same sun looked down on Annie–somewhere. Bertha had never been asked to carry a heavier burden for another soul. Papa was right. She didn't share his notion that she'd done the best she could, but it was over.

She brought her attention back to his anxious face. "I know it's time to let it go, Papa. And I promise I'm going to try."

CHAPTER 26

Monday, February 5

Sarah stepped out of the barn and brushed her hands together to clean them from the dust of the feed bin. Her back ached, her head throbbed, but when hadn't they during the last two dreadful weeks?

Fourteen days had passed since Henry's trouble in town, and he hadn't snapped back as fast as she'd expected—from his injuries or his mood. Not being able to do his work made him even meaner. Thomas and some of the other neighbors pitched in where they could, with the plowing in particular. Sarah shouldered the rest of her husband's chores on top of her own.

She prayed daily for grace to live with Henry. He had taken on most of Dandy's more trying traits, but Henry bested the mule in cantankerousness. And despite the fact she ministered to him every spare minute, he had adopted the mule's same distaste for her.

To make matters worse, the weather turned from bad to horrid since the day of his injuries. Heavy snow had fallen in Jefferson—by far the most bitter pill for Sarah, since Henry had dangled warm winters to entice her to come south. Not much she hated more than being cold, and working outside in the snow the last few days had chilled her to the bone.

She took a lingering look at the house and groaned. She longed to go inside by the fire, take off her boots, and prop her bruised and swollen feet on a kitchen chair. But one glance at the wood box this morning told her she'd be gathering firewood today. The cookstove and fireplace had gobbled every stick she could find over the two-week cold spell. Best to get the box filled now and get back in time to start supper. Henry's appetite had made a full recovery.

She glanced toward the stand of trees. Gathering firewood wasn't her favorite chore. When she first took the job from Henry, she'd found a treasure of small, easy-to-carry branches and sticks, those that Henry would pass right over. Now all the suitable pieces she could bundle up in her apron were gone from the nearby places. This forced her to wander farther each time, which meant a longer walk back with her burden.

The days had grown a little warmer since the snow fell, but white patches still lingered in areas shaded from the sun. She decided to walk as far out as she intended then gather as she made her way back. That way she could pretend she just decided to go for a walk.

May as well find some pleasure in the task.

She stepped back inside the barn and lifted her coat from the hook. The dog lay on his side, his body stretched to full length, in a hay pile near the door. She paused beside him. "I'll be right back, Dickens. Thought I'd let you know I was going, since you're the only living soul on the place who cares."

Sound asleep, he moaned and rolled to his back with his hind legs straddled and his front legs folded to his chest. She sighed. "No, I don't need any help. But thank you kindly for asking."

She slipped into her coat, tied on her scarf, and struck out. No need carrying a hoe or a snake stick into the woods today. Too cold. Which meant snakes had more sense than people.

At the edge of the yard, she ducked under the fence and slipped into the coolness of the surrounding forest. Despite being bone-tired, despite the way her man was acting, Sarah found herself enjoying her walk in the woods. On the trail worn there by Henry's feet, she saw a few gathering birds and chasing squirrels, but the rabbits and deer were in hiding. She loved the wildlife in Jefferson—except the coons. They were funny to look at, yet true to their markings, they were bandits, every one. The rascals spent all their time stealing food from her garden, the feeding troughs, or Dickens's dish.

The sun had dared to peek through the clouds a couple of times during the past two weeks, its warmth a welcome relief. It seemed inclined to shine a bit today, but the overcast sky put up a stiff fight. A pity, since now the wind had picked up.

Sarah walked until she came to a small clearing. The last storm had littered the area with fallen limbs. There were ample good-sized pieces for her to collect and fold into her apron, with plenty left for the next time. She'd have to try to remember the spot.

She stood up to get her bearings. Unless she was mistaken, the Marshall Road lay to her right with Polk Street Bridge just a little ways up, which meant she was south of the Big Cypress Ferry. That put town straight ahead.

She pulled up her collar and fastened the top button of her coat. The sun finally quit on her altogether, and the cloudy sky pitched the thickly wooded grove into near darkness. A chill crept up her spine that had little to do with the weather. The chattering squirrels had disappeared. The birds, too, if the silence meant anything. She found herself glancing up, willing the light to come back, because when the sun left, the joy went out of the walk. Sarah reckoned she'd best stop fooling around and finish gathering so she could get on back home.

She spotted a perfect-sized limb near the ridge of a slight hill and bent to retrieve it. Then another she could reach without straightening. And one more just ahead.

Still stooping close to the ground, Sarah's hand closed around the crumbling stick as her eyes scanned the grassy mound ahead. Her body stopped so fast she jerked; then she fell back on her hands and crab-scrambled away.

Dear God in heaven, don't let it be!

She felt helpless, defenseless down on her behind, so she fought to her feet, ripping the hem of her coat as she stood.

Jesus, close my eyes! I don't want to see this!

If not for the wood bugs crawling on its eyes and from its nose, Sarah might've sworn the body was sleeping. Dressed like a lady, it rested on its back with one arm folded across its stomach. That was all Sarah took time to see.

She longed to break and run but knew she mustn't. Whoever did it might be watching. She forced herself to turn and walk away as if she hadn't seen. Certain at any second the killer would lunge from behind, she pulled her chest forward until her shoulder blades popped. It seemed as if she could see, hear, smell a thousand times better as her darting gaze searched the woods.

Just a little farther and she'd reach the Marshall Road. Just a few more steps to safety. She went a little faster. Three steps. Faster. Two more steps. Run!

She burst onto the road with legs so weak she tripped and fell. A horse and rider came at her from the corner of her eye as she went down, and dread slammed into her chest. All the strength left her body just when she needed it. Limp, she tried to crawl, desperate hands clutching at woody stobs and tall tufts of grass to pull herself along. With the last ounce of might she could muster, she thrust her body from the ground and staggered away from the road in a panic.

"Sarah!"

She didn't know the voice.

"Sarah King!"

He knew her name.

She froze, swiping tears from her eyes with dirty palms to see. If she didn't know his face, if he came for her, she'd outrun him if it meant sailing off into the bayou.

"Sarah, come here, girl. Are you all right?"

William Sims. The colonel's son. Lived in a big house on Friou Street in town.

She didn't realize she held her breath until white spots swirled past her eyes and blackness loomed. She lifted her chest and gulped. Air flooded her lungs. Giddy, she went down hard on her bottom. "No, sir," she gasped. "I ain't all right a'tall. I need help."

He got off his horse and hurried to her side. "Are you hurt?"

She motioned toward the woods with a trembling hand. "Mr. Sims, there's a lady laid up in those woods. She's dead."

His head jerked toward the grove. "Dead?"

"Yes, sir."

"You sure?"

She nodded.

He stood up and started for his horse. "Just sit right there. I'll go for help."

She reached a grasping hand toward him. "No, sir. Please don't leave me here alone."

He pointed his finger. "You do like I say. Stay here so we can find you. You'll have to show them where it is."

Sarah ran up on the road and stared after the galloping horse. "Oh, please don't leave me here," she whispered. She whirled in a circle, searching the ditches, the bushes, the trees. When her eyes lit on the woods at the place where she'd burst through, she retreated to the opposite side of the Marshall Road, her eyes still fixed on the spot. Pulling her gaze away, she turned and ran a few feet, pressed her body against a tree, and slid to the ground. How would she ever go back in there?

Well, I can't! I won't.

She could leave. Run on home to Henry. Cook his food. Do his chores. Put this nightmare right out of her mind.

But Mr. Sims knew who she was. And Mr. Sims told her to stay put.

It seemed three lifetimes before clamoring hooves hit the Polk Street Bridge. Three men appeared on the road in front of her, Mr. Sims and two others.

"Well, where is she?" one of them growled.

Mr. Sims pushed back his hat. "I told her to stay here."

Sarah knew she'd better show her face. She stood. "I'm over here."

The big man scowled at her from across the way then motioned with his hand. "Well, come over here, then."

She pushed the brush aside and hustled over the road on shaky legs. The official-looking man looked straight at her but spoke to Mr. Sims. "What'd you say her name was?"

"Sarah," he said. "Sarah King."

The man tipped his hat. "Sarah, I'm Justice of the Peace C. C. Bickford, also the ex-officio coroner for Marion County. You can call me Judge Bickford."

She didn't know what all the words meant, but the way he said them made her feel more and less afraid at the same time. Unable to speak, she stared up at him.

He pointed at the man riding the other horse. "This here's my constable, Mr. A. J. Stambaugh."

Sarah nodded at the constable.

Judge Bickford cleared his throat. "I understand you ran across something amongst those trees."

She nodded again.

"Speak up, now. If you think you found something, say so."

"I did find something. A dead woman."

He narrowed his eyes. "And you're certain of that? It couldn't have been an animal? A deer or wild hog? A bundle of trash, maybe?"

"I'm right sure of what I saw."

Looking none too happy, he pointed at the tree line. "Sure enough to have us traipsing all over those woods?"

Anger easing her fear, Sarah shook her head. "I can walk you straight to her."

The man chewed the inside of his lip, studying her hard, and then sighed. "All right. Let's go."

Leading a parade of white men on horseback into the woods had to be the most peculiar thing Sarah had ever done. Though less afraid in the company of the officers, she still checked over her shoulder every few steps to make sure they were still with her.

Glad she'd taken the time to get her bearings before she found the body, Sarah retraced her steps. She stopped within a few yards of the place where the woman lay and pointed ahead of them and to the left. "She's over on that mound yonder. Do I have to go any farther?"

They didn't answer, just got down off their mounts and walked in the direction she'd pointed. When they stopped and leaned over the woman's body, Sarah moved closer to the horses. She found comfort in the animals' warmth and size, knowing they'd be the first to sense trouble.

After the men looked around a bit, they hurried back. Mr. Sims looked sick to his stomach. The judge took off his hat, spat on the ground, and wiped his mouth with his sleeve. "How close did you come to the body?"

"Not close." Her voice faltered. "From here to that tree."

"Did you touch anything?"

She shuddered. "No, sir."

"What's the first thing you did after you found her?"

"I didn't stay there at all. I left in a walk."

The constable laughed. "Likely the fastest walk ever performed in Jefferson."

The judge gave him a stern look, and he turned away, still smiling.

Sarah couldn't stop shaking. She clasped her hands together to keep them still then pressed them to her chin. "Can I go now?"

The judge shook his head. "Not yet. I have to summon a jury and hold an inquest."

More words she didn't know. "What's an inquest?"

"An inquiry of sorts. We'll have to carry out an official investigation."

Her heartbeat quickened. "When?"

"Right now."

"Where?"

He lifted his head to motion behind him. "Right over there."

Panic clawed at her throat. "And I have to stay?"

"I need to ask you more questions. With the jury present."

"But, Judge, my husband needs me at home. He's ailing. I didn't even tell him I left." She hadn't remembered any of these details until she spoke them aloud. "Please, sir, can't I go? This trouble ain't got nothing to do with me."

"It does now. You're an official witness. When we find out who did this, there's going to be a trial. You'll be called on to testify."

The overhead trees swirled. Sarah's stomach took a sickening dive. White spots danced before her eyes again, and bitterness rose in her throat. The judge noticed, because he offered his arm and helped her sit on the ground. "I'm real sorry, Miss. . .now what was your name again?"

She swallowed bile. "Sarah."

"Sarah. That's right. Just settle yourself there and try to get comfortable, Sarah. This will all be over soon, and you can go see to your husband."

It wasn't over soon. Judge Bickford found men to serve as his jury, but it took them forever to arrive. The judge, constable, and some other men searched the clearing, collecting things from the ground and writing them all in a book. Dr. Eason came, and she wanted him to tell the judge about Henry, but he barely took time to nod in her direction before he hurried over to kneel by the body.

By the time the judge got around to questioning Sarah in front of the jury, she was faint from so many hours without food and water. He asked the same questions he had before, going round and round until her head whirled.

Night approached, making it so murky in the grove that they stumbled over each other in the dark. Judge Bickford made the decision to bring in a hack to move the body to his office, where he would take up with his inquest the next day.

At long last, Sarah was free to go—and she couldn't get away fast enough. She took the road instead of the woods, but after going just a little ways, she realized she was alone in the dark.

And the killer began to play games. He crept alongside her for a few steps, hiding in the trees to her right, his feet rustling grass and snapping twigs. He bobbed through the brush on the other side with a rattle of bare limbs and crunch of dry leaves. When he darted across the road in front of her, hunched over close to the ground, Sarah froze.

Common sense whispered that the sounds were the critters she loved, startled from their wallows by her shuffling feet, and the darting figure was nothing more than a wild boar. But her shattered nerves and wounded spirit wouldn't accept it.

She turned to run back to the comforting voices and circles of lantern light bobbing through the forest but realized they were coming out of the woods behind her, heading in the opposite direction. The tears came then, flooding her eyes and causing her nose to pour. She didn't dare cry aloud for fear the killer would hear and come after her. Pulling up her skirt, she started to run, the wind rushing past her ears, her long legs pumping in time with her heart. Sarah ran as fast as she could, sobbing the whole way, until she staggered onto the back porch.

Henry opened the screen door with a crash and folded her into his arms. He squeezed her so tightly against his chest she feared he'd hurt his ribs. Or hers. "Where were you? Girl, I been out of my mind."

"Henry!" she wailed. "I tried to come back. They wouldn't let me." She reached for his face and found it wet.

"Who? Who wouldn't let you?"

"Judge Bickford and his men."

Henry held her in the light streaming from the kitchen and studied her face. "Tell me where you went, Sarah."

"To fetch firewood." She buried her face against his chest to block out the memory of crawling wood bugs. "There was a body. In the woods. I found it."

He lifted her into his arms and carried her inside the house, though it must have caused him terrible pain. She let the tears come as loudly as they wished now. She was safe.

CHAPTER 27

Tuesday, February 6

Bertha marked another X on Mama's big wall calendar then stepped back to count the number of days since she'd last seen Thad. Sixteen. The age she'd been when she first set eyes on Thaddeus Bloom—a brash, giggly sixteen-year-old to his quiet and confident eighteen. Tomorrow she'd scratch off the seventeenth day. The age she was when he left town. The day after that, when she stepped up to the wall with her thick pencil, it would be eighteen days since Thad rode away without saying good-bye. Eighteen. The age she turned today.

"Happy birthday, sprite!"

Bertha leaped right out of her musings and almost out of her bloomers when Papa roared behind her.

Laughing, he danced up and kissed the back of her head then hooked his finger around the tasseled shade and pulled it out for a peek. " 'Tis a fine day for it, too. Will ye look at that? The sun's out."

Mama bustled into the kitchen and grabbed her apron from a hook. "Well, it wasn't shining eighteen years ago. We were shoveling snow that year, if memory serves."

"And they've been shoveling since, Emeline. It's forever snowing in Maine."

Mama gathered Bertha for a tight hug and answered Papa across the top of her head. "I'll ignore your derision for now and just say I'm glad we came south." She took Bertha by the shoulders and gazed at her face. "Happy birthday, dear daughter. And many happy returns of the day."

"Thank you." Bertha smiled and sent up a silent prayer of thanksgiving. She loved her mama before, but liked her much better now. It amazed Bertha the difference love could make in a woman's heart if she allowed it to come in.

Mama glanced at the newly crossed square on the calendar page, and a tiny frown perched on her brow. "Did you sleep well?"

"Yes, ma'am. I believe I did."

Her face softened and she nodded. "Francis, go gather eggs. I need three of the freshest you can find."

He winked at Bertha. "And they say slavery's been abolished."

She laughed as he slipped on his coat and went out. Mama gathered measuring cups and spoons, flour, sugar, butter, and milk and arranged them around a big bowl on the counter. Then she stood with her finger pressed to her lips. "Where is my saleratus of baking soda?" She turned to Bertha. "Though I regret asking you to do extra on your special day, would you mind rolling out biscuits for breakfast? I've gotten a little ahead of myself, I think. But I wanted to get this done."

Bertha pretended not to know what she meant. "Get what done?"

"Your cake, silly. For today's celebration." Her eyes danced with excitement. "We're going to have a high time. "I've invited Magda's family, of course. And the minister, along with our friends from church, our nearest neighbors, and your young friends from school. Oh yes, Moses and Rhodie Pharr. Can you think of who might be missing?"

"Only one."

Mama paused from sifting sugar into her bowl. "Oh, Bertha. I considered the possibility Thad might turn up but thought it best not to mention it. I want only your happiness today."

"I know you do." She lifted one shoulder. "I'm sure he wouldn't be able to leave school this soon anyway. Only wouldn't it be nice if he could be here?"

"It would at that." Mama tilted her head and gave her a pleading look. "Try to put Thad out of your mind, just for today, and have a good time."

Bertha bit her bottom lip and nodded. "Yes, ma'am. I'll try."

Mama reached for her mixing spoon. "While you're at it, make an effort to act pleased with Papa's gift. He tries so hard every year, and he means well."

At the look on Mama's face, Bertha's hands stilled on the rolling pin. "It's even worse than usual, isn't it?"

Mama hunched her shoulders and tittered. "Infinitely."

"Tell me."

"Words fail me, dear." She leaned to check on Papa's whereabouts then motioned for Bertha to wait while she crept down the hall. She returned with the latest copy of *Harper's Weekly* and spread it open on the kitchen table. After another glance out the window, she started flipping pages.

"*Harper's Weekly*?" Bertha laid aside the biscuit cutter and wiped her hands. "There are lovely gifts in there." She hurried around to peer over Mama's shoulder. "Books of poems. Leather cases for gloves and handkerchiefs. And look! Fur-lined collars from New York!"

Mama turned right past all the ads Bertha mentioned, as well as the ones for Tiffany & Co. and Decker Brothers' pianos. Riffling back a few pages, she stopped and placed her finger under a tiny drawing of a white skeleton.

Bertha frowned and leaned close to read the text aloud. " 'The Performing Skeleton. Fourteen inches in height. It will dance in perfect time to any tune.' " She skipped ahead a bit. " 'Seemingly endowed with life.' "

Mama took up where Bertha left off. " 'Never fails to delight, astonish, and produce a decided sensation.' "

They stood up together. Mama pressed both hands over her mouth in a useless attempt to stifle her laughter. Bertha pointed at the ad. "The astonish part is working already."

Mama gave up her fight for composure. "Oh, Bertha," she howled.

"For pity's sake, I'm eighteen. I can't receive a dancing skeleton at my eighteenth birthday party, witnessed by all of my friends."

A rattling noise from outside straightened Mama's face and sent them both scrambling—Mama to her room with the magazine and Bertha back to her biscuits. Mama came out sober and empty-handed and scurried to her mixing bowl. "What was that?"

Bertha shrugged and glanced toward the window. "I think someone's here."

Papa called a greeting, and Bertha nodded across the room at Mama, who smiled back. Neither stopped what they were doing to receive a guest. Bertha knew her mama assumed, as she did, that Papa's friend from the house behind their place had come to visit. The old man always came calling through the backyard and never ventured inside.

A high-pitched keening, like the cry of a wounded panther, ripped holes in the comforting silence, exposing every nerve in Bertha's body. She jumped back, and the sheet of biscuits slid to the floor.

Mama dropped her spoon then snatched it up, brandishing it like a weapon. Her frightened gaze left the widow and fixed on Bertha's face. "Oh my soul. Bertha, go find the source of that appalling sound."

What on earth?

Sarah rolled over in bed to find bright light streaming through her bedroom window. She raised one arm to shield her eyes and squinted at the curious sight. Each day since her first one in Jefferson, her feet had hit the floor and plodded to the kitchen long before daylight dawned. She threw back the covers and tossed her body off the opposite side of the bed, feeling around with her toes to find her shoes.

"Henry!"

No answer. Something was wrong. She just knew it. Why else would she still be in bed at this hour? Some vague memory tugged at the fog in her mind, something dark and dank with fear. She could get no better grip on her recall than her toes could get on her slippers. "Henry, where are you?"

Sarah gave up trying to reach under the bed with her feet. Padding barefoot, she crossed the room and snatched her raggedy robe from the back of a chair. Tying the belt around her waist, she reached for the bedroom door. It opened before her fingers touched the knob.

"Did you decide to join the rest of the world?"

She scowled at his grinning face. "Where were you? What were you thinking to let me sleep all day?"

He chuckled. "Seven thirty ain't exactly all day. The sun ain't been up ten minutes. Besides, you needed to rest."

"Rest?" She lifted the pitcher from the dressing table so she could fetch hot water for the basin. "I'll rest in heaven. Did you forget I have your chores, too?" Opening the door, she stared back at him. "I know you meant well, but you've put me so far behind I'll be working past midnight."

"Sarah, wait."

Sarah, wait? Sarah, sleep? She didn't have time for either. She hustled down the hall mumbling under her breath. When the passage opened onto the kitchen, she scarcely believed her eyes.

Arabella, Thomas's shy, pretty wife, stood at the sink washing dishes. Their newest baby sat up on the table while her eight-year-old sister spoon-fed scrambled eggs into her wide-open mouth. Between bites for the baby, the young girl picked through a pile of dried beans scattered across the tabletop. The oldest girl swished a broom near the door. They all gave Sarah timid smiles then went back to their work. Her work.

She looked over her shoulder at Henry's grinning face. "What's going on here?"

He took her arm and led her toward the table. "Thomas brought 'em by first thing this morning. They heard in town what happened, so they come to help. The boys are outside now, feeding the chickens and tending the mule."

The fog swirled away in a whoosh, and the thing she'd shoved aside slipped out of the darkness and faced her down. She shuddered in its presence then peered at Henry's face. Still so much she didn't understand.

He winked down at her. "Ain't it shore enough nice of them to come? They good people, Sarah."

She nodded and shared another smile with Thomas's wife.

"You hungry, ma'am?"

She nodded. "I believe I am."

Arabella took a wrapped plate from the counter and set it on the table. Then she plopped the baby on one hip and took her to the sink to wipe her mouth. "It's still warm," she said, nodding back at the plate.

Sarah sat down in front of the breakfast. She couldn't remember the last food she ate that she didn't cook. "Thank you kindly, Arabella. It looks real good." Digging into the plate of pan sausage, cream gravy, moist scrambled eggs, and biscuits, she found it *was* good. Better than hers, though she hated to admit it.

"Where's Thomas?" she asked with her mouth full.

Henry cleared his throat and took too long to answer. "He'll be back directly. He left to haul Jennie Simpson over to the Biddie house."

Sarah took another bite of her biscuit. "What for?"

Surprise lifted Henry's brows. "Well, you know." He pointed out back. "The body. In the woods."

She knew. Why would he go on about it in front of the children? She raised her brows back at him then tilted her head at the baby. "We ain't gon' discuss it right now. Besides, what does any of it have to do with Jennie Simpson?"

He shot her a worried frown. "She jus' wanted to be the one to tell Miss Bertha on account of she knew how worried little Bertha's been."

Sarah felt as vacant as a plowed field, yet every person in the room stood staring at her. "Tell Miss Bertha what? Stop talking in circles, Henry."

Henry cast a desperate glance at Arabella. She lowered her gaze, so he turned and met Sarah's eyes. "Are you saying you don't know?"

Her middle did a flip. "Know what?" She stood up so fast her chair tipped, scaring the baby and making her cry. "Stop it, Henry. I don't know nothing."

He came over and gripped her shoulders. "Sarah, that poor woman you found. . ." He stopped and swallowed hard. "The body in the woods. . .it's Miss Annie."

Thomas's boys hit the porch like twin bulls, their thundering feet shattering the hush that fell alongside Henry's news. "Mr. King!" one of them cried. "A lawman's pulling into your yard."

Wiping her fingers on a towel, Bertha hurried to peer out the window.

Thomas Jolly sat in the driver's seat of a wagon parked out back. Jennie Simpson sat beside him with her face clutched in her hands. The unearthly sound came from her.

Papa stood waving his arms at Jennie to shush her while his panic-stricken eyes stared toward the house.

Bertha took off her apron and willed her feet to move. She opened the door and stepped out with Mama right behind.

As they approached, Jennie dabbed at her eyes with her palms as if blotting out a scene she couldn't stand to see, her mouth twisted in grief. "Oh, Mista' Francis, it's jus' so awful." She moved her hands, and when her eyes opened, she jumped. "Why, hello, Miz Biddie." She jerked her gaze to Bertha. "And there you is, you pitiful little thing." The sight of Bertha set her off again. She clutched her face and wailed.

"What's going on out here, Francis?"

Papa raised his brows at Mama and licked his lips. A bad sign. He walked straight to Bertha and picked up her hands. "There's dire news, me girl."

Bertha's trembling knees tried to buckle. She steeled herself and searched for truth in his eyes. "Thad?"

He looked startled. "Heavens, no, darlin'. Nothing about your Thad."

Behind them Jennie cried louder. Thomas reached to pat her shoulder, but she wouldn't be comforted. "Po' Miss Bessie," she cried, rocking back and forth. "Po' dear, sweet chile."

Bertha shifted her gaze from Jennie's outburst back to Papa. "Something happened to Annie?"

He squeezed her hands until her fingers ached. "They found her, Bertha. She's been murdered."

Mama moved behind Bertha and held on to her shoulders. "Where?"

"In the woods. Somewhere off the Marshall Road."

Bertha fought to understand. "They found her here? In Jefferson? That's impossible. She's been gone for weeks."

Jennie's full lips trembled. "It's the Lawd's honest truth, Miss Bertha. You know Sarah King? Live in the woods down off Polk? She found her body while she out fetching firewood."

"How do they know it's Annie? It could be anyone."

Papa shook his head. "It's her, darlin'."

She pulled free of his hands and backed away. "It's not true. It can't be."

"It's her, Miss Bertha," Jennie sobbed. "It's really her. I done seen with my own two eyes. She's laying over at the coroner's office. Looked jus' natural, like she's sleeping. It's Miss Bessie, all right. Your Annie, I mean. Still pretty as a picture, but jus' as dead as she can be."

Bertha turned to run for the house. She made it three steps before the blackness that chased her brought her down.

CHAPTER 28

Sarah let go of Henry and clung to the edge of the table while he stepped out onto the porch. After talking to the lawman in a low, respectful voice, he opened the screen and motioned for her. Sarah's broken heart lurched. Now what?

She picked up the half-eaten biscuit from the table and put it back on her plate, lifted the overturned chair and pushed it in, then crossed the room and ducked out the screen door to stand beside her husband.

Constable Stambaugh sat tall and self-important on a buckboard. "Sarah King?"

She started to tremble, and it showed up in her voice. "Yes, sir?"

"Judge Bickford sent me to fetch you. You need to come with me into town."

"What for?"

"Girl, you know what for. He told you last night his inquest would commence again today." His face lit up in a broad smile. "And you're our star witness."

Sarah couldn't decide if he meant to be nice or make fun. "Do I have to?"

He gave her a piercing look. "Oh yes. You have to."

She felt Henry step close to her back. "Can I bring her?"

The constable grunted. "I'm taking her with me when I leave." His eyes shifted to Sarah. "Hurry and get dressed."

She looked down at herself, amazed that she'd walked outside in her robe. She hurried past Henry and the boys on the porch, past Arabella and the girls in the kitchen, and into her room. She barely got the door closed before Henry opened it again.

"I'm going with you."

"Will he let you?"

His jaw tightened. "He ain't stopping me." He caught her whizzing past in her rush to dress and whirled her around to face him. "You all right?"

She peered into his worried brown eyes. "I'm not sure I can do this, now that I know who—"

"You can do it. I'll be there with you. Arabella said she and the girls can stay all day if need be."

Sarah pulled her best frock down from a hook. "You think it'll take all day?"

He shrugged. "Never been to nothing like it before. I guess we'll find out."

She touched gentle fingertips to his side. "Don't you need to stay here and rest?"

He placed his hand over hers and squeezed. "Knowing you're all right is the only rest I need. Hurry up, now. Let's get this over and done."

When he released her hand and started for the door, she caught his fingers again. "Why didn't you come for me?" She blinked back tears. "Yesterday, I mean?"

Henry looked startled at first then tilted his head and closed his eyes.

Her bottom lip trembled, but she managed to finish her question. "I stewed on it all night, when I wasn't wrestling with my memory, but I never did come to a sensible excuse for you." He lowered his face, and she met his gaze. "Henry, even if I was mad, even if I didn't love you no more, I'd still search for you if you went missing." Her eyes brimmed until tears slipped over the edges and streamed down her face. "Don't you know if you'd been there, I wouldn't have been so scared?"

He closed the distance between them and gathered her into his arms. "You silly woman. You ain't got the sense God give a goose."

Sarah's temper flared. She pushed on his chest, but he held her fast and stroked her hair.

"When you left the house after making my dinner to go out and do my work, I watched you head for the barn looking like the whole world rested across your back. I got so mad at my sorry self, I felt sick. The only way I could stand myself was to go to sleep. So I did."

She relaxed against him, his words a salve to her pain. She thought he hadn't noticed how hard she'd worked.

"I woke up and saw it was dark outside, and still laid up like a big old pouting boy. I waited for you to call me to supper, only you never did. When I went in that kitchen and saw no lights and no fire in the stove, I got so scared. I thought Dandy kicked you and left you laying out there hurt. . .or worse. I hauled tail to the barn, but you weren't there. Or anywhere."

His intense gaze bored into her heart. "I figured you got your fill of me and left. I didn't know if Miss Jennie took you in or maybe you found a way to book passage to St. Louis. I jus' knew I had to find you before I lost you for good. So I saddled Dandy and led him out, and that's when I seen lights flickerin' in the woods. Right out in the middle, where they don't belong." He drew a shaky breath. "Sarah, I thought. . ." He clenched his eyes shut and turned away.

Sarah pressed her face to his back. "What, Henry? What did you think?"

He shuddered. "I thought those hateful men got out of jail and come for me. I figured they seen you outside and took you instead, jus' for spite. I jus' knew they had you out there in those woods and. . ."

Sarah spun him around and pulled him close. "Hush, now.

Hush. I'm all right, Henry. None of that happened."

"I ran back to the house to fetch my shotgun, and that's when I heard you on the porch. The whole time I tended you, until you fell asleep in my arms, Dandy stood outside in the yard, saddled and ready to go. After I saw you were down for the night, I went out and put him up. Out there in the barn, I dropped to my knees and thanked the good Lord for taking care of you again, when I couldn't."

He gave her a wobbly smile. "Good thing He's there to watch over you, since I keep making such a mess of it."

She pressed his face between her palms. "Stop that. Nobody could've known what waited for me in that grove. Somebody had to find poor Miss Annie, and I guess that somebody was me."

"Henry? Miss Sarah?"

Arabella's voice behind the door gave Sarah a start. Henry pulled it open, and she stood looking ready to run away again. "That man out there's getting mighty edgy. Says you best put a move on."

Henry nodded. "We coming." He glanced at Sarah over his shoulder. "Hurry, now. I'll go stall him as long as I can."

When he closed the door behind him, Sarah shimmied out of her robe and into her best blouse and a skirt, smiling despite everything that swirled around her when the skirt's button barely fastened.

A curious notion crept into her head, and in an instant Sarah made up her mind. Kneeling, she took the unfinished white dress, full of pins and basting stitches, from the middle drawer of the chest and wrapped it in her good shawl. Then she tucked the bundle inside her coat, slid on her shoes, and joined Henry in the kitchen.

"Ready, now?" Henry grinned and jerked his thumb toward the porch. "Those boys doing they best to distract that lawman, but they running short on tricks."

Sarah gave a shaky smile and tried to still her trembling legs. "We best rescue him, then." She glanced toward the open door. "Let's go, while I still have the courage."

Henry wrapped his arm around her shoulders and tucked her close. "Long as I'm by your side, that's all the courage you need."

Thanking God to have her husband back, she gazed up at him. "Then whatever you do, Henry King, stay close by my side."

Bertha steeled herself as the hinges of the bedroom door squealed behind her. Why couldn't they do like she asked and just leave her be? She understood good intentions, even their need to comfort, but she had no use for empty words of solace or promises the pain would pass. These were poor substitutes for absolution.

"I brought you some tea, dear. Chamomile. Your favorite. And look who's come to see you."

When she didn't turn, Mama plowed ahead. "Look, Bertha. Magda's here."

A tray slid onto the table beside her. Liquid trickled into a cup, and a spoon clinked on china. "Sit up, dear. I have your tea."

She squeezed her eyes tighter and willed them away. After a long pause, the cup and saucer settled onto the tray with a rattle, and Mama sighed.

"She's been like this since this morning," Mama said, as if Bertha weren't right there in the room. "Hasn't said a word to anyone."

"I'll talk to her, Mrs. Biddie."

The door opened. "I'll leave you with her, then. Oh, and there's a sandwich and slice of cake for each of you under the cup towel. I went ahead and finished her cake. Hated to see the ingredients go to waste, and besides, I needed some way to busy my hands. Try to get her to eat something, won't you?"

Magda's skirts rustled as she settled in a chair by the bed. "Yes, ma'am. I'll try."

The door closed. Bertha gritted her teeth, waiting for Magda to beg her to get up, to snap out of it, to eat something, to come to her senses and go on with her birthday celebration. Instead, Magda abruptly stood up, moved to sit down on the bed beside her, and began smoothing her brow. "This isn't just about losing a friend, is it, sugar?"

Sudden tears seared Bertha's eyes. She tried her voice but managed only a squeaky whisper. "I failed her, didn't I?"

"Oh, Bertha, you didn't."

She clenched her fists, the words coming easier now that the dam had burst. "I was Annie's last hope. I let her down. I let God down."

"How can you say such a thing? You sacrificed everything to help her. You gave your all."

"Did I? I had so many chances to say the right thing, yet it seems I never did. Even that last night I let myself get distracted, allowed my heart to be divided. All I could think about was getting back to Thad." She sobbed into her pillow. "If only I'd known it was her last night on earth. . ."

Magda leaned closer. "Her last? How do you know that?"

"It's the only thing that makes sense. Abe killed her the very next day. That's why he came back to Brooks House without her." She twisted to look back at Magda. "He must've caught her sneaking back to their room on Saturday night, and it was the last straw." She buried her face in her hands and cried bitter tears. "Oh, Magda, don't you see? While trying to help Annie, I got her killed instead."

Judge Bickford's inquest would haunt Sarah's dreams for the rest of her days. Living through finding Miss Annie's body in the grove was hard enough. Reliving it time and again while twelve stern-faced men looked on proved taxing to her very soul. Several times during the questions, Sarah felt close to losing her few bites of Arabella's eggs and biscuit, so she found herself grateful that Henry's news about Miss Annie had cut her breakfast short.

Henry stayed as close as the officials would allow and kept a watchful eye on her the whole time. She had only to seek his eyes to find the strength to carry on. So it seemed odd, now that the inquest was over, that she would need to find a way to slip away from him a bit.

Outside the coroner's office, she reached to touch his arm. "Henry, I need to go back inside. I left my coat."

He glanced at the door. "Wait here. I'll fetch it."

She wrapped her fingers around his wrist. "No, don't." At his surprised look, she loosened her grip and managed a smile. "I mean, you'll never find it, and I know right where it is." Both true statements, since she'd folded the shawl-wrapped bundle into the coat and stashed it under a desk the first chance she got.

Henry frowned down at her then back at the building. "You sure?"

She patted his hand. "Just go get Dandy and pull him around. I'll be right back."

He gave her a curt nod and set off down the boardwalk. They had to park the rig a good ways down because the coroner's office had turned into a spectacle that rivaled the county fair. Judge Bickford had left the body exposed for public viewing, and hundreds of curious citizens had come for a chance to see.

Her heart so far up her throat she could taste it, Sarah opened the door and slipped into the building. Knowing she had little time, she hurried down the hall to the office where she'd left the coat. Though her own things lay beneath, she felt like a thief skulking beside the desk, waiting for a chance to take them.

Her gaze darted around the room. None of the clustered groups of men took any notice, as if—after all their questions—they'd forgotten she existed. After a deep breath, she ducked down and back up fast with her prize in her hands.

Sarah found the room that held Miss Annie's body by walking the corridor alongside the parade of people that stretched from outside to an unmarked door. She unwrapped the white dress, laid her coat and shawl across a nearby chair, and marched up to the door carrying the folded garment in front of her. Breathing a sigh of relief when she saw a colored woman posted outside, she sashayed over and peered down her nose at her. "Open up. I need to take this in."

The woman looked her over then knocked with one knuckle.

A young girl peered out and scowled at them. "Can't come in. We's undressing her."

Pushing down her fear, Sarah nodded at the frock in her hands. "I know. That's why I'm here."

The girl glanced at the soft, shimmering cloth, stepped aside, and reached to touch it as Sarah passed. "Ain't that purty?"

The door closed behind them, and Sarah's horror knew no bounds. Too scared of what she might see if she didn't, she kept her eyes on the floor.

"Well, well. If it ain't the very person who found our pretty customer."

There'd be no mistaking the sultry voice of Isabella Gouldy. Sarah remembered the last time she'd seen her, ducked in an alley clinging to a man. She only hoped Belle had been too far into her cups to remember the disgusted look on Sarah's face.

"Come for another little peek, Sarah?"

Before she could answer, Belle cut her off. "If you come for a job, you're too late. They're paying me and Mollie here, and these four girls."

Mollie Turk and three other women stood beside the young one who opened the door. Sarah lifted her eyes to Belle Gouldy's face. "Paying you?"

She nodded. "To strip off her things and list the items we remove for the trial. Me and Mollie get paid extra for making her burial clothes."

Sarah resisted the urge to scurry out of the room and let them get on with it. She held up the dress. "I have the grave clothes right here."

Belle cursed. "Those no-count dogs promised the job to us."

Sarah held up her hand. "You still get paid the same, because this one isn't finished. It's only basted together and still needs a hem."

Belle stared at first then gave a bawdy laugh. "Well, that makes our job easy, don't it, Mollie? Don't expect the old girl will need more than basting stitches. She won't be putting much strain on her seams." She smoothed her hand over the bodice and whistled. "Sure is a fine cut of cloth to throw down a hole on a corpse."

Sarah stiffened. "You just see that it gets on her. I'm sure to find out if you don't, and I'll tell Judge Bickford." The tone of her voice surprised Sarah. Belle and the rest, too, by the looks on their faces. But her bluff worked. No one needed to know Judge Bickford had no knowledge of Sarah's mission.

Belle drew back her hands. "All right, all right. Seems a pitiful waste, though."

Sarah handed her offering to Mollie Turk, who took it to a small bench where her sewing basket waited. Sarah's eyes went to the bolt of rough material laid out on the table and shuddered. She tried to imagine the lovely, kindhearted Miss Annie in heavy black moleskin, but the picture wouldn't come. Peace settled around her heart as she left the room. She'd done the right thing.

CHAPTER 29

Wednesday, February 7

The wind skimmed across the surface of the murky bayou at Sarah's feet. The last traces of drifted snow, bright white against the dark sludge, looked more like icy lace where the water had lapped patterns at the surface. She pressed her hands to her swollen middle, raised her face to the warmth of the sun, and thanked God she wasn't in St. Louis.

Today, Jefferson would lay Miss Annie to rest. The townsfolk had donated one hundred fifty dollars to pay for her burial in Jefferson's Oakwood Cemetery. Perhaps now the kindhearted beauty with haunted eyes would find peace.

Footfalls came over the rise behind her and paused. Sarah smiled without looking around. "Back already?"

The familiar stride continued down the hill, not stopping until it reached her; then arms circled her from behind. "Naw, I ain't made it back yet."

"Is that a fact? So a handsome stranger holds me in his arms?"

He chuckled, his barrel chest rumbling against the back of her head. "How you know I'm handsome? You ain't looked yet."

She giggled and squeezed his wrists. "I know handsome when I feel it, and you feel mighty handsome to me."

Henry leaned to nibble her neck. She gave him a playful slap on the arm. "I wouldn't go getting fresh. My husband's a big man with a mean jealous streak. You wouldn't want him finding out."

He held her without answering for a spell then bent close to her ear. "While we're on the subject of husbands finding things out, I got a question for you."

She swayed back and forth, pulling him along with her. "Go ahead and ask. I might even answer."

He held her still and took a deep breath. "Did you ever get around to making yourself a dress with that pretty white cloth I bought you?"

She tensed in his arms. No matter what, she wouldn't lie. "Yes and no."

"Girl, that ain't no kind of answer. You either made a dress or you didn't."

She swallowed the knot in her throat. "I made one, just not for me."

Catching her hair in the stubble on his chin, he nodded against her head. "What if I told you there's a story around town about a fancy white dress showing up yesterday on Miss Annie's body?"

She cringed. It hadn't crossed her mind that she'd owe Henry an explanation. "Well, I. . ."

He turned her around and placed a gentle hand over her mouth. "Before you strain that little noggin, let me finish. As the rumor goes, a certain Sarah King hauled that dress straight into the coroner's office, as if sent there by Judge Bickford himself, and insisted Isabella Gouldy use it for Miss Annie's grave clothes–which means today when they lay her to rest, your white frock is going down with her." He peered closer. "All that sound about right?"

She cut her eyes to the ground. "Are you mad?"

He tilted his head to the side and cupped her chin in his palm. "Not mad. Curious. Why would you do such a thing, after hankering so long for that cloth? You hardly knew Miss Annie."

Uneasy, she toyed with the button loop on the front of his shirt. "I'm not sure I can explain it."

He caressed her hand. "Jus' do your best."

"Something about that woman touched my heart. Made me count my blessings."

"How so?"

"Since that day in my kitchen, when Jennie told me how mean Annie's man treated her, I couldn't stop thinking about how different our lives were. For all her fine clothes and big diamonds, Miss Annie cried more tears in a day than I have in a year. Yet with all that pain, she took the time to show genuine love for folks."

"She did at that, God rest her soul."

"Henry, I felt pressed to give the dress, as if the Lord Himself wanted her to have it." She waved her hand. "Oh, I know that don't make no sense, considering how Miss Annie lived her life, but it's how I felt. And I don't regret giving it."

"Reckon it was for your own benefit? Like laying down a sacrifice?"

She rested against his chest while she mulled over his words. "That could be. He's been dealing with my heart on several matters lately."

"That may be the answer to the other thing I've wondered about."

She leaned back to look in his eyes. "Which thing?"

"You mind telling me why you're so different lately?"

She smiled. "Me different? How so?"

A splash on the surface of the water pulled his gaze away from her face. He held her, staring at something over her head. "You seem quiet inside. Like a body who's made her peace."

She twisted around to face the water. Mindful of his ribs, she leaned her head gently against his chest. "I guess I have made peace. With life here in Jefferson. With God. With myself. I'm just done struggling."

He tightened his arms around her. "How'd you come to that place so fast?"

"Like I said, Miss Annie showed me a better way than hate. I think she crossed my path for that reason. And the day hate almost got you hanged, I decided not to give it one more second of my time."

He tensed. "I wish I felt that way."

She patted his hands. "There's nothing right about the way things are in Jefferson, and I won't say it don't grieve my heart. But I learned something that terrible day. Most of these folks care about us deep down, but the old ways cloud their minds, the things they learned from their folks. The others, like those horrible men, don't deserve the time it wastes to hate them."

Henry sighed. "Life can't go on like this forever. Something has to change."

"I hope it will someday. But please don't let it change you, Henry. Peaceful, loving folks like you and Miss Annie are Jefferson's hope. We've already lost her to senseless cruelty. Don't let three black-hearted strangers take you, too."

Henry stood still for a long time, until a tear fell from overhead and landed on Sarah's chest. As he relaxed against her, she sensed he'd finally let go of his pain.

After a time, he wiped his eyes on his sleeve. "Ain't you going to Miss Annie's funeral?"

She shook her head. "I don't need to. I've already said good-bye."

He sniffed then chuckled. "So Sarah's dress will be there, but she won't?"

She grinned. It was time to tell him. Until now she'd kept her secret suspicions to herself. She needed to be sure before she broke the news.

Heart pounding, she took his big, calloused hand in her own and slid it down over the front of her skirt. "Before long that little dress wouldn't have fit me nohow. Even after I deliver, I don't expect that tiny waist would ever go all the way around again." He tensed, and she flushed with pleasure. "They claim a woman's body changes after birthing a baby."

Henry let go and moved around to stare at her with furrowed

brows. He opened his mouth to speak then closed it again, reminding Sarah of the poor befuddled fish that once took a swim with his overalls. She pressed his hand tighter against her waist. "Speak up, Papa. How do you expect to teach my daughter to talk if you can't?"

He found his voice. "You mean it, Sarah?"

Smiling so hard her face hurt, she nodded.

He took off up the hill whooping so loudly he flushed a mess of wood thrushes from the nearby brush. After he tromped up and down a few times, shouting and bashing everything in sight with his hat, he ran back to her so fast she dodged for fear he'd run her down. He caught her before she got away and swung her off the ground. "Henry King gon' be a papa! You hear me, world? Henry gon' have a son!"

As if remembering her delicate condition, he stopped short and set her down gently. She took his cheeks in both hands and gave him a fierce look. "Now we have good reason to make things better in Jefferson. This baby is part of us, and she'll be part of this town."

Henry's eyes blazed. "My son gon' walk these streets with his head up, Sarah. I won't allow nobody to treat him how they done me. Or steal his self-respect like they done yours."

She shook her head. "You want change, Henry? Well, Jefferson may never change, but we can. If we raise our daughter to always look to God, her head will always be lifted, now, won't it? I refuse to pass on a legacy of hate."

They glared at each other for a spell before they both started to laugh. He nestled her under his arm and walked her up the hill. "You jus' forget that daughter stuff right now. It's a boy, and that's all there is to it."

"Hush up, Henry King. I need me a little girl to make white dresses for."

At the top of the rise, he hauled her around to face him. "I tell you what. . .if you give me a son this time, next time you can have a girl. But after that, all boys. We need brothers for Henry Jr."

She nudged him and started for the house. "Humph! Sisters, you mean. For my little Annie."

Papa followed the horse-drawn hearse along the winding, tree-lined paths of Oakwood Cemetery.

The warmth of the day had long since given way to a chilly afternoon breeze, so Bertha raised her collar higher and bundled into the wool blanket Papa kept for her under the seat.

"You holding up all right, wee girl?"

She lifted her trembling chin in his direction and nodded.

Mama begged Bertha not to attend Annie's funeral, but she had insisted.

Papa stood up for her, saying, "The obligation of a friend doesn't end until the last clod hits the casket." The way Bertha had it figured, she'd not get off so easy. She fully expected the debt she owed would follow her to her own grave.

Since Annie's death, the yoke had altered but not lessened a whit. The burden of hope had become a load of guilt; one so heavy Bertha stumbled beneath its weight. And though she tried, Magda hadn't said a word to make her feel better. Before she left, she asked Bertha to pray, but she couldn't. God wasn't interested in a word she had to say.

As for Thad, she had given up on him, too. After all, she didn't deserve happiness, and Thad didn't seem to care, so why should God intervene in the details of their lives?

The hearse came to a stop in front of them, and Papa helped her down. When her feet touched the ground, she swayed a bit, so he wrapped his arm around her shoulders. "I haven't called it wrong, have I, sprite? Will this be too much for you?"

She straightened her spine. "It would be too much for me to miss it. I have to do this, Papa."

He squeezed her tight. "That's me girl."

The men hired to bear the casket were walking away from the hearse toward the open grave. Except for Mr. Stilley, Dr. Turner,

Dr. Eason, Sheriff Bagby, and a few other townsfolk, curious strangers made up most of the hushed gathering. A small band of colored residents stood off to the side, including most of the staff from Brooks House–Jennie Simpson, Thomas and his wife, and the one they called Cook.

Papa nudged her forward. "Let's go, Bertha. I'll be right here holding you, and I promise not to let go as long as you need me."

She gripped his steady arm. "I hope you mean that, because I need you."

The six men who carried Annie's casket gently lowered it into the ground with ropes. The assembled mourners crowded closer, and the minister opened the service with a prayer. Bertha struggled to focus, but her mind swirled with thoughts of Annie and the times they'd shared–their long talks about crushes and corsets and candy–and every other childish wasted word that kept her from saying the only thing that mattered. The words of faith Bertha had managed to spout seemed weak and trite. Not nearly enough to save her friend.

Bertha lowered her face to her hands just as Papa's arm lifted from her shoulders. She felt him step away, and it shook her back to the present. She felt cold and alone without the comforting weight around her neck and more than a little cross. Hadn't he promised not to leave her as long as she needed him? Yet he'd left her the second she needed him most.

She turned to see where he'd gone. He stood behind her, his features alight with a sappy smile. Confused and hurt, she faced the front again just as another comforting arm, another warm body, took Papa's place from the opposite side. Startled by the surprising familiarity, her gaze jerked to her consoler's face.

Thad!

His expression remained solemn except for the barest of smiles and a tiny wink. She glanced over her shoulder again. Papa beamed and raised his thumb.

The rest of the service became a blur of questions and scattered feelings. The poor minister might've yodeled the rest of the message for all she heard. That is, until his booming voice read the closing passage of scripture. " 'What man is he that liveth, and shall not see death? Shall he deliver his soul from the hand of the grave?' " His burning gaze swept the circle of mourners. "That's why, dear children, it becomes imperative that we who have been enlightened with the truth persist so diligently to obey the admonishment in James 5:20." He held the book aloft and began to read. " 'He which converteth the sinner from the error of his way shall save a soul from death, and shall hide a multitude of sins.' "

Bertha spun away from Thad, brushed past Papa, lifted her skirts, and ran. She ran through the idle curious, providing more than their money's worth of morbid entertainment, and past the grieving staff of Brooks House, who stared with sympathetic eyes. She passed up the wagon and didn't stop until she'd barreled through the front gate, thundered a good ways up the road, and crashed into a heavy thicket standing between her and a winding trail.

The branches clutched at her sleeves and tore long scratches in her ankles. Cruel briars crisscrossed in front, and in back her skirt caught around the thorns of a tall devil's walking stick growing up through the brush. If she attempted one more step, she'd fall facedown on the briars or be pulled back on the spiny stick. Trapped, she couldn't move an inch. Her dilemma reminded her of her life. Thad's return stirred hope in her heart, but guilt over failing Annie left her at a standstill.

Too distraught to cry, she looked around to weigh her options. If she could possibly sit down without ripping the flesh from her palms, she might manage to free her skirt from the cruel spike. She leaned to lower her body onto one arm when a hand shot out and latched onto her waist. "Don't move, Bertha. That's stinging nettle beneath you."

"Oh, Thad," she wailed. "I'm stuck."

"I can see that. Let's get you unstuck." He held her up with one hand and carefully freed her skirt with the other. When the last piece of cloth inched free, he lifted her from the thicket and set her down on the road. "Are you all right, sugar?"

With trembling fingers, she smoothed her tattered skirt. "I guess so."

"Good. Now tell me what just happened. Why did you run off like that?"

Bertha averted her gaze. "I believe I need to sit down."

Thad scanned their surroundings then took her by the wrist. "Can you walk?"

"Yes, I think so." She wasn't pretending feminine frailty. Her legs trembled so much she feared they might fail her.

Thad led her to a clearing where a big tree lay, felled by the wind in a recent storm. He took off his overcoat and spread it over the bark then helped her to sit. Settling beside her, he inched a bit closer. "I missed you, Bertha."

Surprised, she raised her head. His simple declaration brought a sweet smile to her lips. She'd expected more questions or a demand for an explanation. "I missed you, too. I'm so glad you're here. How did you hear about Annie?"

He studied his twiddling thumbs. "I didn't. Not until I got into town today."

She frowned, considering his words. "Then why did you leave school?"

"I didn't." He raised his head, and something flickered in his eyes. "I never made it to school."

Bertha couldn't trust her ears. Of all the bewildering events of the past few days, this confused her the most. "What are you saying? You've been gone for two weeks. If you weren't at school, where have you been?" She bit back the important question. If he hadn't gone to school, why had he left her?

"I spent some time down in Houston."

"Houston?"

"I got on the train in Longview with every intention of going to Bryan. When it pulled into the station, I couldn't make myself get off. I stayed on and rode it clear to Houston."

She stared up into dark brown eyes with long blond lashes and a sprinkling of tiny freckles at the corners and tried to sort out what he was telling her.

"I was plenty scared at first, but the trip gave me time to think. By the time the train hit Houston, I'd made up my mind. I won't be going back to Bryan. I'm never going to college, Bertha."

Her heart raised its head. "Does your papa know?"

He answered with a somber nod.

"What did he say?"

"It's not what he said this time; it's what I said. I told him I appreciated his intentions, but they were misplaced, that Cyrus should be going to school, not me. I told him to apply the money he'd saved for my education on sending Cy to Texas AMC." He shrugged. "The old man bucked a little at first. When he saw I meant business"—Thad snapped his fingers—"just like that, he set his dream on Cy, where it always belonged."

By now they were both smiling.

"How does Cyrus feel about that?"

Thad shook his head, remembering. "You never saw a happier boy in your life."

Bertha touched his arm. "What took you to Houston?"

He caught her hand and squeezed it. "Just north of there, in a little town they call Humble, is where our future lies. I can't explain it now, but as soon as we can be married, I'll take you there and show you."

A shock surged through her. She cringed and slid her hand away as surprise replaced the confident joy in Thad's eyes.

"What's wrong, sugar?"

"I don't know. I'm confused."

He swallowed. "About me?"

When she didn't answer, he pushed off the log and paced in front of her. "I don't know what there is to be confused about. Two weeks ago you said you loved me. How could that change in such a short time?" He stopped to glare, but his eyes glistened with unshed tears. "If I'd known you don't really care for me, I would've stayed down in Humble and saved myself a trip."

She sprang up and stood with him. "I never said I don't care for you."

Bewilderment replaced the pain. "What, then? This frog-hopping has to stop. You need to pick a toadstool and light, Bertha." Then his mouth opened. The look in his eyes said he thought he'd figured it out. "Wait a minute—I know what's wrong. You want a proper marriage proposal, and you deserve one."

He plowed ahead before she could deny it. "A proper proposal suits me fine, Bertha Maye Biddie." He dropped down on one knee. "I've already proved I'll wallow in the dirt for you."

"Wait! Please don't kneel, Thad. That's not it."

He howled and gripped his head. "Girl, you're driving me mad. If you care for me, what's there to be confused about? You'll either marry me or you won't."

"It's not a matter of will or won't," she shouted. "I can't."

Thad tugged her down in front of him and laced his long fingers through her hair, his grip too tight around her head. "That's crazy. I won't hear it. You already said you love me."

"I do love you."

His voice trembled. "All right, then. You said loving each other should be what matters most." He pulled her closer as his darting gaze roamed her face for answers. "What happened to that?"

Bertha lowered her gaze and gave in to threatening tears. Thad let go of her hair and rocked her, murmuring comfort in her ear. A few yards south, a train rumbled past on the way to the station on Alley Street. The whistle blew as the engine approached the Line Street crossing, and the woeful sound filled Bertha's chest, mourning with her and echoing her grief.

When she quieted, he patted the top of her head the way he had the last time she saw him. It hurt to remember that day, the day he said he loved her but had to leave. Now she understood how he must have felt.

He pushed her back to look at her. "I think I know what's ailing you, sugar. You don't want to marry while losing Annie is so fresh. That's all right. I can wait. For as long as it takes to grieve your friend, I promise I'll wait for you."

She shifted her eyes to his. "I don't deserve such a promise. Or hope for such happiness."

"What?" He stood to his feet, pulling her up with him. "Bertha, what's going on? Why would you say something so foolish?"

She straightened her spine and looked him in the eye. "Because I caused Annie's death."

Thad gripped her shoulders and gave her a shake. "Don't you say it again. You had no part in her death. That madman killed her for spite and greed. How could you think anything different?"

"No, it's true. Abe got mad because Annie snuck out the night before. I asked her to slip away and meet me. If I'd left her alone, she'd still be alive."

Thad stared at her so long she squirmed. With a groan, he crushed her to his chest. "Poor, sweet girl. How long have these tiny shoulders borne such weight? You need to lay it down, Bertha."

The same words Papa had said to her.

"I have no right to lay it down." She tried to pull away, but he held her.

"You had no right to pick it up. I saw how Abe treated Annie. He was bound to kill her eventually. Honey, if Annie wouldn't get away from him, there was nothing you could do to stop it."

She remembered Annie's tortured face the night they met in the alley.

"He hurt me. He always hurts me."

She saw Annie's twisted arm, the tattered gown, the fear in her eyes at just the mention of Abe's name. She ducked her head. "But I—"

Thad raised her chin with his finger. "It is not your fault."

"You really think so?"

"I know so. The only person who could've saved Annie from Abe was Annie."

His words were a balm, each one a drop of warm, soothing ointment bringing the pardon she needed. Her heart opened a crack and light poured in—except in one dark, haunted corner.

"That explains why the Lord sent me on a mission to save her.

I brought about just the opposite. I failed Him miserably."

"Now you've failed God, too?"

She tensed. Was he making fun? "Yes, Thad. I let my feelings for you distract me. Because of me, Annie died without God's forgiveness."

"How do you know that?"

She reached for the hankie she'd folded into her sash, but it wasn't there. "I just know."

He took her hand and led her back to the log, easing her down on his knee. "All right. What exactly do you think God told you to do?"

"He told me to tell Annie about His grace." She felt for the hankie again. Had she lost it in the briars?

"And you had no chance to tell her?"

"I tried."

"When?"

"The night before she died."

"Did she listen?"

Bertha swiped the back of her hand under her nose. Unattractive, but necessary. "I don't know. Maybe."

"Did she run away from you or stick her fingers in her ears?"

"Of course not."

"Then she heard you, Bertha. After that, the burden fell on Annie."

"But it's obvious I didn't say enough."

"What else might you have said?"

"That's just it. I couldn't say anything more."

He scrunched his brow. "Why's that?"

"Because. . ." The truth dawned, and Bertha raised her head. "Because she wouldn't allow it." For the first time since Annie's death, she remembered. Annie had backed away, refused to hear.

Thad drew her next to his chest. "Don't you see, goose? You did exactly what the Lord asked of you. Suppose God sent you to say those things to Annie knowing it was her last chance to hear? In that case, did you fail Him?"

His compassion broke her heart anew. Tears rolled down her cheeks. "No," she whispered.

"And did you fail Annie?"

"When you put it like that, I guess not."

He shook out a red bandanna and wiped her eyes then put it in her hands so she could blow her nose. "Sounds like you've been too hard on yourself on all counts."

The train whistle blew again in the distance, one short moan followed by a long, heartrending wail. This time it mourned for Annie. "Thad, it breaks my heart to think that after her miserable life, Annie missed heaven."

"Sweetheart, you may never know how God used your words in Annie's heart. All we can do is obey and trust Him with the rest."

"Can you trust God with the details?"

Papa had asked that question concerning her future with Thad. And look at the wonderful way God had worked out the details of their relationship.

Releasing the weight of guilt from her chest, Bertha drew in a deep breath and felt her heart surrender the last shadowed crevice to the light. She wrapped her arms around Thad's neck and urged him close. His hands tangled in her hair, and his cheek slid along hers until their lips met.

"I love you, Bertha," he said in a husky voice.

"I love you, too."

"Will you marry me?"

"Yes, I will."

"And live with me in Humble?"

"Whenever you say."

He withdrew to look at her. "You mean it?"

When she nodded, he got up and stood her to her feet. "It's rough country, sugar, and that's all I can promise you. You won't have the comfort and convenience you're accustomed to. We'll be scratching out a life from nothing." He studied her eyes. "It'll be hard work, and you'll be leaving behind everything you know. It might change you."

She cocked her head at him. "Do I have to wear fancy shoes all the time?"

"You don't have to wear shoes at all, unless you want to. There's no one around to care."

She raised her hands. "Hallelujah! Humble won't change me. It'll set me free."

His expression turned grave. "Now the important question. What would you say to a yard full of bloodhounds?"

She giggled. "Woof, woof?"

Laughing, he picked her up and hugged her until her sides hurt. Then he set her on her feet and kissed her cheek. "We'd best go. I told your papa I'd find you and bring you home. If we don't show up soon, he'll send a posse." He grinned. "I don't want to get on the bad side of Francis Biddie. Especially tonight."

She grinned, too. "What's so special about tonight?"

"If you must know, we men have a lot to talk about. I plan to ask your father's permission to marry his lovely daughter." He winked and offered his arm. "I think I'll wait until he says yes before I tell him about Humble."

Bertha slid her arm through his and winked back. "Considering who we're dealing with, you'd best wait until after the wedding."

CHAPTER 30

Saturday, March 10

Bertha gazed around her bedroom one last time. The dressing table, cluttered since her youth with sundry items necessary for her toilette, looked oddly bare with everything packed away. It reminded her of the front window last Christmas after Papa took down the tree.

Remembering her cameo brush set still in the bedside table drawer, she lifted it out as she'd done a thousand times before, only this time she'd never put it back. It would soon be on its way to a place called Humble, Texas, in the company of Mrs. Thaddeus Bloom.

Shoving the brush and comb deep inside her velvet drawstring bag, Bertha set it near the rest of her luggage then smiled at the container of tooth powder, the one thing left behind on purpose. She caught sight of her image in the looking glass and backed away from the dressing table to see more. Preening a bit in her dress of white dimity with matching wedding bonnet, she jumped when Magda cleared her throat.

Bertha looked back and grinned. "Fiddlesticks. You caught me."

"It's all right to admire yourself today, sugar. You're a lovely bride." She pointed toward the hullabaloo in the dining room. "Everyone out there agrees."

Bertha gave a playful laugh. "It's unanimous, then." She held her dress out to her sides and twirled. "It's because I'm so happy, don't you think?"

When Magda didn't answer, Bertha glanced up. Her friend sagged against the door frame, both hands hiding her face.

Bertha hurried over and gripped her shoulders. "Don't you dare. It's bound to be bad luck for the maid of honor to cry at the wedding party."

"I'm not crying," Magda protested from behind her hands. "There's something in my eye."

She swiped her thumbs across Magda's cheeks then held them up for her to see. "Which one? They're both leaking."

Laughing, they fell against each other and stumbled over to fall down on the bed. Magda rose up with red, watery eyes. "I can't believe you're going, that's all. I've had you all to myself, and just like that, you'll be gone. I've tried to be happy for you, but I'm going to miss you too much. How will I cope?"

Bertha kicked off her shoes and sat cross-legged on the bed. "I know a remedy for that. Come with me."

"Come with you? Where?"

Bertha grabbed her hands. "To live with me in Humble."

"Don't be daft. I couldn't."

"Why not? You wouldn't have to come right away. You can wait a few months until we settle in a house."

Magda shifted on the bed. "Papa would never allow it."

"Oh, I think he would if Thad promised to look out for you." She squeezed her fingers. "So you're considering it?"

Magda flinched. "I didn't say that."

"You didn't have to. If you've gotten to what your papa might say, you're entertaining the thought."

Magda shook free of her grasp. "Forget about it. It's a scandalous notion. I wouldn't think of intruding on you newlyweds."

Bertha leaned close and widened her eyes. "Don't be so hasty, dear. There's a lot going on in Humble. A world of opportunity for a single girl."

Magda tilted her head like a befuddled hound.

Bertha leaned hers back and laughed. "Men, sugar. Thad claims there are scores of unattached men. Mostly well-heeled gentlemen and businessmen looking for a place to settle. A few rough-and-tumble frontiersmen, too." She winked. "And very few women to balance things out."

Magda leaped to her feet and stood at attention. "You'll find me on the next train."

Bertha clapped her hands together. "Well, I should say so! After all, your piece of wedding cake had a ring inside. That means marriage within a year, so you'd best get busy."

"Oh, pooh. It's a silly tradition. Pretty little Rhodie got the thimble. There's no way she'll wind up a spinster. I think our pieces got switched." She held up one finger. "Although when that rascal Charles Gouldy bit into the coin, it gave me hope. He's sure to be prosperous someday, if it means he has to steal it."

They heard a knock and turned. Mama stood smiling in the open doorway. "Such boisterous laughter coming from this room! What am I interrupting?"

Bertha waved her in. "Nothing that won't keep. Come in."

"I don't need to come in, dear. You need to come out. Your new husband has scoured the grounds for you, perhaps remembering the last time you vanished." She pointed toward the front of the house. "I left him straining his neck at the parlor window. Come put him out of his misery, won't you?"

Bertha scooted off the bed and rushed to hug her. "Oh, Mama! I'm so happy."

Mama beamed down at her. "It becomes you. I've never seen you more lovely." She wiped her eyes with a lace hankie and kissed Bertha's cheek. "Your guests are waiting for you to present your gifts, and you have such beautiful things." She clasped her hands together. "There's the most stunning appliquéd Rose of Sharon quilt from Thad's mother. I understand she made it herself. Do hurry, love. I want you to see it."

Unexpected tears stung Bertha's eyes. Though Papa called her "love" quite often, it was the first time Mama ever had. She linked arms with her. "Let's go, then. Shall we?"

Bertha offered her other arm to Magda, and the three of them filed down the hall to the parlor.

Thad stood across the room, staring into the fireplace. In his dark suit, with flickering light on his face, he looked more handsome than she'd ever seen him. He glanced up, and Bertha sent him a little wave. A thrill tickled her spine when it seemed his breath caught at the sight of her. He waved back and moved toward her, stopping along the way for a quick word or a handshake with a guest. He finally reached her side, and Bertha's own breath caught when his hand slid down her back.

"Where've you been, Mrs. Bloom?" he whispered. "I've missed you."

"I'm sorry. I've missed you, too."

She took his hand and made her way to the center table piled high with wedding presents. The men feigned interest at first then settled in the corner discussing the weather. The women circled the table, complimenting Mama's embroidered pillow slips and sighing over Mrs. Bloom's quilt.

A commotion in the corner caught her eye. Papa had spotted her and stormed her way. "So here's the bonniest bride on two continents. Come along, daughter. It's time to pronounce me blessing on this fine union."

He took the newlyweds, one on each side, then stuck his fingers in his mouth and blew a sharp blast. All activity ceased, and the company crowded around them in a circle. Papa placed one hand on Bertha's head. To the delight of his audience, he reached the other hand toward Thad's, shrugged, then called for a chair. Satisfied, he began to speak. "Great God, one true God, I bring these precious souls before You, entrusting them into Your care."

His fingers tightened on her head. "Bertha Maye Biddie Bloom, may your life be filled with plenty and your womb suffer no lack. May the love of your husband warm your heart and brighten your days. May the peace of the Lord Jesus Christ follow you all the days of your life." He patted her head.

"Thaddeus Abel Bloom, may the wife of your youth bring you joy. May your pockets be blessed and your quiver full. May God shine His face on your journeys and prosper the work of your hands." He motioned for Thad to stand. "Friends and family, I give you Thaddeus Bloom and his wee wife, Bertha."

A riotous outcry and boisterous clapping ensued. The guests surged toward them, shouting congratulations and pounding Thad on the back. After Julius Ney and his wife wished them well, Rhodie Pharr stepped up and took their place.

Bertha smiled, happy to see the beaming girl. "Hey, Rhodie."

"Hey, Bertha. You sure make a lovely bride."

"Why, thank you."

Rhodie held up her thimble. "Guess I'll never be one."

Bertha took it from her hand. "Rubbish. A clear case of mistaken identity. You must've cut in front of someone."

She grinned and glanced at her brother. "I did, actually. I jumped ahead of Mose."

Mose blushed and lowered his head. Bertha always suspected the boy was sweet on her, but likely no more than on every other girl he met.

"Hey, Bertha, whatever happened to that pretty necklace my brother gave you?" Rhodie blurted. "You know, the one that looked like woven metal straws?"

Mose blushed from the roots of his hair to his turned-down collar. He leaned to yank Rhodie's long red braid. "Dumb girl. I said not to mention it today."

Bertha's own face grew warm. Rhodie meant the filigreed cross. Since Mose found it and gave it to her, Bertha didn't know how he'd react to hearing that she'd given it to Annie. "I haven't seen it for quite some time." She asked God to forgive her if the vague answer was a lie by omission. She just couldn't bear to hurt Mose's feelings.

Bertha wanted the necklace back in the worst way. Not because Mose gave it to her, but as a remembrance of Annie. Thad helped her search for it after the funeral. It never showed up at Brooks House, and the coroner's office assured her it wasn't with Annie's body when they found her, a fact that broke Bertha's heart.

She had prayed every day that it would somehow turn up. Finally, she'd had to agree with Thad's opinion that Abe Monroe, who was in fact Abraham Rothschild, son of a wealthy Ohio jeweler, took the cross when he took Annie's diamonds.

Rhodie twisted around to gloat at Mose. "See, I told you. I knew it was Bertha's. I'd know that thing anywhere."

Bertha squeezed Thad's hand. "Rhodie, what are you talking about?"

Too busy winning her argument to heed Bertha's question, Rhodie put both hands on her hips and thrust out her chest. "You owe me a nickel, Moses Pharr."

Thad, who towered over Mose, took his arm and hauled him around. "What's your sister talking about?"

The boy looked up with frightened eyes then scowled at Rhodie. "Aw, she thinks she saw that worthless trinket I gave Bertha."

Thad gave him a little shake. "I got that part. When did she see it?"

Rhodie squeezed between Thad and Mose. "Yesterday," she provided. "I saw it yesterday."

Bertha's heart pounded so hard she heard it inside her ears. "Where, Rhodie?"

Mose eased free of Thad's grip. "She claims T-Bone Taylor's sister wore it to school on Friday."

Bertha met Thad's knowing glance. Beau and T-Bone Taylor. The little scoundrels who ran thieving raids along the banks of the Big Cypress. "Theresa Taylor has my cross?"

Rhodie snorted. "Sure does. She pranced around the classroom bragging to anybody who'd listen. Said her brothers found it." She cocked her head at Bertha. "You must've dropped it somewhere, huh? That's too bad. I guess it's finders keepers, just like when Mose gave it to you, right, Bertha? Because I'll tell you this: Theresa Taylor will never give that necklace back."

Bertha clutched Thad's arm. "We have to go find it."

He nodded. "Don't worry; we will."

"No, I mean now."

He blinked and glanced around at the guests. "We can't go just yet, sugar. We have to wait until the party's over."

She shook her head. "Theresa won't give us the necklace, but her brothers can get it. We have to find them, and it may take all afternoon to track those two down." She cast a desperate look around the room. "We have to do something, Thad. I won't rest until I know if it's mine."

"Don't forget, sugar, our train leaves Jefferson in about three hours."

She tried to put her feelings into the determined look she gave him. "I won't get on it until I find out."

He sighed his surrender and kissed the top of her head. "Wait here. I'll go fix it with your folks."

Thad crossed the room and took Papa aside. They huddled a few minutes before Papa motioned for Mama to join them. He spoke quietly to her; then they hurried over while Thad turned to his parents and Cyrus.

Bertha met Mama with a tearful hug. "Are you angry with me?"

"Of course not, dear."

"Papa?"

"Go do what you must, sprite. Just try to spare time for a proper good-bye before you leave."

"I will. I promise. Please pray our efforts pay off."

Magda linked arms with Bertha. "I'm coming along to help you find them."

Rhodie squealed. "Can we come, too?"

Bertha nodded. "I'd like you and Mose both to come, if you will. We need all the eyes we can get."

After she made her apologies and accepted another round of hearty congratulations, Bertha found herself seated next to Thad in her new father-in-law's phaeton buggy amid a shouting circle of well-wishers. Mose, Rhodie, and Magda sat behind them in Mose's wagon waiting for them to pull out.

Charles Gouldy shoved his way through and crowded close to the rig. "Hey, Thad! Wait up. Are you leaving so soon?"

Thad leaned to take his offered hand. "What are your plans for the next hour or so?"

Charlie shrugged. "You tell me."

Thad hooked his thumb. "Climb in back of Mose's rig. They'll fill you in."

On the way to the Taylors' tumbledown shack, Thad looked over his shoulder and frowned. "We would be there already on horseback."

"True, but I could hardly ride the back of your mare in this dress. And those four won't fit in the saddlebag."

He snorted. "I thought you wanted to find the Taylor boys. When we roll up there in a wagon train, they're sure to bolt."

She unpinned her wedding bonnet and folded it on the seat between them. "We'll find them. You can bet on that."

"I don't know, sugar. Those rascals are slippery as greased otters."

She peered up at him. "Maybe so, but I prayed."

Thad laughed. "They don't stand a chance, then. God knows where they are."

The wagons turned down the rutted road leading to the faded cypress hovel that housed Gladys Taylor and her three unruly offspring. Hardly more than an overgrown trail, the lane ran alongside the bayou all the way up to the property. Bertha scanned the water and spotted the boys' blue dinghy gliding up to the dilapidated pier in back. She nudged Thad and pointed just as they moored the boat and crawled ashore.

Even from a distance, their gangly arms and legs looked as brown as beans, probably from time spent near the water where the hot sun reflected off the surface, baking them twice. Dodging and sparring, they ran straight up the bank and into the barn without a glance toward the approaching wagons. Behind them, the little boat bobbed low on the surface of the water, likely filled to the brim with pilfered loot.

Giddy with excitement, Bertha clutched Thad's arm. "Park right here. We'll slip around and catch them in the barn."

Thad shook his head. "We'll knock at the front door, thank you. Slipping around anywhere on this place will get you a buckshot shower." He applied the tip of his whip to the horse's rear end, and the buggy sped toward the house with Mose hot on their tail. Thad rolled to a stop and bailed out, ran around to help Bertha, then ushered her up the crumbling walkway. The others got down off the wagon but waited at the foot of the path.

The door opened before they reached it. A disheveled Gladys Taylor met them on the porch with her shotgun, staring dumbly at Bertha in her wedding dress. "What madness is this?"

Thad positioned his body between the wild-eyed woman and Bertha.

She stayed put but peered around him to see.

He took off his hat. "Morning, ma'am. We don't mean to bother you. Just came by to see your boys for a minute."

Suspicion sparked in her faded blue eyes. "My boys?" Her voice came out cracked and shrill, sounding too old for her age. "What fer?"

Thad held up his hands. "Just to talk. We're hunting information about a necklace Theresa wore to school on Friday."

When her eyebrows drew together, Bertha nudged him in the ribs.

He glanced at her and changed his tactic. "We intend to offer a generous reward."

Gladys lowered the gun onto her hip. "A reward?" She seemed to chew on the word. "For the necklace or the information?"

Bertha brushed past Thad. "Mrs. Taylor, I understand the boys found a cross on a silver chain?" She cleared her throat. "I really need to see it. If it's the piece of jewelry we're looking for, it's not worth very much, except in sentimental value."

Thad put a protective arm around her shoulders. "Ma'am, I'll pay good money for a short talk with the boys. Or Theresa, for that matter."

Gladys seemed to mull it over then shook her head. "They ain't here. Ain't none of 'em here."

Bertha opened her mouth to protest, but Thad tugged on her sleeve. "How about you, ma'am? Do you know anything about a silver cross? Maybe you'd be interested in trading some information for a few dollars."

She raised her chin. "I don't get in my children's business or rifle through their personal things. We stay friends thata way."

Frustrated, Bertha bristled. "With all due respect, Mrs. Taylor, you'd do well to keep up with their things. Because most everything in their possession doesn't belong to them."

Thad hauled her back. "Bertha. . ."

A thundercloud formed on the woman's face. She opened her mouth ready to spew, but before she let fly her venomous rant, T-Bone and Beau rounded the house, still shoving each other and laughing. They saw Thad and Bertha at the same time and froze like startled deer. Then they spun, clinging to each other for balance, and shot out of sight.

"Get 'em, Mose!" Rhodie screamed.

Springing past them so fast his image blurred, Mose vaulted into motion. When he disappeared around the house, Thad took off after him, with Charlie and Gladys Taylor close behind. Bertha, Magda, and Rhodie followed as fast as their skirts would allow.

"No!" Gladys Taylor's bloodcurdling howl rocked the secluded cove. "Don't you hurt my boys!" Seconds ticked past, bogged in molasses, as she raised her shotgun at Thad's back.

Bertha, Magda, and Rhodie screamed and scuttled forward. Bertha lunged for the gun and shoved the exploding barrel to the sky. Rhodie and Magda piled on Gladys and wrestled the weapon from her hands. She sank to the ground, rolling and screaming like a banshee.

The two boys had reached the boat and were paddling furiously down the bayou. Mose shot alongside them on the bank, running full out, with Thad and Charlie on his heels.

"Please, God, don't let them get away," Bertha prayed aloud. "We'll never find them in those woods."

Rhodie, so excited her freckles stood out, gave her head a vigorous shake. "My brother won't lose them. Mose can track a gnat in a whirlwind."

Just as the skiff disappeared around a crook in the bayou, Mose dove, but Bertha didn't see if he landed in the boat or the water. With a burst of speed to the end of the bank and a gangly soar, Charlie followed him in. Thad, his long legs hurdling fallen logs and briar patches, tore around the bend on dry land.

"Let's go," Rhodie shouted. "They'll catch them at the low crossing."

Bertha glanced at the boys' hysterical mama and decided to return her shotgun later. She hurried after Magda and Rhodie, stashing the gun in the buggy's boot before she climbed aboard Mose's wagon.

Rhodie snapped the reins, and they took off faster than Bertha believed the tired old horse could run. They rumbled past a good stretch of piney woods before Rhodie cut over on a logging road toward the bayou. At the end of it, she reined in the horse, and the three of them jumped down without regard to modesty or decorum.

Rhodie pointed ahead of her as she ran. "Through here."

Bertha and Magda followed, though branches and prickly bushes tore at their clothes. Bertha wished she'd heeded wisdom instead of vanity when she decided to stay in her dress.

They broke onto a sandy clearing at the water's edge. Just as Rhodie predicted, the rascals were caught. Thad, still in his suit, sat on the ground holding little Beau in his lap. It took Mose and Charlie, both soaking wet, to pin T-Bone to the ground. The whelps howled like wounded hounds, kicking and beating at their captors with flailing hands and feet.

"Be still, now," Thad shouted. "We don't plan to hurt you none."

Bertha kneeled on the ground next to the oldest boy and touched his arm. "T-Bone, listen to me. We just want to ask you some questions. You have my word we won't harm you or your brother." She tried to soften her eyes to a plea.

He stilled and stared back at her, his frantic gaze roaming her upswept hair and fancy dress.

Thad nodded at Mose and Charlie. "Let him go."

They pulled away from T-Bone and he sat up, scooting to rest his back against a sapling. His tongue flicked nervously over his lips as he glanced at his brother. Thad let go of Beau, who scurried on his backside like a crab to press against his brother.

Bertha crawled closer to the two frightened boys. "Rhodie saw a cross necklace that you found and gave to your sister. Do you know the one I mean?"

The question stirred visible fear to the surface. T-Bone shot Beau a warning look then stared at the ground. "We ain't gave Theresa no necklace."

"Did, too," Rhodie cried.

Bertha held up her hand to silence her. "Boys, listen to me. It's very important that you tell me where you found it."

T-Bone shook his head. "Sorry, ma'am. Don't know what you're yapping about."

Thad stooped down beside Bertha. "I'm real sorry you boys don't trust us. We could've kept you out of a heap of trouble, what with Sheriff Bagby so interested in talking to you two about that missing gold jewelry."

Beau squirmed around to look at Thad. "Gold jewelry? That's a crock. We just had one necklace, and ours was silver."

His brother whirled on him. "Pipe down, you stupid little toad." Unable to contain his fury, he took him by the throat and wrestled him to the ground.

Charlie grinned. "Nice work, Thad."

Thad lifted T-Bone by the back of his drawers and set him down hard. "I'm done playing with you, son. Start talking."

Little Beau sat up crying, his nose red and running. "We didn't kill that lady. We just wanted to have a look. Ain't never seen no dead body before. Anyway, *she* was in *our* secret hideout." An angry look came over his face. "She didn't have no business there in the first place."

Bertha pressed her hands over her mouth to stifle a sob.

T-Bone scowled but didn't go after his brother again.

Thad rested his hand on T-Bone's shoulder and spoke in a gentle voice. "We know you didn't kill her. Shoot, everybody in Jefferson knows who did. So why don't you just tell us what happened."

T-Bone's tough demeanor crumbled, and he became a scared little boy. "We didn't mean no harm. We saw her laying in the woods and ran over to help. I bent down to shake her, thinking to wake her up. That's when I saw blood on her head." He ducked his head and ground his fists in his eyes.

Thad squeezed his shoulder. "Just take your time, son."

The boy lifted his trembling chin. "I wanted to leave." He gave his little brother a careful glance. "But Beau remembered seeing that same woman in town. He said folks called her Diamond Bessie on account of all the diamonds she wore."

Beau glared at T-Bone, his eyes like a feral cat's, but T-Bone kept talking. "Beau started searching all over her fingers and ears."

Beau stood up. "Did not!"

T-Bone pushed him down and crawled over him with balled-up fists. "Yes, you did." He faced Thad again. "I swear I never touched her after that first time." He shuddered. "I couldn't."

Thad seemed to weigh T-Bone's words for several seconds before he leaned over his brother's head. "I want the truth, Beau. Lying is a useless talent. When the truth comes out, and it always does, folks tend never to trust you again." He touched the little boy's arm. "A man's word is his most valuable possession, Beau. Didn't your daddy teach you that?"

Bertha elbowed Thad, but it was too late.

T-Bone spoke up behind them. "We ain't got no daddy. Never have."

Thad mouthed an apology to Bertha. Scooting closer to Beau, he set him up. "What do you say, partner? You ready to tell us the truth now?"

Beau gulped hard. The shadows under his hollow, darting eyes made him seem eighty instead of eight. "T-Bone's right. I done it. I figured since she was dead, her diamonds would do us more good than her. Only there weren't no diamonds. I looked all over. Just when I gave up looking, I seen that silver chain. I pulled on it and that purty cross fell out." He got up on his knees in front of Thad. "I never would've took it, but I looked down and the clasp was right in my hands. So I undid the hook and it slid right off her neck."

Bertha shoved past Thad and yanked Beau toward her. "Did you say off her neck? Not from her pocket? Or out of her hand?"

Her intensity scared the boy, and he screwed up his face. "No, ma'am. It was around her neck."

She shook him. "You're sure?"

He started to wail. "I swear it!"

The minister's words from the funeral were emblazoned in her mind. " '*He which converteth the sinner from the error of his way shall save a soul from death, and shall hide a multitude of sins.*' "

Bertha crushed him to her and kissed the top of his tousled head. "Beau, you wonderful little boy. Thank you!" She lifted her face. "Dear Lord, thank You." When she released him, Beau scuttled back to his brother, staring at Bertha like she'd lost her senses.

Magda rushed over and fell beside her. They toppled in a heap, laughing and crying at the same time. Charlie, Mose, and Rhodie stood gaping at them on one side; Thad, Beau, and T-Bone on the other.

Bertha struggled to her feet and ran to Thad, burrowing into his chest. "I'll explain later. Right now I need to get my hands on that silver cross."

Thad twisted around so both of them faced the boys. "I give

you my word of honor no one here today will ever mention what we know. But that necklace belongs to my wife, and I want it back."

T-Bone's Adam's apple rose and fell. "We'll go fetch it."

"I'll go with them," Mose offered. "Make sure there ain't no funny business."

Thad pulled Beau in front of him and patted him on the chest. "I don't expect any more funny business out of these fine lads, but go ahead and ride with them if you like. We'll meet you in front of their house."

Mose motioned to Charlie. He shook his head. "What about that shotgun?"

Bertha grinned. "Don't worry—I took care of the gun. We can send it to her later, after she calms down."

Mose and Charlie herded the boys toward the boat. On the way, Charlie slipped his arm around T-Bone's scrawny shoulders. "Say, I'm in the market for a new fishing partner. You boys like to fish?"

T-Bone shrugged. Little Beau peered up at him from the other side. "Shucks, yeah. You know any good spots?"

Charlie rested his other arm around Beau's neck. "Good spots? Why, I know the best honey holes in East Texas."

Charlie's offer to teach them the words to "Old Dan Tucker" was the last thing Bertha heard before they piled in the boat and pushed off toward Gladys Taylor's place.

Bertha, Thad, and the rest climbed aboard Mose's wagon with Thad at the reins. On the way, Bertha explained the significance of Annie wearing the necklace.

Rhodie, her mouth ajar, leaned between them, listening. When Bertha finished, Rhodie gazed up at her. "You're right, Bertha. If Annie felt unworthy to wear the cross, something happened to change that or she wouldn't dare put it on."

Thad smiled over at Bertha. "Only one thing can make that kind of change. So you know what that means."

Bertha thrilled at the confirming words. "It means Annie heard me. She died at peace with God."

Magda scooted beside Rhodie and looked up at Bertha. "I do have one question. You told me Annie was drunk that last morning in Kate Woods's restaurant."

"Yes," Bertha said. "I thought about that, too. Only Frank Malloy told Papa that Abe plied Annie with drink. Perhaps she didn't want it but was too scared to refuse. I mean, how could she explain what happened to her to someone like Abe?"

Magda inhaled sharply. "That makes sense. D. P. McMullen saw them, too, on Austin Street headed for the bridge. He said Annie handed her bottle to Abe, made him take it from her. I don't think she wanted it."

Up ahead, Mose, Charlie, and the Taylor boys stood on the road in front of the house. Thad pulled up beside them and set the brake.

Mose approached the wagon and held up a flash of silver. "Here it is, Bertha. I think it's the same one I gave you."

Thad took the chain out of Mose's hand and offered it to Bertha. When she cupped the delicate cross in her palm, she remembered the words she'd shared with Annie.

"The gift this cross represents is more powerful than any laundry list of sins you may be guilty of, no matter how heinous. The cross covered them all. You just have to accept it for yourself in order to be free."

Sometime after the last time Bertha saw her, Annie Moore came to believe those words. The woman who rode into their lives a misguided sinner left the world a beloved saint. Bertha had trusted God with the details—of her life and of Annie's—and just like Papa said, God had proved Himself worthy.

Thad wrapped her in his arms and pulled her close. "We have a train to catch, Mrs. Bloom."

She smiled at him through happy tears. "And adventures to chase, if I know you."

Grinning, he leaned to whisper in a breathy voice, "And a honeymoon to get started. . .if that's all right."

On a mission to mop the confident grin from Thad's face and light a fire in his dark eyes, Bertha had set out to learn the secret of

Annie's sway over men. Gazing into his face, aglow with love for her, she realized she'd had the power within her from the start.

She tilted her chin and gave her husband a saucy wink. "Me darlin', I thought you'd never ask."

Dear Reader:

This story is woven around the actual murder of Annie Stone, aka Bessie Monroe, aka Diamond Bessie, on January 21, 1877, in Jefferson, Texas. The ill-fated Diamond Bessie left a mark so deep during her brief visit that she's still a household name in Jefferson today. I chose to call her Annie in the book, because I believe if not for one early, impetuous mistake, she'd never have needed these aliases or the others I didn't mention.

I researched for months to learn why Annie made such an indelible impression on the town. From the considerable distance of 130-plus years, I found it impossible to get an accurate look at her. Even the opinions and attitudes of her day were conflicting. Some judged her a disease-ridden prostitute without morals or conscience. Others considered her an unfortunate young girl who lost her way. Jilted and abandoned by an older man at fifteen, possibly disinherited by her family and left to her own devices, (emphasis on vices) then abused and victimized by Abraham Rothschild, she unquestionably had a rocky start.

As I stood over her humble grave in Oakwood Cemetery, I found myself in the same dilemma as Bertha Maye Biddie, the heroine of this book, who asks, "Devil or angel? I couldn't tell." I feel certain of one thing, however. From Annie's vantage point, whether resting with angels or contending with devils, she would heartily approve of using her life to share my witness.

In my cast of characters, many—too numerous to list here—were actual denizens of 1877 Jefferson and key players in the drama that unfolded before, during, and after the murder of Annie Stone. Their names are still bandied about the streets of Jefferson, especially during the annual play, *The Diamond Bessie Murder Trial*, a reenactment.

Despite the notoriety Sarah King gained from finding Annie's body, I found no further information on her, even after searching the library and the courthouse records and speaking with local historians. With apologies to her descendants, I've used creative license in writing her story.

On December 30, 1880, after three indictments and two trials, Abraham Rothschild was pronounced not guilty. He boarded the train out of Jefferson, some say for the last time. Others believe he returned at least once. According to the caretaker of Oakwood Cemetery, a handsome elderly gentleman came asking the whereabouts of Annie's grave in the 1890s. He laid a wreath of roses near her headstone then knelt and said a prayer.

In his book *The Abe Rothschild Story*, historian Fred McKenzie includes a marriage license he uncovered in Vermillion County, Illinois, showing that twenty-four-year-old Abe Rothschild married twenty-two-year-old Bertha Moore on January 10, 1877, a few days before Abe and Annie began their journey from Cincinnati to Jefferson. According to Mr. McKenzie's research, Abe went on to become a "con man, flim flam artist, and snake oil salesman" as well as "a diamond thief of the first water."

Blessings,
Marcia Gruver

Discussion Questions

1. Annie Monroe glided off the train in Jefferson, Texas, looking like no one Bertha Biddie had ever seen before. How would you react if you met such a woman in your hometown? How do you think most people would react to a woman living a lifestyle like Annie's?
2. What should we as Christians do when we encounter people in situations that are in stark opposition to what the Bible teaches? What did Jesus do when he encountered the woman who was about to be stoned for adultery?
3. How can you become more aware of those around you who are dealing with serious problems? Do you seek out those who are hurting because of their life choices, or do you ignore them? Why?
4. What do you think was the turning point in the relationship between Bertha and her mama? How was it different from that of Bertha and her papa?
5. Where did Thad go wrong in his dealings with his papa?
6. Sarah experienced various forms of loss throughout the story. How did this affect her relationship with Henry? With God?
7. In what ways are Bertha and Sarah alike? In what ways are they different?
8. Although Bertha loved Thad, she stood him up to go help Annie. Why do you think she did this? Was her concern for Annie greater than her love for Thad?
9. Are we to obey God—even when it costs us something?
10. Bertha found Annie's confession difficult to hear, yet she held her ground, more determined than ever to help her. Annie's list of sins might have caused a different person to deem her a lost cause. Does God make throwaway people?

Texas Fortunes *Book No. 2*

Marcia Gruver

Dedication

To my daughter Tracy, my inspiration and my noblest creative endeavor.

Acknowledgments

To Mr. Lee Allen Gruver and Mr. Jerry Lee Ritter for your patience, your unwavering faith, and the generous loan of your names.

To Eileen Key, who nursed this manuscript in its infancy, and Elizabeth Ludwig, who held its hand and brought it home.

To the ladies in the Humble Museum and the Octavia Fields Branch Library in Humble, Texas, for answering my endless questions.

CHAPTER 1

Humble, Texas
January 1905

A plaintive cry of *purty, purty, purty* sounded from the treetops overhead. Charity Bloom glanced up and frowned. The redbird's compliment once caused her to flush with pleasure. Now it just made her mad.

Hush, deceitful scoundrel! I don't believe you anymore. Pretty was the last thing she felt and might never feel again.

Without the sun to warm her, the threadbare fabric of Charity's dress did little to prevent the north wind from biting at her back. Only sparse, mottled beams of light fought through the canopy of pine, so the trail into town hoarded the morning chill. She pulled her shawl closer and told herself the cold was the reason for her shivers. Relieved, she reached the trailhead and took her first grateful steps into the light.

The rapscallion cardinal hopped to a lower branch and made one last attempt to convince her before she moved out of range. She ignored him and pushed his song from her mind.

It wasn't long before another voice took its place. "It's too soon, daughter," Mama had cautioned. "You'll wind up lashed to the spit and roasted. Fresh scandal's scarce around these parts. Them spiteful cats are bound to gnaw on yours 'til the hide's wore off. Folks feast on others' misery."

Charity forced the words and the shame they conjured to a dark corner and covered them with righteous determination. Humble, Texas, was home, and they wouldn't drive her away. After all, she'd done no wrong–unless love and misplaced trust were sins.

She defiantly lifted her chin, only to lower it again and sigh as Main Street came into view. Humble was indeed her home, but the landscape had changed so much over the last week she hardly knew it. Scowling, she gazed eastward to Moonshine Hill with its towering oil derrick, the culprit to blame. Strange how the unrest in Humble rivaled the recent upheaval in her life. Otherwise unrelated, both events had landed in her lap with the force of a runaway train.

Reflected sun from a row of tin roofs across the way stabbed at her eyes. She shielded them with her hand then ducked into a strip of shade along the front of the dry goods store and headed for the Lone Star Hotel. Where the crowd became as thick as Mama's grits, she raised her elbows, steeled her resolve, and surged into the multitude.

Hordes of tents spread in an ever-widening circle from the heart of town, their occupants swarming like insects. The mingled voices, all shouting to be heard, made a deafening din, and Charity resisted the urge to hold her ears until she passed. Scores of men, women, and children spilled onto the street in droves, making it hard to gain any progress. She tried to stay head-down, mind on her business, but before long the meddlesome stares and huddles of pointing, whispering people weakened her resolve along with her knees. Mama was right. She was a hardheaded girl on a foolhardy mission.

"Hush now. Here she comes."

The words filtered back from just ahead on the boardwalk. Charity glanced up in time to see Elsa Pike bury a bony elbow in her daughter's ribs. The women strolled ahead of her, Mrs. Pike tall and thin next to the decidedly round Amy Jane. The pair put Charity in mind of the number ten. Taken together, they were ten times the trouble no matter how she ciphered.

They slowed their pace and waited while Charity caught up. Why hadn't she listened to Mama?

Mrs. Pike turned with a smile as sweet as caramel corn. "Hello, Charity. What a shock to see you in town. Feeling better so soon?" Amy Jane wore a sugary smile, too—as if seconds ago they weren't crouched, feeding on her misfortune.

She fought the urge to turn tail and run but braced herself and met them head-on. "I'm feeling fine, ma'am. Thank you for asking."

Mrs. Pike took Charity's hand in her long, gloved talons. "I want you to know how awfully bad we feel for you, dear."

Charity eased her hand free. "There's no need."

Mrs. Pike clucked her tongue then lowered her voice to a whisper. "Your poor mama. I hear she took in boarders to buy material for your wedding gown."

"And what an exquisite dress!" Amy Jane added, her voice too loud. "All that fandangle and fancywork. Your mama really outdid herself."

Charity cringed. A picture swam into her mind of Mama hunched in a circle of lantern light drawing a needle through tiny sequins with work-weary hands. More than once Charity found her asleep the next morning, her face pressed to the hard kitchen table.

She could manage disgrace and every indignity heaped upon her, but the memory of Mama's fingers, blistered for naught, dealt her shame. She lowered her head. "Yes, she worked powerful hard on it."

"You looked lovely in it, too, dear, with your hair swept up, black as pitch against all that lace." Mrs. Pike wagged a bony finger in Charity's face as if she were the culprit. "Your young man should hang his head for all the trouble he's caused."

"He's not my young man." Her correction came out a whisper neither woman seemed to hear.

A brisk wind had picked up, a low moan at first and then a howl through the center of town. It whistled under the boardwalk and gusted around them, plucking at Mrs. Pike's tall, jaunty hat and Amy Jane's balloon sleeves, frills she knew Mr. Pike could ill afford.

Charity held a tender spot for Shamus Pike, her departed papa's oldest friend. How many hours of backbreaking labor had it cost the poor man to provide his two peacocks their gaudy feathers?

Mama Peacock seemed in need of extra wings as she struggled to hold her bonnet while protecting her modesty and that of her daughter from the blustery wind. "But then, men never think of such things," she said from under the flapping brim. "I'm sure Daniel never gave a thought to your mama's sacrifice."

Amy Jane stepped closer and licked her lips, eyes wide in her round, freckled face. "About the dress. . .will you be selling it? I would dearly love to have it."

Mrs. Pike whirled on the girl. "Amy Jane! How utterly crass."

"What, Mother? I didn't leave Charity at the altar. I'm sure she has no use for it now."

The wind stopped as quickly as it had come, leaving behind a palpable hush.

Charity looked over their shoulders, past the low row of buildings, to the backdrop of tall Texas pine, longing to be at home in her room.

"What on earth would you do with Charity's dress?" Mrs. Pike asked.

"Wear it, silly. Did you forget I'm getting married in three months' time?"

"It won't fit you, dear. You're quite a bit larger than she is, you know."

Charity's head jerked up at this. *Poor Amy.*

Amy Jane looked indignant. "I've starved myself, or haven't you noticed? I'll be much smaller by then. And Mrs. Bloom could let it out for me." She glanced at Charity. "Couldn't she?"

Mrs. Pike shook her head. "Amy Jane, there's not enough material on that tiny dress to cover your backside, never mind the rest of you."

Charity fought the smile tugging at her lips as she watched them spit and spar, her presence forgotten. Amused, she slipped past and continued on her way. She felt a mite guilty for walking off without saying good-bye but had no stomach for the direction the conversation had taken. Besides, a peek over her shoulder at their waving arms and lively faces told her they hadn't noticed she'd gone.

"Charity Bloom! Wait right there, sugar."

Charity groaned. She didn't have to glance to see who'd

shouted, didn't need a look to know who charged her way. *Serves me right for having a laugh at Amy Jane's expense.*

It wasn't that she minded seeing Magdalena Dane. In fact, she loved Mama's old friend. She just didn't relish an encounter with her in the middle of town.

Mother Dane lifted the hem of her stylish blue dress and sashayed into the street, to the delight of the locals gathering behind her. Oblivious to them, she picked her way across the ruts and bore down on Charity. When she reached the boardwalk and stepped up, Charity attempted to speak, but the older woman pulled her so tightly against her ample, satin-covered bosom that just to breathe was enough. "My spunky girl!" Mother Dane cried. "Imagine that, you coming out so soon. Are you all right, precious?"

"I'm fine," she said, her words muffled by yards of cloth and copious flesh. "At least I will be when you turn me loose."

Mercifully, Mother Dane eased her grip and stepped back. "Don't put on a brave front for me. Go ahead and cry if you like. You have every reason to." Her anguished eyes searched Charity's face. "I haven't called on you, dear. Please forgive me. I didn't know what to say."

Charity reached for her hand. "I understand, I really do, but Mama laid out her deck of cards on Monday."

"She did?" Mother Dane's eyes grew wide and wet. The prying cluster of busybodies across the way mumbled and shuffled when she pulled a lace handkerchief from her bodice. "Dear, sweet Bertha. I thought she wouldn't ever want to see me again, much less play cards."

"Mother Dane, you know Mama better than that. She wouldn't cast off a friendship of thirty years' standing over something like this." She winked. "Much less a game of penny candy poker."

"Stop it, now! Honey, how can you jest? I've been distraught. Grievously vexed. How's your mama taking it?" She fanned herself with her hankie. "Bertha's my touchstone. I don't know what I'd do without her."

"Yes, ma'am, she knows that. You're hers as well." *And a more unlikely pair there never was.*

"She's been on my mind every second. You both have. If there's anything I can do, anything at all. . ."

"Goodness, no, you've done enough. Sending Nash out to the house with her wages was far too generous."

The truth was, Mama nearly split a gut when Mother Dane's hired man turned up with a fistful of money for the days she'd missed, but there was no need to mention that now. "Mama plans to work off every penny, but I'm ever so grateful. Having her home the last few days has meant the world to me."

"Of course it has." Mother Dane enveloped her again. "I shrink in my boots to think my own daughter caused you such pain—and after all you've meant to each other. She always was selfish and headstrong. But you already know that, don't you?" She moved Charity to arm's length and peered at her again. "Was there any warning? Any sign Emmy and Daniel might do such a thing?"

The question brought fresh the memory Charity had struggled for days to forget. In that instant she stood again at the altar of Free Grace Church, clothed in yards of sequined lace, while Daniel Clark walked away from her.

She watched again as Emmy's lovely silhouette stepped into the aisle, took two deep breaths, and ran—not toward Charity as she expected, but out the door on Daniel's heels. That was when she knew. Given the collective gasp from the assembled guests, they knew it, too.

Her cheeks flamed at the memory, and she cast an embarrassed glance across the street.

"Emily has disgraced our family in the past, that's for sure, yet no more than we expected," Mother Dane was saying. "But this! Leave it to my Emmy to be in the right place at the right time. She always was an opportunist."

The harsh words tugged at Charity's heart. "Maybe we should give her a chance to explain."

"Don't." Mother Dane held up her satin-gloved hand. "Don't you defend her, dear. Not after what she's done. Lord knows I love my daughter, but let's be frank. She'd not extend you the same courtesy."

Charity hesitated then had to nod.

"Besides, how can she explain when she's not talking? She's holed up in her room and won't let me in. Mind you, she doesn't have a thing to tell that I don't already know. All of Humble knows her guilty little secret."

Charity shook her head, not ready to accept what the words implied. "Whatever happened, I refuse to believe she meant to do me harm."

Pain flashed in Mother Dane's eyes. "I'm afraid the days for pretense are past, dear. We know Emmy's heart best, you and I. She may be confection on the outside; inside she's a festering sore."

For the second time that morning Charity longed to cover her ears. "Please don't."

Mother Dane lifted Charity's chin with her knuckle and gazed into her eyes. "It's true, though it hurts me to say it. I prayed she might be more like you, wished with all my heart you might influence her with your goodness." She shrugged, her countenance the picture of despair. "I guess it wasn't to be. I fear my only child is bound to deal me heartache."

Charity drew the teary-eyed woman into an embrace. Over a padded blue shoulder she noticed that the interest of the locals had drawn a crowd. Now a collection of curious strangers stood alongside her friends and neighbors, and Charity grew warm under their scrutiny. She fished a handkerchief from her skirt pocket and dabbed her friend's cheeks. "There now, you just brighten up some. Emmy will be fine. You'll see."

Mother Dane drew herself up and managed a shaky smile. "There you go fretting about me in the midst of your own suffering." She squeezed Charity's hand. "You're a good girl, Charity Bloom."

Charity summoned a wry smile. "If that's so, then I need to finish my errands and get home before Mama starts to worry."

"All right, darling. You run along. Do give Bertha my love."

"I will."

"And, sugar?"

Charity sighed and turned. She'd almost made good on her escape and wanted nothing more than to flee. "Yes, ma'am?"

"Before you go, may I offer one last word of encouragement?"

"Of course."

With eyes like thunderheads, Mother Dane cast a withering

glance at the gathered snoops. "Don't let these tongue-wags get at you. They're spewing nonsense. This was all Emmy's fault. . .and Daniel's. It had nothing to do with your mama."

"Mama?" Charity closed the distance between them. "What are they saying?"

Mother Dane's chin shot up. "Never you mind. That highfalutin Eunice Clark may consider her son too good for you, but Daniel's cut from different cloth. I don't believe for a minute he feels the same."

Charity's heart sank, because she knew the truth of it. The cloth Daniel was cut from didn't fall far from his mama's bolt. Though smitten with her, Daniel had been troubled that his fiancée was the daughter of a widowed servant. It didn't help that folks believed Mama to be mad as a hatter.

"What Daniel feels doesn't concern me anymore," Charity said with a lift of one shoulder. "It's over. There's no use trying to make sense of it now. I just want it behind me if this town will allow it."

Thankfully, Mother Dane's gaze held compassion, not pity. "Are you so certain it's over, dear? Daniel could have a change of heart."

Charity's spine stiffened. "But I won't."

Tears snuffed the flicker of hope in Mother Dane's brown eyes. "It's such a tragedy, then. Daniel was a good match for you, honey. All we might've hoped for. He could've given you so much."

"Hush, now," Charity soothed. "Don't worry about me for another minute. I'll be fine."

Mother Dane wiped her eyes. "Yes, you will. You're Bertha Bloom's daughter, aren't you?"

She squared her shoulders. "I am, and glad of it. Speaking of Mama, give me a kiss and let me be on my way. I left her elbow-deep in chores."

"Now there's a dear girl. Tell Bertha to take a few more days off and to look for me come Monday. Tell her to lay out those poker cards again. I got my hands on some candy corn."

Charity smiled. "You won't make it home with any, you know."

Mother Dane sniffed. "That remains to be seen. You just tell her, you hear?"

"Yes, ma'am."

She wagged her finger. "Don't forget."

"No, ma'am, I won't."

Charity moved away, painfully aware that those around her were reluctant to disperse. She wasn't sure what they'd hoped to witness between Emmy's mama and herself, but they seemed sorely disappointed by what they saw. Charity wanted only to finish her business and get home, so she quickened her pace and headed for the first of the only two stops on her list she still planned to make. The rest of her errands could wait for a better day—sometime next year perhaps.

Stubby Morgan had taken to fetching her mail from the commissary post office at Bender's Mill. Then he left it with Sam, the hotel clerk, saving Charity a trip out to the mill. Rumor had it that Stubby went to the trouble because he was sweet on her. She didn't think it so.

Inside the new hotel, she crossed the lobby, raising an eyebrow in greeting as she passed the huge portrait of Pleasant S. Humble, the town founder. Uncle Plez, as he was known by the locals, stared down at her from his place of honor, and she would have sworn she saw one bushy brow twitch.

Sam had the mail in his hands before she reached the front desk.

Charity thanked him and stepped aside to sort it. She tried not to think about Daniel, but his face and Emmy's, too, swam in her head, making it impossible to concentrate on the letters. What they'd done was sure to hurt later. Right now she felt only anger. Which influence had Daniel finally given in to—his mama's constant braying about marrying beneath himself or Emmy's pale ringlets and haunting blue eyes?

Hang Daniel. . .and Emmy, too. They deserve each other.

"Excuse me. . ."

Charity jumped so violently she nearly took leave of her shoes, and the stack of mail flew in every direction. She whirled to find a stranger in a wide-brimmed hat beaming down from a considerable height. She pressed her empty hands to her heart. "Goodness me! You startled me out of my wits."

"I sure did, didn't I? Such a start this early in the morning can't be good for a body."

Charity struggled to settle her pounding heart. "Sir, I'm now qualified to assure you it isn't." She gazed around at the letters and mail-order catalogs scattered over the lobby then scowled up at the man.

He stepped closer and tipped his hat. "Please forgive me, ma'am."

They were the proper words and gestures, all right, but Charity reckoned he'd seem more contrite if he could straighten his grinning face.

CHAPTER 2

The handsome young man laid aside his overstuffed bag and bent to retrieve Charity's mail. He was tall and lean-muscled, the padded shoulders of his brown jacket making him seem as broad as Shamus Pike's bull. His long legs sported slim trousers, full at the top and held up by blue suspenders. Fawn-colored hair, longer than she was used to seeing, curled out from under his hat, and except for a scruffy shadow, he had no facial hair. Even inside the dimly lit hotel, she could see that his eyes were green like hers and Mama's.

Watching him bob for letters like a child on an Easter hunt, she ducked her head to smile then laughed in spite of herself. He heard and glanced up, so she leaned to help, grateful for something to do until the heat cooled in her cheeks.

When they stood up together, he still beamed like a roguish boy. Feeling silly about catching his infectious grin, she sobered and cast him a guarded look. "Have you just arrived in town, sir?"

He took off his broad, stiff-brimmed hat and held it to his chest. "Yes, ma'am, I have. Name's Buddy Pierce."

She offered her hand. "Welcome to Humble, Mr. Pierce."

His work-roughened fingers enveloped hers. "Little lady, I won't mind a bit if you call me Buddy. In fact, I'd prefer it."

Charity paused to consider. His earnest face and clear-eyed stare seemed honest, genuine, and not a bit forward. "Very well. Buddy it is. Isn't that a sobriquet?"

He released her hand. "Beg your pardon?"

"Buddy's a nickname, am I right? What's the name your mama gave you?"

He managed to frown and smile at the same time. "Never you mind about that."

She wrinkled her nose. "It's that bad, is it? Well then, welcome to Humble, *Buddy*. I'm Charity. Charity Bloom."

"I know who you are." He hooked a thumb in Sam's direction. "The clerk told me all about you."

"He did?" She shot a look at Sam, her cheeks warming again. Surely he didn't mean. . .

The little man behind the desk watched her over the top of his glasses while pretending to write in his register. Watched *over* her might be closer to the truth. Since Papa died, Sam had made a habit of keeping an eye on her and even more diligently since strangers took possession of their streets.

"Charity's an unusual name, if you don't mind my saying. Real nice, though."

His deep, rumbling voice pulled her attention to the stranger's face—and such a nice face. When had he moved so much closer?

She took a tiny step back. "Thank you. It's from the Bible."

"Is that a fact? Let's see, how does it go? 'Charity suffereth long, and is kind.' Does that describe you, Miss Bloom?"

She met his mischievous eyes and raised her brow. "Not on most days, if I'm to be honest."

His smile revealed deep dimples. "Well, Charity-from-the-Bible, I'm about to test the measure of your kindness. It seems the procurator of this fine establishment can't accommodate me, so he suggested I speak with you. Is it true your mama lets rooms on occasion?"

So that's all Sam told him.

Relieved, she took the mail from his hands and added it to her pile. "That all depends, Mr. Pierce. Have you come to Humble chasing oil?"

He cocked his head to one side, his grin widening. "What makes you ask?"

She waited to see if he was joking. He wasn't.

"Mister, throw ten stones in the air and nine will land on some money-hungry dreamer come to get rich."

He nodded and motioned toward the street. "And all those people are here because of the strike."

It was a statement, not a question, but she answered anyway. "Most everyone you see, except for the locals kept here by stubbornness or greed."

Buddy laughed, and she liked the sound of it. "Do you fall into one of those categories?"

His directness put her off balance. As casually as possible, Charity faced a nearby desk and busied herself straightening the letters so they'd fit in her drawstring bag. They were all tucked inside before she glanced over her shoulder and answered him. "I failed to mention the rest—those too poor to get out." She shrugged. "Besides, where would I go? I've lived here all my life."

She scolded herself for such boldness with a stranger. What was there about the friendly cowboy that made her tongue clatter like a snake's rattle?

He worked an envelope from under the counter with the toe of his boot, picked it up, and placed it on her stack. "To answer your question, Miss Bloom, it seems you've got me pegged. I have to say yes, I've come here looking for oil." He held up one finger. "But if it hurts my chances for a room, I'll deny ever saying it." He wriggled his brows and grinned. "I could use a hot bath and a meal."

"My goodness, of course you could. Listen to me groaning about the boom when that's what brought you to town. Not to mention holding you here with a hollow stomach and no place to lay your head. I hope you'll forgive my rudeness."

"Nothing to forgive. Besides, I owe you after the fright I gave you."

"Yes, you do," she scolded then smiled up at him. "Have you traveled far?"

He lifted his chin. "All the way from St. Louis, Missouri."

Charity stopped fidgeting with the mail and gaped. "Where they held the World's Fair?"

"Ah! The Louisiana Purchase Exposition. Quite a show."

"You were there? How wonderful! My dearest friend—that is, a girl here in town—and her mama went. They came home filling our ears. I would love to see such a thing."

He cocked his head to one side. "Is that so? I got the notion you don't like crowds."

She rolled Mama's Sears catalog and shoved it into her bag. "It's not crowds I mind, Mr. Pierce. I just don't like tripping over people in my own backyard."

He laughed. "If I promise to steer clear of your feet, can you find room in your backyard for one more wayward soul?"

The man had positively no sense for the proper amount of space to allow between them, and somehow his nearness affected her breathing. She shifted her weight away from him then tilted her head to meet his hopeful gaze. "Truthfully, we're out of the boardinghouse business, but there's a chance I might be able to help. Mama will have the final say though." She gathered her courage and blurted her brazen offer. "I have one quick stop to make at the general store; then I'll be going home. Would you care to follow along and ask her?"

Buddy dropped his hat on his head and hitched up his bag. "Yes, ma'am, I surely would."

She held up her hand. "Just one more thing. I'm afraid Mama don't take kindly to oilmen. How are you at dodging rotten eggs?"

His eyes grew wide. "Not too good, I reckon. I make for a sizable target."

Charity laughed and made for the door. "Come on. You'll be safe with me."

In front of the general store, Buddy took one look through the window at the jostling mob and said he'd wait for her outside. She left him leaning beside a barrel of brooms, one booted foot braced against the wall.

Despite impatient moans and grumbles, the beaming clerk allowed Charity to slip to the front of the line with Mama's list. She felt bad about it at first then decided there should be some recompense to the locals for the loss of peace and quiet.

Outside, Charity motioned to Buddy, and he fell into step behind her. She moved deftly through the crowd but had to stop and wait for him a time or two when his large frame and overstuffed bag caused a jam on the teeming boardwalk. She stole a few discreet glances while she waited. Buddy Pierce happened to be easy on the eyes.

"Nice little town you have here," he shouted as he drew near.

"It used to be," she said and pushed ahead of him again.

He said something else Charity didn't hear, so she just smiled and shrugged her shoulders. While they passed in front of the noisy tents, they gave up any attempt at talking.

Buzzards circled above the towering wall of trees up ahead, and Charity wondered what lay dead or dying on the forest floor. So many harsh, greedy men had come to town she knew it could as likely be a man as an animal, though the thick trees and underbrush would not easily give up the information.

Farther out away from the tents it grew quieter, and Buddy tried again. "What changed?"

"Excuse me?"

He came alongside her. "You said it used to be nice. What changed?"

"Mr. D. R. Beatty hit himself a gusher." Her mouth twisted like she'd sucked a lemon. Less than pretty, no doubt, but she couldn't help it. The sound of that man's name boiled her insides. "The multitude flocked here like Humble was the Promised Land. You've never seen the like."

"And there went your town."

"Yes, there went my town. Now our sons and brothers rub shoulders with men who'd plant a knife in your middle for a fifteen-cent bottle of booze. Two-bit saloons and gambling houses built from spit and sawmill scrap sprang up overnight. Not to mention those *other* houses set on fleecing our men of their dignity as well as their hard-earned money."

She blushed but noticed he did, too. "Forgive my candor, Mr. Pierce, but Humble used to be peaceful, filled with simple, good-hearted folk. A perfect place to live"—she glanced up and their eyes met—"if you like that sort of thing. I suppose you prefer the excitement of the big city."

Buddy flashed his teeth and winked. "There's where you're wrong. I'm a country boy at heart."

She smiled back. "A country boy with a lust for treasure?"

"Lust? No, ma'am, not me. I wouldn't turn away a blessing, but the Good Book teaches not to lay up treasure here on earth."

"Oh, you read the scriptures?"

"I try to make it a habit."

"Well, it's a good habit to have. However, I must confess that now I'm confused. Back there you said you were here because of the oil. From what I hear, striking oil brings more than a blessing. It can make a man mighty rich."

He nodded. "True enough, but I'm just a working man earning my way. I'm here to represent another fellow. A wealthy operator out of Beaumont. It's men like him who wind up with all the money."

"I see." She wasn't sure why the information made her feel better about him. His affairs were certainly none of her business.

"I'll be heading up a crew of his men that are due into Humble today."

"Today? Won't they need a place to stay, too?"

He laughed. "They're smarter than me. They had the foresight to reserve rooms."

Just ahead, Charity's mama bolted through the yard onto the dirt road, juggling a white chicken. She tripped on the hem of her faded skirt but righted herself before she went down. Long strands of salt-and-pepper hair had worked free from her disheveled bun, streaming out behind her as she ran. Feathers dotted her head and clung to her glowing face, and she was missing a shoe. A dark substance covered both feet and soaked the hem of her skirt. The distressed chicken appeared to have been dipped to the drumsticks in tar.

"Charity," she called. "Come a'runnin', baby. The chickens are loose again."

"Blast those infernal coons," Charity said and then drew up her skirts and ran.

"Raccoons?" Buddy Pierce had come alongside, his bag bouncing against his legs as he loped. "I thought she said chickens."

"The coons have learned to break into the coops. . .after the feed. There's no lock that'll keep them out."

"Really? Clever creatures."

"Indeed. Trouble is, they lack the proper manners to close the door behind them when they leave."

Charity ran past her mama then stopped and looked back.

Mama stood staring up at Mr. Pierce, the escaped chickens forgotten. "Well now, who you got here, sugar?"

Mr. Pierce held out his hand but drew it back after a quick glance at Mama's black fingers. He nodded instead. "Buddy Pierce, ma'am."

She cocked her head. "Bertha Bloom. Nice to meet you, sonny."

Charity watched her take a long, slow reckoning of Mr. Pierce. She felt a sudden affinity with whatever unfortunate creature lay in the stand of pines watching the carrion birds circle overhead, drawing nearer with every pass. She braced herself for what was bound to come out of Mama's mouth.

"Where'd you turn up this one, Charity? He's a big 'un. Right pretty, too."

Charity groaned. It was worse than she'd expected. "Mama, behave. Allow me to apologize for her, Mr. Pierce. She's become quite bold, if not brazen, in her old age."

"And rightfully so," Mama said. "Contending with body parts that drape south and wayward facial hair gives me leave to be naughty on occasion. Don't you think so, Mr. Pierce?"

Buddy's mouth worked hard at stifling a grin. "I can see your point, and that's for sure, Mrs. Bloom."

Mama leaned in as close as the chicken and her short stature would allow and presented her top lip to Mr. Pierce. "Look here, I'm sporting a 'stache to rival Teddy Roosevelt's. Pert near as impressive as the first lady's." She threw back her head and cackled in concert with the chicken.

"Oh, Mama, you're just plain scandalous. Pay her no mind, Mr. Pierce, or she'll only get worse. And where on earth is your shoe, Mama? You'll catch your death."

Buddy Pierce was paying little attention now to her mama's tomfoolery. He had focused on the hen, his hands edging in its direction, as if eager to take hold of it. "Mrs. Bloom, if I could just have a closer look at that chicken. . ."

Mama sized him up with a glance then passed him the flustered hen. "Ain't you never seen a yard bird before?"

"One or two, but none as interesting as this one. Where did you say you caught it?"

"Back yonder." She gave a toss of her head toward the rear of their place. "In the bottom."

"The bottom of what?"

Charity interpreted for him. "Out back of our property, in the low spot."

Mama nodded. "Blasted piney-woods rooters got it all dug up out there."

"Rooters?"

"Hogs, mister. Wild hogs. You might be a pleasure to look at, but you sure don't know much."

"Mama!"

Mr. Pierce continued unperturbed. "Do you own this property, Mrs. Bloom?"

Mama propped her hands on her hips, pressing gooey impressions of her fingers onto her skirt. "Why, yes, I own it. My man, Thad—God rest him—held it free and clear before we ever married. This place has been mine for nigh on to twenty-eight years."

"Do you mind if I take a look?"

She frowned. "Ain't nothin' back there 'cept swamp water and Texas gumbo. Mud," she corrected for Buddy's benefit. "Black Texas mud." She pulled back her skirt and thrust out her bare foot as evidence, squeezing her toes together until thick sludge oozed from between them.

Mr. Pierce examined her foot and nodded. "If it's where you've been chasing this chicken, then I'd sure like to see it."

She shrugged, her bony shoulders pulling even with her ears. "Young man, I can't imagine what you find so interesting about a fool chicken and an old woman dim-witted enough to chase it through a bog, but suit yourself. Anyways, you can fetch out my shoe. Follow me."

CHAPTER 3

It took Buddy Pierce ten minutes flat to see what he wanted to see down in the bog. Then he'd taken off for town like a branded cat. He was back now, having hauled two flustered men with him. Charity heard them crashing through the yaupon thicket, shouting and laughing as if they'd taken leave of their senses.

Mama watched from the rickety stoop, hands on her hips, her head bobbing like a demented bird as she followed their movements through the brush.

Charity crossed the yard to the edge of the porch and gazed up at her. "Where's your bonnet?"

Mama groped the top of her head, her eyes still trained on the bushes. "Must be in the bog."

A riotous shout gave Charity a start and pulled her gaze back to the thicket. "What will happen, Mama?"

"Cain't say, baby. Too soon to tell."

"Mr. Pierce said we got oil back there."

"That's what he said, all right."

"How can that be?" Charity's voice took on an edge. "How could oil have been there all along, and we never knew?"

"Sometimes you cain't see what you ain't looking for." Mama turned startled eyes her way. "Hush now. Here they come."

Buddy strode through the cut ahead of the other two men. All three were covered in mud. Of the lot, it would be hard to say who wore the silliest grin. One of the men, every bit as tall as Buddy but gawky and rawboned, carried several bottles of the black muck, each sealed with a cork. When Charity glanced his way, his smile widened, and he nodded a greeting. Up close, despite being awkward and thin, he was every bit as handsome as Buddy, too.

"Mrs. Bloom, where's the deed to your property?" This from the stocky, dark-haired man who balanced an odd-looking instrument on his shoulder.

Mama looked him over. "Who's asking?"

Buddy stepped forward, still beaming, and gestured to his companion. "Mrs. Bloom, this here's Mr. Lee Allen." Then he pointed at the lanky young man. "That's Jerry Ritter. These are the gentlemen I told you about."

Mama nodded at each one in turn.

Mr. Allen advanced a step so he could rest his load on the rail. He gazed up at Mama with kind blue eyes. "Ma'am, just see to it your deed is safe. There are desperate and unscrupulous men in this town. You ladies living out here alone. . .well, I wouldn't want you taken advantage of, or worse."

Mama looked at Buddy. "Is that this feller's way of saying you got good news for me?"

Buddy preened. "We can't be certain yet, but it sure looks good. Ain't that right, Lee?"

Buddy's excitement rekindled the spark in Mr. Allen, spreading a broad smile over his weathered cheeks. He nodded at Buddy then at Mama. As quick as it came, the smile disappeared. "Mrs. Bloom, is there someplace in town you all could stay?"

Charity cut around Mr. Allen and his equipment to face him squarely. "Why can't we stay right here?"

"It's ain't safe, ma'am." He answered Charity's question, but his eyes searched her mama's face.

Mama regarded Buddy with a raised brow. "When I said you could look for oil on my land, you never said nothing about us leaving. Forget it. We ain't going." She snorted. "Besides, I got nothing to fear in my own home. The Winchester my man left me warrants that."

Buddy stepped forward. "There's another reason besides the

danger." He glanced at Charity, his eyes pleading for support she couldn't give. "Mrs. Bloom, you agreed that if I saw the need, you'd allow me to bring a crew onto your place. There'll be men and equipment scattered so thick you'll be tripping over them. It'd be best if you were out of the way."

"Out of the way?" Mama's eyes blazed. "This here's our home. We got nowhere else to go."

Mr. Allen smiled again, creasing the skin around his gentle eyes. "Chances are good you'll soon afford to live wherever you choose. For now I firmly suggest you stay with family or friends. A hotel, perhaps. You can arrange a more permanent solution later."

Mama jutted her chin at Buddy. "What about you? Where will you stay?"

"Don't worry about me, ma'am. My two friends here booked rooms at the hotel. I can bunk with one of them for a few days."

Charity swallowed hard. "What about our house?" Her voice rang shrill in her ears. "Our things?"

"Pack up what you need for now; then lock it up," Buddy said. "We'll try to keep an eye on the place for you. Later on, you'll have plenty of help with moving your belongings."

Charity couldn't speak. Speaking required an intake of air, but an elephant straddled her chest.

For the last two years, after speculators drilled the first well near Jordan Gully, crooks and shysters had sniffed around their land like hounds on a hunt. Mama had taken the broom to all of them. Charity watched her now, waiting for her reaction.

She won't be pushed around by these men.

"We'll need time to pack," Mama announced. "And a ride into town. I got no horse and buggy, and it's too far to carry our things."

Buddy nodded. "I'll see to it that you get settled, ma'am."

Charity shoved past the men and rushed onto the porch. "What are you saying, Mama? We can't leave home. Where will we go?"

Mama gently pushed her aside. "Come back for us in an hour, Mr. Pierce. We'll be ready."

Not since Papa died had Charity felt so lost. In fact, the way he left was easier to bear—there one day and gone the next—but in a manner she understood. Mama had disappeared standing right in front of her.

The men tipped their hats and made for the front yard. At the corner of the house, Buddy Pierce glanced back. A puckered brow had replaced his grin, and his questioning eyes stayed on her until he disappeared behind the house.

Charity reckoned his frown was a reaction to the look on her face. Just what did her expression reveal about the goings-on inside her? She wanted to call him back and ask. Lord knew she couldn't figure it out.

She should be happy. She and mama would be better off, maybe even rich like Mother Dane and Emmy. Like Daniel. Why did that make her feel so strange?

"Rangeland," Mama said behind her. The single word made no more sense than anything else she'd said that day.

The silence that followed stood like a wall between them. When Charity could take it no longer, she glanced over her shoulder. "What'd you say, Mama?"

The stubborn little woman stood shading her eyes with one hand, staring at the oak tree behind the house as if she'd never seen it before. "You asked me what would happen. I'm answering your question. We'll buy rangeland. Acres of it, and cover it with cattle. I always wanted to raise me some beef stock." She turned without waiting for an answer and went inside.

Charity crossed to the porch rail and gazed about, seeing the tall, paint-chipped dwelling and weed-strangled plot with new eyes. In the side yard stood a row of pens where Papa had sheltered prized bloodhounds. Except for slight weathering and the need for a coat of whitewash, the pens looked the same as they had when filled with braying dogs. She could almost see Papa bent over the long basins pouring out water for squirming red pups.

She was here on the porch that day, five years ago, when Mama stepped out the back door and told her Papa was gone. He'd been swept off his feet by the current while fishing near the banks of the San Jacinto River. Mama sold the bloodhounds soon after because she couldn't afford to feed them.

Tears sprang to Charity's eyes. She'd been born in this house, lived here all her days. Just like that, her mama had agreed to walk away from everything that held them together after Papa died.

The screen door opened behind her, and the squeal of the springs set her teeth on edge.

Mama stood grim-faced in the entry. "Come inside now. There's a mess of packing to do, and we're running short on time."

An urge came over her to refuse, to scream and run headlong into the woods. Instead, she lowered her gaze to the rotting boards beneath her. "Yes, ma'am. I'll be right along."

The door closed. Charity looked at her fingers, white from gripping the weathered rail. She fought to still her trembling lips then lifted her chin and went inside.

Rustling noises drifted down the hall from her mama's cluttered bedroom. Charity found her bent over a satchel, rummaging through her clothes. The dimly lit room smelled of the pressed and dried magnolia blossoms Mama kept in her dresser drawers, but the odor had never put Charity in mind of a funeral before now.

Arms buried elbow-deep in the bag, Mama twisted around to look at her. "No time to dawdle. They'll be back directly and expect us to be ready."

"But where are we going?"

"Where do you think?" Mama averted her eyes and went back to her task. "We got no one but Magda. She'll take us in."

Charity's heart leapfrogged. "For crying in a bucket! I can't go to Mother Dane's house. Not after Emmy. . ."

"You got a better idea, let's hear it. Magda would front me the money, but there ain't no rooms left in town. Remember, that's how Mr. Pierce came to be on our place." She stood upright, her hands filled with faded undergarments. "It's amazing how the good Lord works His will, daughter. If you hadn't brought Mr. Pierce around here, I would've run him off, just like I done all the rest."

Charity groaned. Why hadn't she left Buddy Pierce right where she'd found him? "And we wouldn't be forced out into the street. I can't go to Emmy Dane's house, Mama. I won't."

This brought Mama around to glare at her with burning eyes. "Yes, you can and you will. Magda's all we got in this town. There's no place else."

Charity put her fists on her hips and planted her feet. "Then I'm staying right here."

"You cain't, daughter. You heard them men. It ain't safe."

"I'll get Sam to stay here with me."

Mama cackled. "Don't talk foolish. Sam has a hotel to run." She bent back down to grope in her bag. "I ain't aiming to deal harsh with you, baby. It's just that some things I know best. So we'll have no more arguments out of you."

Charity's legs wouldn't hold her. She sank to the side of the rumpled cot and covered her face with her hands. "Why are you doing this?" The ragged words tore at her swelling throat.

"Are you crying, daughter?" Mama hurried over and plopped beside Charity on the bed, gathering her up in skinny arms. "Don't, baby. You'll have me blubbering." Mama rocked her, patting her hair and murmuring comfort until Charity finally sat up.

"I don't want things to change again, that's all."

Mama nodded. "You've had more'n your share of unwanted change, sugar. But this is a good thing. Cain't you see that? It's an answer to prayer."

Startled, Charity looked at her. "You prayed to get rich? That's against the Good Book."

Mama raised a brow at her rebuke. "No, daughter. It ain't a sin to have money. The sin is in loving what you have more than God who gave it." She settled back and crossed her arms. "A better life is what I prayed for. If the good Lord has chosen to send me the money to buy one, then by golly, I want it."

Charity wiped her nose with the back of her hand and nodded. "So you don't have to be Mother Dane's cook anymore."

Mama sat up straight and pushed Charity to arm's length, her eyes fierce with emotion. "No, child. So you won't wind up Emmy's."

Buddy left Lee Allen and Jerry Ritter standing on the boardwalk in front of the Lone Star Hotel. They had agreed to meet there for lunch as soon as Buddy secured a rig for transporting Mrs. Bloom and her daughter into town.

Mrs. Bloom's daughter. . .

CHASING CHARITY

There was something about that girl. Something besides skin like fresh cream against piled-up black hair and a waist so tiny he knew he could reach his hands around it. Something besides pond-green eyes and full lips that turned up at the corners even when she frowned. He'd seen pretty girls in his time, but Charity Bloom was different, and he planned to find out why.

He sure didn't know what to make of her reaction to good fortune. He'd found oil on a lot of folks' land, but she was the first he'd ever seen scowl about it. If he didn't know better, he'd think it made her mad.

Dwelling on Charity Bloom caused him to pass right by the livery. He caught himself and laughed aloud, then backtracked and entered the stables, still chuckling as he passed through the wide doors.

"Kin I help you?" A runt of a man with rowdy gray hair stepped out of the shadows wiping dirty hands on the front of his vest. An intolerable stench filled Buddy's nostrils, growing stronger as the man approached. Buddy realized the smell of sweat, dung, and rotgut whiskey emanated from the proprietor and not from his animals.

"Yes, sir." Buddy shoved his hands deep into his pockets to keep from holding his nose. "I'm looking to hire a buggy for the afternoon. Oh, and three saddle horses that I'll need for a few weeks." In St. Louis, he had grown accustomed to the motorcar his employer provided, but it was hardly a practical conveyance for the muddy streets of Humble.

The fellow cleared his throat and spewed a brown stream in the general direction of a spittoon in the corner. Then he leaned against a splintered rail with crossed arms, looking Buddy over. "New in town, ain't you?"

"Yes, sir."

"You got kinfolk in Humble?"

"No, sir."

The old man continued to examine Buddy through narrow, beady eyes. "Anybody local who can vouch for you?"

Buddy choked back a protest. It would do him no good. "Well, let's see. I guess that'd be Mrs. Bloom and her daughter. They're the only townsfolk I've met."

The man's brows shot skyward, the pull on his eyelids widening his eyes. "Crazy Bertha?" He shook his head. "Mister, I can't give you a rig on the weight of an association with her."

"Who?" Buddy's mind scrambled to understand. "You mean Bertha Bloom? Why do you call her that?"

The old coot twisted around and fired another shot at the slimy, stained pot. "Stranger, if you have to ask, then you don't really know Bertha. But on account of you mentioning her daughter, maybe I can oblige." A leer distorted his wrinkled face. "Just how well acquainted are you with that pretty little gal?" He winked and grinned, exposing a gap in his teeth.

Buddy wanted to widen it. He stood taller and stared the man down. "How much do I owe you?"

The little man shrank under Buddy's gaze. He lowered his eyes and rubbed his stubbled chin. "Tell you what. Let's settle up when you come for the horses."

"Fine by me," Buddy said. "Get the buggy ready. I'll be back in twenty minutes."

At the hotel, Buddy found Lee and Jerry seated on benches in front of a long table laden with baskets of brown rolls and pitchers of frothy milk. The men waited their turns at huge platters piled high with sliced pot roast followed by steaming bowls of mashed potatoes and assorted vegetables. The smell of the room set off a fierce growl in the pit of Buddy's stomach.

He sidled up beside Lee on the bench, tucked a napkin into his collar, and nodded at the men. "Shovel it in fast, gentlemen. We need to get the Bloom womenfolk settled before nightfall. There's more than a few roughs in this town." He remembered the uncouth demeanor of the liveryman and scowled. "More than a few scoundrels, to boot."

Lee passed him a bowl of thick creamed corn. "Say, Buddy, what do you figure was stirring young Miss Bloom?"

Buddy's hand paused on the bowl. "You saw it, too?"

"Saw what?" Jerry asked.

Lee regarded him with one raised brow. "Son, I don't expect you took much notice of Miss Bloom's behavior. How could you? You were too distracted by her other attributes."

Jerry set down his mug with a bang. "High rickety, ain't she a huckleberry?" The flush on his young face and the wide, milk-ringed grin told Buddy more than his words.

"A huckleberry, is she?" Lee forked a serving of roast and smiled at Jerry. "Let's see now. Two days ago you used that term while referring to an oil rig. The week before, I believe a newfangled motorcar earned the same accolade. I think Miss Bloom might consider herself lumped with unflattering company. Don't you agree, Buddy?"

"I do indeed. But what can you expect from an Oklahoman?" Buddy dropped his gaze and shoved a bite of food into his mouth to keep from smiling.

Jerry sat up straighter. "By golly, I'm a Texan and you know it. Born and raised in Wichita Falls."

Buddy shrugged. "Same difference. You couldn't slip a hummingbird feather between Wichita Falls and the Oklahoma border. They may as well claim you."

Jerry drew his mug and plate closer and turned away, offering them one bony shoulder. "There ain't no call for that kind of talk."

Lee laughed aloud and pounded him on the back. "Aw, come on, Okie, don't take on so. We're just having some fun."

"Eat up, boys," Buddy said. "We don't have time for high jinks. We're burning daylight."

Across the table, a thin, balding man leaned forward and cleared his throat. "Excuse me, gentlemen. Did I hear you mention getting the Bloom women settled? Something happen out at their place?"

The three men exchanged uneasy looks. "No, sir," Buddy said. "Nothing worth talking about."

Though no one sat near them, the little man looked to his left and then his right. "Does it have something to do with the wedding?" he whispered.

"Wedding?" Buddy and his men asked together.

"The wedding that never was, I should say." The man's mouth widened at their blank stares. "You haven't heard, then?" He seemed thrilled by the fact.

Lee put down his fork. "If there's something we need to know, get on with it. Whose wedding are you referring to?"

"Why, Miss Bloom's, of course."

Troubled green eyes and a furrowed brow stole across Buddy's mind. "Miss Charity Bloom?"

"Yessir. One and the same. She was all set to marry Daniel Clark, the son of the richest man in town, don't you know. Almost done it, too. Made it all the way to the altar before things turned sour." He tried on a sad look that didn't fit. "Poor little thing, standing up there in a pretty white dress with tears in her eyes. . ." Fixing them with mournful eyes, he shook his head. "I reckon a crying bride is the most pitiful sight there is."

Jerry leaned across the table, nose to nose with the man. "What happened?"

He licked his narrow lips, all but smacking them over what would come next. "Miss Bloom's intended walked right out of the church, practically on the arm of her childhood friend, Miss Emily Dane." He raised both hands in the air. "Now there's a lollapalooza. Young Mr. Clark might've cut a fat hog when he took up with her. There's a slim chance that boy will ever tame a girl like Emmy."

Jerry's brown eyes widened in disbelief. "Are you saying some featherbrain had Miss Bloom corralled then cut her loose? Who would do a fool thing like that?"

The man shook his head. "It's a poser, all right."

Surprised and a little embarrassed for Charity, Buddy felt heat crawl up his cheeks. He stood up and threw some money on the table. "We got no more time for loose talk and speculation about other folks' business. The lady's not present to defend herself, so I suggest we hear no more."

Lee stood with Buddy, hitched up his trousers, and nodded at the man. "You have a good day, sir."

Jerry still leaned in, about to ask another question, but Buddy hooked a finger around his suspenders and drew him up. "Let's not keep our friend from his fine meal. Besides, we'd best get moving. We don't want to keep the ladies waiting."

CHAPTER 4

For Charity, the ride to Mother Dane's house felt like a walk to the gallows.

While packing the buggy, Buddy Pierce and his men were helpful but oddly subdued. It hadn't escaped her notice that Buddy never met her gaze. The other one, the tall, skinny man with eyes that matched his russet hair, stared at her for much of the evening. When told of their destination, Buddy reacted as if Mama had suggested he drive them off a cliff. They had something stuck in their craws, and that was for sure.

Charity put it aside. Her own woes had her so tightly wrapped that she had no time to ponder what might be ailing them.

Now they stood before the Danes' front door, bags in hand, to beg entry to the enemy camp. Mama had no sense for propriety, that was nothing new, but it had never stung Charity so cruelly before. Behind them, the men mumbled and shuffled their feet, overly preoccupied by something in the distance.

A loud ruckus came from inside, dominated by Mother Dane's deep, commanding rumble and punctuated by Emmy's shrill pleas. When the massive oak door began to open, it was all Charity could do not to turn and bolt. As if she read her daughter's mind, Mama tightened her grip on Charity's arm.

Mother Dane's broad smile greeted them. "Why, Bertie, bless my soul, what a pleasant but thoroughly unexpected surprise."

Her considerable girth, clad in fashionable big sleeves and full skirts, took up most of the doorway and prevented Charity from seeing around her. Forced to cast manners aside, she rose on her toes and peered over Mother Dane's shoulder.

"We need shelter, Magda," Mama said.

Mother Dane stepped aside. There would be questions later, but she'd heard all that was necessary for now. Mama needed her.

"Set those bags at the foot of the stairs, gentlemen; then hang your hats in the hall and have a seat in the parlor. I'll fetch some coffee. You all look like you could use it."

Mother Dane hadn't really asked, just issued the order. Like everyone else in Humble, the men complied without hesitation. After a tearful hug with Mama, Mother Dane hurried to the kitchen to keep her end of the bargain.

A quick, furtive check of the room told Charity that Emmy wasn't present. Whether upstairs or hiding in an adjacent room she couldn't tell, but sooner or later a confrontation would be unavoidable.

Like Cleopatra awaiting Mark Antony, Mama settled onto a plush, button-tucked divan and held court with a broad smile. The servant waiting to be served. Long graying strands streamed down each side of her face, and Charity wished she'd learn to pin up her hair.

The men sat stiffly across from Mama on the matching couch. Charity sank into a big green chair and willed it to swallow her whole.

"See? I told you, sugar," Mama said. "I knew it'd be all right. Magda wouldn't turn us away just because of Emmy and that no-account Daniel Clark."

All three men shifted their gazes to Mama, waiting to hear what she had to say next. Charity tensed, prepared to save herself from humiliation if it meant swooning at their feet.

"Here we are." Mother Dane entered the room as she always did, like an actress on cue. She approached them smiling, but a brief, nearly imperceptible frown directed at the top of the stairs told Charity that Emmy had escaped to her room.

"That was quick," Mama exclaimed.

"Already had it brewed. I'm used to making a big pot for Willem and me. When he's on the road, it's too much, but I don't know how to make it taste good otherwise." She set the tray on the low table and looked around at her guests. "Now it won't go to waste."

After seeing everyone properly served, Mother Dane lowered herself to the divan beside Charity's sprawling mama. "Now then, what's this all about, Bert?"

Mama passed Mother Dane her cup then sat forward and rubbed her hands together like a child with a secret. "You won't believe what's going on out at our place." She narrowed her eyes and jabbed her bony finger at Buddy Pierce. "That one. That boy right there has the gift, Magda. He can take one look at the ground and find treasure."

Now she had Mother Dane's rapt attention. "Treasure? Oh my, honey. Do go on."

Mama's dancing eyes returned to Buddy. "Tell her, son. Tell Magda what you found on my land."

Buddy leaned forward and smiled. With his hands clasped in front and long arms propped on his knees, he began to talk. He told about when he first caught sight of Mama's chicken, and how he realized the goo on its feathers must be oil. He explained how he rushed back into town, praying the whole way his crew had arrived with their equipment so they could do their tests.

He lit up as he talked, and Charity wondered at the source of his excitement. Was it the thrill of discovery or the joy of helping someone less fortunate that stoked a fire in his eyes?

Whatever inspired his zeal, she enjoyed watching and listening to him very much. His deep voice and dulcet tones so soothed her, drowsiness set in and she found it hard to sit upright. Snuggling deeper into the plush green upholstery, she laid her head against the overstuffed arm while Buddy's muted rumble became a nest of bees in her head.

"Charity? Wake up, dear."

She bolted straight up, swiping the back of her hand across her mouth and searching the room for Buddy and his men.

Mother Dane offered the crook of her arm to pull up on. "They're gone, honey."

"Oh my. I fell asleep."

"You sure did."

She looked back at the big chair and pictured herself lying there. "Did I do anything. . .unladylike while I slept?"

Mother Dane laughed, not out loud, but Charity knew because her bosom shook. "Child, you snored so rowdy-like you ran those nice young men plumb out of the house, and all the while your mouth was wide and drooling like a hound at suppertime. We couldn't make polite conversation for all the racket, so they left."

"Mother Dane!"

"Got quite a kick out of it, they did. Especially that good-looking one."

"Did not!"

The shaking grew violent, and Mother Dane's hearty laughter filled the room. She pulled Charity close for a hug. "Come on then, sleepyhead. Your bed is made and calling for you."

"Where's Mama?"

"Upstairs in my bed. It's more comfortable. I set up a cot in the room for me in case she needs anything. Bert was plumb tuckered out, so I promised I'd see to you. I put your things at the opposite end of the hall like always."

Just like Mother Dane. Always tending to Mama.

"Did Emmy. . .?"

"Never graced us with her presence. She'll be down soon enough, though, or starve. I certainly won't be taking up a tray."

Charity rested her head on Mother Dane's shoulder. "Oh, it's all so awful."

"That it is, sugar, but time has a way with these things." She held Charity at arm's length. "Besides, it's not all bad news. Young Mr. Pierce said you and Bertha may come by some money."

Charity grimaced, and Mother Dane took her by the chin. "Mercy, what a face."

"I don't want those filthy oilmen's money. Mama said she didn't either. She said they come in and lease up all the land, getting rich off good-hearted people who don't know any better."

"Uh-uh, sugar. Not this time. Mr. Pierce told Bert she could drill out the oil herself and keep the money."

The words caught Charity off guard. "Mama? Drill oil? That's crazy talk. She don't know the first thing about it."

Mother Dane laughed again. "Sweetie, you're wide-eyed as a hoot owl. That young man didn't mean for Bert to do the work herself. He meant she could finance it and keep most of the profit."

Charity blinked. "Finance it? With what? It would be easier for Mama to do the drilling than to come up with that kind of money."

"Mr. Pierce is going to help her get it done. He has a plan. Something about leasing some of your land to pay for it."

All Charity could do was stare.

Mother Dane gathered her close again and patted her back. Then she turned her to face the stairs and urged her toward them. "Come now, child. I'll walk you up. I know it's a lot to take in, especially when you're still half asleep. I promise things will look better by the morning light."

"I declare, Mother Dane, I don't see how."

Alone in the big four-poster, Charity marveled that it seemed as grand as it had when she was a girl. In this very room, she and Emmy had wrestled, giggled, and whispered until the wee hours. Emmy started out in her own bed, but when the household fell silent, she would sneak down the hallway and throw herself, all gangly legs and tousled hair, into bed with Charity. In those days, they had no notions about rich or poor, fidelity or deceit.

She couldn't remember a time when Emmy wasn't a part of her life. Their mamas grew up together in East Texas. When Mama married Papa and moved to Humble, her best friend soon followed. Even after Mother Dane married into money, the two were inseparable. It took Mama eight years to conceive her only child. She liked to claim she held on to Charity until Mother Dane could meet Uncle Willem and hang up her old maid hat because the girls were meant to be reared side by side.

So they had been, and they'd loved each other since Emmy first toddled close and touched Charity's face. How could Charity bear life without her best friend?

She pictured Emmy lying in her bedroom at the end of the

hall, and her eyes flooded with tears. She almost wished the door would fly open and Emmy would sail into the room. The desire to reconcile consumed her. The pain caused by what Daniel and Emmy had done paled in comparison to the hollow ache in her heart.

I could forgive her.

The thought struck like a blow. She lay in the darkness and reeled from it.

When the next idea came, it took her breath. She could tiptoe down the hall and climb into bed beside Emmy. They would whisper and giggle tonight and save the serious talk for morning. It would be harder by the light of day, but they'd work it out. They always had.

Before she changed her mind, Charity slipped from the bed and opened the door. The polished brass banister reflected the moonlight shining from the gabled windows, providing a lighted marker along the corridor. Outside Emmy's room, she paused. Her heart pounded, but she wouldn't allow herself to go back. Turning the knob, she winced when the hinges creaked then drew a sharp breath when a rush of frigid air hit her face. Emmy's bedroom was colder than the guest room had been. Much colder. Charity shivered in her thin nightdress.

The outline of Emmy's body lay still under the quilt, so she hadn't heard the door. Charity approached the high bed, her mind awhirl with all she planned to say. She smiled in the darkness, imagining her friend's reaction, though if she couldn't stop shivering, she'd scare Emmy awake.

A stiff gust of wind lifted the curtains. *For pity's sake, no wonder. She'll have us frozen by morning.*

Charity backed away and tiptoed to the window to close it. Her hand rested on the sash when something in the garden below caught her eye. The full moon revealed a lone figure dressed in nightclothes and wrapped in a long white shawl. She stared at the fair-haired apparition in disbelief.

Crossing to the bed, she threw back the quilt. Three plump pillows mocked her. She whirled and rushed to the window, prepared to call out, but something about Emmy's lovely profile stopped her. The upturned, moonlit face held a look of longing so intense it pricked Charity's heart.

Emmy feels what I feel. Her heart is so broken she can't sleep.

She considered the trellis. She wasn't afraid of heights, but climbing the rickety framework in her nightdress seemed foolhardy. Nevertheless, she pulled the garment high and prepared to swing her leg over the windowsill just as another figure emerged from the shadows.

Emmy rushed to meet Daniel. He took her in his arms and pressed her head to his chest, her long nightdress billowing about their legs. Charity tried to turn away but couldn't. A single tear fell and splashed against the windowsill.

"I hate you, Emily Dane." She knew she whispered, but the words thundered in her head. "Oh, how I hate you."

In the moonlight, the couple seemed to merge into one, and the scene burned into Charity's eyes. Careful to be quiet, she lowered the heavy window and turned the lock. Blinded by tears, she stumbled across the room and slipped into the hall, easing the door closed behind her.

CHAPTER 5

Charity swept through the kitchen door to find her mama in front of Mother Dane's cast-iron stove. At the dawn of a new day, Cleopatra had traded her couch for an apron and skillet. Dwarfed by the huge black contraption, she looked even smaller than usual, reminding Charity of a little girl playing house.

Barefoot as usual, Mama stood like a crane, one foot propped against the opposite knee. She gazed out the window, a shaft of light bathing the side of her face, and her eyes squinted against the rising sun. Without looking, she took an egg from a basket on the sideboard and cracked it into a big yellow bowl. Lifting the bottle of milk, she poured a dollop over the eggs, never spilling a drop.

Anyone else might think the view past the checkered curtains held her fancy. By the dazed look in her eyes, Charity knew the confines of the carnation-weave wallpaper held her body, but her mind and spirit soared somewhere in the distance. Drifting off that way, among Mama's many other odd habits, had led the townsfolk to think her peculiar at best. Some even called her insane.

Charity took a deep breath and gathered her courage. "I'm leaving, Mama. I will not stay in this house another minute."

Mama glanced over her shoulder. "You hush now. And close that door. They'll hear you."

"There's no one awake to hear. Besides, I don't care." Charity swept past the threshold and did as she was told. The careful way she eased the door shut contradicted her bold statement.

The frustrating little woman chuckled and went back to her task. "There's no one awake because they were up half the night. Made quite a ruckus, they did, pounding on doors and spitting like cats."

Charity squirmed. "They weren't the only ones up all night."

Mama kept a stiff back to her, but the motion of beating the eggs set her thin frame to dancing. "Couldn't sleep, huh? Is your conscience sore, daughter? The Good Book says, 'The wicked are like the troubled sea when it cannot rest, whose waters cast up mire and dirt.' " She chuckled. "Sounds like our bog, don't it?"

Charity banged her fist on the table. "No, it doesn't. It's nothing like our bog. Mercy! You sorely vex me sometimes. When you talk like that, I go to thinking—"

Mama turned, her movements slow and deliberate. "Go on and say it."

Charity felt her stomach fill with mush. She couldn't meet those burning eyes.

"What's the matter? Lost your nerve?" Mama's work-worn fingers had gone white around the spatula. "Let me finish for you, then. You go to thinking I'm loony like this town has me pegged. Now ain't that so?"

Charity fixed her eyes on a crack in the floor. "I'm sorry, Mama. I know you're not loony. Only sometimes you act so strange."

Her long silence made Charity nervous, but Charity knew enough to stay still and wait.

"Come over here, daughter."

She dared a quick glance at Mama's face. "Ma'am?"

"Do as I say."

Eyes still downcast, Charity crossed the room. Her mama laid down the spatula and faced her. "Now then, you look me square in the eye."

Charity's head hung lower.

Mama hooked an index finger around her chin and raised her red-hot face. "Go on, take a look. Look deep in my eyes, clear past the faded skin and wrinkles. That's it. All right, tell me what you see."

She searched the soft green eyes. "What do you mean? I don't see anything."

Mama released her chin. "And there's your problem." With that she picked up her utensil and returned to the eggs.

Frustration crowded Charity's throat, making her voice come out shrill. "You're not making any sense."

The spatula went down again, and Mama wiped her hands on her apron. "Let me tell you what you missed." She raised a finger and thumped herself hard on the chest. It rang hollow in Charity's ears like the sound of a ripe melon. "Underneath this pruned-up skin, back behind these tired old eyes, I'm still just a girl. No different from you, except on the outside."

Charity shook her head. "Don't be silly. You don't have pruned-up skin or tired eyes. You're not yet fifty."

Mama placed both hands on Charity's shoulders. "It's the road I'm walking, but it don't matter none to me. Just because I've got a few years under my belt, folks expect me to act like I swallowed a bucket of starch. Well, I won't. That ain't me."

Charity knew Mama wanted some sign that she understood, but she could only stare back and nod.

"Baby, these bodies age, and there's nothing to be done about it. If we're lucky, if we don't fight it, our souls stay young forever. I won't put no face on for the world. I tried for your sake, but I cain't do it no more. It plain stifles me."

She reached around to set the skillet off the fire. "I'll tell you something else. Your papa never tried to change me. Never once made me feel crazy. But then, I reckon he was the last soul on earth willing to accept me just how I am." Her gaze jumped back to the checkered curtains, and Charity's heart pitched and dove for her feet. She suddenly knew exactly where her mama's thoughts had been when she entered the room.

She held out her hand. "That's not true. I—"

"Bertha Maye!"

Mother Dane's strident voice struck panic in Charity's heart. She spun toward the kitchen door. "I have to go, Mama. I have to leave right this minute."

"Just where do you think to go?"

"I pondered that all night. First, I'll check the hotel. If they don't have a room for us yet, I can put our names on the list."

"And then?"

"Home. I want to go back home. At least for now."

Mama put a hand on her hip and turned back to the scorched-smelling eggs. "I sure thought a daughter of mine could stand up to trouble better than this, but you go on. I won't stop you."

Mother Dane trudged into the kitchen, still wrapped in her dressing gown. "Here you two are," she announced, swiping her forehead with the back of her hand. "It's a blessing for Emmy her daddy's out of town; else we'd be planning a wake this morning." She glanced toward the skillet, sniffing the air. "You burning those eggs, Bert?"

Mama faced her. "Magda, can Nash fetch Charity into town this morning?"

"Sure thing, honey. I ain't going nowhere." Mother Dane ambled to the counter, her attention on the platter of crispy bacon. "Where's she running off to this early?"

"On a fool's errand."

Perhaps weary from her own nocturnal battle, Mother Dane didn't press. "Let me go dress and tell Nash to square the rig. That is, if I can find him. How something as bodacious big as that man disappears with such dependable regularity beats all I ever saw."

Charity eased toward the exit. "Don't trouble yourself, Mother Dane. I'm already dressed. I'll go tell him myself."

The kitchen door closed behind her, and Charity ran for the foyer, careful not to look toward the stairs. On the way, she hoisted her bag from behind the chair where she'd left it and burst onto the wide porch—straight into the arms of Buddy Pierce. They collided, and her bag jerked loose from her hands and skittered across the porch.

"Whoa, there!" he cried, pressing her against him to keep her upright. At such close proximity, his voice sounded deeper than usual and seemed to rumble from his broad chest.

"Morning, Miss Bloom. So we meet again." He squinted when he smiled, crinkling the corners of his eyes. "Not that I don't enjoy these encounters, but a simple hello would do. Unless you need a good fright to start your heart in the mornings. Have you tried coffee?"

She pulled free and peered up, raising the brim of her bonnet so she could see. "Mr. Pierce, where on earth did you come from? You simply must stop creeping up on me."

He had the starch to grin. "My sincere apologies, ma'am. I'm getting right good at it though."

She brushed at her dress and tightened the ribbon holding her hat while she fought to regain some dignity. "If you're truly sorry, you can rescue my bag from that hedge."

Buddy glanced behind him then walked to the edge of the porch and bent down. She watched him hesitate before poking in a lacy bit of cloth and closing the latch. She bit back a smile when he returned red-faced.

He held up her satchel and studied it. "Didn't I tote this inside just last night?"

"You did."

"And now you're bringing it out again?"

"Give it to me, please."

"You seem in an awful big hurry to get somewhere."

"That's because I am." She snatched the upraised bag from his hand. "In fact, I'm about to give you an opportunity to repay me for ambushing me at every turn. You may give me a ride into town."

Buddy looked at the door. "I'd be happy to, but. . ."

Charity followed his gaze. "I see. You have business inside. Very well, I'll wait for Nash." She started for the steps, but he grabbed her sleeve and hauled her around.

"Not so fast. My only business is to see that you and your mama are settled and to offer my help with moving the rest of your things."

"Is that all? In that case, you needn't worry. We're just fine."

He cast another doubtful peek at the house. "Well, if you say so. . ."

"I do." She took his arm and urged him toward the steps. "Shall we go?"

He settled his hat lower, studying her from under the brim.

"Well, yes, ma'am," he said, allowing her to lead him from the porch. "I guess so."

In the distance, a high bank of black clouds closed on the horizon, a dark swirling wall with a fluffy white top. It snuffed out the light as it inched forward, pulling a curtain over the bright, sunlit morning. Buddy wondered what more rain might do to the rutted streets of Humble. The lowland area of Southeast Texas suffered frequent flooding, but he'd heard more thunderstorms than usual had rumbled through the small town in recent weeks.

He glanced at Miss Bloom, who had remained silent for most of the ride. Quite out of character for the spirited young thing he'd first met in the hotel. He found it odd he hadn't seen that woman since, except for a glimpse on Mrs. Dane's porch.

Buddy pulled up to the crowded boardwalk in front of the Lone Star Hotel and set the brake. Hopping down, he made his way around the wagon with the mire sucking audibly at his boots. Necks craned as he helped Miss Bloom down, careful to keep her dress out of the mud. When he offered his arm, she took it, and he led her through the mob to the door of the hotel.

Inside, he intended to hang back a respectable distance to allow her to conduct business in private, but she clung to his arm and steered him straight to the counter.

"Morning, Sam." She beamed at the clerk. "I'm going to need a room for a few weeks for Mama and me."

Sam frowned. He seemed loath to be the bearer of bad news, especially to her. "I'm dreadful sorry, child. There are none to be had."

She bit her bottom lip. "Hmm, I expected as much. When do you suppose that will change?"

The little man shook his head. "Not in the foreseeable future."

"I see." Her slender fingers drumming a rhythm on the countertop, she stared at a large portrait dominating the far wall as if the mustachioed man in the frame might lend her wisdom.

The aging clerk pushed his wire-rimmed glasses higher with a palsied hand. "If you don't mind my asking, has something happened out at your place?" His anxious expression and the way he hovered near Charity reminded Buddy of a brood hen and her chick.

The pretty hatchling smoothed her fluff and released a weary-sounding breath. "It's quite complicated, really. You see, Mr. Pierce here saw black stuff on Mama's chicken and–"

Buddy took hold of her shoulders and pulled her back, upsetting her balance as well as the angle of the blue feather protruding from her straw hat. "What the lady's trying to say is"–he stared into her startled eyes, using his to flash a warning–"there are much-needed improvements going on at their house. It's not the safest place for them just now."

Sam eyed Buddy, his frown deepening. "As I recall, you're not a registered guest of the hotel, so why do I see your face in my lobby most every day of late?"

Buddy nodded. "Nothing gets past you, does it? You're right, of course. I'm not official." He grinned and held out his hand. "Name's Buddy Pierce. I guess you might say I'm a guest of a guest."

Ignoring Buddy's hand and his explanation, the man turned back to Charity. "Is there something else I can do for you, my dear?"

She stepped to the counter again, adjusting her hat and frowning at Buddy before she answered. "I understand there's a waiting list."

"Why, yes, there is."

"Can you put us on it?"

"I can, but I warn you, it's long." He pulled a ledger from under the counter and slid it toward Charity. Names filled the page from top to bottom on several sheets. "Might be weeks before we can get to you." He tilted his head toward the window. "The boom, you know."

Buddy watched Charity, waiting for her reaction. The news was sure to upset her.

"Very well." She took the pen in her gloved hand and scratched her mama's name on the last line. Following suit with the others, she added the number two and circled it then pushed the book back to the clerk and nodded. "Thank you, Sam."

The old man's gaze swept Buddy. His Adam's apple bobbed several times before he finally squeezed a question past his throat. "I don't mean to pry, little miss, but have you found adequate shelter for you and your mama until we're able to accommodate you?"

"As a matter of fact, we have. Mama will be staying at Magdalena Dane's house. I've decided on a more sensible arrangement for myself." She fixed Buddy with a determined glare. "You heard right, Mr. Pierce. I won't be going back to Mother Dane's."

Before Buddy could react, she walked away. He caught up to her near the door and offered his arm again. She took it, and he swept her through the crowd outside. At the wagon, he helped her swing up onto the seat then watched her until she began to squirm.

"What are you waiting for?" she asked, looking down at him from the rig. "Let's go."

Buddy blinked. "Fine. Where to?"

"Home." She dared him with her eyes and sat up straighter, plucking at the folds of her dress. "I'm going home, and there's nothing more to be said about it."

His mouth dropped open. He closed it fast and swallowed. "I'm sorry, you can't do that."

"Oh, but I can. I declare, Mr. Pierce, you're forgetting yourself."

Buddy hurried around the wagon, swung up beside her, and studied her angry face. "Didn't your mama tell you?"

From the look of her, it was clear she'd heard those words before. She leaned toward him, her speech slow and deliberate. "Tell me what?"

"She leased the house. To the oil company as living quarters for the roughnecks."

Thunder boomed overhead and lightning marbled the darkened sky. A quirky wind bore down on them, pushing back Charity's hat and raising tendrils of black hair to the heavens. Against the angry backdrop, she reminded Buddy of a snake-tressed Medusa.

"What did you say?" Her eyes narrowed, heightening the illusion. "Just when did she do that?"

"We worked out the deal last night, while you were. . .um. . . resting. That's why I showed up this morning. I knew you'd need a hand with your things."

Charity's gloved fingers clenched and unclenched in her lap, and her chest heaved. "That infuriating old woman. That's why she let me go so easy." She whirled on Buddy, balled fists going to her waist. "She can't do this. It's my house, too. If she can lease it without telling me, then I can unlease it. You tell that oil company the house is no longer available." She drew herself tall, obviously pleased with her stand. "That's right–the deal's off. Now take me home this instant."

Buddy shoved his hat back with his knuckles and scratched his head with his thumb. "That won't exactly be possible, ma'am."

"And why not?"

"It's too late. When I left your house this morning, twenty men were eating breakfast at the table."

Thunder sounded again, closer this time. Charity leaned toward him once more, staring hard, as if that would help his words sink in. Her big green eyes, so near he could see tiny flecks in them, flooded with tears that spilled over and down her cheeks. When she collapsed against him sobbing, Buddy couldn't decide whether to comfort her or hide her from prying eyes. He chose the latter.

Righting her hat, he pulled it low to hide her face then clucked at the horse to pull away from the boardwalk. He scrambled for the reins, fighting hard to concentrate on his driving instead of the weeping girl clinging to his side.

Buddy steered the horse down a side street that ran alongside the railroad tracks and parked the rig. Setting the brake, he pulled Charity closer and patted her shoulder while she cried. He searched his mind for comforting words but came up painfully short. "There now. It can't be all that bad."

"Yes, it is!" she wailed. "How can you say that? I'll be sleeping in the streets tonight."

He tried not to focus on how small she felt against him, how soft. "I'm right sure that won't happen."

"It has happened. I have nowhere else to go. I can't stay at Mother Dane's. I won't." Her wail became a sob, and she hid her face in her hands. "Don't ask me to explain. You wouldn't understand."

He cleared his throat. "Oh, I don't know so much about that. I might understand a lot better than you think."

Charity grew still against him. "What are you implying, sir?" When he didn't answer, she leaned to stare up at him, her face a swollen mess. "You know, don't you?"

Buddy raised his brows. "Any way I answer that question makes me a cad. If I say yes, I risk embarrassing you. If I say no, I've deceived you. Which do you prefer?"

She burrowed into his chest again. "I could just die. Oh, please don't look at me. I'm so ashamed."

"There's no need to be."

"Yes, there is. I'm a jealous, spiteful shrew."

Buddy couldn't help but smile. He was glad she couldn't see him. "I'm sure you're neither of those things."

"I am. You don't know what I've done."

He patted her on the back. "I can't imagine you doing anything wrong."

She tilted her head and peered up at him. "Last night Emmy climbed out a window to be with Daniel. I locked her out of the house. . .in her nightdress."

One look at her guilty expression should've been all the warning Buddy needed to keep a straight face, but his callous sense of humor betrayed him. He was going to laugh whatever the cost. He held her and roared until his sides ached.

When he dared to look up, he was shocked to find Charity beaming. Her nose was still red, her eyes bright with tears, but mirth lit her glowing face. By golly, the Okie was right. She was the prettiest thing he'd ever seen. Her big eyes held his for a heartbeat, and he forgot to breathe.

"You are a cad indeed, sir." Her rebuke might've stung if not for her broad smile.

He took off his hat and placed it over his heart but couldn't stifle a smile of his own. "I guess I owe you another apology."

"Well, don't you bother. Though I'm touched by your sincerity."

"Miss Bloom, I sense you doubt me."

She waved her hand. "Please, call me Charity. Now that I've bared my soul and given you a glimpse of my lower nature, I believe we can dispense with formalities."

Hat still at his chest, he bowed his head. "I would be honored."

Huge raindrops began to fall, pelting the top of Buddy's bare head. Instinctively, he held his hat over Charity.

She leaned from under the brim and peered up at the sky. "Now do you see how awful this is? I can't even get in out of the rain. There's no place for me to go."

"Wait a minute." He should have thought of it before. Or had she just inspired him? "I think maybe there is."

"But where?"

The rain came down harder, soaking them to the skin. Buddy handed her his hat and took up the reins, whirling the horse into the street. "Hang on," he shouted. "You'll find out when we get there."

CHAPTER 6

Bertha lay curled at the foot of Magdalena's green-striped divan, one finger dead center of a checker. Magda sat across from her, propped against the flower-print pillows at her back. Earlier she had raised the sash to ease the cloying stillness. Now the scent of rain wafted in on a lively breeze that pestered the curtains and flapped the shade. Though it put up a brave front, the morning sun had lost its battle with a murky sky. The shadowy corners crept so close they'd soon need to trim a lantern or abandon their game altogether.

Magda squirmed and sighed. "That's it, Bertha. You've made your move. It's my turn."

"Hold your horses. I ain't let go yet."

Another huffy exhale from across the board brought Bertha's attention to Magda's face. "You mind to stop all that blowing? You're about to scatter these checkers." She scowled and leaned away some. "Besides, you ate onions this morning, didn't you? Your breath could peel the paper from these walls."

Magda lifted her chin. "You know I like a few diced on my scrambled eggs."

"Humph! A few would mean you could still taste the eggs."

Reaching around to the side table, Magda picked up her coffee cup. "Just hush and play, would you?"

Bertha looked up as big Nash came through from the kitchen

carrying one of Magda's dining room chairs. On the way he banged it against the doorpost and bumped everything he passed.

Magda grimaced. "Land sakes, Nash. There won't be nothing left."

He glanced up and smiled as if he'd just noticed them in the room. "Maybe so, but whatever left gon' stand up straight. I fixed that wobbly leg you been fussing 'bout so long." He set the chair down and pushed it up to the table.

Bertha saw right away that the back of the chair stood four inches shy of the other five in the set. "Lookie there, Magda," she hooted. "You called it right. There's hardly nothing left."

Magda scooted forward to look. "Nash! What on earth have you done?"

He flashed another big smile and gave the chair a good shake. "See there, Miz Dane? She's steady."

Slumping against the sofa, Magda shook her head. "Never mind that fool thing. Have you seen Charity this morning?"

"No, ma'am. I ain't seen her since last evening. I would'a reckoned she'd be in the parlor with you all."

Bertha gave him a pointed stare. "Do you see her in here anywhere?"

He gazed about the room. "I don't see her in here a'tall. Is she s'posed to be?"

Magda winked at Bertha. "I thought you saw everything that happens around this place." She took another sip of her coffee. "Where've you been all this time?"

"Where've I been?" He stood taller and squared his shoulders. "Doing what I s'posed be doing, Miz Dane. Caring for old Rebel and tending chores. So unless Miss Charity come out to the barn, I wouldn't be likely to see her, now, would I?"

"Well, keep an eye out for her, you hear? She wanted a ride into town, but since the buggy never left the yard, I can't imagine how she went. I don't guess you hauled her on your shoulders?"

His grin returned. "No, ma'am."

"Did you turn Rebel out to graze?"

"No, ma'am, he's still in his stall. It's coming up a powerful blow out there. That old sky black as pitch. The pasture ain't safe for old Rebel jus' now." With that, he tipped his battered hat and backed out the way he came.

Magda sighed and settled again onto her pillows. "I just can't figure it. How did Charity leave if Nash didn't drive her, and where did she go?"

Bertha's heart lurched, but she kept her peace.

Magda cast an accusing glance. "You reckon she knows about the house?"

"She's bound to by now."

"Then where could she be, Bert? And in this storm? She's been gone an awful long time."

Bertha let go of the checker. "Hush and play. It's your turn."

Outside, what started as a heavy patter on the porch became a ruckus of hard-driving rain. Magda heaved herself up and rushed to close the window. "Honey, I think that's hail. I sure hope we don't get us a tornado."

"Me, too, but I wouldn't be surprised. A good twister's long overdue."

Magda released the tasseled shade and spun around to face her. "Charity's out in this! Aren't you the least bit worried?"

Bertha shrugged. "She'll turn up by suppertime." Magda's hard stare from across the room weighed her down, but she kept her attention on the game.

"Sometimes you're too harsh with that girl."

She looked up. "I don't go to be. Life is cruel. I want her fit to handle it."

Magda bent close to the window and took one more peek at the weather. "There's a limit to what a person can take." She turned and held up one finger in a cautionary gesture. "Mark my words–keep it up and she'll turn on you."

Bertha struggled to keep her voice even. "She already has."

"Tommyrot. That child loves you more than life. She's a good girl, to boot. Count your blessings, Bertie. Suppose you had to contend with my–"

"Emmy!"

Magda froze at Bertha's cry then followed her nod to the head of the stairs where Emmy reclined against the newel post. "Well,

well. So you decided to come out of hiding. How long you been standing there?"

The girl didn't answer. Hand in front of her face, she studied her tapered nails as though they held the answers to all of life's questions.

"Emily, I'm talking to you." Magda walked to the lower landing and stared up. "You may as well come on down. You can't eavesdrop on folks once they know you're there."

With an angry swish of her skirts, Emmy flounced down the stairs. On the bottom step, she turned a surly face to her mama. "I'm hungry. Were you planning to let me perish?"

Magda snorted. "There was no danger of that."

Sucking in her middle, Emmy looked down and wrapped her hands around her tiny waist. "Whatever do you mean? Why, look at me wasting away. I haven't eaten a bite for days."

Her mama raised an eyebrow. "Stolen provisions don't count? What about the food you've pilfered from my kitchen every night?"

"Mama, take that back! I never did."

"Emily, gnawed drumsticks don't naturally sprout from hedges, nor do lamb chops spring up in front yards. You've littered the place with your leavings. Did you think no one would notice?"

Emmy raised her chin and turned away. "Why blame me? There's no telling what's subject to spring up around this house." She flashed a pointed glance at Bertha. "Or who."

Not one to be trifled with, Magda advanced on Emmy, her voice a threatening growl. "After the shenanigans you've pulled, young lady, it would serve you best to lower that nose and act civil." She pointed. "Get over there and apologize to Bertha; then march into that kitchen and fetch yourself some food. No one will be serving you today."

Emmy dashed over and curtsied. "Sorry, Aunt Bert." Skirts rustling, she scuttled into the kitchen.

Watching her go, Bertha grinned. "Them rosebushes sure tore up that pretty face."

"Looks like she hit every one. The very idea, skulking about the windows of her own home trying to break in. She scared the dickens out of me. Served her right to meet the business end of a thorn or two."

Bertha leaned against the chaise and chuckled. "Now who's being harsh? Still, I bet it'll be quite a spell before she tries it again."

Magda grunted and picked up her cup. "It better be." Thunder shook the house as she settled on the divan to finish their game.

Bertha stole a casual glance at the window, her heart crowding her throat.

Magda moved as if to play her turn, but her hand crossed the checkerboard instead and gripped Bertha's fingers.

Startled, Bertha looked up into caring brown eyes. . .and felt her armor slide. "Oh, Magda! Where could she be?"

Emmy found a fresh loaf in the bread box and cut thick, crusty slices from the end. The corner pantry behind her yielded a jar of muscadine jelly. She scooped fat globs onto buttered bread and spread it clear to the edges. Her mouth watered before she could close the sandwich and get it to her lips. Grateful for something besides fried meat, she took a huge bite and rolled her eyes toward heaven. After pouring a tall glass of milk, she leaned against the counter and stared out the window at the storm, her thoughts turning to Daniel.

Her need for Daniel Clark rivaled her need to breathe. She wondered where he was at that moment. Did he think of her even now, yearn for her as she did for him? No one had ever made her feel the way he did. One glance from him and all was lost—her upbringing, her morals, her family. . .even her best friend.

Remembering Charity, the next bite of sandwich stuck in her throat. She gulped her milk to try to coax it down then lay the food aside. Lightning struck and thunder pealed with a crash that rattled the kitchen window. Emmy leaped away from it, and her stomach lurched. She'd heard them say Charity had gone missing, might be out somewhere in the storm.

Well, I won't think of it! I just won't!

Emmy turned from the window and picked up the sandwich

and milk. She'd finish them later, up in her room. Though she was loath to go back inside her dungeon, anything was better than spending the day with those cackling hens in the parlor.

She paused at the door. To get upstairs, she had to pass them one more time. After that, she'd hole up in her room until nightfall. Under cover of darkness, she'd sneak back down to the kitchen and pillage for more rations. After all, a girl had to keep up her strength.

CHAPTER 7

Charity clung to Buddy's steadying arm as the wagon raced up the street, spewing muddy water in its wake. The heavy rainfall had emptied the boardwalk in front of the hotel, making it easy to pull close to the door.

Buddy hauled back on the reins, took one look at the quagmire on his side, and then crawled over Charity to descend, dragging her and her bag off behind him. They ran into the lobby, laughing so hard they had to hold on to each other to stay upright, their sodden clothes leaving puddles on the polished wood floor.

From behind the desk, Sam stared with an open mouth before loudly clearing his throat. "Say, there. . .Miss Bloom. . .are you all right?"

Charity stopped giggling long enough to look over Buddy's shoulder at Sam then fell into more laughter at the astonished look on his face.

Before she could regain her composure, Buddy answered for her. "No, Sam, she's not all right. Can't you see she's soaked clean through?" He took her arm and led her to the counter. "The lady's in dire need of dry clothes. As a matter of fact, so am I." He held out his hand to Sam, his soaked sleeve dripping rivulets on the counter. "The key to Mr. Allen's room, if you please."

Sam recoiled as if Buddy's hand was a snake. "I'll do no such thing. How dare you attempt to besmirch this girl's reputation.

Sir, I won't allow it."

Buddy's earnest face relaxed into a slow grin. "Pick up your jaw, Sam. I have no lascivious notions toward our Miss Bloom." He extended his other palm. "That's why I also need Mr. Ritter's key. For myself."

He gestured at the guest book. "While you're at it, scratch Lee Allen's name from your registry and replace it with the lady's. Mr. Allen has surrendered his reservation to her, effective immediately."

Sam leaned into the counter. "On whose authority?"

Buddy's eyes twinkled, but his jaw was set. "Just the man who pays the tab. You see, the current occupants of those two rooms work for me, and I foot the bill for their housing. We'll find a corner of Mr. Ritter's room to lay another bedroll. I'll continue to pay for the other room as long as Miss Bloom needs it."

Charity whirled to face him. "Oh, Mr. Pierce, I couldn't."

He pointed at the register where Sam had drawn a line through Mr. Allen's name. "The deed is done, ma'am. Your protests won't change it."

"B–but I simply won't t–take his bed from under him and leave the three of you to one room." Yet even while she objected, she shivered so violently her words came out through chattering teeth.

Buddy smiled. "Rest easy. The three of us have bunked in closer quarters, I assure you." He nodded at Sam. "Have someone show the lady to her room while I tend to the buckboard." With that, he gave her a saucy wink, laced his thumbs behind blue suspenders, and strutted to the door.

"Buddy," Charity called after him. One glance at Sam's frowning face and she amended. "Mr. Pierce. . .I can't tell you how grateful I am."

Buddy tipped his soggy hat then turned and dashed outside.

Daniel Clark huddled in a corner of the hotel lobby among a group of men who had ducked in out of the rain. Feeling a mixture of disbelief and something else, an unsettling, uncomfortable emotion he couldn't shake, he watched the exchange between Charity and the strange man.

He'd never witnessed this Charity before—her delicate face framed by damp ringlets of coal and her wide eyes flashing, her head thrown back and her soft lips drawn in a smile full of gleaming white teeth. In all the time he'd known her, she'd never laughed so freely in his presence or clung to him weak-kneed with glee. Seeing her that way stirred something inside him that quickened his breath.

And then she was gone. Vanished from the top of the stairs, still laughing and chattering like a schoolgirl. Her absence left him as hollow as a gourd.

The fog in Daniel's head cleared enough to realize that the men crowded around him were staring, amusement dancing in their eyes. Clearing his throat, he pushed through his mockers, feigning interest in the weather past the front window. "Well, gentlemen, looks like it's beginning to clear."

Their snickers and whispers were lost on him as he hurried to the door and slipped out. Casting a glance at the offending stranger who had run into the hotel alongside Charity, he lowered the brim of his hat to block the persistent light sprinkle and hurried down the boardwalk toward home.

Charity released the bottom hook of her skirt and let the drenched fabric fall in a soggy heap at her feet. She stepped free and ran to the corner where she had tossed the wet satchel. Wrinkling her nose at the musty smell the rain had coaxed from the heavy canvas, she slid the bag over the floor then lifted it to the dressing table. Rummaging inside, she pulled out dry undergarments and her last clean dress. Shivers shook her from the draft blowing in around the window frame and under the door, and her teeth chattered until she could hear them.

There were clean towels and soap beside the basin of hot water Sam had sent upstairs. She freshened up and dressed as fast as she could. The water warmed her some, but her teeth still rattled. Jerking the blanket from the bed, she draped the soft folds over her shoulders.

The boar-bristle brush in her bag came from Mama's vanity set, an expensive gift she'd received as a girl in Jefferson and brought with her to Humble. Charity ran it through her hair, feeling guilty for having taken so precious an item without permission.

With her curls pinned up, the mirror over the basin reflected the image of her old self. So why didn't she feel like herself?

Charity leaned to study her face, so clean her nose reflected the light coming in under the shade. A fire she couldn't name lit her eyes from within and colored her burning cheeks. She put a hand to her trembling mouth to quench the smile she saw there and pushed the truth from her mind.

She turned from the mirror to look around, and her heart swelled in gratitude to Buddy. The room was small but cozy. From the blanket that covered her to the crisp sheets, the embroidered pillowcases, and the lace curtains at the window, everything smelled fresh and new.

The gleaming floors were of the same polished wood as the door, windowsill, and corner table that held the basin. Floral paper in shades of blue and green adorned the walls, and a rag rug beside the bed cushioned her feet.

Noise from the street below drew her to the window. A light rain still fell, but clustered strangers milled about the boardwalk again. She shook her head. A far cry from the days when she recognized every face in town. She feared the discovery of oil would cause Humble to become as bustling and sprawling as nearby Houston. Why couldn't the confounded oil companies pack it in and leave for good? She wished they'd all hop the first train out and go back to where they came from.

All. . .except Buddy Pierce.

Charity fell onto the bed and stared at the ceiling. Just who was he anyway, this bull of a man who met her at every turn, the handsome stranger who rescued her and knew all of her secrets? Remembering his teasing and spirited laughter, she hugged herself and smiled.

Had she ever seen such eyes? Green as a bitter apple and rimmed in brown, they looked right through her. And the size of him! When Buddy pulled her to his chest, she felt small and safe. His arms wrapped around her stirred a peculiar sensation in her middle, pleasant and unpleasant in equal measure. Warm butterflies tumbled in her stomach now just thinking of him.

She lurched upright. How could she possibly entertain such scandalous musings when only days ago Daniel had stood at her side, Daniel had held her?

Perched on the edge of the bed, staring at her troubled reflection in the frosty windowpane, she admitted that it hadn't been the same. She'd never once thrilled to Daniel's touch or come to life in his presence the way she had with Buddy.

How can that be? I almost married Daniel Clark.

Yet she hadn't once grieved for him the way she had for Emmy. Hadn't they both betrayed her?

Charity remembered Emmy's mournful face turned to the light, pining for Daniel while she grieved over shattered trust. She pictured Daniel emerging from the shadows, saw Emmy embracing him in the moonlight.

How could I have ever loved that wicked girl?

Yet her heart was her undoing. Whatever the cost, whatever the fool her devotion made her, she loved Emily Dane more than herself. The faithless girl was the sister she'd never had, and one never stopped loving a sister.

"Oh drat!" In her angst, Charity had twisted her dress until the thin fabric ripped. Fingering the ragged edges, she wondered if she could fix it. She had only one other outfit not too worn or frayed to wear. Juggling between three dresses made her weary.

Washing them every week became a challenge. Scrubbing wore down the nap more each time. Every washday there were buttons to replace and tears to mend. If only Mama could afford more material. They had tucked away money for that purpose, but the infernal wedding gown had sapped every penny and then some. She toyed with converting the gown into something suitable, but the idea wasn't practical. The fabric proved too fine for everyday use.

Amy Jane Pike's offer to buy the dress struck Charity's mind like a thunderclap. She could afford material for three, maybe four dresses with that kind of money.

As fast as she remembered Amy Jane, she realized something else. She was on her own now. In order to survive, she would need every penny that fell into her hands for necessities. Nothing more. The thought filled her with regret. . .and fear.

"Young Mr. Pierce said you and Bertha may come by some money." Mother Dane's words came to her unbidden.

If oil truly lay under their land, buying clothes would never be a problem again. She could buy a trunk full. And Mama would never need to scrub another floor. She could replace her straggly teeth with a store-bought pair and afford fancy combs like Mother Dane's for her hair. Charity imagined her mama gussied up like Mother Dane, and the picture made her laugh out loud.

Having money could do all those things and more, but she pushed the temptation from her mind. Such thoughts opposed how she felt about the oil boom in her town, not to mention her convictions about the evils of too much wealth.

A moan from deep within Charity's stomach reminded her she hadn't had breakfast, though the hour was well past noon. Her immediate fortune lay in selling her wedding gown. She would go see Amy Jane and then find some food. . .as soon as she warmed up a bit.

She lay back and snuggled deeper into the feather mattress. Drawing the soft blue blanket against her face, she breathed in the fresh, new smell. Clouds darkened the sky outside the window, casting the small room into shadows, while overhead the light patter of rain on the roof pounded out a muted lullaby.

CHAPTER 8

Two minutes of high wind and scattered hail and the tempest was spent. Thunder and lightning in a pitch-black sky had been the worst of it. One of those storms that make empty threats.

By the time Buddy drew near the stable, he had made up his mind. A light drizzle still fell, but what of it? He was already wet, and Charity's mama would be worried sick if he didn't set her mind at ease.

The horse had the smell of the stall in his nostrils and showed reluctance when Buddy made him turn.

"Giddap, you lazy beast. You ain't worth your weight in sour oats. Cut dirt, or I'll trade you for a gasoline engine."

The horse laid back his ears but plodded past the livery door. In no hurry to part with his feed bag, he shivered with irritation while Buddy shivered from the cold. A damp chill had penetrated his bones, and he ached all over. Scraping his knuckles and picking up a splinter on the jagged wood, he groped beneath the seat and found a spare saddle blanket. The stale covering would cause him to smell like the stockyard but might save him from the grippe.

The trail to the Danes' house felt farther than it actually was, even after the horse accepted his plight and picked up the pace. With tremendous relief, Buddy finally pulled up to the house and climbed down. The rain had stopped completely. He shrugged off the blanket and headed up the walk.

The door opened before he reached it, and Charity's mama blew out of it raving. "Where's my girl? Was it you hauled her away from here?"

He held up his hands. "Your daughter's fine, Mrs. Bloom." The feral gleam in her eyes brought to mind the liveryman's estimation. She looked like Crazy Bertha.

"I said where is she? Why'd you take her, and what've you done to her?"

Flustered, Buddy glanced at Mrs. Dane, who had come to stand behind her friend. The big woman took one look at his face and came to his aid.

"Bert, let the boy get a word in. It appears he has something to say. Let's hear him."

"Talk fast, stranger. Magda, fetch me your shotgun for if'n I don't like what he has to say."

The cold left Buddy, driven away by fear of the tiny, wild-eyed woman. "Ma'am, on my honor, Charity's safe. I got her in out of the rain, and I'm sure she's warm and dry by now. Don't worry, I left her in good hands."

"Where at?"

"In town. I put her up at the Lone Star Hotel."

A shrill scream exploded from Mrs. Bloom's tight lips, and she charged him, head down, like a bull. He caught hold of her forehead before she could ram him and held her off. She swatted at him with both hands, connecting only with the air.

"Bertha!" Mrs. Dane caught her around the waist and hauled her back. "Let the boy explain."

Bertha thrashed against her friend's grip. "You heard him. He's done took her to the hotel and tarnished her."

Buddy rocked back on his heels. He'd never heard such talk from a lady before, and her words stunned him. Then he got mad. Being accused of the same thing twice in one day was quite enough.

"No, ma'am, I did no such thing." He had to shout over her screams. "I wouldn't do anything to hurt your daughter. Last I saw, she was standing in the hotel lobby where I left her, soaking wet and exhausted—a condition she came to be in through no fault of mine."

Mrs. Bloom ceased her struggling and stared up at him, no longer Crazy Bertha, just a guilt-ridden, heartbroken mother. She dropped her gaze before his accusation. "Why didn't you bring her here, then?"

"She refused to come back. No disrespect intended, ma'am, but you have a stubborn daughter."

From behind Bertha Bloom, arms still locked around her waist, Mrs. Dane nodded. "An inherited trait."

His fiery indignation cooled, Buddy pushed back his hat and stepped closer. "I only did what I thought best for Charity."

Mrs. Dane chimed in again. "He got her off the streets, Bert. You should be grateful for that, anyway."

Mrs. Bloom pursed her lips in thought, pressing her finger against them. The conclusion she came to smoothed her furrowed brow. She nodded then looked over her shoulder at Mrs. Dane. "Turn me loose, Magda. I got my right mind now."

"You sure?"

"I'm sure. Now let me go."

Mrs. Dane cautiously complied but held her arms at the ready, just in case.

Mrs. Bloom looked up at Buddy. "You swear on all things holy that you ain't hurt my daughter?"

"I don't hold with swearing on holy things, ma'am, but you have my word as a Christian gentleman. I'd cut off my arm before I'd hurt her."

Bertha Bloom folded her arms, stock-still except for her tongue, which slowly traced circles in her cheek. She tilted her head. "You mean that, don't you, son?"

"Ma'am, I sure do."

"Will you help me bring her home?"

He chewed over his next words then decided to take the risk. "I don't mean to interfere in your business, Mrs. Bloom, but don't you think you're asking a lot of Charity? To stay here, I mean?"

She weighed and measured him with a glance. "You know a few things about us, don't you, boy?"

"I know enough. I believe your daughter feels she doesn't have a home. Provide her one, and she'll come."

She jutted her chin. "Fine—then help me."

Buddy cocked his head and frowned. "Me, ma'am?"

"Who else? You're the only one that can."

"How so?"

She looked into the distance and drew a long, ragged breath. "I never trusted no oilman before. I've hated and shunned the lot of you. But something about you rang true from the beginning."

She fixed him with a stern gaze. "You're the one who talked me into leasing my house and half my property to pay for this well. Now get yourself over to my place and find oil. Else clear off so I can take my daughter home." Mrs. Bloom's direct stare was a challenge.

Buddy answered it with a nod. "There's oil beneath your land, all right. A lot of it. I'd stake my reputation as an oilman on that."

"Then go coax it out of the ground so I can buy my daughter a place to live. I'll give you two months to look. If you don't find anything by then, you clear out and I reclaim my property."

Despite the fire of his enthusiasm, the cold had begun to creep back into Buddy's limbs. He couldn't control the shivers that took him. "I'll g-get on over there f-first thing."

Mrs. Dane latched onto his sleeve. "Not so fast, young man." She held him at arm's length and looked him over. "Soaking wet and chilled to the bone. You won't be able to do anything if you catch your death."

Her grip tightened and she started for the house. He had no choice but to follow. "You need to get into some dry clothes. My husband's about your size, only shorter. 'Course, he's fleshy around the middle, not muscled up like you. I guess some of his things will have to do."

She paused and wrinkled her nose at him. "If you don't mind my saying, you need a good washing. You smell worse than a buffalo herd."

In one last desperate attempt, Buddy pulled free of her grasp. "Yes, ma'am. I reckon that's true, so I'd best get on back to town."

Mrs. Dane linked arms with him, but not in the delicate, genteel manner of a lady. In fact, she nearly wrestled him to the ground. "Don't make me take you by the ear, young man. Dry clothes and a warm tub is what you need, and I'll be taking no sass on the subject."

She dragged him past the front door and into the parlor. "You might as well save yourself the twenty-five cents. That's what a soak in hot water costs in town, you know, plus fifteen cents for a shave." She winked over at Mrs. Bloom. "I'm offering fifty cents worth of scrubbing, two dollars worth of duds, and a plate of vittles if you're hungry. . .and it won't cost you a plug nickel." She chuckled. "And, Mr. Pierce, 'free' is a bargain you can't afford to pass up."

Satisfied with the angle of her hat in the vanity mirror, Charity pulled on clean gloves and stepped into the hall. Two rooms down, a man stooped next to the keyhole struggling to fit his key into the lock. After a closer look, she realized it was Buddy, though something about him seemed different. She closed her door hard to get his attention.

He leaped and whirled as if she'd shot him, then spun without a word and went at the lock with a vengeance.

Planting her hands on her hips, she feigned anger. "So there you are. First you help a lady and then you run out on her."

Buddy's frantic fingers stilled. He straightened slowly and turned, one chestnut brow arched to the sky. "You know, a man can run into a heap of trouble in this town for that very thing."

Stunned by his angry face, Charity clasped her hands at her chest. "What very thing?"

He abandoned the stubborn key and charged like a bantam hen with chicks. "Trying to help a lady, that's what. Do you have any idea the humiliation I've suffered?"

For the first time she noticed his manner of dress. He wore a white shirt, suitable for Sunday service but made for smaller shoulders and a wider waist. Gathered folds allowed the sleeves to fit his big arms, but they ended far shy of his wrists. A woman's sash of robin's egg blue held up black trousers six inches too short and miles too big around the middle.

She stared, trying to take it all in. "Oh, Buddy! What in the world?"

"See what I mean?" He held his arms out to his sides. "This is my reward for the good deed of the day."

Charity ached to laugh, but the look on his face warned her not to. She pointed at his waist. "Is that. . . ? Why, Mother Dane has a sash exactly like that."

"Not anymore, she doesn't."

"Oh no!"

His gaze jerked to her handbag and his scowl quenched her grin. "Where do you think you're going? I've just wrestled a bobcat over putting you up in that room, and now you're leaving?"

The breath caught in her throat. "Mama."

"As bad as she was, your mama wasn't the worst of it. I'd sooner face Custer's Indians than deal with that Dane woman again. She had me shucked and in a tub before I could say Jack Sprat. Then she trussed me in this getup and left me no choice but to ride into town looking as queer as a pig in a parlor."

Charity jerked a hand to her mouth, glad he couldn't see behind it, and tried to look appalled. "How scandalous! They're a couple of ruffians, those two. Oh, Buddy, I should've warned you. Would have, too, if you'd bothered to tell me where you were going."

An elderly couple appeared at the head of the stairs, saw Buddy, and openly stared. Charity guessed they'd caught sight of him downstairs and were still in a stir. As they passed by, the grinning old man pointed at Buddy's bare ankles and whispered something about floodwater. In front of their door, they looked back with amused eyes, collapsed into giggles, and scrambled inside.

Buddy slouched and hung his head. "I'll have to fight every man in Humble before I live this down."

"Why on earth did you go to the Danes'?"

"Why do you think? You ran off without a thought for anyone. In a storm yet. For all they knew, a twister had you in a Louisiana swamp by now."

She stared into his eyes and knew his claim to be true. Ashamed, she dropped her gaze and leaned on the wall. "If not for you, it might've."

Buddy drew a deep breath then released it along with his air of indignation. He leaned against the wall beside her—too close—and lifted her chin with his finger. "Hardly accurate, since there was no twister. And stop changing the subject. Where are you off to?"

"I have business outside town."

He shook his head. "Whatever it is, it'll keep until tomorrow when I can go with you."

She raised her brows. "I'm grateful for the offer, but I've conducted business on my own for some time now. I think I can manage."

"And I gave my word to your mama that I'd watch out for you. I don't need you getting into mischief that I'll have to answer for later. Besides, you won't make it back before nightfall. I get the feeling Humble isn't the same safe town it was before."

Buddy was right. The streets grew wilder every day. She could count on one hand the times she'd been in town after dark, even before the boom. She stood upright and faced him. "Fine, you win. But why can't we go right now?"

"I'm exhausted and hungry, that's why. As soon as I change out of this silly garb, I'm finding myself something to eat and going to bed."

Her heart sank. At the mention of food, the rumble in her stomach picked up something fierce, but she wouldn't be eating until she sold her dress. Planting her feet, she got ready to take him head-on, though she felt dwarfed by his looming size. "I'm sorry, but I must go now. If you can't go with me, I'll be forced to go by myself."

"Why? What could be so all-fired important?"

She wilted a bit. "I can't say. It's personal."

"You have to give me more than that if you expect me to jump to your bidding."

Reluctance to answer his question knocked the air right out of her bluff. She gave a careless toss of her head. "Very well, then. Will you take me first thing tomorrow?"

"I have business of my own in the morning."

Her hungry stomach lurched. "I see."

"I should be finished sometime after lunch. We'll go then."

She burned with curiosity but wouldn't ask. She didn't hide it well, though, and he volunteered the information.

"I happen to be headed out to your place."

Her head jerked up. "Whatever for?"

"I promised your mama I'd get things moving along out there. First thing tomorrow I'll be riding out to see if I can't speed up those drills." He ambled over to the door and set to work struggling with the lock again. "Blast it all. What's wrong with this infernal thing?"

"Buddy?"

He turned.

"Take me with you."

"That's not a good idea."

"Why not?" She pouted, irked that he returned to the lock, dismissing her.

"It's no place for you. The yard is crawling with roughnecks and buried under equipment. Besides, I'm not taking the rig."

"I'll walk with you."

"Too muddy to walk. I'm going by horseback."

"I can ride."

He exhaled and shifted his weight to the other foot. "Why do you want to go out there anyway?"

Was he irritated at the lock or with her? "Just do. I'm curious."

"Well, the answer's no."

She crossed her arms and leaned against the door. He still fought with the key. After a bit she eased over to him. "You know, I think that must be the wrong one."

He straightened and frowned as though the thought hadn't occurred to him. "You think so?"

She watched him figure it out. He'd have to go downstairs, and he'd sooner be poached and pickled.

"Charity, could you. . . ?"

"Exchange it for you? Of course." She took the long brass key from his hand and dangled it between them. "In exchange for a favor."

His hopeful eyes narrowed. "You wouldn't bushwhack me like that."

She smiled her sweetest smile. "Such a harsh word."

He threw up his hands. "Who spawned the hardheaded women in this town? Go on, then. Get my key. But you'd best be ready to head out first thing in the morning."

"I'll be ready. I promise." She rushed to the head of the stairs and then turned. Blast pride–she was desperate. "Buddy?"

"Now what?"

"I haven't eaten all day, and I'm faint from hunger."

"Lucky for you, I am, too. We'll rustle up a bite downstairs before we turn in."

"Wonderful idea." She lifted the hem of her skirt and started down the stairs.

"I just hope you can keep up tomorrow," he called after her. "Because I won't be coddling you."

CHAPTER 9

The fiery red and gold horizon, visible between fat, knotted trunks, belied the cold of the morning as Charity followed Buddy out of town. The horses' steady footfalls were quiet on the pine straw blanket, and the creak of leather and occasional snort of a horse were the only sounds to break the stillness. In the chill air, their breath, and that of their mounts, came out in smoky billows of mist. Charity shivered and drew her shawl closer, her attention on Buddy's back.

His spine as rigid as a tomato stake, he sat tall in the saddle on the big bay. As for his vow not to coddle her, so far he'd failed to keep his threat. While she couldn't claim Buddy had pampered her, he had certainly tended to her needs.

After staring hard at her denim britches, he wouldn't allow her to go with him to the livery, insisting she wait inside the hotel instead. In no time he returned with a gentle horse for her, shortening the stirrups before taking her elbow and helping her aboard. Then he led her through the swampy streets, guiding the little mare past the mud holes and deepest ruts before handing over the reins.

Charity blushed remembering how Buddy looked at her when she opened the door dressed in men's pants. She guessed the women in St. Louis wore split skirts or riding habits, but Humble afforded no such luxuries. Women here made their own by cutting worn-out frocks up the middle and sewing them into flared legs, or they borrowed jeans from a man. Thankfully, she'd packed an old pair handed down from her slip of an Irish grandfather.

She stared down at her legs. A mite snug and hardly the latest fashion, but the pants served her well for sitting a horse. "It's mighty cold, isn't it?" she asked then cringed, waiting for Buddy to order her to return to her room. She needn't have worried.

The quarrelsome man hadn't said ten words to her all morning. He'd had even less to say at dinner the night before.

She itched to get him talking again and searched her mind for something to draw him out. "Hey, what's that over there?"

Buddy looked over his shoulder, and she pointed near the edge of the trail. "Are those coyote droppings?" She winced at her choice of topic but forged ahead anyway. "You know, I think they are. He left some tracks, too. See? In front of the droppings. One paw in front of the other, as clear as day."

He acknowledged her findings with a grunt and turned away again.

"Coyotes don't usually come in this close to town. Wonder what drew him?"

Buddy shrugged. It seemed the most he would give, so Charity gave up. They rode the rest of the way in silence.

A quarter mile from her property, a commotion the likes of which she'd never heard reached Charity's ears. The sound grew louder as they neared the house, yet Buddy seemed unconcerned. She longed to ask about the source of the racket, but her offended pride wouldn't allow her.

As they rode up even with the yard, the hullabaloo frightened the horses. Buddy's mount sidestepped, prancing and bobbing his head until Buddy dug in his heels and coaxed him forward. Charity's skittish little mare fell in behind. They picked their way to the rear of the house and reined in at the edge of chaos.

Sludge-covered men darted to and fro, dodging wagons, equipment, and each other. Oxen strained against carts filled with pipe, their massive hooves slinging mud as they pawed the rain-soaked ground. Rigs loaded with timber sat off to one side. She recognized these as belonging to Bender's Mill. More stacks of lumber lined the bog in staggered piles. At least Charity thought it was the bog. Everything looked so different she found it hard to get her bearings.

A clearing stretched in a wide circle from the edge of the dense woods beyond the bog all the way to the scrub bushes behind the house, creating an open area that hadn't been there before. Heavy black boots had trampled the yard to mush, leaving very little grass—only a few tufts along the fence line.

Charity's stomach tightened. How odd to see strangers pouring in and out at the back entrance. Someone had tied the screen door open with a rope, an invitation to swarms of flies and mosquitoes. Muddy tracks crisscrossed the steps and porch. She shuddered to think what the floor inside must look like. Mama would be fit to bury!

Well, so be it. It was justice served. When all the nonsense was over and they returned to this mess, Charity wouldn't lift a finger to help clean.

"Morning, Miss Charity!"

She turned in her saddle to see who shouted the greeting.

Stubby Morgan grinned up at her, his copper hair and matching freckles stark against his pale complexion.

"Why, good morning. What are you doing way out here this time of day?" She glanced toward the mill wagons. "They got you making deliveries now?"

"No, ma'am. Don't work out at Bender's no more." He pointed over his shoulder with a grimy thumb. "I signed on with this outfit."

Stunned, Charity gaped at him. Stubby had gone to work for Bender's Mill the year his papa died. He was only fourteen at the time. Charity, barely ten when it happened, felt sad when he never returned to school.

His dappled face flinched under her searching gaze, and he shuffled his oversized feet. "The pay's good, Miss Charity." He brightened. "Three dollars a day! More'n twice what I brought home from the mill. In my family, that's too good to pass up."

She found her voice. "But don't you see? It won't last. I can't believe you quit your steady job to work for a company that'll be long gone in a matter of weeks."

A puzzled look lit briefly on his upturned face before he flashed an angelic smile. "Why, sure it'll last, ma'am. Humble's a boomer town now." He gestured over his head at a group of men standing nearby. "Just ask them fellers over yonder. Zeke there helped me land the job. He put in a good word for me with the drillers."

Charity followed his nod. Ezekiel Young and his son Isaac, her nearest neighbors to the north, stood in a long line of men passing boards from the wagon to the clearing. Charity understood their presence. The Young family had lost their cotton crop to boll weevils, and with Isaac set to wed Amy Jane Pike in three months, there'd be another mouth to feed.

Shamus Pike himself huddled with another group of men shouting to be heard over the ruckus. Despite Elsa's fancy airs, Shamus always worked extra jobs between crops. He had no choice. His wife and daughter scooped up money as fast as he raked it in. If the oil company paid so handsomely, Elsa would see to it that Shamus was first in line.

Charity leaned over in the saddle so Stubby could hear. "You've worked that mill for ten years." She frowned and nodded at the melee behind him. "Don't throw it away for this. I'll bet they'd let you change your mind if you asked."

Stubby shrugged his narrow shoulders. "Why would I change my mind? Like I said, Miss Charity, the pay's real good." He peered up at her, shading his eyes from the sun. "Don't worry none about your mail. I can still run out and fetch it for you every Saturday."

She shook her head at the kind-faced young man. "I won't have you go out of your way like that for me. I'm grateful for the offer, but don't trouble yourself about it anymore."

"You sure?"

She smiled. "Real sure."

A man near the house called Stubby's name. He grinned at Charity, tipped his battered hat, and ran off. Her gaze drifted past him and over the scope of her land, taking in every violation, every unspeakable change, every heavy-footed stranger tromping through her yard.

Her room sat tucked behind those mud-spattered walls. She pictured the quilt on her bed, a gift from Grandma Leona Bloom in Jefferson, covered in sludge. Remembered her diary with its too flimsy lock, left out on her desk. Nausea settled in the pit of her stomach, coupled with something akin to rage.

These men rode into Humble like a gang of roughs and thieves, turning everything upside down with their silly oil. They had disrupted her life and defiled her home. Hiring her friends and neighbors to take part in it dealt Charity a staggering blow.

She felt Buddy's gaze on her and glanced his way. He watched her from astride his horse with the same puzzled look she'd seen two days before. What must he be thinking?

Who cares what he thinks? This is his fault. All of it.

"I'm going," she spat. "I've seen enough." She whirled the mare and dug her heels into its flank, leaving Buddy in a spray of mud.

Charity hoped the horse knew the way back. She was too upset to think about where she was going. Clinging to the saddle horn, she let the mare take her where it would, while the trees on both sides of the trail passed in a blur.

Her life was a fine mess. In a week's time she'd lost her fiancé, her best friend, her home, and her mama, in that order. The only good had come to her at the hands of a stranger, a man at whom she'd just flung dirt.

Guilt niggled at her conscience. How could she be cruel to Buddy Pierce? He'd offered her nothing but kindness since the day they first met. If not for him, she would be homeless.

Forgive me, God. I've acted shamelessly. I should turn around and apologize.

Before Charity could act on her decision, a pause in the mare's stride broke the monotony of her plodding and a shudder coursed through her body. Her ears fell back, and she cantered to the side.

"Easy, girl. What's your trouble?"

The horse's breath came quicker and her head shot up. Eyes wild with fear and nostrils flared, she edged away from the right side of the trail, and it was all Charity could do to hold her. A low growl came from the bushes just before the mare reared, her legs pawing the air. Charity hit the ground hard and rolled in the mud, away from the flailing hooves. She fought to draw breath into her lungs but couldn't. This scared her almost as much as the scraggly beast crouching at the edge of the path.

The wolf, no longer interested in the fleeing horse, stalked Charity in short, quick bursts. His body lay low to the ground, his hollow haunches trembling from the effort. He bared his teeth in a wide, feral grin, and stringy spittle ran in rivulets from his mouth.

She struggled to get up, to breathe. Twenty more feet and he'd be on her. She groped the ground for a weapon. Desperate, scrambling fingers closed around a clump of muddy grass, and she tensed to hurl it at him.

Fifteen feet.

Ten.

Leering, taunting her, the wolf rose for the last advance. Sure of his kill, he swayed closer.

Charity met his eyes and saw evil. She dug her heels into the ground and scrambled away. Willing air into her lungs, she hurled the fistful of mud at his face. He wouldn't take her without a fight.

Still, he came. Almost upon her, he snarled and gnashed his teeth—the promise of things to come.

God, help me!

The wolf took two more steps then froze midstride. He crouched again, his attention drawn to an approaching rider.

Buddy reined in between them. "Don't move." His voice was grave with warning. "He's rabid."

Buddy's horse trembled, no happier than the mare to be so close to the snarling creature, but Buddy held him steady.

Charity struggled to her feet. Her lungs had somewhat eased, and she sucked in short, gasping breaths. She longed to leap for the horse but knew if she did, he might bolt.

The wolf held his ground, too blind-insane to be afraid.

A shot rang out from a nearby wooded grove. The wolf yelped and lunged, straight for the legs of Buddy's mount. The big bay reared, but Buddy held the saddle. The wolf died midleap and fell on the muddy trail with glazed eyes, teeth still bared. His tongue lolled to the side, and bloody foam rimmed his muzzle.

Charity shuddered at the sight. Buddy rode his frantic horse a few feet away, leaped off, and ran to Charity. Oblivious to her mud-covered clothes, she threw her arms around his neck and hid her face against his chest.

He held her and rubbed her back with both hands. "Are you all right?"

"My legs won't hold me."

"Don't worry, I've got you."

She nuzzled closer and shuddered. "I was so scared."

"Me, too," he whispered, "but it's over now."

She raised her head and sought his eyes. "I'm sorry for being mad at you, Buddy."

He cupped her chin with his finger and laughed down at her. "Were you mad at me? Funny, I thought I was mad at you."

She smiled and pressed her cheek against the rough fabric of his shirt, for the first time aware of the clean, woodsy smell of him. He held her tighter.

"You know," he said, his breath warm against her hair, "next time you get peeved at me, you might want to let me in on it. Seems a shameful waste of anger if I don't know."

She rose up and nodded at the wolf. "What happened? Who shot it?"

He tilted his chin toward something behind her. "I think there's your answer."

Charity looked over her shoulder. Three riders emerged from the trees, one of them Daniel Clark. He came alongside them, a rifle balanced across his saddle.

"You all right, Charity?" His blue eyes moved over her, dark with an emotion she'd never seen there before.

Aware that Buddy still held her, she drew a breath and moved away from him. "I will be."

Sidney Anderson spoke up. "We been trailing that wolf all day. Rabid, you know."

Buddy moved toward them, planting his feet carefully to give wide berth to the dead animal. "Yep, we figured that out."

Daniel motioned at the ground with his chin. "Sid, take a shovel and bury that critter. Put him deep. Cover the blood, too. Last thing we need around here is an outbreak of rabies. And, Jack"—he pointed down the trail—"follow Miss Charity's horse and make sure it gets back to the livery."

Buddy nodded at Daniel. "Much obliged. I'm grateful you

showed up when you did."

Daniel flashed a broad smile. "Oh, I reckon you could've handled the situation. We just came along at the right time. We've tracked that thing for miles."

Buddy grinned. "So you said."

Daniel leaned in the saddle to offer his hand. "I don't believe we've met. I'm Daniel Clark." He seemed to chew on the next part but said it anyway. "A friend of Miss Bloom's." His eyes shifted to her when he said it.

She could tell he wanted to catch her reaction. She forced herself not to have one.

Buddy seemed not to notice. He reached up and shook Daniel's hand. "Buddy Pierce. I work for an oil company here in town."

"Glad to know you, Mr. Pierce." Though he spoke to Buddy, Daniel stared at Charity. "Can I give you a ride into town, honey? You could use some cleaning up, and I'm headed that way."

The endearment stiffened Charity's spine. Daniel Clark was cockier than a man had a right to be. No matter how black his hair or broad his shoulders, there were some things you just didn't do. Besides, how did he know she was staying in town?

She took a step closer to Buddy. "No, thank you. Mr. Pierce will take me."

Daniel's dark eyebrows rose; then his gaze swept to Buddy. "I'll leave you in his capable hands then." He tipped his wide-brimmed hat and turned his horse.

"Daniel. . . ?"

Leather creaked as he shifted his weight to look at her.

She swallowed the ache in her throat and met his eyes. "Thank you. For shooting the wolf, I mean."

He held her gaze until her cheeks grew warm. Mischief teased the corners of his mouth. He glanced at Buddy. "I'd shoot a wolf for you any old time, sugar." He winked then spurred his horse and rode away.

Sidney fetched a shovel from his pack and bent to scoop up the carcass. Charity spun away from the gruesome sight. She doubted she'd ever forget the big animal standing over her, its trembling legs coiled and ready to spring.

Buddy's hands gripped her shoulders from behind. "I'm sorry you had to go through that, Charity. I feel responsible."

She reached to touch his fingers. "You? Nonsense. How could it be your fault?"

He stepped around to face her. "If I hadn't pouted like a schoolboy this morning, I would've taken a closer look at those tracks you found." He glanced over at the wolf. "I expect they belonged to our friend there."

Charity shook her head. "It's nobody's fault. And like you said, it's over now."

He smiled, mostly with his eyes, and nodded. "Let's get you back to town, then." His arm went across her shoulders, his grip firm.

Tucked against him, she felt safe. She allowed him to guide her to where the bay stood pawing the ground. On the way, she saw his hat, saved from the mud by a thatch of tall grass. She bent and picked it up, brushing it off before handing to him, but his curious gaze followed Daniel up the trail.

"That your Daniel?"

She halted, nearly tripping him, and dashed his hat to the ground. "He's not my Daniel! Why does everyone keep saying that?"

Buddy's forehead crumpled. "Ease up, little lady. I didn't mean to pry." He leaned for his hat, wiped the fresh mud from the brim onto his jeans, and walked on ahead.

Charity cringed and pressed her knuckles to her eyes. "Buddy, please wait."

Whatever she meant to say next, the words were lost when he stopped short and turned. Embarrassed, she spit out the first thing that came to mind. "Goodness, but you're a cantankerous man. You keep me in a constant state of gratitude or regret. I never know whether to thank you or say I'm sorry."

He lifted a brow. "Which one you offering this time?"

She winced. "Definitely the latter. I'm sorry. I truly am. I'm not the least bit mad at you. It's that insufferable Daniel Clark." She glared up the trail. "Have you ever witnessed such arrogance? Why, the nerve of him."

"He did seem mighty friendly, considering."

A blush crept up her cheeks.

Buddy brought the horse around and motioned for her to climb on. When she lifted her foot to the stirrup, he frowned at her mud-covered pants. "Reckon it's too late to whistle for old Daniel? I'm not sure I care to cozy up behind those all the way into town."

She swung into the saddle. "Don't tease. It's not funny."

He climbed up behind her and leaned to take the reins, so close his breath tickled her cheek. "It's none of my business, but if you ask me, Daniel Clark is a man having some regrets."

She squirmed around to glare at him. "Whatever do you mean?"

Buddy flicked the reins. "Like I said, Miss Bloom, it's none of my business."

CHAPTER 10

Emily Dane sprawled in her four-poster bed, idly gnawing a drumstick. Barefoot and still in her nightdress, she lay propped against goose-down pillows, one long leg crossed over the other. With her free hand, she twirled one of the blond ringlets framing her face while admiring the smooth, bare skin of her knees.

"You're downright scandalous in your impropriety, Emily Dane."

Mama's stern voice in her head made her giggle. That's what she'd say, all right, but what of it? According to Mama, she was forever downright scandalous in one silly thing or the other.

Emmy froze midbite and stared down at the greasy poultry until her eyes crossed. *Gracious! If I keep this up, I'll be prime pork and ready for the slaughter.* She extended her leg and stared, examining it from every angle before she smiled. *Then my thighs won't be quite so fetching, now, will they?*

Deliberately, and with great satisfaction, she flicked her wrist, tossing the half-eaten chicken leg through the open window. "There you go, Mama. Another pretty rose for your garden."

Emmy wiped her fingers on the lace napkin in her lap then gaped at the dark oily spots left behind. She had smuggled the fried chicken to her room wrapped in one of Mama's best linens. Holding the square of delicate cloth aloft, she surveyed the mess. "Oh bother! They'll hear her clear to Montgomery County if she gets wind of this."

She rolled onto her stomach and slid to the edge of the bed, peering into the dark recess between the floor and her lumpy mattress. Fighting to keep her balance, she leaned further in and worked at a tear by the nearest slat until she had removed a handful of fluff. Then she tucked the soiled cloth deep inside the hole. After stuffing the cotton in after it, she pushed upright and lay back with a satisfied smile.

There. Now she won't need to fret.

A thought flitted past, changing her smile to a frown. It was Mama's own fault, after all, for opening the door to Charity and Aunt Bert. She left Emmy no choice but to rummage like a thief in her own kitchen, so she'd have to live with the occasional missing napkin, now, wouldn't she?

She flopped on her side and stared at the floral wallpaper. During her confinement, she had memorized the line of every petal and every shade of pink. She knew how many blooms adorned each wall, as well as the numbers facing left and right. She had stared at the big ugly roses for days now, and they'd stared right back, silent witnesses to her frustration.

In truth, her history with the flowers started more than mere days ago. The horrid walls had been her constant companions for the past eight years, since Papa hired her room remodeled the summer she turned twelve. No one had touched it since. For Emmy, the youthful decor had long since lost its charm.

No matter. Soon she'd be mistress of her own big house, filled with brand-new rooms to look at, to decorate however she saw fit. Daniel had built it for Charity, but Charity would never live there. Emmy would marry Daniel, and the pretty, brick-fronted structure with its wide columns and a porch that wrapped all the way around would be hers. And there wouldn't be a pink rose in sight.

Hugging her pillow, she rolled to the other side of the bed where her vanity table beckoned. She knew she should dress and freshen up, but why go to all the trouble? Why wash her face, pin up her hair, get all gussied up for these four walls?

Hooves pounded up the drive. She leaped from the bed and rushed to her second-floor window, arriving just as the horse and rider passed from sight, hidden by the tangled branches of the oak outside her window. She peered out, using the lace curtain for cover, and caught a quick glimpse of muddy boots as the caller moved under the portico.

Next came the strident, angry voice of Auntie Bert. "You got a lot of nerve coming around here, Daniel Clark."

Emmy gasped. *Daniel? What in the world. . . ?*

"There ain't no need for that shotgun, ma'am."

Shotgun! Emmy's heart pounded so hard she feared they'd hear it downstairs.

Daniel's familiar voice rumbled, but she couldn't make out his words. Desperate to see, she leaned over as far as possible, but the front porch roof hid all but their feet.

Aunt Bert's voice became shrill. "Did you say wolf?"

"Mad with rabies, Mrs. Bloom. I shot it dead."

"Is my girl all right?"

"She's safe enough—from any four-legged threat, at least."

"What do you mean by that?" This from Emmy's mama.

"Mrs. Dane, there are prowling wolves of the two-legged sort that can be just as dangerous."

Aunt Bert's voice took a hard edge. "You can say that again. I'm looking at one."

Mama shushed her.

After an edgy silence, Aunt Bert piped up again. "What is it you're trying to say to us, boy?"

"If you're really aiming to know, I'll tell you."

"Get on with it, then."

Emmy strained to hear, but Daniel's next words escaped her. She considered shimmying down the trellis and listening from behind the hedge but feared they'd catch her. She leaned so far out she had to tangle the fingers of both hands in the ancient vines to keep from toppling headfirst out of the window.

"Mrs. Bloom, you don't even know where Charity is, do you?"

"Not that it's any of your business, but I know exactly where she is. She's over at the Lone Star Hotel under the watchful eye of a friend."

Daniel cleared his throat. "I suppose by *friend* you mean Buddy Pierce?"

"Yep. I got that nice boy looking out for my Charity. If it weren't for the likes of you and her so-called best friend, she'd be here with me where she belongs."

Emmy cringed, but Daniel let it pass. "Well, ma'am, that nice boy you speak of is a stranger around these parts, ain't he? Just how much do you know about him?"

Aunt Bert was quiet for so long Emmy wondered if she'd heard Daniel's question.

"I've had about enough out of you!"

She heard, all right. Fury boiled from Aunt Bert's mouth, so fierce it singed the fuzz on Emmy's ears.

"I ain't answering no more questions from a polecat. I trusted you with my girl once, but you turned out to be a fizzle. Don't come around here now telling me who to trust with my own daughter."

"Pour it into him, Bert. He ain't good for nothing but telling lies and shaming young girls."

Emmy's grip tightened on the vines. *Oh, Mama! How could you?*

Daniel's raised voice echoed beneath the vaulted roof. "What you think of me don't change the facts, Bertha Bloom. You ought to know I just parted company with Charity and Mr. Pierce. Your nice boy there had his hands all over Charity, right out in the open in the bright of day."

Tension charged the air, like the second before lightning strikes. Emmy felt the hair on her scalp lift.

"I don't believe you." Aunt Bert's voice crashed the answering thunder.

"Ask Sidney Anderson and Jack Mayhew. They'll tell you it's true."

"No! I'm saying I don't believe you had the brash to march up here and spout something like this about my Charity, after what all you done to her." Aunt Bert's pitch might've shattered glass.

Another weighty hush.

Daniel shuffled his feet. "I didn't come here to fret nobody," he finally said. "I just thought you'd want to know."

"All I want to know is you in your saddle, riding away from here."

More silence. Emmy imagined them staring each other down.

Then Daniel's parting words floated up, as chipper as if they'd gathered for a Sunday social. "I'll take my leave then, ladies. You two have a pleasant day now, you hear?" Emmy pictured him tipping his hat, turning a rigid spine to the old biddies and walking away.

She withdrew a bit when Daniel stepped down off the porch and headed for his horse. He mounted up then rode out from under the oak tree and down the drive, slinging mud in his wake.

The women were still on the porch muttering dark curses at his back. Emmy leaned out again to better hear what Aunt Bert was saying.

"Why, if I weren't a lady, I'd kick him into a pulp."

"I'd tie him up and hold him for you. What you think he's up to, Bert?"

"No good, I'd say. Seems to be pulling some kind of a bluff."

Her mama paused for a bit before asking the question plaguing Emmy's mind. "You don't think there's any truth to what he said, do you?"

Aunt Bert's tone chilled Emmy's spine. "Magda. . .there'd better not be."

More shuffling feet, and then the door closed behind them.

Emmy pulled her head inside and made a mad dash for her clothes, dressing as if the house was on fire. On the way to climb out the window, she cast a glance at her image in the mirror over the dresser.

Drat! Her hair needed pinning, but there was no time to do it right. She had to catch Daniel.

He would take the trail out. She could catch him if she cut across the fields on Rebel. She wouldn't dare try it if Papa was home. Oh, there'd be trouble if she got caught. Terrible trouble. But she could outrun Mama.

In the barn, she paused before saddling old Rebel. Papa prized the palomino, still the fastest horse on the place, over most things in life, sometimes even her and Mama. Only there was no time to weigh the consequences. Daniel was riding away.

Five minutes later, Emmy raced across the field. She urged the horse through a tight thicket then over a marshy low spot to Jordan Gully. Despite her wishes, he slowed to pick his way across a deep ditch on the row of planks fashioned into a makeshift bridge. At the trail, she saw Daniel and laid a switch to Rebel's flank.

"Daniel! Oh, Daniel, wait."

He turned in the saddle and reined up his horse. As she approached, he drew alongside, and the press of his leg against her thigh took her breath.

"Emmy, what in blazes are you doing out here?"

The sound of her name in Daniel's long drawl raised gooseflesh on her arms. "I came to talk to you."

"Where'd you come from? I was just at your place."

"I know. I heard everything. Wasn't it dreadful?"

Daniel nudged his hat up and checked the trail behind her. "Come on. We'd best get you out of sight." He took the reins from her hand and led her horse into the cover of trees and thick underbrush.

They dismounted, and Emmy threw herself against him. "I had to come, sugar. I just had to. Please don't be cross." She pulled away to look at him. "I'm appalled by the hateful way Mama spoke to you. It made me feel sick to my stomach."

Daniel squirmed in her arms and didn't return her embrace. "If she catches us together, she'll have my hide and yours, too. I'm hardly in her good graces just now—or Bertha Bloom's, for that matter."

"Who cares? It's not fair. How dare those cackling crones treat you so shamefully! Would they rather you'd married Charity when you love me? What sort of life would that be for either of you? I say it's a blessing you woke up in time."

Her arms were tight around his neck, her body pressed close, but Daniel stood stiff as a plank with his arms to his sides.

She wiggled impatiently. "Hold me, sweetheart, and don't you fret. Things will turn out right in the end. We'll make them understand it was for the best. You'll see. Mama will finally come around to our way of thinking. Charity, too, for that matter."

At the mention of Charity's name, Daniel's body tensed, and he pushed her away. "I just don't know anymore, Emmy."

The tone of his voice, his gruff manner, even the sick-cow look on his face were all new to Emmy, and they frightened her. "What, sugar?" She tried to get a look at his eyes, but his head was lowered. "What don't you know?"

"It won't be that easy now. There's more to consider."

She drew back a step. "More to consider? Like what?"

Daniel took off his hat and used his arm to wipe the sweat from his brow. Then he propped the toe of his boot on a fallen tree and leaned into it, staring off into the woods.

Emmy watched and waited.

He cut his eyes around to her. "It's Mama."

Emmy knew they'd have her own mama's ruffled feathers to contend with, and Aunt Bert's, too. The mention of Mrs. Clark came straight out of nowhere. "Your mama? What about her?"

Daniel's foot slid off the tree and hit the dry leaves with a crash. He straightened and faced her, and his piercing blue eyes sliced her to the bone. "Emmy, she don't feel the same about you. She don't want us together."

Emmy's jaw dropped. Icy fingers of fear gripped the nape of her neck. She recovered and tried to smile, but her mouth quivered. "Don't be silly! She likes me. You've told me so a dozen times." She clutched her skirt in bunches to still her trembling hands. "Of course, you didn't need to tell me. I could see it for myself, whenever I was with her." She swallowed, trying to force the shrillness from her voice. "It's Charity she don't approve of, not me. She said I'm a much better catch than Bertha Bloom's daughter. You said so yourself."

Belligerence set Daniel's lips in a hard line. "That was before we shamed her in front of the whole town and tarnished her precious reputation. She's singing a different tune now, and it ain't a lullaby." He dashed his hat against his leg so hard it made her jump. "All because you chased me from the church house like a lovesick heifer. Why didn't you just keep your behind on that pew, Emmy? Couldn't you act like a lady for once?"

Emmy closed her gaping mouth and swiped her hand across it. "You'll take up for me, won't you? With your mama, I mean?"

He lowered his eyes and turned his back on her.

She rushed him and wrapped her arms around his waist. "You'll take a stand for me—for us—won't you?"

Daniel's body went rigid again. Even his voice came out stilted.

"Maybe we need to let things cool down some. Give folks time to forget."

She released him and withdrew. "The other night under that oak tree you didn't say anything about cooling down."

"Don't talk like a trollop. Besides, it ain't like that."

"What's it like, then?" Emmy felt like a shrew. She heard the harsh, strident tone of her voice but couldn't stop. "You can't even look at me, Daniel? I've risked everything to be with you. What will you risk for me?"

He didn't answer, didn't turn to face her.

She nodded at his obstinate shoulders. "All right, then. I don't need a pine knot to fall on my head. I guess this is good-bye."

Daniel whirled and caught her by the arm. "Come here now. Where do you think you're going?" He jerked her against him and tightened his grip on her waist. "I'm sorry, sweetness. Don't pay me no mind. I'm just confused by all the voices in my head—yours, Mama's, Charity's—all telling me different things. I can't think straight no more, that's all."

Emmy stiffened. "Charity's? You got Charity's voice in your head?"

Daniel looked like a hound caught in the coop. "Aw, now, not like you're thinking. I'm just mighty worried about her, that's all. She's been carrying on, all giggly and loose, with some stranger in town. It ain't like her."

"Stranger? Oh, you mean Buddy Pierce."

His eyes darkened again. "You know about him?"

"Well, I saw him. He was out at the house last night. Those two old guineas dragged him inside and gave him a bath."

Daniel blinked his disbelief. "A bath? I get the loud end of a shotgun, and that outsider gets a bath?" He glared as if she'd drawn the water herself. "Is there anyplace in town he ain't horned in on?"

Wary, she watched his angry face. "I can't tell why you're letting him get so far under your skin."

Daniel seemed to remember himself, but the dark storm remained on his face. "Ain't nobody under my skin. I just feel responsible for Charity, what with it being so soon after. . .well, you know. I feel like we drove her to act that way."

Emmy walked off from him a ways, hands on her hips, one side of her body angled toward him, the other side in retreat. She raised her head and sought his eyes. "And you're sure that's all that's bothering you?"

He gathered the ends of the reins and led the horses to where she stood. "Let me help you mount up. You'd best be getting back before they miss you. I got all the trouble I want right now. I don't need the sheriff down my neck."

Emmy snorted. "Those two wouldn't call the sheriff. They'd load up and hunt you down themselves."

Daniel made a stirrup for her with his hands and swung her up onto Rebel. "Then get home quick. I'd sooner face the sheriff than Crazy Bertha with a loaded gun."

He took to his own saddle, then eased past her and rode out to scout the trail before whistling the all-clear.

She followed and found him studying the sky. "It's getting on to the noon meal. They'll be looking for you."

"And they'll find me."

They measured each other with guarded looks. Daniel broke the silence. "Give me some time, Emmy. I'll set things to right."

She bit her bottom lip. "You know I'm not the patient sort."

He nodded.

Emmy nudged Rebel and they trotted away a bit. Then she yanked on the reins and pulled him around. "Daniel?"

He sat in the same spot, watching her. His lifted chin bade her speak.

Pulling one foot close to the saddle, she fiddled with her bootstrap. "Is she all right?" Her gaze flickered to his face then returned to her boot. "Charity, I mean? Did that wolf hurt her any?"

"Never touched her. Charity's fine."

Emmy nodded, still not meeting his eyes. "That's good."

"Go on, girl. Get home."

She found her stirrup again. "I'm going."

Emmy dug her heels into Rebel's side. He responded by breaking into a gallop and then a run. She rode hard and didn't look back, fleeing the bitter truth before it surfaced and ruined everything.

The big horse tried to slow before the gully, hesitant to cross the plank bridge. She laid the switch to his side and he leapt for it. They landed with a jarring thud and his hooves beat against the boards, sending vibrations through her body. The wind whistled past her ears as they flew over the marsh. Rebel stumbled, bogging down and tripping over roots. She urged him faster. He risked falling, breaking a leg, but still she pushed him.

On the far side of the swamp, she sent him barreling headlong into the brush. Tangled branches tore at her skirt, exposing her bare legs to deep scratches. Rebel threatened to buck, so she pulled him out again and sent him crashing into a grove of young trees instead. Somehow he made it through, and she drove him toward the house as if the hounds of hell chased them.

Inside the dark, cool barn, she worked feverishly to unsaddle the old horse. Rebel heaved and blew, his body lathered with foamy sweat that ran red from deep scratches. Blood matted his long white mane, now a tangle of sticks and twigs.

Emmy dropped the saddle on the ground and stared at the terrible sight. "Oh, Rebel. What have I done?" Guilt consumed her. She had punished Papa's horse for Daniel's sins.

Her tingling legs began to throb and sting. She pulled up her dress and gasped at the state of her torn and bleeding flesh. Her thighs weren't so comely now. Unlike Rebel, she knew she deserved it.

As if confirming her thoughts, a shadow loomed from behind, blocking the warmth of the sun. Startled, she whirled. Mama stood at the barn door, glaring at Emmy's bare skin.

"You wicked girl." She spoke quietly, matter-of-factly.

Emmy dropped her skirt. "I'm sorry, Mama."

"Where have you been, Emily? What have you been up to that put your legs in that condition?"

"It's not what you think."

"So it has nothing to do with Daniel Clark? That's what you're telling me?"

Emmy couldn't summon the right answer.

Mama shook her head. "Just as I thought." She caught sight of the horse and rushed inside the barn. "For heaven's sake! What happened?" She ran her hands over the bloody cuts. Rebel flinched, and tears sprang to her eyes. She spoke without looking at Emmy, her voice jagged iron. "Find Nash and have him come tend to this animal. Then get upstairs to your room. This time I say when you come out."

"Yes, ma'am." Emmy hurried toward the barn door, but Mama called her back. She turned slowly, dreading what she might hear.

"There won't be no hiding this from your Papa. No telling what he'll do to you, but I won't lie to him on your account."

Emmy forced herself to look at her mama's face. "No, ma'am," she whispered.

Mama nodded. "As long as we understand each other. Now git."

Even more than having Papa find out, Emmy dreaded telling Nash. She could already imagine the look on his face. He had tended Rebel since the horse was a colt.

She found him and delivered the message, careful to avoid his eyes. Then she trudged to the house, feeling like she'd sooner face a noose. Not that she minded going back inside her rose-covered prison. Her actions merited worse. The part she couldn't bear was being shut in with the memory of what had just happened between her and Daniel.

CHAPTER 11

The morning dawned clear and milder than days past. The sun, bright and hot outside the window of the Lone Star Hotel, arched warm, hazy rays through the open shade, chasing the chill from the room.

Not ready to leave the soft cotton mattress, Charity lay on the bed and watched the sky, enjoying the heat of the sunshine on her feet. A pleasant day in the middle of January was common for Texas and a welcome change from the one before.

Buddy never took her to see Amy Jane like he'd promised. After the wolf encounter, he hustled her to town instead and delivered her straight to her room. Then he ordered a bath brought up and made her promise to take to her bed right after. She found the special treatment downright silly, since she'd only sustained a few bruises and muddy knees, but he insisted. She didn't argue long. Buddy's determination and size made him a formidable opponent. Satisfied he had her settled in for the night, he headed back out to her place, and she hadn't seen him since.

Wide awake now, Charity stretched then winced at the pain.

I guess we can add rattled bones to bruises and muddy knees.

It seemed Buddy was right after all. She had hit the ground harder than she thought. With great care, she rolled to the side of the bed and sat up.

Patting her hollow stomach, she felt more than heard the

familiar growl. Buddy had paid for her breakfast the day before. She wouldn't allow him to do it again. Today she became mistress of her own fate.

Amy Jane Pike had expressed interest in her wedding dress. Charity intended to find her first thing and speak to her about buying it. If things went the way she hoped, she could soon afford to pay for her own breakfast.

Aware of every sore muscle, she stood and hobbled to the basin of water. Cold, but it would have to do; she couldn't wait for more. She tended to her toiletries, pinned up her hair, and pulled on a faded day dress. The comfortable jeans had beckoned, but they were a mess. Besides, she wouldn't be traveling on horseback today. She'd have to rely on her feet instead.

When all was in order, Charity limped into the hall. On impulse, she knocked at Buddy's door. He didn't answer. Up and gone before daylight most likely.

She shuffled past his room and made her way to the stairs. Halfway down, she noted that each step came easier than the last. Moving and using her taut muscles warmed and relaxed them, bringing some relief.

Sam looked up as she tottered past the front desk. "Miss Bloom, will you come here, please?"

Too late, she realized Buddy had likely set the old clerk to watch out for her. If so, she might never get out the door.

Balderdash! Let him try to stop me.

She steeled herself and turned on her brightest smile. "Morning, Sam. Lovely day, is it not?"

He glanced toward the window. "Yes, I reckon it is."

She approached the desk, determined to move with grace. It wouldn't do for him to notice her stiffness. "Did you wish to speak to me?"

"Surely you're not going out?" He posed it as a question. Implied it as a fact.

"But I am." She raised her brows. "Is that a problem?"

He gestured toward the dining hall with a palsied hand. "You haven't had breakfast, miss. Mr. Buddy says I'm to make sure you eat. Said to put it on his tab."

Mr. . . .who?

She focused on Sam's face. If she allowed her gaze to follow where he pointed, she'd be undone. Her nose would take over and chase the wafting aroma of biscuits and crisp bacon down the hall to the dining room.

"I'm not"—to say she wasn't hungry would be false—"ready to eat just yet." A contradiction rumbled in her inward parts, but at least she'd spoken the truth. She would be ready to eat when her own money lay in her hand.

Sam grew agitated. "Mr. Buddy will be cross with me if you don't eat something."

There. He'd said it again. Her brows rose higher than before. "Mr. Buddy?"

"Yes, miss. That nice Mr. Pierce."

"Two days ago you were ready to string him up. Now he's *nice Mr. Buddy*?"

Sam grinned so wide his mustache fanned out above his mouth. "Well, you see, that was before."

"Before what?"

"Before I came to know what a fine young man he is. He's taken right good care of you during your"—he cleared his throat—"financial inconvenience."

That much was true. Buddy had tended to everything out of his own pocket, all for a woman he'd met only days before. It reminded Charity of a Bible story, the tale of the Good Samaritan. Except this battered traveler was all better now and ready to make her own way.

"Mr. Pierce has been more than kind." She leaned in and furrowed her brow. "I'm grateful. Don't think I'm not. I just can't let him do it any longer. It's not fitting. I won't eat another meal I haven't provided for myself."

"But, Miss Charity, breakfast is included in the cost of your lodging."

"And thereby you've made my point, Sam. I'm not exactly paying for my lodging, am I?"

His wide eyes challenged her over the top of wire-rimmed glasses. "Mr. Buddy won't like it."

"Then don't tell him." She pressed a gloved finger to his mouth. "Sam, I mean it. Now if you'll excuse me, I have to be about looking after my own needs for a change." She left him there, still scowling his disapproval, and sauntered outside to the boardwalk.

The sun seemed bent on drying up the mud. Except for a few shaded puddles, only the deepest holes still held water. Charity gathered her shawl about her, ducked into the noisy, milling crowd, and allowed herself to be swept eastward in the general direction of Moonshine Hill. Where the walkway ended just past the hardware store, she took the two steps down to the ground and set out for the Pikes' place. She breathed a sigh of relief when the drier streets and thinning crowd made her walk to the edge of town easier than she'd anticipated.

Moonshine Hill, a thriving community two miles east of Humble, sprang up overnight amid the clamor for oil and the clatter of drilling rigs. It had fast become bigger than Humble, the town that spawned it. Shamus and Elsa Pike owned a fair-sized patch of land northwest of there. Not as far from town as her own place, but still a good long stretch.

The midmorning sun warmed Charity's face. If not for a brisk north wind, she could have removed her shawl. The day felt crisp and clean with no hint of the oppressive Gulf moisture that often saturated the air. She found herself enjoying the walk.

Where the path leveled out for a good distance, Charity lifted her face to the sky and closed her eyes. She followed the sun blindly, until the bright light turned the backs of her eyelids white. When she opened them again, for fear of veering off course, shadowy squiggles darted about in her field of vision. She smiled and blinked them away.

Turning north, she found the trail leading to the Pikes' house suitably dry as well, so long as she dodged the deeper ruts in the dark, crumbling clay. Overhead a woodpecker knocked on a tree trunk, while a frenzied crow swooped by with a meal in his beak, a contender for the prize hot on his tail. She stopped to watch, curious about the outcome.

A buck stepped into the clearing a mere thirty feet in front of her and checked the air for danger, his nose tossed to the sky.

Charity was still and stood downwind of him, so he took no notice of her. When he crouched and lunged from the brush then sprang into the forest on the opposite side of the trail, it had nothing to do with her. Something had startled him and sent him darting for cover—something already chasing him.

The thicket from where the buck had first emerged began to shudder and sway, pulling her attention from the quivering undergrowth that had swallowed him on the other side. With a jolt, she realized another creature had taken the deer's place. A piteous whine, unmistakably canine, arose from the scrub, followed by a mournful growl. Charity stared hard at the bushes, her heart hammering apace with the woodpecker's beak.

Don't be silly. The wolf is dead. Daniel shot it. You saw it yourself.

Charity reversed her steps, determined not to turn her back on the devil that lurked in the brush.

Then what? A second wolf? Something worse?

She cast around in her mind for a way to protect herself. Could she outrun it? Not likely in a dress. Should she climb a tree? The tall straight pines nearby afforded no low branches. Would the Pikes hear if she called out? She filled her lungs and opened her mouth to scream. By golly, she'd make sure they heard.

The bushes rustled then parted to reveal the long velvet ears and wrinkled snout of the Pikes' bloodhound. Red pushed onto the trail, still dragging his ears, his frantic nose snuffling and sweeping the ground. He sensed or smelled Charity and jerked up, eyes alert, body tense. When he recognized her, he wriggled from head to tail. Torn between tracking the deer and greeting his guest, he finally ambled in her direction, grinning up at her through droopy folds.

Charity released the breath burning in her lungs, and weakness flooded her limbs. "Red, you old scoundrel. You scared me half to death."

The big hound wagged his tail and pushed his muzzle into her hand. Red was one of Papa's, or had been. Six years ago when Doozy birthed nine pups, Shamus Pike set his cap for the pick of the litter. Or, as Mama liked to say, he downright coveted Red. But Papa loved the little whelp from the moment he was born and wouldn't turn him loose. A year later Papa died, and Mama couldn't afford to keep the dogs. She sold the rest but gave Red to Shamus in memory of their longstanding friendship. Shamus had cried openly.

Charity knelt on the trail and pulled Red's big head close to give him a good scratching behind the ears. "Truth be told, darlin', I've never been more glad to see you."

Red accompanied Charity the rest of the way. He marched her through the yard and delivered her to the house, circling and collapsing in a panting heap as soon as they stepped on the porch.

Charity raised the brass door knocker and let it fall. It struck her as odd, considering Shamus and Papa's close ties, that she had seldom visited the Pikes' home.

In fact, despite Papa's friendship with Shamus, Mrs. Pike had always regarded Charity and her mama with an upturned nose, due in part to Mama's scandalous behavior but mostly because she envied Mama's relationship with Mother Dane. Elsa considered Magdalena Dane's influence in Humble society to be a prized feather for her cap, so she had sought Mother Dane's favor for years. Mama she could do without, and she had never found Charity worthy either before her betrothal to Eunice Clark's son.

Biting her bottom lip, Charity knocked again. She hadn't considered that they might not be home, which would mean the long walk was for naught. . .and her stomach would remain empty.

While she waited, she looked around the place. Fronted by trees and bordered by acres of plowed ground, the house was smaller than Mother Dane's but somewhat larger than her own. The Pikes farmed cotton. Shamus, with the help of hired men, planted every spare inch of his ground and leased more from other landowners, including Charity's mama. If not for the money he paid to farm their best ten acres, they wouldn't have survived after Papa died.

In three directions, the fields were plowed under in preparation for spring planting, with the exception of a patch of winter vegetables behind the barn. The bare, harrowed ground butted up against the tree line, with no other homes in sight. It seemed a lonely existence.

She raised her fist and knocked again, sure now she'd come all the way to the Pikes' for nothing.

"One moment, please."

The muted voice behind the door would be Mrs. Pike, because in the distance Amy Jane stepped out of the barn and headed up the path leading to the back door. She carried a galvanized bucket and moseyed along like someone in no kind of hurry. The pail contained milk that sloshed with every careless step, soaking her dress and leaving frothy white puddles on the ground.

Her attention on Amy Jane, Charity jumped when the door jerked open with a flourish.

Elsa stood with both hands clasped to her chest and a huge smile on her face. "Charity, dear! How grand."

She suppressed a smile. One would think royalty had come to call. Quite curious that Elsa Pike, who claimed to be descended from nobility herself, still seemed to consider Charity of social importance, despite her breakup with Daniel. Perhaps she thought it wise to hedge her bets, in case they reconciled.

Charity gave in to the smile and extended her hand. "Good morning. I apologize for the early hour."

"Nonsense. We've been up since dawn." Elsa stepped back and widened the opening. "Come right in." She wrinkled her nose and cast a disparaging glance at the ever-optimistic Red. He had risen halfway when she appeared, his droopy eyes hopeful. She shooed him with the hem of her dress. "Scat! Scat, you filthy beast! Charity, don't let him near you, honey. He stinks to high heaven."

Charity had to admit an impressive stench emanated from Red. She sidestepped the fleeing dog and crossed the threshold. "You're very kind to receive me without notice."

"We're glad to have you. Right this way, dear."

Charity followed Mrs. Pike along a dim, narrow hall adorned on both sides with framed tintypes of Elsa's supposedly blue-blooded ancestors. Staid men trussed up in dark suits and sporting handlebar mustaches scowled at her from the wall. Demure women with upswept hair and high-buttoned collars censured her as she passed. Charity made faces at them before turning her attention to Elsa's back.

She had dressed in a gown fit for a party, yet it gaped where she'd left two buttons unfastened. It appeared the crooked sash at her waist, inside out and mismatched, had been snatched up and tied on at the last minute. The state of her explained why she'd left Charity standing so long on the stoop.

They came to an arched doorway on the left, and Elsa waved Charity inside. "Have a seat in the drawing room, dear. Make yourself easy while I pour you some tea."

"Please don't trouble yourself, Mrs. Pike. I can't stay long."

"No trouble at all. There's a pot left from our morning repast, along with fresh blueberry scones. Would you care for one with your tea?"

Charity's mouth watered. *A buttered scone!* Such a casual offer of so dear a morsel. The only thing better would be manna served by the hand of God.

She gave a slight nod. "I might nibble at one if you don't mind, while I wait for Amy Jane."

Elsa clasped her hands again. "You've come to see Amy Jane? She'll be so pleased." She pointed behind them. "She's just outside in the. . .in the garden resting, poor lamb. She didn't sleep well last night. As you know, my Amy's quite delicate. Her aristocratic bloodlines, you see. The slightest thing throws her right off kilter."

Charity couldn't judge her thrown-off kilter, but the six-foot tall, big-boned Amy Jane was anything but delicate. She covered her mouth and feigned a small cough to hide her laugh. Mrs. Pike seemed not to notice.

"Make yourself at home, dear. I'll run out and get her then fetch your tea." With that, she spun and scurried from the room, slamming the back door on her way out.

Still smiling, Charity stepped inside the parlor. The room hadn't changed a whit since the last time she'd been inside, and that was a couple of years before Papa died. The same long divan dominated the small space. Across from it, the same low table and high-backed chairs. Curtains of yellow lace, a wedding gift from the old country, still graced the windows. Behind the divan, the colorful braided rug in front of the stone fireplace gave the room a warm, cheery glow.

She bypassed the chairs and walked to the window. By her calculations, Amy Jane and her bucket could've made it to the house three times by now. Charity was curious about where she'd gotten off to. She lifted the edge of the heavy shade and took a peek.

Amy Jane stood near the garden fence, staring out across the field, the bucket of milk at her feet forgotten. Her body gently swayed, as if to music, while her long hair kept tempo behind her. Mrs. Pike came into sight, bearing down on her with a vengeance. The serenity on the girl's face changed to shocked annoyance as her mama descended.

Elsa plucked at her—untying her apron, straightening her skirts, fussing with her hair—as though she had ten hands, all the while chattering like a frenzied squirrel. Charity couldn't hear her words, but the bossy tone was clear. She heard perfectly, however, when Amy Jane shouted, "Stop it, Mama!" and slapped her hands away.

Elsa took up the pail and herded the girl through the gate. When they disappeared behind the house, Charity whirled and bolted for the divan, feeling guilty for having spied.

In her haste she upset a small worktable and overturned it. The drawer slid out, spilling folded papers and a writing set onto the rug. Charity righted the spindly-legged piece, shoving the items deep inside the dovetailed drawer. She returned Shamus's pipe stand and tobacco box to the bottom shelf, sending up a prayer of thanksgiving they weren't broken. Scrambling to the divan, she sat down just as the back door opened.

After a whispered squabble in the kitchen, mother and daughter appeared on the threshold. Amy Jane sported fresh-pinned hair and a bonnet. Elsa carried a tray laden with a silver tea service, a platter of deep-fried scones, and a collection of jams and spreads. Pushing Amy Jane into the room ahead of her, she placed the tray on the table in front of Charity. After surveying her bountiful spread, Elsa gave a contented sigh and settled into one of the ornately carved chairs. Amy Jane dropped without ceremony into the opposite chair.

The aroma of hot blueberries and fresh-churned butter made its way to Charity's nose, setting her stomach to growling. She pressed her arm against her middle, but too late. Both women glanced at her and then looked away.

Elsa bent over the tray. "Here, dear. Let me serve you a scone. Amy

Jane, pour our guest some tea. She's just had a very long walk."

Amy Jane slouched in the chair with her arms folded, her jiggling knees a sign of her impatience. She watched Charity with wary eyes and pretended not to hear her mama. "What brings you way out here anyways?"

Elsa fired a horrified look at Amy Jane. "Mind your manners, child. She's come to see you, of course."

Unconvinced, the girl watched Charity with one raised brow.

Charity took a large, somewhat indelicate bite of scone and chased it with a sip of tea before she answered. "Actually, I'm here on business."

"Business?" Elsa's brow shot higher than Amy Jane's. "I thought–"

The girl cast a smug look at her mama.

Elsa made a face then moved her seat closer to Charity. "What sort of business, dear?"

"I've come to offer my wedding dress for sale."

The daughter's mouth fell open. The mother choked on a sip of tea. While they recovered, Elsa sat and stared, and a smile stole over Amy's face.

With a rattle, the older woman put down her china cup. "Are you serious?"

Charity nodded. "Yes, ma'am. Quite."

"Dear girl, your mama made that gown for you with her own two hands."

Amy Jane scowled. "Hush, Mama. Charity wants to sell the dress. She don't need you reminding her who made it." Her greedy eyes swept the room. "Do you have it with you?"

"No, but if you're interested in buying, I can return with it today."

Amy's hands went to her flushed face, and her eyes brightened. "Mama, could we? You know how I love that dress. It's absolutely perfect and prettier than any we've seen in the catalogs. Oh, please buy it for me."

Rubbing her eyes in circles with her forefingers, Elsa slumped in her chair. "I don't know, Amy Jane. It would have to be altered a great deal. Even then it might not fit you."

"It will, Mama. You'll see. I've been eating less than the chickens."

Elsa gave her oversized daughter a doubtful glance and sighed. Then her eyes met Charity's. "It's settled, then. Come what may, we'll take the dress."

Charity beamed and reached for a second scone. "I just know you won't be sorry, Mrs. Pike."

Elsa picked up her crocheted napkin and shook it. With a glance down at her mistake, she used the toe of her shoe to brush the scattered crumbs beneath the table. "Dear, there is one last detail."

Charity pressed her fingers to her mouth and swallowed the big bite she'd taken with a self-conscious gulp. "And that is. . .?"

Crossing her hands over her chest, Elsa swiveled toward her. "While I'm reluctant to discuss business—it's a man's job and one I don't envy—we must come to terms on the worth of the garment. Do you. . .um. . .have a price in mind?"

"I do, in fact. After giving the matter careful consideration"—Charity sat up taller and cleared her throat—"I'm asking thirty dollars for it." Her hopeful heart faltered a bit when Elsa's face blanched. "I know it's a lot, Mrs. Pike, but the gown is worth every penny."

Elsa plucked the napkin from her lap to fan herself, oblivious this time to the resulting shower of crumbs. Looking like she'd swallowed a pincushion, she shook her head. "Oh, I don't know, dear. Thirty dollars? My, that's a lot of money for a single item of clothing. After all, it is just a dress."

Amy Jane looked anxious. "Not *just*, Mama. It's the perfect dress. And I'll get lots of wear from it."

Elsa whirled on her. "Just where do you intend to wear a thing like that, and you married to Isaac Young?" She gathered her napkin into a wad and flung it on the silver tray. "Every time I think of it, I get the vapors. I'll never approve of your marrying a dirt-poor farm boy. Mark my words, if not for your hardheaded papa, it wouldn't be happening. Why, I—"

After a mortified glance at Charity, Amy Jane shot her mama a pointed look.

Elsa caught the warning. She cleared her throat and turned with a plastered smile. "We'll buy your wedding gown, Charity. Against my better judgment, we'll buy it. However, I can't pay you everything at once. I'll give you some now, some later, until we've paid it off."

Amy Jane wrung her hands. "That'll take weeks. I need the dress right now." Tears gathered at the corners of her lashes. "You know alterations take time."

"Well, I'm sorry, Amy Jane! We don't have that kind of money!"

Elsa's raised voice echoed in the stillness that followed. A raspberry tinge flushing her cheeks, she settled deeper in the chair and fiddled with a thread on her sleeve. Seconds passed before she licked her lips and addressed Charity, speaking in measured tones. "I meant to say money's a mite scarce just now. My husband's varied investments take all our ready cash. The end return is worth it, of course. However, we're forced to scrimp some during the dry spells." She gave a self-conscious laugh. "So I have only a few silver dollars in my purse. Oh, and a jarful of commissary tokens from Bender's Mill."

Charity saw her sale slipping away and along with it her independence. She scooted to the edge of her seat. "I have an idea. Suppose you give me some of the money now, like you said."

Elsa's eyes flickered with interest.

"Whatever you can manage. And I don't mind commissary tokens. They're as good as cash."

The flicker ignited to a flame. "Go on."

"I'll give you the dress now and trust you to pay the balance."

Amy Jane gasped and bit her knuckles.

Elsa leaned toward Charity. "You would do that for us?"

"Of course I will." *I must do it. . .for me.*

Amy Jane bounced in her chair, squealing like a cornered hog.

Despite the quick glance at her furniture and the disapproving look she sent her daughter's way, Elsa's smile remained in place. "Shall we shake on it, then? That's what the men do."

Charity set down her cup and wiped her mouth with the napkin. The three women stood together and took turns exchanging hearty shakes and broad grins.

Outside on the porch, Charity felt somewhat better about what she'd done. She had a full belly plus five dollars in silver coins and commissary tokens in her pocket, with the promise of more to come. Amy Jane was a happy bride-to-be, looking forward to wearing the wedding dress of her dreams. Overall, it had gone quite well for Charity's first business transaction.

She was almost clear of the yard when Red appeared at the edge of the trees and loped across the field to meet her. Dodging just in time, she followed Elsa's example and shooed him with the hem of her skirt. "You can't come with me, boy. Go on, git."

The big dog ducked his head and slunk out of reach but seemed determined to follow. She stamped her foot. "You hear me, now? I said git. You can't go home with me." She laughed at herself. "I can't go home myself, come to think of it."

All the way into town, Red tracked her. Charity threw sticks and small stones at him, but he persisted. Even when she couldn't hear or see him, she knew he was there, stalking her from the brush. Papa always said the only thing bloodhounds were better at than deer-trailing was man-trailing. She decided there was nothing she could do about it, so she ignored him and trudged ahead.

Only part of her plan had succeeded. She still had to make the trek to Mother Dane's house to get the dress then take it to Amy Jane. She dreaded the thought of all that walking. Worse, she dreaded telling Mama she'd sold the dress. She'd sooner face another rabid wolf.

CHAPTER 12

Daniel Clark sat propped against the outer wall of Sterling's Feed Store in a rickety ladder-back chair, his booted feet crossed high atop piled bags of grain. In the company of several men, Daniel was in no mood for talking, so he kept to himself and pretended to sleep.

He would have slept, too, but for the stretched-out hole in the cane-bottom seat. Half his backside protruded through it already. If his body relaxed, he'd wind up in quite a pickle.

A stiff southern breeze blew up the rain-soaked street, whisking the chill from the mild winter morning. The warmth of the gentle wind swept over him, bringing with it the pungent aroma of horses and mud—animals and land, the smells he loved best. The fragrance of his heritage and his future.

True enough, timber had made his daddy rich. Not Daniel. He sought his fortune in ranching, and the effort had padded his pockets. Lately, he dreamed of a different sort of gold. Black gold, they called it. If he showed the same knack for finding oil that he had for raising livestock, he'd put this mud-sucking town on the map. Better yet, he might move his talents to a bigger city. Somewhere on the Gulf, Galveston maybe. He reckoned he wouldn't mind seeing the ocean.

The uncommon stillness of the men seated about him pulled Daniel from his thoughts. Their endless trite chatter about weather and crops had ceased. Sidney Anderson chuckled under his breath. Ezekiel Young laughed outright. When they began to hoot and catcall to someone, Daniel opened one eye and took a peek.

Charity stood in the street with one hand resting on her hip, scolding a big red dog with the other. The hound cowered beneath her wagging finger and rolled over, his long ears splayed and his legs tucked submissively. The second Charity turned, he was up chasing after her skirts. The men beside Daniel roared, pointing at the girl while slapping their legs and clutching their sides.

Daniel grinned, too, when Charity whirled on the hound again, shouting and stamping her feet. The dog ran a short distance away and sat down to watch, as if waiting for her next move. Charity cast a few more words of warning in his direction, punctuated by pointed finger jabs, before stalking away.

The persistent creature perked his ears at her departing back. He squirmed to his feet then paused, took a few steps, and froze. He stayed put until Charity passed Rogers & Grossman's Dry Goods Store, but as soon as she disappeared around the corner, he shot to his feet and loped after her.

Jack Mayhew pulled a dirty handkerchief from his overalls and wiped the tears from his eyes. "By golly, I ain't laughed that hard in years. That old dog sure knows what he wants."

"He sure does," Sidney agreed. "Beats all I ever did see."

Ezekiel Young, the oldest of the men, squared around to offer his opinion. "I got a feeling he'll keep tracking her, too. Ain't nothing bound to stop him. Weren't no give-up in that animal."

Daniel let Zeke's words sink in a bit before he leaned forward, dropping the chair's front legs with a bang. He stood up and hooked his thumbs in his suspenders, his gaze fixed on the spot where Charity and the bloodhound had disappeared. "Gentlemen, a man could take a lesson from that old dog."

Ezekiel turned questioning eyes to Daniel. "What you 'bout to do, son?"

Daniel didn't bother to answer. Taking the two steps down to the street, he strode across in long, purposeful strides.

"What do you mean I can't have it?"

Charity hadn't meant to raise her voice. Giving Mama sass

wouldn't go very far in persuading her. Besides, the last thing she wanted was for Emmy to hear and find out she was there.

Mama glared. "Don't take that tone with me, girl. What do you mean marching up here demanding things what ain't your'n?"

Mother Dane appeared at the door behind Mama. "Don't leave Charity on the stoop like a common peddler, Bert. Bring her in."

"I already asked her in. She ain't having it."

Mother Dane reached past Mama and took Charity's arm. "Well, sure she is. Come take a load off, honey. You look plumb tuckered. Let Mother Dane fix you some lunch. You must be starved."

No match for the strength in the sturdy woman's grip, Charity was over the threshold before she could gather her wits. Heart in her throat, she cast a quick look around for any sign of the enemy.

"Don't bother looking," Mother Dane said. "You'll not be seeing her today. She won't be leaving her room for quite a spell, I can promise you that."

While she spoke, she herded Charity to the parlor. "Go on now. Sit and talk with your mama. I'll go scare us up some grub, if Emmy spared us any, that is. I guess I could always pick a bouquet of drumsticks from her pretty leftover bush." She hooted at her own joke then headed for the kitchen door, still chuckling under her breath.

Charity stared after her. "Leftover bush?"

"Never you mind," Mama said. "We got our own fat to fry." She pointed Charity toward the divan then perched across from her in the big green chair, arms folded over her chest. "Now then. Get to telling me why you need a wedding dress in such an all-fired hurry."

Charity widened her eyes. "Heavens! I'm sure it's not what you're thinking."

Mama looked away. "I don't know what to think. Whether you care or not, I've got a new crop of gray in my hair—with your name on every strand. You disappeared for two whole days. I had to find out secondhand that you were set on by a crazed wolf."

The strain in her voice squeezed Charity's heart. "Oh, but

I'm fine, see? He didn't hurt me none. They told you that much, didn't they?"

Mama shrugged. "I reckon so."

"All right, then. None of the rest matters."

"It matters a heap to me."

Charity reached to pat her hand. "I'm sorry, Mama. I truly am."

Mama's sorrowful gaze locked on her. "Just what is it you're sorry for? That's what I really need to know."

Surprised by her intensity, Charity slid to the edge of her seat. "What sort of question is that? What are you asking me?"

The probing green eyes found hers again, and tears welled there. "I'm asking what you've been up to, child."

Stunned, Charity sank back against the cushions. "What do you think I've been up to?"

Mama chewed her bottom lip and watched, saying nothing.

"Mama? Tell me what you mean."

After drawing a deep breath and rolling her shoulders back, Mama squirmed forward until their knees touched. Her suspicious glare pinned Charity to the sofa. "The word I got has you flouncing about town acting pert and chipper with Mr. Pierce."

The last possible words Charity expected out of her mouth.

"Pert and chipper? I don't understand."

"Don't play thick, daughter. You was seen in public snuggled up to Buddy Pierce with his hands all over you."

Charity felt rage. Indignation. She shot to her feet, no longer worried about Emmy or anyone else hearing. "I never did that! Who said such a vile thing?"

Mama seemed not to hear. "How you think it made me feel to have a snake like him come telling dirty stories on you? He said you had your arms around that man right out in plain sight, in front of half the men in town."

"Who, Mama? Who told you that?" Charity spewed the words in white-hot fury.

Mama shouted right back. "That dirty scum ex-feeancee of yours!"

At first Charity couldn't breathe. She groped in her mind

for an anchor that would hold. Something to help make sense of Mama's words. "Daniel?" she finally whispered. "Daniel said those things?"

"Do you deny it?"

She had to sit down. . .or fall. "Yes, I deny it. You don't believe him, do you? I thought you knew me better."

"I thought I did, too, seeing as how I raised you right. Two days ago I would've swore you'd never run out on me. Yet you did." Mama's voice broke, and she slumped over, hiding her face in her hands.

Charity pushed off the couch and knelt at her feet. "I didn't run out on you. I had to go, don't you see?" She held her, rocking back and forth. "I couldn't stay in Emily Dane's house after what she did. I couldn't bear to face her."

Mama sat up and wiped her eyes on her dress. "I knowed it'd be hard on you to come here. It was hard on me, too." She sniffed. "I never done it to hurt you. If it was a wrong decision, I'm sorry. I didn't see no other way at the time." She gave Charity an accusing glance. "We would've made out all right if you hadn't gone and made everything worse by locking Emmy out of the house."

Charity sat back on her heels."You know?"

"Let's just say I guessed before. Now I know. What'd you do it for?"

Charity pointed toward the front of the house, her voice grim. "She was in the garden with Daniel. They were. . .together. I saw them through the window." The memory of the offense stirred righteous ire to the surface. She pointed again, as if they were still there, all of her wrath boiling from the tip of her trembling finger. "Let me tell you, those two make pert and chipper look like a spinster soiree."

Mama nodded. "Calm down now. I suspected as much. And Magda's no fool either." She pulled Charity close for an embrace. "Still, that don't justify what you done. Vengeance belongs to the Lord, sugar. He don't need our help in settling accounts."

Charity rested her head on her mama's thin shoulder. It felt so good she wanted to cry. "You're right. I don't know what came over me."

"It weren't like you to do such a mean-spirited thing."

Charity leaned back and searched her mama's face. "You don't believe that tommyrot Daniel said about me, do you?"

"If you're denying it, I don't." She cleared her throat. "Only he did name two other men who could back up his story. Said they seen it, too."

"Just two?" Charity smiled. "A minute ago half the men in Humble were witnesses."

Mama shrugged one shoulder. "Might as well have been. The whole town's heard by now."

Charity shook her head. "Then they've heard lies. You know I'd never–" The anchor Charity sought dropped with rattling chains and a heavy thud, dragging her words to a halt. She saw it now, clear and bright, as if the sun had just come up.

"Wait a second." She pulled herself to her feet and sat on the table in front of Mama's chair. "I know exactly what Daniel Clark saw. When the wolf attacked me, he was there, along with Sidney Anderson and Jack Mayhew."

"Yep, he mentioned them fellers."

"They rode up after Daniel shot the wolf. Buddy Pierce had just helped me up off the ground."

"Go on. I'm starting to get the picture."

"Buddy held me, all right, and I clung to him, too shaken to stand on my own. That's what they saw. Daniel made it ugly out of spite."

Mama leaned against the chair and closed her eyes. "It makes perfect sense. I believe you, daughter."

Charity picked up her mama's hands and squeezed them. "You do? Oh, I'm glad. Does that mean you're done scolding me?"

"No, just resting a bit. Give me a second to catch my breath."

Laughing, Charity kissed the backs of her hands. "Oh, you! What am I to do with you?"

Mother Dane swept into the room, carrying a tray piled high with food. "I heard laughter, so I figured it was safe to come in."

"It's safe enough, Magda, but we ain't talked everything out yet. We still need to have us a powwow about a certain wedding dress. You can stay here and referee."

For her part, Charity preferred to eat before any more discussions. The offerings on Mother Dane's tray looked downright tantalizing, and Mrs. Pike's blueberry scones had worn off halfway to town. The long walk, not to mention shooing Red every few feet, had worked her up a man-sized appetite. Not that she ever succeeded in chasing off the stubborn mutt. Most likely when she left, she'd find him waiting outside the front door.

No matter how hard she tried to pull her gaze away, the plate of piled-up sandwiches held her in a trance.

Gratefully, Mother Dane noticed and intervened. "Now, Bert, surely that skirmish can wait until after we eat a bite."

Charity jumped up to clear a place on the table. Her mouth watered at the sight of thick slabs of smoky ham wedged between chunky slices of bread, fresh-baked if her nose knew its business. Not to mention a platter of cold fried chicken, a bowl of potato salad, and a whole buttermilk pie.

Scrunching in beside Mother Dane on the divan, Charity ate until her eyes glazed over. She tried to make polite conversation but failed because her mouth stayed too full to speak.

When she reached for a second sandwich, Mama spoke up. "Charity, tell me you're not shoveling food like a field hand because you're starved. Buddy Pierce swore he'd look out for you."

Charity swallowed her bite and lowered the sandwich. "He has, Mama. Buddy's bought my every meal with money from his own pocket until today."

"What makes this day any different? Looks to me like you needed to eat today, too. Why wouldn't he feed you?"

She steeled herself. "I won't let him do it anymore, that's why."

Mama glared. "And he put up with that?"

"He doesn't know."

Mama lowered her sandwich to her plate. "What do you mean he don't know?"

"He's been buying my meals on his hotel tab, through Sam. I told Sam I won't eat any more meals Buddy pays for."

Mama sat back, considering her words. Then she raised one eyebrow. "You two have a falling out?"

"Of course not. I want to make my own way, that's all. I can't let Mr. Pierce continue to do for me." While she talked, she worked on getting a huge slice of buttermilk pie onto her plate without spilling a morsel. "To be honest, I don't know why you allowed it in the first place."

Mother Dane cleared her throat and shot a warning glance. Charity softened her tone. "I mean. . .we're beholden to a complete stranger, aren't we? Mr. Pierce is a very nice man, but he's not family. Not even an old friend. Yet he's shelling out a dollar per day for my room and board." She balled her fist and brought it down on the couch. "A dollar a day, Mama. How will we ever repay that kind of money?"

Mama stiffened. "I'm good for it. I'll give him back every penny."

"Oh, really? How?"

She sniffed and raised her chin. "When my well comes in."

Charity tried not to roll her eyes. "That well is just speculation, not a sure thing. Suppose it never comes in. Then what?" Before Mama could answer, she forged ahead. "Besides, how you reimburse Mr. Pierce is not the point. We just met him a few days ago, yet you've totally entrusted him with my care." She held up a creamy forkful of pie, poised to take a bite. "If you want to give this town something to talk about, let them get wind of that."

Mama lowered her brows and shifted her lips to the side. "I never looked at it that way. 'Course they're bound to talk anyways, what with a young girl living alone in a hotel when she has kinfolk alive to care for her. It just ain't done, daughter."

"It'll seem a lot more respectable if I'm paying my own way instead of living off a stranger. Besides, I'm hardly his responsibility."

"You're right about that. You're mine." She pushed up from her chair and came to sit beside Charity on the divan, resting the plate of food she'd barely touched on her lap. "Come back and stay with me, sugar. I'll set things straight before long. Buddy said that oil in the bog holds the promise of a future for us—of a day when I can put you in a big, fine house and take care of you myself. Living here might be hard for a spell, but—"

Charity slapped her hands over her ears. "Please don't."

Mama gulped, swallowing the rest of her words. "Don't what?"

"Spout one of those senseless things you always say."

Mama set her plate on the table then gave Charity a long look. "Well, for heaven's sake, what things?"

"Things like, 'It's never easy to blaze a new trail.' Or 'We gotta wrestle it through to the end.' "

Her mama heaved a sigh and slumped back on the divan.

Ashamed, Charity took her hands from her ears. "Oh, go on, then. Spout away since you're busting to."

Huffy, Mama leaned to retrieve her plate. "Well, I cain't now. You done took all my good 'uns." Eyes narrow and sulky, she picked up her sandwich and took a bite.

Laughing, Mother Dane slid one arm around Charity's shoulder and squeezed. "Your mama's right, though, darlin'. You need to come stay where you belong. I know it'll be hard to face Emmy, but you'll have to someday. You girls can't stay at odds forever. We're family."

Charity hugged Mother Dane. "I appreciate the offer; I really do. Right now I have a place to stay. All I need is this one bit of help so I can make my own way for a while longer."

Mother Dane looked puzzled. "What bit of help is that, sugar?"

Charity twisted to face her mama. "Permission to sell my wedding dress."

Mama's eyes flew as wide as the dish on her knees. "You want to sell the dress I made?"

Charity talked fast. "Lord knows I don't want to, but I got a real good price. Mrs. Pike agreed to pay me thirty dollars. Can you believe it? That's all the money I need to get myself out of this fix and to hold me until things get straight. Don't you see? It's the only way."

Mama slung her sandwich, missing the table and scattering greasy bread and chunks of ham over the rug. She stood to her feet. "If it's the only way, then you're sunk, little miss. You ain't about to sell that dress." That said, she swept past them to the landing and stomped upstairs, tackling each step as if it were a bitter enemy.

Charity started after her. "Mama, wait!"

Mother Dane grabbed her arm and lowered her to the divan. "Let her go, honey. She ain't mad. She's hurt. Bertha's dangerous when she's hurt."

Charity's mouth went dry as dirt. Fear tickled her insides like a swarm of scurrying spiders. "I have to talk to her."

"If you don't give her time to cool down, she'll say things she don't mean. Once said, they'll hang between you."

"You don't understand. I need that dress."

If a look could bare the soul, Charity's lay stripped to the bone before Mother Dane's probing eyes. "I'm afraid to ask, honey. Why so desperate?"

"Because. . .I've already sold it."

Mother Dane's jaw fell slack. "Oh, honey, you didn't."

Charity turned out the pocket on her skirt, displaying the bright silver coins. "Mrs. Pike gave partial payment. We shook hands."

Mother Dane stared at the money cupped in Charity's palms. Instead of offering a glimmer of hope, the expression on her face made Charity's insides hurt. She released the pocket, and the coins slid out of sight with a lighthearted jingle, an outlandish sound in the midst of such gloom. "I guess I should've known better, I know how mulish Mama can be. Now what am I to do?"

Mother Dane pulled her close and gave her a little shake. "Don't take on so. This will require a bit more time to figure, but we'll think of something. Go on and finish your lunch. Afterwards, we'll sort it out together."

Charity squinted at her plate. The slice of pie, so appealing a moment ago, caused her stomach to lurch. She passed the food to Mother Dane, stood, and picked up her shawl. "I have to go."

"Honey, don't leave. That'll just make matters worse. Her Irish temper will cool in a bit."

Charity pulled on her gloves with such force the seam of one finger busted. "I don't have time to wait for that cantankerous old woman to cool. If I'm to fend for myself in this world, then I need to be about it, don't I? Thank you for lunch, Mother Dane. If you'll excuse me, I have to go find a way out of this mess Mama's landed me in."

She rushed to the door. Red lay curled on the porch sound

asleep, his eyes hidden under saggy bags of skin. When Charity moaned at the sight of him, he jerked alert, his tail thumping a rhythm on the smooth stones. She was not so pleased to see him.

Mother Dane hustled up behind her. "Where are you going? What will you do?"

Charity stared at her in silence. Where would she go? "I don't know yet. I need time to think. Good-bye, Mother Dane."

There was no way around the big dog panting up at her, as persistent and immovable as the cut of ancient rock on which he lay. So Charity tiptoed over him, stepping wide to clear his bulk. Instead of making her way to the path, she jumped off the side of the porch and made a beeline for the front garden. Shaking all over, and still drained by the squabble with her mama, she stumbled into Mother Dane's shaded arbor and sat down in front of the fountain. She needed time to ponder, to get her bearings before starting the long trip back to the Pikes'.

Red had followed, and he promptly laid his nose to snuffling the soft clay around the trees and shrubs. Leaving him to his own devices, she leaned against the cold iron bench to think.

It would be easier to send Red home than to get that obstinate old woman to change her mind. In fact, if it came to a match between the two, Mama was more dog-stubborn than the dog.

A sound reached her ears over the whining and snorting of the big hound—a relentless tapping that penetrated the whirlwind in her head and plucked her from the pit of dismal thought. Annoyed, she looked around to find the source.

The rapping grew louder, followed by the rattle of a windowpane. Red lifted his head and growled deep in his throat. Thinking it had to be Mother Dane, Charity looked at the house, but a quick check of the lower windows proved her wrong.

Mama perhaps?

Expecting to see the crabby old grouse, she followed the noise to the upper floor. . .and came face-to-face with Emmy, peering down from her bedroom. Charity tried to look away, but the girl's wide-eyed stare held her fast.

Red trotted over and nudged her with his nose, demanding attention.

Her willful, disloyal gaze still fixed on the tortured blue eyes above, Charity's fingers found and caressed the dog's soft, bristly muzzle. The irony of the moment struck her. They had changed places, she and Emmy. Now Emmy watched from above while Charity embraced a mongrel in the garden.

With a start, she realized Emmy still wore her nightdress. Her flaxen curls, always pinned and perfect, fell past her shoulders, dull and matted. The lovely pale face Charity knew so well gazed down without expression, her breath misting frosty puffs on the glass. Without warning, she raised one hand, pressing her palm to the window. Leaning in, her face crumpled with grief.

Charity spun and bolted from the garden. With Red on her heels, she lifted her skirt and sprinted for the thick woods that lined the property. When she reached the cover of the trees, she dove in as fast as she could, dodging bog holes and saplings until she came to the trailhead. A good way up the path she stopped, completely spent. Bent over at the waist, one hand at her throbbing side, she gasped for air and fought the sobs crowding her throat.

Red left her side and trotted ahead a few paces to greet someone emerging from a thicket just off the path.

Startled, Charity jerked upright. "What are you doing here?"

"Waiting for you," Daniel said. "We need to talk."

CHAPTER 13

Her hand still pressed to the window, Emmy watched Charity reach the edge of the yard and dart into a sparse crop of seedlings. Plowing through their spindly branches, she fought her way to the mouth of the trail then ducked behind thick brushwood. Emmy caught only glimpses after that, until Charity finally disappeared into the trees.

Emmy knew what she must do. Even to her fevered mind the act seemed foolish, but there was no time to think it through. She opened the window and crawled over the ledge, deftly gaining a foothold on the rickety trellis. Hanging there, suspended between right and wrong, she wondered if her rose-infested tomb had driven her quite mad.

Dressed only in her gown in the bold light of day, she scrambled to the ground. When her bare feet touched the cold red clay, her mind went to Nash, the only person on the place besides Mama and Aunt Bert. No matter. She trusted him. Even if Nash saw her streak across the grounds in her nightdress, he'd sooner cut off his arm than snitch on her.

She gathered the hem of the cotton garment and lit out, feeling Mama's eyes on her back from every window in the house. She knew exactly at what point the trees would hide her from sight—the same place where they'd swallowed Charity—and she didn't breathe until she reached that spot.

CHASING CHARITY

Daniel had followed Charity down the trail then hung back when he saw where she was headed. He had a feeling she wouldn't be staying long, so rather than face the two clamorous shrews crouched on the back side of Mrs. Dane's door, he'd hunkered down behind a juniper tree to wait. The sight of Charity through spiny branches told him his hunch had paid off.

He couldn't wait to speak to her, to tell her he still loved her. He imagined the look on her face when he said it. Her dark brows would lift in surprise and the corners of her full, red lips would twitch with pleasure. Maybe she'd toss her head and laugh the way she had that day in the hotel.

Heart thumping, he moved closer. "Did you hear what I said, honey? We need to talk."

Her hat in her hands, her long black hair disheveled and freed from its pins, she looked wild and beautiful. . .and furious. She lifted her chin and her eyes flashed. "Oh, you're right about that, Daniel Clark. We need to talk, and that's for sure."

He took another step forward.

Charity matched it with one step back. "What are you doing out here anyway, skulking behind bushes, waiting to spring out on lone women?"

Daniel ignored the last part and reckoned the answer to the first should be obvious. He summoned the patience to respond. "Like I already said, I was waiting for you. I followed you all the way from town."

"Is that a fact?" She watched him from beneath her dark lashes.

Daniel's hands began to sweat. Things weren't going well. Her look remained guarded, not at all what he'd expected.

She held her unyielding stance and raked him with glaring eyes. "Maybe you weren't waiting for me at all. Maybe you were lurking out here until I left Mother Dane's house so you could slither up and spread more lies." She glanced around at the bushes and tall grass. "I don't see Sidney and Jack. Won't you need your two deceitful witnesses?"

So that was the burr in her britches. Well, it explained her fury.

"Now, honey, don't be mad. I didn't go to hurt you none. I was only trying to protect you from that oil company fellow."

His heartfelt words brought a curious reaction from Charity. Her eyes flew open, and her body recoiled like he'd struck her. Daniel realized afresh that he'd never understand women.

Scorn blazed in her eyes. She spoke, her tone low and mean. "Tell me something, Daniel. Why do I need the likes of you to protect me from anything?"

He rested his hands on his hips and stared at the ground. "I guess you don't. Looks like I had this figured all wrong. Turns out it might be me who's needing you."

Daniel held his breath, waiting for her reaction. When it seemed he could reach out and touch her silence, he glanced up and found her staring. Some other emotion had replaced the anger, one he didn't recognize. Whatever its source, it left Charity's face as blank as a new slate.

"Why would you say something like that to me?" she finally asked. "After all that's happened."

He edged closer, longing to touch her. Charity's body tensed, and the hound beside her stood up and growled. Daniel glanced at the dog but held his ground. "I said it because it's true. I love you, sugar. I know it now. I'd wrestle a bull to win you back."

Astonishment replaced her empty expression. Daniel bit off a smile and watched, waiting for it to turn to pleasure. "Please, Charity. Let me come close. I need to hold you. Let me soothe away the pain I've caused."

Her lips curled. She tilted her head and laughed, but not the way he remembered. "You think you can smooth things over just by holding me?" Her dark brows lifted—in contempt, not happy surprise. "I guess I should be grateful you got my name right. It must get rather confusing dangling two women on the same line." One brow rose higher. "Assuming there are just two of us."

"Now, honey, you know better."

"Do I?"

He dashed his hat against his leg. "Yes! I ain't never loved nobody but you."

"What about Emmy, Daniel? Can't you make up your mind

which one of us you want?"

This was all wrong. She should be in his arms by now. Angry at himself, frustrated with Charity, Daniel raised his voice. "Can't you see I made a mistake? I don't care nothing about Emmy. It's you I want. Emmy don't even matter no more."

Charity cringed and covered her face. "How can you say such a cruel thing?" She hurled the question, the accusation, at him in a low moan. "Emmy does too matter. She matters to me."

It was his turn to raise a brow. "Why? Lord knows she don't deserve it. That girl's not fit to kiss your feet. Shoot, she's not fit to pour out your chamber pot."

Charity lifted her face, her features set in stone. "Get out of my way."

"Just wait a minute. We're not done talking."

"Yes, we are." She tried to shove past, but he grabbed her shoulders.

"No, now! Please listen. I can't eat. Can't sleep. You're all I think about. All I care about. Don't go like this."

The dog advanced, hackles raised. The warning growl he gave was no bluff, so Daniel turned her loose. She lurched away from him and called off the dog.

Daniel gripped his head with his arms. He had to think, had to find the right thing to say. At the sound of hurried footsteps, he looked up to find that Charity had run up the trail, well away from him.

He cupped his hands over his mouth and shouted after her. "You just need time to ponder what I said. You'll come around, and when you do, I'll be waiting."

She didn't answer or even look behind her. Instead, she picked up her pace, stumbling along the rutted trail as if he were chasing her. Daniel followed, but not too closely, because every so often the old dog stopped and checked over his shoulder, making sure he kept his distance.

Emmy knelt in the brush, watching Daniel's broad back until he reached the far end of the trail. When he made the turn toward town, she gave in to trembling legs and dropped to the ground on her behind.

A large dung beetle attached to the side of her knee and walked the length of her bare leg, coming to rest at her thigh.

Emmy stared down at it, smiling at the irony, and accepted the reproach. She shivered at the feel of its barbed legs against her flesh but couldn't summon the will to brush it away.

She wished the numbness she felt extended to knees pressed too long against the cold, hard ground. She noted the indention of a pinecone etched into one, leaving a blue-black imprint in her flesh. It hurt, but not like the ache crowding her chest. An intolerable throbbing had started down deep and pushed up her throat in waves that kept time with her heartbeat.

"Emmy don't even matter no more."

"Emmy does too matter. She matters to me."

Emmy fell against the hard ground and surrendered to the pain. She lay in a hollow, a spot wallowed out in the tall brush by hogs. Certain she deserved the sharp sticks and knobby roots biting into her flesh, and the stale, fetid stink left by the last pig to sleep on the dead grass, she started to cry. As she stared up at the cloudless blue sky through a canopy of soaring pine and a blur of hot tears, something Aunt Bert had said years before echoed in her mind—words that had come to her more than once of late, but she'd pushed them away.

"Don't live your life for the devil, Emmy. Old Slue Foot plies his wares like they're treasures. Then when you least expect it, he trips you up and leaves you flat on your back."

She'd laughed when she heard it. The words had conjured a picture of the vendor carts at the St. Louis World's Fair, only Aunt Bert's peddler hawked his goods wearing horns and a forked tail.

"Don't live your life for the devil."

She mulled the words over again, feeling as if God Himself had bent to whisper in her ear.

Yet how unlikely that a holy God would stoop to where she'd fallen or speak to someone sprawled on the ground, laid worthless and bare.

Would You, God?

The swaying branches overhead swam into a cluster. Emmy felt, more than heard, a low moan starting in her throat, becoming a high-pitched wail as she cried out her shame. Clutching her face, she rolled over, drawn into a tight ball of misery.

The sensation that someone knelt beside her persisted. Emmy didn't understand one thing about it, but she knew in her heart that she wasn't alone. Something powerful swept over her, carrying her high above the rebuke of pain and the stench of swine, leaving ease and sweet release in its wake.

When she sat up, she couldn't tell how much time had passed. She thought she must've slept a bit. What else but sleep, though she'd never slept so well or found such peace at rest.

The sound of an approaching wagon roused her, striking fear in her fragile heart. It had to be coming from home. Theirs was the only house this far down the trail. Maybe only Nash, headed into town on an errand.

"Emily Bertha Dane! Where are you?"

Mama!

Emmy pressed close to the ground and willed herself small. The rig had pulled alongside her now, and she prayed the brush was thick enough to conceal her white nightgown.

"Where could she be, Bertha? I've seen that girl pull some high jinks in her day, but even I can't believe this one."

"That makes two of us. You sure he said she was in a nightdress?"

Nash, you no-'count scoundrel.

"Yes, and in broad daylight! I'm going to put her in a convent, Bert, I swear it."

"You ain't Catholic, honey."

The rig rattled past, drawing the voices out of earshot. Keeping low, Emmy rolled to her sore knees and parted the high grass to peer out. Well beyond her now, they headed in the direction of town. Nash wasn't with them, so Mama held the reins, and Aunt Bertha rode beside her. The women sat tall on the seat, the motion of the wheels on the rutted trail tossing them to and fro.

Emmy watched them, Mama's head turned to the left, Aunt Bert's to the right, searching the woods on both sides of the trail.

Low in the distance she heard Mama call out to her again. "Emmy? Emily Dane! Land sakes, child, answer me!"

Her eyes fixed on the distant wagon, Emmy backed out of her hiding place and slipped into the woods. She would have to make it home through the trees without being seen, even by that traitor Nash. Once safely there, she'd figure a story to tell them they'd believe.

At the edge of the clearing, she crouched behind an overgrowth of honeysuckle vine and watched for Nash. Seeing no sign of him, she dashed across the field to the yard. Reaching the trellis, she scrambled up like a hounded cat and tumbled over the windowsill, landing on the floor with a crash.

"Why you ain't jus' took the door, little miss?"

Whirling, she came face-to-face with a haughty, indignant Nash.

"No call to sneak no mo'. They's onto you."

She struggled to her feet and grabbed a quilt from the bed to wrap herself. "What are you doing in my room?"

Nash, who towered over tall men and loomed over her, filled the room with his presence. His bulk intimidated most people, but Emmy knew him to be as meek as a lamb. He jabbed his chest with his thumb. "What am I doing in here? What I'm s'posed to be doing. Waiting for you, like I's told." He gestured at the quilt. "Ain't no sense hiding what you done showed the whole world. That'd be like tying up the gunnysack after the kittens crawl out."

"Why'd you tell on me?"

He lowered his gaze. "Didn't want to. Didn't when I first seen you shimmy down that trellis in your altogethers. I jus' shook my head and mind my own business. I guess I be used to your shenanigans by now. But then I heard you squealing like you being skint."

Emmy gasped. "Did you tell that to Mama?"

"No, missy. Didn't want to scare her no more than I had to. But I was beholden to tell her something in case you was in trouble."

She flung herself back on the bed. "Oh, Nash! I am in trouble now. Mama will skin me herself."

He nodded. "Yep. When she find out you ain't dead, she jus'

might kill you. That be a murdering even old Nash can't spare you."

Emmy bolted upright, her fingers clasped under her chin. "But you *can* spare me. In fact, you're the only person who can."

Eyes wary, Nash eased toward the door. "Naw, now. Uh-uh. Don't you start in on me. I tol' you if you didn't quit flying out that window, you'd lose some of them fancy tail feathers. Now your behind's showing, and jus' like always, you expect me to help you cover it." He held up a restraining hand. "You may as well turn aside them bewitchin' blue eyes. They ain't doin' you no good this time."

"I wasn't doing anything bad, Nash. You believe me. I know you do. Help me think of something to tell Mama."

His brown eyes widened. "Miss Emmy, I loves you like one of my own. You know I do. Only I got to make myself scarce on this one."

"You can't! Not this time. Please, I need your help."

Doubt flickered in his eyes. He wagged his head, but his voice wavered. "You gon' lose me my job, Miss Emmy. I got mouths to feed."

She had him. Lowering her long lashes, she let her shoulders slump and her arms go slack. "Of course. I understand. Don't you worry about me none. I'll be fine." Trudging to the side of her bed, she plopped back down on the mattress. "I've grown accustomed to living in this room."

Like a convicted man offered a reprieve, Nash jerked open the door and started out. . .then paused on the threshold and sighed. "I reckon if you was to tell your mama she heard me wrong 'bout you running for the woods. . .if you was to tell her I found you in the barn tending old Rebel. . .I wouldn't say you was lying."

Emmy wanted to run and wrap her arms around him but remembered her state of undress and stayed put. She tried to convey the depth of her gratitude in the fervor of her quiet response. "Thank you, Nash."

He glanced at her with hooded eyes. "I'm plain weary of breaking commandments for you, girl. You've kept me sorrowful before the Almighty till my drawers be worn at the knees. Try and behave yourself for a spell."

She gave a dutiful nod. "I will. I promise."

He waved a bony finger in her face. "If you really want to thank me, stay on this side of that window from now on, leastwise while wearing your scanties." Looking around, he added one last thought. "If your mama don't nail it shut, that is." His scowl disappeared, replaced by a wide grin. He closed the door behind him, still chuckling as he made his way down the hall.

Emmy dropped the quilt and spun in a circle, then fell across her bed. She'd done it again—worked Nash with the skill of a puppeteer and had him prancing to her will. With the aid of her reluctant marionette, Mama would believe her. Oh, she'd call Emmy reckless, lecture her on modesty, and that would be that.

As she lay staring at the ceiling, an unfamiliar sensation wormed its way into her chest, not unlike the feel of the dung beetle on her thigh. The usually sweet victory bittered in her mouth like an underripe persimmon. She wasn't herself somehow and wondered if it showed. Curious, she scooted to the edge of the bed and leaned to stare hard at the mirror.

Her familiar image peered back at her, just the same as before, save a few sticks and leaves in her matted hair. Exactly the same. . . except for the eyes. Eyes that gazed back, guilty and troubled, in a way they'd never done before.

"Oh, pooh!" she told her reflection. "I'm being silly. Nothing has changed." She'd plied her tricks like always and managed to save her hide.

She picked up her brush and worked it through her tousled hair, pushing aside the scattered emotions that made this time feel different. Because the difference was, if Emmy admitted the truth, her game had lost its pleasure. . .and made her feel like she'd wallowed with the hogs.

CHAPTER 14

Charity didn't slow down until the trail opened out onto town. With a frightened glance at Daniel, still following in the distance, she dashed through a rain-soaked clearing, slip-sliding through the mud in her haste.

Sensitive to her fear, Red trotted stiff-legged beside her, the hair along the ridge of his back flared like porcupine quills.

Her dread of Daniel seemed unreasonable. Yet the chill she'd felt while staring into his brown, soulless eyes had oozed around her, encasing her in fright the way sap envelops a bug. His effect on Red didn't help.

Before they made the turn alongside Rogers & Grossman's Dry Goods Store, Red stopped for one last throaty growl aimed in their pursuer's direction.

In her heart, Charity knew it wasn't the first time she'd noticed Daniel's callous behavior toward others. The confusion came from his ability to turn it off in an instant while his winsome ways and aching good looks lulled her into believing she'd imagined the whole thing. Indiscretions too blatant to overlook, she'd explained away as a onetime occurrence, a momentary weakness. Until today.

"Charity, wait. What's got into you, girl?"

Her heart lurched. Daniel's long-legged stride had nearly closed the distance between them.

Red's growl deepened to a vicious snarl. Charity tapped his

head and sped up. "Let's go, boy." Wheeling too sharply around the corner of Rogers & Grossman's, she drove straight into the middle of Jerry Ritter, one of Buddy's men.

The poor man shouted, "Whoa!" then grabbed her and spun around to keep her from falling.

Buddy stood behind him on the boardwalk wearing a surprised grin.

Mr. Ritter beamed down, aglow with delighted surprise. "Well, shucks. Hello there, Miss Bloom. Are you all right?" He held her wrist and helped her gain her footing. "Best be more careful, ma'am. You're liable to get yourself hurt."

Buddy took the two steps down to the ground. "I thought you reserved that manner of greeting for me. Looks like running folks down in the street is just your little way of saying howdy." He chuckled. "I have to admit, I'm a mite disappointed." He sobered, his brows knitting together. "Say, aren't you supposed to be resting?"

She shot an anxious glance behind her. "I'm sorry, gentlemen. I'm in a terrible hurry."

Buddy drew near and pulled her close, his gaze following hers to the corner. "What's wrong? You look like the devil's chasing you."

Daniel rounded the building. Red whipped in front of her and crouched, baring his teeth. He cut loose with frenzied barking, his deep bray piercing Charity's ears. Daniel froze, but the dog didn't seem to be the thing holding him this time. In fact, despite the fuss Red was making, Daniel appeared not to notice him. His gaze seemed fixed on Buddy's hands resting on Charity's shoulders.

A curse spilled from his sneering mouth and he spun in the opposite direction, his frantic gait from earlier slowed to a cocky swagger.

Charity released her breath. The muscles in her legs, tensed so long in flight, relaxed in a rush of warmth. It left them trembling so hard Buddy's hands, still on her arms, were the only things holding her up.

Lee Allen, whom she hadn't noticed before, bounded down to stand beside Jerry, his attention on Daniel's back. "Was that fellow giving you trouble, ma'am?"

Embarrassed to admit how much, she shook her head.

Bristling as much as Red, Jerry puffed like rising dough and glowered after Daniel. "If he does, we'll sort him out for you." He sniffed and hitched up his britches. "Shouldn't take but a minute."

"It's nothing I can't handle myself," she protested, not sure whether she told the truth.

Buddy pinned her with a no-nonsense look. "Did he hurt you?"

She glanced away. "Of course not."

"Threaten you in some way?"

Squirming, she raised pleading eyes to Buddy's.

He gave an answering nod. "You boys go ahead without me. I'll catch up later."

Mr. Allen hooked his finger in Jerry's suspenders and hauled him around. "Let's go, Jim Jeffries. You retired from the ring this year, remember?"

A blank expression wiped the scowl from Jerry's forehead. "The champ's retired? Who told you so?" Meek as a baby bird, he followed Mr. Allen up to the boardwalk, still pecking for information. "Huh, Lee? Jim Jeffries quit boxing? Why didn't anybody tell me?"

Buddy stared over Charity's shoulder until their banter and heavy footsteps faded. His chin hovered so near, she noted wisps of whiskers too fine to shave at the edges of his mouth. They were golden brown like the hair curling from under his hat, only several shades lighter. The longer ones curved around his top lip, and she wondered if they tickled.

His gaze swept back and caught her looking, his soft green eyes turning her heart to pudding pie. He smiled. "Want to talk about it now?"

The compassion in his voice made mush of her insides.

Oh no! I'm going to cry.

She covered her face. . .too late. Buddy sheltered her under his arm and gently guided her. . .somewhere. When they stopped, he turned her against the front of his shirt and let her weep.

Though it felt so nice to be there, Charity composed herself as fast as possible and pushed free from his tender embrace. Wiping her eyes on the handkerchief he offered, she stole a quick glance at him. "I can't imagine what you must think of me. All I do is pout and squall." She blew her nose, mortified that it honked like a prodded goose. "I hope you'll believe me when I tell you this is the most I've cried since Papa died. Things are so awful now, no matter which way I turn." She sighed. "I guess I'm finding it hard to cope."

Rocking back on his heels, Buddy shot her a piercing look. "You didn't lock your friend outside again, did you?"

She gasped. "Absolutely not! Don't talk foolish."

He grinned. "Sorry. Just trying to make you smile. I've decided I don't like seeing you cry."

Charity returned his smile. "I've given you plenty of chances to come to that conclusion, haven't I? You must be sick of me."

Buddy cupped her chin in his double-portioned palm and pulled her head up, snaring her with the intensity in his eyes. "Sick of you? Oh no, ma'am. Not by a long shot."

A peculiar weakness, accompanied by the same warm sensation that afflicted her whenever she thought of him lately, nearly buckled her knees. Except this time the power of her feelings nearly swept her away. When the sky tilted, she refocused to find that the world consisted of little beyond the brim of Buddy's hat. Shocked by a bold urge to caress the fuzz on his lip, she lowered her eyes and backed away.

Determined to shake off his spell, Charity raised her head and looked around. He had led her around by the rear door of the dry goods store behind a mountainous pile of empty crates. The stack formed a half circle that butted up against the woods, creating a private, cozy den of sorts. The pine boxes held the mixed odor of whatever wares they'd last held. Some smelled strongly of coffee, some tobacco, and a few reeked with the pungent, clingy tang of onion. Red worked his way along the line, busily sniffing out any odors she had missed.

By the look of the cigar butts and empty liquor bottles littering the ground, they weren't the first inhabitants, but the secluded nook was nice.

Buddy pulled down several crates, testing them with his weight until he found two he trusted. He placed them next to the stack, facing each other, then bowed at the waist and motioned for her to sit. "Milady?"

Laughing despite her unease, she gingerly sat, straightening her skirt around her legs. Red trotted over and curled up at her feet, while Buddy pulled his seat a little closer and perched on the edge, watching her without saying a word.

Just as the silence grew heavy, he spoke. "I think the reason you get teary-eyed so often is because you haven't let it out."

Charity jerked her gaze to his earnest face.

He blushed, but his eyes held steady. "I'm serious. Maybe you just need to have yourself a good cry. A stomp-your-feet, pound-on-something, bawl-for-all-you're-worth sort of cry."

"Very well, if you insist."

He held up both hands. "Whoa, now. I didn't mean right here and now."

His panic amused her, and she grinned. A twinkle lit his eyes as a slow smile replaced the fear. She started to laugh, and he laughed with her.

When they were quiet again, she gave him a shy glance. "I suppose you want to know about Daniel."

He eased back a bit. "It's none of my business really."

She scooted forward, bothered by the distance he'd put between them. "That's not so. After all, you have quite a stake in me by now. One I'm bound to repay."

His head swung from side to side. "Nonsense. You don't owe me a thing. I only hope I've earned your friendship."

She tilted her chin. "Oh, Buddy, you've earned more than that. You have my eternal gratitude."

Brows drawn in concentration, he mulled over her words. As if he'd made up his mind, he suddenly leaned across the dog and took hold of her hand. "If that's so, I hope I've gained your trust as well."

Surprised at the direction he'd taken, she squeezed his hand. "You know you have."

He squeezed back, sending a jolt along her spine. "Will you answer one question for me, then? I've no right to ask, but it concerns a matter that's hounded me since we met."

Hesitant, because she had no idea what he might be about to say, she steeled herself and nodded. "Go ahead and ask."

"Why were you so angry the day we found oil on your land? It wasn't just about leaving your house, was it?"

He had noticed. She knew it that day. Scattered emotions crowded to the surface, all struggling for release.

What's wrong with me? I will not cry again!

She swallowed hard. "I don't want the oil."

He scrunched his brow and lifted his chin.

"Well, not the oil itself," she hurriedly explained. "I mean the money, I guess."

From the deeper scowl lines on his face, she reckoned Buddy was truly puzzled now.

He cleared his throat. "Most folks are right happy to get their hands on more dough. Especially that much."

She drew up her shoulders and pulled her hand free. "No amount is worth what it's doing to our town. I detest the sight of those derricks. Especially Mr. Beatty's number two well—the way it stretches to the sky, belching smoke and steam. It's an ugly old eyesore."

Doing a poor job of stifling a grin, Buddy slumped over and braced his arms on his knees. "Ma'am, that well pumps over eight thousand barrels a day from a depth of seven hundred feet. I hate to contradict, but she's considered quite a beauty around these parts."

"I don't care. I hate her." With a forceful swipe of her arm, Charity brushed at her skirt as if dashing Mr. Beatty and his well to the ground. If only she could so easily rid her lap of all the problems clustered there lately—all caused, directly or indirectly, by the oil boom.

Buddy angled his head. "That's a harsh tone from such a pretty little mouth."

"It's true. I hate her. And let's not insult my gender—that hulking stack of iron is no lady. I don't want to add to the unsightly display in Humble by erecting one like it in my own backyard."

Buddy patted her clenched fists. "Dear girl, don't you understand yet? The boom is here. There will be oil derricks stretched across this land as far as the eye can see. In a year or less, they'll be so thick you can jump from one to the other and make it clear across town without ever touching the ground. What's one more going to hurt?"

She stared at him a moment then pressed her knuckles against her temples. "Oh, Buddy, I hope not. And I sure don't want Mama to have any part in it."

He curled his finger under her chin and lifted her face. "It's going to happen, Charity. With or without your mama's well. You can't stop it, so you may as well reap something from it to make a better life for the two of you."

She pulled away. "Why do people keep saying that? We've always been poor. It's all we've ever known. But we were happy with the life we shared, at least before Papa—" She cut off a ragged sob just in time. Only an odd little hiccup escaped to give her away.

Buddy stood, pulling her up with him. He nudged Red's flank with his boot, startling him awake and sending him scurrying aside. Then his arms went around her again, and she melted against him.

"You miss him, don't you?"

She nodded against his chest. "He was a wonderful man," she said when she could speak. "I don't say that because time has sweetened the memories. He really was special."

"Why don't you tell me about him?"

She searched his eyes. "Really?"

"Yes, I'd like to hear."

Before she realized it might not be proper, she traced circles around the top button on his shirt with her index finger while memories flooded to the surface. Suddenly self-conscious, she jerked her finger away. "Papa was funny. Always teasing. When he came into a room, he brought life through the door. Back then our house seemed fit to burst at the seams with love, joy, and laughter"—she grinned up at him—"and long-eared dogs. Papa bred the finest bloodhounds in the state. They were his passion." She tipped her head toward Red, falling asleep again beside her crate. "He was one of them. Papa's favorite. He belongs to Shamus Pike now."

"How'd you wind up with him?"

She grimaced. "It's a story you don't have time for. Suffice it to say, I can't get shed of the old rascal."

Buddy grinned. "He's a fine specimen, all right. I heard about him in town. A lot of folks still boast about Thaddeus Bloom's prized hunting dogs. What happened to the rest?"

Her finger wandered to the button again. "Mama sold them. Every last one." Aware she sounded like a resentful child, she softened her tone. "I told her I would take care of them, but she said we could barely afford to feed ourselves, much less a pack of hungry hounds."

"And you were sorry to see them go."

She sighed. "It felt like losing Papa all over again."

"It may have been for the best, though, don't you think? It would've been a lot of hard work for a—"

Her hand came up. "Don't dare finish that sentence. I'll have you know I stood toe to toe with Papa from the time I could walk. There was nothing girlie about me growing up."

He gave her a skeptical look.

"It's true! Papa always wanted a son. When he wound up with me instead, he taught me to hunt, fish, and tend the hounds. I was a scandalous tomboy." She smiled, remembering. "He even called me Charlie."

"Charlie?"

"Sort of a play on Charity, I guess. But he did have a best friend named Charlie back home in Jefferson, so who knows."

"I think I like it. It suits you."

Her cheeks warmed, so she changed the subject. "Papa loved to fish most of all, and no man in the county was better at it. He always took me with him. . .except on that last day."

Buddy cleared his throat. "The day he died?"

She nodded. "He didn't wake me that morning. I've always wondered why. If I'd been with him, I could've done something."

"Weren't you still just a child?"

"Almost fifteen. Hardly a child."

Gentle fingers caressed the base of her neck, smoothing circles of comfort into her skin. "There was nothing you could do. You know that, right? If you'd gone with him that day, you'd likely be lost to us, too. Sounds to me like God intervened because it wasn't your time."

His words tumbled into her head and ricocheted. When they

settled, a light flickered somewhere in her mind. Charity had never considered such a possibility. It held the promise of absolution but conflicted with the guilt she'd carried since Papa's death. She'd need more time to sort it out. "I just know that the day he died, everything changed, and it's never stopped changing since." She ground tears from her eye with the heel of her hand. "I feel like I can't catch my breath."

Buddy lifted his head and stared over her shoulder into the woods behind them. "As an eagle stirs up her nest, flutters over her young, bears them on her wings. . ."

Her gaze jerked to his. "Excuse me?"

He took her arm and helped her to settle down on the crate. "I've felt the way you describe. I didn't quote it right just now, but I didn't find peace until I found that scripture."

"What does it mean?"

"I didn't understand either until someone taught me about eagles." He puffed his cheeks and released a long breath. "Let me see if I can explain." He pressed closer and played with her fingertips while he talked. "You see, a mother eagle works hard to build a good nest for her young. She makes it nice and thick, pads it real good. It's so comfortable, in fact, that her young would never venture out of it without her help."

Charity made a face. "Don't tell me. She pushes them."

"She doesn't have to." He grinned. "Old mama eagle's smarter than that. She flaps her big wings over that nice cozy nest, stirring up all the soft padding until the sticks and straw are exposed. Before long, sticks and straw is all that's left of the nest, and it doesn't take much convincing to coax those little fellows over the edge."

"Why would she do such a cruel thing to her own children?"

Buddy quit playing with her cold fingers and enveloped them in his warm hands. "Well, because"—he lifted tender, caring eyes—"it's the only way they'll ever learn to fly."

Unsettled by his comparison, she stood to her feet. "It's getting late, and I still have a long walk ahead. I have a pressing errand east of town."

He stood, too, bouncing the heel of his hand off his forehead. "That's right, your errand. I promised to help, remember?"

"Don't fret. I can manage."

"How will you get there?"

"The same way I got here—on foot."

"Now, Charity, there's no need for that. Let me take you, or hire you a buggy at least."

"Don't you think you've done enough? I appreciate the offer, but there's still plenty of daylight and. . ." She paused then continued. "Like I told you before, my errand is of a personal nature, so if you don't mind. . ."

He blushed and took a step back. "Of course."

As she brushed past him, Red came up from a sound sleep and loped toward her.

Buddy reached for her arm. "Charity, wait. About the drilling. . . you're not angry with me, are you?"

"Angry?" She gave him a warm smile. "No, not anymore."

He took off his hat and gave her a wry look. "But you were."

She dropped her gaze. "How did you know?"

"Wasn't hard to figure. That first day out at your place you were cross about something. Then after that old wolf got after you, you apologized for being mad at me. Didn't know why at the time and never dared to ask. Knowing how you feel about the well, I'm just putting two and two together."

Took you long enough.

"All right, I confess. I blamed you at first. You know. . .because you found the oil in the bog."

"Fair enough. How about now? Do you blame me still?"

Charity shook her head and gave him a warm smile. "Not very much." Laughing at his grimace, she placed her hand on his arm. "I don't blame you at all. And I could never be mad at you again."

He gave the top of his head an absentminded scratch. "Well, at the risk of changing that, I have one last question."

She groaned inside. Buddy Pierce was one truly exasperating man. "Which is?"

"Don't you want to see your mama's financial burden lifted? Wouldn't your papa want that, too?"

The air between them crackled.

Charity sucked in a breath through her nose and held it, but it didn't seem to meet her need to breathe. She'd have to be more careful in the future what she claimed she could never do again. "I really must be going. I'll see you back in town."

"I'm sorry, Charity. I didn't mean. . ."

After a few paces she turned, nearly tripping over Red. "To answer your question, I wish more than anything I could ease my mama's burden. I hate watching how hard she works, and I intend to help her just as soon as I find a way to earn some money. However, there's simply nothing I can do for her now, considering I'm left to provide for myself without a penny to polish."

She whirled to leave. As she passed the pile of crates, the corner of her pocket caught on a nail and tore away. Coins and commissary tokens tumbled in a sparkling shower, spilling over the ground. Charity spun, clutching at her ripped dress and staring at her secret scattered in plain sight between them.

Confusion masked Buddy's face. He bent to pick up a bright silver piece and held it out to her. "I think I see your point, Miss Bloom. Why fritter away time polishing pennies when your pockets are filled with these nice, shiny dollars?"

CHAPTER 15

The coin in Buddy's outstretched hand glinted in the sun like a circle of quartz. Beyond it, Charity stood like the statue of St. Louis of France—only pretty.

"It's not mine," she finally said, her wide eyes shifting like she'd been caught at something. "At least, not anymore." She flapped both hands in frustration. "I mean, it never really was." She pointed behind her. "In fact, that's my pressing errand. I'm going to return that money to its rightful owner."

Buddy didn't speak. She made so little sense he didn't know how to respond. Even worse, his eyebrows hovered somewhere in the vicinity of his hairline, and he couldn't coax them down.

She balled her fists and jammed them onto her hips. "Don't look at me like that, Buddy Pierce. I can assure you I didn't steal it."

When he couldn't answer, she stalked past and perched once more on her recently vacated seat. "I may as well tell you. You know every other humiliation I've endured—why not this?" She leaned to pat the opposite wooden box. "What are you waiting for? Sit down. I don't have all day."

Wordlessly, he pointed behind him at the coins on the ground.

She waved her gloved hand. "Leave them. They're not going anywhere."

He forced his brows to relax then sidestepped the dog, who sat with his head tilted toward Charity, looking as confused as

Buddy felt. Squeezing between her full skirt and his crate, Buddy sat down. Red trotted over and settled at Charity's feet with a groan of resignation.

She drew a breath and dove in. "The money belongs to Elsa Pike."

Buddy frowned and rubbed his chin. "Now where have I heard that name before?" Before she could answer, he held up his finger. "Oh, right. The duchess."

This earned him a smile. "She's not really a duchess. Folks call her that in jest. She claims she descended from royalty."

"And she really didn't?"

Charity shrugged. "No one knows for sure. Her husband acts embarrassed when anyone mentions it. Mama thinks Elsa made it up."

Buddy chuckled at the mention of Charity's feisty mama. "She could be right."

"So anyway, about the money..." She began to fidget. "I arranged a little business transaction with Mrs. Pike that fell through." Her tiny frown became a scowl. "Actually, it was run through by Mama's sharp tongue. That ornery woman can't abide to see me happy."

He laughed. Her head jerked up, so he traded his tickled grin for a sympathetic smile. "Sorry. You were saying?"

"It's my dress, after all. Oh, she made it, true enough, but she made it for me. I should have the right to do with it whatever I please." She glanced up and sought his eyes. "Don't you agree?"

He shook his head. "I'm sorry, I don't follow. You sold a dress?"

"My wedding dress. Haven't you heard a thing I've said?"

"I'm trying, sweetheart." The unexpected endearment slipped from his mouth, as natural as drawing a breath. Still, he blushed when he realized what he'd said.

So did Charity.

He tried again. "Let me see if I have this right. You sold your wedding dress to Elsa Pike, but your mama didn't approve so you're on your way to fix it."

She did a jaunty point with her finger. "Exactly."

He grinned. "See, I was listening. What if Elsa won't give it up?"

"We never got that far. I still have the dress, or rather Mama does. She's buried her talons and refuses to part with it. So I have to return Mrs. Pike's money and somehow. . ." She sighed. "Somehow break the news to Amy Jane."

Grateful she could so easily explain the money, Buddy felt the tension ease from his shoulders. "Is that all?"

Charity stiffened. "What do you mean, 'Is that all?' "

"I mean I don't see what's so scandalous about selling a frock."

She looked at him as if toadstools had sprouted from his ears. "Not just any frock, Buddy. My wedding gown. The one I wore for the hour it took to ruin my good name in this town."

He shot forward, startling Red, and wagged his finger. "Now you see? There's your problem. If you ask me, you set too much stock by what folks around here think. About you *and* your mama." He slouched back and pushed his hat off his forehead. "I thought you were about to bare your soul again, maybe tell a story as lively as your last confession. I have to say, I'm a little disappointed."

Charity's lips parted; then she swelled like a colicky horse. "Well, forgive me for letting you down. Hopefully my next calamity will provide you with more entertainment." She turned a frosty shoulder in his direction. "Perhaps the severity of my problem escapes you. When I hand this money over to Mrs. Pike, it means I won't be eating supper tonight."

Buddy bristled. "You know full well I'm not about to see you miss a meal. It's only when you're headstrong that you wind up with a hollow belly, not to mention a heap of trouble." He bent to give her the eye. "Now ain't that so?"

Charity stood. "I won't bother to answer such a ridiculous question." She leveled a withering glare at his outstretched legs. "If you'll be so kind as to move aside, I'll be going now."

Buddy lifted one pointy-toed boot to her crate, totally blocking the way. "No, ma'am, I won't excuse you. Not until you promise I can take you to the Pikes' in my rig."

The startled look in her bright eyes became a hooded challenge. "I've asked you kindly to remove your feet."

He took off his hat and fiddled with the band. "I'll be happy to. As soon as you agree."

With a swish of her skirts, Charity pivoted to face the rickety stack behind them. Chin held high, she seemed to weigh the danger of squeezing through the tight space. Obviously finding it too risky, she turned around and crossed her arms over her chest, so stiff she appeared to grow six inches in stature. "Why, Mr. Pierce, did I mistake you for a gentleman?"

He tucked his hat back on his head then pushed it up to see her face. "That's an impressive show of indignation from the same *lady* who bamboozled me a couple nights back. I consider this an act of justifiable recompense."

"Bamboozled? Why, I never–"

"You don't recall the matter involving me in a monkey-suit and you with a certain room key?"

Charity's scandalized expression disappeared, and her defiant chin lowered to her chest. She laced her hands behind her back and traced circles in the dirt with her shoe. "I didn't bamboozle you, Buddy. I wouldn't." She bit her bottom lip, but a tiny smile fluttered at the corners. "Besides, I believe the word you used then was 'bushwhacked.' " The smile widened into a grin. "And I've since decided your estimation of my actions was entirely too harsh."

The girl enchanted him. Before he could stop himself, he was on his feet with his arms around her, laughing like a man with no sense. He knew he didn't imagine it when she returned the enthusiasm of his embrace. When he could, he held her away from him and gazed at her beaming face. "Pardon my zeal, Miss Bloom, but has anyone ever told you how endearing you are?"

She affected a coy look. "Oh yes. Every day."

"I'd tell you every day if I could." Heat warmed his face, matched by a rosy flush on her cheeks. With her eyes cast down, all he saw were dark, sweeping lashes curled up at the ends. He longed to kiss each one but knew he'd gone too far already.

She lifted her gaze. "If you're sure you don't mind, I suppose you can give me a ride. If you still have the time. . ."

Buddy stepped aside. "After you, ma'am." He sighed. "That is, if you can hurdle that overgrown hound."

Charity smiled. "It wouldn't be the first time I've had to jump him, though I'd rather not." She nudged the dog with her toe. "Get up, Red."

He reluctantly stirred then followed them sleepy-eyed to the rig.

Buddy handed Charity aboard then scuttled back to pick up her assorted loot before swinging up onto the driver's side. One brow raised, he handed the money and tokens to Charity. Without a word, she snatched them then opened her one good pocket and let them tumble inside.

They rode quietly at first. Charity, whether staring off in the distance or watching Red trot alongside, seemed lost in thought.

Probably rehearsing her speech to Mrs. Pike.

Buddy was busy rehearsing a speech of his own. He noisily cleared his throat.

As he'd hoped, Charity's head swung around. "You have something you wish to say to me, Buddy?"

"I don't want to intrude on your musings."

She made a face. "Believe me, they bear intrusion."

"I just wanted you to know, although your situation appears bleak at the moment, I believe things will work out in the end."

A slight frown creased her forehead. "On what do you base such confidence?"

He grinned. "The Bible does say, 'Charity never faileth.' "

She didn't actually return his smile, but the slight deepening of her dimples gave her away. "I know you're probably right. It's just that things seem so hopeless."

"Hopeless? I haven't turned you out in the street yet, have I?"

She patted his hand. "That's because you're a wonderful man. Except I can't in good conscience allow you to continue what you've been doing. It's outlandish."

"I really don't mind." How could he admit that not only didn't he mind taking care of her, but he wanted to? How could he tell her that tending her needs just felt right somehow?

"I'm sorry–it's out of the question. If I can't pay my own way, I'll be forced to check out of the hotel in the morning."

Surprised, he spun on the seat. "And go where? To the Danes'?"

"Never!"

"Then where, I'd like to know?"

The dejected slump of her shoulders told him she couldn't answer his question.

They continued the ride in silence. Buddy's mind roamed in circles until he had crossed off every possibility and exhausted his imagination. He turned to prayer, where he should've started in the first place.

As they rattled down the road leading to the Pikes' farm, the solution darted up and hit him squarely between the eyes. He reined up and faced her on the seat. "I know what we can do."

Her eyes brightened. "There's a remedy to this predicament?"

"Indeed there is. It's simple really. The oil company owes your mama a fair sum for the lease of your house, isn't that so?"

She nodded, but the mention of the oil company dampened the expectant light in her eyes.

"Just listen now. If Bertha agrees, I believe I can arrange to charge off whatever money I've spent on you against her check. They'll deduct my portion and hold it for me. When she gets the balance, she can take over from there. Then you won't be taking anything from me."

Charity clasped her hands. "Oh, Buddy. Will the check be enough for all that?"

He nodded. "With money left over to hold you through the month. They're fairly free with their purse."

She sneered. "They can afford to be, can't they?"

Buddy picked up her hands. "Listen, I'll be the first to admit that drilling oil—like anything else involving fast money—attracts a bad bunch of men. Sure, there are depraved, greedy souls who take advantage of good folks to make a dollar, but we're not all bad."

She cringed and pulled one hand free to cover her mouth. "Oh, Buddy, I didn't mean. . .that is. . .well, you're not, of course."

"Not just me, Charity. If you took the time to get to know a few more of us, you'd find that the majority of men in the oil business are decent, hardworking, and honest." He gave her other hand a firm squeeze. "I intend to hang around long enough to prove that to you. I'll have you trusting oilmen again if it's the last thing I do."

She offered a brave smile and turned away, but not before he saw the flicker of doubt in her eyes.

CHAPTER 16

After more than two months, waking up at the Lone Star Hotel still felt peculiar even after Mama moved in. Rather, especially after Mama moved in. The feisty rascal refused to share the room until she could pay her own way, but the minute she got the first oil company check, she turned up at Charity's door with a bag of clothes and a stubborn mind-set. "Ain't no daughter of mine living in a hotel by herself as long as I can help it," she'd insisted. "Thaddeus Bloom would spin in his grave if he knew."

Living with her in their spacious, high-ceilinged home had been challenge enough. Sharing a space no bigger than Rebel's stall proved downright trying. Mama alternated between talking nonstop when awake and snoring down the rafters while she slept, so peace and rest became scarce in Charity's life. For that reason, when an uncommon stillness settled over the room, she rolled over in bed to look around.

Her rowdy companion was gone, though a sleepy glance at the window told Charity the sun had barely risen. She yawned and stretched then swung her feet to the cold floor. Usually by the end of March the weather was warm, but a recent cool snap had penetrated the smooth boards, turning them to ice beneath her toes.

At home she kept a pair of Papa's thick woolen socks in a dresser drawer for chilly mornings, but only heaven knew where they were now. Wearing them never failed to warm her heart right along with her feet, so she considered the lack of them one more casualty in a string of losses. She shuddered, picturing them mud-soaked and stretched over the big, smelly feet of a roughneck.

Not yet committed to rising, Charity reached behind her and pulled the warm blanket around her shoulders. She sighed, aware she'd awakened with the same confused feelings she'd taken to bed. Elation and despair, a miserable mix, fought for vantage in the pit of her stomach.

Last night, from out of nowhere, Mama announced they were going home. "Those men have searched for the bottom of that hole for nine weeks now," she'd said. "If they ain't found it yet, I expect they ain't likely to. We'll head out there first thing in the morning and tell them to clear out."

The unexpected words had pierced Charity's heart, unleashing a flood of forgiveness, relief, and joy. They were going home, to the house where she'd been born, to the only life she'd known before the specter of oil had curled sticky black fingers around Humble.

There was only one problem. The marauding invader employed a most agreeable representative in the person of Buddy Pierce.

During her stay at the hotel, Buddy had made a point to see Charity every day. Most evenings he made it back to town in time to clean up and take supper with her and Mama. If his work at the house detained him past their meal, he'd find some reason to knock on their door. For propriety's sake, he and Charity would stand in the hallway and whisper or sit in a secluded corner of the lobby and talk until bedtime. Mama noticed his attention and delighted in teasing her.

As if summoned by her thoughts, Mama jerked open the door and swept in like a gusty wind. "Get up, little gal, and shake that floor," she crowed. "Your old mama's running circles around you already." She came and perched on the side of the bed. "I've done been down to the livery and back. Hired us a rig for the trip out to the house. Ain't nothing fancy, but it'll get us there. The old man was hitching it up when I left. Said he'd deliver it to the hotel himself." She gave Charity a sharp slap on the leg. "What do you think about that?"

Her boisterous mood at the early hour rattled Charity's nerves.

She winced but offered a sleepy smile. "Morning, Mama," she mumbled, rubbing her eyes. "Gracious, but you're lively. How long have you been up?"

"Long enough to see your beau and his men leave for work before the cock ever crowed. He looked about as spry as you do. You two might want to consider trading some of that late-night talking for sleeping."

The wound-up little woman crossed to the window and peered down to the street. "Wahoo! Come on, gal. The wagon's sitting out front right now." She spun around laughing. "Took me a spell to convince that old possum to let me take it, but when he saw the color of my money, he couldn't find his pocket quick enough."

She came back and stood over the bed, brandishing a bony finger. "And that there's what I've been saying all along. Money makes a difference in people's lives, even oil company money."

Unwilling to wade those precarious waters, Charity bit her lip and nodded.

Oblivious, Mama continued, "Shame our cash is about to run out just when I'm getting used to having it." She heaved a sigh. "Even more of a shame that boy couldn't make good on his promise. Now we'll never know what it's like to make ends meet without stretching the life out of a dollar."

Charity's heart lurched. Buddy's question about easing Mama's burden came to mind. She hadn't yet lifted a finger in that direction, and in fact had only created a heavier load. Not to mention the fact that her disastrous wedding had put a terrible strain on Mama's purse. . .with no well-heeled son-in-law to show for her trouble. "I'll pitch in soon. I promise. I hear Elsa's looking for help around the house after Amy Jane marries. If she'll have me, after all the hullabaloo, I can work for her."

Mama scrunched up her face. "I reckon I'd rather see you slave after Emmy the rest of your life than work for Elsa Pike." She sat beside Charity on the bed and gripped her shoulders. "We'll deal with all that later. Right now, the only thing holding us here is you, so don't just sit there under them covers. Hurry and dress so we can get packed and eat a bite before we head home."

"Does Buddy know?"

"What? That we're coming? I started to tell him our plans this morning, but I don't need him trying to talk me out of what I know is right. I reckon the sight of us on the porch with our belongings should show him we mean business."

Pulling her chilly feet beneath her, Charity sat cross-legged in the bed. "But where will they go? The men, I mean."

"That ain't our concern now. We had a deal. Two months and no more. Their time is up."

Charity pictured the house and shuddered. She remembered the mud, tracked so thick on the porch she couldn't see the boards, with heavy-footed men traipsing in and out all the time. The kitchen had to be fly-spotted from leaving the screen tied back. No telling in what condition they'd find their beds. "Mama, the whole place is a in a muddle. How will we ever set it right again?"

Mama waved her hand. "Never mind about that. We'll just wrestle it through to the end."

Charity groaned and scratched her nose with the blanket. "That's fine for you to say. You haven't seen it."

"Don't worry, honey. The two of us will find a way. We always have, ain't we?" She cocked her head and stared dreamily. "Almost hate to leave here though. I think I might miss seeing that Lee feller around. He sure is nice. Makes me wish I was ten years younger."

"So it's *Lee* now, is it?"

Mama bristled, her face crimson. "Don't look so surprised. I ain't buried yet."

"I'm only surprised by what you said. You're not ten years older than Mr. Allen. A couple of years, at most."

Mama gazed at her, weighing her words. "Just two? You reckon so?"

Beaming, Charity swung her feet to the floor. "So you are sweet on him."

Dimples deeper than her own creased Mama's cheeks. "Hush up. We got no time for silly talk. Dress yourself, daughter, unless you've acquired Emmy's fondness for parading outside in your nightdress."

Charity laughed and pushed off the bed. Standing in front of the tall pine wardrobe, she picked through her clothes, studying them one by one. Besides her three old dresses and the bridal gown pushed to the back, two brand-new frocks hung there, one green and one blue. Not handmade like most things she owned but ordered straight from the catalog. Another good thing to come out of the oil company money, she grudgingly had to admit.

She held them up. "Can I wear one of these?"

Mama stood by the bed, shoving her clothes into a bag, not bothering to notice whether they were clean or dirty. She glanced back. "Out to that filthy place? Whatever for?"

"I want to, that's all. I'll change out of it before we start to clean." She tilted her head and pouted her lips. "Please?"

Mama gave her a knowing look. "Go on, then. Look nice for Buddy. But you'd better be careful. There won't be no more big checks to buy dresses once we take the house back."

Charity twirled and squealed. "Thank you, Mama! I promise not to muss it." She chose between the two outfits and returned the other one to its peg. Reaching to the back, she ran her fingers down the sequined bodice of the wedding gown. "Do you suppose Mrs. Pike and Amy Jane will ever forgive me for going back on our deal?"

"Sure they will. Time takes care of such things."

"They won't even speak to me, and they avoid me on the street."

Mama snorted. "Count your blessings."

Charity caressed the silky sleeve once more before gently tucking it back in place. "I must say, I'm glad it wound up this way. It's such a beautiful gown. I just hope I get to wear it before it yellows with age."

"Don't be silly, child. The way things are going with you and Buddy, you'll wear it, and soon I'll wager. You two are as cozy as turtles on a warm rock." A smug look crossed her face. "If I play my cards right with Mr. Allen, maybe I'll get a chance to wear it first. 'Course I'd have to shorten the hem by six inches at least." She hooted at her own daring then held up Charity's shoes. "Sit down and I'll help you put these on."

Charity slipped on her stockings then pulled out the chair in front of the dressing table. Sobered, Mama stooped to help her with the laces. "How long you reckon it'll take them men to clear off our land?"

Charity shrugged. "A few hours at most."

Mama breathed a contented sigh. "Tonight I'll actually get to sleep in my own bed. Never thought I'd choose it over all this finery, but I do."

Charity bent to squeeze her hand. "Me, too."

"Reckon we'll get the house clean by bedtime?"

"Not like it was, I don't expect, but if I have to sleep there tonight, I'm eager to get started. Only. . ."

Mama peered up at her and waited.

Charity extended one leg and feigned an interest in her shoe, trying hard to sound casual. "Does this mean Buddy will leave?"

Mama shook her head and went back to the laces. "Don't borrow trouble, honey. There's plenty of oil business in Humble to keep him right here. Besides, I get the feeling he's not so eager to leave town just yet. You keep batting them pretty eyes and I expect he'll be around for a good long while."

It was just a tiny bit of hope, but she latched onto it. "You really think so?"

Mama dropped Charity's foot on the floor and stood. "I do. Now let's go scare us up some grub before I perish."

They followed the aroma of food to the dining hall, where Sam saw to it they started their journey with a good breakfast. After a hearty platter of bacon, fried eggs, biscuits, and grits, they climbed aboard the hired rig and set out, their hearts as full as their bellies. They barely cleared the hotel before Red bounded up and fell in beside them, tail high, ears alert, as if he counted himself their personal escort.

"Fool dog," Mama murmured, casting him a withering look.

Charity just laughed and shook her head.

The cool of the morning persisted, though the sun had come up bright, casting long shadows over the trail. The countryside only hinted of spring, but there were patches of early wildflowers and tender new growth on a few bare limbs.

Charity closed her eyes and thanked God for a beautiful new day. In her estimation, life couldn't be better. The two things for which she had fervently prayed seemed close enough to reach out and touch.

Not only were they going home, but her heart stirred with

the possibility that Buddy might care for her enough to stay on in Humble. Since the latter part was too important to trust to Mama's scattered observations, Charity determined to find out for herself. She would see him in another half mile. She decided to be bold and watch him closely. If he truly cared, she'd know. She'd see it in his eyes.

Charity hoped she looked as good as she felt. She had worn the green dress. It was the prettiest and matched the color of her eyes. After Mama helped to pin up her hair and fasten her bonnet, Charity pulled long strands free, winding them into dark curls around her face. A splash of lavender water at the crook of each arm finished her off.

"You smell nice, baby. Just like springtime."

Startled, Charity glanced up. It was uncanny how Mama picked up her thoughts. "What a nice thing to say. Thank you."

"You look right pretty in that new frock, too. I'm glad you wore it."

Smoothing the fabric against her lap, Charity smiled. "I do love it. I'm so glad you bought it for me."

Mama turned her head to the trail again, but not before Charity saw tears glistening in her eyes. "I wanted to buy you lots of new things."

Charity leaned close and hugged her. "Don't you dare fret. I know you're disappointed, but what you're giving me today is worth more than ten new dresses." She squeezed her tighter. "We're going home, Mama! That's all that matters. I'm content without all the rest–honest, I am."

Red barked, loud and unexpected beside them, causing them both to jump. Mama shouted an insult at him, a coarse offense she'd picked up from Mother Dane.

"Mama!"

"I'm sorry, daughter. He scared me."

The dog ducked and cowered in shame, but his sense of obligation overshadowed his disgrace. He trotted alongside them, big head swaying to and fro, alert eyes sweeping the brush-lined trail. Evidently, whatever he had barked at earlier wasn't important enough to pull him from his self-appointed duty.

Obviously eager to get home, Mama kept the horse moving at a brisk pace. Determined to keep up, though he drooled and panted profusely, Red kept apace with the horse. Charity figured she might feel sorry for him if he weren't so pigheaded.

"Why do you suppose that stubborn old hound persists on following me wherever I go?"

Mama glanced down at Red and smiled. "Oh, I reckon I know why."

Her words, spoken with quiet assurance, surprised Charity. "You do?"

"Don't you?"

"No, ma'am. Enlighten me, please. Then maybe I can put a stop to it."

"That ain't likely." She ducked low and leaned in like a little girl sharing a secret. "He senses your daddy in you."

Charity frowned. "Papa?"

Softness settled over her mama's face the way it always did when she spoke of him. Like a magic wand, it blurred the faint lines around her eyes and lit a dreamy glow within their depths. "Red worshipped the ground he trod. You have his same spirit, Charity. All the good residing in Thad he left here with you when he passed." She faltered and pressed a hand to still her quivering lips. "You're so much like him, daughter. Did you know when you sit with me in a darkened room I feel he's there instead?"

Charity's eyes stung. "I'm really that much like him?"

"The breath and soul of him. You even love the Almighty the same. Thad worshipped the Lord free and joyful, like King David himself."

How could such beautiful words hurt so much? Charity swallowed hard against the tight knot in her throat and nodded. "I can still hear Papa's voice in my head: 'Let God do His work, honey. Confess your sins and let 'em go. Don't cling to your guilt. Enjoy the gift of freedom Jesus gave you. After all, it cost Him all He had.' "

Mama nodded. "You took them words to heart."

The tears flowed then, running down Charity's face and splashing onto the crisp green fabric of her dress. "I did, Mama. I pinned all my hope on them."

They embraced again. Since he barked the last time they hugged, Charity remembered Red. He wasn't on either side of the wagon, so she turned in her seat to look. He still followed, straggling a good way behind them. His panting had worsened, to boot.

"Stop the wagon, Mama."

"Why?"

"I want to put Red in the back."

"What for?"

Mama sounded doubtful, but she pulled on the reins nonetheless. Charity jumped to the ground and waited for Red to catch up. When he did, she lowered the tailgate and ordered him inside. Too tired to jump, he only managed to plant his two front paws on the rig. She stooped and wrapped her arms around the dog's body to give him a boost. Red scrambled inside, squirming with pleasure.

Mama threw up her hands. "Charity Bloom! Now you'll smell like that old rascal, and after you promised not to soil that new dress."

To show his gratitude, the drooling dog licked Charity from chin to eyebrows before she ever saw it coming.

"Heavens!" Mama shrieked. "Now you'll stink of dog breath, too. What on earth were you thinking?"

Charity closed the tailgate and dusted her hands. "I'm thinking a creature with Red's brand of devotion deserves to ride."

Mama cast a warning glance. "Don't lose sight of the facts, honey. That ain't our dog no more."

Scratching Red's wrinkled snout, Charity smiled. "Try telling that to him." She sauntered to the front of the wagon, the swish of new petticoats adding to her pleasure. Seated beside Mama once more, she nodded toward the horse. "Let's go. I'm anxious to get this over and done."

"That makes two of us."

Red groaned and fell to his side before stretching the length of the wagon bed and closing his eyes. Mama laughed and nodded. "I stand corrected, dog. I guess that makes three."

She shook the reins and clucked at the horse, setting him in motion. Pulling her foot up to rest the sole of her boot on the rail, she looked about her with a big smile. "The good Lord sure gave us a fine day for it, didn't He?"

"That He did."

"I reckon your sweetheart will be right disappointed in us when we get there."

Charity hadn't considered that possibility. She flashed her mama a worried look. "You think so?"

Mama nodded. "He sure wanted to find oil on our land. I expect he'd drill clear to China if we didn't stop him."

"You don't think he'll be mad at us, do you?"

Mama opened her mouth to answer, but if she said anything, Charity never heard it. A deafening explosion rocked the area, sending shock waves through the ground so violent they rattled the wagon. The horse reared and got set to bolt, but Mama held the reins, shouting at him to hold steady.

Over the treetops a column of mud blasted to the sky and then spewed in every direction. There followed a greenish-black surge that rushed into the air for eighty feet before raining down over the surrounding pine. Black ooze fell straight down, pelting them and bombarding the trail in giant globs, spooking the crazed horse even more. He threw himself back on his haunches again, his front legs pawing the air.

"Get off, Charity!" Mama cried. "I cain't hold him!"

Charity's feet hit the side rail, and she was on the ground, running for the horse's head. She clutched his harness, holding on for all she was worth. "Get down, Mama! Jump!"

Mama dropped the reins and shot to her feet. One leap and she was clear. . .and just in time. A wet wad of mud landed on the horse's back, and no power on earth could have held him. With glazed eyes and foaming mouth, he bucked just as Charity fell back and turned him loose. Then he burned up the trail, blindly running in the direction of the very thing he feared. As the wagon thundered by, Red, stiff-legged with fright, stood staring at them from behind the tailgate.

Mama lay on the ground where she'd landed then rolled. Propped on both elbows, she stared at the roaring apparition overhead.

Charity rushed to her side. "Are you all right?"

She lay slack-jawed with dread. "What's happening, Charity? What is that thing?"

Before Charity could answer, a lone horseman cut around the runaway rig, elbows high and flailing as he urged his mount. He didn't bother to stop the wagon but headed straight for them, riding hard.

Her mama still gazed at the sky. "Is it Armageddon, daughter?"

Charity pointed at the rider. "I don't know, but look."

Mama gaped as the man bore down on them whooping and hollering, covered head to toe in muck. He reined in his horse so fast the animal spun to the side, kicking up a cloud of dust.

Mama looked him over then turned to Charity. "Is that a man?"

She nodded. "I think so."

"Who is it, then?"

Charity leaned down and pulled her to her feet. "I'm not sure, but I think it's Buddy."

The dark figure leapt to the ground and came at them, laughing so hard he ran in a crooked line. "We did it!" He grabbed Mama in a bear hug and whirled her off her feet. "We got us a gusher!"

Charity gaped at the mess he'd made of her mama's clothes and backed away. He set Mama on the ground and smeared a sloppy kiss on her cheek. "No more cooking and scrubbing floors, little Bertha. You can hire your own help now."

Catching his mood, Mama started to laugh. She turned and pointed at the sky. "So that's what that thing is? Oil?"

"Oil, Mrs. Bloom, and plenty of it. Enough so you'll rest easy all your days. Charity, too, and her children's children."

At the mention of her name, he came at Charity, ready to grab her, too, but she screamed and darted away.

"Buddy Pierce, don't you dare touch me!"

He halted in his tracks, his arms still reaching for her. "And why not?"

She pointed. "Look at what you've done to Mama. She's covered in that stuff."

"Covered in gold, sugar. Come and get you some." He leered jokingly and came at her again.

She screeched and lit out for the trees, finding a big one to put between them.

He chased her around it laughing like a madman while Mama hooted from the trail.

"You stop right now—I mean it. This is my new dress, and I promised Mama I'd stay clean."

He paused long enough to nod at her arm, his grin crazy-white against the sludge on his face. "I hate to be the one to tell you, Miss Bloom, but it's too late for that now."

Charity followed his gaze to the greasy spatter on her sleeve, made worse every second by the shower of oil falling around them. "Oh no! Just look at that. It's ruined."

No longer smiling, Buddy stared at her around the tree trunk. She clutched the cool, rough bark and stared back.

"You still don't get it, do you, sweetheart? You're rich, Charity. You can buy a new dress every day of the week if you want. The whole shop, if you've a mind to."

And there it was. The thing in his eyes she had set out to find. Love offered up from the deep green depths, there for the whole world to see. Her knees grew weak. She had no choice but to allow Buddy to catch her before she hit the ground. With both arms clutching his neck, she watched over his shoulder with wide eyes as the roaring black spout rocked the sky.

CHAPTER 17

"Which one are you looking at now?"

Charity sat at the dressing table, pinning her hair and watching her mama through the big looking glass. Mama sat cross-legged in the middle of the bed, bent low over the catalog in her lap. At the question, her head came up, one finger held steady on the page to mark her place. Her eyes met Charity's in the mirror.

"It's the Henke-Pillot."

Charity pointed to the toppling stack wedged against her side. "And those?"

Mama picked up the topmost book. "This here's the Sears Roebuck." She pointed down at the pile. "That one's John Deere. The rest are old Harper's Weeklies. I'm studying on the adverts."

"John Deere? I thought you were set on raising cattle, not crops."

Her attention divided between her daughter and the catalog, she turned another page. "Ain't looking for me. Widow Sheffield's plow is held together by prayer and a wad of spit. I reckoned I might fetch her a new one when our money comes in."

Charity smiled at Mama's reflection. "I might've guessed. You haven't a greedy bone in your body."

Mama shook her head. "It ain't that. If God intends to bless me when I don't deserve it, how can I do less than bless others? I've always said money in the right hands does more good than harm. Now I aim to prove it."

Instead of returning to her browsing, Mama watched while Charity fussed with her hair, peering so intently that Charity started to squirm. She put down the brush and squinted back at the brooding image. "What now? You're staring."

Mama frowned. "You're mighty flushed, sugar. You ain't taking sick, are you?" Tossing the catalog aside, she wiggled to the edge of the bed and hurried over to press her palm against Charity's forehead. "Gracious, I reckon you're a mite warm, too."

Cheeks flaming, Charity caught the groping hand and pulled it away from her face. "I'm fine. It's a warm day, that's all."

Mama slid both arms around Charity's neck, resting her chin on top of her head. Their gazes locked in the glass. "Don't you get sick on me, you hear? Not now, when everything's about to change for the better."

Charity patted her hand. "I won't. I promise."

Relieved when her mama crawled to the center of the bed and took up her books again, Charity returned to taming her hair. She dared not confess the little meddler had caught her mooning over Buddy, an activity that warmed her cheeks quite often lately. He'd been gone for two whole days now, and Charity missed him something fierce.

They'd never made it home that day. Charity had begun making peace with the possibility they never would. Back in the hotel, Mama overflowed with plans to build a new house every bit as grand as Mother Dane's, with a stove like hers and a balcony attached to each of their bedrooms.

Buddy's lesson on the eagle had come to Charity on wings of mercy. She'd spent a lot of time pondering her death grip on the past and decided not to let it steal her future. Papa had been an immovable rock in her young life. When the floodwaters washed him downriver, they'd swept her sense of security along with him. Thanks to Buddy, she understood she'd been clinging to all the wrong things. The only constant in anyone's life was God. As long as He hovered nearby, she could soar above a few sticks and straws.

After the gusher blew in, Buddy commandeered every available freighter then hired men eager for work to drive wagons loaded with oil to Port Arthur. He said a refinery there would pay top dollar for every barrel they could haul.

The morning the makeshift caravan departed, Buddy had leaned down and pressed his lips to the corner of her mouth before swinging up on the lead wagon. That quick, stolen kiss consumed her thoughts far more than his parting words—the promise to return with so much money Mama couldn't spend it in a year.

Mama had spent the last few days trying. She haunted Rogers & Grossman's Dry Goods Store, bent on seeing, touching, and smelling every item for sale. Back in their room, she pored over catalogs for hours, making endless lists. Charity teased her about it but had to admit she'd jotted down a few notes of her own.

Buddy planned to take them to Houston when he got back, to the Kennedy Trading Post and Market Square. Mama had journeyed to Houston once when Papa was alive, but not by rail. Charity had never left Humble, much less set foot on a train. She and Mama awaited Buddy's return like children counting down to Christmas.

It amazed Charity to realize she'd known him for only a short time, yet it seemed she'd soon perish without him. His absence caused an ache deep inside that grew worse every day. Thinking of him was like scratching an itch—to do so made the problem worse, but she couldn't stop.

She glanced at the mirror to find her face bright red again. She looked away and struggled to compose herself before Mama noticed. Thankfully, a loud knock jarred them both, jerking Mama's attention to the door.

Charity's heart pitched. Had Buddy returned early?

Evidently the same thought had come to Mama. She cleared the bed in half the time it took her to root off of it before and crossed the room a split second ahead of Charity. She yanked at the door and slung it wide, her giddy grin saying she expected Buddy to be on the other side.

Shamus Pike stood in the hall clutching a scruffy hat. His hesitant smile revealed he hadn't expected the elaborate reception. "Afternoon, Bertha. Miss Charity."

"What in tarnation are you doing here?" Mama had never perfected the fine art of polite banter and wasn't one for beating around the bush.

Shamus's smile disappeared. "I come to discuss important business, Bert." He nodded into the room. "Can I come in?"

Mama waved him through but surprisingly left the door propped open. Concerning herself with the rules of respectability was not her usual behavior.

"This about the land lease money? It ain't due for two weeks yet, but I'll take it if you insist." She held out her hand and chuckled at her own wit.

Shamus shook his head, and color flooded his face. He wouldn't meet Mama's eyes, and his Adam's apple bobbed several times. Finally, he cleared his throat and got to the point of his visit. "Now, Bertha, don't think what I come to tell you means you won't be taken care of, you and Charity. I owe a debt of friendship to old Thad, God rest him, so I wouldn't have it any other way."

Mama dropped her head to the side the way Red cocked his and stared while getting scolded.

Charity didn't understand Shamus's words either, but the anxious way he blurted them flipped her stomach.

Mama motioned to the chair in front of the dressing table. "I reckon you're trying to tell me something, but I guess you'd better sit down and start over, because I ain't understood a word so far."

Hat still wadded in both hands, Shamus sidestepped to the chair and sat. A thick-middled, broad-shouldered man, he looked out of place seated on the delicate furniture. Mama and Charity perched together at the edge of the bed and waited for him to continue.

"What I come to say is hard for me." Shamus stared at the bare stretch of floor between them while he talked, his big hands working the old hat like dough. "I got no wish to hurt you, wouldn't do that for the world, but sometimes the dealings between men bring pain to their families. It's the way life is."

Mama scooted closer to Charity and took hold of her hand. "I'll thank you kindly to get to the point, then."

Shamus squirmed in the chair until Charity feared it would collapse. Finally, he looked up and rushed ahead as if he needed to get it said. "It's about your land, Bertha. Fact is, it ain't your land no more. At least it won't be soon enough."

Mama sat up straighter and stared him down. "What are you saying to me, Shamus Pike?"

He dropped his gaze again but kept on talking. "You know yourself old Thaddeus had a gambling problem once. A right reckless problem."

Mama tensed. "I ain't denying it, but that was a long time ago."

Charity's head jerked around.

Her mama shrank five inches under her searching gaze. "Sorry you had to hear it like this, baby. I'm afraid it's true. Games of chance always had a strong pull on your poor papa. He kept his weakness in check by teaching me and Magda how to play poker for fun. 'Course, we never bet nothing serious. Just harmless things like buttons, matches, hard candies sometimes."

Charity had always wondered how their weekly poker game came to be.

"After you was born, he changed," she continued. "Promised he'd never place another bet—a promise he kept as far as I know."

Shamus snorted. "He made one last wager. Thad gambled away your property before he died. To me."

Mama's fingernails dug into Charity's hand. "How so?"

Shamus leaned over and considered her with probing eyes. "You want the details?"

"I sure do."

He sat up again, watching them. "All right, then." He rubbed his palms down his trouser legs and swallowed hard. "Six months before he passed, Thad and me was in town together of a night, both feeling our oats, me liquored up and him just feeling spry. The bet was Thad's idea." His bloodshot eyes fixed on Charity. "Somehow it come to him to gamble on whose daughter would marry first, Amy Jane or Charity there. The stakes we put up were our homesteads."

Charity couldn't tell if the trembling in their clasped hands was Mama's or her own.

"Thad wouldn't do a thing like that. He told me he was finished with gambling." Though her voice quivered, Mama's words were forceful.

Shamus glared her way. "He not only done it; he goaded me

into it whilst I was drunk!"

His expression softened when Mama drew back. He ducked his head and cleared his throat then continued in a quieter voice. "Later on Thad's conscience got the best of him. He tried to get out of it, but I wouldn't allow him to welsh on a bet. I'd sobered up by then and had some time to think. Old Thad thought he had a sure thing, what with Amy Jane so big and plain and Charity so fetching. But I reckoned I might be able to turn things around on him. I figured I had a fair enough chance, considering men around these parts need a good sturdy woman—one who can bear lots of babies and help shoulder the load. As pretty as Charity is, I figured Amy Jane stacked up better in that respect."

He glanced Charity's way again. "No insult intended."

She nodded, speechless.

"When Daniel Clark started up courting Charity, I got real nervous. Took a gun to my head when he proposed." He sat back and exhaled. "Good thing I didn't pull the trigger."

Mama grunted. "Good for who?"

His eyebrow spiked. "Say again?"

She waved him off. "I wouldn't have come after your land even if Charity had got married to Daniel. First off, I never heard any of this before now." She lifted her chin at him. "And second, only a heartless reprobate would snatch a person's home right out from under them."

Shamus sputtered. His ears turned purple, and his chest heaved. "That's because you're a woman, and women are weak. You can't understand the ways of a man. Sometimes we got to do things we don't like to make our way in this life. That includes taking risks."

He opened his mouth to say more, but Mama stopped him. "No, sir. That don't apply to Thad. He was a good man. Better than most. I can boast about him in this company, because we all know it's true." She shifted toward him, prepared to do battle. "You'll never convince me he risked our home. He wouldn't do that to us."

Shamus leaned forward and met her charge. "He would on a sure bet."

Charity couldn't stay still. "If such a bet existed, Papa's death canceled it out."

Shamus wagged his graying head. " 'Taint so, Charity. In the weeks leading up to your wedding, I figured I'd lost it all and I was bound to give it. When Amy Jane steps to the altar, I'll accept no less from you." He slouched in the chair and folded his arms, his eyes hard on Mama's face. "Bertha Bloom, I expect you to honor your dead husband's word."

Charity didn't wait for Mama's answer. She pointed at Shamus. "That's why you pushed Amy Jane's marriage to Isaac Young, even against Elsa's wishes." She knew it was true, but it felt odd to say it. In other circumstances, she'd never speak so boldly.

Shamus glared at her finger through narrowing eyes. "I'll thank you to pull in that claw and mind your tongue, little cat. This here's betwixt me and your ma."

Mama stared at Shamus like he'd turned green. "You're telling me if Charity had married Daniel, I'd own your whole place right now? Shamus, that's crazy talk."

"It might be crazy, but in a few days I'll hold your deed."

Mama jumped to her feet. "I don't believe it! You got no proof."

"Oh yes, ma'am, I do." Shamus stood. As if he'd been waiting for the chance to do so, he reached into the hip pocket of his overalls. Producing a square of paper, he waved it in her face. "The proof is right here." He undid the folds and crossed the small room to stand before Mama, his thumb pressed to the bottom of the page. "Ain't that your Thad's writing?" He looked from Mama to the paper then to Charity, his eyes bulging, his voice shrill with emotion. "And that's his very own John Hancock signed in ink right there at the bottom. Now you can't deny that."

Mama trembled as she took the paper. She handled the scrawled signature with a reverent touch, and tears sprang to her eyes. "Them's his marks, all right. I'd know them anywhere." She handed the paper to Charity and slumped back onto the bed. "Read it to me, daughter. Real slow."

The tears in Charity's own eyes blurred the page. She swiped at them with the back of her hand and tried to focus on the words. "It says, 'I, Thaddeus Horatio Bloom, square of mind and in possession of my good sense, do hereby enter into a bound agreement with one Shamus P. Pike–' "

"No, Thad!"

Charity jumped at the tortured cry that tore from her mama's throat, her plea directed at Papa as if he were right in the room uttering the terrible words himself. Mama fell onto the bed with her hands over her ears and wailed. "Don't read me no more. I cain't stand to hear it!" She reached for a pillow and buried her face in it. "Read it to yourself, daughter; then tell me it's not true. Please say my Thad didn't do this to me."

Charity read on, searching for some shred of hope. She read clear to the bottom without finding it. The room swirled and seemed to inhale sharply, sucking the air from her lungs. Shamus still hovered just above her face, and though she couldn't bring him into focus, she became acutely aware of the smell of him–manure, the open field, burnt oil.

Oil!

She pushed to her feet, forcing Shamus to stumble away. Glaring at him, she shook the paper in his face. "I understand it all now. I know why you're doing this."

His determined gaze grew wary.

"You don't want our land," Charity spat. "You're after what they drilled on it."

At the mention of their gusher, Mama moaned and wailed louder.

Shamus set his jaw. "It's a fair bet between me and your pa, Charity. Neither of us knew the future when we made it."

He snatched the document from her hand, blotting at the tear-smudged ink with a filthy rag before cramming it into his pocket. "This paper will hold up under the law, too. I already checked. So consider this official notice. I'll be taking possession of your place directly after Amy Jane's wedding. Make sure you're cleared out by then."

He shoved his hat down on his head and marched to the door, pausing on the threshold as if something had just occurred to him. "You should count yourself lucky that well came in before the wedding. At least you'll get something out of it before you lose it."

He left, leaving the door standing open behind him. Charity jumped up to slam it, desperate to shut him out along with the terrible news he'd brought in with him, but it was too late. One look at Mama told her the damage was done.

She had scrambled to the middle of the bed and pulled her knees close to her body. Deep, heartrending sobs ripped from her throat, loud enough to disturb the other guests. Charity crawled onto the bed behind her and shielded the tiny body with her own.

"Don't you cry, Mama. Don't you fret now, you hear?" Charity cradled her, rocking and stroking her hair. "Hush now. Everything will be fine. You'll see. Everything will be just fine. I promise."

Too angry to pray, she rocked until Mama slept while her mind whirled with a plan that would help her to keep her promise.

CHAPTER 18

With a grunt, Daniel heaved a feed sack onto the growing stack he'd raised in the corner of the barn then propped his arms against the burlap bag and leaned his head to rest. The pungent odor of jute mingled with grain assailed his nostrils, reviving him a bit. Up since dawn, he'd tackled and finished a long list of chores, though it wasn't yet ten in the morning. For a man to be bone-weary two hours shy of midday was just plain no good.

He'd found little rest the night before. The minute his body grew still enough for sleep, his head kicked up, filling his thoughts with long black curls and a wide, laughing mouth. He fared no better with the morning. Charity had come to him in his waking hours, just as she had throughout the night, teasing, taunting, hovering just out of reach.

Longing for her one minute and cursing her the next, the weight of conflicted emotions had bruised his insides. Whether he felt more anger toward Charity, Emmy, Buddy Pierce, or himself he couldn't tell and grew weary from trying to sort it out.

Daniel jerked up from the feed and forced Charity out of his mind. He'd have to work harder, stay too busy to think. Better worn out and sore than tormented by his own thoughts.

He rubbed the stiffness from his aching shoulders and headed out to fetch another bag from the wagon beside the barn. When he stepped outside, the Dunmans' dogs across the road were barking, so he glanced up to see what had caused the commotion. Not that their braying was uncommon. Those two set up a ruckus with very little goading, but he could tell from their excitement something unusual was afoot.

He shaded his eyes and peered closer. What he saw set his heart to racing, though good sense told him his bleary eyes were seeing things. He rubbed them with the heels of his grimy palms and took another look. . .and there she was. The phantom that robbed his sleep at night and plagued his soul by day stood just outside the gate.

Down off her horse, Charity hovered near its flank, bent over with her back to Daniel.

Hesitant, he crossed the yard. He couldn't think what to say to her when he got there, couldn't imagine her answer. Still, he walked.

She jerked around when he opened the gate. "Goodness, Daniel! You gave me a start."

He smiled and nodded. "Sorry. Didn't mean to."

Reaching down, she cradled the horse's hind foot and ran her hand around the shoe, her long fingers moving gently over the soft inner flesh. Daniel waited for her to speak. When she didn't, he latched the gate behind him and eased closer. "What you got there? A rock?"

Charity answered without looking up. "She was favoring one side a bit. I thought I'd better check." She let go of the mare's hoof and dusted off her hands. "Whatever it was seems to be gone now."

"What brings you out this way?" Even with hope frolicking inside his chest, he hated himself for asking.

She stared across the street at his neighbors' shuttered windows. "Mama sent me to the Dunmans' on an errand, but from here, it looks like no one's home."

He shook his head. "Took the train to Houston to visit kinfolk. I've tended their dogs all week."

Charity glanced at him. "Is that so? Well, that's odd. Mother Dane usually gets wind of such things before anyone else."

He nodded toward the house. "They left in a rush. Sickness in the family, I heard."

Daniel didn't quite know what to do with his hands. He finally rested them on his hips, but then, feeling like an old woman, he let them drop to his sides. "I see you got shed of that old red hound." He winced and cursed himself for reminding her of that day.

Charity glanced around her legs, as if she might find the dog there. "It seems I have. For now, at least."

She smiled slightly and Daniel returned the expression, ashamed of the joy it stirred in his heart. His mind reeled. Why were they discussing horses and neighbors and dogs with all that lay between them?

"I guess I'd better head on home." She took the horse's reins in her hands and prepared to mount.

Daniel surged forward and clutched her wrist. "Charity, wait. I know why you're here."

Her body stiffened. "Whatever do you mean?"

"I mean I've thought of you night and day since I saw you last. Now fate has set you right outside my gate. It's meant to be, sugar. Can't you see it, too?"

She relaxed her shoulders and faced him. Was that a smile tugging the corners of her mouth? He felt sure of it, and the sight quickened his heartbeat.

"Fate, Daniel?" It was all she said, but the way she said it, and the fact that she seemed not the least bit eager to mount the horse, told him volumes. . .and gave him courage.

He stepped closer. "You've missed me, too. Don't deny it, Charity–I can feel it."

She stood between him and the horse, staring at the ground by his feet, her big eyes veiled by long, dark lashes. She had on a blue dress he'd never seen before and wore her hair pinned up in back, though several dark curls had escaped, teasing her delicate face. He was near enough to smell her, and it made him dizzy.

When she didn't retreat from his advance or react to his nearness, he let eager arms encircle her waist. She tensed up a bit but didn't pull away. Too far gone to control himself, he buried his face in her hair and drew in her scent while he had the chance. When his lips brushed the soft skin of her neck, she withdrew, alarm in her eyes.

"I'm sorry, honey." He took an unsteady breath. "I've just missed you so. I've gone mad thinking of you."

She nodded then looked around his shoulder toward the house.

He followed her gaze. "Don't fret about Mama. She's not at home. Besides, I don't care anymore what she thinks."

Charity closed her eyes and reached trembling fingers to his face. "You really mean that?"

He clutched her hand and drew it to his lips. "I never meant anything more in my life. I want you for my wife, Charity. I want to be with you forever."

She sagged against the horse, but Daniel caught her and pulled her close, laughing as he held her. "Oh, sugar, I know. You're as relieved as I am. We're together again now, and I promise to do everything in my power to make it up to you."

"Anything, Daniel?"

With her face pressed so tightly against his chest, Daniel barely heard the muffled question. He rested his cheek against her head, thanking his lucky stars for such good fortune.

"Anything, sugar. Anything at all."

Charity rode away from Daniel's house with shattered emotions. It amazed her how easily she had deceived him, how effortlessly she'd slipped into the role of a jezebel. At the same time, it frightened her how natural it felt. Mother Dane's long-held hope that Charity's behavior would rub off on Emmy may have worked in reverse. Emily Dane herself couldn't have carried out what Charity had just accomplished.

It was settled. She and Daniel would marry in three days' time.

"The sooner the better," he had said.

Yet how hard it had been to embrace him, to let him hold her. She'd had to close her eyes and imagine Buddy standing there, Buddy's arms around her, Buddy's cheek beneath her fingers. A brazen device, still it would get her through the coming days. After the wedding, she'd have to put such faithless thoughts out of her mind, and Buddy out of her heart forever.

Daniel had balked when Charity asked him to keep their plans a secret, insisting no one could know there was a wedding afoot until they were officially husband and wife. He believed she feared his mama would stop the marriage. She let him think what he wanted, so long as he complied with her wishes.

I did it, Mama. Now everything will be fine. Just like I promised.

She knew her mama wouldn't be happy at first. It would require some fancy talking to get her to go along with the scheme. Charity would just have to convince her there was no other way. In the end, she'd come around to Charity's way of thinking. She had no choice.

"You done what!" Mama slammed the brush on the dressing table and whirled on Charity, her face so red with rage that Charity expected fire to blast from her nostrils.

"Mama, just listen for a minute."

"I ain't having it, Charity. Do you hear me? I'll go to my grave poor and homeless before I'll see you married to that uppity, no-account scalawag."

Charity tried to stay calm, but hysteria crept into her voice. "Surely you see this is the only way?"

"To have you marry a lying, cheating fool? The only way for what? To ruin your life? I won't let you do that for me."

"After all you've done for me? It would be an honor to ruin my life for you, but that's not what I'm doing. I'm saving us."

Mama's eyes flashed. "I already got me a Savior, daughter. He don't need no help from you."

"You know what I mean. It'll save our home. Besides, Daniel loves me. He really does. I can feel it."

Mama's eyes became slits, and she grunted. "Then what was that foolishness with Emmy?"

Charity flicked her hand, as if the gesture or her next words could ever take the sting out of what those two had done. "Emmy turned his head for a bit, that's all. You know Emmy can do that to a man. But Daniel's in his right mind now. He knows what he wants, and it's me."

"You don't say? And what do you want?"

She averted her eyes. "I almost married him once, with your blessing. It must be my fate." Daniel had used the same word. Now it rang hollow in her ears.

"A fate worse than death." Mama spat the bitter epitaph and scowled like she could taste it.

"My goodness. Straighten that terrible face." Charity wrapped her arms around her mama's waist and whirled her around the room. "Come on now. Just think of it. I'll be all set. A proper married lady. Plus it will keep Shamus Pike's conniving hands off of our land. It's a perfect plan, and you know it."

Mama broke free and backed away. "I asked you a question, Charity."

Busying herself at the dressing table, she shrugged. "What question?"

"I asked what you want, except I reckon I already know the answer. There's a bigger, better man in your thoughts than that dirty scum of a Clark boy. A real man, one worthy of you."

Charity turned her face away, but Mama took hold of her arms and shook her. "I'm dead right," she cried. "I can see it right there in the mirror. You're in love with Buddy Pierce. How can you think of marrying anyone else?"

She fought the tears. That would be all it took to have Mama forbid her. Forcing a smile instead, she measured her words. "Like I said, it's my fate to marry Daniel."

"Honey, no! Why not just marry the man you love?"

Charity turned from the mirror and pulled her mama close. "Because he's never asked me, that's why." She bit her lip hard to hold back a sob. "Anyway," she said, staring across the top of Mama's head through brimming eyes. "Buddy's not here right now, is he?"

CHAPTER 19

Emmy paused to wipe her feet on the tattered rug at the back door. Mama said it would stop Nash from tracking in half the barnyard, and it worked when he remembered to use it. Emmy had a good share of the outdoors on her own shoes, so she took care to wipe them well.

Easing the door open, she slipped through to the kitchen, ears alert. She didn't relish another confrontation with her mama and avoided her whenever she could. Things hadn't gone well between them since the day Emmy climbed out of the window in her nightdress.

Mama had listened to her claim that she'd been in the barn tending Rebel. She even sat quietly through Nash's version, but it was clear she wasn't convinced. She'd cast long, suspicious looks at the conspirators before sending Nash outside to work and Emmy to her room. And for the first time in her life, Emmy felt bad about telling a lie.

The events of that day had strained their relationship more than ever, to say the least. It vexed Emmy to no end and caused an ache in the pit of her stomach. The only bright spot of late had come in the form of a telegram from Papa. Urgent business held him up north for six more months at least. So he never needed to see what she'd done to his horse, and Mama wouldn't tell. Despite her reprieve, Emmy faithfully took care of Rebel, though it was Nash's job. She felt it was the least she could do, and the old horse seemed pleased by the arrangement.

Commotion from the parlor caused her to pause midstride. She recognized Auntie Bert's voice, and she sounded upset, so Emmy tiptoed to the door and listened.

"What am I to do, Magda? I cain't let her throw her life away on that boy. It just ain't right. Especially now that she loves someone else."

Emmy's heartbeat quickened. Were they discussing Charity? Charity in love with someone besides Daniel? Impossible! If so, on what boy was she about to throw away her life?

The way she saw things, this could only work to her advantage. She eased closer and pressed her ear to the door.

"When did all this come about, honey?" Her mama's voice was low and soothing, in that tone she only used with Aunt Bert.

"This morning. Charity broke it to me over at the hotel not an hour ago. Poor little thing, acting so cheerful for my sake when I know her heart is breaking."

Was Aunt Bertha crying? Emmy's pounding heart lurched. She'd never heard her cry before. Mama said she cried buckets when Uncle Thad passed, but Emmy never saw it.

She suddenly wailed from behind the door, dispelling any doubts and sending a chill through Emmy's veins. "I had to get out of there. I couldn't stay in that room another second and watch her put on a brave face. I know she's doing it for me, and I cain't stand it."

"Don't let her do it, Bert."

"I don't want her to. You know that. I tried my best to sway her, but that stubborn girl's mind is set like flint. She says after Shamus takes our place, we'll lose the oil company money, too, and then we won't be able to afford the hotel. We'll have nowhere to go."

"You and Charity ain't at the mercy of Shamus Pike. You can live with me. You know I would take care of you both 'til the day I died."

After a lengthy silence and a sniff, Aunt Bert finally answered. "I know you would, honey, but that ain't right, neither. And with things turned inside out between our girls, it won't work. Charity's not about to stay here, and this time I won't stay without her."

"So what, then?"

Aunt Bert sighed before she answered. "I guess I can see it clear now as bad as it tastes in my mouth. We got no choice. I pray the good Lord will show us another way, but meanwhile we got us a wedding to plan."

"What about Buddy?"

"I'd wager he feels the same about my girl as she does for him, but he ain't here to ask. By the time he comes around again, it won't make no difference. She'll be married to someone else."

So Charity was in love with Buddy Pierce. It answered the first part of Emmy's question. A twister spun into her chest. If Charity loved Mr. Pierce, exactly whom did she plan to marry?

"It makes me see red, though," Aunt Bert continued. "That other one ain't nothing but a cheating scoundrel. I'd sooner see him dead than married to Charity. Daniel Clark don't deserve my little girl."

Emmy reeled from the door, hoping they hadn't heard her gasp. She reached for the table to steady herself and fell into the nearest chair. Lowering her head, she clutched her face so tightly her fingernails bit into her flesh.

Daniel was going to marry Charity. After all they'd meant to each other, after what she'd sacrificed. She could no longer tell herself he hadn't meant what he'd said that day on the trail. He meant it, all right. She didn't matter to him and never had. He loved Charity instead, and she would be his bride.

"Emily Bertha Dane, how much did you hear?"

She shot upright, wiping her eyes on her sleeves. Mama and Aunt Bert loomed over her, their faces tight with rage.

"Why, she heard it all, Magda. You can tell that by looking at her."

Her mama took her by the wrist and jerked her to her feet, causing the chair to tip over and hit the wall with a bang. Strong hands dragged her away from the table, and her anklebone took a sharp rap against the carved wooden leg. She howled in pain to no avail. Mama hauled her into the parlor and forced her to sit on the divan, then stood over her with Aunt Bertha.

Emmy stared up at them, more afraid than she'd ever been in her life. She didn't recognize the squint-eyed women crouched above her like bobcats on a rabbit.

"Emily, I asked you a question. How much did you hear?"

She drew back, desperate to put distance between herself and Mama's red face. "I didn't hear anything. Honest!"

"Don't you dare lie!"

"Why?" Emmy shrieked. "Why does it matter so much what I heard?"

Aunt Bertha beat Mama to the answer. "Oh, it matters all right, little gal. It matters a heap."

Emmy's wide eyes shifted to her mama. "Won't somebody please tell me what's going on?"

"Emmy, I'll sit on you for three days if I have to, to make sure you don't ruin this for Aunt Bert and Charity. You've dealt them enough pain as it is. Come to think of it, you're the cause of all this trouble."

The weight of the words struck them dumb as the truth hung heavy in the room. Then Emmy started to cry. Deep, wracking sobs rolled up and out from her middle, breaking the painful silence.

Her mama eased down beside her and pulled her close. "There, there, now. I didn't mean to hurt you, baby. I just can't understand why you insist on doing what you know is wrong. Listening behind doors, for instance. How many times have I warned you about it? I told you it would catch up to you someday."

Still rigid with emotion, Aunt Bert sat down on the other side. "This here's that day. Emmy, I need you to tell me what you heard us talking about. It's important."

"And no more lies," Mama added.

Emmy wiped her eyes and sat up. Whatever was going on, she'd never seen the two of them act so strangely. She took courage from Mama's arms around her and decided to try the truth for a change.

"I heard you say Charity's in love with Buddy Pierce, but she's fixing to marry Daniel."

Mama and Aunt Bert shared a grim expression.

"And I heard something about Shamus Pike taking your land."

Aunt Bert leaned forward and slapped her legs with both

hands. "Well, that's it, then. Our goose is cooked."

Mama released Emmy and scooted around to glare at her with one raised brow. "No, it ain't, because she won't tell. Will you, Emmy?"

"Tell what? Land sakes, you two are talking in riddles."

The older women sat in tense silence, obviously deciding whether to enlighten her or not.

Emmy gathered her nerve and dared to ask the only question she wanted answered. "Why is Charity marrying Daniel if she's in love with Buddy Pierce?" She looked back and forth between them, waiting for one of them to speak.

Aunt Bert fixed her with a piercing stare. "Emmy, do you love your Aunt Bertha?"

"Yes. Of course I do."

"Do you have any feelings left for Charity?"

"You know I do!"

"Then sit up and listen good, because I'm about to trust you with our very lives. What I'm going to tell you ain't ever to leave this room."

Aunt Bert gave her a look so intense the force of it pressed Emmy against the couch. "I won't tell a soul, Auntie Bertha. I promise."

CHAPTER 20

Buddy stepped out of the stable, tired but elated after leaving his horse strapped to a feed bag in the liveryman's care. Hungry himself, he intended to belly up to breakfast just as quick as the dining hall of the Lone Star opened for business.

He stood on the already bustling boardwalk in the cold gray dawn and tried to work the miles out of his backside. It had been a long, tough pull, but he made the ride from Port Arthur in record time. And no town ever looked so good to a man as Humble looked to Buddy that morning.

He shifted the weight of the saddlebag on his shoulder and patted its bulging pockets. Bertha Bloom would be mighty happy to see the contents, but not nearly as glad as he would be to see her beautiful daughter.

Thoughts of Charity pushed aside the empty gnawing in his stomach and replaced it with the now familiar ache he got whenever she came to mind. The only remedy was to have her near—medicine he planned to swallow in large doses as soon as the sun rose a bit higher.

He smiled, imagining the look on her face when she saw him back ahead of schedule. To accomplish it, he'd left it up to Lee and Jerry to return with the wagons and bought himself a horse. An irresponsible move, no doubt, but he couldn't wait another week to see Charity.

If things went according to plan, if she accepted the ring in his vest pocket, no matter where his work took him next, they wouldn't be split up again. She could go along wherever he went, at least until they started a family. Then he'd find a way to spend as much time as possible at home. He imagined Charity in the family way, her round belly ripe with his child, and his face glowed with pleasure at the bold thought.

Mind still fixed on the future, Buddy drew in deep of the clear morning air and stepped off the boardwalk into the path of a big black horse pulling a loaded wagon. The wild-eyed creature reared, and the driver cursed, jerking the reins to the side. Buddy scrambled out of the way just before the front wheel ran him over.

The rig lumbered to a stop, and the man leaped down. Buddy saw right away it was Daniel Clark. Daniel, who didn't seem to recognize him, closed the distance between them in quick, angry strides. A scowl as black as a thunderhead darkened his face. "By golly, I almost hit you, mister. Didn't you hear me coming? What in tarnation were you thinking?"

Buddy took off his hat and offered his hand. "Accept my apologies, sir. My mind is elsewhere this morning."

Daniel wiped his palm on his trouser leg before taking Buddy's in a firm grip. "Whatever has your mind, I hope it's worth your life. It almost got you killed." He leaned in for a closer look. "Well, if it ain't Mr. Pierce. I didn't recognize you under all that dirt and facial hair. Can't tell if you've had a hard ride or been rode hard."

Giddy with fatigue and pure joy, Buddy ignored the sarcasm. "If you said both, you wouldn't miss it by much. Truth is, I'm at the easy side of a long, hard ride, but it was worth every mile considering what's waiting for me on this end."

Daniel raised one brow. "Do tell? Sounds like a woman to me. Got a little gal waiting for you?"

Buddy felt reckless. "Not just any gal. The prettiest in Texas." He knew he sounded cocky, but he wasn't in a mood to consider Daniel's feelings. After all, the foolish man had trifled with Charity's heart.

Unaffected, Daniel returned his smile. "Well, I don't see how that could be, partner, since I'm about to marry the prettiest girl in Texas."

Daniel getting married? Buddy felt like scratching his head. Could he mean Emily Dane? Charity claimed he was done with her. One thing was for sure—the man's swagger got more annoying by the second.

"That's right, Buddy, old boy. You need to check your facts and try again. The sweetest prize in the county fair is spoken for, and the blue ribbon goes to me."

Something about the way he said it brought heat to Buddy's neck. Clark was enjoying himself too much. He offered another handshake, determined to hide his fear. "I guess congratulations are in order, then. Who might the lovely lady be?"

Daniel gripped his hand, too tightly to be mistaken for goodwill. His eyes burned with anticipation like a cat ready to pounce. "Oh, you know her quite well."

Buddy fought to control his breathing. He wouldn't let the man see him rattled. "That's not likely. I don't know that many women in Humble."

"I reckon you're well acquainted with this one." Daniel stepped so near that Buddy smelled barber soap on his face. "Charity and I have reconciled. She's consented to be my wife. In a few days, Charity Bloom will be Charity Clark." He lowered his voice and affected a conspiratorial tone. "I'll thank you kindly to stick that under your hat though. We've decided to keep it quiet for a spell."

Buddy jerked his hand free and glared at him. "I don't believe you."

Daniel smirked, blatantly enjoying Buddy's pain. He whirled away with a laugh and ran both hands through his hair, preening. The cat cleaning his paws after the kill. When he faced Buddy again, his smile had turned cold. "I can see how you might not want to believe it, seeing as how you've gone sweet on her, but it's true. What say we ramble on down to the hotel, and you can ask her for yourself?"

Buddy longed to knock the sneer off Daniel's face. There wasn't much doubt he was telling the truth. He didn't seem the type who could pull off a bluff. He was too shallow and easy to read. If he intended to walk Buddy straight to Charity, he couldn't be lying.

Daniel interrupted his thoughts. "I don't mind waiting for you to make up your mind. Just don't take all day. You see, I have a house to make ready for my new bride." He took two deliberate steps forward and looked Buddy dead in the eye, his leer leaving no doubt of the intent behind his boast. "And when I carry her over that threshold. . .no one can stop me. . .from making her mine."

Buddy didn't remember what Daniel said next. He barely recalled passing him the saddlebag with instructions to give it to Bertha. He didn't think about anything until he found himself on the boardwalk in front of the depot. Pausing briefly at the door, he crossed the threshold and approached the counter to book passage on a southbound train. Plenty of work awaited him in Houston. Lee and Jerry could handle things here. He would wire instructions and word of his whereabouts when he arrived at Union Station.

Bertha's trusting face drifted before him, but he pushed it aside. Unlike him, she'd be fine. He had left her in the capable hands of two men he trusted. As for Charity, he couldn't allow even the thought of her into his mind for fear of bawling like a boy in knickers.

He paid for his ticket and stepped outside just in time. The Houston, East & West Texas engine roared into the station, wheels churning, stack belching. It barely stopped before passengers boiled out in a great wave, jockeying for position on the platform. Those waiting to board pressed against the tide of people trying to get off.

He hoisted his bag to one shoulder and stormed into the flood, grateful for the distracting noise and clamor. Pushing his way to the door, he handed his ticket to the conductor and swung his bag on board. He followed it without a backward glance at the accursed town of Humble, the black hole that had swallowed his heart.

Daniel burned with satisfaction as he watched the big engine roar to life with short bursts of smoke. The wheels began to turn, picking up speed as the train pulled out of the station. . .hauling Buddy Pierce out of Charity's life. His gamble had paid off. Daniel's future with Charity was wrapped up and tied with a big red bow. She would be his, all legal and proper, with nothing to stand in his way.

The HE&WT disappeared down the tracks in a shimmering cloud of dust.

Daniel smiled slow and easy and tipped his hat. *You have a nice trip now. You hear?*

He turned on his heel, ready to strut up the boardwalk to his rig. The tune he whistled died on his lips when he saw who stood blocking his way. "Well, hello, Emmy."

"What did you say to him?" Her eyes were hard, her lips white-rimmed and tight.

"Good morning to you, too. You're up and about early, ain't you, sugar?"

She bristled. "Come now, Daniel. It's utterly boorish to pretend things are right between us after all this time."

Daniel held up his hands in surrender. "Fine. If that's how you want it." He had dreaded this confrontation for weeks and needed to get it done, but why this morning, when things were going so well?

Emmy edged closer. "I asked you a question. What did you say to that man?"

He held his arms out to his sides, making a show of looking around at the crowd. "Which man? As you can see, there's no shortage of men in Humble this morning. No proper place for an unescorted lady, I might add."

He glanced past her shoulder. "And you are without escort again, I see. Question is, are you a lady?" He leaned into her angry face. "Tell me, *Miss Dane*, does your mama know you're following me around again?"

Something flickered in her eyes besides fury. Whether pain or shame he couldn't tell, but he had waded too deep to stop now. "Ah, well, probably not. She don't always know where you are—or what you're up to—now, does she?"

Emmy pointed up the track behind him. "I just saw Buddy Pierce get on that train bound for Houston, and I get the feeling it was an unscheduled trip. You said something to make him leave, didn't you? And I know what it was. You're not so good at keeping secrets, are you?"

Daniel grabbed her arm. "Maybe you don't know as much as you think you do, sugar."

Her eyes went to the saddlebag slung over his shoulder and darkened. "I saw him hand you that bag. Would you like for me to deliver it to Aunt Bertha?"

He tightened his grip, causing her to wince. "You won't mention Buddy Pierce *or* this bag to anyone. You hear me?"

"Let go, Daniel. That hurts."

Daniel checked the jostling crowd for witnesses before he jerked Emmy close and breathed a threat against her startled face. "Just know this. If you do one thing to spoil things between me and Charity, I'll kill you with my bare hands."

She stared up at him, disbelief in her eyes, but he knew his threat had found its mark. He shook her once for emphasis. "You messed it up for us before, flaunting yourself, pressing against me until I couldn't think straight. I won't let you do it again, Emmy. You hear me? Be warned. I won't let you ruin this for me." He turned loose of her arm, despising the feel of her flesh.

"Don't you dare talk that way to me." The words were an angry snarl, but he saw fear in her eyes.

"Like I said, Emmy—be warned."

Emmy backed away, rubbing her arm. She ignored the curses and complaints of those she bumped into, her eyes never leaving his face. Not until she'd put considerable distance between them did she lift the hem of her skirt, lunge for the less-crowded street, and run. She dashed across, dodging mud holes, horses, and a team of oxen. Racing along in front of the far boardwalk, she scurried to the first side street and disappeared from sight.

Daniel sucked in deep through flared nostrils and realized he'd been holding his breath. He looked down at his clenched fists and willed them to relax. Emmy flashed through his mind—cowering in fear, rubbing her mottled arm.

"Let go, Daniel. That hurts."

Flushed with shame, he covered his face with trembling hands.

"You all right, mister?"

The gentle hand on his shoulder, the sudden voice in his ear, hurled Daniel's heart to his throat. He spun and clutched the stranger's wrist in a cruel grip.

Startled by Daniel's reaction, the old man lost his balance. Skinny arms flailing like disjointed sticks, he fought to gain purchase with his cane. "Let go, mister!" he cried. "I meant you no harm!"

Daniel eased his hold and the man pulled free, teetering a bit before leaning hard on his walking stick. With his other hand on the cane, he had no way to rub his wrist, so he rolled it against his vest. Pain etched deeper lines in his weathered face.

"I thought you might need a doctor or something, but hang you if'n you do. You're no better'n a mad dog." He staggered away, giving Daniel wide berth, and limped down the boardwalk muttering to himself.

A mad dog? Is that what he'd become? Perhaps, but he saw no cure except in marrying Charity—and, by golly, that's what he aimed to do. Maybe then he could return to his right mind.

No one, be it Emily Dane, Buddy Pierce, or Charity herself, had better try to stop him.

He squinted as the sun's first rays cleared the rooftops and hit him square in the eyes. Morning had hardly begun, yet he'd had a week's worth of trouble already. Well, so be it. But let any trouble that lurked in the remaining hours find and fall on someone else. He'd had more than his fair share for the day.

Bertha stood on Magdalena's front porch, hesitant for the first time ever to open the big oak door and step inside. She sorely needed to jaw a spell with Magda but reckoned she wasn't up yet and didn't have the heart to rouse her. The big house loomed dark, with no light behind the drawn shades, and Bertha couldn't bear the thought of sitting inside alone.

Mopping beads of sweat from her top lip with her sleeve, she gazed around the yard. In their part of Texas, a body couldn't always tell the difference between spring and summer, and the hazy morning foretold a sultry day. Just a few days before, they had awakened to downright cold mornings. Thad always said if a fella didn't cotton to

Texas weather, all he had to do was wait a minute.

Despite the heat, Nash was already hard at work in the side yard, bent low over a wagon wheel. If he wasn't the biggest man Bertha had ever seen, he sure was in the running. As if he heard her thoughts, he stood upright and stretched, like a bear rising to full height. Shading his eyes with his arm, he balanced a wrench in his other hand and absently scanned the horizon. When his gaze passed over the house, he took a backward glance and squinted Bertha's way, until his eyes lit on her there in the shadows.

She waved.

He grinned and waved back with the rust-colored tool before crouching down by the wheel.

She stifled a yawn. Thanks to Charity she'd been awake for hours, long before first light. The girl had kept her up half the night, moaning and panting as if something chased her. When Bertha gave up on sleep and got up, Charity kept to her bed, but just barely. The way she pitched and rolled, it wouldn't be long before she threw herself to the floor.

It hurt Bertha so fiercely to watch, she had to get plumb out of the room. She'd left Charity a note saying where she'd be and struck out on foot before sunup, headed for Magda's place.

Now that she was here, she felt a mite silly. There was no sense in bothering Magda again. No matter how many times they hashed it over, they came up with the same answer.

The die was cast. The milk spilt. Tomorrow her only child would become one in the sight of God with a man not fit to touch her. Bertha didn't reckon she could bear it.

Careful to steer clear of the rosebush, she stepped on a crate and pulled herself up to sit on the rail. The haunting smell of the red blossoms wafted up, wrapping her in scent as heavy as her sorrow. She leaned her head against the post and settled in for a good cry, but the sudden sense of another presence raised the hairs on her arms. She took a slow, careful look behind her.

"Squeeze that rail any harder and you'll snap it in two."

She shrieked and leaped to her feet, nearly twisting her ankle.

Magda stood on the threshold in a blush-colored dressing gown, her hair let down to her waist.

Bertha fell against the rail, one hand over her pounding heart. "Land sakes, Magda, you scared me right out of my bloomers."

Unruffled, her friend regarded her with doubtful eyes. "Honey, Humble ain't ready for that one."

"You ought not to sneak up on a body. With your hair all loose and flowing, I thought you was a spirit."

Magda grinned. "A ghost in a pink sheet? Get in here out of the dew, honey. I reckon it's soaked your brain." She made a sweeping motion toward the door. "Well? What are you waiting for? This calls for scrambled eggs."

Bertha held up her hand. Long scratches dotted with tiny drops of blood ran the length of her forearm. "You ain't getting no eggs out of me. Look, you made me brush up agin' those blasted thorns."

Magda dismissed her wounds with a glance. "Well, we can summon the doctor if you like, but I believe I can patch that up myself." She held the door wider. "But not with you on the porch. Get yourself inside."

Bertha allowed herself to be herded into the house. Just before Magda closed the door, she leaned out and searched the yard for Nash. When she spotted him, she shouted orders in his direction, loud enough to be heard in town. "Nash! Leave what you're doing and fetch us some eggs. Get a whole mess, and we'll scramble some for you."

Nash laid the wrench aside and stood up smiling. Remembering how damp grass rusted out a tool, he stooped to pick it up again, wiping it on his trousers before laying it in the wagon bed.

Fetch some cackleberries, you say? Yes, ma'am! I'm gon' fetch plenty, and right this minute.

He headed for the chicken yard, stomach rumbling under his belt. Wasn't much he liked better than those two cooking up something in the kitchen. He'd never say it to Ophelia, didn't dare, but Miz Bloom stirred up the best pan of biscuits he ever tasted. When she drizzled on bacon-fat gravy and paired them with eggs, there wasn't no better eating this side of the river.

At the coop, he shut the gate behind him and hurried up the slanted ramp into the henhouse. Right off he sensed the birds were restless. All around in the dim, dank-smelling house they shuffled and squirmed, making the low, throaty babble that always brought to mind the foolish chatter of women. "What be wrong with you old gals?" he cooed. "Has something done crawled in this here house?"

His mind went to a chicken snake, making him think twice about poking his hand in the nests. He loathed the slithery beasts and didn't care to run across one today. "If an old snake was in here, you'd be stirring up more of a squawk, now, wouldn't you? Maybe we got us a rat instead."

Nash cocked his head and stared about, willing his eyes to adjust. "Mistah Rat, is that you? Come on now, don't tease old Nash. Who be in this henhouse besides these tetchy hens?"

He waited. Not that he expected Mr. Rat to answer. In fact, that'd be the last thing he'd want to hear. He only hoped the sound of his voice would drive the intruder away. Hearing nothing except more chatter and babble, he smiled around at the small, dark space. "Look like it just be us chickens. Now, ladies, if you don't mind, I need to borrow me some breakfast."

He shifted the basket down his arm and eased his other hand under the first hen. His fingers closed around two warm eggs, and he pulled them out, testing their weight to see if he'd picked up the laying egg. Before he got them to the basket, a quiet sniffle drifted from the corner behind him.

Nash spun toward the sound, dropping his prize. The real one landed at his feet with a splat. The marble laying egg hit the floor with a thud then wobbled away. "Who that now! Who be in here with me?"

A loud wail was his answer. One he'd heard before.

"Miss Emmy!" He tossed the basket aside and took a step in her direction. "That's you, all right."

The rightful dwellers of the house set up a squawk to match the girl's mournful caterwauling. Some ran in wild circles, getting nowhere fast in the closed-up space. Others sailed past his head, beating their wings in his ears like giant hummingbirds.

"Come on now. Stop that howling—else these hens ain't never gon' lay another egg. They'll all wind up in a pot of dumplin's, and it'll be all yo' fault. Here, let Nash help you up off that nasty floor."

He lifted Emmy to her feet, but when he turned her loose, she fell again. He caught her and held her upright. "What's ailing you, Miss Emmy? What you doing hiding in the henhouse?"

She clung to him, still bawling like a lost heifer, and Nash could feel her trembling.

This gal's jus' a child, he thought as he held her. A *wayward child, and that's for sure, but a child no less.* He wondered what she'd gotten herself into now.

"Talk to me, girl. Did some fool hurt you? If they did, they's gon' answer to Nash."

He realized she wore her town clothes and knew in his soul that her mama reckoned her still in bed. "Where you been, Miss Emmy?" he asked in a low voice. "What done happen to you?"

"Oh, Nash!" She was crying so hard he scarcely understood. "It was awful. Just awful."

CHAPTER 21

Bertha sat in the big green chair, pinned between the padded arm and her padded friend. Wedged in beside her, Magda brandished a sewing needle, determined to tease the dark tip of a thorn from Bertha's hand. Bertha struggled to get free, but Magda hoisted a leg over both of hers, ending all hope of escape.

"Stop your wiggling and let me get it."

"Not yet, I told you. It's too fresh. Let the bleeding stop first."

"I never saw a body take on so over a tiny bit of blood. Hush now. I've almost got it."

Bertha squirmed again. "Get up, Magda. This chair won't hold us both. The legs are bound to cave."

"Then you'd best let me get this done."

"Let me up," she shouted. "I cain't feel my legs no more. You got 'em wadded in a knot."

"Bertha, hold still!"

The front door burst open. Emmy tottered on the threshold, fully dressed this time, but covered in feathery tufts from head to toe, her indigo day dress dotted with splotches of white. Red face swollen from crying, she seemed past caring what they thought.

The sight of her struck Bertha dumb. She reckoned Magda, still holding the needle aloft and staring at Emmy, suffered the same. Without a word, Emmy flew past them and up the stairs. The stench that lingered in her wake left no doubt about the nature of the white splotches. They had come from the same place as the feathers.

The two women gawked until Emmy passed out of sight and her bedroom door slammed shut. After a brief silence, the sound of hysterical crying reached their ears.

Magda broke the spell. "Well, if that don't beat all. Where the devil has she been this time of the morning?"

Bertha's disbelieving gaze swung her friend's way. Magda couldn't be that dumb. "Where you think she's been?"

Poor Magda aimed vacant eyes at her. "She looked like she just came from tending the chickens, but why would she get all gussied up for that?"

Maybe she was that dumb. "Honey, Emmy ain't been tending chickens—she's been wallowing with them. She ain't just come *in* from the henhouse. She came home *through* the henhouse. There's the difference. She's been hiding."

Magda blinked once, twice. "From what?"

"From us. She seen us on the porch and tried to wait us out in the coop."

To Bertha's great relief, despite the crushing and pinching of her body it caused, Magda struggled up from the chair. She faced Bertha with her hands on her hips. "What are you telling me?"

Bertha stretched to work the kinks from her side and lowered her tingling legs to the floor. "She's been with Daniel."

After a stunned silence, tiny wrinkles formed between Magda's brows. "Come now. You don't really think that, do you?"

"Think it? I know it."

Fire blazed in Magda's eyes. "Bert, I'll skin her. I mean it."

Bertha shook her head. "Leave her be. What's done is done. By the look of her, I'd guess Daniel didn't say what she wanted to hear, though I almost wish he had. Whatever passed betwixt them two, I reckon come tomorrow we'll still be having us a wedding."

Magda spun and glared up the stairs. "I can't believe the unmitigated brash of that girl. And after we warned her. . ." She looked back at Bertha and shook her head. "No, sir. I've had all I can take. I'm going up there to reckon with my wayward child. By the time I finish with Emmy, she'll swear she's seen the wrath of God."

"You'll do no such thing."

"She gave us her word!"

Bertha curled her legs into the cushioned seat and patted the space in front of her. "Get over here now. I need you to pluck out this here thorn. After all, it's your fault I got it."

Magda pressed the heels of her hands to her forehead. "What am I to do with my daughter, Bertha? Lord knows I can't control her no more. Should I send her up north to stay with her pa?"

"It ain't too late to turn Catholic."

"This ain't funny, Bert. I've reached my wit's end."

Bertha smiled. "And that was a trip hardly worth packing for." She patted the chair again. "Come sit, honey, and let's talk. That's right. Come on now."

Magda ambled over and slumped beside her so heavily Bertha feared her prediction about broken legs would come to pass. She bit back her fear and wrapped her arms around Magda instead. "Give her some time, honey. We been so het up about Charity's happiness that we plumb forgot about Emmy's. That girl's in love, whether she has the right to be or not. Right now she's hurting."

Magda sighed. "It's hard to feel sorry for her. Her own willful nature got her into this mess. What will become of her, Bert?"

"Oh, she'll be fine."

"What do you base that on?"

"She's your daughter, ain't she? Besides, we gave our girls to God a long time ago. Don't go taking Emmy out of His hands just when she needs Him the most. Leave God room to work."

Magda released her breath in a ragged sigh. "I pray for her, Bert. All the time. I actually thought I saw her beginning to change. She's been different lately. I can't explain how exactly, but it seemed a change for the good. Did I imagine it?"

Bertha shook her head. "No, I seen it, too."

Magda's eyes filled with tears. "I felt so good when she broke down and cried over what she'd done to you and Charity. Before that day, I wondered if the girl had a conscience."

Bertha nodded and rocked her gently. "Do you recollect how pretty Emmy was as a baby? I never seen a more beautiful child, before or since."

Magda smiled, a faraway look in her eyes. "She was a delightful child. So precocious." She shook her head and the smile left. "I reckon we encouraged that for our own amusement. . .and look where it got us."

Bertha leaned to hug her tight. "Oh, honey, she's still that same sweet little gal. Under that vinegar and sass, she's still our very own Emmy. We just need to find some way to coax her back to the surface."

Magda let slip the slightest of grins. "How do you propose to do that? With a bull whip?"

Bertha roared with laughter. "I wouldn't tote no bull whip into that room tonight! Not with Emmy in need of some way to ease her frustrations."

Magda laughed along with her then sobered straightaway, her gaze fixed on the landing. "Do you think I should go to her?"

"I wouldn't. If she don't come down by suppertime, maybe you could duck in. You'll just upset each other now."

Magda nodded.

A commotion in the kitchen caught their attention.

Bertha pushed against Magda with her feet. "Let me up. That's Nash coming in the back door. I reckon he's got me some eggs to scramble. I'm so hungry I could eat a bushel."

As they struggled to rise, the truth crept up on Bertha. A tickle in the back of her mind at first, then clear in a sudden rush. Magda stilled, too. From the look on her face, the same thought had dawned on her. Emmy had been hiding in the chicken house–and Nash had just come from there.

"Reckon he knows anything?"

Magda set her jaw. "If he did, he wouldn't tell. Them two are in cahoots. That blasted disloyal Nash takes her side over mine every time. I should fire him and be done with it."

"Fine. Then Emmy would have nobody. You leave Nash to me. If there's something to be pulled out of that man, I can do it with my cooking."

Magda grinned. "That might do it. Nash goes weak in the knees at the mention of your biscuits."

"Go on, then. Move your mountain so I can get up. After I get us fed, Nash can take me back to town. I need to see how Charity's faring."

Halfway to the kitchen with Magda close on her heels, she stopped midstride and almost fell when Magda bumped into her from behind. She spun and gripped her friend's arms, peering up into her eyes. "Magda, you know what I just realized?"

"What's that, sugar?"

"This is my last day to look after Charity."

Magda gave her a tender smile and pulled her close. "I doubt that. You'll be trying to look after Charity for the rest of your life whether she's married or not."

Though Bertha suspected the words were true, they brought her no comfort. "Oh, Magda, hurry. Help me get breakfast over and done. I want to spend time with my baby whilst she's still mine."

The swinging door opened behind them. When Nash saw them embracing, he lowered his head and started back out again, but Magda's deep voice stopped him cold. "Get that wheel finished while we cook breakfast. After we eat, I need you to drive us into town."

Nash's head whipped around. He stared like Magda had spoken Chinese, then shuffled his feet and worried his shirttail before he answered. "Um. . .yes'm, Miz Dane. Only that old wheel be plumb shot. I was about to ask could I run it on in to the blacksmith. It needs a good patchin'."

"You saying it won't take us into town?"

He took a step forward, avoiding their eyes. "No, ma'am, that ain't what I'm saying. It'll get us to town, all right. But whilst we there, I s'pose I needs to haul it over to the smithy. See if he can do something to make it las' longer." He brightened a bit, as if he liked what he'd just said. "Yes'm, that's right. It jus' need to las' longer this time."

With one glance, Bertha saw he didn't fool Magda either. They followed him into the kitchen, Magda eyeballing him all the way. She stopped him before he got to the back door.

"Nash?"

He turned, his smile too bright. "Yes'm, Miz Dane?"

"You feeling all right?"

"Oh yes, ma'am. Fine and dandy. Be a sight better when I'm chomping on Miz Bertha's biscuits and gravy."

Magda cocked her head, watching him.

His smile floundered and died. "All right, then. I'll go see to that busted wheel now."

"You do that, Nash."

"Yes'm. I'll do that right now."

When the door banged shut behind him, Magda hiked her brows at Bertha. "He's up to something."

Bertha pulled the heavy iron skillet off a hook on the wall. The weight of it pulled her close to the floor before she hefted it up onto the stove. "That he is."

"What you reckon?"

She lit the gas burner and poured bacon fat into the skillet from an earthen jar. "He's a man, ain't he? No telling what he's up to. And don't waste your time trying to find out. It'll come to light soon enough. It always does. Men ain't worth spit at covering their tracks."

Daniel sat tall on the buckboard seat, his gaze sweeping the wide expanse of open field in front of him. So much land. His land. He had bought the property, cleared it, even built the house himself with the help of a few hired hands. The knowledge warmed his insides.

He paid cash for it, every cent his own, earned with sunbaked flesh and a busted back. Raising cattle wasn't the easiest way to earn a dollar. He refused to let the old man put a nickel toward building the house and was mighty glad of it now. He'd never bucked his folks before, so he couldn't predict their reaction. One thing was sure as sunrise—marrying Charity without his mama's blessing spelled trouble. But even if they disowned him, stripped him of his inheritance, they could never take his ranch.

Daniel turned his attention to the house. He took particular pride in the tall structure, two stories high and fronted with brick shipped from up north. Whitewashed columns graced the front entrance, beams as thick as a man's waist, supporting a gabled overhang. The portico extended to a wraparound porch, which led to an attached gazebo in the rear garden.

He had cleared the surrounding pine, leaving the house nestled in an oak grove. Crafted big and fine, the dwelling bore enough modern trappings to make any woman happy, yet he'd furnished it with the simple things Charity grew up with, things to please a country girl's heart.

Daniel had built the house for Charity, and tomorrow she would live here. A thrill shot through him at the thought. Followed by a chill at how close he'd come to losing her.

And for what?

He leaned and spat on the ground then wiped his chin on his sleeve. What on earth attracted him to Emmy Dane in the first place? He'd never chased her in school, fawning over her, panting for her attention like the other boys. Oh, she was pretty, all right. Always had been, but only on the outside. Unlike Charity, Emmy's insides stank like rotting flesh.

Despite Charity's pure heart, he'd seen another side of her lately, a fiery depth she'd never revealed before. Now that he'd noticed, her innocence coupled with this smoldering fire had nearly driven him mad. He wondered at the source of the mysterious flame. Had it always been there? How had he missed it before now? He pushed from his mind the fact that he'd only glimpsed it while she was in the company of that spineless Buddy Pierce.

Well, no matter. Fate had granted him a second chance. Tomorrow Charity would be his. He'd have a lifetime to find out all there was to know about her.

He heaved a sigh of relief and looked back at the contents of the wagon. He had hauled in the furniture weeks ago; it was time now to lay in supplies. Tools for her garden, staples for her pantry, sheets for her bed. All the things necessary to turn Charity's house into a home.

Charity reached deep into the wardrobe and pulled out her wedding gown. Stepping in front of the mirror, she held it against her body and turned from side to side in order to see it from every angle. Such a lovely dress, the prettiest she'd ever seen. Even more precious given the sweet hands that made it.

She clutched the fabric to her face and breathed in the smell. A mixture of sweet magnolia, infused there from spending so much time in Mama's room, mingled with the scent of pine picked up from weeks of hanging in her closet at home.

Home. The word conjured a picture of the big house she loved, fronted by the very magnolias she smelled on the dress and flanked by the towering pine from which Papa had cut wood for the closet. But it was her home no longer and would never be again. Even if she and Mama moved in today, Charity couldn't stay long enough to take off her shoes.

Tomorrow she would go to live with Daniel, and the thought made her feel lost. His was a lovely house, built just for her. She'd walked through it with him, laughing and planning the day they would share it. There'd been a time she thought that day would never come.

When she understood about Daniel and Emmy, she had grieved for the house, mourned the fact that it would be Emmy's things adorning the rooms, her clothes in the closets, her children playing in the yard.

Now the fickle house had changed mistresses again, only this time Charity couldn't imagine herself living there. Her vision of blue-eyed children running over those grounds had gone, replaced by a ruddy-cheeked, sandy-haired brood that scampered among sweet magnolia and pine, gazing up at her through smoky green eyes. Her mind couldn't conceive of any other way.

She groaned and lifted her face to God. *I've never asked You for anything this important before. Can You? Will You?*

A shrill voice in the hall interrupted her tortured prayer. "Charity! Where are you, baby?" Mama burst through the door and flew at her, her breath coming in labored gasps. She wrapped Charity, dress and all, in her arms and squeezed her so tightly it hurt.

"Mama, for heaven's sake! I'm right here where you left me. What on earth?"

Mama didn't answer, just held her, rocking back and forth.

Mother Dane lumbered in, more breathless than Mama, and shut the door behind her. "Pay her no mind, sugar. She's just being Bertha."

Charity smiled over the little woman's head. "Well, that explains a lot, but not nearly enough. Why is she breathing like this? Has she been running?"

"Up the stairs. I tried to stop her, but I couldn't catch her."

Mama, her swollen eyes squeezed shut, still grasped at her, straining to get a better hold.

Charity pulled her loose and held her at arm's length. "Stop it now. What's ailing you?"

Mother Dane sprawled on the bed, her chest heaving. "When I catch my breath, I'll give you the long version. The short of it is, it finally dawned on her that you're getting married tomorrow."

"Oh, mercy. Come here." Charity pulled her weeping mama close and held her while she cried, fighting hard to push aside her own bitter tears.

CHAPTER 22

Charity stretched out on a knotted rag rug across from her mama and Mother Dane. Mama sat cross-legged on the floor in front of the bed chattering like a schoolgirl while Mother Dane wound her long mane into a proper bun. Charity smiled each time Mama mindlessly held up a hairpin when Mother Dane wiggled her fingers, never missing a beat in her story. Yet Charity's mind was on anything but hair and idle babble.

Every footstep on the stairs was Buddy, every word in the hall his voice. She watched the door until her eyes hurt, ears straining for the sound of a knock that never came.

"That reminds me, Magda," Mama said, "did you check on Emmy before we left?"

Mother Dane scrunched her lips and sniffed. "A lot of good it did me. She just curled up and moaned. Didn't even bother to answer."

Charity sat up straight. Their conversation had taken an interesting turn. "What's ailing Emmy?"

It took too long for them to answer. Mama caught Mother Dane's finger and pinched it before she let go of the next hairpin. Mother Dane gave an answering tug on her hair.

Mama winced then smiled up at Charity. "She ain't herself today, baby. That's all."

"What's the matter? Is she sick?"

"No, not sick, really. More like a bit out of sorts."

Charity crossed her arms and looked from one to the other. "What are you two keeping from me?"

Mama's shoulders drooped. "All right, then. Emmy found it out, and she's grieving."

"Found what out?"

"That you're marrying up with Daniel." Mama's eyes widened. "We didn't tell her though. She snookered us."

The words sent Charity's mind reeling. *Emmy grieving? Over Daniel?*

"She loves him, then?" It eased her heart to know it. It meant Emmy hadn't toyed with their lives just to ease her boredom.

Mother Dane turned kind eyes her way. "Don't you fret over Emmy, pet. The Good Book says we reap what we sow. If Emmy's heart is heavy today, it's because it's harvesttime and she's finding her crop hard to swallow." She went back to pinning Mama's hair. "You have enough grief to bear, Charity. Don't throw Emmy's weight on your shoulders." She heaved a deep sigh. "Anyway, I reckon she's my load to carry. Speaking of which, I need to head on back and see about her. What time of the day is it getting to be?"

Charity pushed off the floor and opened the shade. "The boardwalk's thinned out and it sounds like the dining crowd has waned. That would make it well past one."

"Could it be that late? No wonder I'm hungry. We plumb missed lunch."

Mama handed up another pin. "Now there's a first, you missing a meal. You ate enough this morning to hold you past noontime tomorrow."

Mother Dane pulled Mama's hair again. "Did not. You rushed us through breakfast so fast that Nash stuffed biscuits in his pockets on his way out of the house." She glanced toward the window. "Where is that ornery man anyway? He said he'd have the rig downstairs in three hours. It's been more like five."

"But, Mother Dane," Charity said, looking over her shoulder then back at the street, "the rig *is* downstairs."

Mother Dane's head jerked up. "It is?"

"Yes, ma'am." Charity pointed. "It's right there. Parked just below us."

Throwing one leg over Mama's head, Mother Dane pushed off the bed. She joined Charity at the window and aimed her gaze along Charity's finger. "Oh, for heaven's sake. That's my wagon, all right. Now why didn't Nash send someone up for us?"

Mama twisted around to all fours and pushed up, rear end first. Shoving her way between them, she craned her neck left and right then looked up at Mother Dane. "He ain't down there, that's why."

Mother Dane strained to see as far up and down the street as possible. "Now where do you suppose that man's gone off to?"

Mama tugged on her sleeve. "Remember how he acted this morning?"

"You think this has something to do with that?"

"Why not? Maybe he's chasing some fast woman."

Mother Dane shook her head. "Nash ain't like that. He's a Christian man, with a family."

"Any man who ain't careful can be snared by easy trash."

"Not any man, Mama," Charity said, "just Clark men." She gasped and put a hand to her mouth, her round eyes fixed on Mother Dane's face. "I'm so sorry. I didn't mean. . ."

Mother Dane patted her shoulder. "I know what you meant, honey. I just pray for your sake Daniel's not such easy prey next time."

Mama sneered. "There'd best not be a next time if he values all his parts." She started for the door. "Let's get down there and find Nash. I'm getting a mite hungry myself. Are you planning to feed us, Magda? I expect they're done serving downstairs."

"If there's any cooking to be done, you'll do it. Otherwise it's finger food."

Mama turned at the door. "Charity, get your things. We'll stay the night at Magda's and get ready for the wedding there." She held up her hand before Charity could protest. "No arguments. You can do this for me. It's only one night. You can stand on your head for one night." She frowned and nodded at the sequined gown hanging on the wardrobe door. "Don't forget that thing. It's not how we planned it, but I expect it'll finally be put to some use."

Downstairs on the street, a jubilant Red leapt up and barked a greeting, dancing around them on his long hind legs. The stubborn dog survived his runaway-wagon ride intact, turning up the day after looking no worse for wear. He'd kept a vigil outside the hotel ever since, lying in constant wait for Charity.

There was no sign of Nash. He had strapped the horse to a feed bag and tied it to a post, as if he planned to be gone a good long while.

Mother Dane stood on the boardwalk, hands on her hips, staring at the rig. "When that man turns up, I should fire him on the spot."

"Let's leave him here," Mama said. "Let him walk back. It'll serve him right."

Mother Dane unfastened the feed bag and tossed it into the wagon bed. "Bertha, that's mean-spirited enough to make me feel better. Hop on, girls. This here conveyance is homeward bound."

Whooping like a raiding war party, Mama clambered onto the seat. "That's telling him, Magda."

Mother Dane pulled herself up beside her. "It ain't telling him half what I plan to when he finally shows himself. That man's due a good tongue-lashing."

Charity looked around to make sure no one was watching before she gathered her skirts and climbed on back. Whining piteously, Red planted his big paws on the tailgate and jumped like an oversized jackrabbit, trying his best to scramble aboard.

"No, boy," Charity scolded. "Not this time. Git now! Shoo! Go over yonder and lay down."

Mother Dane turned the horse's nose toward home. The wagon bounced along the rutted street until they reached the trail, where Charity braced for a rough ride home. Red heeded her commands no better than usual and followed them all the way. When the wagon came to rest in the yard, he stared at her from the ground, his long dappled tongue lolled to the side and a wide grin on his face.

She shook her finger at him. "You're a bad dog, Red Pike. Or is it Mr. Bloom these days?"

He wagged his tail.

"So that's what you think, is it? That you've wormed your way in? Well, get such thoughts out of your head, old man. Despite your noble beginnings, you're numbered with the enemy now. They'll make you slink home to join their ranks one day soon, and don't you forget it."

The dog wriggled so violently he was bound to get dizzy. Charity hopped down and cupped his big head in her hands. "You haven't heeded a word I've said, have you? Be still now. Keep that up and you won't be able to walk a straight line."

While Mother Dane unhitched the horse, Charity took the dog by his baggy scruff and led him to the house. At the door, she ordered him to lie down. He dropped and curled at her feet.

Mama chuckled as she stepped over his long legs to get into the house. "I ain't seen him pay you no mind before. I guess you scared him with that talk about sending him home. Get him some water, sugar. His tongue's dragging. We'll have to rustle him something to eat in a bit."

By the time Charity tended Red and joined Mama in the kitchen, Mother Dane was coming in at the back door. "Get to shaking that skillet, Bert," she called. "I've worked me up a raging hunger. This is the longest I've ever waited for lunch."

"I'm moving as fast as I can. Pull out the ham and slice it. That coffee we made this morning's strong enough to stand up and holler by now. Thought I'd use it to stir up some redeye gravy. Charity, hand me the coffeepot, sugar."

Mother Dane rubbed her hands together. "Now you're talking."

While Charity fetched the pot, Mother Dane hurried for the covered charger that held the smoked ham. Balancing it on one hip, she carried it to the table.

"Emmy must be faint from hunger," Mama said from the stove. "When I get everything ready, you can carry her up a plate."

From behind them came a gasp. Charity and Mama turned in unison to look.

Mother Dane stood over the pan with the lid in her hand, staring down at the meat. "That won't be necessary," she announced. "Believe me, that girl ain't hungry."

"What is it, Magda?"

"Just Emmy up to her old tricks."

Mama set down the coffeepot and joined Mother Dane at the table. "What are you going on about?"

"As you can see, Emmy's already eaten, and eaten good by the look of it. This ham's been whittled to the bone."

Mama whistled. "There's enough meat cut from that shank to feed her for a week, and Nash to boot." Mama shook her head and headed back to the stove. "And here I was worried about her empty stomach. Magda, if there's anything left, whack it off and lay it on a platter. We'll eat it with bread. That'll stretch it."

CHAPTER 23

Bertha lounged on Magda's green-striped sofa and watched her lumber down the stairs. She could've tracked her progress with her eyes closed by the groaning of the old floorboards. Never a small woman, Magda had fattened up considerably over the years. Fretting over her daughter drove the poor woman to eat. In the place of corn liquor, Magda drowned her sorrow in corn pone, corn pudding, and corn on the cob.

Bertha had battled her own bouts of distress since Thad died. She wondered if her scattered emotions during the year of bone-numbing grief that followed had hastened all the vexing maladies plaguing her these days. If so, she wouldn't mind trading places with Magda. She'd rather contend with a wider girth than droopy skin and whiskers.

She glanced at the tray Magda had carried in earlier from the kitchen. "Are you still planning to eat this sandwich? It's your third, you know."

Magda trudged the last few steps and plopped down on the divan. "I didn't bring it out here to look at it. And I can count, thank you. Where's Charity?"

Pain echoed through Bertha's chest. "She went to lay out her wedding dress. How's Emmy?"

Magda reached for her food. From the look in her eyes, she nursed the same heartache. "I poked my head in, but she wouldn't answer. Just laid there with the quilt pulled over her face. I let her be. I only hope she's asleep and not pouting. At least her belly's full and she's not bawling."

Bertha nodded. "Her belly should be full. I never seen a body eat so much food, except you, when you were carrying her."

Magda choked on her bite of sandwich. When she recovered, she stared at Bertha with bulging eyes.

Bertha shook her head. "Honey, don't even think it. That would be a tragedy worthy of Shakespeare's quill. Emmy put in the family way by Charity's husband?" She shuddered. "None of us could bear it."

Magda blotted her glistening neck with the napkin in her lap. "How can we be certain? After all, she's acting so desperate."

"I give Emmy credit for having more sense than that. She's willful, not stupid."

"I'm glad you think so. I'm not so sure anymore. Judging by the stunts she's pulled lately, you wouldn't know Emmy had any sense at all."

Compassion tugged at Bertha's heart. "She's suffering for it now, though, poor little thing. Despite all she's done, a body can't help but pity her."

"Pity?" Magda's lips took a dubious turn. "I'm not sure she deserves it."

"Listen to you!" A small shred of ham rested in the hollow of Magda's chin. Bertha snatched the napkin from her hand and plucked it off with a lacy corner. "And after you told me I dealt too harsh with Charity."

"I don't mean to sound harsh, Bertha. I love Emmy. Trouble is, my bullheaded daughter thinks if she wants something, then everyone should just understand and get out of her way. If she gets moon-eyed over her best friend's fiancé, why, that's reason enough to set her cap for him. After all, hasn't she always got whatever she wanted?"

Bertha smiled. "And whose fault is that?"

Returning her food to the plate, Magda wiped her fingertips. "I already admitted we spoiled her. Don't forget, you had a hand in it, too. But what she done to Charity she never learned from me.

I had a spell of mooning over Thad years back, but it never once entered my mind to try the stunt Emmy pulled."

Bertha fell against the button-tucked cushion and stared. "Magdalena Dane, are you telling me you was swimmy-headed over my Thad?"

Magda's cheeks flushed a bright pink. "For about one minute. Then Willem came along and that was the end of it."

Bertha scooted to the edge of her seat. " 'Til Willem came along? Honey, that was a year before we had our babies. You'd known Thad seven years by then. That's a heap more'n a minute."

Magda sat mute, studying her hands.

"All this time and you never told me?"

"Didn't see no reason to."

Bertha couldn't get past it. Magda sweet on Thad for that long but never once letting on. It explained a couple of things—why Magda was an old maid before she finally married, and why Thad's death hit her so hard.

"You and Thad. Honey, if I'd only known. . ."

Magda shook her head. "If you'd known, things would be just as they are. It was never me and Thad. The two of you belonged together from the start, just like Willem and me. I've had no room in my head for anyone but him from the first day we met." She winked. "Despite Thaddeus Bloom's winning ways and powerful good looks."

Bertha gazed at the ceiling, remembering. "He sure was a fine figure of a man."

Magda grinned. "*Ein hübscher Mann*, as my mama used to say. As handsome as you were pretty. You two made a lovely couple."

Bertha returned her grin and nodded. "I had good teeth back then and nice skin." She traced her fingers over her cheek and frowned. "Hard work and old age be hanged!"

Magda hoisted her glass of milk. "Hear, hear!"

"I don't think Thad would know me if he come back now."

"Balderdash. He'd still cut you out of a herd."

Bertha tilted her head. "You reckon?"

"I do."

She leaned to pinch off a corner of Magda's ham sandwich and poked it into her mouth. "I never was as pretty as Charity," she said, her mouth full. "And nowhere near the likes of Emmy."

Magda sighed. "I only wish Emmy acted pretty." She pointed her finger at Bertha. "Besides, you're mistaken. You were more fetching than the two of them put together. Don't you recall being chased about town by Moses Pharr and the rest? Every boy in Jefferson, Texas, wanted to court you." She chuckled. "You led them a merry chase. . .at least until Thad come along."

Nudging a greasy piece of ham deeper between the two thick slices of bread, she picked up her sandwich. "Are you forgetting you were twice the rascal that Emmy can be? Never made no sense how I wound up with my girl and you with yours. If I hadn't watched you deliver a month before I birthed Emmy, I'd vow those two got switched."

Bertha slapped her legs, laughter bubbling up from her belly. "Weren't no mixing them babies, what with Charity's black hair and Emmy's crop of white curls."

"Still as white as the day she was born. I blame Willem's seed for that curse. A curse it's been, too, since men are bound to make fools of themselves over fair-haired women. And Emmy's too weak in character to resist the attention."

Bertha shook her head. "Don't sell her short. That girl's strong-willed and smart. She's just learned to use what she's got to get what she wants."

Magda snorted. "Trouble is, most times what she wants belongs to someone else. That brings sorrow to everyone concerned."

Bertha patted her friend's knee. "The Lord uses our mistakes to guide us." She nodded toward the top of the stairs. "Emmy's feeling the sting of her own actions, but she'll be the better for it. It'll teach her to count the cost before she jumps next time."

"Sugar, I hope you're right. If Emmy learned to love others half as much as she loves herself, it sure would save me some grief."

Bertha offered a sympathetic grin. "I don't think she sets out to cause you pain. Do you?"

Magda took a big bite and waved one hand absently at Bertha. "Not really," she said with bulging jaws. "She just gets in over her head sometimes."

Emmy took another bite of her sandwich and waved one hand absently at Nash. "This ham is divine. Packing a lunch was the best idea you ever had."

Nash seemed not to hear. He sat hunched in the seat across from her with his face pressed against the passenger car window while the countryside scrolled past. Emmy could see his reflection in the glass. His wide eyes danced back and forth, trying to take in everything at once.

She held out a sandwich wrapped in paper. "Here. Eat some before it goes bad."

He shook his head and answered without turning. "Got no time for to be eating. Ain't never rode me no train before, and I don't aim to miss it."

Emmy grinned. "So you like it, do you?"

"It's jus' like I reckoned."

Emmy giggled at the wonder in his voice. "And you were scared to come. I knew you'd love it. Didn't I say you wouldn't be sorry?"

He faced her then. "Love it, I do. Sorry is what I'll be when your mama finds out. Sorry, no 'count, and out of work–if I ain't lynched first."

"Oh, Nash."

"Don't you 'Oh, Nash' me. How long you reckon before Miz Dane jerk back that quilt and see them pillows sleeping in yo' bed instead of you? Probably already did see. I bet all my wages she's got the sheriff dogging us now. Most likely a posse on horseback chasing this train."

Emmy wiped a greasy thumb on the paper around her sandwich. "Don't be silly. I don't want to hear that foolish talk."

Eyes bulging, he gawked at her. "You ain't gon' be saying silly when he catch up to us. Jus' how silly you gon' feel watching me swing from a rope? I still cain't figure how you got me into this mess." He shook his head. "Mm, mm, mm. No, sir. I sho' can't figure it."

Emmy cast a nervous glance at the surrounding passengers. Raising her nose a bit higher, she ignored their angry glares. She had obtained permission for Nash to ride up front by insisting she needed her *boy* for protection and to carry her bags. It made Emmy's stomach ache to say such a hurtful thing, and even more so when Nash lowered his head, but there was no help for it.

She frowned across the aisle at him. "Shush now, before someone hears. You'd be in worse trouble if you'd have let me come alone. You know it yourself."

He glowered. "There now, you see? Hanged if I do and shot if I don't. You done hauled me into a full-sized mess."

"Oh, pooh. Quit your squawking. We had to come, didn't we, if we want to save Charity?"

The memory of Daniel's threat made her shudder. "I still can't believe how he fooled me. . .fooled us both." She rubbed her wrist, still feeling his cruel grip on her arm. "Of course, he wouldn't dare lay a hand on Charity until after they're married, but by then it'll be too late. You want to help me prevent that, don't you?"

Nash didn't answer. He perched across from her, too busy wading through deep indignation to answer, sullen to the point of pouting. He spared her a look. "What good you reckon finding Mistah Pierce gon' do?"

"Gracious. Don't you ever listen when I speak?"

He shook his head. "Not so much. Generally gets me in too much trouble."

Emmy wadded her sandwich wrapper and shoved it inside the sack. "It may not help at all. But if there's any truth to what I heard. . ." She leaned close and lowered her voice. "If Mr. Pierce feels one spark of affection for Charity, then he's our only hope. It's a gamble, but a gamble we must take."

Nash's tense hands worried the tattered hat on his lap. "You reckon they know we's gone by now?"

"Maybe." Emmy considered her answer for a minute and then nodded. "Most likely, in fact." She shook her head to dislodge the thought and handed Nash a sandwich. "Eat this and don't talk about it. What's done is done. There's no going back."

Nash took the wrapped offering in one hand, shooing her words like pesky flies with the other. "Naw, missy. Ain't nothing done yet. I could go back, all right. I could get off this contraption and walk home. Tell Miz Dane I ain't seen hide nor hair of her wayward child."

Burying his face in the paper, he took a huge bite of the sandwich and proceeded to talk around it. "That's right, I sho' could. In fact, I jus' might."

Emmy shrugged. "Suit yourself, but you're in for a mighty long walk, considering we're pulling into the station. We're here, Nash! We're in Houston!"

He narrowed his eyes at her. "Miss Emmy, don't you try to fool old Nash."

She pointed out her side window. "See for yourself."

He squirmed in his seat, trying to see through every glass at once. "No, we ain't! That fast?" A grin spread over his face, wider than the grease on his cheeks. "Now don't that jus' beat all?"

Emmy stood, fighting to keep her balance as the big engine rolled to a jerky stop. She grabbed her reticule and handed Nash her leather bag. "Stop that gawking and follow me."

She moved into the aisle and started for the exit, helped along by the surging crush of people. When she looked back and found herself alone, she stepped aside before the disorderly stampede pushed her right out the door.

Nash still hovered over her seat, trying to gather the remaining sandwiches with one hand while juggling their bags with the other.

"Leave that, Nash. It's trash now. It won't last in this heat. We'll find something to eat later on."

Nash dropped the bundle with some reluctance and pushed his hat down on his head. He pressed into the aisle and came toward her, glancing back several times at the food.

"Stop dawdling over that trifling ham," she shouted past the scrambling passengers. "Don't worry, I won't let you starve."

"But, Miss Emmy, we ain't got us no money."

The rush swept Emmy along. She had no choice but to step down off the train into bedlam. Gentility and manners had vanished with the coming of the oil boom, along with every trace of decency and order. Those waiting to board merged with those departing, becoming a blur of frantic people. Emmy broke free and shoved her way to the side, adjusting her hat and smoothing her rumpled skirt while she waited for Nash. He appeared on the threshold at last, holding their bags aloft.

"There's no need to fret about money or food," she called up to him. "I have my ways."

A burly man pushed past Emmy in his rush to board, jostling her so rudely she would've toppled and been trampled underfoot had Nash not leaped to the platform to offer a steady hand. He cast a dark look at the surrounding horde. "I ain't so sure even your wily ways gon' help in this place."

Emmy followed his gaze. A most curious assortment of people milled about on the boardwalk. Not even in Humble, where the boom had brought thousands of strangers to her town, had Emmy seen the likes of this lot. Work-roughened, sin-coarsened men loomed on every side. Whatever lured them, whether the promise of excitement or unbridled greed, they allowed themselves to be driven like cattle toward the train.

Three women elbowed past, shouting and laughing, holding their own with the men. By the look of them, they were headed to find work in the saloon at Moonshine Hill, or perhaps to ply a different trade on the outskirts of Tent City. The stale odor of toilet water, whiskey, and bad breath hung in the air behind them. Emmy's stomach lurched. Sudden panic washed over her, and she groped for Nash's arm.

Next to her, a drunken man in a cleric's collar clung possessively to the sort of woman Aunt Bert called a "painted lady." The woman stared at them in a brazen way, her bloodshot eyes going to Emmy's hand on Nash's sleeve. Then she leered, as if they shared a secret, her loose crimson mouth vulgar against her yellow teeth. Emmy shuddered and turned away.

"Come along, Miss Emmy," Nash said. "Let me take you out of this mess."

He tucked her behind his back, using his body as a shield as he pushed through the rush of people. Along the tracks, men heaved burlap bags of feed, crates filled with sacks of pinto beans, and boxed canned goods onto the cars, supplies bound for Humble. These days everything from heavy equipment to sewing needles found its way there by train. Provision for the boomers.

Rail bosses hurled orders laced with vile curses in loud, angry voices. Emmy covered her ears as Nash guided her past the men. Those who noticed her with him cast angry glares at Nash or looked her over in such a way that she yearned for her quilt from home to wrap up in.

Nash pulled her along in zigzag fashion until they reached the far end of the platform. Here the mob thinned out a bit, though the laughter and cries of the jostling crowd, mingling with the din near the railcar, stirred a rush in Emmy's chest that made her head spin. She found it unsettling but exhilarating at the same time.

She guessed Nash felt it, too. Despite his nervous darting eyes, a smile stretched over his face. "Whoo-ee!" he cried. "These the most folks I ever seen in one place."

"In one place? Oh, Nash, it's the most I've seen in my life."

He flashed his grin her way. "Me, too. Reckon they all live in Houston?"

Emmy barely heard. Near the spot they'd just left, a man on the swarming platform caught her attention.

"Nash, look!"

"Look where?"

She pointed. "Right there. There's something familiar about that gentleman. I know him from somewhere."

Nash shaded his eyes and stared. "Which one? There's a whole mess of gentlemen over there."

Emmy's head bobbed as she strained to get a better look at the long-legged fellow.

Behind her Nash grunted. "Miss Emmy, you got me looking for a boll weevil in tall cotton. I don't see nothing but a whole mess of bodies."

For the space of two seconds, she had an unobstructed view of a handsome young face. Her mind scrambled to place him. "Oh my! I think. . ."

Emmy gripped Nash's arm. "Yes, by golly, it's him!" She pointed a trembling finger. "That man works with Mr. Pierce." She craned her neck to search the milling throng. "That means he must be here somewhere." Joy filled her heart, so full she could taste the sweetness. "See the goodness of God? He's led us straight to Buddy Pierce."

Glancing up, Emmy found Nash watching her. She squirmed under his searching gaze but steeled herself and met his eyes. "What are you gawking at?"

He shoved his hat aside and scratched his curly head. "If I didn't know different, I'd think I's gawking at Miss Charity. Them words sound like they come right out of her mouth."

Feeling petulant, Emmy raised her brows. "Stop your meddling and get yourself over there before Mr. Pierce gets away. Now hurry! Find him and bring him back here."

Nash squinted hard, shaking his head. "I can't bring what ain't there. I reckon you seeing things. You said yourself Mistah Pierce was alone when he left on that train."

Emmy longed to thrash him. "That man over there knows where he is now. And look! He's leaving!"

"Miss Emmy, stop all that bouncing. Ain't ladylike. Show me what face you know in all them faces, and I'll fetch him for you."

She aimed her finger again, so excited she barely held it straight. "There. The tall, thin man with bushy hair. Hurry, he's getting away."

Mumbling under his breath, Nash scurried in the general direction she'd pointed. Emmy gathered her skirts and lit out after him. She lagged a few steps behind when he reached the young man's side.

"Suh? Excuse me, suh. I don't mean to trouble you none, but the little lady over there. . ." He turned to point at Emmy, then frowned and adjusted his words when he found her on his heels. "This young lady right here sho' hankering to have a word with you."

The gentleman took off his hat and turned a shy smile her way. Confusion mingled with admiration in his warm brown eyes. He bowed slightly. "Yes, ma'am? What can I do for you?"

Emmy turned on her brightest smile. She knew the power wielded by her full lips and deep dimples. She'd learned at an early age how to use them to gain advantage over men. "Good afternoon, sir." She tilted her chin up at him. "Forgive my boldness, but I need your help."

Confusion won over admiration. "My help? I'm afraid I—"

"Don't trouble yourself trying to remember. We haven't been introduced. Still, I know who you are. You work with Buddy Pierce, isn't that so?" She expected the mention of Buddy's name to reassure him. He stiffened instead.

"Yes, ma'am, I sure do, but—"

In her excitement, Emmy cut him off again. "I need to speak to Mr. Pierce right away. Will you take me to him?"

A glimmer of suspicion crept into his eyes.

Emmy pressed closer and turned up her smile. "Heavens, where are my manners?" She extended a gloved hand. "I'm Emily Dane, daughter of Willem and Magdalena Dane of Humble. This is our man, Nash."

The young man offered a hesitant smile and accepted her hand. She watched him try to work it out in his mind. "Name's Jerry Ritter. It's a pleasure to meet you, miss."

"Mr. Ritter, you were a guest in my home awhile back. You came there with Mr. Pierce."

His frown deepened.

Emmy felt her smile fade a bit. "We didn't meet that day. I was. . .feeling poorly, so I never joined you. But I saw you from the landing. You were there on behalf of Bertha and Charity Bloom."

A flicker of recognition shimmered in his eyes. When he smiled, she rushed ahead. "Mr. Ritter, I must find Buddy Pierce. It's a matter of extreme urgency."

His young face grew serious. "Well now, it looks like we've got that much in common. I'm trying to locate him myself."

Emmy's heart lurched. "You mean he's not traveling with you?"

"Well, he was. Then he took off for Humble on his own, carrying a saddlebag stuffed with money. Me and Lee—that's our partner—we got worried about Buddy traveling alone with so much currency, so I lit out after him. Never did catch him though. When I got to Humble, Buddy had already come and gone. One of our roughnecks claimed he saw him leaving town, so I hopped the first train bound for Houston, and here I am."

Understanding dawned on Emmy. "You were on the same train we rode in on, weren't you?"

"If you pulled in just now, then I guess I was."

Desperation weighted Emmy's heart. "Do you know where in Houston Mr. Pierce might go?"

"Not exactly. I just know it ain't like him to be so unpredictable." He looked away, but not before concern flickered in his brown eyes. "That man's as honest and God-fearing as the day is long, but there was an awful lot of money in that bag. It's got me right anxious."

Emmy decided to show her cards. "Mr. Ritter, I know exactly why your friend took an unscheduled trip to Houston, and it had nothing whatever to do with money."

He shifted his weight toward her. "Keep talking."

"Mr. Pierce found out Charity Bloom is set to get married tomorrow, to Daniel Clark."

He winced and nodded. "That explains a lot. Buddy was carrying a ring in his pocket that he hoped to slip on her finger."

Emmy felt a rush of excitement. "That can still happen. Charity doesn't love Daniel. The truth is, she's in love with Mr. Pierce. It's him she wants to wed."

His eyes widened. "Then why is she getting hitched to someone else?"

"There's no time to explain right now. Just know Charity's being forced to marry in haste for her mama's sake. She's tried to wait for your Mr. Pierce, but she's running out of time."

Mr. Ritter's eyes twinkled and his cheeks flushed red. He'd caught her enthusiasm. "Miss Dane, are you sure about all of this?"

"Yes, that's why we're here. We have to find Buddy before it's too late for both of them. Oh, please! Can't you help us?"

He pressed a finger to his chin and nodded. "Maybe I can."

"Then you know where Buddy is?"

"I have a few ideas. Grab your bags and follow me."

CHAPTER 24

Charity stood before Mother Dane's stove pouring hot water into a skillet of golden-brown flour. When the liquid hit the smoking pan, it sizzled and steam rose to the ceiling. Elbows waving, Charity clutched the heavy black handle and went at the mixture in a stirring frenzy. Still, the bubbling gravy inched toward the top, until Mama stepped beside her and lowered the gas.

Waving her hand to dissipate the billowing moisture, Charity glanced over her shoulder. "Thanks, Mama. I'm not used to this newfangled cooker. I'm beginning to appreciate Mother Dane's attitude toward it."

"Keep your eyes on that fire, or you'll see another side to her attitude. If'n that blue flame turns red and yellow, this whole place will fill up with smoke." She wrinkled her nose in distaste. "Leaves a black mess on everything it touches."

Charity regarded the stove with newfound respect, her eyes trained on the dancing blue blaze. The cast-iron behemoth stood a foot taller than her and took up one whole corner of the kitchen. She still marveled that it was fueled by gas, the first such contraption of its kind in Humble. Uncle Willem had borne it home along with a good supply of fuel after a trip to the Midwest. He claimed he had a close call somewhere in Kansas, where he averted a mishap just in time to avoid blasting a hole in the earth the size of the Grand Canyon, sending him on an untimely journey to meet his Maker.

He bought the stove as a birthday surprise for Mother Dane, who despised the thing. She cursed it often, using words that burned Charity's ears. She lamented her old box stove with the same fervor and swore to make Uncle Willem's life wretched until he brought it home.

Charity gave the gravy another stir and lowered the burner still more, easing the heavy lid onto the skillet. "Mercy, all they do around this house is eat. It's a wonder you stay so slim."

Mama scraped a pot of buttered mashed potatoes into a serving bowl before she answered. "The Danes do love their vittles, daughter. When they ain't eating, they're talking about it. I reckon when folks can hire their work done, there ain't much left to do but sit about and eat. Besides, Magda always did like her grub. Even as a girl, they had to shoo her away from the table."

Charity peered out the window over the sink. "Speaking of Mother Dane, where do you suppose she's gone off to? It's getting dark out there."

Heavy boots hit the porch with a thud, and Mother Dane muttered to herself while she scraped them on the rug. When she opened the door, her ashen face gave Charity such a start that she dropped her ladle on the stove with a clatter and rushed to her aid. "Oh my! You're pale as paste. Are you all right?"

Winded, Mother Dane leaned against the doorpost, wiping her glistening face with her apron. "I'll be fine, sugar. Just need to rest a spell. Tending that horse sure takes it out of me." She drew a deep, shaky breath and took Charity's arm for help over the threshold. "I guess this old body's seen better days."

Mama turned from mixing salt into the potatoes. "You need to shed that weight, Magda, and you know it. You cain't carry it like when you was young."

Mother Dane gave her the eye. "Now I'm fat *and* old. Thank you, Bert."

Chuckling, Mama went on stirring. "Did you tend them squawking chickens?"

Mother Dane shook her head. "I fed Rebel and that's about it. The rest of those critters can fend for themselves for one night. I got no tending left in me."

Handing off the bowl to Charity, Mama led her friend to the table. "Come take a load off them feet. Me and Charity can ramble out and finish up later. Still no sign of Nash?"

Moaning, Mother Dane sank into a kitchen chair. "Not a peep. I guess he's gone for good this time, though I can't imagine why. We treated that man like family." She sniffed, and her bottom lip trembled. "He let me down bad this time. With Willem gone and Emmy too frail to help out, I'm left with the whole thing in my lap. He sure picked a bad time to skedaddle."

Charity hurried over to set the gravy boat on the table then rested a silver spoon at its side. "Nash isn't gone for good. He'll be back. You can count on it."

Mama turned from the stove. "You reckon so, baby?"

"Yes, ma'am, I do."

"Then where's he at?"

"I couldn't venture to guess. I'm certain he'll have a lively excuse when he shows up."

Mother Dane drew herself up in the chair. "This time he'll tell it to the wind whilst I sweep his sorry hide off the porch."

Charity smiled at Mama, and Mama winked. The Dane household would soon founder without strong, capable Nash, and they all knew it.

From the cupboard as familiar as her own, Charity pulled down a heavy mason jar filled with the green beans she'd helped Emmy put up last summer—not that Emmy had weighed in on the task. She spent most of the morning sitting cross-legged on the table singing silly ditties and telling stories. In short, trying to do all she could to keep Charity too entertained to notice she hadn't lifted a finger to help with the canning.

Charity wrapped a cup towel around the mouth of the jar and pried the lid off with a satisfying pop, then drained the beans and poured them into a warming pan. She tossed in a strip of salted fat and put on the lid. Mama took up the golden-brown pork chops that Charity had just fried and layered them on a cloth-covered platter to soak up the grease. Snuffing the fire under the skillet, Charity turned to the table to take inventory.

Still slumped in her chair, Mother Dane pressed a hand to her back and groaned, her face a tight grimace. "I'm bushed, girls. Let's eat quick so I can turn in and get an early start on tomorrow."

Mama crossed to the table, her arms loaded with the platter of breaded chops. "You cain't turn in yet, Magda. I had my heart set on a round of cards."

Mother Dane frowned her disapproval. "At this hour? Honey, it's too late."

Concern pinched Mama's face. "Since when did you ever think it was too late to play cards? Are you feeling all right?"

"No, I'm not. I'm right fizzled out, if you really care to know."

"Aw, come on," Mama wheedled. "You got enough steam left for one or two hands."

Mother Dane picked up a piece of meat, then winced and tossed it at her plate.

"Careful, they're hot," Charity called from the stove.

Shoving her finger and thumb inside her mouth, Mother Dane spoke around them. "Blast it, Bert, I'm tired. Why do you suddenly want to play cards so all-fired bad?"

Mama cut mournful eyes at Charity before she answered. "I ain't in any hurry to get to bed, that's why. Tomorrow will come soon enough as it is."

Watching Mama's face, Mother Dane nodded. "Sure thing, sugar. I guess I can make it for a hand or two."

"You'll join us, won't you, daughter?"

Charity looked at them through a blur of tears. "Of course I will. I'm not all that anxious myself to see this day end."

Mama wiped her hands on her apron. "It's settled, then. What say we serve up this food and get it ate?"

Charity joined them at the table, her eyes still damp. "Won't Emmy be starved by now, Mother Dane? I can fix a nice plate for her, and you can take it up before we sit down."

Mother Dane and Mama stared until Charity's cheeks began to warm. She didn't know how to explain it, but the idea that Emmy loved Daniel had patched her wounded heart and replaced her anger with pity. After all, she found herself in much the same state–devoted to a man she couldn't have.

Mother Dane motioned her closer for a hug. "The Creator ran

short on love after making you, Charity. Your mama named you right, that's for certain." She patted Charity's hand. "Don't trouble yourself. I'll take something up in a while."

Mama slumped into a chair, piled her plate high with mashed potatoes, and passed the bowl. "That child ain't sat down to a decent meal in days. Don't that worry you none?"

Mother Dane's eyes bulged. "Are you forgetting the ham, Bert? She's been eating better than we have. Didn't even throw food in the yard this time."

Mama chuckled. "She could've thrown something out, Magda. Don't forget, Red's out there somewhere. He'd make quick work of ham scraps."

Charity gasped and laid down her fork. "I forgot to feed that worrisome old dog." She looked around at the scraps on their plates and brightened. "I'll toss him these pork chop bones after dinner. He'll be glad to see them."

"Tomorrow early, I'll tie him in the wagon and cart him home," Mother Dane said. "Shamus may have to pen him for a spell to keep him there."

Mama grinned and nodded. "If they don't pen or tie him, he'll be waiting for you on the porch when you get back."

They finished the meal amid laughter and light chatter. Afterward, they rose together to clear the table. Even Mother Dane stayed in the kitchen to help, as if reluctant to leave their company. With everything covered and put away, the big stove scrubbed clean of greasy splatters, and Red offered his feast of bones, Charity followed the older women into the parlor.

While Mother Dane set up the game table, Charity and Mama brought in three chairs from the dining room. Charity pushed hers into place then took a step back and squinted. "What happened to this one?"

Mama winked at Mother Dane as if Charity wasn't looking right at her. "Something wrong with that chair, you say?" She perused the item in question with one hand on her hip and the other rubbing her chin. "I don't know. It appears just fine to me. Don't you think so, Magda?"

"It sure does."

Charity frowned and held one hand over the backrest of each seat to gauge the height. "No, look. This one's much shorter than the rest."

Mother Dane chimed in. "Are you trying to convince us that chair shrunk?"

"Don't be daft, Magda. Furniture don't shrink. Maybe Charity growed instead." Mama lifted the chair and studied it, her glee scarcely contained. "Wait, I see what you've done, daughter. You've hauled in the milking stool."

"Oh, Mama!"

"Hush and behave yourself, Bertha," Mother Dane called from the sideboard. "Old dependable Nash leveled that chair for me, Charity. I'm just glad he didn't fix them all, or we'd be sitting with our knees around our ears." She opened the door to the shelf where she kept her parlor games. "Now then, ladies, name your poison."

Still grinning, Mama slung her arm around Charity's waist. "How 'bout dominoes, girls?"

Mother Dane raised an eyebrow at Charity. "Did she say dominoes?"

Shrugging one shoulder, Mama sat down and made a show of dusting the table. "If Emmy felt better, we could play euchre. Takes four to make a good game of euchre." She tapped a finger against her lips while she pondered then held it up in the air. "Wait, I know. We'll take turns at cooncan. There, it's settled. Bring out the cards, Magda."

Mother Dane nodded at Charity. "Go over and feel her forehead. I believe she's come down with the fever."

Mama glared. "Leave off me, woman." She jabbed her chest with her thumb. "This here's the new Bertha. No more gambling. You might as well get used to it."

Mother Dane, her eyes as wide as Charity's felt, joined her beside the table. Speechless, they stared down at Mama, who sat rigidly in her chair.

"Pick up your jaws. It's true," she affirmed in a sullen voice. "I don't know why I ever gambled in the first place. It's brought us nothing but heartache and loss. Charity wouldn't be in this mess if Thad hadn't made that silly bet. I don't know how he could do such a sorrowful thing, but at least it's opened my eyes. I vow on his grave I'll never lay another wager as long as I live."

Charity dropped a kiss on the top of her head. "Don't swear, Mama. You're not supposed to."

"I promise, then. I promise you won't see me gamble no more. I know it always grieved your tender conscience, and I'm sorry."

Across the table, Mother Dane cleared her throat. When Mama's wet-rimmed eyes swung toward her, she glanced away and pulled out her chair. She kept her head down and her attention on the table while she dealt the cards, but mirth teased the corners of her mouth.

Mama gave her an angry glare. "Don't think I didn't see you rolling those eyes, Magda. And wipe that grin off your face. Whether you believe it or not, I'm dead serious."

"Don't be silly, sugar. I never doubted you for a minute."

Muttering under her breath, Mama directed her attention to the game. She picked up her cards, studied them, and then gave a low whistle. "I'll be hanged if these wouldn't make a right fine hand of poker."

Charity met Mother Dane's astonished eyes across the table before they both collapsed into laughter. Charity howled until she cried, wiping her eyes on the sleeve of her cotton dress. Mother Dane's deep belly laugh all but rattled the windows. Mama watched them, furious at first, until a huge grin lit her face and she fell over in a fit of giggles.

After several more outbursts, laced with Mother Dane's side-clutching and her mama's moans, they settled into a companionable silence. Charity couldn't stop smiling until Mama broke the spell.

"If you don't mind my saying so, daughter, I never expected to attend so many weddings in your honor." She looked up from her cards and gave Charity a sweet smile. "I always reckoned one day to lose you to some addlepated upstart, and that would be bad enough." She shrugged her shoulders. "But I never, ever expected things to turn out like this."

Mother Dane frowned a warning. "You talk like tomorrow is Charity's last day on earth. She's not dying, for pity's sake. She's getting married."

Mama bristled. "To Daniel Clark! Dying would be more tolerable, in my opinion."

"Bertha!"

"Well?"

Charity sighed. "That's all right, Mother Dane. I know what she means. It would be different if we were planning a real wedding."

Mama nodded. "Like if you was set to marry Buddy, you mean."

His name conjured the dear face Charity had pushed from her mind all day. Crushing pain struck deep in her chest like she hadn't endured since Papa died. Mama was right. This wedding felt like a funeral.

She laid down her cards and scooted her chair back. "I think I'll go on up now. I'm feeling tired."

Before Charity could stand, her mama dropped to her knees beside her chair. "Baby, I'm sorry. I never meant to hurt you. I don't know why I spew such blether. I just don't think."

"You didn't–"

"Yes, I did. I made you sad. I know you're grieving over Buddy. I know how much you love him." She clutched Charity's hands. "Daughter, you don't have to go through with this wedding. Your feller will be back soon. He'll come riding into town looking for you. Don't let him find you in Daniel's house."

Charity's heart leapt at the words, but she pushed it back down and pulled free. "Hush now. It's all decided."

"But I changed my mind. I don't want you doing this fool thing." She swatted the air. "I don't care about the house. We'll get by without it. Ain't nothing more important to me than your happiness."

Charity took the familiar little face in her hands. "You listen to me. I'm going up those stairs to bed. I need my rest because tomorrow is my wedding day. I'm marrying Daniel, just like we planned, and you're going to be there, happy and smiling, to give us your blessing."

Mama seemed struck dumb by Charity's calm, forceful words, a favor for which Charity felt grateful. She had no confidence in her own strength and didn't know how long she could hold out.

She gave Mama's tearstained cheek a tender kiss. "Move now.

Let me out of this chair so I can go to bed. I suggest you two do the same. The hour is late."

Mother Dane came around the table and helped lift Mama from the floor.

Charity couldn't bear to see her mama's stricken look, so she averted her gaze and brushed another kiss on her forehead as she passed. One foot on the bottom step, she forced a bright smile and turned. "Good night now. Get some rest. I need you fresh tomorrow."

Mother Dane wrapped Mama in a bear hug from behind, laying her cheek against the top of her head. "Too late for that, child. This old thing ain't been fresh for many a year."

Though her heart was shattered, Charity couldn't help but laugh.

The awful pain returned as she made her way up the stairs. She wanted to get to her room before she broke down and cried, but on impulse she paused near the top landing.

The two of them, still hugging, still staring up at her, hadn't budged.

"There is one more thing."

Mama leaned forward. "What's that, baby?"

"Where's Papa's Bible? I thought I'd read a bit before I turn in."

Mama's eyes melted into dark pools of sorrow, as her heart swelled up and broke there.

Charity despised her own weakness. She shouldn't have asked for the Bible. It only served to reveal the depth of her pain.

"It's in Magda's room. On the table by the bed. You want me to fetch it for you?"

The anguish in Mama's voice matched the agony in her eyes. Charity longed to rush down and hug her again but knew it would only make matters worse. Instead, she turned and took the last two steps up the staircase. "Don't trouble yourself. I'll get it. Good night, Mama. Good night, Mother Dane."

"Sleep tight, sugar," they called in unison.

The worn leather book lay open beside the bed in Mother Dane's room, just as Mama had said. Charity closed it gently and tucked it under her arm.

In the hallway, she turned to stare at Emmy's door. A force she couldn't understand pulled her toward it. Perhaps it was the desire to escape the present, to go back in time to simpler days, when she and Emmy were young, carefree girls. Perhaps her battered heart sought comfort from the person who knew her best, a person whose own heart was wracked with grief. Whatever the reason, Charity found herself standing outside Emmy's room, her trembling hand clutching the knob.

The pounding in her chest seemed audible as she opened the door. The gaslight in the hall poured a shaft of light across the floor in front of her. Charity held her breath and ducked inside. Shadows etched the room. She could just make out Emmy in the center of the high, four-poster bed, the covers drawn over her face.

In that moment, everything in Charity's life seemed caught in a ludicrous dream. Tomorrow she would marry a man on whom she'd set her cap for years, yet she'd rather be drawn and quartered. Marrying him would bring heartache to a person she loved with all her heart, a person who lay a mere six feet away, yet she dared not call her name.

It was more than Charity could bear. She clutched the Bible to her chest and fled, taking no care to be quiet. She ran down the hall with her hand pressed against her mouth to suppress a wail, knowing once she gave in to it, she'd bawl like a motherless calf.

CHAPTER 25

Buddy leaned against the bar, tracing ever-widening circles with the base of a tall, sweaty mug. He gripped the handle and took another drink, wondering again why he'd stormed into a place like this only to embarrass himself at the last minute.

Under the scrutiny of every man in the place, he had turned up the glass and taken a long, deliberate swig, as if the sticky-sweet sarsaparilla was his intention all along. He had no taste for strong liquor and wanted no part of it, despite how bad he felt.

Something about the dank, smoke-filled saloon brought Buddy a measure of comfort, even a sense of camaraderie with the men. Perhaps due to the feeling of shared hopelessness or the sight of his own pain reflected back from their hollow eyes.

None of the long faces seemed interested in conversation; Buddy reckoned the other patrons swirled in pits of their own trouble. He felt isolated and anonymous but at the same time accepted into a curious brotherhood of suffering.

A wizened old man strengthened this notion when he stopped to pat Buddy's back on the way out the door. Buddy had never felt such misery. It seemed fitting to hole up in the most miserable place he'd ever been.

He had walked in on impulse a couple of hours past noon. Driven from his room by hunger, he left the hotel to scout out a bite to eat. Instead, he barged into the saloon. He wasn't sure how long he'd nursed his wounds in the dimly lit room. Long enough to watch the bright square of light above the swinging doors fade to orange and then darken.

Having never been inside a saloon in his life, Buddy couldn't believe he'd passed so much time there. He spent much of it comparing Charity to every woman he'd ever known and had been forced to admit her attributes were not his imagination. She was in fact the most wonderful woman he'd ever met, a conclusion that only added to his misery.

The rest of his confinement passed in a blur of strange faces, cigar smoke, the stench of stale liquor and unwashed bodies, and more sarsaparilla than he'd consumed in a lifetime.

"What in blue blazes. . . ?"

The familiar voice pulled Buddy's attention to the mirror behind the bar. Lit by the gaslight on the wall, in sharp relief against the dark opening, the reflection of a familiar face topped by an unruly shock of hair stared back at him from the door.

Buddy spun around grinning, confused but immensely glad to see Jerry Ritter. "Well, lookie here! You're a welcome sight, Tumbleweed. When'd you blow in?"

Jerry reluctantly left his place at the door and pushed into the room, leading a curious and unlikely parade. One of the prettiest women Buddy had ever seen followed him in like she belonged there, though she clearly didn't. On her heels, his posture afraid and defiant at the same time, came big Nash, Magdalena Dane's oversized handyman.

Buddy's head reeled at the sight of them strolling in together. He couldn't have guessed the reason for it if he'd tried.

"What's he doing in here?" The barkeep glared hard at Nash. "Can't y'all read?" He pointed at a sign nailed over the door. "That boy can't come in here. No darkies allowed."

Stepping in front of Nash with a swish of her skirts, the tiny woman tilted her chin and faced the bartender. "This man is with me, sir. We'll only be a minute, and I'll see he does no harm. You have my word. You can do a lady one small favor, can't you?"

The slightest movement of her head caught the glow from the gaslight, causing pinpoints of fire to ricochet through her hair.

She reached a finger to twirl one glittering curl, and the effect was mesmerizing. Every eye in the room held an answering light, and Buddy found himself falling under her spell. He stared at the lovely face, convinced her smile would sweeten day-old coffee.

The allure of plump lips and bottomless dimples weakened the barkeep's will. It was obvious women like her seldom graced his establishment. Looking like he'd swallowed the pickle barrel, the poor man managed a nod.

By the scowl on Jerry's face, he might've swallowed one himself. "Well, if this ain't the last place I expected to find you. . ." His narrowed gaze fixed on Buddy's glass.

Buddy raised the mug. "Don't worry, partner. I'm still a teetotaler."

Jerry leaned to smell the offending drink, his face set in a grimace. When he rose up, his countenance had brightened considerably. "Why, that's sarsaparilla!"

Buddy set the mug down and shoved it away with one finger. "That's what it is, all right. I should know. I've swallowed buckets of it. I don't reckon I'll drink another for the rest of my natural life." He shuddered and turned from the bar. "How did you find me?"

"We weren't planning to look in here, I can tell you that." Jerry flashed his teeth and nodded. "Though it's a good thing we did. We were headed to the hotel next door. I remembered staying there the last time we came to town."

The lady elbowed past Jerry. "Gentlemen, please. We have no time for idle chatter." She held out her hand. "Mr. Pierce, my name is Emily Dane. I can't tell you how glad I am to meet you."

He nodded and returned the gesture. "So you're Emily. I might've guessed." While he couldn't imagine a man letting go of a woman like Charity Bloom, the sight of the pretty little thing before him answered a few hard questions about Daniel Clark.

Buddy's gaze traveled from Emily to Jerry then to Nash. He leaned to rest his elbows on the bar, amused by the improbable grouping. "So what's going on here? Where did you three meet up, and what in tarnation are you doing in Houston?"

Emily's expression was grave. "We came to find you, Mr. Pierce. I have a matter of utmost importance to discuss."

Buddy smiled and winked at Jerry. "In that case, you'd best call me Buddy."

She held his gaze. "All right, then. . .Buddy."

His grin widened. "Well, go ahead. Say what you traveled all this way to tell me. You have my undivided attention."

She wasted no time getting to the point. "Charity's in trouble and you're the only one who can help her."

Buddy bolted upright. His head reeled, his stomach churned, and it had nothing to do with the sarsaparilla. At least he didn't think so. "What kind of trouble?"

Emily's sober expression revealed little emotion, but her bright eyes blazed. "She's about to marry Daniel Clark."

His heart eased and he slumped on the bar stool, wholly defeated. "Miss Dane, I'm afraid you came all this way to tell me what I already know. Forgive my boldness, but you and I are the only poor souls who find that news disquieting." He spun on his heel. "Now if you'll excuse me. . ."

She clutched his arm. "That's where you're wrong, Mr. Pierce. Charity's plenty disquieted. She may be set to marry Daniel, but she's in love with you."

Buddy twisted to look over his shoulder. "What did you say?"

"It's true. Trust me. I heard it from a reliable source."

"Then why?"

"I'll cut straight through the fat. Charity has to be married by day's end tomorrow or Bertha loses her home to Shamus Pike. She felt she had no choice but to marry whoever was handy, so she hoodwinked Daniel and got him to propose. You weren't there, and she feared you wouldn't make it back in time."

"But I was there."

"I know. I watched Daniel drive you out of town."

Buddy flushed at her rebuke. "Didn't you tell her?"

Emily lowered her eyes. "She's not exactly speaking to me just now." Then she raised her head, her expression fierce. "I figured it would mean more to her if I show up with you by my side."

"You don't think Daniel said anything?"

Emily sneered. "What do you think?"

"But I gave him a saddlebag full of money for Bertha. Didn't he give it to her?"

"No, and he won't until after the wedding or they'll know you came back. That's information he'll play close to his chest until Charity says, 'I will,' tomorrow."

Tomorrow! The word caused a jolt to his middle. He stood, tall and determined. "Charity won't be saying, 'I will,' to Daniel ever, if I have anything to say about it." He turned and counted out money onto the bar then strode past Emily toward the door.

Jerry called to him, but it didn't slow him down. Outside on the boardwalk, Jerry burst out of the saloon behind him, his voice frantic. "Buddy, wait up. Where do you think you're going?"

"I have a train to catch."

"Not tonight, you don't."

Something in the way he said it made Buddy stop and turn. Jerry ran into him. Emily and Nash weren't far behind.

"Why don't I?"

"We came in on the last run from Humble, that's why. There won't be another one out until tomorrow morning."

Buddy glanced around at their faces. When Emily nodded, he continued down the boardwalk with the three of them fast on his heels.

Jerry ran to catch up. "Slow up a mite, big fella. What do you aim to do?"

"I aim to hire me a horse and ride to Humble."

"Aw, Buddy! Now you have me wondering if sarsaparilla is all you've had to drink. Riding to Humble is a foolhardy idea. By the time you can get there, the whole town will be rolled up for the night."

He whipped around. "I have to see Charity."

"What for? To wake her up?"

"Then I'll go see Clark first and set him straight."

Nash's eyes widened. "No, suh. That'll just land you in irons."

"I don't care. I'll do what I need to if it'll stop that marriage."

Emily tugged on Buddy's shirt. "The wedding's not until noon tomorrow, if that helps."

Buddy knew she meant to comfort him, but the words caused

a band to tighten around his head. "Miss Dane, if you'll take a closer look at our situation, you'll realize that's not much time." He freed his shirtsleeve from her fingertips and hastened down the boardwalk.

The livery was shut up tight and padlocked when they arrived. Buddy grasped his head and moaned then pounded on the doors until the proprietor stepped out of a side entrance with a large key ring dangling from his hand.

"Sorry, folks. We're closed. You'll have to come back tomorrow."

Buddy hustled his direction with Jerry and Nash on his heels. "Sir, this won't take much of your time. I need a horse right away."

Emily crowded in between them. "He means four horses."

Keys jingling, the pale, scrawny man scratched his armpit. "Yep. You and half of Houston. I ain't got none available. Might have a couple in the morning though."

Buddy shifted his weight to peer between the cracks in the boards. "I can't wait that long. You must have something in there I could ride."

"Something *we* could ride," Emily corrected, bobbing and weaving beside him, trying to see inside the stable.

The liveryman sniffed, wiping his nose on the back of his hand. He regarded Emily as if trying to guess her weight. "I got one broken-down nag. She's along in years and swaybacked. Couldn't handle anyone heavier than this little gal here."

All eyes swung to Emily. Her throat worked up and down, but she took a bold step forward. "We'll take her."

Buddy held up his hand. "What good will that do?"

She frowned her opinion of his question. "I could ride ahead and tell Charity you're coming."

Nash chuckled. "That old mare gon' wind up riding you into town."

Jerry grinned. "We'll wave at you in the morning as our train passes you by."

Buddy steeled his jaw. "It's out of the question, Miss Dane. Too dangerous."

Nash sobered. "He's right, Miss Emmy. I cain't let you do it."

The liveryman finished locking the side door then leaned

against the wall. "Sure wish I could help."

"Thank you kindly, sir," Buddy said. "Maybe you still can. Do you know anyone who might be willing to sell me a horse? I'm willing to pay handsomely."

The old fellow's eyes lit. He pointed behind him. "Like I said, I got this mare—" After a glance at Buddy's scowl, he shrugged. "Sorry, mister."

"That's the best you can do?"

"Haven't you looked around? This town's gone mad since they struck oil in Humble. Makes a man wish he had a hundred horses. Even then, I don't guess I'd have any for you folks tonight."

Buddy had heard of men keeling over from grievous frustration. Thankfully, they were much older, or the rate of his heartbeat would concern him. He hit the wall with a balled-up fist, rattling the doors and arousing a muffled whinny from the lone horse inside. "Blast it! Now what?"

They all stared at him with startled faces. The liveryman took a broad step in the other direction.

Emily gripped his shoulder. "We'll think of something, Mr. Pierce."

Without waiting to hear what the pretty lady's *something* might be, Buddy tore off down the street.

Jerry rushed to get in front of him, walking backwards while he talked. "Listen, Buddy, the train pulls out at dawn tomorrow. You can rest tonight and still make it in plenty of time. That makes more sense than riding hard all night and arriving bushed. What do you say to that?"

Buddy slowed his stride, considering Jerry's suggestion. "I don't think so."

Emily nodded toward Jerry. "He's right, Mr. Pierce. Something could happen to you on the trail at night. You could be ambushed or your horse might break a leg. Then you'd never make it in time to save Charity."

He stopped walking. "That's the first thing anyone has said that makes sense."

"Besides," she continued, "you don't know what you'll be walking into when you get there. You'll want to be fresh and clear-minded."

Buddy's gaze traveled from Emily to Jerry then back to Emily. "None of it sits well with me, but it appears I have no choice."

Jerry slapped him on the back. "Now you're talking. Let's see the lady tucked in for the night and go get us some shut-eye."

Shut-eye was the last thing Buddy would get with every muscle twitching to get back to Charity. "I plan to be the first man on that train in the morning. You hear?"

Despite Jerry's smaller size and Buddy's dragging feet, Jerry hustled him down the boardwalk toward the hotel. Emily ran alongside, panting from the effort to keep up, and Nash lumbered along behind them. Inside, Buddy arranged rooms for the three of them and inquired about shelter for Nash.

At the door to Emily's room, she reached to touch Buddy's arm. "Mr. Pierce, you won't leave without me tomorrow, will you?"

Buddy met her haunting blue eyes. "I don't mind you stringing along, Miss Dane, but I won't wait for you. I suggest you arrive at the station on time if you plan on riding into Humble with me." He tipped his hat. "Good night now."

He left her staring after him and made his way down the hall to his room.

CHAPTER 26

A single moonbeam, slipping through a broken slat in the shade, bored behind Daniel's eyelids. He pitched and tossed on the wide bed, trying in vain to escape the pesky glow. Not that the amount of light in his room had changed. He'd lost his talent for sleeping through a hurricane. The air was heavy and hot, insufferably so, but he dozed at last, until sweat trickled past his ear, tickling him awake. Stirring, he cursed and punched the lumpy pillow into submission before flopping over onto his stomach.

Charity came to him then. She hovered over the bed and whispered through pouting red lips, so close her soft breath in his ear raised gooseflesh on his neck. He rolled onto his back and her long dark hair fell over him, caressing his face, his chest. He could smell her skin, taste her breath as she drew closer. Ecstatic, he reached to encircle her waist with his arms, convinced she was there.

His pounding heart jerked him awake and Charity was gone, her vivid presence replaced by deep loneliness, his faithful companion for much of the night.

Why had he excused himself and gone up to bed early? So far sleep had eluded him, and now, after the dream, there was no hope of rest.

He sat up on the side of the bed. When his bare toes hit the floor, it gave him a shock to realize the room he thought stifling hot was in fact quite nippy. Straining to reach it with his heel, he dragged a sock beneath his feet. Only his feet were cold. In the predawn chill, his stirring blood continued to warm his body and torture his mind.

He would have to get up. There was no help for it, though it made him frustrated and angry with himself. He needed sleep. The day that lay before him would be taxing enough with a rested body.

He had decided to tell his parents about the wedding, but only at the last minute on his way out the door. If they were willing to accept Charity, if they wanted to witness the marriage of their only son, they would be welcome to ride with him to the church. That prospect warmed his heart.

The other possibility scared him witless. His parents could very likely disown him today, shun him, and strip him of his inheritance. If so, it would be his mama's doing, but Papa would go along with her to keep the peace.

Daniel grimaced. If that's how things went, then blast them both! He didn't need them. He'd proven that. And Charity was worth it. He would lose anything to gain her. Why hadn't he realized that before? At any rate, he would face heaven and earth—worse, his mama's wrath—to take a stand for her today.

He shivered. Whether chilled by his thoughts or the icy floor he couldn't tell, but the cold had started to penetrate his body. He turned up the lamp in order to locate his other sock and smiled when he discovered he'd slept with it wadded among the covers. He reached for the one under his feet, pulled them both on, and then crossed the room to stand before the tall, mirrored wardrobe.

Peering closer, he rubbed his stubbled chin. "Funny, you don't look like a groom," he muttered to his rumpled reflection. "Look sharp, old boy. Today's your wedding day."

The words broke the spell. The bleak mood that had hovered through the night lifted, and Daniel had to laugh at the simpleton grinning at him from the mirror.

He would hurry and dress, then pack the rest of his clothes and hide them with the other belongings he'd stashed in the buckboard. After that, he would get started on his chores. It was too early yet to feed the stock, but there were things he could do, tasks done so many times he could manage them in the dark.

Stunned, Daniel realized it was the last time the responsibility would be his. Overseeing his father's property would fall to someone else tomorrow because Daniel would have chores of his own. From now on, the affairs of his house, his and Charity's, would occupy his time. The thought brought a thrill that shot right through him and roared in his ears.

He eased from his room, pausing to peer down the hall toward his parents' bedroom. No light shone from beneath the door and no sound came from within. He tiptoed past, mindful of the squeaky boards, and headed for the landing.

A hearty yawn watered his eyes as he descended the stairs, sleepy at last. Smiling, he shook it off. Too late now. Any rest he got would have to come later, after Charity became his bride.

"Come on, Miss Emmy, this ain't no Sunday stroll. You best hurry now or you gon' be chasing that train down the track."

"For pity's sake, Nash, I'm coming." Out of breath, Emmy strained to close the gap between them. "No one in God's creation can keep up with your gait, much less a body saddled with my short legs. I'm doing the best I can."

Despite the weight of both their bags, Nash breezed along ahead of her, still a good distance away until he stopped short to stare. "You best hush all that fussing and save your breath for running. That train's coming now. I can see it."

The sun glinted off a speck of metal in the distance, and a thin plume of smoke spiraled into the air. Emmy picked up her pace, turning her attention to the station platform. "Do you see Mr. Pierce and Mr. Ritter?"

"Not yet, I don't. Ain't likely to, neither, what with all these folks flocking around. I reckon we won't see them two men again 'til after we's boarded. Maybe not even 'til we get home."

Emmy's eyes lit on a rumpled head of brightly colored hair. "Oh, but you're wrong." She pointed toward the far edge of the platform. "There's Mr. Ritter now."

They pushed through to where the young man stood craning his neck at the crowd. When he saw them, he flushed with pleasure and waved frantically until they reached his side.

"Where's Buddy?" Emmy asked, only to hear her question parroted back. She stared up at him. "What do you mean where's Buddy? Isn't he with you?"

Mr. Ritter gaped at her, his face a picture of her own confusion. "I thought he was with you."

The first flicker of panic flashed in Emmy's chest. Heart racing, she studied the melee around them. "Well, he must be here somewhere."

Mr. Ritter shook his head. "I was one of the first men on the platform this morning. I've watched every person come and go since."

"You must be mistaken. He was so determined to catch this train."

The words were hardly free of her mouth when the big engine roared into the station, belching black smoke in rhythmic blasts. The mob surged toward it in one massive heave, bumping and jostling Emmy as they shoved past. She sought Buddy in the swirling sea of faces and then remembered Nash, who stood head and shoulders above the rest. She tugged at his sleeve. "Do you see him, Nash?"

"No, Miss Emmy. I don't see hide nor hair of Mistah Pierce."

"Oh, do look harder. He must be here. If he's not, then. . ."

"Something's wrong," Mr. Ritter finished for her. "Come on, let's go."

Emmy fell in behind the men as they raced down the near-empty boardwalk, headed for the hotel. Despite the early hour, Mr. Ritter paused to peer into the saloon. From what Emmy could see, there wasn't much going on in the shadows behind the swinging doors, and Buddy was nowhere in sight.

The long-legged rascals ran ahead of Emmy, leaving her trailing behind. Inside the shabby hotel lobby, she saw Mr. Ritter already on the stairs with Nash right behind him. She glanced at the clerk, prepared to hear him raise a fuss about Nash going upstairs, but some matter in the other direction held his attention. Emmy heaved a sigh of relief before raising the hem of her skirt and barreling after the two men. She caught up with them just outside Buddy's room.

"Why did you leave without him in the first place?" she demanded of Mr. Ritter, who stood pounding with the palm of his hand.

He gave another hard whack. "I knocked this morning, but he didn't answer. I figured he left without me."

"You really believed he wouldn't wait for you?"

Mr. Ritter glanced over his shoulder. "You heard him last night, same as I did. He wasn't planning to wait for nobody."

Nash doubled his massive fist and hit the door several times, so hard the frame rattled, then pressed his ear against the polished wood. Stepping back, he shook his head. "He ain't in this room, that's for sure. We could've raised the dead with all this ruckus."

Several occupants along the hall stuck out their heads and glared their way. Nash jumped behind Emmy and Mr. Ritter in a feeble attempt to hide his bulk. "We best get on out of here," he whispered. " 'Fore we winds up in a mess."

Emmy shook her head and rattled the doorknob. "I won't leave without Buddy. He's the reason we came. Help me get this open."

Mr. Ritter placed his hand over hers on the knob. Compassion had softened his gentle eyes. "Buddy's not here, ma'am. Come along now. Maybe he's made it to the station by now."

Nash shook his head. "If'n he did finally make it to the station, we'll never know it. He'll be somewhere on that big old train."

Emmy spun around to face him. "And we won't know whether to board or not!" She moaned, pressing her knuckles to her throbbing temples. "Oh my goodness, we're just too addlepated for words. One of us should've waited on the platform. Now what are we going to do?"

She cast around in her mind for a solution. There had to be something sensible. If she could just get one moment to catch her breath, she knew it would come to her. Trouble was, they were fresh out of moments. That train wouldn't wait.

Jerry started for the stairs, waving them on with his hand. "Let's go," he called. "There's nothing more to do here."

With some reluctance, Emmy moved to follow. Just as she gave in and turned away, just as her hand released the knob, she heard a sound from inside. It was a man's voice, weak and faint, yet desperate in tone. She whirled toward the stairs. "Mr. Ritter, come back! He's in there. Buddy's in this room."

Jerry stopped and stared at her. He hooked his long thumbs in the waistband of his trousers and let his shoulders slouch in defeat. "Ma'am, I understand your frustration–I really do. But I'm growing a mite impatient with you now."

Emmy stomped her foot. "I tell you he's in there and he's in trouble. Get over here right now. Both of you."

Like boys responding to their mama's no-nonsense voice, the men dashed to her side and pressed their ears to the door.

"You right, Miss Emmy," Nash whispered. "Somebody's in there."

Jerry nodded. "I hear it, too." He stood up and rapped hard twice, then placed his mouth next to the jamb. "Buddy, is that you? Open up."

Emmy felt her panic growing. "Nash, you're going to have to break it down."

Always ready to oblige, Nash backed up and prepared to charge. Before he could make his move, Jerry lunged in front of him.

"Now just hold on there. We can get inside without leveling the wall. I can't afford to replace it. You two wait here and don't move. I'm going after a key." He wagged a finger at Nash as he jogged by. "Don't get any more ideas about busting down doors."

Emmy pressed her face to the inlaid panel. "Hang on, Mr. Pierce. We're here to help you. Mr. Ritter's bringing the key."

She heard a loud groan in answer and thought to have Nash proceed with the original plan, but Mr. Ritter appeared at the top of the landing with a brass key dangling from his hand. He ran the last few steps toward them, and Emmy backed out of his way.

"I'm here, Buddy. Hang on," he called as he worked the key in the lock.

When the door swung open, the three of them burst inside the room. An unbearable stench met them first, and Emmy covered her nose with her sleeve. Buddy sprawled across the mattress, on top of the covers, dressed in the same clothes he'd worn the day before.

"What in the world? Why, he's not even made it to bed properly." Mr. Ritter approached his friend and peered down. "What's up, old man? What happened to you?"

Buddy's eyes were bloodshot and glazed, his face the same shade of green as the blanket on which he lay. Nash nodded at the gruesome washbasin on the floor beside the bed and backed toward the exit. "He sick, that's what. Powerful sick. Something done turned his stomach inside out."

Tears flooded Emmy's eyes. How could Buddy be sick? He was the one person in the world with any hope of saving Charity, but he had to be in Humble to do it.

Buddy raised a trembling hand toward Jerry. "Get me to the station," he whispered.

Jerry shook his head. "Sorry, my friend. You're in no condition for a train ride. You've taken ill."

He motioned Jerry closer. "Not ill. Just a little weak in my gut. Too much sarsaparilla on an empty stomach."

Jerry stared hard at him then doubled over and roared with laughter. "Are you telling me you got this way from drinking sarsaparilla?" He hooted and slapped his leg. "I never met a feller who couldn't hold his sarsaparilla before. Maybe you should've stuck with whiskey."

Grabbing the front of Jerry's shirt, Buddy pulled him down against his chest and ground out a threat. "Ritter, you'd best get me down to that station right now, or I'll. . ." He fell against his pillow, too weak to finish.

Jerry paled. Whether from Buddy's anger or his foul breath, Emmy couldn't tell, but the man had his attention.

"Have you lost your senses?" he wailed. "How am I supposed to get you anywhere when you can't even stand up?"

"Carry me," Buddy gasped. "Hog-tie me with a rope and drag me–I don't care. Do what you have to do to get me on that train."

Backing out of Buddy's reach, Jerry crossed his arms. "I won't do it. You're far too sick to be moved."

Buddy lunged at him. "Get me on that train, Jerry! I tell you I can make it."

"No, sir. I'm sorry. You can't."

"Oh yes, he can!"

Buddy's determination had lit a fire in Emmy. She pushed Jerry out of the way. "Nash, come over here and help Mr. Pierce out of this bed. Hurry. This man has a train to catch."

CHAPTER 27

Bertha lay in Magda's big bed with the covers pulled up to her chin. Awake for hours, she'd heard the creak of every settling board and the hoot of every barn owl. She was also privy to the snores, snorts, and sleepy ramblings coming from her roommate. Not to mention that Magda's every toss and turn wrought a symphony of rattles and groans from the makeshift bed in the corner.

Thankfully, Magda stirred at last and eased out of bed. Bertha knew she should be up, too, and already down in the kitchen with a good start on breakfast, but she couldn't convince her body to move.

When Magda tiptoed past for the third time, Bertha rolled onto her side and cleared her throat. "I ain't asleep, you know. You can stop all that creeping about and light the lamp."

In the dim room, Magda leaned to look at her from behind the wardrobe door. "Did I wake you, sugar? I tried real hard to be quiet."

Bertha propped up on one elbow. "I hate to hear that, because you made enough noise to wake Rebel clear out in the barn. You never could tread softly worth a hoot."

Magda came over and sat on the bed beside her. "I know. That's why I was leaving the room." She reached to touch Bertha's forehead. "Are you feeling all right? You never sleep this late."

Bertha took Magda's cool hand and held it to her cheek. "No,

I ain't feeling one bit all right."

"Are you taking sick?"

She nodded. "Heartsick, I guess."

Magda patted her face. "I know, sweetie."

"Charity's run out of time."

"I know," Magda cooed.

"I'm her mama. I should be able to save her, but I'm not smart enough. I don't know how to help her out of this one."

Magda squared around on the bed and faced her. "Maybe you're not supposed to. Did you ever consider that? Maybe Daniel's the man God intended for Charity all along. Remember, she wanted to marry him once and with your blessing. The thing that turned you against Daniel is his jilting her, which he's trying to make amends for."

Bertha sat up and shook her head. "I don't know, Magda. There's something about that boy that ain't quite right. I always sensed it."

Magda gave her a piercing look. "Is this one of those *feelings* you get?"

She crossed her arms. "Don't you go discounting my feelings again. They've served me well over the years. I believe they're from God." She jabbed Magda in the arm with her finger. "Anyway, look who's talking. It was you who said he weren't good for nothing but telling lies and shaming young girls."

Magda nodded. "He did those things and that's a fact—but, honey, people make mistakes. I do things every day that I regret. If Daniel really loves Charity, don't you think he deserves another chance?"

Bertha took Magda by the shoulders and stared into her eyes. "Let me ask you this: If Daniel really loves my girl, how could he hurt her by tossing her aside like trash in front of the whole town? If he respects her, why did he spread lies about her virtue?"

Magda shook her head.

"Thad never would've done that to me. Willem couldn't have treated you so shamefully either, and you know it. On my wedding day, I had no doubt Thad loved me, even cherished me. I want the same for my little girl."

Magda nodded. "I remember your wedding day like it happened yesterday. You were a beautiful bride. Thad was so proud." She got a faraway look in her eyes. "Honey, the way that man looked at you—" Picking up Bertha's hands, she squeezed them hard. "Oh, Bert, you're right. If we let Charity marry Daniel, it could ruin her life. What're we going to do?"

Bertha set her jaw. "I don't know just yet. One thing's for sure—we need to pray like we've never done before."

Charity came awake with a gasp. Her wide eyes sought something to ground her, to still her pounding heart. Recognition came slowly, one familiar sight at a time. First, the broad water stain on the ceiling in the shape of a woman's boot—or the country of Italy, depending on how you looked at it. Just below the boot were the tall spires of a four-poster bed with a backdrop of bright yellow wallpaper. Her eyes quickly swept the other furnishings, and she released her breath. She had awakened in the Danes' guestroom, in a bed as familiar as her own. Mother Dane and Mama were just down the hall.

So why did she feel so lost?

She moved to sit up and realized Papa's Bible lay open across her chest. It came to her then in a rush, as the rising sun flooded the room. Her gaze jerked to the window. It looked like a beautiful morning, hardly a fitting start for the darkest day of her life.

When that same sun rises tomorrow, I'll be married to Daniel Clark. Daniel. Not Buddy.

The thought of it crushed her, and she regretted waking. Rolling onto her side, she fought to return to unconscious oblivion, but sleep eluded her. The light was too bright, the truth too harsh to shut out. It didn't help that her wedding dress hung on a peg near the window, mocking her.

The day before she had clutched the dress to her face and asked God for help. The words of her prayer came back, and she whispered them aloud. "I've never asked You for anything this important before. Can You? Will You?"

He could, of course: God could do anything. It would be a small matter for Him, a tiny miracle in the great scheme of things. The problem was, He hadn't. For whatever reason, it appeared

God wanted her to marry Daniel.

Disturbed by the thought, she picked up Papa's Bible and sat upright in bed. Crossing her legs to cradle the worn book, she let it fall open in her lap. Then she closed her eyes and pressed her index finger to the page. Feeling foolish, yet afraid of what she might see, she opened her eyes and looked.

"Greater love hath no man than this, that a man lay down his life for his friends."

Her heart pounded. Was that the answer? Did God expect her to lay down her life, her future happiness, for her mama? Could she do it? Could she give up her dreams for love and contentment and never grow to resent it?

If God had truly called her to such an unselfish act, He would have to help her. It seemed beyond human strength, no task for mortal flesh. What sort of love was that anyway? And what was the source?

She remembered the passage in Corinthians from which Mama had taken her name. "Charity" in that text meant "love." Mama always said love was the only fitting name for a child born to her and Papa.

Charity knew the verses by heart. She'd heard them often enough. Still, she thumbed her way to the scripture.

"Charity suffereth long. . ."

Well, that part rang true. She had suffered every day since Emmy fled the church with Daniel.

"And is kind. . ."

She had tried to be.

"Charity envieth not; charity vaunteth not itself, is not puffed up, doth not behave itself unseemly. . ."

These might require more diligence on her part.

"Seeketh not her own. . ."

That part felt like divine direction, but she didn't like it much. She read on.

"Beareth all things, believeth all things, hopeth all things, endureth all things. Charity never faileth."

The last part gave her pause. Love never fails. That's what it really said.

She felt as if God had tossed her question back at her. "Can you? Will you?"

Charity closed the book, careful to tuck back all the mementos Mama kept inside. Scraps of paper, clippings and lists, pressed magnolia blossoms, and little notes from Papa, yellowed with age, were scattered throughout his Bible.

She wriggled one of the notes from between the delicate pages and smiled. Papa preferred lead to ink for writing and carried a pencil with him always. He once read that George Washington used a three-inch pencil when he surveyed the Ohio Territory in 1762 and that Thomas Edison kept one in his vest pocket to jot down notes. "Sugar," he liked to say, "what's good enough for George and Tom is plenty good for old Thad."

She held the page closer to the window and strained to read the faded words, barely visible now. She could make out only, "Love always, Thad," scratched at the end.

The words burned in her heart. Despite the fix they were in, despite evidence that Papa had caused it, she knew how much he had loved them. She knew he would sacrifice his happiness for Mama without a backward glance.

Charity fell against the bed and stared at the ceiling. The written words of both her earthly father and her heavenly Father conveyed the same message—a lesson on love—and she would do her best to listen.

Mother Dane and Mama were stirring down the hall.

Charity swung her legs over the side of the bed and stood up. It was high time to get started, to quit stewing over things she couldn't change. It was her wedding day.

CHAPTER 28

The whistle blew, followed by a shout for all to board. Emmy's body tensed, and she picked up the pace, ears strained for the chug of the engine or the screech of turning wheels. She couldn't see the platform for the row of buildings yet to pass, but she knew they were out of time.

She whirled to check the progress of her companions. The three struggled along several yards back, poor white-faced Buddy Pierce held up between Nash and a panting Jerry Ritter.

"Do hurry," she shouted. "The train is leaving."

"We is hurrying, Miss Emmy. It ain't easy toting a grown man, and this one is a mite overgrowed."

Emmy found it hard to feel compassion while saddled with a burden of her own. Thankfully, Nash had stowed Buddy's bag under his free arm, but the task of toting her own luggage and that of Mr. Ritter had fallen to her. Unaccustomed to carrying so much weight, she had to stop and shift the load a bit to ease her aching fingers. "Oh pooh. You could carry two more like him and you know it. Stop your bellyaching and come on."

They rounded the corner of the last building together. Emmy sighted her mark, an open passenger car, and bore down on it just as the car began to move. The bespectacled conductor leaned halfway out of the door and watched her.

"Wait, sir!" she called to him. "Stop the train."

The man shook his head. "Sorry, little lady. Can't do that."

"Oh please, you must!"

Emmy dropped the bags and ran. The man's mouth was moving, but the churning wheels carried him away too quickly for her to hear. She gathered her skirts and ran faster. Nash shouted something, but she couldn't make out his words either over the roar in her ears.

"Come on!" she screamed back at them. "Pick up your feet. We can still make it."

Nash caught up with her then, lifting her away just as the last car rumbled by shaking the ground at their feet. He carried her some distance from the tracks and set her down hard on the platform.

"Miss Emmy, that was the most foolhardy thing I ever seen. Is you trying to get killed?"

Emmy turned toward Jerry, who stood pale as death staring her way, and Buddy, who sprawled in the dust where Nash had dropped him.

"I'm sorry, I. . ."

"You what?" Nash shouted. "A lunatic? Yes, you is. Now get over there away from these tracks."

Without waiting to see if she complied, Nash headed for the scattered luggage. He retrieved the bags in short angry jerks, all the while rolling his eyes and muttering dark curses under his breath.

Emmy trudged to where Jerry stood and looked down at Buddy. "I'm very sorry, Mr. Pierce. Are you all right?"

Squinting against the rising sun, he peered up at her. "I reckon I will be. If I live."

She glanced over her shoulder at the silver speck wending its way in the distance. "We missed it. Now what?"

Jerry pivoted toward the depot. "When's the next one?"

She shrugged. "I don't know. They're never on time."

"Forget going by rail." Weakness strained Buddy's voice. Or maybe desperation. "The Rabbit is slower than cold honey. We'd never make Humble by noon."

Jerry nodded. "Makes you wonder why folks gave it that name."

Emmy laughed. "Certainly not because of its speed. The old-timers claim she used to make unscheduled stops along the tracks so passengers could shoot jackrabbits. Most believe she earned the name by how she jerks and hops."

Straightening his elbow, Buddy propped himself higher. "Thank you for the timely history lesson, Miss Dane."

She curled her top lip at him.

"Either way the train's out. I'm telling you, we need to hire some horses."

"You can barely sit upright. How would you ride clear to Humble?"

"I'll find a way, Jerry. I have to."

Nash returned and handed the bags to Emmy, all of them this time, then helped Jerry lift Buddy off the ground. "Let's get this poor ailing man a place to sit. After that we can figure what we gon' do."

They found a bench against the outer wall of the depot and lowered Buddy onto the paint-chipped slats. A more natural shade had replaced his alternating green and sickly white pallor.

Emmy hoped it was a good sign. "Mr. Ritter, I think a bite to eat would benefit your friend greatly. Why don't you go see what you can find for him while we try to solve this problem?"

A grin eased the worried frown from Jerry's face. He patted his stomach. "I could use a bite myself, ma'am. How about you?"

At the mention of food, Emmy realized she was famished. "I wouldn't mind it a bit." She nodded toward Nash. "Him, too. We took no time for breakfast."

Jerry nodded. "I'll fetch us all something, then."

Seated between them on the bench, Buddy's glare followed Jerry and then Emmy. "Hold up. Have you two forgotten why we're here? Charity's clock is ticking. We don't have time for a family picnic."

Emmy patted his shoulder. "Mr. Pierce, I'm anxious, too. But it won't take long to eat, and we'll gain strength for the journey."

Buddy scowled. "A journey that needs to get started." He yanked a small pouch from his vest pocket, pulled out money, and handed it to Jerry. "Get jerky and hardtack, and any other food we can eat on the road." He pointed at something behind them. "When you get back, you can hustle over there and get me a horse."

The livery stable perched directly across the tracks. The towering building with its wide facade looked different by morning light. The grounds teemed with animals and people, from the holding pens on each side of the slung-back doors to the trampled areas in front. By the look of it, the liveryman did all right by himself, and the railroad company wasn't the only venture in town to profit from the boom.

A wagon rumbled over the tracks beside them, the driver sharply reining his two-horse team into the muddy yard.

Emmy gripped Buddy's arm. "I have a better idea."

Buddy waved Jerry away to buy the food while his gaze remained fixed on her face. "I'm listening."

Emmy pointed at another passing rig. "What about one of those?"

"You want to buy a wagon?"

"Not buy. Hire. That way, you can rest in back until you're feeling better."

Nash rubbed his dark chin and nodded at Buddy. "That may not be a bad idea, Mistah Pierce."

Buddy's brow furrowed. "Good thinking. If they don't have a rig for hire, we can book passage on one bound for Humble. I'll pay the asking price to anyone who can get me there before noon."

Emmy stared down the boardwalk in the direction Jerry had gone, shading her eyes to see better. "Then it's settled. When Mr. Ritter comes back, he can make inquiries."

Buddy shook his head. "I say the two of you go now. I get the feeling you're just as capable, and there's no time to waste."

Emmy searched his earnest green eyes. "But you'll be left on your own."

"I'll be fine. Besides, Jerry will be back soon." He didn't give her time to argue but shooed her and Nash with a backward wave of his hand. "Go on now, and hurry."

Though reluctant to leave him alone, Emmy opened her parasol and motioned for Nash to lead the way. "You heard the man. Let's find us a ride home."

Nash led her past the depot and along the boardwalk to a well-traveled crossing. Her determination faded a bit as they approached the front of the livery. Up close, they found it even busier than it appeared from the station. Wagons of every size and description boiled out of the stables and onto the rutted road, some passing far too close to suit her.

It didn't take long to learn there were no rigs left for hire. Together they walked the grounds, asking questions and checking wagons. The majority of travelers headed for Humble seemed more than willing to help, but their conveyances were too full to accommodate a traveling band sitting upright, much less a man the size of Buddy lying flat of his back.

Fighting the urge to wring her hands, she looked up at Nash. "What do we do now?"

Nash drew a deep breath that lifted and filled his broad chest. "We don't give up, that's what we do." He cut his eyes down at her. "Don't fret now. We'll find something."

"You saw for yourself. Not one of these people has room for us." Emmy bit back tears and tried to still the tremor in her voice. "It can't be God's will for Charity to spend her life with someone like Daniel. Why are we having such a hard time trying to save her?"

Nash's roaming gaze came to rest on her face. "Whoa, now." His rumbling voice was a gentle rebuke. "Is that what we doing here? Saving Miss Charity? If so, you can count me out. I ain't fit to save myself, much less Miss Charity. Child, that be God's business."

Something behind her caught and held his attention. A smile lit his eyes. "And the Almighty might jus' have a little trick up His sleeve."

She followed his pointing finger in time to see a stocky young man toss a faded satchel into the bed of an otherwise empty wagon. He walked to the rear and closed the tailgate, then hurried around to help a tall, gray-haired woman onto the seat.

Emmy let out her breath in a rush and clutched his shirt. "What if they're not going to Humble?"

"Ain't but one way to find out."

"You're right. Let's go ask them."

She started forward, but Nash caught hold of her arm. "Where you going?"

"To negotiate a ride, of course."

"No, you ain't. You staying over here. Them's my people, Miss Emmy. We stand a much better chance if you let me do the talking."

"That's ridiculous."

"No, missy, it ain't. You jus' stay put this time. I'll be back directly."

In a casual, unhurried stride, Nash approached the wagon with his hat in his hands. The kind-faced woman smiled and nodded a greeting. The young man beamed and quickly extended his hand. Nash talked with low tones and quick gestures, lifting his chin toward the wagon and jabbing his finger back toward her. Emmy saw the man's wide grin fade just before he cast a frown her way. Nash stayed a few seconds more then turned and hurried across the yard.

"What'd they say?" Eager to know, she called out the question while Nash was yet halfway back.

He waited to answer until he reached her side. "Them be good folks, Miss Emmy. They headed for Humble, all right, and the boy, he say we can ride. Don't want no money for it neither. Only. . ."

Her excitement had soared higher with every word until the last. Something in the way he said it foretold bad news. "Only what? Speak up, Nash."

He cleared his throat and looked away. "He say he ain't about to put his old mama in the back of that wagon, not for you or nobody else. Not for no amount of money."

Emmy looked across to where the two strangers huddled close together. It appeared the woman gently scolded. The boy answered with a firm shake of his head before he jumped from the seat and walked away.

Emmy blinked up at Nash. "Of course he won't put her in back. Why, I don't blame him. Tell him we accept his terms, only we will indeed pay them for their trouble. Mr. Pierce said so."

"But, Miss Emmy. . ."

"Go ahead, tell them."

"Well, but. . ."

"What now?"

He pointed behind him. "That there rig ain't but a one-seater, which puts you riding in back." He lifted both dark brows. "With all us men."

Emmy saw his point. She had to swallow before she could answer but tried hard to sound nonchalant. "So?"

"So it won't look proper. 'Sides that, it's a long, bumpy ride, and that bed ain't made for comfort. Yo' mama gon' skin me good if'n I haul you through Humble throwed off in the bottom of a wagon like a sack of potatoes." He took a quick look over his shoulder and leaned closer. "Worse yet, whatever they been hauling in that thing be long past burying."

Emmy tried not to pause, tried not to ask. "Are you saying there's a bad smell?"

Nash shook his curly head. "You gon' wish it jus' bad. Truth is, that smell done took a turn toward evil." His expression was guarded, watchful.

She made up her mind. "It doesn't matter. What's a little odor to contend with for Charity's sake? You tell them yes. I'll let Buddy and Jerry know we have our ride."

Emmy turned to go. Nash reached to stay her, and she looked back at him with questioning eyes. The way he squinted down at her made her insides pitch. She glanced away. "What is it, Nash? Why are you peering a hole through me?"

"I'm wondering what done changed you, that's all."

She forced a laugh. "Don't be silly. I'm no different."

His hand on her elbow held her fast, but his voice was kind. "Yes'm, you different. Nothing I can point a finger to, but I see change all over you."

"Don't talk foolish."

"Ain't nothing foolish. Don't forget I've known you quite a spell. I watched you learn to toddle. In all this time, I ain't never seen you cross the road to help nobody, much less be willing to wallow in stink. Don't tell me you ain't different."

She met his stare, trying to maintain a steady gaze. "I don't know what you're talking about."

He laughed and wagged his head. "You can't fool old Nash that easy. You know jus' what I'm talking about. Them big blue eyes telling on you."

Emmy flinched and could've pinched herself for it. She pulled free and stalked away. "I know this—we don't have time to discuss it. Get on over there and tell those folks to wait for us. Inform them we'll be back with two more passengers. Then hightail it back to the depot so you can help with Mr. Pierce."

Five minutes later, Jerry Ritter, the young stranger, and Nash—mostly Nash—had Buddy loaded into the bed of the wagon. They propped him against the dilapidated tailgate of the old freighter, the wood so battered by time and pocked by beetles that Emmy feared he'd wind up riddled with splinters.

It seemed a fitting backdrop for a man so broken and battered himself. Too weak to sit up, Buddy sprawled over most of the rear, crowding Jerry into the far corner. Emmy perched at Buddy's feet on a cushion of feed sacks Nash had gathered for her, and Nash sat by her side.

Buddy insisted he felt some better, yet his green pallor had returned. Emmy wondered if she ought not secure a bucket for him, but thought better of it when she considered their traveling companions. She hadn't missed the look that passed between them when they learned Buddy was ill. In lieu of offering him a bucket in case his stomach resisted the jerky he had eaten, Emmy sent up a quick prayer that Buddy wouldn't need it, then cringed and prayed harder when she remembered Nash had predicted a long, bumpy ride.

CHAPTER 29

The odor Nash warned of rose like a specter from the wagon bed, becoming unbearable when the wind died down. Emmy began to lose faith in her prayer, convinced even divine intervention couldn't lessen the effect of that powerful stench on a sour stomach.

She leaned toward Buddy and stared. "Are you all right, Mr. Pierce?" Though she whispered, the woman riding up front glanced back with a troubled expression.

Buddy nodded grimly without opening his eyes. "I'll be fine."

The tremor in his voice belied his confident answer. Emmy settled down and prepared for a difficult ride.

Nash had introduced the young man as Benjamin, the woman as Miss Lucille. They seemed to be decent people, especially the mother, though her son rode stiffly on the seat and said little. Emmy wondered if he felt uncomfortable about his decision to put her in the rear.

While the right thing to do for Miss Lucille's sake, it took courage on Benjamin's part, especially when the locals stopped to glare as they made their way down the street. Emmy made a point to smile and wave as she passed. It served to take the edge off their collective indignation, but only a bit, and no one in the wagon relaxed until they were well out of town.

Emmy heard Miss Lucille let go of a deep sigh. Nash, too, exhaled loudly and grinned, and Jerry's good-natured smile returned.

Nash sat up straighter and broke the silence. "Whoo-ee! We going home, and I sure is glad. I seen the big city now and don't care much for it. Ain't no fit way to live, all that coming and going and everybody a stranger. I expect old Nash gon' stay put from now on."

He tilted his chin and looked up at Benjamin. "Son, you folks from around here?"

"No, suh," Benjamin answered without looking back.

Miss Lucille turned in the seat, her lovely face set in a serene smile. "We come to Houston by way of Louisiana, Mr. Nash. After Benjamin's papa, God rest him, went to be with the Lord."

Nash lifted his battered hat. "Sure sorry, ma'am."

She bit her bottom lip and nodded. "He's in a better place now, but thank you kindly. So anyways, when Benjamin heard them oil companies was hiring folks in Texas, he figured they'd be plenty of work for a man with a strong back." She patted her son's shoulder. "My Benny here is one of the strongest men around."

Emmy considered the empty wagon bed. "Where are your belongings, Miss Lucille?"

Nash cleared his throat and pressed his elbow against Emmy's ribs.

Miss Lucille gave him a tender glance. "That's all right, Mr. Nash. I don't mind."

When her dark eyes returned to Emmy, humiliation swam in their brown depths. Emmy felt like she'd been caught in the woman's underwear drawer. "Sorry, ma'am."

"Don't fret, child. You meant no harm. The truth is, we own the clothes on our backs, a few things in that bag under the seat, and little else. Took selling everything we had to buy us this wagon. Benny got a good deal on it, though, down at the stockyards."

Emmy and Nash exchanged knowing looks. Miss Lucille smiled and pulled a square of cloth from her waistband, handing it back to Emmy. "Here, baby. Hold this against your nose; it'll help some. It's what I do when there ain't no breeze to take the edge off." She laughed. "You wouldn't think so, but you get used to it after a while."

Emmy reached for the cloth, handing it down to Buddy instead. "Thank you, ma'am, but if you don't mind, I think he needs it more."

Buddy took the tattered fabric from Emmy's hand then nodded weakly toward the flask strapped to Nash's side. "You think I could have a sip of that water?"

Nash bent to hand it over. "Why sure, Mistah Pierce. Help yourself."

Buddy pushed himself to a sitting position. He drank deeply, wiping his mouth with the cloth when he was done. Passing the flask to Nash, he took in his surroundings as if aware of them for the first time. "What time you reckon it is?"

Nash dipped his head at the sun, still low in the sky. "It's early yet."

Buddy nodded. "I think we'll make it in plenty of time, don't you?"

"Don't know about plenty, but yes, suh, we gon' make it."

Buddy took one more look around, then pressed the rag to his face and hunkered down. The motion of the wagon soon lulled him to sleep. Whether from the cloth, the water, or fervent prayers on his behalf, Buddy did look some better. The color had returned to his face, and he looked peaceful at rest. Beside him Jerry dozed sitting upright, while his head lolled about in a comical fashion.

Emmy felt herself drifting off as well, until Miss Lucille began to hum a haunting melody. Her lovely warble didn't startle Emmy awake but rather the familiar hymn. She'd heard it many times, and not just at Sunday service. Aunt Bert, Charity, even Mama sang it often, though never with the depth of emotion she heard in Miss Lucille's rich voice.

Nash closed his eyes, nodding slowly up and down, and then leaned his head against the seat and took up the words.

" 'Amazing grace, how sweet the sound that saved a wretch like me.' "

His deep baritone rumbled in Emmy's chest, sending a chill through her body and raising the hairs at the nape of her neck. Miss Lucille harmonized with Nash in a high, clear voice, and even Benjamin joined in. Their blended voices became an angel chorus as their song swelled about her.

" 'I once was lost, but now am found, was blind, but now I see.' "

Emmy had never paid any mind to the lyrics before, despite the many times she'd heard them. She closed her eyes and listened, attuned to them for the first time. They rolled over her like the warm, salty surf on a Galveston beach, each wave heavy with import just for her, each word filled with meaning, like a precious gift discovered. They filled her with peace and an unfamiliar emotion that lifted and thrilled her in ways her trysts with Daniel never had. She raised her face to the sun, surrendering the whole of her being to the overwhelming feeling, allowing it to carry her away.

"Miss Emmy?"

She opened one eye. Nash stared down at her, and she smiled at his worried frown. Still warmed by the joy bubbling inside, she leaned toward him and lowered her voice to a whisper. "Do you believe in God?"

His eyes widened. "You know I do."

"No, I mean really believe that God exists. That He's not just something to say grace to or an excuse to pass the offering plate. Do you think He's actually out there somewhere. . .listening when we talk?"

Nash sat up straight and narrowed his eyes. "Girl, what's got you pondering such things? It ain't like you."

"Because I believe it, Nash. I really do." She cut her eyes up at him. "Don't you dare laugh."

He shook his head. "I ain't doing no laughing."

Benjamin and Miss Lucille still crooned just over Emmy's head. They had switched to a spiritual, singing now about crossing the Jordan, the two of them oblivious to anything else.

Emmy glanced to see if Buddy and Jerry were still asleep then scooted closer to Nash and lowered her voice even more. "Do you remember the day I crawled out the window in my nightdress?"

Nash rolled his eyes toward heaven. "How am I gon' forget that day?"

She placed a finger to his lips to shush him. Shifting around in front of him, she continued. "Something happened to me out there in those woods. Something so bad I wanted to die from the hurt and shame."

Suspicion erased the grin from Nash's face. "That Clark boy spoiled you, didn't he? Jus' like I figured." Murderous rage seethed in his eyes.

"No! Not that way. And keep your voice down." After a quick look around, she continued. "What Daniel did, he did to my heart, to my soul." The bitter taste of his name drained the joyful warmth from her heart.

"He spoiled me, all right, but with cruel words and callous indifference. The worst part is, I helped him do it. When I realized how he tricked me, used me, I was so ashamed. I hid out in the brush and prayed for the ground to swallow me whole and a fat oak tree to fall in behind me. I never wanted to draw another breath."

Nash averted his eyes. "You ain't got to tell me none of this."

"Yes, I do. Daniel made it look like I chased him, wooed him away from Charity. I promise you on Mama's life it was the other way around. Everywhere I turned, he was there. He made sport of it. He'd catch Charity not looking and wink at me or sidle up and whisper things he shouldn't. Once he caught me alone in the kitchen and kissed me full on the mouth. He worked me that way for weeks, until he had the blood boiling in my veins."

Nash frowned and shook his finger in her face. "Hush now. You don't s'posed be saying such things."

"It's just the truth. Everyone blamed me–Mama, Charity, Aunt Bert. Even Daniel acted like he never said he loved me. Oh, Nash, I hated him so!"

Nash shifted his gaze to something over her shoulder. He grimaced and his brows shot up. "You want to be lowering your voice. You got all these folks watching you."

Emmy realized with a start that Benjamin and Miss Lucille had stopped singing and were staring over their shoulders at her. She whirled to find Buddy raised up on one elbow and Jerry watching, bleary-eyed and openmouthed.

"Go ahead and look, all of you!" she shouted at their blurring faces. "See if I care. I've been gawked at all my life."

Buddy closed his eyes and settled down. Jerry cleared his throat and turned over.

Emmy burst into tears, and Nash drew her to his shoulder. She hid her face against the rough fabric of his shirt until Benjamin and Miss Lucille returned to their song. When she finally dared to peek, Buddy slept again and Jerry, his eyes squirming and lashes fluttering, pretended to.

Unable to rest until she knew Nash understood, she peered up at him. "I didn't want to die because of what Daniel did to me," she whispered. "It was because I saw the darkness of my own heart. Charity, who knew me best, somehow loved me most, yet I betrayed her. I shamed my folks and hurt my aunt Bert." She swiped her nose with the side of her hand. "Even you, Nash. I've treated you just awful."

Emmy watched his face for a reaction, any sign of ridicule. Instead, he pulled a discolored hankie from his pocket and pressed it into her hand, then waited for her to continue.

"I never wanted to listen when you all talked to me about sin. It made me feel funny inside, so I closed my ears to it. But that day I saw myself as a sinner. I talked to God for the first time in my life, and He heard me. I know it, because afterwards I didn't hurt so bad and I didn't want to die anymore." She shook her head. "Oh, I'm making a mess of telling this." She gripped his hand. "Something happened to me out in that thicket. Something real."

Nash sat taller and grinned all over. If he'd been a dog, his tail would've been wagging.

She wanted to stop and ask what he found so funny, but her words spilled out too fast. "When I got to the house, I was so blind-afraid of Mama, I put it out of my mind, but when I woke up the next morning, I felt different. About Daniel, about myself, about everything.

"And here's the strangest part," she said, poking his arm for emphasis. "A lie don't set easy with me at all now. When we told Mama I was in the barn with Rebel instead of in the woods, I barely got the words past my lips."

He laughed then, and she grinned along with him but quickly sobered. "The thing I did to Charity pressed me so hard I knew I had to see her, to beg her forgiveness. That's where I was headed the morning I ran into Daniel in town, and. . .well, you know the rest."

Nash still beamed. "That explains what's so different about you." He snapped his fingers. "I knowed it had to be something."

Annoyance tickled her brow. "I'm glad you understand it. Now explain it to me."

"Don't you see, child? You found religion. The real kind."

The simple words sounded so important. So final.

"I found what?"

"You found Jesus, Miss Emmy."

She shook her head a bit to let the words sink in. "I did? Are you sure?"

Nash laughed. "I reckon the truth is, you got still long enough for Him to find you."

Emmy fell against the splintered board behind the seat, her attention glued to his face. "If what you say is true, what does it mean?"

"It means God always gon' be your heavenly Father."

Papa's stern face came to mind, and Emmy had trouble imagining how that could be a good thing.

Nash tried again. "It means you been accepted into the family of God, and you gon' go live in heaven someday."

Heaven. That mysterious, illusive place Mama swore Emmy would never see if she didn't mend her ways. The prospect of missing it hadn't bothered her one fig. Mending her ways to live in a place she'd never understood required too much energy on her part, and she'd long ago abandoned all hope of ever seeing it. "What if I don't want to go? Why do I need to live somewhere else? If God really cares to make Emily Dane happy, he can let me live on in Humble, Texas, for all eternity."

Nash fell back and roared with laughter.

Emmy feigned a stern look but giggled despite herself. "Now look what you've gone and done. You woke Mr. Pierce again."

Nash slapped his leg and crowed louder. "I cain't help it. You something else, Miss Emmy, and that's the truth. How you gon' compare those rutted trails in Humble with streets of pure gold?"

She lifted her chin. "Unless I can bust them up and spend them, what good are they?"

Nash sobered and wiped his eyes on his shirtsleeve. "Jus'

what you gon' buy with your busted-up streets? Ain't nobody got nothing for sale to measure up with what's waiting for you in heaven. Someday you'll know that to be true."

A smile sweetened Buddy's face.

Emmy smiled in return, wondering how much he'd heard. "Go back to sleep, Mr. Pierce. There's a long ride ahead of us yet. I'll try harder to keep this thoughtless man quiet."

Buddy nodded and turned over. The still-groggy Jerry settled his head onto his arm.

Emmy closed her eyes and leaned against the backboard, trying to imagine Humble's trampled, muddy streets paved with gold. She decided it would be a shameful extravagance and sat up prepared to say so when the look on Nash's face stopped her cold. "Gracious, what's wrong?"

He had to swallow first, his jutting Adam's apple rising and falling just over her head. "Miss Emmy, we might be about to see heaven a mite sooner than we expected." He pointed, his terrified stare fixed on something behind them.

Dread of the unknown settled in the pit of Emmy's stomach. She tracked the line of his muscular arm to the tip of his trembling finger. At first she saw only a flurry of motion in a raised cloud of dust. As they drew nearer, she made out the silhouettes of what had to be men on horseback hastening their way, but they didn't look quite right somehow.

"What on earth, Nash? Are those men?"

"Miss Emmy, I got me a good hunch they's devils." He gripped the toe of Buddy's boot and gave it a shake. "Wake yourself, Mistah Pierce. We got company."

Buddy came up fast, turning to look behind them to where Nash pointed. "You think they're coming for us?"

Emmy took comfort from the strength in Buddy's voice, but his words made her chest ache with fear. The approaching men shouted and whooped like Indians on a raid. They were near enough now to count. Six. . .no, seven riders, closing fast.

Jerry, fully alert, gripped the edge of the tailgate. "We might have a delay in our trip."

Nash scrambled to his knees and leaned forward. He rubbed

his eyes hard, as if he couldn't believe what he saw, and then rubbed them again. "Naw, suh, Mistah Ritter. We got us worse than any delay. We got a mess of pure trouble." His voice came out strained, as if his throat had gone dry.

Buddy glanced at him. "Calm down, Nash. Probably just young bucks on a lark."

Emmy had never seen Nash's eyes so wide. Even the whites bulged from his face.

"Naw, Mistah Pierce, them ain't bucks on a lark. They got sheets on they heads. We all dead men."

Miss Lucille found her voice. Ice filled Emmy's veins at her words, shot through with fear. "Help us," she hissed. "Lord, help us all!"

CHAPTER 30

Lord, help us all!"

The tortured cry rang through the parlor like a pronouncement of doom. Charity's head jerked up. Mama hovered at the head of the stairs, the picture of overstated tragedy. Still barefoot, she had at least donned the pale blue dress Mother Dane had bought for her to wear to the wedding.

Mother Dane exchanged a quick smile with Charity before she crossed to the bottom landing. "What's the matter now, Bertha Maye?"

Charity drew up her shoulders. Mother Dane must be feeling exceptionally brave.

Mama scowled down at her. "What do you think is the matter? I declare, you must be sleepwalking half the time." She caught their smiles and descended the stairs in a huff, fussing and muttering the whole way.

She had never looked so nice. Charity knew Mother Dane had pinned her hair, because every strand lay perfectly in place. The lace-trimmed skirt of her new dress stood out, starched and crisp. Another of Mother Dane's interventions, since Mama never pressed her clothes.

Still frowning, she joined them in the parlor, her busy fingers pulling at her collar and plucking at her skirt. Mother Dane slapped her hands away when she reached for her hair.

"Stop fidgeting and leave that alone. You're determined to muss it before we get out the door. Can't you let yourself look nice for a change?"

"I cain't help it. I'm plain miserable trussed up like this."

"It's a special occasion, Bert. You can let yourself fall apart again as soon as it's over."

"Special?" Mama hissed. "A funeral's an occasion, too, but I wouldn't call it special."

Mother Dane ignored her comment, stepping in front of the hall mirror to primp. "Where's Emmy? I thought you said you could coax her down."

Mama patted her piled-up hair. "I tried. Didn't get very far. She's still curled up in bed, pouting, by the look of it. Wouldn't even speak to me."

"Is that a fact?" Mother Dane balled her fists and glared up the stairs. "Well, if you'll pardon me, ladies, by golly, I think I can persuade her out of that bed."

Mama grabbed her sleeve. "Don't do it, Magda."

The storm on Mother Dane's face blew with full fury. "This here's Charity's wedding day. Emmy ought to be there. Charity should mean more to her than some scalawag of a man."

"Go easy on her now. Daniel Clark is a scoundrel, but I guess our Emmy's in love with him. Don't you see what that means, honey? The man of her dreams is marrying her best friend today. It'd be right cruel to make her stand and watch."

Mother Dane faltered a bit. "Well, it don't seem right."

Mama took Charity's hand. "It is right, and Charity agrees. Don't you, honey?"

Fighting back tears, Charity nodded. "Leave her be. I understand. I really do."

But did she? She never imagined her best friend would be absent from her wedding. Who cared if Emmy found it hard to watch? It was a miserable day for everyone concerned.

Except Daniel, of course. Somehow he always got what he wanted. Right now he wanted Charity. She had to wonder how long it would last. The one thing she knew for certain, with Emmy present or not, she would get married today. Only a miracle could save her now, and no miracles were visible on the horizon.

She put her arms around Mother Dane and Mama, her gaze going from one dear face to the other. "So that's it, then. Let's get going, ladies. It's time."

Mama pulled her close. "Oh, daughter! I can hardly bear this. It feels like doomsday."

Charity rubbed her back and kissed her cheek. "It's the only way, Mama. It's God's will, I think."

Mama sniffled. "You don't sound too sure."

She made a wry face. "I'm afraid it's the best I can do."

Staring down at Mama's feet, Mother Dane sighed. "I thought I felt those long toes underfoot. You going to your daughter's wedding without shoes, Bertha?"

" 'Course not. What do you think I am, some loutish hick? My boots are on the back porch. I left them there last night after I fed the chickens."

"Bertha!"

"Well, I couldn't bring them in after I stomped around in the coop. They was covered in poo. I'll slip into them on the way out the door."

Mother Dane held her ground. "You'll do no such thing."

"Why? They're dry now. A little beating and scraping should take care of the droppings." She rubbed her chin. "Ain't much I can do about that smell though."

Mother Dane gaped at Mama, her jaw slack.

A giggle rippled in Charity's chest, exploding into a laugh. She doubled over and laughed so hard she couldn't tell if mirth or madness had taken her–and she didn't care. First Mama, then Mother Dane caught it and howled along with her. The three of them clung together in the middle of the parlor, gasping for breath and struggling to hold each other up.

Mama straightened first, her face a broad grin. "We'd better take care now. Last time this happened we ended up bawling."

Charity struggled to compose herself. She stood up, smiling and wiping her eyes. "Not this time, Mrs. Bloom. Only happy tears allowed on my wedding day."

At the stricken look on both their faces, she hurriedly explained.

"Listen, you two, my fate is in God's hands. I'm all right with that. If God doesn't want me to marry Daniel Clark, it won't happen. Can't you put your faith there, too?"

Mama gazed up at her and nodded, then whispered the words she had uttered from the top of the stairs, only this time they were more of a prayer. "God, help us. God, help us all."

Mother Dane snatched Mama's arm and turned her around. "You march up those stairs and put on the shoes I bought for you."

"They hurt my feet."

"Too bad. You're not wearing smelly boots to your daughter's wedding. Now go. We'll wait for you in the rig."

The mention of the wagon seemed to remind Mother Dane of another weighty cross she bore. "Blast that infernal hired man of mine. He should be here to drive us into town today. I can't help but wonder where he could be." She released a long, shuddering sigh. "After all these years. . .well, I just don't understand it, that's all. I guess I'll never forgive Nash for the way he's let me and Emmy down."

"Miss Emmy!" Nash shouted. "Get yourself up under that seat!"

For once the girl seemed too scared to argue. Nash would be sure to thank the good Lord just as soon as they were out of this mess. He only hoped he wouldn't be thanking Him in person. Miss Emmy scrambled under the buckboard seat, and Nash covered her in burlap bags.

"Benjamin, hand your mama back this way so's I can get her hid."

Mr. Ritter shot forward to help Miss Lucille swing her legs past her son. Together, he and Nash pushed her down to lie beside Emmy.

"Sorry, ma'am," Nash said softly before he spread a smelly bag over her face.

Mr. Pierce turned from watching the riders close the gap between them. He nodded toward the women. "I'm not sure how much good that'll do. They've seen them by now."

Ignoring him, Nash whirled toward young Benjamin "Son,

you best drive this rig like you ain't never drove before." Though he shouted, his voice echoed in his ears like it came from the bottom of a rain barrel. He skittered up behind the boy's tense back and yelled louder. "Don't you stop no matter what. You hear me now?"

Benjamin answered by laying his whip across the lead horse's flank. The animal leaped forward and strained at the harness, his hooves pounding the hard-packed trail. The other horse had no choice but to speed up, too.

They hit a rut that nearly tossed everyone over the sides, bringing a loud wail from one of the women. The next hole was worse, and the sharp crack of splitting wood came from under the bed.

"It's no good," Mr. Ritter hollered from where he sat. "If that was the axle, this thing won't hold together. We have to stop."

"He's right," Mr. Pierce called, his eyes fixed on Nash. "We can't outrun those riders. We'll have to face them sooner or later."

Fear clawed Nash's throat. He had to make these fool men understand. "Easy for you to say, Mistah Pierce. They ain't aimin' to hurt none of you white folk."

"I won't let them hurt you, Nash."

"Then they gon' hang you, too."

Mr. Pierce had the audacious brash to smile. "Those men won't be hanging anyone. They're just trying to scare us a little."

"You ain't from the South, is you, mistah? We already scared, and they know it. No, suh. If they catch us, they's gon' kill us."

A bullet whizzed through the back of the buckboard, narrowly missing Mr. Pierce and wiping the grin clean off his face.

Before Nash could recover from the shock, a hooded rider on a fast horse caught up and pulled alongside. Nash braced for a bullet, but the man passed them by without a glance. To his horror, the rider swung from his mount onto the back of the lead horse and struggled to rein him in.

Benjamin stood up and lashed at the intruder with his whip, showing courage Nash knew he didn't have—courage or the foolishness of youth. Nash had lived longer than young Benjamin, long enough to learn how harsh the penalty for such an act, and how cruelly delivered.

No matter how hard Benjamin struck, the man held on and eventually stopped the horse. The wagon pulled up with a shudder.

Amid the mad laughter and shouting of the veiled gang, Nash thought he heard Miss Lucille let go an agonized whimper. He wondered if the dread in her heart matched his own, wondered if Benjamin knew enough to be afraid.

Mr. Pierce lurched to his feet and faced the riders. "Whatever you men are looking for, you won't find it here."

One of them spurred his mount forward. "I ain't so sure about that, mister."

"You've made a mistake. We're carrying nothing of value."

Through holes cut in the makeshift hood, the man aimed a hard stare at Nash. Nash dropped from his knees to his backside and willed himself small, thinking it better to pose no threat.

"Ain't no mistake," the flinty-eyed devil sneered. "I'm looking at what we're after. But you're right about one thing. It ain't worth much."

The other men hooted and catcalled, and all of them edged closer to the wagon.

Mr. Ritter stood up beside Mr. Pierce and turned his pockets inside out. "We got no money. See?"

The man cocked his gun and leveled it at him. "You just keep those hands still."

Mr. Ritter frowned and answered boldly, but Nash heard the tremor in his voice. "We don't want any trouble. We're nothing but a band of travelers headed for Humble to look for work."

The stone-cold eyes swung to Nash again. "Well, you see, that there's your problem. Me and the boys don't much care for your choice of traveling companions."

The lone rider who had stopped them jumped down from Benjamin's horse and sauntered back to where Benjamin still stood with the whip in his hand. Violence and hatred marked his haughty stride. "That's right," he said. "We don't care for them at all. Especially this one."

"This" spewed out like a curse as his hands closed around the boy's leg and pulled, jerking him off his feet. Benjamin fell down hard, crying out in pain when his back struck the buckboard seat.

Miss Lucille screamed, a mix of fear and rage in her voice. The hateful man jerked off his hood and hopped onto the side of the wagon, a loathsome grin on his face. "Well now, what we got here?"

Nash saw he was no more than an overgrown boy, which explained his reckless manner.

The lead rider growled in frustration. "What are you doing, Jackie? Put that back on."

"Why? It don't matter none if they see me. They won't be around long enough to talk about it." He pushed dirty blond hair from his eyes and leered at Nash. "Ain't that right, boy?"

Nash hung his head and tried to come up with the answer they wanted. A hard kick against the side rails rattled the rig and brought him to quick attention. "Yes, suh, that's right."

"You best pay attention when I'm talking to you, boy."

Nash raised his head, but it was hard to bear the contempt on the smug young face.

The brash fool looked over his shoulder. "See there, fellers? He knows I'm right. I can see it in them big eyes of his. He knows he won't be around to tell any tales."

His cruel laugh chilled Nash on the inside. When he turned again, his face had changed, and Nash wished the hatred and cruelty would come back. In its place he saw dark mischief and the glint of evil desire.

His smile widened. "Now then, Big Eyes, let's see what you got stashed under that seat."

The boy swung aboard the wagon and pulled the burlap off the women in one quick jerk.

Miss Lucille screamed again. Dread whitewashed Miss Emmy's face.

"Well, I'll be!" he shouted then winked at Mr. Pierce. "And you said you weren't carrying nothing of value."

He grabbed Miss Emmy's arm, so hard she yelped, and dragged her from under the seat. As he pulled her past Miss Lucille, she glanced at Nash, her eyes pleading for help. It was the last thing he saw before his world faded into white-hot rage and swinging fists.

CHAPTER 31

Charity looked around the small chapel. The room hadn't changed, though it held less people than the last time she'd been there. Her gown was the same, but this time, instead of feeling like a bride, she could hardly stand to look at the dress–a sentiment that extended to the ecstatic groom at her side.

A smiling country preacher stood ready to sign the marriage license, the same diminutive man who had gazed at her with pity on that other wedding day. Charity knew by the way he beamed at her now, he considered the impending ceremony to be reconciliation, the righting of a terrible wrong. Well, it was true, wasn't it? Marrying Daniel would make things right, but in a way the preacher might never suspect.

He lowered his pen to the document with a flourish, oblivious to Charity's misery. Desperate, foolish thoughts filled her mind as she watched him sign her doom.

Why couldn't he sign in pencil the way Papa always had? Then I could erase the signature legalizing this union. . .and use the same eraser to rub the smile off Daniel's face and the misery from Mama's eyes. After that I would use it on my mind to obliterate all memory of this wretched day.

Maybe that's why Papa preferred a pencil. Ink was so final, so permanent. It left no room for changing your mind.

Daniel nudged her alert with his elbow. She struggled free of her musings to find both men gazing expectantly at her.

The preacher cleared his throat. "Would you like for me to repeat that?"

She warmed clear to her toes. "I guess you'd better."

He adjusted his glasses and glanced at his notes. "Very well, then. Charity Bloom, will you take this man to be your lawfully wedded husband, to have and to hold. . ."

Despite herself, she lost focus again. Something niggled at her from just beneath the surface. A matter of great importance, to be sure, but she couldn't quite get a bead on it.

This time Daniel buried his elbow with some force, hard enough to make her gasp. "Wake up, sugar. You're supposed to say something here."

She stared up at him but couldn't see his face for the vivid image that, until that moment, had lurked in the dark recesses of her mind. A picture that loomed before her now, bathed in white light.

"Daniel, I–"

"Just say, 'I will,' Charity. That's all you have to say, and then it'll be my turn." His eyes begged her to speak.

She spun on her heels instead and sought her mama's face.

Mama stood as if pulled by an overhead string.

Charity stepped off the platform and swept up the aisle, her eyes locked on her mama's as she passed. She had a second to wonder if the gaping mouth and raised brows signaled panic or relief.

When she bolted for the door, Daniel followed. He caught up with her there and latched onto her arm, pulling her up short. "Why are you doing this? You want to hurt me, is that it?" He whirled her around to face him. "That's it, right? You're taking your revenge for what I've done."

"That's not it at all. I just need some time."

His expression turned pleading. "Honey, please don't do this. I said I was sorry for hurting you. I'll do anything to make it up."

Charity narrowed her eyes. "If that's so, then turn me loose. There's something I have to do first. I'll be back within the hour. I promise."

Hope washed over his face. "And then you'll marry me?"

She lowered her voice and told the truth. "I don't know yet."

The words sharpened his tone and fanned a blaze in his eyes. "Hold up there, little girl." His fingers dug into her arm. "I gave up everything for you—my parents, my inheritance, my whole life. What do you mean you don't know?"

Charity winced and tried to pull away. "Stop it, Daniel. You're hurting me."

"Turn her loose, boy," Mama growled behind them, "if'n you value your life." Her tiny body trembled with rage, and her mottled face held a warning. Mother Dane stood with her, adding weight to the threat.

The preacher stepped around the women and glared at Daniel's grip on Charity's wrist. "I don't know what's going on here," he said in a low voice, "but, son, you'd be well advised to let go of her arm."

One by one, Daniel's fingers lifted, revealing white marks on Charity's skin.

She spun and raced for the chapel entrance. Before her hand fully closed around the knob, someone jerked the door open from the other side. She gasped and heard the sound repeated in unison behind her by Mama and Mother Dane.

Frantically swiping the tears that prevented a clear view of his dear face, Charity tried to say his name. It came out an incredulous whispered question. "Buddy?"

His eager eyes looked everywhere at once, taking in her dress, the chapel, and those gathered behind her. When they finally settled on her face, they held a mixture of panic and pain. "Tell me I'm not too late, Charity. Please tell me you didn't go through with it."

In two steps she met him on the threshold. Her gaze locked on his, and she touched his battered cheek. "What happened to your face?"

He pressed her hand to his bruised flesh then pulled her palm to his lips for a soft kiss. In his eyes blazed the same emotion she'd witnessed that day on the trail when the well blew in. This time fear mingled with his passion, so the fire raged even hotter.

Charity started to speak, but a shrill voice, as recognizable as her own, broke the spell. "Wait, Charity! Don't do it!"

From across the churchyard, a peculiar apparition staggered in their general direction, twice weaving off course before correcting itself. Charity watched in fascination as the figure stumbled up the steps and lunged for Buddy, using his body to prevent falling headlong through the door.

The creature clung to Buddy and peered around him from the threshold. It spoke again, Emmy's unmistakably familiar voice emanating from a decidedly unfamiliar form. "Don't tell me we're too late!"

Unable to believe her ears, Charity gasped. "Emmy?"

The pale, gaunt face, scratched and dirt-streaked, with one eye swollen shut, hardly resembled her. Bits of hay and woody debris tangled her hair, the blond locks half pinned, half flowing free. Her frock fared worse, the skirt so filthy it made the color uncertain, the bodice stained by a substance that resembled dried blood. The dress was torn in several places, and muddy water darkened six inches of the hem.

Full of questions, Charity drew a deep breath and opened her mouth. An unspeakable stench snaked around her like a fog, so dense it seemed tangible. With every breath it grew stronger, more caustic. Incredibly, it seemed to emanate from Emmy and Buddy, so awful Charity couldn't imagine the source. Whatever the cause, the horrid smell threatened to turn her stomach.

Mother Dane stepped forward and squinted. "Why, Emily Dane. It is you. Have you been tipping the bottle?"

Mama took a step back and pinched her nose shut with two fingers. "Pee-yew. What have you two wallowed in to take on a stink like that? Emmy, this rivals your recent trip to the henhouse."

Mother Dane rested her hands on her hips. "What have you been up to, little miss? And how did you get in this condition? When I left you an hour ago, you were still in bed."

Charity jerked her gaze to Emmy. It didn't seem possible to wind up in such a state between the Danes' house and the church. She recalled the night she had slipped into Emmy's room, ready to bare her soul to a carefully arranged pile of pillows.

You little trickster! You were never in your room. You weren't even in the house!

Her head reeled. Emmy had somehow gone after Buddy and brought him back.

"Pierce!" In the midst of Charity's revelation, a strident voice bellowed at her back. "I might've known you had something to do with this."

Daniel! Charity had forgotten him in the commotion. He stormed from the center aisle to stand at her elbow, his face a furious mask.

Buddy took a step forward. "You're right, Clark. I have everything to do with it." His blazing eyes swept toward Charity and instantly softened. He took her shoulders in his hands and pulled her close in a protective gesture. Unlike Daniel's harsh hands, Charity found Buddy's touch gentle, his fingers a light caress on her skin.

His earnest gaze searched her face. "Emmy told me everything, honey. You don't have to marry Daniel. I'll marry you right now, if you'll have me. And not just to save your land. I love you, Charity. More than I can say."

Daniel swelled like a blowfish and lunged, his fingers clamping down on Buddy's arm. "Get your filthy paws off my bride."

Buddy froze, his gaze locked on Daniel's hand. "Is that so, Charity? Are you this man's wife?"

The preacher stepped from behind Mama and Mother Dane and cleared his throat. "There have been no vows exchanged here today." He spoke the words with authority, in a tone that contradicted his small stature. The pronouncement made Charity's heart soar.

Daniel wailed like a wild thing. He whirled and jerked up a nearby chair, then rushed Buddy with it.

Distracted by Charity, Buddy never saw him coming. She screamed, but it came too late for him to move.

A shadow loomed behind them and a long arm shot out, catching hold of the chair just before it came down on Buddy's head. Jerked from Daniel's grasp, the makeshift weapon rose over their heads and sailed past Daniel, where it shattered to kindling against the wall.

Chest heaving, Nash jutted his chin at Daniel. "You jus' step on back now, Mistah Clark. I done walloped me one mess of fools today. I got no qualms 'bout adding you to the pile." Behind

Nash stood Jerry Ritter. Two people Charity had never seen before hovered just outside the door.

Charity marveled at the change in docile, mild-mannered Nash. He stood with fists clenched at his waist, his feet planted in a determined stance. His big hands were cut and swollen, but from the look in his eyes, that wouldn't deter him from using them again.

Daniel seemed to make the same assessment. His eyes traveled from Nash's hands to his somber face and back again. For all his bravado, it was clear Daniel wasn't ready to take on big Nash, but the ugly snarl and menacing look he shot him made Charity queasy.

"You'll live just long enough to regret this day, boy," was all he said before he shoved past them and out the door.

Nash watched him, his expression grave. "He prob'ly right about that," he whispered. "They gon' hang me now for sure."

"Nobody will hang you for defending a man," Buddy said. "That's all you were doing. I'll make sure no one lays a hand on you."

Mama elbowed her way closer. "You reckon we're finally shed of that varmint?"

Buddy glanced toward the door. "I doubt it, Mrs. Bloom. We'll face that trial when it comes." He held out his hand to Nash. "Meanwhile, sir, I owe you a debt of gratitude."

Nash grinned and stood taller. "Call us even, Mistah Pierce. I wouldn't be here now if'n you hadn't waded in and helped me back yonder." He nodded at Jerry and the younger man. "Same goes for you two."

A huge smile overcame Buddy's grave expression. He pulled Emmy to stand among them. "Don't leave out our Miss Dane, here. She darted in and delivered a fair lick or two of her own."

The little band of misfits exchanged wide, knowing grins. Charity burned with curiosity, but another more pressing matter consumed her. She touched Buddy's arm. "Though I would dearly love to stay and hear more of this adventure, I desperately need to get somewhere, and fast. Mother Dane, may I take your buggy?"

"Sure you can, sugar. It's right outside. Nash can drive you." She glowered at him with flashing eyes. "If he's still working for me, that is."

Nash looked like she'd caught him with an empty pie tin. His shoulders, so broad and proud just seconds ago, rounded to a slump. "Yes'm, if you'll have me."

"All right, then. Take Miss Charity where she needs to go. Mind you, I have a few things I need to say to you, but I guess they can simmer a mite longer." She aimed raised brows at Emmy, who wilted before her searching gaze. "And don't think you've gotten away with anything. There's too many unanswered questions to suit me. We'll have a set-to, the lot of us, when the smoke clears."

"Yes'm, Miz Dane," Nash said and backed out the door.

Charity smiled. Facing an angry fist, even a charging bull, was a whole different matter for a man than standing up to Magdalena Dane.

"Wait just a second now." Buddy touched Charity's shoulder. "I hate to be a pest, honey, but I just proposed marriage to you. You haven't said yes, though I don't recall you saying no, either." He gestured around him. "I mean, we are standing in a chapel." He nodded toward the reverend. "And this fine gentleman came ready to perform a ceremony. The way I see it, there's no sense wasting a perfect arrangement."

Charity's heart swelled. "Oh, Buddy. Yes, I want to marry you. More than anything. I will, too, but there's something I have to take care of first."

Mama had stood quietly long enough. "Charity, what on earth are you saying? You go on and marry this boy. Ain't it just what we wanted? It'll solve everything."

She shook her head. "Not everything, Mama. Let's go, Nash."

"I don't understand. Where are you going?" Buddy asked.

"To the Pikes' place."

Mama gasped and laid a hand to her heart. "Straight into the devil's jaws? Daughter, you cain't."

"I have to. If my hunch is right, it'll pull our bacon out of those jaws for good."

Mama took a determined step forward and locked arms with her. "If you're going to see that nasty, no-good Shamus Pike, I'm going with you."

Buddy latched onto her other arm. "Me, too."

Charity smiled down at Mama then up at Buddy. "I guess there's no talking you two out of it, so let's go."

As they passed Emmy, her burning stare caught and held Charity's attention. Charity never expected the tenderness she saw in Emmy's blue eyes or the grief etched on her battered face, and it pierced her heart. Pent-up tears welled, and Charity reached to take her hand, but her overeager companions herded her out the door.

Mother Dane and Mama crowded up front with Nash, while Charity and Buddy climbed onto the back of the wagon. Emmy, Mr. Ritter, and the two strangers piled into the other rig and struck out after them. Though warmed by Buddy's presence and thrilled by his hand clasped tightly over hers, she was too preoccupied to enjoy it fully. As hard as she tried to focus on Buddy or what lay ahead at the Pikes', she couldn't keep her mind off the mournful look on Emmy's face. The girl was busting to tell her something, but she didn't get the chance.

Behind them, Emmy sat tall in the bed of the old wagon, her back against the tailgate, arms draped casually over the rail as they bumped along the trail. The fact that Emmy climbed into the rear surprised Charity. The sight of her so comfortable there astonished her. She couldn't help but smile.

Charity never intended to arrive at the Pikes' in a caravan, but the situation had spun out of control. Given the gravity of the accusation she was about to make, a few more witnesses wouldn't be a bad idea. The closer they came to Shamus Pike's place, the better she felt about having some company. When they turned down the long drive and headed in the direction of the house, she was downright glad of it.

CHAPTER 32

"Goodness. What's all this?"

Elsa Pike, stationed at the entrance of her home like a dowdy sentry, stared past Charity, her gaze shifting from face to face. Evidently quite confused by the unlikely assembly, a frown replaced her customary smile.

Charity bit back a chuckle. Lo, the would-be queen of Humble society caught at her worst and too surprised to care.

She'd been baking again, her apron a testament to the different ingredients. Flour had somehow wound up on her head, perhaps while scratching an itch, and mixed with sweat to become tacky pearls of dough strung in her hair. The bejeweled strands hung in damp gray rings about her face, as limp as the dignity she fought to regain.

Charity held out her hand. "Good morning, Elsa. My apologies for barging in like this, but I'm here on urgent business."

Elsa took Charity's hand then cringed at the mess left by her fingers. She nodded at Mama and Mother Dane in turn while she offered Charity the end of her apron.

"Bertha. Magdalena. It's so good to see you."

Amy Jane appeared behind her mama, her customary frown intact, edging her thick brows even closer. Unlike Elsa, she seemed oblivious to everyone but Charity. She gasped and pointed an accusing finger. "Will you look at that! She's wearing my dress."

Her smile restored, Elsa reached around to swipe at Amy Jane. She missed. "Well, so she is. What's going on here, Charity, dear?"

Amy Jane pushed closer. "She's come to rub my nose in it, that's what."

Elsa whirled on her. "Amy Jane! Charity has not donned that silly dress and hauled all these people onto our front lawn just to get under your skin. Hush now, and let her explain herself."

She returned her attention to Charity. "Forgive my outburst, child. Go ahead, then."

Now that she actually stood on the Pikes' porch, Charity's confidence waned. She reached for Buddy's supportive hand. "I've come to see Shamus."

"Shamus?" Elsa failed to hide her disappointment.

"Yes, ma'am," Charity said. "My business is with him." She peered past them but detected no movement in the deep shadows of the house.

Elsa untied her apron and whisked it off. "I'm afraid he's not here at present, but I expect him back real soon. Would you care to wait?"

"If you don't mind."

Curiosity had crowded Elsa's manners aside. Her eyes strayed back to the odd assortment of people, mostly strangers, dotting her front lawn. Unable to contain herself, she asked one more eager, leading question.

"Isn't there something I can do for you in the meantime?"

Too anxious to stand on formality, Charity forged ahead. "Mrs. Pike, I know I'm taking disgraceful liberties, but I have no choice. Will you permit me to examine something in your parlor?"

Visibly relieved to be back in the center of things, Elsa swung wide the door. "Of course, dear. I have nothing to hide. Come in, all of you."

Charity's grip on Buddy's hand tightened, and they walked inside, Charity aware that a parade of people slipped in behind them. First Mama and Mother Dane. Mr. Ritter and Emmy came next. She imagined Elsa and Amy Jane brought up the rear. Elsa's invitation didn't likely extend to poor Nash and his friends, and they doubtless waited beside the rig. In the close confines of the narrow hallway, the smell that arose from Buddy and company grew so fierce that Charity feared Elsa might order them back outside as well.

How peculiar the stern expressions on the wall had seemed to Charity the last time she'd walked the dimly lit passage, and how comical Elsa in her unbuttoned, disheveled dress. Now the bedraggled characters who filed past the framed faces made all that seem proper by comparison.

Once inside the cheery parlor, Charity wasted no time. She headed straight for the mahogany working table and yanked out the bottom drawer.

Her mama gasped. "Charity Bloom, what on earth? I raised you better than that." She shot a nervous glance at the parlor door, but Elsa hadn't yet made it inside. "You can't go snooping through drawers without permission, whatever the reason."

"I know, Mama."

"Close it, then."

"Yes, ma'am, in a second." Charity stooped to better see inside, while her frantic fingers searched the contents.

Behind them Elsa cleared her throat, and Mama lost her patience. "Charity Bloom!"

Charity stood, careful to keep her back to the group clustered at the door. Her gaze swept the papers in her hand, taking in the information as fast as she could manage. Then she faced the assembled group, holding aloft the documents and Shamus's writing set.

"I knew it," she said and then drew a deep, cleansing breath. "I just knew it."

Mama's scorching gaze traveled from Charity's face to her upraised hands. "What is that you're holding?"

"Our freedom."

"Explain yourself."

"Mama, I stood beside Daniel and watched that preacher sign our marriage license, wishing he would sign in pencil the way Papa always did, so I could erase it. That's when these two documents came to mind as clear as day." She waved each one in turn. "One in pencil, one in pen, both in Papa's handwriting."

She watched the circle of familiar faces, waiting for them to catch on. "This one"–she passed it to her mama–"is the only one Papa actually wrote."

Mama took it from her and scanned it front and back. "Thad always did prefer a pencil for scratching on paper."

Charity held up the other. "This one, the document Shamus brought to our hotel room, was traced out in ink by someone else."

Buddy stepped up and took both papers. "What's the difference between them?"

Charity smiled. "A big difference." She faced Elsa. "Mrs. Pike, did you know about this?"

Elsa's cheeks had lost their rosy glow. "I must say I'm at a loss. I make it a rule not to plunder through my husband's things, so I haven't a clue what those"–she waved toward Buddy, who stood over the lamp studying the writings–"scribblings might be. Enlighten me, please. Just what is it you think you've pulled from my Shamus's drawer?"

Her eagerness dimmed by the fear she read on Elsa's face, Charity cleared her throat and started again. "Are you aware of a bet between Shamus and my father?"

"A bet?" Elsa frowned and shook her head. "Between Shamus and Thad? I don't know anything about that."

"Did you know Shamus had plans to take our home?"

Mama sputtered. "Take it? More like steal it right out from under us."

Elsa whirled on Mama. "Bertha Bloom, bite your tongue. My Shamus was Thad's closest friend. I'll thank you to remember that."

Mama glared back at her. "He's been no friend to me or my daughter, Elsa Pike. That's what I'll remember." She nodded at the documents in Buddy's hands, her eyes searching Charity's for understanding. "Do those papers mean what I think they mean? Your papa never made no bet at all?"

"He did, but not for our home. Papa only put up the ten acres Shamus leases from us. Nothing more."

"But why would Shamus put his whole place up against ten acres? That ain't sensible."

"He didn't. He only put up ten acres to match Papa's bet. Shamus lied about that, too."

Buddy held up the copy he had taken from Charity's hands. "Then where did this other one come from?"

Before she could answer, the back door slammed, followed by heavy footfalls in the hall. The already tense muscles in Charity's back contracted with dread, and her legs trembled so hard she feared falling. Afraid to turn, she heard him before she saw him.

"What's going on in here?" The booming voice gave them all a start. Shamus hulked in the doorway, hat in hand. His gaze swept Charity, from the hem of her dress to the flowers in her hair. His dark eyes narrowed to slits when they reached her face. "Well now, ain't you a sight."

He tilted a tight jaw toward Elsa, his gaze still locked on Charity. "What are these people doing here?"

Charity's throat constricted and all the moisture left her mouth, but she held her ground. She glanced at Buddy for strength before she took the papers from his hands and approached Shamus. "Mr. Pierce here just asked the origin of this forged document." The confident, steady tone of her own voice surprised Charity. She had expected it to match the way she trembled inside. "You can answer that question for him, can't you, Mr. Pike? I do believe you know."

One glance at the evidence Charity waved in his face stirred a flicker of fear in Shamus's eyes. He shook his head and brushed past her. "You're speaking in riddles, girl. I don't know anything about a forged document. Now tell me what you're doing here or clear out."

Mama squinted and jutted her hip. "Just look at him. Fidgety as a bag of cats. He's guilty, all right." She squared off in front of Shamus, blocking his way. He seemed to shrink before the tiny woman, and Charity knew Mama's size didn't hold the big man in check.

Mama took a bead on Shamus with her eyes. "To think I spent the last years guarding my land from crooked strangers, when all the time the knife was coming at me from behind. Shame on you, Shamus Pike. You've trod on Thad's memory and betrayed our long friendship. I curse the day that river swallowed him up, but at least he ain't here to see what you tried to do to his family."

Tears flooded Shamus's eyes, and he lifted one hand toward Mama. "Bertha, I can explain."

She drew back with a hiss. "Don't you bother. I wish the dead could come back so Thad could haunt you. As for me, I don't care to ever lay eyes on you again."

She glanced around the hushed room. "Well, that's it, then. We're done here." Her head swung in Charity's direction, her eyes bright with tears. "Come on, daughter, and bring them papers with you."

Charity fell in behind her as they filed out of the parlor, but she turned at the threshold to glance back at Shamus, who stood staring down at the floor. "We won't need to call the sheriff about this. That is, so long as you leave us be."

He nodded without looking up.

Buddy's hand at Charity's back urged her out the door. At the wagon, the little group huddled around her and her mama, and Buddy's hand became a firm, comforting arm encircling her waist. Admiration shone from his eyes. "How did you know?"

"Good question, boy," Mama chimed in. "How did you know about them papers, sugar? Or even where to find them?"

Charity gathered the silky folds of her wedding dress in both hands. "Would you believe it? I owe it all to this gown."

Lifting her thin shoulders, Mama peered vacantly at the frock. "To that thing? How so?"

"You see, the day I came out here to offer it for sale, I stumbled over that table and knocked it to the floor, along with the contents of the drawer. I shoved everything back so quickly I had no time to look them over. But I guess the sight of Papa's handwriting on those documents got stuck somewhere in my mind."

Mama nodded thoughtfully. "I never understood Thad's stubborn partiality to a pencil. Not sure he did either." Her eyes brightened. "I reckon God understood. It was for this day, so Shamus couldn't steal from us."

"It's a miracle. An answer to prayer." Emmy, standing just outside the circle of friends, had breathed the awestruck words.

Charity smiled and moved in her direction. "Yes, a miracle. One of many."

Emmy took the last few steps to meet her, a plea in her smoldering blue eyes. "I have something to say to you, Charity Bloom. Something you need to know."

The diminutive Emmy, though shorter than Charity, had never seemed childlike. Yet standing there wringing her hands, her upturned face streaked with dirt, she bore an innocence Charity had never seen in her before.

She nodded. "You'd best go ahead and say it."

"I know you think I lit out after Buddy and brought him back so I could have Daniel for myself, but it just isn't so."

"Then why would you do such a thing?"

"It was for you. I did it for you." Once started, something broke loose in Emmy, and a rush of words followed. "I discovered the truth about Daniel." She grasped Charity's fingers. "You don't really know him. Neither did I—that is, until a few days ago. He hoodwinked us both. Beneath all that charm and polish lies a cruel and vicious man. Please take my word for it. I've seen his dark side, and I love you too much to see you married to him. I set out to bring Buddy back no matter what the cost."

In tears now, she took hold of Charity's arms. "I know it won't earn your forgiveness. I mean, how could you forgive the things I've done? Even so, I had to save you from that mean, no-account scoundrel. I simply had to."

Emmy let go of Charity and fished a lace hankie from her bodice, likely the only clean piece of cloth left on her body, and wiped her eyes. "Of course, it must seem hypocritical of me to call Daniel cruel after the pain I dealt you. What I did was reprehensible."

"Yes, it was."

"Wicked."

"Quite."

"Completely selfish."

"You left out disloyal."

With each agreement, Emmy's tirade grew less impassioned. She glanced up at Charity with uncertain eyes before faltering ahead.

"So like I said, you could never be expected to forgive me."

Charity grinned. "Yes, I could."

"I'd walk over hot coals to make it possible, though I know you could never. . ."

"I can, Emmy. I already have."

Emmy looked as if she dared not hope. "What did you say?"

"I said I forgive you."

"After I betrayed you, humiliated you? No, you couldn't. I've ruined our friendship for good."

"Emily Dane, you've done no such thing. We'll be friends forever."

The words brought Emmy's wringing and squirming to a halt. She stared at Charity in wonder. "But how?"

Charity raised her hands out to her sides. "To be honest, I don't know! Maybe I love you too much, Emmy. Or maybe I discovered I'm capable of hurtful, spiteful things myself."

She pointed toward the house. "All I know is back there I looked at Shamus Pike and saw true regret. He let greed get the better of him, and now he's sorry. I expect he wishes more than anything to undo it, to make it right again." She placed her hands on Emmy's shoulders. "I see that same look in your eyes."

Emmy's fingers clenched into fists that she tucked under her trembling chin. "I am so ashamed. I would do anything to make it up to you."

Charity took Emmy's face in her hands. "Goodness, by the look of you, you already have." She laughed and wiped a smudge from Emmy's face. "Do you know you're an absolute mess?"

"Yes, and I always have been."

Charity laughed. "Honey, I didn't mean. . ."

"It's true, and you know it. I made a mess of my whole life then tried to ruin yours, too."

Charity lifted her chin. "Emmy, it's all right. Besides, if you think about it"—she cast a pointed glance at Buddy—"you did me quite a favor."

She opened her arms, and Emmy walked into them. They held each other in the midst of the damp-eyed circle of witnesses and wept.

Mother Dane and Mama stood arm in arm, sniffing and wiping their eyes, Mother Dane on her lace hankie, Mama on her sleeve.

A tearful Mother Dane motioned to Emmy. "Come over here, sugar pie, and let your mama hug you, too."

Emmy rushed over and fell against her ample bosom. "Does this mean you're not cross with me anymore?"

Mother Dane grunted. "I never said I wasn't cross, little girl. You still have some explaining to do. But we'll worry about that later." She made a face and held Emmy at arm's length. "Land sakes, what foul mischief have you rolled in?" She held up her hand. "Don't tell me. Just climb up on that wagon and let me get you home and in a washtub. You're wanting a good scrubbing."

Buddy's warm hands settled on Charity's shoulders and turned her around. "Can I talk you into that wedding now? I don't imagine that preacher has gotten too far away."

Smiling, she caressed his filthy, swollen face. "As handsome as you are today, how can I refuse?"

When he beamed, she patted his broad chest. "Yet I must."

His smile died and his chest deflated. "This is no time for jokes, Charity. Don't you love me?"

The hurt in his eyes struck deep. Charity took his hands in her own. "Buddy, I love you very much, but I don't want to remember my wedding as the day I was supposed to marry Daniel Clark. I think I'd rather plan our own, wouldn't you? And do it up right from start to finish?"

Buddy's arms went around her again, strong and secure. "You just set the date, ma'am. I'll be there." His brows gathered in a mock frown. "Don't make me wait too long now. You hear?"

From behind them, Charity's mama gave a huge sigh. "So be it," she said then crooked a finger at Nash. "Come on and get me home. If there ain't to be no more weddings today, I need to get shed of these boots. They're killing me."

Mother Dane spun around. "Tell me you didn't–" Without waiting for an answer, she bent and raised the hem of Mama's dress. "You did! Bert, how could you?"

"Magdalena Dane, take your hands off me before you're left

with a stub. I told you those shoes pinch my feet." She raised her foot up off the ground and waved it in the air. "I cleaned these up real nice. They don't even smell."

Mother Dane looked at Charity and shook her head. "Honey, I tried, but you can't dress up a mule's behind to look like anything else."

Mama spit and sputtered. "Least I ain't a mule's behind sashaying around in frilly hats and lace hankies. Don't forget, I knew you long before you married money."

Charity laughed and hugged her mama, her heart so light it seemed she could rise to her toes, lift off the ground, and soar over the treetops. "Don't you worry, Mother Dane. Have I mentioned the fact that my mama is oil-rich? She can afford to buy as many shoes as she pleases. We're bound to find her a comfortable pair to wear to my next wedding." She glanced over at Buddy and smiled. "My *last* wedding."

Mother Dane sniffed. "You might find a pair to suit her, but it'll take some time and likely every cent she's got."

Mama grinned at Charity. "I'd still have a good pair if that feller of yours had ever found the one I lost in the bog." She cocked her head and cackled. "It likely blasted to kingdom come and back when that well blew in. It's probably wedged in the top of a pine tree right now."

Mother Dane turned from giving Emmy a hand up onto her rig. "I can't think of a more fitting end to that old piece of leather. You've worn that pair since you married Thad. I was glad to see them go." She held out her hand to Mama. "Now come over here and let me help you up so we can go home. I wouldn't mind stepping out of my own shoes for a spell. I got a corn on my great toe that's ready to sprout ears."

CHAPTER 33

Charity stood on the top landing of Mother Dane's staircase, holding her breath. The steps spiraling down to the parlor and to the unavoidable confrontation with Mama seemed far too few. Heart pounding, she prepared to take the first one then paused to wait out a brief bout of vertigo. When it passed, she breathed a shaky laugh and steeled herself to try again.

You can do this, Charity. You can do this. . . .

"Charity!"

The strident voice startled her severely, and she almost lost her balance.

Mama stared up at her from the bottom step with horror-struck eyes. She pointed behind Charity. "Get back in there this minute and take that thing off."

Charity clutched at her bodice. "You scared me right out of my skin."

Mama's expression turned hard. And determined. "I mean to scare you right out of that dress. Go take it off. You can't wear that infernal thing again."

Charity lifted the hem of her wedding gown clear of her feet and started down the stairs. "Of course I can."

Mama, turning red now, watched her descend. "Daughter, go take it off like I said. Put on that store-bought one that we picked out."

Charity reached the bottom step and twirled. "What's wrong with this one?"

Shrinking away from her, Mama pointed a trembling finger. "You know what's wrong with that thing. It's hexed. You've worn it for two weddings now, but you still ain't married."

Charity jumped flat-footed to the floor. She felt lighthearted and somewhat daring, as young and carefree as a child. "That fact alone makes it a blessing in my book. Besides, how could something so lovely bring bad luck?" She picked up her mama's tiny hands and caressed the bent fingers. "Especially considering it was fashioned in hope by these dear hands, with love sewn in every stitch."

Mama tried to wriggle her hands free. "I thought we already decided you weren't to wear it."

"You decided. I just went along to save you from fussing. But now I've changed my mind." Charity kissed each of her mama's palms and drew her close for a hug. "The dress was made for this day," she whispered against her mama's hair. "We just didn't know it before now."

Mama raised her face, and Charity's heart caught at the measure of love that shone from her eyes. "This day is all I ever wanted for you, baby. God sent Buddy to us."

"I know, Mama. God is so good. He knows just what our hearts need."

Emmy stood up from the divan and crossed the parlor. "I was about to come up and help with your hair, but, oh my, I see you didn't need me." Her eyes brimmed, and a single tear tracked down her cheek. "You're a vision, Charity."

Charity laughed and pulled her into the hug. "Stop it now. You'll just get me started, and I don't want to cry today."

Mother Dane pushed herself up from the big green chair. "You do look exquisite in that gown, sugar, but I think your beauty has more to do with the joy on your face than how you're dressed. Right this minute you'd look good in a feed sack. There's nothing more beautiful than the glow of a bride in love."

Mama beamed. "The glow of a bride in love? Now that's something she ain't wore to a wedding before." Her bright smile faded. "I just wish your papa was here to see how pretty you are. He'd be so awful proud to strut you down the aisle."

Charity gently tugged a lock of Mama's hair. "We're not going to cry today, remember?"

"You're right, sugar," she said, wiping her eyes. "He wouldn't want us to."

Nash opened the kitchen door behind them. "The rig's out front, Miz Dane."

Mama spun to face him, her tears forgotten. "Well, get in it. You're coming to my daughter's wedding, ain't you?"

Nash looked aghast. "Miz Bloom, you know I cain't hardly do that."

"Oh pooh! Why not?"

He stepped into the room, fidgeting with his suspenders while he searched for something to say. "Miz Bloom, that's a white man's church. How could I do such a thing?"

"Because I asked you, that's how. I don't give two hoots what this town thinks of it, neither. It's the least they'd expect out of Crazy Bertha. We might as well give 'em something new to jaw about." She winked and jutted her chin. "Since Buddy reclaimed my money from that Clark rascal before he took off to Galveston, and since there's plenty more where that come from, I'm rich enough to do whatever I want."

She leveled her finger at Nash. "So you put on your Sunday best and come, you hear? Bring that nice Benjamin and Miss Lucille, too. Today's special. I want to share it with my friends."

"But, Miz Bloom–"

Mama jerked her finger up again. "No buts now. I'll expect to see you there."

Charity slid her arm around Mama's waist and smiled in his direction. "Please come, Nash. Buddy would be so pleased."

Nash looked from face to face, a desperate plea in his eyes. His gaze finally settled on Mother Dane, who offered him no help at all.

"You go on and do like she says, Nash. It'll be all right."

"Yes'm, Miz Dane," he whined. "I'll do like she say. But this family gon' get me hanged." He backed out the way he came in, muttering and shaking his head.

Mama lifted one foot high in the air, struggling to maintain her balance. "Look, Charity," she crowed. "I'm wearing my new shoes."

"I'm proud of you, Mama. They're stunning. How do they feel?"

She frowned and squirmed a bit. "Well, they do pinch my big toes."

Mother Dane donned her wide-brimmed hat, securing it with a long gilded pin, and then lifted her parasol. "Charity, make sure Bertha's hem is long enough to cover them toes. She'll be barefoot before you can say, 'I do.' " Smiling, she opened the front door with a flourish. "Let's us go to a wedding, ladies!"

Charity gazed around the little chapel and tried to commit the scene to memory. It would be the last time she stood among family and friends to say her vows.

Mama sat on the second row with Mother Dane and Emmy by her side. Jerry Ritter and Lee Allen were there for Buddy, sitting tall and beaming with pride.

Mr. Allen's presence presented quite a dilemma for Mama. Torn between staring at him or her daughter, she was bound to develop a crick in her swiveling neck. Even more surprising were the shy glances passing between Emmy and young Mr. Ritter.

Nash and Benjamin stood against the back wall near the door, whispering and twisting their hats. Miss Lucille sat on the last pew with a beautiful smile on her face, clearly at home in God's house, wherever she found it.

The preacher came to stand before Charity and Buddy, his hands clasped at his waist. He smiled at them, but Charity's cheeks still flamed. What must he think, presiding over three weddings in a row, all for the same bride?

He nodded at her and Buddy in turn then cleared his throat. "Before we begin, I'm going to need your full names for the marriage certificate." He paused and ducked his head. "Well, the groom's at least. I have the bride's name filled in."

Behind them Mama cackled. "I reckon you know it by heart by now." She grunted then nudged Mother Dane. "Keep them elbows to yourself, Magda."

Charity wondered how red her face must appear against the

white wedding gown. Buddy smiled in delight and squeezed her hand. Good thing he and Mama were having such a grand time.

The preacher nodded again at Buddy. "And the groom's name?"

"Buddy Pierce." Buddy's voice rang out clear and strong, but he squirmed when he said it and refused to meet the preacher's eyes.

The man frowned. "Buddy's a nickname, isn't it? What's your given name, son?"

"Well, sir, never you mind about that."

His words gave Charity a start. She had asked him the same question on the day they met. His answer then had been the same. She looked at him in disbelief. Was she about to marry a man whose name she didn't even know?

The preacher lifted the paper toward Buddy and jabbed at it with a long, bony finger. "This here's a legal document. I can't put a nickname on it. It won't be official."

Buddy released Charity's hand and stepped closer to the man. She watched in disbelief as he lowered his head and whispered something in his ear. At first, the man of God looked like he'd swallowed a pinecone. He gaped at Buddy until Buddy nodded; then he chuckled and shook his head before he wrote it down.

When Buddy returned to Charity's side, she stared up at him. "Buddy?"

He smiled at her. "Yes, Charity-from-the-Bible?"

So he remembers, too.

"We're about to be married. Don't you think I should know your name?"

"Buddy will do for now."

"When are you planning to tell me?"

"I can't see how you'd ever need to know."

Charity heard scattered laughter behind her and turned to look. The room had stilled, and every person watched.

"I see," she said, lifting her chin stubbornly. "And what shall I call our firstborn son?"

"What's wrong with Junior?"

The assembled guests erupted in delighted titters, Mama loudest of them all.

Charity was done tiptoeing. "For crying in a bucket! Just tell me." She crossed her arms and turned her back on him. "I refuse to marry you until I know your name."

Mama gasped and stood up. "What did she just say?"

Mother Dane groaned. "Surely she didn't."

Mama and Mother Dane pushed out into the aisle and stormed forward, with Emmy just behind them. With each step, the slap of Mama's bare feet on the smooth wooden floor echoed through the hushed chapel.

She clambered onto the podium and latched onto the reverend as if to prevent his getaway. "Don't listen to this foolish girl, Preacher. She'll marry this man or answer to me." She spun around to point at Benjamin and Nash. "Block the door, men. No one leaves this room." Then she gave the man of God a shake. "Stop messing about and get on with it."

"Wait a minute, Mama," Charity said. "I didn't say I would never marry him. Just not until he tells me his name." She whirled on Buddy. "I don't see one thing funny about it, either."

Buddy held up both hands. "All right, sugar, if you insist. Just remember, I tried to warn you. It's a heavy cross to bear. Don't blame me if you really do change your mind after hearing it." He whispered in her ear then stood back grinning.

Charity blinked up at him, sure she'd heard him wrong. "You didn't say Wigglesworth?"

He placed his hand over his heart. "On my honor, Miss Bloom, that's my handle."

She shook her head. "No one would burden a child with that name. Not with a straight face."

"Oh, I doubt my mother had one. Her sense of humor rivaled her passion for poetry, especially the works of Michael Wigglesworth, the seventeenth-century poet."

Mama gave Charity a grave look. "Buddy was right, baby. Some things is better kept quiet."

Lee Allen slapped Jerry Ritter on the back. "Wigglesworth, is it? After all these years, it took a woman to get it out of him. I'd say that's true love, wouldn't you, Jerry?"

Mr. Ritter grinned and nodded. "Can't say I much blame him for holding out."

When the laughter in the room died down, Charity peered into Buddy's eyes. "So you're telling me the truth?"

His expression never wavered.

She nodded and sighed. "Junior it is, then. We owe it to our son to spare him the pain."

The preacher stepped forward, containing his mirth with visible effort. "Shall we proceed? Or is this wedding called off, too?"

Still smiling, Buddy looked at Charity, his expressive brows raised in question. She latched onto his arm and squared around to the front. "Go ahead, sir. I'm ready now."

"Very good." He directed a look over his spectacles at Mama, Mother Dane, and Emmy. "Now, ladies, if you'll please take your seats, we'll commence to marrying these two young folks."

Mother Dane and Emmy filed back to their pew, but Mama held her ground. "If it's all the same to you, Reverend, I'll stay close by until they're hitched." She tilted her chin at Charity. "Just in case."

The preacher nodded and adjusted his glasses. "I guess that'll be all right, but I think it's safe for you to turn loose of my arm now."

Mama stepped back after a warning glance at Charity and a sheepish grin for the preacher. He cleared his throat and began.

"Dearly beloved, we are gathered here today, in the sight of God and man, to join this couple in the bonds of holy matrimony. . . ."

EPILOGUE

Shamus Pike stood on the road outside the church. Red strained at the tether in his hand, pawing the ground and whining to get free.

Before Charity could stop her, Mama stomped off the porch and across the chapel lawn. Charity tightened her grip on Buddy's hand and hurried down the steps with the others falling in behind. "You're too late, Shamus," Mama spewed. "They're married now. Whatever you hoped to gain by coming here won't work. We're onto your tricks."

Shamus held up his hands in surrender. "No tricks, Bertha, I swear."

"That'd be a stretch to believe. What are you doing here?"

"I come to bring little Charity there a wedding present." The strain on his face turned his weak smile into a grimace. "Found this old dog here over to Magda's again yesterday morning and hauled him home."

The grimace grew wider, and he chuckled. "Weren't even lunchtime before he was right back over there. Ain't no rope will hold him, and I just can't see penning him up all the time."

Mama took a step forward, her fists clenched. "We ain't interested in your present or your story. Now clear out."

Charity gripped her arm. "Wait. Let him speak."

Shamus turned haunted eyes on Charity. "Red's always looking for you, gal. He's powerful spoilt to you of a sudden. I figure this hound has his heart set on where he wants to be, and I can't fight it no more." He held the rope out to her. "You'd be doing me a favor if you'd just go ahead and take him."

Thunderstruck, Charity fumbled to speak. Shamus parting with Red was unthinkable. "Are you sure?"

His expression looked more like a smile now. "Consider him a wedding gift from me and my girls. Please take him, Charity. I think it would've pleased Thad."

"Don't speak his name," Mama hissed. "You ain't worthy of it."

Charity pulled her back. "Mama, don't–"

Shamus held up his hand. "No, let her talk. It's the truth, and she's got every right to say it."

The anguish on his face made Charity's insides ache.

He turned to Mama. "Just let me explain a few things, Bertha; then I'll be on my way."

Charity slid her arm around her mama's waist. "Go ahead, Mr. Pike. Have your say."

Before he spoke, Shamus eyed Mama as if waiting for her to protest. "I don't know if you all know this, but my wife is descended from royal stock."

Mother Dane nodded. "I reckon Elsa's mentioned it once or twice."

Mama grunted. "Once or twice a day."

Shamus lowered his eyes. "Oh, she wallows in it, all right, but it's true enough. Her great-grandpappy was the ruler of some foreign country I can't even pronounce. A real blue blood who left behind plenty of money. 'Course the family pretty much disowned Elsa after she run off with a poor farmer like me."

He got a faraway look in his eyes. "I guess my Elsa loved me in the early days. Back then she made me feel like I was a king myself." He shook his head. "But I ain't never provided for her the way she was accustomed to. Not like she deserved." He sighed. "I told myself if I could just do more, work harder. . ." He faltered and looked away.

Charity met Mother Dane's eyes over Mama's head.

"Folks all around me were striking oil and getting rich, and not a drop to be found on my whole place. You have to understand, it made me feel doomed to failure."

Shamus dropped his shoulders and cried great, gulping sobs that tore from his throat and sent chills up Charity's spine. He cried so hard it forced him to his knees, and he knelt there and sobbed out the rest. "Bertha, I'm so ashamed. I told myself it was for Thad, that a woman alone couldn't manage the kind of money you'd come into, that I would still provide for you and Charity." He covered his ears with his hands as if he couldn't stand to hear his own words. "The truth is, I wanted it for my girls. I needed to see them proud of me again."

Peering at Mama with grief-stricken eyes, he began to plead. "I know it's no excuse for what I done to you and Charity, Bertie, but Lord knows, I'm sorry. Could you ever find it in your hearts to forgive me?"

When Charity started toward Shamus, Red surged forward, pulling free of Shamus's hand. He reached Charity and leaped, prancing around on his hind legs.

Buddy caught the rope just in time to keep the dog off her dress and handed him off to Nash. Then he helped Charity lift the sobbing man to his feet.

Charity wrapped her arms around Shamus. "There now. Please don't cry, Mr. Pike. Of course we forgive you."

Mama planted herself in glaring defiance. "Don't you dare speak for me, daughter. I do no such thing. I ain't forgave nothing."

Whipping around, Charity stared at her in disbelief. "Mama, look at him!"

"I don't care."

Motioning for Emmy to join her, Charity walked to where Mama stood, all tight fists and rigid back. She placed Emmy between them and pulled her into a tight embrace from behind. "Mama, you've always tried to live your life according to God's Word, and you taught me to do the same. Now isn't that true?"

She bit her bottom lip and nodded.

"Don't you remember the passage that says, 'Ye thought evil against me; but God meant it unto good'? Look around you. This day would be so different if Emmy hadn't done what she did. I'm not saying she did a good thing, but God turned it around and used it to bless us. If I hadn't forgiven her, if she wasn't here to share it with me, this day would hold far less meaning."

She gave Emmy one more squeeze then took hold of Mama's shoulders, pointing her to where Shamus cried unashamedly next to Buddy. "He made a terrible mistake, but Shamus was Papa's dearest friend. He came here today to ask for mercy."

Mama shrugged and swayed like a stubborn child. "Maybe someday I'll give it. Just not today. The hurt's too fresh."

"He's asking today."

"I want to," she whispered, slanting her eyes up at Charity. "I just cain't. What he done was too bad."

Charity gave her a pointed look. "And where is that written in scripture?"

Still sullen, Mama stared off down the road for a time before she answered. "I guess it ain't."

"And what is? You've said it to me a thousand times."

Mama dropped her shoulders and sighed. " 'If ye forgive not men their trespasses, neither will your Father forgive your trespasses.' "

Shamus staggered forward, a plea in his hollow eyes. "I can't live with myself no more, Bert. Please grant me pardon. I won't go home 'til you do. I'll hound you worse than Red's done Charity."

Charity slid her arm around her mama's waist. "I think your someday has come. Today is a perfect day for forgiveness."

Mama tensed in Charity's arms. She shuddered and sighed once more before her body relaxed. Pulling free, she turned to smile at each expectant face. "We've laid a feast for my daughter's wedding party over to the Danes' house. I expect to see all of you there."

She squared her shoulders and started across the yard. As she passed by Shamus, she paused, her eyes still aimed straight ahead. "Nash laid a wild hog and some backstrap on the pit. Seeing you're partial to smoked meat, why don't you fetch Elsa and Amy Jane and come on by the house."

Shamus reached as if to touch her arm but didn't. "Thank you, Bertha. I know right well I don't deserve it."

As if they were the words she needed to hear, Mama met his eyes at last. "None of us do, Shamus. None of us do."

She peered up at him for several minutes, one hand on her hip, the other shading her eyes from the sun, until she seemed to come to a decision. "Say, do you know anything about raising cattle?"

The man's shame-laden eyelids widened in surprise. "Cattle, you say? I reckon I know some."

"Tell you what," Mama said. "Let's you and me have us a little powwow on the subject after this shindig, all right?" She waved over her shoulder at Mother Dane. "Come along, Magda. Quit lollygagging about. We got us a feed to put on."

Buddy slipped up behind Charity. "We'd best get started, too, honey. It's a long way to St. Louis, and that's after your mama turns us loose."

Emmy took Charity's hand and squeezed it. "I'm going to miss you so much."

"I'll miss you, too, just dreadfully. But I have to meet my new in-laws, don't I?" She patted Emmy's fingers. "Don't worry, the month will go by fast and we'll be home again. We won't stay a day longer than we planned. Buddy has to get back and help Mama run the oil business."

Buddy shook his head. "We won't have that reason to hurry back, sugar." He put one arm around Lee's shoulder and the other around Jerry's. "We're leaving your mama in capable hands."

Charity considered their warm, open faces and decided Buddy was right. Not all oilmen were bad, after all.

Buddy nodded at Red. "Now I guess we'll need someone to keep your old dog in line. Nash, do you mind keeping an eye on that flop-eared critter until we get home?"

Nash grinned all over and tightened his hold on the rope. "Why sure, Mistah Pierce. I'll be more'n happy to."

Charity pressed against Buddy and let him take her in his arms. "So, dear husband, how does the idea of raising champion bloodhounds strike you?"

Buddy smiled. "Harder than raising a brood of kids, I'd wager."

"If they're all as stubborn as Red, you'll win that bet," she said, laughing. "He's just a big old baby himself."

At the mention of his name, the dog strained against the rope in Nash's hand and drew a slow, lazy tongue over Charity's fingers.

Emmy laughed and pointed. "Look at that. He kissed your hand."

Charity frowned and pulled a lace hankie from her bodice. "Goodness, he's forever doing that."

"Sure he does," Nash said, leaning to scratch Red between the ears. "This old boy's a true Southern gentleman. A gentleman gon' always kiss a lady's hand."

Red lowered himself to the ground and stretched his legs out in front. With a contented sigh, he rested his head, letting his big ears puddle in a wad, and closed his droopy eyes.

Nash chuckled. "Least he don't too much mind sharing Miss Charity. You're in luck there, Mistah Pierce."

Buddy frowned. "I guess it wouldn't matter if *I* minded some, now, would it?"

When the laughter died down, Charity feigned anger. "You all make me sound like some old bone to be fought over."

Buddy leaned to kiss her cheek. The way he cupped her head, tangling his fingers in the hair at the base of her neck, thrilled Charity to her toes.

"Not just any old bone, little wife," he whispered. " 'Bone of my bones, and flesh of my flesh,' which leaves old Red there out in the cold."

Charity blushed and pulled away. "Well, at least he's finally calmed down some. Look at him. Just lying there as meek as a lamb."

"That's because his heart be at rest," Nash said. "He finally caught up to what he been chasing."

Buddy pulled Charity close again and tilted her face to his, love so evident in his eyes. "I know how you feel, old boy." He directed his words at Red, but his gaze remained locked on Charity's face. "I know just how you feel."

A stiff breeze picked up, gusting over the church grounds, mussing Charity's hair and flapping her skirts. Unafraid, she raised her face to greet the sheltering wings and welcomed the changing wind.

Discussion Questions

1. After being jilted at the altar, Charity Bloom braves stares and whispers from the locals in Humble, Texas. Why do you think the innocent victim often pays a higher price for the sins of others?
2. Though Charity loves her quirky, outspoken mama, she's a source of frustration and embarrassment at times. How do you think Charity handled her temptation to be ashamed of her mother? How can we best love, honor, and show patience for the eccentric characters God places in our lives?
3. The nature of Buddy's job in oil exploration requires a close association with those seeking fulfillment from the accumulation of easy money. Charity's negative reaction to the possibility of newfound riches confuses him. Money can be the source of comfort, security, and pleasure, but is it absolutely necessary for our happiness?
4. Despite Emmy's terrible betrayal, Charity realizes she still loves her and wants to continue their longstanding relationship. Have you ever been surprised by the depth of your love for and willingness to forgive a person who caused you great pain?
5. Charity mistakes her attraction to the handsome, charismatic Daniel for lasting love. When she realizes she's more hurt over Emmy's betrayal than Daniel's, she questions her feelings for him. After her powerful response to Buddy, and later when she falls in love with him, she sees the difference and knows she almost made a terrible mistake. How many failed marriages and broken relationships might be linked to the same self-deception? Without gossiping, share what you have witnessed.
6. It's been said that "we don't know what we've got till it's gone." Easily lured from his commitment to Charity by Emmy's blond curls and dimples, why did Daniel find Charity so irresistible once he saw her with Buddy Pierce? After succeeding in winning Emmy's heart, why did Daniel's game lose its thrill, and why did his desire for her turn to disgust?

7. Daniel Clark is skulking behind a juniper tree, a symbol of evil in legend and folklore, waiting to declare his fickle love for Charity. What significance can be seen in the dung beetle crawling on Emmy's leg in the hollow?
8. In a quest for God, we dress in our Sunday best, drive to church, sit on pews, and pray. Wracked with pain and shame, Emmy cries out to God from a dank, moldy hog wallow, and He's faithful to meet her there. Why do we restrict our dealings with God to buildings of brick and mortar when He longs for intimate relationship?
9. After her appointment with God in the hollow, no one is more surprised than Emmy by the manifestation of her new nature. Though sincere in asking God's forgiveness, it took accepting Nash's explanation for her to come to terms with the import of the encounter. It seemed God had stood waiting for the first possible chance to step in and heal Emmy's life. How far will God go in His eagerness to reconcile with man?
10. In desperation, Charity takes her situation out of God's hands and tries to "fix" things by tricking Daniel into marriage, when all the while God had the solution already worked out. How is this similar to the patriarch Abraham and his wife Sarah's efforts to work out the details of their problem? How is it different?
11. Though absent in the flesh, Thaddeus Bloom, Charity's papa, is a strong presence in the story. Through Bertha and Charity's memories and Bertha's revelation that his essence lingers in his daughter, we get a fairly good picture of him. In what ways do those we've lost in death continue to live in us?

Texas Fortunes *Book No. 3*

Marcia Gruver

Dedication

To my grandfather, Thomas A. Cooper–
May my efforts to carry on in your footsteps bring honor to your memory.

Acknowledgments

To Rebecca Germany and Barbour Publishing for the chance to write the books of my heart and for your continued care and support. I'll be forever grateful.

To my dear friend Elizabeth Ludwig, word maestro extraordinaire. Thanks for rounding out my rough edges. You helped make this book sing.

To Tracy Jones, my collaborator and plot consultant.

To Nina Gracia and Robert Gonzalez, my Spanish language consultants.

To Bert Lee Bell, for his kind assistance and for providing the wonderful historical resource entitled Memories of Peter Tumlinson Bell, *compiled by Verner Lee Bell.*

To Nelta Coggins and Jim Marmion for providing invaluable reference material.

To Pete Wilson, my cattle consultant.

They shall not hunger nor thirst;
neither shall the heat nor sun smite them:
for he that hath mercy on them shall lead them,
even by the springs of water shall he guide them.

Isaiah 49:10

CHAPTER 1

Humble, Texas
August 1906

The stagnant well appeared bottomless, as dank and murky as a grave. Emmy rested her arms on the cold, jagged stones and leaned to peer into the abyss. Mama's embroidered lace hankie, shimmering in the meager light, hung from an outcropping of rock about six feet down. Narrowing her eyes, she peered at the spot of white that stood out from the surrounding darkness and heaved a sigh, stirring the fetid air below and raising a noxious odor that took her breath.

She pushed up her sleeves and blasted a droopy blond ringlet from her eyes with a frustrated puff of air. There was no help for it—at the risk of certain death, she had to retrieve that handkerchief.

A figure loomed, drawing alongside her with a grunt.

She jumped, and her heart shot past her throat. Chest pounding, she wasted a glare on the dark profile, noticing for the first time a scatter of lines around his eyes and tiny gray curlicues in his sideburns.

"Nash! I nearly leaped over the side." She swatted his arm. "I've asked you to stop sneaking up on me. I've a good mind to fit you with a cowbell."

A chuckle rumbled from his chest, as deep as the chasm. "I didn't go to scare you, Miss Emmy." He bent his lanky body so far she feared he'd tumble headfirst into the never-ending shaft. "Say, what we looking for inside this hole?"

"We're not looking for anything. I've already found it." Emmy clutched his shirtsleeve and pulled him away. "Go fetch me a lantern, and be quick about it." She tucked her chin in the direction of the palomino pony lounging under a nearby oak, nibbling at the circle of high grass around the trunk. "Take Trouble. He'll be quicker than walking."

Nash frowned and rubbed the knuckles of one hand along his temple, as if an ache had sprung up there. "What you need a lantern for, with the sun up and shining the past five hours? There's plenty of light to see."

She braced herself and pointed. "Not down there."

Nash's sleepy eyes flew open. His startled gaze bounced along her finger to the circular wall of weathered stones. "Down there?" He took a cautious step back. "What's in this sour old pit that might concern you?"

Emmy swallowed hard. She could trust Nash with anything but dreaded his reaction all the same. "It's. . .one of Mama's hankies." She squeezed her eyes shut and ducked her head.

His shoulders eased, and he ambled over to gaze inside. "Is that all?"

If only it were. Emmy risked a peek at him. "You don't understand."

He winced as if she'd spoken a bad omen. "Uh, uh. Not from her good batch? Them she's always cackling about?"

Emmy cringed and nodded.

The delicate, lacy linens held an uncommon depth of meaning for Emmy's mama. Hand embroidered in Germany by her grandmother then brought to the Americas and placed in Mama's hope chest, they represented heart, hearth, and homeland to Magdalena Dane. In equal measure, they represented distress, discontent, and discord to her only daughter, because the bothersome bits of cloth seemed determined to cause Emmy grief.

Nash's stunned expression hardened into an accusing glare. "Why, Miss Emmy? Why you done brought about such misery? You ain't s'posed to touch 'em, and you know it." His graying brows fluttered like two moths bent on escape. "There's scarce few left, and your mama blames you for them what's missing."

She moaned and flapped her hands. "I didn't mean to take the silly thing. It was warm when I rode out this morning. I knew I'd likely sweat, so I snagged a hankie from the clothesline. I never looked at it until a few minutes ago. That's how this terrible mishap came about. I held it up as I rode, staring in disbelief. Trouble was galloping across the yard when the wind caught it and. . ." She motioned behind her. "The willful rag drifted down the well before I could stop the horse and chase after it."

Emmy lowered her eyes then peered up at him through her lashes. "None of this is my fault, Nash. Papa should've covered this smelly cistern months ago, and those wretched handkerchiefs have a mind of their own."

The hint of a smile played around Nash's lips. "If so, they harbor a mighty poor opinion of you."

She wrinkled her nose at him.

Wagging his head, he rested the back of his hand on his side. "In all my years of working for your family, of all the fits I've seen your mama pitch, the worst have been over the loss of them fancy scraps of cloth." He shuddered. "Miss Emmy, I'd be mighty grateful if you'd wait and break the news to her after I leave for the day. She gon' be powerful upset."

Emmy held up and wiggled a finger. "On the contrary. I won't be upsetting Mama."

"How you figure that?"

"Because there's no need to tell her."

Nash propped his elbow in one hand and rubbed his chin with the other. "Missy, I thought you was done telling lies and scheming. Don't forget you're a saint of God now."

A saint of God. Yes, she was, through no fault of her own. Like Elijah's fiery chariot, God had swirled into Emmy's life in a weak moment and delivered her from herself. Not that she minded His day-to-day presence. In fact, she rather enjoyed the peace He brought. It was during times of temptation when she found the constant stirring in her heart to do the right thing a bit of a bother. Yet no wonder, really. In the past, she'd had precious little practice in doing the right thing.

She blinked up at Nash. "I have no plans to lie, and I won't need to scheme. We're simply going to return Great-grandmother's hankie to Mama's clothesline, washed, rinsed, and fresh as a newborn calf."

Nash stared then shook his head. "No, ma'am. You jus' forget about what *we* gon' do. Question is how are *you* gon' pull it off?"

"I'll show you." She shooed him with her hands. "Run fetch that lantern like I asked and leave the rest to me."

Still shaking his head, Nash mounted Trouble and laid in his heels. The horse bolted across the yard to the well-kept shed tucked behind Emmy's two-story house. With a furtive glance toward the porch, Nash eased the door open and slipped inside.

While she waited, Emmy watched a rowdy band of crows swarm Nash's cornfield. The black bandits bickered and pecked for position before settling in for a meal, oblivious to the mop-headed stick Nash had dressed in a ragged shirt and floppy hat and then shoved in the ground. She dared not call his attention to the culprits or he'd bluster after them, shouting and waving his arms like a demented windmill, leaving her to cope alone with her pressing dilemma.

She jerked her gaze from the birds when Nash rode up and slid off Trouble to the ground, a lighted lantern in his hand.

Handing over the light with a flourish, he lowered one brow and pinned her with a squinty look. "Here's what you asked for. Jus' be sure to leave me plumb out of the story when you go explaining yourself to your mama."

He turned to go, but Emmy caught hold of his shirttail. "Not so fast. I'm not done with you."

Nash covered his ears and reeled away. "Don't tell me no mo'. I ain't seen nothing, and I ain't heard nothing. If anybody needs me, I'll be feeding the chickens."

Emmy aimed a haughty laugh at his back. "It's too late for that. You're in up to your hat, and it's no less punishment than you deserve for sneaking about all the time."

Nash dug in his heels and stood facing the grove of loblolly pine at the edge of the yard, his body stiff as a post.

Repentant, she softened her voice to a plea. "I'm sorry, Nash. I had no call to utter such a thing. It's just. . .I can't do this without you."

Arms dangling at his sides, he tipped his head toward the sky and whispered something, a prayer no doubt, before turning to face her. "What you want me to do?"

She peppered him with grateful kisses then grabbed his hand. "Come over here." Hauling him to the gaping cavity, she lowered the lamp. "See? There it is."

They gazed at the only bright spot in the oppressive gloom, their ability to see inside the shaft made no better by the frail circle of yellow light.

Nash shrugged and drew back from the side. "Too far down. May as well wave it good-bye then go 'fess up to what you done."

Emmy gripped his arm. "Nonsense. We can get it out of there."

"How, short of fishing it out with a cane pole? And I got no hooks." He scratched his head. "I reckon I could take my hammer and pound a bend in a nail."

She shook her head. "Too risky. If the hankie slips off it'll settle to the bottom, and that'll be the end of it." She drew a determined breath. "I have a better idea."

Nash's eyebrows rose on his forehead, reaching new heights, even for him. "What sort of idea? Harebrained or foolhardy? Them's the only two kinds you have."

She swallowed hard and fingered the wooden bucket sitting on the wall. "I'm going to straddle this, and you'll lower me down to fetch it."

The shaggy brows bested their last mark. "You cain't mean it, Miss Emmy."

"I do so."

"Then your idea is both harebrained and foolhardy. You must be plain tetched up under them pretty white locks. S'pose that rope snaps in two?"

"Oh, pooh." She patted the heavy hemp coiled around the crank. "This rope is thick and sound." She pointed over her shoulder at the horse. "You could lower Trouble down that well."

He nodded. "Yes'm. That's exactly what I'd be doing." He jerked off his weathered hat and dashed it against his leg. "Don't ask me to put you in that kind of danger. No, missy. I won't do it. Not for nothing in this wide world."

Touched, Emmy smiled at the man who'd been like a father to her over the years, far more of a parent than her own papa, who didn't stay home often enough to have much practice at the role. She took Nash's hand and squeezed it. "I won't be in any danger. As long as you're holding the handle, I know I'll be safe." She peered up into his sulky brown eyes. "You know if you don't help me I'll just find a way to do it myself. I have to get that hankie."

He gaped at her. "The silly thing ain't worth dying for, is it? Your mama has fussed at you before, and you lived to tell the tale. Why is this time so all-fired special?"

She squared around to face him. "I can't have her angry about anything just now. I'm planning to ask permission to go to St. Louis when Mama travels with Aunt Bertha to South Texas. It'll be hard enough to convince her as it is. If she gets in a snit, my plan is doomed."

"Why they going off so far?"

"It's Aunt Bertha's idea. Now that she has money, she's determined to go into the cattle business. She's bent on learning all she can. Papa knows a very successful rancher down south who's willing to teach her everything he knows."

"Cain't you jus' stay home?"

"They'll be gone for a month or better. Mama refuses to leave me here alone for that long, and I'd much prefer going to see Charity."

Nash smiled and nodded. " 'Specially with her jus' done birthing the little one."

Emmy beamed. "Exactly. I can help Charity bring him home."

A thrill coursed through her at the thought of seeing Charity and Buddy's new baby boy. Emmy and Charity were as close as twin sisters, best friends like their mamas had always been. Emmy's mama and Aunt Bertha had grown up together in Jefferson before moving to Humble.

Last year, a handsome young oilman came to town and found oil on Aunt Bertha's land. Charity wound up married to him and soon left for St. Louis to meet his parents. When Buddy found out she was expecting, he kept her in the city so she'd be close to good medical care.

Not a day had passed that Emmy didn't think of Charity and long to see her. She was coming home next month, bringing little Thad to meet the family.

Nash narrowed his eyes. "You ain't jus' trying to sneak off to St. Louis to see that oilman friend of Mistah Buddy's, are you? Don't think I didn't see you making eyes at him the whole time that preacher was trying to marry off Miss Charity."

Emmy whirled. "Who? Mr. Ritter?" She dismissed the thought with a wave of her hand. "Jerry Ritter was just a passing fancy."

Nash raised a cynical brow.

"Oh, pooh, Nash! You stop that!" She fiddled with the row of tiny buttons on her sleeve. "Besides. . .Aunt Bertha claims Mr. Ritter was recently betrothed to a childhood sweetheart." She flicked off an insect from the cuff of her blouse and dashed away her humiliation with the same resolve. "Therefore, my desire to be in St. Louis has nothing to do with him. I just need to see Charity. If I get into any more trouble, Mama's bound to haul me with them to that dreadful desert town instead. If she does, I'll just dry up along with it and perish. I mean it!"

Grinding the toe of his oversized boot in the dirt, Nash sighed and shifted his weight. "I don't know, Miss Emmy. . ."

Emmy stifled a grin. She had him. "I'll be just fine. I promise. Now help me climb up."

Still mumbling his objections, he offered an elbow to Emmy so she could pull up and sit on the uneven stones. Unfastening the buttoned flap on her split skirt, she swung her legs over and settled on the side, trying hard not to look past her boots. "Turn your head while I sit astride the pail. It won't look so dainty in this outfit."

Nash gazed toward the field, obviously too distracted to notice the raiding crows.

Still clinging to his arm, Emmy held her breath and pulled the dangling rope closer, guiding it between her legs. "All right, I'm ready. Lean your weight into the handle. I'm about to push off."

Nash shifted his gaze to the sky. "Oh, sweet Jesus. Please protect this chil'."

Holding her breath, she scooted from the edge, squealing when her body spun and dipped about a foot. "Nash! Have you got it?"

"I've got it. Stop squirming now. You heavier than you look."

Emmy forced herself to still, more afraid than she'd expected to be. She felt more than saw the yawning gulf, a great gaping mouth poised to swallow her whole. "Hand me the lantern and then you can lower me. But go slowly, for heaven's sake."

She breathed a prayer as she spiraled past the opening and descended. Glancing up, she bit her lip and watched the rope unwind from the wobbly reel, outlined by a circle of light. Misguided but determined white roots that had pushed through cracks in the mortar groped at her, snagging her hem and sleeves. Crisscrossed nets of taut, silky threads offered whispers of resistance before giving way and sticking to the exposed parts of her legs. Emmy held the soft glow of the lamp closer to the side, shuddering when eight-legged bodies skittered in every direction. She gritted her teeth, suppressing a shriek and the urge to order Nash to haul her out of the wide-awake nightmare.

You can do this. Just a little more and you'll be there. Three more turns and you'll have Mama's hankie in your hands. This will all be worth it then.

Exhaling her relief, she drew even with the jutting rock that had caught the precious heirloom. Holding the lantern out of the way, she swayed her body until the motion brought her closer to the wall.

She snatched at the white spot. Instead of soft linen, she felt thick, sticky padding. In place of the crush of a napkin gathered in her palm, there was the unmistakable writhing of something alive.

CHAPTER 2

Carrizo Springs, Texas

"You will find what you seek in the fire, Isi."

Diego Isi Marcelo ducked his head and cast a dour look at his walking companion. "Please, Mother. I've asked you never to call me that in town. Around here I'm known as Diego."

A rolling tumble of weeds skipped across the windblown street and bounced through the heart of Carrizo Springs, dodging pedestrians, horses' hooves, and ox-drawn carts headed for the fields. Diego sidestepped a laughing boy rolling a barrel hoop with a stick, his face the color of buttonwood leaves in the fall. A skinny dog and three other sun-baked children chased behind him.

Diego's mother clutched his arm and pinned him with endless brown eyes. "Diego is the name your father bestowed to appease your grandmamma. Still, *Señora* Marcelo never forgave him for marrying a Choctaw." She nudged him and smiled. "There's nothing wrong with Little Deer, Isi. It's a fine Indian name. Besides"—her wounded expression erased the smile, and she swept her upturned palm toward the crowd of men in wide sombreros, short jackets, and ruffled shirts—"which of these prancing *charros* delivered you under his skirts beneath a desert moon?" She jutted her chin. "I would think my opinion should concern you more."

Laughing, Diego raised both hands in the air. "I surrender. Call me what you will." Wrapping his arm around her shoulders, he snuggled his tiny mother close. "Now then, what's this about finding what I seek? In the fire, you said? Sounds like more tribal superstition."

She shot him a warning glance. "You'd do well to heed my visions, son. And even better not to scorn them. They come to me from *Chihowa Palami*."

Diego sighed. "I would think the Almighty had more pressing matters to concern Him." He tucked his thumb inside his belt and affected a saucy strut. "Actually, I don't need anything your fire might bring. I like my life just fine the way it is."

Her short, dark lashes fluttered, the motion almost hidden by high cheekbones and deep-set eyelids. "Your posing may work on John Rawson and his *vaqueros*. Some days you manage to conceal your disquieted soul even from me. Just don't think you can fool the Great Spirit."

He grinned. "Now, Mother, I know for a fact God's Spirit is too busy to worry about Diego Marcelo's disquieted soul. He has His hands full hiding Pancho Villa from the *Rurales*." He leaned close to her face. "Oh, and keeping Theodore Roosevelt from shooting off his toes."

Her lips tightened into a determined line, and her fingers brushed his hand. "I don't wish to astonish you, Isi, but God is more concerned about your future than I am."

Diego feigned shock. His mother waved off his teasing then raised her strong chin and stared into the distance. "Chihowa Palami sees you on the inside. He's in every beat of your lonely heart. God's love for you is great. Many times He has whispered of you in my dreams. Your future will appear in a whirlwind of smoke and rise to meet you in flames brighter than the beard of my Irish father."

He leaned closer and whispered next to her ear. "That future wouldn't happen to have blond hair and blue eyes, now would it?"

She elbowed his ribs. "If so, she wouldn't be the one you speak of."

His brows lifted. "Not the lovely *Señorita* Rawson? Are you certain? I find myself disappointed."

There was a slight pause in her stride before she recovered. "You fancy Greta Rawson?"

Diego guided her up the steps of the boardwalk. "So there's something about me you don't know? *That* astonishes me, Mother." He winked and caressed her head between her dark braids. "As a matter of fact, I'm having serious thoughts about asking Mr. Rawson's permission to court his fair daughter."

She tilted her head to look at him, her eyes guarded. "Careful, son. Once outside the gate, you must ride the horse you're sitting."

He chuckled. "What sort of Choctaw proverb is that?"

"Only the wisdom of a concerned mother. Good sense speaks every language, except in matters of the heart. If you shame Greta Rawson, you shame her people. You'll wind up the foreman of a different ranch." She shot him a weighty glance. "In a different state."

"Shame Greta? You know me better. My intentions are honorable."

"Because you are honorable, Isi. I only meant that when you discover she's not the right woman for you, you'll have to end the relationship or live in misery for the rest of your life."

He gave her a piercing look. "*When* I find out? You talk like you know something you're not telling me."

She tightened her grip on his arm and focused on something in the distance. Diego smiled and shook his head. Watching her noble, determined profile, he wondered what secrets she kept and what mischief lay ahead for him.

A curse rang out from inside the grocer's shop as they passed. Hurried footsteps brought the man who'd uttered the vulgar words onto the walkway behind them. "Whoo-ee! I thought my eyes was playing tricks, but sure enough, that's a real red-skinned Injun squaw."

Diego stopped walking so fast he nearly tripped his mother. He spun, his arm tightening around her shoulders.

Smiling widely, the jovial-looking, raw-faced fellow stood ten feet away, both hands on his hips. "Look at her, prancing down the street like she belongs there. If that don't take the biscuit."

Cuddy Rawson, the son of Diego's boss, ducked out of the store behind the man. He shoved his hat on his blond head, his eyes round pools of disbelief.

Several others, with expressions similar to Cuddy's, followed him outside.

The senseless dolt on the boardwalk cupped his hands around his mouth. "Hey, Pocahontas. . ." Laughing now, he pointed north, presumably toward the Indian territories. "Your tribe went that way."

Diego left his mother and approached the grinning *bufón*. "I'm feeling generous today, mister. I'll give you one chance to apologize to my mother, but make it quick."

The stranger furrowed his brow. "You mean that little buffalo muncher is your mama? Sorry, Cochise. I figured you fer a local."

Cuddy rushed him at the same time as Diego, but Cuddy got there first. Catching the man by the scruff of his neck, he whirled him into the waiting crowd, who surrounded him and hustled him down the street.

"Hey," he cried to his captors. "What the devil do you think you're doing?"

"A *muy* big favor, *señor*," one of them answered. "We're saving your life."

Cuddy gripped Diego's arms, holding him until the gang of men rounded the corner behind the livery. When his fists uncurled and his breathing slowed, Cuddy released him then shrugged and grinned. "Sorry, Diego. I had to step in and help him out. He's new in town. Poor man had no idea what kind of trouble he was in."

Diego drew a trembling hand through his brown curls and gave a shaky laugh. "It's for the best, my friend." He worked tense kinks from his neck then tugged his leather vest into place. "I suppose God watches out for fools."

Cuddy glanced toward the spot where the crowd had disappeared. "He sure enough rescued that one."

Diego winked and patted Cuddy on the back. "I was referring to myself."

Cuddy tipped his Stetson at Diego's mother. "Melatha. Good to see you're feeling better."

Diego's mother smiled and nodded. Diego rejoined her and she slipped beneath his arm, her face void of expression. "I appreciate what you meant to do, but there was no need."

"No need? He insulted you."

"With empty words? No, Little Deer, he insulted himself and his people. If not for Cuddy, you would have done the same." She patted his hand. "I do wish you'd learn to control your temper, son. A public brawl is no fit way to settle a quarrel. Remember, your ancestors were tranquil people."

He drew back. "Tranquil? You're forgetting a few ancestors, Mother. The Spaniards on my father's side had lively dispositions, as did your father's Irish relations, whose tempers boiled the blood in their veins. Both of those men would've avoided a public brawl, too. They'd have shot him where he stood."

"I'd prefer you sought the way of the Choctaw. The way of peace."

He wagged his finger in her face. "There, you see? If my soul is disquieted, there's your reason. How could I know the proper way to conduct myself? I'm a mixed breed. A mongrel. A man without a past."

Her brows bunched in disapproval. "Nonsense. Your past is rich in culture."

"Which culture would that be? The blood is so mixed in my veins, I've lost all notion of who I am."

"Tradition is stronger than blood, Isi. You learned this at your mother's knee, and I've strived to teach you well. More to the point, only one bloodline really matters—that of Chihowa Ushi, the blessed Son of God."

Melatha sat alone at her roughhewn kitchen table, gazing through the window at the rear entrance of the bunkhouse. Isi had disappeared through the door the minute they returned from town, his mood brooding and restless. His state of unease would add many prayers to her lips come nightfall.

Her gaze shifted past the vaqueros' quarters to the field where wind-ripples danced through the tall grass like spirits playing tag. Scattered cactus stood with upraised arms, offering dark purple pears as sweet, juicy sacrifices. The fluffy white vine that young Cuddy called "old man's beard" grew along the barbed wire fence in mounded clumps like the piled-up snowdrifts back home.

The Bible spread open on the table pulled Melatha's attention to the present. She finished the passage in chapter 8 of Solomon's Song.

"Love is strong as death; jealousy is cruel as the grave: the coals thereof are coals of fire, which hath a most vehement flame."

She shuddered. The ancient words struck her heart with another confirmation of her fiery vision.

Chihowa Palami, bow my son to Your will. A bent reed turns to iron in the Father's hand.

As she always did before closing the worn leather book, she read the words inscribed in bold script in the center of the first page: *Melatha Rhona Flynn, daughter of Kelly Míchéal and Hatabushik Loosa Flynn. May you ever heed the truth revealed within these pages.*

"Ah, Isi," she whispered, her fingers tracing the letters, "your grandfather's words are your heritage, the connection to the past you seek. Though you can't see it yet, they're the path to your future as well."

His restless soul filled with longing, Isi had run so fast from himself he'd landed them both in Carrizo Springs near the border of Texas and Mexico. But no matter how far he'd run, his destiny perched on the horizon, determined to overtake him.

As for Melatha, she didn't mind where her son's desperate flight had driven them. She loved South Texas, the land Isi called "God's country," and had plans to settle in for good.

When they first arrived, the Rawsons had welcomed her into a room in their home but soon realized she needed her own space. Mr. Rawson graciously offered the northeast corner of the yard where Isi built her a spacious *jacal* out of mud and sticks. He'd seen to it that the walls were sturdy and sound, and Melatha blessed the day she'd first set foot beneath its humble thatched roof.

There was a spare corner in the house for Isi's bed, but he insisted on sleeping in the drafty bunkhouse with his men. He claimed he needed their respect more than his own comfort, and he'd never ask them to do anything he hadn't first done himself.

The strength of her son's character and his willingness to take a stand in such matters was the reason Mr. Rawson promoted him from a greenhorn to foreman in only three short years.

Strength of character failed her son when the odor of griddlecakes drifted from her hearth in the mornings, or roasted ears of corn at night. For meals he left his charges to eat Cook's grub in the bunkhouse and joined his mother at her table–a fact that warmed her heart as hot as her coals and kept her skillet sizzling.

Melatha had no knowledge of the life Isi had lived during their five years apart, and she had never asked him. Her interest lay in his future, not his past.

God's Spirit had shown her this future while she prayed. Not a clear image–only hair as white as the vine tangled along the fence and eyes like a fair summer sky.

EMMY'S EQUAL

A lively young filly would come to her brooding son from the north. Their hearts would meld in a whirlwind of fire, and their passion would restore Isi to life.

CHAPTER 3

Emmy couldn't open her hand fast enough. . .or sling the hideous spider far enough. Chest aching, she realized it had been a matted web she'd seen all along. Mama's hankie likely floated atop the foul pool below—forever lost.

"Nash!" a shrill voice called from above her head.

Emmy grew rigid. *Mama!*

She heard a muffled gasp from Nash then the rattle and whir of the crack as she plummeted wildly. Before she could think, scream, or pray—before she stood facing her Maker—she came to a jarring halt with a jerk and twang of the rope.

The ancient bucket collapsed beneath her, parts of it scraping and pinging off the rocks before landing with a splash. She gasped and tightened her legs on the remaining slats, gripping the rope so tightly the rough hemp burned her palms. Bile rose in her throat, made worse by the rancid smell of the water, much closer now. Even more disturbing, the plunge had snuffed her light.

Something cold sailed out of the darkness, landing on her bare skin then slithering up her leg. Not a snake, the thing had tiny grasping feet.

Frantic, Emmy brushed it off before clinging to her lifeline with trembling fingers. She opened her mouth to cry out to Nash, but Mama got to him first.

"Here you are. For corn's sake, where've you been all morning?

I've scoured the place for you."

The fact that Mama stood somewhere above, her deep, strident voice echoing in Emmy's ears, scared her nearly as much as the fall.

Get shed of her, Nash! And hurry!

"You been huntin' me, Miz Dane?" Nash's strained words tumbled down the hole. "Why, I been right here all along."

"I've called and called. Why didn't you answer?" Mama's tone meant her hands had gone to her hips.

" 'Cause I ain't heard nary a one of them calls until now. I 'spose you might've yelled louder."

"Oh, never mind. Have you seen Emmy?"

After a tense silence, Nash began to sputter. "H-Have I seen Miss Emmy? Now, that's a good question. I did see her right after breakfast, sure 'nough. 'Course I saw her yesterday, too, and—"

"Just tell her this when you see her—Willem is on his way home. He'll arrive by train tomorrow. He's decided it ain't safe for me and Bertha to go south alone, so he's coming with us."

Emmy's heart lurched. Papa going with Mama to South Texas? The new development made it infinitely more important that she avoid the trip. Emmy's relationship with her papa wouldn't exactly inspire sentimental sonnets. On the rare occasions when he happened to be home, he spent all of his time correcting her, perhaps to make up for lost time, or ignoring her completely as if she made him uneasy. If given a choice, she preferred the lectures to his silence.

"Yes'm, I'll tell Miss Emmy jus' what you said. When I see her, that is."

Emmy prayed with renewed vigor for the strength to wait Mama out. Busting her skull or drowning in stinky water might definitely impede her plans to visit St. Louis. Dying in a well or emerging from it a raving lunatic covered in newts and spiders meant she'd never have the chance to see Charity's baby. However, all of these possibilities were more enticing than an extended trip with her papa or facing her mama's wrath. She tightened her grip and held on for all she was worth.

"What are you doing out here anyway?" Mama said to Nash. "There's no time today for lollygagging. You have work to do."

"Yes, ma'am, I sho' do."

"Get on with it, then. What are you waiting for? The stalls won't sweep themselves."

"Um. . .yes'm, Miz Dane. Jus' as soon as I finish drawing a bucket for Miss Emmy's horse."

"Emmy's horse? Well, I'll be switched and tickled, there he is. What's Trouble doing out here?"

"I. . .brung him out to get a drink."

Emmy could almost hear the gears churning in Mama's head. "So, you're telling me instead of taking water to the horse you brought the horse to water? To a hole full of putrid water, in fact?"

"W–What I meant to say was," Nash stammered, "I didn't remember this well being bad till I got out here."

The hush meant more whirling parts in Mama's head. Emmy thought she could smell the smoke.

"I see. So, why's he saddled?"

"Hmm. Yes, ma'am, he's saddled all right. I can see why you'd ask that question, too. I reckon it's because Miss Emmy wants him ready to ride when I'm done watering him."

Mama blew out her breath in a whoosh that rattled all the way down the well to Emmy. "That's enough out of you. I don't know what you and that girl are up to, and I don't have time to ponder. Go on and get to those chores. Take Trouble with you. He can drink from the trough the way a critter's meant to."

"But I ain't done hauling up the bucket." With each word, Nash's voice climbed the scale toward a soprano.

"Move aside. I'll take care of it."

"I cain't let you do that, Miz Dane. It be too heavy for a lady."

"Nash, give me the crank."

"No!"

Heavy, cloying silence oozed down the shaft. Emmy hung surrounded in it until Mama recovered enough to speak.

"What did you say to me?"

"I said no. I mean, no, ma'am."

"Jonas Nash. . ."

Emmy cringed. She'd gotten Nash into terrible trouble. Mama had used his Christian name.

"I reckon I pay you fair enough wages to get a 'yes, ma'am' to most anything I ask you to do around here. Especially something as trifling as this. Now give me that handle."

Taller than most men and as solid as a boulder, Emmy's bossy, controlling mama was a formidable opponent. The tumble of russet curls pinned up on her head made her appear even larger, like the ruffled feathers of a bird facing down a rival. Grown men cowered before her no-nonsense voice, and few of them in Humble, least of all Nash, had the pluck to stand up to her when she got angry.

Even so, surely he'd never relinquish his hold and scurry off to do her bidding, leaving Emmy to plunge to her death in the gloomy deep. She held her breath and wondered at the depth of the lapping water, hoping she'd break her neck and die on the way down rather than drown in the nasty stuff.

A scuffle ensued—Nash desperately pleading, Mama as mad as a whole nest of hornets.

Emmy felt the exchange of hands on the crank when she dropped a foot lower. She started to cry softly and pray with all of her might.

"Don't let go, Miz Dane. Please, ma'am. Don't you dare let go."

"For pity's sake! What have you got at the end of this rope?"

Her mama cranked the handle and Emmy eased up a few turns. With a grunt, Mama laid her weight into it, and Emmy shot toward the circle of light in jerky bursts. She cleared the top in time to see the backside of Nash scurrying toward the barn.

Mama yelped and let go of the handle briefly before latching onto it with both hands. "Emily Bertha Dane!" she screeched. "If this ain't the last place I expected to find you." She glared toward Nash, who broke into a trot after one last anxious glance over his shoulder. "I'll deal with him later. As for you, climb out of there and explain yourself."

Emmy held out her hand.

Mama grasped it and pulled her to the side.

Emmy longed to kneel and kiss the ground, but the look on her mama's face told her she'd best save her knees for prayer.

Mama glared at her. "Do you realize you could've been killed?"

Trembling from head to toe, Emmy could only nod.

Still scowling, Mama pulled the busted bucket over the wall and rested it on the opposite side of the well. A puzzled look crossed her face before she leaned to pick something up from the ground. Holding her hand-embroidered handkerchief aloft, she gaped at Emmy in surprise. "Would you look at this? It's one of my hankies." She cocked her head and stared at it dumbly. "How do you suppose this wound up way out here?"

CHAPTER 4

Emmy's heart sped up as Daniel Clark's arms slid around her waist, his grasping hands cruelly biting into her flesh.

"Stop," she whimpered. "You're holding me too tight."

Instead of loosening, his eager fingers curled, digging deeper in her back. Emmy cringed and started to cry.

Lightning crashed overhead. "Forget about Charity," Daniel whispered. "She doesn't matter."

Emmy lifted her gaze and stared into the haunted hollows of Daniel's eyes. "She matters to me."

He stepped away from her and raised a pistol to his head.

Panic struck and sobs wracked her body. "No, Daniel!"

Anger, hatred, and blame burned in his eyes. "Time to get up, Emmy," he called, his voice shrill and distant.

"Don't do it, Daniel. Please. I said I'm sorry."

He tilted his head to the swirling black clouds and closed his eyes, his finger tightening on the trigger.

Charity stepped from the shadows and wrenched the gun from Daniel's hand. Pushing past him, she raised the barrel of the gun and aimed it straight at Emmy's chest.

Emmy's heartbreak turned to terror. "Charity, what are you doing? It's me."

Charity smiled. "I said get up right now. You hear me?" The pistol exploded with a crash that rattled the house.

Emmy opened her mouth to scream and. . .

EMMY'S EQUAL

"Emily Bertha Dane!"

Emmy's eyes flew open.

The bedroom door that had hit the wall with a resounding bang swung back toward Mama. She stood on the threshold, her plump arms folded across her buxom chest. "You'd best shake that floor, little miss. I've been shouting for ten minutes."

The bright, cheery room enveloped Emmy in a rush of yellow wallpaper and lace curtains. The shock of normalcy and light crashed against the darkness of her dream in a collision that hurt her head. She squeezed her eyelids together to block out the sun.

"Oh, honey." Mama crossed the room and sank onto the side of the bed, pulling the mattress down and rolling Emmy against her thigh. "You had the dream again, didn't you?"

Struggling to sit upright, Emmy shuddered. "How did you know?"

Mama tilted her head and sighed. "If the fright on your face hadn't told me, your tears would've given you away." She smoothed back Emmy's hair. "Did Daniel kill himself again?"

Halfway through a nod, Emmy stopped and shook her head. "No. He started to, but it was different this time." She frowned. "Charity appeared and turned the gun on me."

"Charity?" Mama crowed. "Why, she'd kiss you before she'd shoot you. You saved that girl's life. Well, from an unhappy life with that horrible Daniel, anyway." Her eyes softened. "Why can't you turn these memories loose, honey?"

Shame drew Emmy's shoulders down. "Maybe because I stole my best friend's fiancé. What sort of person does that?"

Mama nodded. "It was a plain awful thing to do, Emmy. But if you hadn't, Charity wouldn't be happily married to the man she really loves."

Emmy scrubbed her face with her hands, trying to erase the last trace of the nightmare. "Still, I actually prefer the way this dream ended. The bullet finally found the true culprit."

Mama patted her hands. "Hush that kind of talk. First off, you needn't worry about Daniel Clark's empty threat to take his own life. He holds too dear the image in his mirror. God and Charity forgave you a long time ago. You need to forgive yourself and get on with it."

"Forgiving myself is hard to do in this town, with Eunice Clark waiting around every corner to pounce."

"Daniel's mama took it hard when he up and left Humble for good. I don't suppose she'll draw in her claws any time soon." Mama's bosom heaved in a sigh. "Don't let her pin the blame on you, sugar. I suspect Daniel had leaving on his mind all along."

Emmy sat up in bed and swung her legs over the side. "Tell that to Eunice, if you don't mind."

Mama swatted Emmy's bare leg so hard it stung. "I just might do that the next time I see her. Which may be today. You and me need to take a run into town."

The forced brightness in Mama's voice set off a warning in Emmy's head. Rubbing the pink-tinged mark on her leg, she peered up past one lowered brow. "What for?"

"We got us a mess of shopping to do. Won't that be grand?" Her tone was far too cheerful, and her gaze waltzed around Emmy's, never once making contact with her eyes. "Your papa wants to buy us a brand new wardrobe."

"New clothes? Our closets are full."

Mama cleared her throat. "He insists we'll need things cut from lightweight fabric. . .since the summer months are so hot in South Texas."

"No!" Emmy shrieked and leaped to her feet. "You said he was thinking of letting me go to St. Louis."

Mama held up both hands. "Calm down, child. He did think about it and decided to say no. It's too far for you to travel without an escort, and we don't have time to arrange a proper chaperone."

"Then let me stay here," Emmy begged.

"Absolutely not. Papa forbids you staying here alone. After the incident in the well, I quite agree. You've been so moody lately. Some time away from Humble will do you good."

"St. Louis is away from Humble."

"Let it go, Emmy. St. Louis is out of the question."

Emmy's hands balled into fists. "Did you tell him about the well?"

"I said I wouldn't, didn't I?"

"Then why!"

"For your own sake. Those dreams you've been having are part of the reason. Besides, your papa would like to spend a few days with you this summer." Mama's eyes turned sorrowful. "Is that so much to ask?"

Emmy groaned inside. Far too much, coming from him. She dropped her gaze. "Can Nash come along?"

"Of course not."

"Oh, please? I need him there. Who will I talk to when I'm bored out of my mind?"

"Someone besides Nash. You know he has to stay here and run things while we're gone. You're not his only concern, Emmy. Nash has a family of his own."

She closed her eyes and let her head fall back. "Oh, bother! When do we leave?"

"Next Monday."

"So soon? That's only a week from today."

"Exactly the reason we'd best get a move on. Chances are we won't find enough suitable clothes for the heat. If we need to hire some things made to fit, a week's not very long." She leaned to kiss the top of Emmy's head. "Hurry down for breakfast, sugar. Bertha made her special biscuits."

"Why does Aunt Bert still make breakfast for us? She has enough money to hire ten cooks."

Mama smiled. "I reckon long-standing habits are hard to break. For both of us. Get a move on, sugar. It's getting late." She started to go then turned. "Don't fret over the trip. You're going to have fun."

Fun?

Emmy frowned as her mama closed the door. Living a week under the same roof as Papa would be less than fun. The word for surviving him while serving a prison sentence in a smoldering wasteland wasn't even in Emmy's dictionary.

Diego rode up even with the porch of the *casa mayor*, the big main house where Cuddy Rawson reclined in a bentwood rocker, his boots crossed high on the whitewashed rail. A tall, sweaty glass garnished with lemon slivers dangled in his hand. His vacant stare and the slight upturn of his mouth meant his thoughts had drifted elsewhere.

Diego cleared his throat.

Cuddy's stricken look and even quicker duck and shift of his eyes confirmed what Diego already suspected. He bumped his hat off his forehead with the leather handle of his quirt. "I'm happy to see you're making a speedy recovery, *amigo*."

Cuddy bit back a grin, pulling his feet to the porch and sitting upright in the chair. He held up his glass. "I owe it to Greta's tender care. She's bent on nursing me back to health."

Diego glanced at the front door. "Would your lovely sister offer a cup of comfort if she knew the reason for your pain?" He nodded at the icy drink. "Lemonade's the latest cure for a hangover, then?"

Cuddy winced then affected an injured look. "Your judgment is harsh, my friend." He cocked back in the rocker again. "How could you suggest such a thing about your most faithful companion?"

"Save your recitals for Greta. This is me you're talking to." Diego dismounted and leaned his back against the handrail while toying with the braided band on his hat. He cleared his throat. "Cuddy, I thought you decided to go easy on the liquor."

A cloud moved across Cuddy's eyes, and he forcefully lifted one hand.

Diego nodded. "Very well, friend. I'll change the subject. For instance, can you explain what you were considering with such intensity when I arrived?"

The shadow passed from Cuddy's face, replaced by a wily twinkle. "You mean before you interrupted my lofty thoughts?"

"I doubt they were very noble."

Cuddy's huge grin brought his countenance to life, restoring some of the color behind his freckles. "We got company coming."

The Rawsons seldom hosted visitors, but when they did, it was cause for celebration—South Texas–style. The prospect of roasting beef on the spit, dancing in the courtyard, singing, laughing, and talking to new faces brought a smile to Diego's face, too. "Bravo! Who are we expecting?"

"Father's old friend, Willem Dane. His wife and her lady friend are traveling with him."

Diego narrowed his eyes. "And. . . ?"

"Isn't that enough for you?"

"Plenty for me, but don't forget, I'm well acquainted with your tricks. A visit from a gentleman accompanied by two old ladies wouldn't set off the look I saw on your face."

Cuddy slapped his leg and laughed. "My, but you're intent on insulting me today."

"Who else is coming, Cuddy?"

He leaned forward and winked. "None other than the fair Miss Emily Dane."

Diego's brow rose.

"Willem's daughter," Cuddy clarified. "Papa claims she's the prettiest little thing he's ever set two eyes on."

"Ah! Now it makes sense. As a devoted son, you'll be standing close by to offer your heartfelt welcome."

"Of course! Only a rank scoundrel would think to do otherwise."

Hinges squealed behind them, stifling Cuddy's bawdy laughter. Greta swept out in a rush of blue skirts and matching hair bows, her hands laden with a silver tray.

Diego took the steps in two leaps. "Let me take that, Miss Greta. I'd hate to see you trip and poor Cuddy here wind up wearing these fine-looking sandwiches."

A flush crept past Greta's high-buttoned collar, staining her porcelain skin a pale pink. "You say such naughty things, Diego, but they're spoken with a certain flair. I can't keep from laughing." She offered the tray with a dimpled smile and the lingering gaze she'd perfected on him lately—the one that had him thinking about her in a completely different way. "Thank you."

He returned her searching look until he felt himself blushing as well. "Of course."

Greta smoothed Cuddy's yellow hair. "Feeling better, big brother?"

Cuddy rubbed his stomach and leaned to gaze hungrily at the tray. "I will as soon as I force down a few bites."

He went for a sandwich, but Diego jerked the tray out of his reach. "Whoa, amigo! None for you." He placed the food on a table out of Cuddy's reach. "Your sister means well, but you know what they say, 'If you stuff a cold, then you're going to have to feed a fever later.' " He aimed his brightest smile at Greta. "We don't want old Cuddy coming down with a fever, do we? I think he needs to rest his frail constitution so he'll fully recover."

Greta clutched the sash at her waist. "Gracious, you may be right. I never once thought. . ."

Diego patted her hand. "Your intentions were admirable, and I applaud them. Besides, just because Cuddy can't enjoy the fruit of your efforts is no reason they should go to waste." Ignoring Cuddy's glare, his fingers hovered above a plump, meat-stuffed triangle. "May I?"

"By all means, Diego. Help yourself."

Cuddy spun around and snatched the roast beef sandwich before it reached Diego's mouth. "I'll take that off your hands, thank you."

Greta scowled. "Cuddy!"

"I'm feeling better, sis. Honest. Diego's company perked me right up."

"Well, if you're sure. . ."

"Positive," he said, with a smirk in Diego's direction.

Before Diego could react, John Rawson rounded the house on horseback with two rugged ranch hands on his heels. The aging *ranchero* sat his horse like a much younger man, with the vigor and authority befitting the owner of a spread like the Twisted-R Ranch. Diego held much respect for the big man and his principles. He'd taken Diego to his heart as a beloved son. In return, Diego loved him like a father.

"Ho! What good fortune to have caught you here together. Now I won't need to waste half the day tracking Cuddy."

Smiling, Diego crossed to the rail. "How may we be of service, sir?"

Still seated, Cuddy snorted. "Speak for yourself, I'm not well, remember."

Mr. Rawson frowned slightly at Cuddy then addressed Diego. "I suppose you've heard we have guests on the way?"

Diego nodded.

"We have a week to spruce the place up. I'll need you boys to help." He leaned to see around Diego. "That means you, too, mister."

Cuddy groaned, but his father ignored him.

"We've gone long enough giving this ranch a lick and a promise. I won't have it going to seed. Just a little effort on our parts and we'll have the place looking natty again. Inside and out."

Diego bit back a smile. Under Mr. Rawson's command, the staff of the Twisted-R kept the house and grounds in immaculate condition.

The gentleman's wife slipped out of the door behind Greta and slid one arm around her daughter's waist. "Focus your energy on the outside, John. Greta and I will take care of the inside."

"Fine, fine," he blustered. "Greta, help Mother and Rosita make preparations in the house. You'll need to wash and air out the bed linens and tablecloths and pull out the best silverware."

"I'll see to it, dear. Did they say how long they'll be staying?"

"No, but I expect it will be several weeks. We'll prepare for an extended visit. Have Rosita bring in her sisters to help with the cooking."

Mrs. Rawson stepped over and leaned on the rail. "Relax, John. I have everything under control."

"Forgive my exuberance, family, but Willem Dane is a very old friend. The last time we broke bread together was around my father's table in Ripponden. You remember, Katherine, the year before we left England."

She nodded. "I remember Willem well. He seemed like a wonderful man."

"Of course, I've seen him a few times since, and we've exchanged letters. Now I'd like to give him a hearty South Texas welcome."

Mrs. Rawson smiled sweetly. "And so we shall. I'm anxious to meet his family." She addressed Greta over her shoulder. "We'll put Mr. and Mrs. Dane in the north corner, Mrs. Bloom directly across the hall. Air out the room that faces east for young Emily. She can withstand the morning heat better than her elders."

Cuddy perked up from where he lounged in the rocker, interested in the conversation for the first time. "Good plan! That room's balcony connects with mine."

His mother's blush brightened her rouge. "Yes, Cuthbert, it does. That's exactly why you'll be bunking with Diego while they're here."

He shot to his feet. "What?"

"It's the only proper thing to do. I won't have Emily uncomfortable."

"That's a ludicrous suggestion."

"Watch your tone, Cuddy," Mr. Rawson warned. "You're speaking to your mother."

"Sorry, Father, but the bunkhouse? Why can't I just switch rooms with Greta?"

Greta spun. "Excuse me? Banish me to that awful hog wallow? I think not! The walls reek of sweat, sour whiskey, and dung-crusted boots."

Diego's brows lifted. *So she does know.*

Cuddy pressed close to Greta's face. "I would expect you to feel right at home in a hog wallow, precious."

She blustered. "How dare you! After I nursed your booze-sodden behind all morning long, waiting on you hand and foot."

"I never asked you–"

"That's enough!"

All eyes jerked toward the bellowed roar and the blotchy-faced Mr. Rawson seated on his horse.

"I'll have no more, understand? Greta Rawson, follow your mother into the house and start the errands I've charged to you."

With a sheepish glance at Diego, Greta hustled inside on her mother's heels.

Mr. Rawson leaned forward in the saddle. "Cuddy. . .in the future, son, you'll conduct yourself like a Rawson under every circumstance. Like a gentleman." He jutted his chin. "Like Diego here. You'd do well to follow his lead."

Cuddy smirked. "I guess that's where I got confused, Father. I didn't realize Diego was a Rawson now."

Anger flashed in Mr. Rawson's eyes. "Not another word, Cuthbert."

Cuddy slumped in the chair, his sullen gaze directed between his knees.

Stern eyes locked on his son, Mr. Rawson turned his horse. "Diego, I'll leave it in your hands to see that everything gets tended. I know I can count on you, son."

Wincing inside, Diego nodded. "Yes, sir."

Mr. Rawson rode off a few yards then left his companions and closed the distance to the porch.

Trepidation in his eyes, Cuddy studied his father's brooding face. "Yes, sir?"

"Do I need to remind you of the proper manner for conducting yourself in the company of a young lady?"

Cuddy stiffened in his chair. "Absolutely not, sir."

Mr. Rawson gave a curt nod. "I didn't think so." He pulled his horse around and cantered away.

Cuddy sat quietly, clasping and unclasping his fingers, his curling knuckles going white. When Diego could stand no more silence, he gripped his friend's shoulder. "I suppose there's a lot to be done, amigo. You ready to get going?"

Cuddy released a long, weary breath. "Sure thing, big brother. I was just waiting to follow your lead."

CHAPTER 5

"You're going on a holiday, Emily, not to a wake."

Mama held up Emmy's least favorite dress, a gray gabardine with puffed sleeves gathered below the shoulders and banded with black appliquéd flowers. Four large, round buttons fastened the long-sleeved jacket in front. Mama gaped at the dress then dropped it on the bed beside Emmy's suitcase and went fishing for more. "This fur-trimmed collar won't do either, sugar. What were you thinking?"

"Do forgive me." Emmy took the garment from Mama's hand and tossed it on the growing pile of rejects. "I'm not up-to-date on the proper attire for a visit to Hades."

Mama slumped on the side of the bed, Emmy's faded flannel nightgown clutched in her hands. "I know your heart's not in this trip, honey, but you're not even trying to be cheerful."

Emmy gave her a glum look. "Cheerfulness wasn't in the bargain, was it? I don't recall that clause when I signed my name in blood."

Mama pointed at her. "Now you're being a pill. Tell me why you're packing these wretched rags and not the new things we got."

"I won't wear my good things to frolic among cockleburs and cactus. I hope to return to civilization one day, and I'd like something decent left to wear when I get here."

Mama scooped up a double handful from the bag. "You'll roast in all of this."

"I don't care. Regardless of what I wear, I'm sure to be thoroughly miserable." Emmy flounced to the mirror. Quite pleased with her image on most days, she leaned nose-to-nose with her reflection and sighed. Her usually pert white ringlets sagged, and dark circles ringed her shaded blue eyes. Scowl lines etched the flawless forehead, and the corners of her pouting mouth turned down.

Snow White dared not inquire of the looking glass today. The dejected toad gazing back wasn't the fairest of any land. She sagged against the dressing table. "I suppose I'm destined to be unhappy until this awful trip is behind me and Papa is back on the road."

An ominous stirring in the looking glass quickened her heartbeat. A distorted image loomed from behind, swirling in a dark cloud of fury like Snow White's evil queen. Emmy should've seen it coming. One could push Mama only so far.

A biting grip on Emmy's arm spun her, inches from Mama's mottled face and blazing eyes. "I've a good mind to give you your stubborn way and let you ride into Carrizo Springs with nothing to wear but tweed and fur collars, though the temperature soars to one hundred degrees in the shade. As your parent and protector, I'll save you from yourself. March your behind downstairs. *I* will see to your packing."

"But, Mama–"

"I said go!"

"You can't pack my–"

"Now!"

Stinging from the rebuke, Emmy fought tears as she bunched her skirt in trembling fingers and dashed from the room, wincing when the door slammed shut behind her. She had seen that much anger displayed by Mama before but never directed at her. Standing behind a barrier wider than oak and hinges, she burned with outrage and guilt–anger because Mama had never understood the rift between her and Papa, guilt because she'd crossed a forbidden line.

"Honour thy father and thy mother: that thy days may be long upon the land which the Lord *thy God giveth thee."*

Pondering the scripture, Emmy touched the doorknob with her fingertips. She supposed it meant her days on earth would be shortened. For all of Mama's vexing ways, she was infinitely easier to honor than the stern stranger in the parlor.

At the landing, she eased down three steps then paused to spy out the landscape. No rustling newspaper spread open in front of the chair, no stocking-covered feet crossed on the arm of the sofa, no odor of pipe tobacco or haze of smoke in the room. She was safe.

Still wary, she took the rest of the stairs slowly, watching for movement by the kitchen door. Near the bottom step, she bent at the waist to peer out the front window.

"What in blazes are you up to, Emily?"

Blood surged to Emmy's head, ringing her ears like a gong. She released her skirt and clutched her chest, at the same time attempting to flee the gruff voice at her back. Tripping on her hem, she fell from the third step and landed in a heap of tangled legs and twisted cloth. Rolling to her back, she propped up on her elbows and stared dumbly at her flush-faced papa.

"Daughter, I've repeatedly asked you not to play games on the staircase."

"I wasn't. . ."

"Don't dispute my words, Emily. I just came down behind you and witnessed your antics." He frowned. "All that creeping about, the stopping and starting. . . What were you doing? I nearly blundered into you."

Feeling foolish, her gaze dropped to his stockinged feet. Well, pooh! No wonder she hadn't heard him. "Sorry, Papa."

He descended with decidedly more grace than she had and offered his hand. "I expect you'll heed my warnings in the future?"

As Emmy latched on and he hauled her to her feet, the warmth of his touch flashed a memory through her mind in a muddled haze. As a child, she'd fallen asleep in the carriage on the way home from an outing and awakened nestled against Papa's shoulder as he carried her inside. The tender way he held her, the warmth of his fingers beneath her hair had so overwhelmed her with feelings of comfort and love she hadn't wanted it to end, so she pretended to stay asleep.

As fast as it came the memory disappeared, leaving behind an ache that swelled her throat. She pulled her hand free and Papa brushed past her to the parlor. "I heard your mother shouting. Are you the cause?"

Cringing, she lowered her head. "I suppose I am."

He settled in his easy chair, as unyielding as the high, straight back of the furniture. "What sort of answer is that? You either are the cause or you're not."

She glanced up and opened her mouth to speak then looked down again as the words stuck in her throat.

He heaved an exaggerated sigh. "Come over here, please."

She complied, standing in front of him with her arms behind her back like a naughty child awaiting punishment. How did he make her feel so diminished?

"Emily, I've tried to be patient with you, but I understand you've been up to one thing or the other the whole time I've been gone, and a couple more escapades since I've arrived home."

Mama told! Emmy's heart plunged and the oft-repeated words sprang to her lips. "I'm sorry, Papa." She sucked in air, her mind scrambling for a good explanation. "I guess I just didn't think it through. I know the well is dangerous, and–"

"The well?" He sat forward. "I was referring to an incident involving your mama's best linens. It seems one of them wound up tossed in the yard. She suspects you are somehow implicated."

Emmy's chin sank to her chest.

Papa snorted. "Just as we thought, and after your mama has asked you numerous times to leave them be."

"I took one by mistake. I thought–"

His hand shot up. "No excuses. You should pay closer attention." He frowned, his brows nearly touching over the bridge of his nose. "Now then, let's return to this confession concerning the well, shall we?"

Dread tensed Emmy's shoulders. "Yes, sir. I, um. . ."

"I meant to tell you, Willem. . . ." Her mama's unruffled voice resounded from the top landing.

Emmy breathed a sigh of relief, her grateful gaze following Mama down the stairs.

"Your daughter put something down the shaft that doesn't belong there." She shifted her attention to Emmy and her eyes softened. "Something quite precious." She swept across the room, skirts rustling, and headed off Papa's next question with a pass of her hand. "Never mind, dear. There was no harm done. We got it out in one piece."

"Even so, wife, it sounds like a foolhardy thing to do and the act of an irresponsible child. One would think the girl had just turned twelve, not twenty-one."

Mama dismissed his insult with a flick of her ruffle-cluttered wrist. "Careful, or we'll turn your game of reversing numbers against you, dear. You're so grumpy of late, one might mistake you for ninety-four."

Thankfully, her teasing tone softened the blow. Papa's face twitched, as if torn between a smile at her clever twist or a frown at her rebuke. The smile won out, of course. As firm as he was with Emmy, he seldom disputed his wife. Unlike most men in town, his tiptoed waltzing around her feelings stemmed from his great fondness for her rather than fear. Emmy's parents had always held each other in the highest regard.

Pausing in the front hall, Mama pulled on her gloves, her vacant gaze fixed on a spot above the doorpost. "Let's see. . .we're all packed and the house is buttoned down. I've prepared a basket of food to sustain us on the train tomorrow. I hope the blasted thing is on schedule. We waited better than an hour for our trip to the state fair last summer." Frowning, she fanned herself. "Positively gruesome in this heat."

She raised her brows at Papa. "I'm assuming you gave Nash the list of his added responsibilities?"

Papa nodded.

"Good. He's a capable man but downright forgetful these days. Must be his age."

Emmy frowned. "He's not that old. You make him sound fit for the grave."

Ignoring her, Mama opened the door. "All that's left to do is wake up and make our way to the station. With the luggage, there won't be room for much else, so Nash will drive us down first then go after Bertha." She regarded Emmy at last. "I expect you to put on the carriage dress I laid out for you and be downstairs and ready for breakfast by six. Understood?"

"Yes, ma'am." She took in her mama's gloves, hat, and the parasol she lifted from the hallway stand. "But, Mama, where are you going?"

"To see about Aunt Bert. If I don't help her pack, she'll do as good a job of it as you did. With Charity in St. Louis, I have to keep an eye on Bertha's shenanigans, or no telling what she'll get up to."

"May I go?"

Mama wagged her head. "No, you may not. What you may do,

however, is sit with your papa and keep him company until I return."

Emmy stole a glance at Papa's face to confirm he was no more thrilled than she at the prospect of an afternoon together. "Oh, please, Mama."

She gave Emmy a pointed look. "Do like I say, Emily. I mean business."

The door closed in Emmy's face. She grasped the knob, her slender fingers clutching with the desperation of a drowning cat. Leaning her head briefly against the cool wood panel, she prayed for rescue. When none came, she turned to find the man she was duty-bound to honor hiding behind his paper. With the sensation of a guillotine falling overhead, she crossed the room and took a seat in the chair farthest from her papa.

Wheeling around the barn with a bucket of whitewash in one hand and a long-handled brush in the other, Diego bumped into Cuddy coming the other way with a pitchfork. "Whoa, my friend!" he cried, sidestepping the sloshing limewater and righting the pail. "You came close to turning a lighter complexion than how you were born."

Cuddy grimaced and held up the tool. "And you nearly wound up dangling from the end of these tines."

Diego set aside the brush and paint and draped one arm around Cuddy's neck. "I've had the feeling all morning that you'd be pleased to see me skewered."

Cuddy ducked his head. "Dreadful sorry, Diego. It ain't about you, really."

His arm still looped around Cuddy, Diego patted him on the chest, laughing when it thudded like a thumped muskmelon. "Forget it, partner. I know what's hung in your craw. I'd feel the same in your boots." He gripped Cuddy's shoulder. "Just don't take it so much to heart. Your father is very proud of you."

Cuddy held up his free hand. "Hold it right there. You're supposed to be whitewashing this barn, not the facts." He sighed and eased gently away. "Don't cry for me, Diego. I'm a big boy. I reckon I can handle the truth when it's dumped in my lap." He flashed a somber smile, shouldered the pitchfork, and rounded the corner of the barn.

Intent on Cuddy's hasty retreat, the *whoosh* of leather on sandy soil startled him. He spun around with balled fists.

Greta had managed to slip up from behind and stood inches away with a wide grin on her face. "I spooked you, didn't I?" She giggled. "I didn't think it possible to sneak up on an Indian, Diego. Melatha will be scandalized."

His hands relaxed at his sides. "Not as scandalized as your mama would be if I had sent you home with a shiner." He grinned. "I almost slugged you, Greta. What were you thinking?"

Her lashes swept down to cover her eyes, as if the truth about what she'd been thinking embarrassed her. "I brought food." She held up a plate covered with a red-checkered dishcloth then leaned to peer around him. "For Cuddy, too. Where'd he rush off to so fast?"

Diego raised the corner of the cloth to find fat rolls of shredded beef wrapped in corn tortillas. He whistled appreciatively. "These could easily spoil my appetite for lunch, Miss Rawson. But they will be well worth it."

She angled her head. "This is your lunch, Mr. Marcelo. I prepared it myself. You and Cuddy missed the noon meal by a half hour."

"We did?" He chuckled and nudged his hat aside. "No wonder these smell so good." He took the plate from her hands and sat on a nearby hay bale, balancing the feast on his knees. "I suppose we got so busy we lost track of time."

Greta perched beside him and offered him a napkin from the stack in her lap. "We figured as much, with everyone so set on getting the place in shape."

He folded the cloth back from the mounded dish and breathed in the aroma of seared beef, spices, and diced chilies. "Yes, ma'am, these look mighty fine." He widened his eyes and lifted his brows, as innocent as a fresh thrown calf. "But where's the rest?"

She blinked twice. "The rest?"

Diego elbowed her and winked. "I thought you made some for Cuddy, too."

Clearly pleased by his appreciation of her cooking, Greta tittered with glee and returned his jab in the ribs. "Oh, Diego. You're such a tease. I bless the day you came to this ranch."

Mid-bite, he twisted to look at her.

Blushing brighter than the red squares in the cloth, she busied herself refolding Cuddy's napkin. "What I meant to say is there was never any fun on the Twisted-R until you showed up." She stole a peek from under her lashes. "Now, we just laugh all the time."

Grinning, he gave an exaggerated tip of his hat. "Glad to be of service, Señorita Rawson. I will happily play the clown for you whenever you wish."

Greta tilted her still-rosy face, nearly blinding him with a smile that revealed tiny dimples he'd never noticed before.

Charmed, Diego stared, forgetting the savory lunch in his lap.

No doubt about it. The time had come for a discussion with John Rawson about his lovely daughter.

CHAPTER 6

Magda stood on her tiptoes to search past the bustling platform for any sign of Bertha then quickly regretted her impulse. The bunion on her left big toe and the bursitis in both knees throbbed a painful reminder that a woman her size ought not to try resisting gravity.

Shading her eyes, she peered along the tracks to the crossroad where Bertha Bloom had best show her irksome behind. . .and soon. The train to take them south was long overdue. Snarling in frustration, she snatched her skirt with both hands, hefted it up, and whirled on the platform. "Where is she, Willem? I sent Nash with the wagon most of an hour ago. They've had enough time to beat us to the station."

Willem arched one brow. "Sending Nash was your first mistake. No one can draw out a simple chore longer."

Magda sniffed. "You've got that right. Still, you'd think Bertha would hurry him along. This was her harebrained scheme. I don't know how she managed to drag me along on this excursion and then persuade you to boot." She curled her top lip. "Cattle of all things. Why can't she learn cattle-raising in Humble? We've got ranchers closer to home than Carrizo Springs, and that's for sure."

Willem latched onto his suspenders and puffed out his chest. "Not ranchers like John Rawson. There's no better man to teach Bertha what she needs to know." A smile plumped his ruddy face.

"Besides, this will give John and me a chance to catch up. It's been quite a spell since I saw him last."

Magda gripped his hand. "I do look forward to seeing John again and meeting his family." She shot a careful glance over her shoulder.

Emmy stood behind them, fiddling with a lock of her hair, a vision in her pale rose carriage dress and matching hat.

Most of the men standing nearby stared openly, eyes wide as if reluctant to blink and miss something.

Catching sight of her mama gazing at her, Emmy flashed a tight smile.

Magda returned it before turning her back to her daughter and lowering her voice. "None of this has made Emily easy to live with, I can tell you that."

One corner of Willem's mouth twitched. "What do you mean?"

"I haven't mentioned it, but she doesn't want to go. I've argued this trip with your daughter until I'm ready to yank out my hair."

"Better your hair than mine, Mama."

Magda's heart leaped and she spun. "Emily! How many times have I asked you not to skulk about?"

Emmy flashed her limitless dimples. "Skulking? I merely walked over to join you. Can I help it if I'm quiet?"

Willem frowned. "Don't sass your mama, girl."

Emmy flinched and bit her lip, suddenly interested in the wide bow stretched across one shoe. "Sorry, Papa. Never meant to sass."

The defeated look on Emmy's pale face fired lead at Magda's heart. She patted her daughter's hand. "Of course you didn't mean to sass, sugar."

"Don't take up for her, wife," Willem growled. "I heard what she said." He scowled at Emmy again. "There will be no more willful resistance to this trip. Understood?"

Emmy sighed. "Yes, sir."

Magda winced, watching her radiant daughter's confidence puddle at her feet. She was still beautiful even with the frown lines that sprang up between her brows. The girl came out of the womb the loveliest creature Magda had ever set eyes on. Tiny tufts of down had caressed her melon-round head, so white it disappeared except in sunlight, with darker lashes so long they rested on her chubby cheeks while she slept. A deep red blush colored her tiny puckered mouth, a mouth still plump and protruding, as if frozen in place from so much time pouting. Except when she smiled.

Emmy's smile was so glorious a transformation, it had the power to stop grown men in their tracks and halt the words on their tongues. When she turned up the full power of it, complete with the crinkle and flash of blue eyes, she mesmerized every man in the room.

Magda's gaze swept to Willem, the only exception. He stared at Emmy, red-faced and sulking, his bottom lip mottled and swollen like an ugly growth.

Squeezing his hand, Magda drew him closer. "Never mind, dear. Let's not spoil our holiday. Emmy's in much better spirits today."

Magda marveled at Willem's change toward their daughter in recent years. From the day she'd come into the world, no one had a greater hand in spoiling Emmy than Willem. He'd encouraged her precocious spirit, pulling her onto his lap and roaring with laughter at her outrageous antics.

When had it changed?

Magda lowered her gaze, pushing aside the disturbing notion that wriggled into her mind whenever she asked herself that question. The answering finger of guilt pointed firmly in her direction. She should learn to keep her trap shut about Emmy's escapades.

Her chin jerked up. "Oh, look. There's Nash with Bertha, and just in the nick of time. Here comes our train."

Nash turned the two-seater at the crossroad and rumbled along the narrow lane beside the tracks. He pulled to a stop next to the platform, then leaped to the ground and helped Bertha down.

Emmy hurried over to hug him good-bye.

The two stood whispering together, until Nash's cautious glance caught sight of Willem's scowl. He patted Emmy's hand and stepped away from her, an uncomfortable smile on his face.

Magda surveyed Bertha. "What on earth kept you?"

"Couldn't find a thing to wear. All my new clothes come six inches too long. Didn't know until after I slipped them on."

At the age of twelve, a sudden growth spurt took Bertha Maye Biddie from the height of four foot eight to four foot ten. After that, she simply stopped growing. Lucky for Bertha, Magda grew tall enough to hand most things down to her. Then Thaddeus Bloom wandered into Bertha's life, marrying her and replacing Magda. After he passed to his eternal reward, washed from Bertha's arms by a raging Texas river, Bertha found herself back where she started. . .in a world filled with out-of-reach places.

In other words, all of her dresses came six inches too long. She should be used to it by now.

Stringy strands had escaped Bertha's hairpins as usual, and the hem of her new frock was crooked.

Magda prayed she'd remembered her shoes. "I see you've been doing your own needlework again."

Bertha glanced down at her dress. "Had to."

Magda took her by the shoulders and turned her in a circle, tracking the erratic path of the fat stitches. "You've made a right mess of it, you know."

Bertha bristled and pointed at the rig. "You try sewing a straight line while riding in that contraption."

Arching her brows at Emmy and Willem to be certain she'd heard right—by the stunned looks on their faces, she had—Magda turned to gape at Bertha. "You hemmed your dress without taking it off?"

Bertha blinked up at her. "Couldn't sit there next to Nash in my corset and knickers, could I?"

Emmy hurriedly covered her smile with one hand, and Willem shook his head.

Magda pinched the fabric of Bertha's dress and raised it slightly to see her feet. Bertha slapped away her hand. "Stop that. I'm wearing them."

"Just checking."

The train pulled up beside them in a rush of blustery wind, smoke, and the loud squeal of brakes, ending the conversation. Magda shouted last-minute instructions to Nash then lifted two of the bulging bags, handing one off to her husband. "Come along, Emily. It's time to go."

With a last hurried kiss for Nash's cheek, Emmy gathered her things and swept onto the train, followed by Bertha, who tripped on the bottom step before righting herself and disappearing inside the car, her luggage thumping up the steps behind her.

Taking Willem's arm, Magda recoiled at the bright red circles staining his fleshy face. She groped for his hand and found his fists clenched. His stormy gaze still locked on Nash, Willem helped Magda on board, handing their bags to the white-coated porter who had appeared behind her.

Watching her husband struggle with his anger, the finger of guilt concerning the rift between Emmy and Willem shifted, lifting the load of blame from Magda's shoulders and replacing it with sudden clarity and a fresh new crop of trouble.

The porter stopped next to a pair of empty seats, motioning with a smile and a nod for Emmy to sit. She groaned. The two wide benches faced each other across a narrow space that barely provided legroom, which meant that for looming endless miles there'd be no escaping Papa's stern glances and constant reprimands. However would she bear it? No doubt she'd arrive at their destination bunched tighter inside than her fists, which were clenched so tightly the tips of her nails stung her palms through the soft leather gloves.

She stole a peek over her shoulder and swallowed hard. Her parents, their mouths drawn like they'd shared a lemon, lumbered through the passenger car behind Aunt Bertha, who chattered wildly to no one in particular.

Wondering what had happened to put the sour looks on their faces, hoping it had nothing whatever to do with her, Emmy settled into a tense wad by the window, leaving plenty of room for Aunt Bertha to spread out beside her.

Mama plodded up and took her place opposite Aunt Bert, storing her parasol and an oversized basket of food beneath the seat.

Unreasonable panic crowded Emmy's throat as Papa settled across from her, a nameless storm brewing on his face. With no forethought, she sprang to her feet and pushed past them into the aisle, her head spinning.

Mama gaped up at her. "What are you doing, Emily? Sit yourself down."

She gripped the back of Aunt Bert's seat for balance. "I won't be a moment. I forgot something." Whirling, she traversed the narrow car, ignoring Papa's bellow—a reckless act of rebellion for which she'd pay dearly.

Praying with all of her might, she brushed past the wide-eyed conductor before he could speak the warning his upraised finger foretold. Nash would be outside waiting for the train to leave. He just had to be.

Eyes sweeping the outer rim of the crowd, she lifted the hem of her garment and helped herself down to the platform. Miraculously, Nash sat atop the wagon right where she'd left him, his expressive brows drawn to the middle of his forehead. Her heart in her throat, Emmy dashed over and clambered up beside him.

He blinked in surprise. "Miss Emmy, what you doing out here? You gon' miss your train."

She clenched her fists under her chin, wincing from the pain of pierced palms against the crush of leather. "I can't go with them, Nash. I simply can't. Please go ask Mama if I can stay here with you."

He slumped on the seat, his voice pitched to a whine. "You know I cain't do no such thing. Your mama's mind is set, not to mention Mr. Willem's. For all your pleadin', you ain't managed to sway 'em none. How you reckon they gon' listen to the likes of me?" He jabbed his finger behind her as if Papa stood there. "Mr. Willem had just as soon fire me on the spot—or worse—if I was to pull off a fool stunt like that." His head swung side to side. "No, chil'. You got to stop asking me for what ain't in my power to give."

Quivering inside, Emmy twined her fingers behind her neck and leaned her head back. "I'm desperate, Nash. I can't see how I'm going to survive a whole month under Papa's thumb."

Nash tugged on her arm until she let go and straightened to face him. His eyes softened to brown puddles of compassion, and he patted her hand. "The good Lord gon' see you through, that's how."

She groaned and fell against the seat. "Very comforting, Nash. Yet another crushing thumb I can't seem to avoid."

The tender pools in his eyes dried up and hardened to flint. "Why you want to say something like that for? Jus' cause you grew up with a stern papa don't mean you got to see God in the same light."

She opened her mouth to defend herself, but Mama's shrill voice turned the words to ash in the back of her throat. "Emily! Get down this instant and come with me."

Emmy was off the rig and standing beside her mama without remembering how she came to be there.

None too gently, Mama took her by the arm. "I don't know what you two are playing at, but just be glad you haven't missed that train.

While you're at it, count your blessings I was able to talk your father into letting me come for you instead of him."

Truth dawned, churning Emmy's insides. Her impulsive act did nothing toward improving the situation. Instead, the threat of a difficult trip had become an impending nightmare. With a last desperate glance at Nash, and with the conductor's final call to board ringing in her ears, Emmy allowed Mama to herd her onto the platform.

There was no hiding. She would step onto the train, face her papa, and reap what she'd sown in her haste.

CHAPTER 7

Isi pushed back his plate and stood. "Thank you, Mother. Muy *bueno*, as usual."

Heart swelling, Melatha beamed. "I'm happy you liked it." She left her own eggs and *frijoles* and rushed to the woodstove where tortillas warmed in a plate. Lifting two of the steaming rounds of corn, she spread mashed beans in a circle. With a square of braided rags, she hoisted the lid from her cast iron roasting pan and tore off chunks of crisp, golden hen, rolling them up in the slathered bread. "Wait, son. You have a long day ahead. Let me wrap these for you to take with you."

Frowning, he hooked his thumbs in the top of his trousers. "You really think I need that?" He chuckled and tugged on his waistband. "I've just eaten enough for two grown men. Thanks to your good cooking, I'm about out of notches in my belt."

She tucked the cloth-wrapped bundle into his rabbit-skin knapsack and slung it over his shoulder. "A woman likes a sturdy man, Isi."

He lifted his brow. "Oh? And which woman are you fattening me up for?"

Melatha chose not to answer. Instead, she took his arm and walked him outside to the porch. Best to let him wait and see for himself.

With disgruntled squawks and a flurry of beating wings, her chickens announced an approaching visitor. John Rawson rounded the bunkhouse and rode straight for them, scattering the frantic fowl in ten directions. He came so close to the steps before reining his horse, Melatha feared the big Appaloosa might stumble and throw him, obliging her to catch the overgrown man in her apron.

His urgent arrival stirred no fear in her heart. The man always scurried about in a frenzy. Though she feared for his health, she greatly admired his vigor.

Isi crossed to lay his hand on the animal's trembling shoulder. "Morning, sir. Care for a bite of breakfast?"

Mr. Rawson patted his bulging middle. "Thank you kindly, but Rosita and the girls fixed me up real good this morning." He nodded at Melatha. "Don't reckon it compares in flavor to your spread, ma'am, but it got the job done."

Isi winked at her. "See? I told you. Your cooking is legendary."

Melatha's face warmed. "Oh, you. . ." Uncomfortable with the attention, she nodded at his boss. "I'm certain Mr. Rawson didn't ride out here to listen to fables."

Mr. Rawson nodded. "Your mother's half right, son. While I'm certain your boasts about her skillet are true, I've come to entrust you with an errand. A very important task."

Isi bowed slightly. "I'm at your disposal. Whatever you need, sir."

A few more straggling chickens scurried past, running from Cuddy, who trotted toward them from the side yard. Stopping at the rail, he rested the sole of one dusty boot on the edge of the porch and brushed the soil and stickers from his bull-hide chaps.

Isi nodded and smiled at him.

Cuddy returned the gestures then tipped his hat at Melatha. "Mornin', ma'am."

"Morning, Cuddy. Would you like some eggs and tortillas? Isi finished the frijoles, but I have a roasted hen warming."

He grimaced. "Sounds right nice, but I believe I'll pass." He swiped his forehead with the sleeve of his white cotton shirt. "Working in this heat takes a man's appetite."

Melatha couldn't help wondering if his recent hankering for hard liquor was the real reason. Concerned, Isi had mentioned it and asked her to pray.

"Not every man." She laughed and pointed at Isi and Mr. Rawson. "Those two pushed away from the table with full bellies."

Cuddy cut around the porch and came to stand beside Isi. Watching Mr. Rawson pay no heed to his son's presence, Melatha's insides squirmed. She released her breath when at last he dipped his head at young Cuddy.

"Our guests are arriving tomorrow. I want you boys to meet them at the station in Uvalde and bring them here. Cuddy, rig up the two-seater. Diego will follow with your horses. After they join you, Mr. Dane can take over the reins and drive his family to the ranch. You'll be their escorts."

He leaned to rest his arm on the saddle horn then regarded them each in turn, his heavy brows flattened over squinty eyes. "You two make sure that family has a safe, uneventful trip. I'll expect to see them pull up in good spirits and in good condition."

Isi squared his shoulders. "You can count on us, sir."

If the warning on Mr. Rawson's face rattled Isi, he hid it well. Melatha's chest swelled with pride.

Casting a pointed look in her direction, the big man lowered his voice, though she heard every word. "Take your rifles. I don't expect any trouble from *banditos*, but Pancho Villa yet rides free. If you ran across him, I doubt he'd wait to hear where your loyalties lie."

Always mindful of her feelings, Isi shot a worried glance over his shoulder before speaking, his voice overly bright. "I doubt we'll have the pleasure of such an encounter. They say he stays mostly to the mountain regions, busy running from the law."

Mr. Rawson straightened in the saddle. "Nevertheless, be cautious. Villa has his share of admirers, young copycats eager to prove their manhood by acting the fool." He shoved his broad-brimmed hat to the back of his head. "It's been some years since I've seen Willem Dane. I don't want an unfortunate mishap cheating us out of a reunion."

An eager smile on his face, Cuddy gave his father a soldier's salute. "Like Diego said, you can count on us."

Mr. Rawson pulled back on the Appaloosa, tapping its sides with his heels. "That's the problem. I am counting on you, Cuddy." He nudged the horse around and scowled at his son. "Don't let me down."

Cuddy's gaze followed his father's broad back until the horse cantered out of sight. A mix of emotions played across his face, from an angry scowl to heavy lids lowered in shame. As he raised his eyes, they burned with a longing so deep Melatha's heart ached for him.

Isi closed the distance between them and wrapped his long arm around his friend's neck. "Wake up, amigo. We got us a ride to make."

Visibly shaking off his father's disappointment, Cuddy grinned. "You bet, brother. I'll go hitch the wagon." He wriggled loose from Isi and bounded down the steps toward the barn.

Isi moaned and dashed his hat on the rail. "Blast it, Mother! How can a man as kind as John Rawson be so cruel when it counts the most?"

Melatha squeezed his rigid shoulder. "There are many ways to be blind, my son. Mr. Rawson suffers the most crippling loss of vision." She turned Isi to face her, using his rumpled collar for an excuse to gather all the comfort she could muster into her nimble fingers and press it into his neck. "Just pray he regains his sight where our Cuddy is concerned, before one of them stumbles and falls."

Emmy lowered her book a smidgen and stole a peek at her papa.

It had taken miles of clattering track for the last bit of color in his cheeks to subside. After sputtering threats and frightening promises, using admirable restraint to hold his volume in check, he'd settled against the seat in a grown man's version of a pout.

Emmy had taken refuge behind her copy of *Little Women*. At first, the story proved a convenient place to hide, but she soon became lost in the characters' lives, due in part to a revelation about her own nature revealed within the pages.

Emmy's temperament too closely matched that of headstrong, outspoken Jo. Like Jo, Emmy's problems sprang from a tongue that was often too quick and too sharp and a mind that seldom engaged before she took action. Jo's sister, the gentle, eager-to-please Beth, behaved more like kindhearted, forgiving Charity Bloom. It was as if Charity and Emmy were Louisa May Alcott's characters in the flesh.

Emmy's heart sank as Charity's pretty face swam in her head. How different she would feel if the southbound railcar on which she traveled was headed north instead, carrying her to St. Louis to spend time with Charity and her new baby.

Sighing, she laid the novel in her lap and leaned toward the window to peer out at the rushing countryside. The rolling hills to the west had given way to flatland as far as the eye could see.

They'd left the station in San Antonio some time ago. The stretch of her legs she'd enjoyed there hadn't been enough to ease the kinks from her bones. When she first heard of it, Emmy had dreaded the upcoming fifty-mile trek by wagon the most. Now, after hours spent sitting on the train, she couldn't wait to get it started. The distance from Houston to San Antonio wasn't the reason the train had trapped them for so long. Rather, it was the lingering stops at countless dingy, uninteresting depots along the route.

Emmy's back ached, not to mention an unmentionable part of her anatomy that had fallen soundly asleep. A mite jealous of the serene expression on her mama's face, Emmy longed for a little extra padding on her posterior region.

Sporting far less cushion than Emmy, tiny Aunt Bertha squirmed on the seat and moaned then pressed her nose to the glass. "Ain't we there yet, Willem?"

Before Papa had time to answer, the conductor appeared at the back of the car to announce Uvalde as the next stop.

Mama grinned at Aunt Bert from across the way. "Ask and ye shall receive, sugar."

"Well, it's a blessing my sore bottom's grateful for," Aunt Bertha announced, and none too discreetly.

Emmy stifled a laugh when Papa's mouth flew open. His head jerked around to nod and grimace at nearby passengers, most looking as scandalized as he did.

Evidently mentioning unmentionable parts in public didn't bother Aunt Bertha one bit. Considering his wife had been friends with the feisty, outspoken woman for going on forty years, one would think Papa would be used to her by now.

The train lurched to a stop with a squeal of brakes. The excited travelers, likely as stiff and sore as Emmy, shuffled into the aisle muttering their relief. Unaware of the stir she'd caused, Aunt Bert squatted to gather her luggage from beneath the seat. Standing, she hoisted the heavy bags and motioned with her head. "Let's go. Ain't none of these folks waiting for us."

Papa followed her with Mama close on his heels.

Grateful to escape the rolling prison, Emmy filed into the slow-moving line, clutching Mama's sleeve to maintain her balance. After so much time spent wobbling and rocking along the tracks, she felt a little dizzy now that the train was still. The crush of people around her made her breathless, and the odor of unwashed bodies in such close quarters pitched her queasy stomach.

Mama glanced over her shoulder. "You all right, baby?"

She nodded, but sweat beaded her top lip and her hands felt clammy.

When had it gotten so hot?

Unconvinced by her answer, Mama stepped aside and pulled Emmy between her and Papa. "We'll be off this contraption in a minute, sugar. You'll feel better after you get a breath of fresh air."

"Do you see 'em, old pal?" Cuddy lumbered to his feet, dipping and swaying as he fought to stay upright.

Diego reached a steadying hand and braced Cuddy against the wagon bed. "Not yet, but I reckon when people actually start coming off the train, it'll be easier to catch sight of them."

His heart aching, Diego studied Cuddy's glassy eyes and unsteady stance, realizing there was no way under heaven to hide his drunkenness from Mr. Rawson's guests. If they complained to their host about Cuddy's sloppy state, it would seal his fate.

Diego had first smelled the liquor on his breath when they were saddling up at their campsite that morning and warned Cuddy to lay off the booze. Nearly to town, Diego caught him turning up a silver flask. Furious, he climbed aboard the rig and forcibly removed it, but by then the damage was done. When Cuddy wasn't looking, he stashed the troublesome container inside the jockey box under the driver's seat.

Cuddy pointed. "Eyes front. There they are."

Diego's gaze followed his wobbly finger. "How do you know it's the Danes?"

"Look at 'em. Three old geezers and a little gal." Cuddy released a whiskey-scented breath in a long, slow whistle, staring with eyes as hungry as a stray dog at the kitchen door.

A jolt shocked Diego's middle. As the party drew closer, the first muddled impression of perfection sharpened to rows of corn-silk curls beneath a jaunty hat, a blush-colored dress that couldn't begin to hide a lithe, perfect figure, and lips the same rosy color, stuck out like a petulant child's.

Lips that begged to be kissed.

"Ain't she something?" whispered Cuddy.

Diego tried to answer, but a lack of saliva had glued his tongue to the roof of his mouth—unlike Cuddy, who swiped drool from his face with his sleeve.

No doubt, she was the prettiest woman Diego had ever seen, but it wasn't just her beauty. Greta was pretty. This girl carried herself like a stallion, fierce and proud, yet her eyes were wide and cautious, like a doe protecting her young.

She followed her three companions across the platform, heading his direction. As she neared, Diego's chest tightened. When they came to a stop in front of the wagon, her roaming blue eyes locked on his, and he sucked air like a drowning man—a condition very difficult to hide. The effort rendered him speechless.

Luckily, Cuddy, who now seemed as sober as a preacher, stepped forward and offered his hand. "You folks must be the Danes."

The older gentleman latched onto his palm and gave it a hearty shake. "That we are. I'm Willem. You must be John Rawson's son."

"Guilty as charged, sir." Nodding at the women, Cuddy lifted his Stetson and pressed it to his chest, using the other hand to run his fingers through his hair. "Welcome to South Texas, ladies."

He tugged on Diego's sleeve, pulling him closer. "This here is Diego Marcelo, our foreman. We've come to escort you out to the Twisted-R Ranch."

A sizable woman with hair the color of coffee beans returned his nod. "Thank you kindly, son. I'm Magdalena Dane." She motioned to the slip of a woman at her side. "Allow me to present Mrs. Bertha Maye Bloom of Humble."

The smaller woman, spry as a barn swallow, bobbed her head like one, and then Mrs. Dane turned to the vision in pink. "This is our daughter, Miss Emily Dane."

The girl offered Cuddy her hand.

He bowed slightly and kissed it.

Diego's hat came off fast when she turned his way. He wet his lips and opened his mouth to speak, not certain any sound would come out. "Miss Dane. I'm honored to make your acquaintance."

"Thank you, Mr. Marcelo. I. . .I'm. . ." The glow of color drained from her face.

Mrs. Dane clutched her daughter's arm. "Emmy, are you all right?"

She nodded. "Fine. I just. . ."

She didn't look fine. She looked green.

Diego stepped forward. "Perhaps the lady could use a glass of cool water? This part of Texas can be hard on a person unaccustomed to the heat."

Swaying toward him, she blinked once before bending over and depositing her lunch in his hat.

CHAPTER 8

Once they left the depot in Uvalde, the scenery shifted and changed like the slow turns of a kaleidoscope. Instead of the miles of desert sand Emmy had expected, acres of waist-high grass covered the landscape, set off by an occasional grove of trees.

Farther along, after crossing the Nueces River, it changed even more. The grass alongside the road grew as high as the rider's stirrups in some places then disappeared in others, choked out by rocks, sand, and brush. Live oak trees lined up next to sapling elms along the riverbank. Wide vistas of patchy grass mixed with scattered scrub brush and squatty trees that sported a tangle of wiry branches. Cacti dotted the landscape, lone sentinels, their fat green arms laden with purple fruit.

This piqued Emmy's interest so much she couldn't sit quietly another second. Scooting to the edge of her seat, she waved her hankie at them. "Look, Mama. What are those lovely bulbs on that cactus? I've never seen anything like them."

Beside her, Aunt Bertha laughed. "That's because you ain't never seen any cactuses, child. Maybe the little ones in pots, but nothing like these beauties."

Papa, who seemed in much better spirits, leaned around Mama for a better look. "Those are cactus pears. Very juicy and sweet on the palate, once you get past the spines, which I understand is very hard to do."

"You mean you can eat them things?" Aunt Bertha's voice was shrill with wonder.

"Yes, you can, Bertha." Papa actually smiled. "According to John, they're regular fare on the Rawsons' table in season."

Mama twisted on the seat, her lips pinched. "No more questions, Emily. You need to sit back and rest."

Emmy's face warmed. "I'm feeling much better."

Mama smiled grimly. "I'm relieved to hear it." She turned to the front, muttering that it wouldn't be much help to Mr. Marcelo's hat.

The heat increased in Emmy's cheeks. The handsome young man rode a short distance in front of the wagon, squinting against the sun. He had pulled the red bandanna from around his neck and twisted it into a rope that he tied around his head. Still, the wind whipped his long curly hair in his face. Guilt squeezed her heart that he battled with the elements while she sat sheltered beneath the canopy of the two-seater.

They made camp at dusk, their two hosts graciously tending their every need, and were up and back on the trail as the sun peeked over the horizon. Emmy could hardly believe it when Papa grunted then nodded at the acres of plowed rows along the road. "We're getting closer now."

Mama shot him a quizzical glance. "How can you tell?"

"We're beginning to see tilled ground. Carrizo Springs is rich in farmland."

Frowning, Emmy voiced her confusion. "How can that be? I thought the south would be barren and desolate."

He shook his head. "Not these parts. The fields are watered by spring-fed creeks."

Aunt Bertha stretched closer to Papa. "What kind of creeks did you say, Willem?"

"Spring-fed. The area sits atop underground fountains called artesian wells. They bubble to the surface and create ready sources of fresh water." He shrugged. "That's not to say it's all lush and green. The ground is still dry in most places."

As if to vouch for his word, the wind bore down and snatched up a puff of sand. Invisible fingers fashioned a whirligig that danced across the open plain.

"Look!" Emmy cried. "Have you ever seen a dust devil so big?"

Grinning, Aunt Bert watched it wend its way toward them until it collapsed ten feet shy of the wagon in a shower of sand. "Will you look at that?" she hooted.

Emmy smiled. "I've never seen anything like this country. Lush here, desolate there. I guess it can't decide what sort of terrain it ought to be."

Mama and Papa laughed, and to her surprise, Emmy joined them. She had determined to despise South Texas, expected to have a miserable ride to the ranch, yet against her will the rugged charm of the land had worked its way under her skin and softened her resolve. Instead of enduring the long journey, the miles and hours swept by unnoticed.

She pointed at a staggered line of brush. "What are those curious spiny bushes?"

Her papa shook his head. "I can't answer that one. Perhaps one of our escorts can shed some light."

To her dismay, he put two fingers in his mouth and whistled. Both men's heads whipped around.

"My daughter has a question, gentlemen."

Since the dark-skinned fellow was closer, the one named Cuddy grinned and waved him over.

Emmy couldn't recall his name from their introduction because her head had started to whirl. She only remembered hair the color of raw sugar on his forehead and matching brown eyes—knowing, thoughtful eyes that must have witnessed things Emmy would never see. Yet the last expression she'd seen in their depths as she bowed her head to be sick was one of startled amazement. Luckily, she got a good glimpse because she didn't dare look at them again.

He angled his horse up beside them. "What can I do for you, miss?"

His voice, as rich as Christmas pudding, drew Emmy's attention to his mouth against her will. When he made an unconscious move to take off his hat—which wasn't there, thanks to her—the gesture broke the spell. Emmy dropped her gaze to her clenched fists.

Thankfully, Papa came to her rescue. "She's asking the name of that scrub brush yonder."

"Those old, straggly trees? Miss Emily, those are mesquite."

So he remembered her name. But then he would. After ruining

his hat, he'd likely never forget.

"Mesquite grows like a house afire and provides a nice habitat for the wildlife," he continued. "Cattle eat the beans when grass is scarce. Many people use them for food, too, as well as medicine."

Aunt Bertha flipped up the brim of her bonnet and gawked at Diego in disbelief. Slapping her leg, she laughed. "Young man, I swallowed that part about picking fruit off a cactus, but don't try to tell me folks around these parts eat trees."

He laughed softly. "Only the beans, Mrs. Bloom. Wood from the larger trees makes good shelter and beautiful furniture. But most mesquite that size grows across the Rio Grande." He shaded his eyes and stared, as if he could see the river. "It also fuels a fine cooking fire. Gives smoked meat a wonderful flavor."

Diego directed the last part to Emmy, so she raised her head and nodded to be polite. His warm smile flashed teeth so white against his bronzed skin it took her breath and delivered absolution to her repentant heart. She couldn't remember ever seeing so handsome a face. Even the no-account scoundrel from her past couldn't compare to this man, and she'd always thought Daniel Clark the best-looking man she'd ever met. . .until now.

Up ahead, lanky, towheaded Cuddy reined in his horse and turned in the saddle. "Hey, Diego!" He pointed toward a distant cloud of dust. The tension in his voice drew Emmy's attention. "Riders. Heading our way."

Diego. So that's his name.

Papa sat forward on the seat as Cuddy wheeled his horse and rode to meet them. "Can you tell who it is, young man?"

Cuddy shook his head. "Not from this distance, but they're closing fast."

"Maybe it's your father coming to greet us? Or someone sent by him?"

"No, sir, that's not Father's mount," he said grimly. "Besides, he sent us to greet you."

Mama gasped when Cuddy unsheathed his rifle and Diego slid a handgun from his boot.

Looking helpless, Papa frowned up at them. "So you expect trouble then? Banditos?"

Cuddy chewed his bottom lip before he answered. "Could be. I guess we're about to find out."

Papa spun toward Diego. "Do you have extra firepower? I'm a fair shot."

Aunt Bert stood up in the wagon. "I can blast a buzzard off a carcass from a hundred yards."

Diego sat straighter on his horse, his pleasing mouth a firm line. "We appreciate the offer, Mr. Dane." He nodded at Aunt Bert. "You, too, ma'am." His watchful eyes remained pinned on the horizon. "But you can be most helpful by sitting down and staying low."

Pulling his attention from the intruders, his comforting gaze settled on Emmy. "Don't you fret, miss. We're prepared to defend you with our lives."

His assurance made her feel better, but she prayed it wouldn't come to that.

Diego tipped his chin at Cuddy. "Let's ride out to meet them, draw them away from the wagon. No need to advertise all the luggage."

He pulled a shotgun from his scabbard and handed it down to Papa. "Keep the rig moving south toward the ranch while we stall them. You're almost there. If anything goes wrong, push this wagon as if the devil were chasing you." He gathered the reins, jutting his chin toward the horizon. "Don't worry about us. We'll catch up." Pausing, he nodded at the gun. "And don't be afraid to use that."

Papa patted the barrel. "If necessary, I'll find a use for it."

Diego tapped his horse's side with his heel and trotted toward the band of four men, closer now than Aunt Bertha's buzzard.

Cuddy followed, his rifle braced across his saddle.

Papa shook the leads and the wagon jerked into motion.

No one made a sound, save that of heavy breathing. Their rapid, shuddering pants reached Emmy's ears despite the creak of the wheels and the pounding of her heart. She had no desire to die that day but, oddly, didn't fear for herself. Her muddled thoughts centered on the safety of the winsome young escort who vowed his life to protect her.

Tension crackled in the air. Papa sat so stiffly on the seat Emmy feared his spine would snap. Mama mopped beads of sweat from her top lip with one hand and worried a tear in the brown leather seat with the other. Beside her, Aunt Bertha's jaw worked in circles, emitting the sound of grinding teeth.

"Watch them, ladies," Papa said. "If they so much as flinch, I'll lay the whip to the horse's back." Even as he issued the command, his head swiveled around three times to look for himself.

All eyes were fixed on the huddle of swarthy men in the distance. Emmy felt fixed in place, as if fear had melded the joints and sinews of her body into stone.

A sudden shout echoed across the plain. Papa's head jerked around and Emmy's legs tensed. She didn't understand the strangely beautiful words, but the tone translated into anger. Papa reached for the whip, and a whispered prayer sprang from Aunt Bertha's lips.

Then Cuddy let out a peal of raucous laughter.

Emmy's gaze flitted to Papa, hoping the laughter meant they wouldn't be scrambling for their lives. He released his breath in a rush and his rigid body slumped with relief. Warmth flooded Emmy's chest, leaving her legs limp and her arms useless sticks in her lap.

"It's all right, sugar. Everything's going to be fine," Aunt Bertha said, though her hand trembled as she patted Emmy's leg.

Papa called, "Whoa," to the team when the horsemen turned their mounts and headed toward them with Diego in the lead. Behind him rode a squat, older man even browner than Diego, with a long, heavy mustache. He rode alongside a slightly younger version of himself in similar clothes. Two men, closer in age to Diego, followed, with Cuddy bringing up the rear.

One of the straggling riders appeared to be the object of a joke. He suffered much teasing from the rest, especially Cuddy. They were all laughing or smiling, except the old man. As he reached the wagon, ridges in his forehead resembled a washboard, and his mustache sagged. Flashing eyes, so dark they appeared black, crinkled into sunburst patterns at the corners.

All of them wore big, peculiar hats sporting wide brims and tall crowns. Cuddy's companion took his off and swiped at him. "Laugh hearty, foolish *gringo*. I know what I saw." Catching sight of Emmy, he clutched the hat to his chest. "But what is this I see?"

He bowed from atop his horse, first at Papa, though he had to force his dark eyes to switch, then at Mama and Aunt Bert. "*Buenos días*, señores. Señoras."

Bowing lower, his gaze swung to Emmy. "Good afternoon, señorita."

They dismounted as Papa climbed down and held out his hand.

"Willem Dane at your service. This is my good wife, Magdalena, her companion, Bertha Bloom, and my daughter, Emily," he said, pointing at each of them in turn. "Happy to make your acquaintances."

Diego, his accent thicker in the company of the men, made introductions all around. Señor Boteo, elder brother to Narcisso, the man who resembled him, father to Francisco, and uncle to Rico, proved to be the link connecting the family. With the old fellow still scowling and the others still snickering, it took no time for the yarn to surface.

"Please to pardon these simpering pups, Señor Dane. They seek to make sport of my son"—he regarded Cuddy over his shoulder, one expressive brow climbing toward his hatband—"when they would do well to sober and heed his warning."

Grinning, Cuddy gripped Francisco's shoulder. "Sober? I doubt you were any too sober when you chased that old bloodsucker off your goat."

The old man made the sign of the cross. "It is unwise to jest about it, son. The stories of *el chupa sangre* are quite real. He has wandered this land for generations, feeding on our livestock, and in rare cases, our people."

Papa stepped closer, his brows meeting in the middle. "Señor Boteo, just what is this creature?"

The old man raised his chin, regarding Papa with intelligent eyes. "An animal not of this earth, señor. A fiend that walks on four legs or two as the mood strikes him. The size of a small bear with spines from his neck to the end of a tail that drags the ground. He has the face and hands of a man, though his eyes are very large and his fingers heavy with thick claws. He doesn't kill with his hands, however, but with two long fangs. With them, he slits the throat of his victim and drains it of blood with his mouth, wasting not a drop. He attacks under cover of night, and his eyes glow like burning embers while he feeds. When the herders or wranglers awaken, they find their animals shriveled on the ground like empty wineskins."

Mama sucked in her breath and he swung her way.

"I beg your pardon, señora." He tipped his hat. "I don't wish to frighten you, but the bloodsucker is quite real as my son can now bear witness. It's rash and dangerous to believe otherwise."

He turned and twirled his leather quirt in the air as if rounding up the men. "Let us be off, and let no more be said about it. We've upset the women enough."

With a shake of his head, Señor Boteo passed the still grinning Cuddy. Stopping in front of Diego, he peered up at him. "Keep your eyes open, son. We'll set a night watch over our flock. I suggest you do the same with your cattle." He held up one finger. "Be vigilant. Never underestimate el chupa sangre. He is swift and smart, and he's avoided capture for centuries."

Diego nodded soberly. "Good advice, señor. If he comes on the Twisted-R, we'll be ready."

Cuddy snorted. "You'll be ready. I'll be snug in my bed. You won't catch me lurking in a pasture all night because a mangy coyote killed a goat."

Jerking his head at Diego, he climbed on his horse and reined it past the rig. "Let's get going, now. The old man will be worried about the Danes. I don't need to wind up on the bad side of a conniption."

As Cuddy rode away, Diego ducked his head and mumbled in Spanish to Señor Boteo. The old gentleman patted him on the back. "Don't trouble yourself, Diego. I overlook him now because he's young, though Cuddy's papa would do well to spend more time on that boy's manners." He led his stout mare around and swung into the saddle.

"*Adios*, amigo," he called cheerfully to Diego and then tipped his hat. "Ladies. . .Señor Dane. . .very honored to meet you." He whistled for his family to follow, and they rode off, leaving swirling clouds of dust in their wake.

Up ahead, Cuddy stood in his stirrups and motioned impatiently with his hat.

Diego mounted his horse and nodded at Papa. "Are we ready, sir?"

Papa unwound the reins from the brake. "As ready as we're going to get, son."

Diego and Cuddy traveled apart for the rest of the way, not side by side, laughing and exchanging good-natured teasing as they had before. For some reason it made Emmy sad.

"We're just about there," Papa announced.

Mama shaded her sensitive eyes and squinted up at him. "Are you certain, Willem? I've had my fill of this wagon."

Papa nodded. "This old horse has ceased his plodding and picked up the pace pretty good. That's a sure sign we're nearing his stall."

"Nice try, Willem," Aunt Bertha muttered, "but I reckon your insight has more to do with that great big house sitting yonder."

Emmy leaned to peer between her parents. Sure enough, a building loomed beyond the sprinkling of misshapen scrub trees Diego had called mesquite. They pulled past the gate under a large scrollwork sign that read BIENVENIDOS AL RANCHO R TORCIDO.

Mama attempted to pronounce the words, craning her neck as they passed beneath until she was nearly in Aunt Bertha's lap. She nudged Papa. "What's it mean, dear?"

He repeated the phrase under his breath then shook his head. "I don't read much Spanish, Magda."

Diego pulled his horse even with the wagon. "It says 'Welcome,' Mrs. Dane, 'to the Twisted-R Ranch.' "

"I see." Mama chuckled. "Well, that makes perfect sense, now don't it?"

A large powder gray creature with big eyes stared from behind a barbed wire fence. He locked gazes with Aunt Bertha as they rode past as if he hadn't witnessed anything quite like her.

Aunt Bert stared back with the same expression. "Will you look at that critter? He looks like a cow that's had his parts took off and put back cockeyed." She lowered her voice to a whisper. "You don't reckon it's one of them bloodsuckers?"

Papa stifled a grin. "It's a bull, Bertha. A Brahman to be exact."

"That don't look like no bull I ever seen. Look at his sad face and droopy ears. Why, his skin hangs slack as a bloodhound's." She pointed wildly. "Land sakes! He's sportin' a hump on his back! You sure he ain't a camel, Willem?"

Papa laughed. "The Brahman's a rare breed from India. Not many exist here in the States. John bought a couple from the King Ranch to start up a breeding program. From the looks of that big fellow, he has succeeded."

The lane stretched for some distance in a line as straight as an arrow from the gate to the front of a large house. They came to a stop when the lane did, and Emmy stared toward the two-story structure fashioned from plastered stone blocks. Posts jutted at intervals from the top beneath a roof as flat as a fritter. Spacious balconies jutted from the upstairs windows where sheer white curtains billowed in the breeze. A covered patio larger than the living area of their home in Humble extended off the side, and a broad door cut from striking, red-streaked wood adorned the portico, opening onto a roomy porch. Two wide steps led down to the ground.

A tiny barking dog pulled Emmy's attention beyond a nearby fence to a field where he chased an orange cat of impressive size to the edge of a pecan orchard then up a tree. The little brown dog danced around the trunk before planting his paws on it, yapping as if to say he was far too busy to entertain such shenanigans. Emmy grinned and spun on the seat to show her mama. Startled, she drew back, clutching her collar.

One of the largest men she'd ever seen, besides Nash, beamed up at them from the ground. He took off his hat and bowed his head. "Welcome, folks! John Holdsworth Rawson at your service."

CHAPTER 9

Diego's chest swelled with pride as the big man approached the wagon to greet his guests. Barrel-chested and broad-shouldered, he cut a fine figure for a man his age.

Born in Europe, Mr. Rawson liked to say he got to Carrizo Springs as fast as he could. At the age of twenty, he'd stepped off the boat in New York Harbor without a backward glance at his mother country. He bragged about doffing his top hat at Lady Liberty then laying it aside along with his frock coat in exchange for a Stetson hat, suspenders, and chaps. In the winter, he added a fringed coat like those worn by his heroes, Teddy Roosevelt and his band of Rough Riders.

He'd laid aside his accent as well, for the most part. Unlike Mrs. Rawson, whose lilting voice flowed like the strains of a haunting melody.

Diego dismounted, his mind fixed on lending a hand to young Miss Dane, but Cuddy beat him to the draw. He stood smiling up at her, one arm held out for her to grip and the other hand hovering near her waist.

Distracted by them, he almost didn't catch Mrs. Bloom when she tripped. By the time he steadied her, the family had reached Mr. Rawson. After hearty handshakes between the men, Mr. Rawson took the Dane women's arms and escorted them to the porch.

A quick glance told Diego his boss had ordered more work done on the ranch in their absence. Someone had swept the ever-present sand from the brick-paved veranda and washed the gray dust from the house and outbuildings, allowing the adobe to gleam in the sun—nearly as bright as Mrs. Rawson's smile, but nowhere close to the spark of pride in her husband's eyes as his arm encircled her waist.

"May I present my dear wife, Katherine Eliza Colbeck Rawson, of the Halifax Colbecks?"

The mistress of the Twisted-R Ranch looked awfully pretty. She'd pinned most of her blond hair on the top of her head, except for one long braid pulled over the shoulder of her new blue dress. She'd done whatever women do to make their waistlines disappear, and the delicate leather shoes peeking from under her hem were definitely not work boots.

Mrs. Rawson smiled. "You'll have to forgive my husband. He hasn't yet embraced the relaxed charm of our adopted country. He behaves as if we're still on the banks of the Ryburn." She held out her hand. "Please, call me Kate."

The elder Dane woman accepted her handclasp. "Magdalena. But you can call me Magda. Willem's spoken quite highly of you, Kate." She took her daughter's arm and pulled her forward. "This is our Emily."

Mrs. Rawson took both the girl's hands. "Hello, Emily. Gracious, how lovely you are."

Emily bowed her head.

With a flourish, Mrs. Dane presented the small woman. "And this is my dearest friend, Bertha Bloom."

"Hello, Bertha. I'm honored to meet each of you. We're so happy you've come. During your stay you must promise to consider this your home."

Mr. Rawson motioned to Cuddy. "Of course you met our boy, Cuthbert."

Cuddy cleared his throat and tipped his hat at Mrs. Dane. "Let's stick with Cuddy, ma'am."

His father frowned. "I've told you before, don't be embarrassed by your name, son. It was good enough for my old papa."

If she was trying to ease his discomfort, Cuddy's mother only made things worse. "Cuthbert is a delightful Old English name." She preened and winked at Mrs. Dane. "It means bright champion, you know." She patted Cuddy's face. "The perfect moniker for you, dear."

A rush of color flooded Cuddy's cheeks. He shot a glance at Emily Dane and so did Diego. Cuddy could relax. The girl seemed oblivious to his humiliation, and in fact to the whole conversation.

She stood with her hands laced behind her back, her chin lifted. The glow of the setting sun had turned her hair and skin the color of crushed peaches. A look of wonder lit her face as she peered around at the grounds.

"And this is our daughter, Greta."

For the first time, Diego noticed Greta standing in the shadows of the portico. At her father's mention, she stepped into the light and curtsied. Having just pulled his gaze from Miss Dane's thick mound of white curls and full ruby lips, Greta's blond hair appeared wispy and dirty by comparison, her lips thin and pinched. Was it only the day before when he found her so attractive?

Feeling guilty but unable to stop, he cut his eyes back to Miss Dane for one more assessment. His breath caught as she lowered her gaze to a goosefoot plant at her feet. Her lowered lashes gave her big eyes a pleasing, drowsy appeal until she raised them and caught him staring. The sleepy look melted into a sweet smile.

The tiny dimples he'd discovered hiding near the outer corners of Greta's mouth were no match for the deep impressions in Miss Dane's cheeks, clearly visible from a distance. He remembered seeing a hint of them even when her expression was sober. Those dimples defied description, as did her smile. Held in its grip, Diego stood rooted to the spot until she lowered her gaze and released him.

Mr. Rawson loudly cleared his throat.

Diego glanced around to find all eyes fixed on him, including his mother's, who had appeared on the side of the house. Her eyes darted over to Miss Dane, wide and wary as if she'd seen a band of restless spirits.

His boss gave an uneasy laugh. "As I was saying, Diego here is our top hand. Couldn't run the place without this boy. . .when his head's not in the clouds, that is."

The rush of warmth to Diego's face surely put Cuddy's blush to shame. He wondered what sort of doe-eyed fool he'd looked gawking across the yard all slack-jawed with his tongue hanging out. Anger followed his embarrassment when no one seemed ready to find something else to look at. Especially Greta, who stood spellbound watching him. Diego's eyes sought hers, but she turned away.

Mr. Rawson's booming voice broke the silence. "Well, don't just stand there, son. You and Diego unload their bags." He spun on his heel and held out wide, welcoming arms to his guests. "So, who's hungry? Kate and the girls have been in that kitchen for days, stirring savory-smelling dishes. Let's go see what they've cooked up."

Mrs. Dane took Mrs. Rawson's offered arm. "I hope you haven't gone to too much trouble on our account."

Her hostess patted her hand. "Nonsense. We love to entertain. Lord knows, we don't often get the opportunity living so far out. Besides, John prepared most of the meat. There's a plump hog roasting on the spit as we speak."

Cuddy passed Diego, stopping just behind him to speak low in his ear. "Don't waste your time staring, big brother. I saw that little filly first, so she's burned with my brand." He shifted closer. "The old man deems me second place in running this ranch, but even he knows I'm good at what I do best."

Diego snorted. "Drunk again, I see."

Cuddy didn't answer, so Diego looked behind him. Shoulders shaking with laughter, the cantankerous boy strolled toward the rig to unload the Danes' luggage.

Diego drew in deeply of the dry, dusty air, picking up the scent of John Rawson's fire pit. Though he loved Cuddy like a brother, at the moment he wouldn't mind seeing him lashed to the spit, spinning alongside the roasting pig.

"Not this one, Chihowa Palami! A lively spirit, yes, but not this unbroken spawn of a cougar. Not this cat with hungry, searching eyes."

Melatha watched as her vision-come-to-life stood apart from the others the way a buck kept his distance from the herd. The girl sized up her surroundings, especially Isi, like a panther before the kill. Her claws unsheathed each time she felt his eyes on her, and she felt them, no mistake about it. She fooled Isi with her slant-eyed glances—drinking him down in great gulps to quench her thirst—but she couldn't fool Melatha.

There was no denying the white curls or her cool, sky blue gaze. Yet how could a girl like this be God's will for her son? Impossible!

Melatha had witnessed disaster when forces of nature collided. Fire struck the ground, splitting trees and burning forests. Dark, swirling whirlwinds thundered from the clouds, uprooting oaks and boulders, leaving a wide path of destruction. This power would be a trifle compared to a clash between White Hair and Isi.

Her attention crossed the yard to Greta standing as straight as a lotebush thorn, her hands clenched by her sides as she watched Isi lean into the wagon bed to gather the Danes' luggage. Emotions warred on the poor girl's face. What first appeared to be seething anger and outrage became jaws slack with fear. For the first time since Melatha met Greta, the mantle of security entitled to her as John Rawson's daughter had slipped, as if she suddenly realized her father couldn't buy her everything.

Dragging her feet, Greta turned and followed her guests inside the house.

"Mother?"

She spun to face him. "You startled me, Isi."

"Who are you spying on? The Rawsons and their guests. . .or me?"

She tucked guilty hands behind her back. "I thought no one could see me."

"No one did, except for me. What are you doing here?"

"Mrs. Rawson asked me to help Rosita and her sisters in the kitchen."

He drew back. "Cooking or serving?"

"What difference does it make?"

He snorted. "A lot. Mr. Rawson asked me to join them tonight. I won't have my own mother serve me at that fancy table when she should be seated beside me. It would be hard enough knowing you're standing in front of the stove."

She grinned. "I stand in front of the stove for you every day, son. Serve you, too. Don't let such high-minded notions trouble your soul." She patted his arm. "I'll gladly lay my hand to whatever task Mrs. Rawson requires of me. It's the least I can do to repay her great kindness."

One of Isi's men barreled past behind them. His head jerked around as he caught sight of Diego, and he drew to a breathless halt.

"He's out again, Diego."

Isi stared over his shoulder. "Again? That's not possible."

The man's eyes shifted to the ground. "*Sí, es* muy *posible*. He's not in the corral or the pasture. Nowhere on the grounds. He's gone."

Isi closed his eyes and let his head fall back. "Saddle my horse. I'll be right there."

He turned and tapped Melatha's chin with his work-roughened finger. "I have to go track that stubborn horse again. Tell Mrs. Rawson I'll be back in time for dinner." He furrowed his brow. "Don't let me return and find you dishing beans."

"What shall I tell Greta?"

Just as she planned, her question caught him off guard. "Leave Greta to me, if you don't mind." He tweaked her nose. "It's none of your business." Winking, he sauntered away, pausing once to tip his hat before rounding the house.

"Humph! None of my business?" Skirting a blackbrush thicket, she made her way to the back of the house, grumbling as she took to the steps. "We will see, my little deer. As surely as the sun sleeps at dusk, we will see."

Not that she believed Greta to be the woman God had for Isi, but after seeing the latest contender for his affection, Greta would do to distract him until the right one arrived.

CHAPTER 10

Magda ran her hand over the multicolored quilt and sighed. Satin, silk, and velvet pieces in vivid jewel tones set against an inky black background offered her fingertips a feast of sensations. "Will you look at this quilt, Bertha? Without a doubt, it's the prettiest thing I've ever seen." She glanced back. Bertha still lingered at the window, staring over the yard. "The grandest thing I've ever felt, too. Come over here and touch it."

Bertha swatted the air behind her. "Leave me be, Magda. I'll feel that thing soon enough. I have to sleep under it tonight."

Magda exhaled dreamily. "I hope ours isn't this nice or I won't sleep a wink for worrying about mussing something so fine." She lowered her voice. "Willem and I have been known to drool." Shifting away from the bed, she slid one finger along the marbled top of the tall, mirrored chest then touched the gilded frame around the glass. "One thing's for sure, most of this furniture came straight over on the boat with Kate Rawson. Handed down from her folks, most likely. You can't find workmanship like this anymore."

A knock at the door caused Magda to jump. Feeling guilty for snooping, she opened it to the young man called Diego.

He grinned and cocked his head. "I have luggage belonging to one of you ladies. Cuddy's on the stairs with more. Can you tell me which bags belong where?"

"Those two are Bertha's, sugar." She pushed aside the shoes

Bertha had kicked off in the corner. "Put them down right there, if you don't mind."

He did as she asked then gave a slight bow and ducked out again.

The Rawson boy appeared behind him bearing Emmy's luggage, one under his arm and one in each hand. He grinned, too. "How about these, ma'am?"

"Those are my daughter's." She pointed. "I believe her room is that way."

He smirked and nodded at Diego before sauntering past.

"That means the two on the wagon belong to my husband and me. You can bring them up and leave them outside our door."

Diego's gaze trailed Cuddy down the hall. "Are you sure? They're pretty heavy."

"Don't worry, young man. Mr. Dane is downstairs with the Rawsons, but he'll carry them in the second he comes up."

Diego mumbled a senseless reply and didn't appear to have the first idea of what she'd said. Laughter between Emmy and Cuddy had drawn his attention to where they stood talking. Each time Emmy giggled, the scowl etched on his forehead grew deeper.

Magda eased the door shut and shrugged at Bertha. "I might as well have talked to his hat. Wonder what put a burr in his bonnet?"

Bertha snorted and nudged Magda with her elbow. "Where are your spectacles, honey? The burr's in his behind, not his bonnet. Put there by your little burr specialist."

Magda twisted to stare at the door. "You think so? That's fast, even for Emmy."

"It don't take that girl long to weave her spells."

Magda tilted her head in thought. "You may be wrong this time, Bert. After all, she threw up in the boy's hat!"

"Maybe so, but that don't change the facts. Did you look at him? He's moonstruck and so is that other one. From where I sit, this situation carries the potential for big trouble."

Chewing on her thumbnail, Magda nodded slowly. "You're right. I'd best talk to Emmy."

Bertha chuckled. "You'll have to wait in line behind them two fellers. I suspect they're making plans to tie up all her free talking time." She yawned and stretched. "I'm ready to touch that fancy quilt now. Reckon I could take a nap before we eat?"

Tossing Bertha's bulging satchel on the bed, Magda shook a finger in her face. "No time for rest, missy. Take advantage of my idle hands and let's get you unpacked. The sooner we settle in, the sooner we eat." She raised her nose and sniffed the air. "I can taste that pig from here."

Unfastening the latch on the bag, Magda upended it and gave it a shake. Currency of every denomination spilled onto the bed in a shower of faded green bills. Dumbstruck, she lifted a tied bundle with two fingers and held it up. "What in the name of everything decent have you done?"

Bertha calmly scooped an armful of the money and stuffed it back in the satchel. "Not this one, sugar. I figured to leave it packed until I need it."

Trying to work things out in her mind, Magda pressed her fingers to her temples. "Are you telling me you hauled all of these greenbacks clear across the state of Texas?"

Bertha snatched the hefty bundle from Magda's hand. "Yep."

"Shoved under the seat in the train?"

"Why do you think I wouldn't let that porter carry my luggage?"

"Over rivers and streams, rocks and cactus, through country crawling with bandits?"

"How else was I supposed to get it here?"

Magda stretched the mouth of the bag and peered inside. "There's enough loot in here to buy your own state! What do you need it for?"

Flustered, Bertha closed the satchel and refastened the latch. "Suppose I find some cattle I want to buy?"

Laying the back of her hand on her hip, Magda studied Bertha's pouting face. "You ever hear of bank checks? Promissory notes?"

Another knock on the door sent Bertha scrambling to shove the money under the bed. After pushing it deeper with her foot, she hopped on the end of the high mattress and tried to appear dignified and nonchalant—difficult to pull off with knees straddled and bare feet dangling.

Magda shook her head and turned the knob.

Willem stood smiling on the other side. "The table is set downstairs. Are you two ready to eat?"

Bertha leaped off the bed and padded to the threshold. "That's a wasted question, Willem. When have you seen your wife not ready to eat?"

Magda elbowed her. "There are worse things than an appetite, you know." She shot Bertha a meaningful glare. "Taking chances with large sums of money, for instance."

Bertha pinched her arm. "What you call taking chances, I call being prepared."

Unfazed by their banter, Willem nodded down the hall. "What about Emmy? Is she dressed for dinner?"

A bell clanged somewhere on the grounds.

Emmy's door jerked open and Cuddy stepped out grinning—until he glanced up at Willem's reddening face. He winced then shoved his hat on his head and offered a weak smile. "Folks, that sound means dinner's served. Around here, if you're late, there won't be nothing left."

He tipped his hat at Emmy, who stood gaping at her papa from the door, and swaggered to the head of the stairs without another glance in their direction.

Emmy had never witnessed such a flurry of activity around a table. Three Mexican girls bearing trays wove in and out on countless trips to the kitchen. When Emmy didn't think another platter would fit between the mounds of stringy pork, tall stacks of tortillas, steaming bowls of beans, and crockery pots filled with spicy-smelling dishes, one of the chattering girls brought in a charger filled with brilliant red slices of yet another food she didn't recognize.

Mr. Rawson forked a piece and held it up for inspection. "Know what this is?" he asked no one in particular.

Papa wiped his mouth and smiled. "I believe I do, but let the womenfolk have a guess."

Aunt Bertha leaned in closer. "Don't reckon I've ever seen such a fancy-colored food before." She shot a look at Mr. Rawson. "Assuming that *is* food."

Mr. Rawson transferred the item in question to her plate. "Why don't you tell me?"

She picked around it cautiously with the tip of her fork then raised her eyes to his. "You sure about this?"

He smiled. "You've eaten a watermelon, haven't you?"

She nodded.

"Well, it tastes a bit like that, only watered down."

Talked into it, she cut a big piece and shoved it in her mouth. Her broad smile pleased Mr. Rawson, if his booming laugh was any indication. "That's cactus pear, Mrs. Bloom. Fresh cut this morning."

"Call me Bertha, and I'll call you John. Is that all right?"

"Why, sure it is." He pointed at a nearby platter. "Those vegetables there are cactus pads, Bertha. *Nopalitos*, we call them. We brush them with oil and toss them on the grill. I think you'll find them delicious."

Mrs. Rawson passed Emmy a crock filled to the brim with a savory-looking dish. "And this is pork stew with *nopales*, a wonderfully tasty addition." She turned to Mama. "Magda, the preserves you just spread on that tortilla?" She nodded for emphasis. "Cactus jelly."

Aunt Bertha reached for another bright-red piece of pear and chewed it thoughtfully. "Let me get this straight. The leaves are a vegetable but the pears are a fruit. All from the same plant? How can that be?"

Their hostess beamed. "It's a versatile commodity in the South, as adaptable as this region and its resourceful people."

Cuddy laughed. "And just as prickly as these people when they're crossed." He had ignored his mother's place cards and planted himself in Greta's chair beside Emmy, earning him a sharp glare from Papa.

Greta didn't seem to mind since it put her opposite them next to Diego.

Emmy had explained to her parents that the door to her room wasn't plumb, so it had swung shut by itself when Cuddy walked her onto the balcony to see the view. Grouchy old Papa hadn't believed a single word.

A hand reached between Emmy and Cuddy to place a dish of deep-green peppers on the table.

Emmy followed the shawl-wrapped arm to find a new face among the servers, this one slightly older. Something about her solemn expression intrigued Emmy. Her serenity and the way she held herself said she was out of place in the role of a servant.

Her presence sparked a peculiar reaction in Diego that Emmy could feel from where she sat. Already somber, when he saw who stood there he tensed and laid down his fork. One side of his jaw twitched, and his eyes darkened with irritation.

One of the serving girls whispered to the newcomer in Spanish. She answered quietly. Mr. Rawson added something to the conversation, and Greta laughed and made a comment, too. Soon, most everyone at the table, including Emmy's bilingual papa, chatted easily in the musical language that Emmy, Aunt Bertha, and Mama didn't understand.

However, Emmy did understand that the soft-spoken stranger seemed overtly interested in her. Each time she looked up, the brooding eyes met hers boldly, until Emmy began to feel uncomfortable. As for Diego, he watched the mysterious lady gather dirty dishes, a frown lining his forehead. Usually skilled at sorting the dynamics of a situation, the scowl on Diego's face and the server's careful appraisal threw Emmy quite off track.

Helping herself to one more glance at Emmy, she picked up an empty tray and turned to go.

Mrs. Rawson held up her hand. "Wait, Melatha. I'd like to introduce you." Standing, she walked around the table and slid her arm around the woman's waist. "Friends, this is Diego's little mother. She's not usually working in our kitchen but has graciously offered to lend a hand today for our special occasion. Melatha's the best cook in South Texas." She tightened her grip. "She's also a dear friend. The Rawsons consider her and Diego a part of our family."

Diego's mother. This time Emmy flashed an appraising glance.

Silent until now, Diego bowed slightly. "I'm honored by your words, Mrs. Rawson. I'm certain my mother feels the same."

The glowing smile on his handsome face flipped Emmy's stomach.

"But if you'll pardon one bold observation," he continued, "isn't it customary for the staff to serve the table while the members of a family dine together?"

"Isi!" his mother hissed.

The light of understanding dawned in Mrs. Rawson's eyes. Flustered, but only briefly, she faced her friend. "He's right, of course! Melatha, put down those things and join us. You've made your contribution for the day."

"I really couldn't, Miss Kate. Besides, I'm not hungry." She gave a tight smile. "All that tasting in the kitchen. . ."

Mrs. Rawson took the stack of dishes from her hands. "That's all right. We're nearly done. I know you're fond of our English tea. Sit and share a cup with us. Allow my guests to benefit from your company."

Diego's mother opened her mouth to protest again, but a short, middle-aged man in dust-covered pants appeared in the archway behind her son. "Excuse me, Señor Rawson." He wadded his hat in his hands. "I need to see Diego, if you please."

Mr. Rawson's moustache twitched. "What now, Pete? Can't you men run things for five minutes without him? The man's having his dinner."

The intruder cut pleading eyes to Diego. "Forgive me. It's important."

Irritation brought out Mr. Rawson's British accent. "What's so flaming important that it can't wait?"

Looking as if he'd sooner lose his tongue, the man swallowed hard then mumbled his answer. "Faron, he's loose again, señor. He's still on the ranch, but none of the men will tangle with him. They call for Diego."

Diego groaned and rolled his eyes. "Not again. That's twice in one day."

Mr. Rawson tossed his napkin on his plate. "Blast that son of perdition!"

Mrs. Rawson gasped. "John! Watch your language."

"Sorry, Kate, but isn't there any fence that will hold that horse?"

Diego patted his boss's shoulder. "Relax, sir. Enjoy your dessert. I'll take care of it."

Worry creased his mother's brow. "Will you return tonight, Isi?"

He flashed a teasing smile. "I suppose that depends on Faron."

"Be careful, son."

He gazed at her with affection. "Don't fret, Mother. I'll come home in one piece." He excused himself and pushed back his chair. "Before I go, sir, Señor Boteo suggested we post a night watch for a few days." His eyes twinkled. "It seems they've had a run-in with el chupa sangre. Francisco chased him off a goat last night."

Cuddy slapped the table. "Come on, Diego! I'm surprised at you for giving that fable enough credence to repeat it."

Greta wiped her mouth then placed her hands in her lap. "Something's killing all those calves and sheep, Cuddy."

He cocked his head to the side and mimicked her. "We do have a coyote or two in Dimmit County, Greta."

Biting back a grin, Diego stood. Folding his napkin beside his plate, he nodded at each of the guests and took his leave.

The warmth of his eyes, lingering on Emmy as he bid her good night, sent chills down her spine. Greta, obviously lost in thoughts she'd not likely share, stared longingly toward a spot past the archway where he had disappeared.

Mrs. Rawson signaled to one of the girls. She ducked into the kitchen and returned with a stack of small plates and a tray filled with sweets. Serving dessert to her husband, Mrs. Rawson raised one tapered brow. "If I may be honest, John, I'm glad Faron got out again. I hope he pulls up lame this time, and you have to shoot him." She passed the tray to Willem then demurely folded her napkin across her lap. "Better yet, perhaps the stubborn thing will bail off into the river and break his hateful neck."

John Rawson paused mid-bite then laid down his fork and stared. "Why, Kate. It's not like you to say so mean-spirited a thing."

She regarded him matter-of-factly. "That animal is the devil himself. I fear I'll live to see him kill you. If not Cuddy or Diego."

Her husband dropped his big hand over hers. "There's no danger of Faron killing anyone, honey. No one can ride him. He's strong-willed is all. I like that trait in an intelligent creature." He leaned to caress her chin. "The very thing that attracted me to you was your feisty nature."

Concern softened her features, and she swatted his arm. "Stop. I'm serious. It makes no sense to keep that stallion on the ranch. He's never been anything but a nuisance."

Papa settled his elbows on the table. "Tell me about this horse, John."

Eyes aglow, Mr. Rawson faced him. "Oh, he's a beauty, Willem. Purebred Spanish. Andalusian, you see. Black as thunder with a heart to match and shrewder than the two of us put together, not to mention the fastest thing on four legs. I admit he's the meanest bundle of horseflesh ever spawned, but"—he twisted around to wink at his wife—"he's worth every second of trouble."

Easing back in his chair, he reached for a small cake to nibble. "The thing is, Faron will only let me near him." He absently waved his hand. "Well, Diego, of course, and he tolerates Little Pete, the man you saw earlier." Leaning in, he nodded for emphasis. "But no man can ride the ornery beast. You should've been here the first time I tried." He chuckled. "The old boy put up a right rowdy kerfuffle."

Aunt Bertha blinked. "That's a good thing?"

The Rawsons laughed so heartily, Emmy's family had to join them, including Aunt Bert.

"Bertha, my dear, let's just say he won the skirmish and leave it at that."

For the first time, Emmy realized Diego's mother had slipped away unnoticed. Though she had gone, the memory of her probing eyes still warmed Emmy's flesh.

Mrs. Rawson placed her delicate hands on Papa's and Mr. Rawson's forearms. "Let's take our coffee on the veranda, shall we? It's a beautiful night."

CHAPTER 11

Diego ran his palm over Faron's trembling flank.

The horse sidestepped into the wall of the stall, snorting his disapproval.

"I know you don't like small spaces, señor, but that's too bad. Perhaps a few days without liberty to move will teach you to appreciate the freedom of your pasture."

Faron kicked at the boards behind him.

Diego laughed. "Spit and sputter all you like, young man. You won't be getting out of here." He brought his ear closer to Faron's nose. "What's that you say? Pretty señoritas throughout the county will be pining for you? I understand completely, for I suffer the same dilemma. Good looks are a curse, are they not?"

Pulling a wilted carrot from his pocket, Diego snapped off the root. "Perhaps this will soothe your battered ego, my friend."

Faron snuffled the offering, lifted it from Diego's palm with his soft lips, then nuzzled for more.

"Hungry, eh? I suppose so, after all your carousing. Tell you what, let's get you something more substantial, shall we?" He chuckled and jumped off the rail to the ground, giving Faron one last scratch between the ears. "Adios for now. Try to behave yourself, sí?" On the way out of the barn, he gave instructions for the horse to be fed and groomed.

As he neared the back door to report to Mr. Rawson, voices from the terrace led him through the hedges instead. A dozen lanterns set along the low-walled enclosure lit the patio while a healthy blaze in the fire pit flickered on the relaxed faces of the Rawsons and their guests. A coffee service rested on the table in front of the women. Deep in conversation, the men took their ease in comfortable padded chairs.

When Emily Dane came into sight, he paused in the shadows to watch her. She sat some distance from the others, balancing a cup of coffee on her knees while she gazed at the starlit sky. With her head thrown so far back, her neck looked impossibly long, and the moonlight turned her skin the same shade as the bone china she held. She sat up and sipped her coffee, the motion pursing the generous lips he couldn't stop thinking about to save his life.

"Diego?"

He leaped, warmth flooding his body. "Greta. I didn't see you there."

"Of course not. You weren't looking for me." She tried to smile, but suspicion crept into her eyes. "Have you taken to skulking in bushes and spying on my family?"

Burning with shame, he laughed to make light of her comment. "I was on my way to speak to your father. I found Faron. Courting a filly in Mr. Tumlinson's pasture."

A genuine smile back in place, she slid her arm through his. "I'm sure he'll be glad to hear. Let's go tell him."

John Rawson's deep rumble held court over his guests as they approached. "Both our families lived in Ripponden near Halifax, overlooking the River Ryburn. An overly impressive name for hardly more than a stream running through the village." He gazed around as if the night hadn't shrouded the scenery in darkness. "Nothing at all like this place."

Mr. Dane lowered his saucer to the table. "Tell us about the region, John."

"South Texas? You could say it's a country inhabited by bandits on both sides of the border. They're locked in a dispute over land rights—a battle as old as Genesis. Which is a whole other story, and I've talked long enough." He glanced up at Greta and Diego. "Here's the man who can fill you in on the landscape. He's chased my horse across it from east to west. Did you find him, son?"

"Yes, sir."

"I knew without asking, or else you wouldn't be standing here. I see you made it back in one piece, but has he?"

"Not a scratch, though that could change by morning. I've locked him in a stall."

Mr. Rawson shook his head. "I hate to hear that." He sighed. "Well, there's no remedy for it, is there?"

"None that I can see."

"Very well, then. Pull up a chair and enjoy the night air. You deserve a rest." He glanced around the terrace. "Where'd that Cuddy get off to? He was here a minute ago."

Emily leaned to look past her father. "Cuddy went into the house, sir. He said he'd be right back."

Diego nodded at the older folks and gave Emily a tight smile before settling into the empty chair next to her. Cuddy's vacated seat, no doubt.

Greta flounced over and dropped onto the chaise alongside her mother. Tight-lipped and sullen, she was obviously angry.

What did she expect? He could hardly stretch his six-foot-three body onto that silly reclining chair between Mrs. Dane and Mrs. Rawson. Peeved, he determined to ignore her.

"I've never seen so many stars." Emily's breathless voice suited the night. Serene yet refreshing, like the pleasant breeze blowing from the west.

Diego gazed at the canopy of pinpoint lights, thicker than lentil stew in places. "Are there no stars in Humble, Texas?"

"Of course, but not like these."

He chuckled. "They are the very same ones, I assure you. It's only the unobstructed view and the absence of light here that makes them seem to jump right out of the sky."

In the near distance, a lone coyote howled, followed by a series of short, high-pitched yips. Its quavering cry was soon answered, the mournful howl even closer than the first.

Emily shivered and glanced behind her.

"Are you cold, Miss Dane? I can fetch you a shawl. Despite the warmth of the days, nights in Carrizo can be quite cool. Especially when the wind blows."

She settled back again. "No, thank you. I'm fine."

He watched her from the corner of his eye. "Are you certain?"

"Yes. It's very kind of you, though, considering. . ."

He angled his chair toward her. "Considering?"

She placed her cup on the arm of the chair and laced her hands in her lap, staring at them. She hadn't yet looked at him straight on, and he found himself wishing she would. After a tense silence, her lashes swept up and she gazed into his eyes. "I never apologized for ruining your hat."

He held up his hand. "No apologies necessary, I assure you."

"I've never done anything so awful before. I won't rest until you say you forgive me."

He grinned. "Well, we can't have that, now, can we? Consider yourself officially forgiven."

Her dimples hit bottom as she giggled and pulled her gaze away. "Very good. Can we start over?"

Diego's heart danced a peculiar jig in his chest. "I'd like that." An uneasy silence passed before he leaned closer. "So. . .how do we go about starting over?"

She turned in her chair and offered her hand. "Let's begin with this, since I spoiled it last time. I'm Emily Dane. Happy to make your acquaintance."

"Diego Marcelo, ma'am." He held out his hand and Emily gave it a vigorous shake.

She laughed merrily and so did he.

"Do me a great favor, Mr. Marcelo, and call me Emmy. It's the name my friends use, and I much prefer it to Emily."

"Emmy. Very nice. I will, but only if you call me Diego."

"I've never heard that name before. I believe I like it." A curious light touched her eyes. "I noticed your mama calls you something different."

Flustered, he cleared his throat. "Yes, she—"

"*¡Oye*, amigo, I see you've kept my seat warm for me."

Cuddy's firm grip on Diego's shoulder startled him, but not as much as the cloying scent of his breath. It angered Diego that he would do so reckless a thing with his father seated a few feet away. He glared up into Cuddy's eyes. "I believe you forgot something in the house, my friend."

"Oh? And what was that?" Cuddy's answer was slurred.

"Your blanket and pillow. It's long past your bedtime, I see."

Cuddy's boisterous laugh was too loud. Diego waited for Mr. Rawson's head to spin around, but the man was engrossed in his friends. Diego swung his gaze to Emmy.

Watching Cuddy with understanding eyes, she held out her cup to Diego. "I could use more of that strong, hot coffee, please. Pour Cuddy some while you're there, why don't you?"

Diego nodded gratefully and took the saucer from her hand. Cuddy slipped into Diego's chair the second he found it free, but Diego didn't mind. Better to have him seated than staggering over the veranda.

As he bent to pour, Mr. Rawson touched his arm. "Here's the man to ask, Bertha. Son, the lady's interested in buying some cattle. Who do we know that may have some for sale?"

Diego returned the pot to the tray without pouring. "As a matter of fact, there's a rancher down Catarina way who's looking to thin his pastures. Started his herd from stock off the Taft Ranch. They're breeding quality cattle down there."

"You know him?"

"Somewhat. I'm acquainted with both of his sons."

"Catarina?" Mr. Dane asked. "I'm not familiar with that town."

"It's not a town, Willem," Mr. Rawson said. "Just a sizable ranch owned by a fellow named Charles Taft. Nowadays they call the whole region Catarina." He looked at Diego. "What's the man's name that's selling his stock?"

"Buck Campbell, sir. His sons are Lester and Joe."

Mrs. Bloom scooted closer. "Can you take me there?"

Diego studied her face. She wasn't joking. "It's a long ride, ma'am. Twenty miles or better over rough terrain. A wagon might bear up on that rugged trail, but it'll slow you down considerably. Can you ride a horse?"

"I reckon so." Looking insulted, she waved at the surroundings. "I may not live way out like this, but we ain't exactly from the city."

Diego bit back a grin. "Yes, ma'am."

Mr. Rawson shook his head. "I couldn't do without Diego around here, Mrs. Bloom, but there's no reason I couldn't take you folks to Catarina."

Emmy's mother frowned and leaned forward in her chair. "Bertha, this is taking a turn toward crazy. I thought you came here to learn about cattle, not carry half of them back to Humble."

"I want me some South Texas cows."

"We have cows back home."

"Not like these. Willem said they breed the finest stock here, and I won't settle for less."

Sighing with exasperation, Mrs. Dane attempted a final argument. "Just how do you propose to get them home? There's no more room in your satchel."

Mrs. Bloom winked. "Why do you reckon that satchel's so full? I already studied on ways to get them home. By rail, for one. They have special cars that carry cattle all over this country." She nudged Mr. Rawson. "Ain't that so?"

"Yes, it's so, and it'll be no problem to load yours at the station in Uvalde. As long as you have the money to pay for shipping."

She leveled him with a gaze. "I have the money."

He lifted his eyes to the Danes.

"She has the money," they said in unison.

"The Humble oil boom," Mr. Dane explained.

Mr. Rawson chuckled. "Very well, then. I suppose you do."

Mrs. Rawson touched her husband's arm. "How do you propose to get them from Catarina to Uvalde, John?"

He sat tall in his chair. "We'll drive them, Katie! By golly, this is still South Texas. The devil's rope be hanged!"

Mrs. Bloom gave an excited hoot. "The devil's rope? What's that?"

"Barbed wire, ma'am. The worst thing to ever happen to a drover." He patted her hand. "But don't you worry. We'll stick to the roads and trails and still get your stock to Uvalde in perfect health." He picked up the coffeepot and poured a cup for himself, then filled the two in Diego's hands. "So it's settled. We'll start planning our trip tomorrow." He wagged his big finger in Mrs. Bloom's face. "But there's no need to get in a hurry. I have plans to show you around Carrizo Springs before we traipse all over Catarina. So sit back and enjoy your coffee."

The swish of shoes on the sandy soil beyond the tile caught his attention. He swiveled in his chair to look. "And here's our Rosita, with *empanadas* fresh from the oven if my nose doesn't lie. Grab one, folks, and eat them while they're hot."

Diego waited until the ladies were served, then wrapped a pie in a napkin and tucked it under his arm. Hustling back to where

Emmy and Cuddy sat, he handed Emmy her coffee. "Forgive me. I was detained." He shoved the other cup and pie to Cuddy. "Eat this," he growled, "and no arguments. You need food on your stomach."

Cuddy reeled drunkenly and laughed. Leaning close to peer into Emmy's eyes, he pointed at Diego. "He thinks I've had one too many."

She drew away and held her napkin to her nose. "I'm afraid he may be right. Please eat something, Cuddy."

He waved his hand. "Nah! Not hungry." He swung to Diego. "I've just been telling Miss Emily about the river. She agreed to let me show it to her tomorrow." He took hold of Diego's shoulder and shook him. "What do you think about that, amigo?"

Diego looked over his shoulder. Mr. Rawson and Mrs. Bloom were huddled together, rambling about cattle no doubt. The others sat talking, not paying the least bit of attention. Except for Greta. She reclined on the chaise, twisting a napkin into a knot and casting doe-eyed glances their way. He sighed. If she would only turn away, he could somehow get Cuddy into the house.

"Diego?"

Emmy's urgent voice sent a jolt along his spine. "What's wrong?"

Her eyes wide with concern, she tipped her head at Cuddy, slumped in the chair and dead to the world. "I'm afraid you were too late with that coffee."

Diego handed off Cuddy's spilled cup to her and knelt to steady him in the chair. "I have to get him to his room without his father's notice."

Her eyes shifted to Mr. Rawson. "How will you manage with him so close?"

"I'll need a favor from you. Can you create a diversion?"

Emmy seemed eager to help. "I'll try." Standing, she smoothed her shirt and, with a grimace over her shoulder at Diego, sauntered toward the others.

"Emily," Mrs. Rawson called, "it's about time you decided to join us." She patted the end of Greta's chaise. "Have a seat right here. I'll serve you one of Rosita's sweet pies. She's renowned in Dimmit County for her empanadas."

Greta snatched her legs away as if in danger of losing them.

Emmy ignored her and delicately perched on the chaise. She

accepted Mrs. Rawson's offering then clutched her mother's arm. "Mama, tell our hosts how oil was discovered on Aunt Bertha's land." She turned a dazzling smile on John Rawson. "I believe you'll find this story quite entertaining."

Grateful for Cuddy's smaller size, Diego slid one arm beneath his shoulders and stood him up. He mumbled incoherently, and Diego shushed him, checking over his shoulder to see if anyone had heard. They seemed to be in the clear, so he hustled Cuddy over the low patio wall and across the yard as fast as he could manage.

Rosita met them in the hall. Without a word, she slipped beneath Cuddy's other arm and helped Diego wrestle him upstairs to his room.

After tucking Cuddy into bed, Diego hurried to rejoin Emmy and the others on the veranda, but when he exited the house, they were standing together bidding each other good night.

Not until he had crawled into his own cot did Diego remember that Cuddy had orders to bed down with the fellows in the bunkhouse. His heart in his throat, he considered going after him but knew it wouldn't be possible. The Danes, Bertha Bloom, and Emmy were settling into rooms off the same hall where he'd have to drag Cuddy's lifeless body.

Pondering the facts, Diego took a measure of comfort from Cuddy's condition. Mr. Rawson needn't fear him slipping across the hall to endanger Miss Dane's virtue or his father's reputation. Tucked beneath his covers, snoring the rafters down, Cuddy Rawson was as mischief-proof as they came. Diego would deal with the rest come morning.

CHAPTER 12

"Well, for heaven's sake! Is that Bertha I hear outside? It's barely daylight."

Willem looked up from slipping on his boot and grimaced. "Who else would be cackling? It's too early for the chickens."

Magda pushed open the patio door and searched the dimly lit grounds below. She followed another loud burst of laughter to where Bertha jumped up and down in the middle of the backyard, holding her side.

Catching a touch of her mirth, Magda grinned. "What's so funny, Bertha?"

Bertha stood with Diego's mother. The drawn-up, somber little woman who served them supper the night before had gone, replaced by a woman with a gleeful expression and dancing eyes.

Bertha pointed. "Look up yonder. On that windmill."

Magda squinted and gazed across the yard. She could just make out the unmistakable shape of a saddle horn and stirrups outlined in the early dawn sky. "Why, that's a saddle! Come see this, Willem. Somebody saddled a windmill."

Emmy stepped onto the balcony from her room. "What's all the commotion out here? They can hear you in Humble."

Diego bounded off the porch beneath them and smiled up at her. "I'm afraid it's my fault." He pointed behind him. "That's a grievous act of retribution directed at me."

"It's his saddle," Bertha cried, obviously privy to the whole explanation. "His men did it to get him back for what he done to them."

Smiling, Willem snorted. "Whatever he did, it must've been bad."

A sheepish look crept over Diego's face. "I guess it all depends on how you look at it. All I did was sweeten their morning ritual."

Bertha winked up at Magda. "With a generous portion of molasses poured down each of their boots. They found out when they pulled them on."

"A sleepy cowboy with sticky boots?" Magda nodded at the windmill. "Son, I'd say justice is served."

A bell clanged, interrupting their fun and signaling breakfast.

Willem patted Magda's shoulder. "Round up Bertha and come to the table. I'm starved."

"You wait for me, Willem Dane. I'm hungry, too. Rounding up Bertha won't take but a minute." She placed two fingers in her mouth and blew.

Attuned to their signal, Bertha's head jerked up.

Magda motioned with her arm. "Come along. You're keeping me from breakfast."

Bertha started for the house. "You won't have to wait on me. I plan to beat you to the table."

Diego stood staring up at Emmy.

Blushing, she flashed him a dimpled smile. "Are you coming, too?"

Greta Rawson eased from behind a trellis and slipped her arm around Mrs. Marcelo. It dawned on Magda that Greta had been standing there in the shadows all along. "He takes his breakfast at his mother's table." She fluttered her lashes. "Don't you, Diego?"

Embarrassed, or maybe flushed with annoyance, Diego nodded then directed his answer at Emmy. "Yes, unless I dine at the bunkhouse. I don't usually eat meals in the house."

Emmy backed away from the rail. "Oh, I see."

Diego took off his hat. "Enjoy your breakfast, Miss Dane." He bowed toward Magda. "And you, Mrs. Dane." His eyes cut back to Emmy. "Perhaps I'll see you tonight."

John Rawson opened the door under Magda's balcony. She couldn't see him but his booming voice rattled the boards at her feet. "You bet you'll see her tonight. We're going to a *pachanga*! You're all invited."

Magda guessed by the wide grin on Diego's face that a pachanga was a good thing.

Bertha required an explanation. She caught Diego by the shirt and spun him around. "A what?"

"*Un partido mejicano*, Mrs. Bloom." He swept his mother into his arms and waltzed her around the yard as the first bursts of light announced the rising sun. "A rowdy Mexican party. We shall eat our fill and dance to a mariachi band."

"Stop, Isi!" his mother cried, giggling like a girl. "I'm getting dizzy!"

He turned her loose and faced the porch. "Whose house, sir? And what is the occasion?"

"Jose Bosques. His daughter's *quince años*."

Diego's face lit up even more. "A *Quinceañera*!" He snatched his unsuspecting mother from behind and whirled her again. "Then we shall dance all night!"

Willem tugged on Magda's sleeve. "There's a plate of ham and eggs downstairs with my name on it. You've kept me from my breakfast so long I won't mind eating yours, too."

She pushed away from the rail. "You won't get the chance." With one last whistle for Bertha, she followed Willem downstairs. At the bottom landing, she spoke her thoughts aloud. "Willem, what is a quince. . .a quincea. . .? What is that thing they said?"

He shrugged. "I don't know, but the mention of it sure stirred things up." They reached the table and he held out her chair, nodding a good morning to Rosita before she scurried back to the kitchen. "One thing's for certain, dear. We're about to find out."

Emmy stood behind the wooden shutters, spying on Diego and Greta. Sneaking about and prying into people's affairs was a habit Mama had worked diligently with Emmy to break. Emmy had tried to mend her ways but found opportunities too frequent and temptations too irresistible. Especially the one taking place in the yard below.

Greta leaned against the adobe wall of a shed, hands behind her back, staring up at Diego. He rested against the wall, too, a respectable distance between them. Greta wore a cotton dress, pale yellow like the ribbon in her hair. Unless Emmy judged her too harshly, she'd spent some time in her mirror tugging the neckline down—not enough to be scandalous but enough to reveal a circle of milky white skin.

Diego's earlier irritation had vanished with the morning dew. He was at ease with Greta, laughing and talking freely, the latter punctuated by pointing, waving, and gesturing with his hands. He seemed in such high spirits, Emmy waited for him to pull Greta into his arms and dance her about the yard. She couldn't help wondering if it was the upcoming party or being with Greta that caused his mood.

His head jerked around to her window as if attracted by sudden motion.

Emmy eased out of sight, wondering what he had seen. Had she moved the shutter and given herself away? Blushing, she hurried to her dressing table, scolding herself for being caught at something she ought not to have been doing in the first place. Sighing, she realized a voice stronger than Mama's had cautioned her to mind her own business. Wishing she'd learn to obey, Emmy whispered a prayer of repentance and one for the strength to change.

After one last glance in the mirror, she stepped into the hall and closed the bedroom door. As she turned to go, a growl from behind nearly jolted her from her shoes. Visions of claws and fangs and goats shriveled to wineskins flashed through her mind as she spun toward the shadows. "Who's there?"

"If it's all the same to you, we can do without slamming doors."

Emmy took a step closer. "Cuddy? Is that you?"

Another moan. "There's no need to shout either."

She smiled. "I'm not shouting. Are you all right?"

He groaned again.

Emmy followed the sound to the dark corner and found him sitting on the floor hugging his knees, his head hanging down. She sat beside him, tucking her legs beneath her and covering them with her skirt. "Is there anything I can do?"

He groped for her hand and held it.

Surprised, she let him. "Why do you do this to yourself, Cuddy? If drinking causes this, why drink?"

He shrugged. "It's fun?"

She shook her head. "You weren't having fun last night, and you're certainly not now. This is more like punishment." Emmy could see him clearly, now that she'd adjusted to the light.

He cut his eyes to her. "You may be onto something there."

She pondered his confession then shook her head. "Why would you feel the need to punish yourself? You're a handsome young man with a wonderful family, a lovely home, and a thriving ranch."

He perked up and grinned. "Handsome?"

"In short, you have everything a man could want."

He snorted. "Miss Dane, 'everything' can be a pretty hefty burden at times. Especially when you're born into a situation you never asked for." He studied her with bleary eyes then hung his head again. "Or when there's someone reminding you at every step that you're not who you should be." He pulled his hand away and wrapped it around his knees again. "But how could someone like you be expected to understand?"

Stunned, Emmy sat quietly, Papa's scowling face looming in her mind. Her heart aching over their shared grief, she reached to caress his fingers. "I understand more than you know."

He raised his head and quirked his brows. She nodded. Smiling sweetly, he twined his fingers around hers and squeezed.

"Emily!"

Emmy pushed off the floor, the stern face she'd envisioned glaring at her from three feet away. She hadn't even heard his footsteps. "Sorry, Papa." Her heart pounded so hard, she knew Cuddy was bound to hear.

He stood, too, and came to her defense. "Emily was tending me, Mr. Dane. That's all. I'm feeling poorly this morning, and she was concerned."

Papa's bottom jaw stuck out, and his breath came in rapid gasps. He pointed behind him. "They're holding breakfast for you downstairs, Emily. See how fast you can get there. We'll deal with this shameless display after we eat."

Emmy stumbled away, casting a nervous glance at Cuddy.

He stared after her with renewed understanding.

Papa herded her to the stairwell, a firm hand at her back. He paused at the landing and turned, his finger aimed at Cuddy like a weapon. "Keep your distance from my daughter, Cuthbert Rawson, or I shall have to speak to John."

"Yes, sir," Cuddy barked, his voice steady and strong.

More sad than frightened, Emmy followed her fuming papa down the stairs. Near the bottom, a gaily hummed tune floated back to her from inside the house. As they rounded the landing, the back of a yellow dress disappeared into the dining room through the arched doorway.

Emmy cringed. She wondered how much Greta had heard and how fast she would tell Diego. It seemed Emmy wasn't the only snoop on the Twisted-R Ranch.

Jaunty footsteps on the stairs and a merry whistle announced Cuddy coming to join them at the table. He breezed through the door and took a seat, flapping his napkin with flair and placing it on his lap.

Astonished, Emmy stared. Evidently, his anger with Papa had shoved aside his misery.

His mother glanced up. "Good morning, Cuthbert."

He grimaced. "Careful with the name-calling, Mother. You'll spoil my good mood."

The creases in Papa's forehead grew impossibly deep. "I thought you were ill." To the casual listener, his tone might be mistaken for concern. Emmy clearly heard the accusation.

Passing Aunt Bertha the gravy bowl, Mrs. Rawson paused. "Oh? Are you all right, son?"

Cuddy flashed Papa a brilliant smile. "Feeling much better now, Mr. Dane. Thanks to your lovely daughter."

Papa blustered and took up his fork, going after his eggs as if they were Cuddy instead.

Emmy shrank five inches in her chair.

Stabbing his fork into a sizable slab of ham on the serving platter, Cuddy lifted his eyes to Mr. Rawson. "Miss Dane is interested in seeing the river, Father. I thought I might saddle a couple of horses and take her out there this morning." He raised his brows innocently toward Emmy's mama. "If it's all right with her parents, of course."

Papa tried to protest, but his mouth was full. He snatched up his coffee to take a drink, but he was too late.

"A splendid idea, son." Mr. Rawson beamed at Emmy and then smiled across the table at his daughter. "Greta will go along to chaperone."

This time Greta sputtered. "The river? Cuddy, there's nothing remotely interesting about that muddy old cesspool. Why, it's hardly worth the ride." He ignored her so she directed her objections to her mother. "You know I don't like the sun. It dries my skin."

Mrs. Rawson shot her a weighted look. "You'll be fine, Greta. Our guest would like to go."

"Can Diego come along?"

Her mother drew back. "Greta Rawson! For pity's sake."

Caught with her knickers inside out, Greta lowered her eyes. "Sorry, Mother. It's just that Diego's so clever and fun. I thought he might make the trip more tolerable."

"Greta!"

Her father held up his hand. "Hush, daughter. Diego is far too busy running this ranch to run off and play."

"But you can spare Cuddy?"

Mr. Rawson tossed a tortilla onto his plate. "Cuddy's a different story."

Emmy checked for Cuddy's reaction to his father's words. He had none.

Taking advantage of the silence, Emmy's papa cleared his throat. "John, I don't think–"

"They'll be fine, Willem. Don't worry. Cuddy knows his way around."

Papa cringed.

Emmy hid her grin behind her napkin. With the boldness of the falsely accused, Cuddy had called Papa's bluff and won most handily. She had to wonder how long Cuddy's victory would last. Willem Dane wasn't used to losing.

Cuddy folded his napkin over his plate. "So it's settled. We'd best get going while it's cool. The ride won't be tolerable in the heat of the day."

His mother swept her arm over the table. "What about all this food? You've hardly touched your plates."

"Have Rosita wrap it and we'll take it with us."

"A picnic?" She beamed. "How fun! You'll have us wanting to join you."

Cuddy stood. "I'm afraid old codgers aren't invited, Mother dear." Grinning, he kissed the top of her head. "Besides, you couldn't keep up with us youngsters."

CHAPTER 13

The Nueces River wound along the back of the Twisted-R Ranch, providing a source of fresh water and a natural boundary. Like an oasis in the desert, an assortment of trees grew along the banks, stretching in a line as far as the eye could see in either direction. As Emmy and the Rawsons drew closer, the sparse ground cover and mesquite gave way to lush green grass and live oak trees, a scene not unlike the banks of the San Jacinto River back home. It was hard to believe the two environments were part of the same landscape. Once Emmy thought about it, she realized the South Texas terrain had been as fickle as a female since she got off the train in Uvalde.

The horses picked up speed as they neared the slope, and Cuddy winked. "They smell the water."

Emmy didn't blame them. If she were on foot, she'd be trotting, too. If Cuddy considered the morning cool, she dreaded the ride home. The sun shone directly at them from above the eastern horizon, already so bright Emmy couldn't bear it in her eyes. Greta had grudgingly lent her a straw hat that Emmy pulled low on her forehead, grateful for the band of shade it provided.

At Mrs. Rawson's suggestion, Emmy had changed into riding britches and a light yellow top. Still, sweat pooled and rolled down her back, tickling her between the shoulder blades. She was relieved to reach the cover of the oaks.

They dismounted and Cuddy tied off the reins. He pulled a carefully wrapped bundle from his saddlebag and handed it to Emmy. "Give this to Greta. Tell her to pick a good spot and spread the blanket."

"I can spread a blanket, Cuddy. I'm capable."

He caught her wrist. "Let Greta, please. And don't wander off by yourself. It could be dangerous."

A chill touched her spine. "Dangerous?"

"Rattlers. They don't play nice around these parts. And the scorpions. . .they'll invite themselves to lunch. You won't know they're there until they sting you."

Her eyes must have conveyed her fear, because he laughed and patted her shoulder. "Stay close to Greta. For all her prissy ways, she's well adjusted to her environment." He took the bundle from Emmy and handed it off to Greta, who had joined them. "Eyes like a hawk. Right, sis?"

She took the pack from him none too gently and stalked toward the bank. "I'm not speaking to my brother, in case he hasn't noticed."

Cuddy widened his eyes at Emmy. "This outing holds promise."

Emmy stifled a laugh.

Though the river hardly lived up to the term *cesspool*, Greta was right in saying there was nothing spectacular about the Nueces. It offered low, murky water and muddy banks, exposed roots along the opposite wall, and stagnant pockets topped by green scum. Still, it was the wettest place Emmy had seen since she'd arrived in South Texas. When she threw in the grass tickling her legs beneath the cover, abundant restful shade, and the wind whistling through the overhead treetops, their little picnic became a refreshing retreat from the heat–and a respite from Papa's broad thumb. She untied the ribbon of her hat and took it off. Shaking her hair out behind her, she turned her face to catch the breeze.

Greta tossed her half-eaten sandwich aside and pushed to her knees. Staring toward the water, she stretched and yawned, then rose without a word and walked away. Spreading her shawl in a grassy spot near the bank, she pulled out a small green book and pen and sat down to write.

Cuddy chuckled. "She's writing scathing insults about me in her diary."

Emmy glanced at Greta hunched over the book balanced on her knees, biting the end of her pencil. "How do you know?"

He winked. "My ears are itching."

Emmy passed him a napkin. "Your ears deceive you. If she's writing scathing insults, they're directed at me." She wiped her mouth. "She doesn't care much for me, does she?"

Cuddy lay back on his folded arms, staring at the brilliant blue sky. "You may not believe it, but Greta couldn't wait for you to arrive."

Emmy gaped at him.

He gave her a fleeting look. "It's true. There aren't many unmarried women her age around Carrizo Springs. She's looked forward to your visit for weeks, made elaborate plans for you two." He rolled onto his side, propping up on one arm. "Truthfully, I got tired of her rattling. To hear her talk, you two should be practically sisters by now."

Emmy scooted around to face him. "So I made a horrid first impression? We haven't shared three words, yet she hates me."

He smirked like a naughty little boy. "It's not that she hates you, sweetheart." He stole a quick look to be sure Greta wasn't listening. "Little sister wasn't prepared for how much Diego would like you."

Heat flooded Emmy's neck. She stared hard at the red plaid blanket between them. "Diego doesn't. . ."

Cuddy pushed up and sat cross-legged, his knees touching hers. "Oh, yes, ma'am. He does." He pulled a long stalk of grass and tickled her hand with the seedy head. "Does that knowledge please you?" He ducked, trying to see her eyes. "I suppose it makes Greta's ill treatment worthwhile, doesn't it?"

Emmy changed her position and brushed off the weedy stalk. "You're the most vexing man I've ever met, Cuddy Rawson."

He flashed a grin. "And you're the prettiest woman I've ever seen, Emily Dane."

She laughed and shook her head.

"It's true, honey." He tapped her on the chin. "Don't try to act like you don't know."

Emmy shrugged. "Some days I know. Some days I'm not so sure." She peeked at him from under her lashes. "I wanted to thank you for this morning."

Cuddy sighed. "The old man is pretty tough on you, isn't he?"

She grimaced. "I wouldn't mind so much if I knew why. Not knowing keeps me off balance, keeps me guessing."

Compassion warmed his pale blue eyes. "That's part of their game, darlin'. To make you doubt yourself."

She studied his face. "I don't think so. Not in my case, at least. I know in my heart there's a reason Papa deals so harshly with me." Her throat swelled unexpectedly. She swallowed. "He wasn't always this way. When I was younger, he was quite affectionate, which makes it even harder." She paused. "You know?"

He scooted closer and pulled her head to his shoulder. "As it happens, I do know."

Emmy's chest ached with unshed tears. "If I could pinpoint the day everything changed, I'd be able to figure out what I did wrong."

She raised her head and they gazed into each other's eyes. Cuddy lifted two fingers and caressed her cheek. "Don't let him change who you are, Emily."

"Diego!" They sprang apart as Greta rushed by. "Look! Diego's here."

Emmy stretched to look past Cuddy's shoulder. Diego sat his horse at the top of the slope, staring down at them. As Greta rushed toward him, he dismounted and walked to meet her.

"You came after all," Greta cooed. "I'm so glad." The change in the girl was astounding. "Come sit with us and share our food. Have you eaten lunch?"

Sit with us? Under different circumstances, Emmy would find Greta's statement quite funny. At the moment, she was busy fretting over how her shared moment with Cuddy looked from atop the rise.

Cuddy whirled around, coming to rest with his arms propped on his knees. "They sent you out here to spy on us, didn't they?"

"Don't be a dolt," Diego growled, a rosy glow on his cheeks. "Your mother feared you might keep the women out in the heat too long. From the look of things, it appears she was right."

Cuddy stood and brushed off his hands. "It is getting late. Pack up, ladies, and we'll head on back."

"There's no need to rush, Cuddy." Greta plopped down and patted the spot beside her. "Sit for a spell, Diego, and have something to eat. We're just now starting to have fun."

Emmy shared a look with Cuddy. He rolled his eyes and she nearly bit her lip in two trying to stifle a laugh.

Diego smiled sweetly and patted his midsection. "Thank you, but I'm still working off Mother's sunflower seed cakes. Besides"—he drew closer to Greta's face—"unless I'm mistaken, the real reason she wants you home has something to do with the pachanga. When I left the yard, she was airing pretty dresses on the clothesline."

Greta spun toward her brother. "Let's go, then. She's bound to be freshening that horrid green gown for me. I don't know why she loves it so. The ruffles make me look like a dowdy schoolgirl."

The mischievous glint in Cuddy's eyes shouted the taunt he bit back. "If you're in such a hurry, pack up these things while Diego helps me water the horses."

Emmy began gathering utensils and tying up the cloth holding the leftover tortillas. To her surprise, Greta squared around to face her, a warm smile on her lips. "I hope you enjoyed yourself this morning, Emmy. I come here often just to think and write in my diary. It's quite a peaceful spot."

Emmy gave her a sideways glance. "I thought you didn't like to come here at all."

Greta blushed and ducked her head. "I suppose I did give that impression." She looked up, regret in her eyes. "I'm sorry, Emily. I've acted the shrew, haven't I? I don't know what came over me. I hope you'll forgive me." She picked up Emmy's hand. "Is it possible that we could start over?"

Shocked, Emmy stared wordlessly at their tangled fingers.

"If we're friends, tonight will be so much more fun. We can help each other dress. I'd love to pin your hair. You have such lovely blond curls."

Emmy's hand rose to her hair. "Why, thank you."

"Did you know I had a quince años party, too?" She dreamily rolled her eyes. "It was a grand affair! Quince años means fifteen years. Of course, it's not our custom, but when I turned fifteen, the locals insisted out of respect for my family."

Greta gazed over Emmy's shoulder with a dazed expression, as if she could see into the past. "I wore the sweetest little dress." She grinned and touched Emmy's arm. "No, not the one with green ruffles."

Emmy laughed to be polite.

"Mama piled my hair on my head," Greta continued, "and wove flowers into the curls like a crown." She sighed. "We danced until dawn. All of my friends attended." A wistful shadow stole over her eyes. She squeezed them shut and shook her head. "They're all married now, except for Mary English. She moved to New York last year to become a journalist. Nearly broke her mother's heart."

Emmy widened her eyes as Greta came up for air. The girl had uttered more words in thirty seconds than she had for two days. Still reeling from the sudden change of heart, Emmy sat speechless.

Smiling prettily, Greta touched her cheek. "I'm elated to see you and my brother are getting along so well."

Ah, Emmy thought, *the reason for the change in her attitude.*

"Cuddy needs someone," Greta said. "He has me to talk to, but a brother won't confide in a sister the way he would a. . .well, a special friend like you."

Greta beamed so brightly Emmy watched for cherubs with harps to alight on her shoulders. She groped for something to say. "We have a lot in common." It was the best she could do.

"We do!" Greta squealed. "I've noticed it, too. We're both fair-haired and about the same age." She nodded matter-of-factly. "You prefer tea to coffee in the mornings just as I do." She wiggled her hand wildly and sat up on her heels. "And look! We're wearing the same colored blouse."

Her cheeks warming, Emmy offered a tight smile.

"Oh." Greta drooped like wilted lettuce and withdrew her hand. "You meant Cuddy, didn't you?"

"Well, I. . ."

"Enough chitchat, ladies," Cuddy called from behind them. "Let's get you back to the ranch. I'd prefer not to incur the wrath of the fair Katie Rawson."

Diego bent to pick up Emmy's hat and gave it to her then offered his hand. She caught a glimpse of Greta's slight scowl as he pulled her to her feet first and took her arm to walk her to her mare. Holding her ground, she lifted her brows and tilted her head toward Greta.

Flustered, he back-stepped to the blanket. "Forgive me, dear girl. I thought Cuddy. . ."

It seemed a struggle for Greta to maintain her serene expression. The tiny creases on her forehead gave her away. "Never assume Cuddy will behave properly, Diego. The poor boy's ill equipped in situations requiring a show of manners." The creases deepened as she glared at her brother. "You see he has none."

Though Greta took out her frustration on her brother, Emmy guessed her irritation had little to do with him. Diego helped Greta onto her horse then turned to assist Emmy. Disappointment clouded his eyes when he found her already mounted.

"Let's ride," Cuddy said, still seeming oblivious. He turned his horse in a half circle and crowded between Emmy and Diego, in effect cutting them off from each other. One look at his satisfied face told Emmy he'd done it on purpose.

CHAPTER 14

Melatha's breath caught in her throat when Isi stepped over the threshold of the jacal. He wore his finest clothes, glossy black pants and a matching short jacket, adorned with shiny buttons in front and on the sleeves. A tanned snakeskin served for a hatband, fastened to the hat by a silver *concha* stamped with the Texas star. He had attached matching conchas to the strap of his best leather boots.

Standing in the shadows cast by the waning light, he looked like Reynaldo on their wedding day, and the sight brought tears to Melatha's eyes. "Oh, Isi. You will leave the Bosques home tonight with the hearts of all the women in your breast pocket."

Wearing a silly grin, he clicked his heels and bowed to kiss her hand. "There's only one heart I care about, Mother, and it's yours."

Snorting, she waved off his teasing. "It's not like you to lie, son. We both know there's another."

He colored and shoved past her. "She's a charming and beautiful girl, but she means nothing to me. Besides, she's already smitten with Cuddy."

Melatha pinned him with an innocent stare. "I was referring to Greta. Who do you mean?"

Caught, he glared over his shoulder. "Why can't you at least leave my thoughts to me? Why must you lay snares with twisted words until you expose my deepest feelings?" He stalked to her and spun her around, fumbling with her apron strings. "And why are you still wearing this? It's time to go."

Melatha turned and caught his hands. "If I have exposed what you feel for White Hair to the light then leave it there, so you might see it clearly." She shook her head. "I recognize her restless spirit, Isi. You have as much hope for breaking that devil, Faron."

He tossed her apron aside and lifted the basket of food she'd prepared for the party. With a haughty grin, he herded her toward the door. "That's encouraging, Mother. You see, I have Faron eating out of my hand."

Diego loaded the vexing little woman and her sloshing crock of frijoles into the wagon and drove to the main house. He pulled in behind Cuddy's two-seater and set the brake. Mr. Rawson had parked his wagon in front of the line.

As the families filed onto the porch, the flurry of activity drew Diego's attention, but his eyes found and fixed on Emmy. She had on a gown of iridescent silk, the top rose-tinted beige, the bottom a shimmering deep purple. Black velvet ribbon crisscrossed the bodice and rimmed the billowing skirt. He feared she'd be too warm until the sun had set and the wind picked up. Frowning, he wondered why the women didn't tell her.

"She looks lovely."

He decided to turn his mother's game against her. "Greta? Yes, she does." Truthfully, he couldn't have named the color of Greta's dress, much less said how she looked. It shamed him that the same girl he'd finagled a chance to spend time with every chance he got now sparked as much interest in his heart as the backside of the barn. In truth, the last two days had opened his eyes to her true nature. Where was the teasing, smiling Greta hiding, and where had the scowling, pouting Greta come from?

"Do you like my new frock, Diego?"

He jerked his gaze to the ground. So Greta's dress was yellow. She wore an awful lot of yellow. "Yes, it's very nice."

Greta twirled. "Perfect for dancing. Wouldn't you say?"

Diego's grip tightened on the reins as Emmy started down the steps on Cuddy's arm. "Um, yes. I suppose so."

To Willem Dane's obvious displeasure, Cuddy escorted Emmy to his rig then climbed up beside her. Mrs. Bloom got into the rear.

Diego's mother nudged him with her elbow. Forcing his attention back to Greta, he smiled down at her. "It's a striking dress and perfect for dancing. I'm sure you'll get the chance to prove it tonight."

Mrs. Rawson paused to stare toward her daughter before climbing aboard the lead wagon with her husband and the Danes. Twisting on the seat, she waved her lace fan. "Greta? Come along. You're holding things up."

"Yes, Mother." She waited to catch Diego's eye one last time before dashing to join Mrs. Bloom on the back seat of Cuddy's wagon just as Mr. Rawson pulled away from the house.

Diego didn't look at his mother, tried not to feel her eyes watching him. They rode to the Bosques ranch in silence.

The sun had begun to slip toward the horizon as they pulled past the gate to the house. Mariachi music filled the evening air with the beat of a lively song. Señor Bosques had brought the band all the way from Cocula, in the Mexican state of Jalisco.

The wagons followed the singing and the laughter to the rear of the house and parked in the grass beside a large wooden dais. Before the party ended, the floor of the platform would be reduced to splinters by hard-driving heels pounding out the rhythm of the dance.

Diego helped his mother down. She stood swaying to the music while he lifted out her contribution to the night, her prized bean soup. Señora Bosques directed him to a line of tables laden with every sort of brightly colored food imaginable. So full was the table, his mother had to help him find a place for the huge pot of beans. She skillfully shifted a few platters and bowls, and he set her offering among them.

Following his mother across the yard, he got his first look at the band. They were dressed in white cotton trousers, loose flowing shirts, and big smiles. Leather sandals graced their feet. One played the five-stringed *vihuela*, blending with the haunting strains of two violins and the strum of the *guitarrón*. The tempo stirred Diego's blood and urged his feet to move.

The thought of dancing brought his mind instantly to Emmy. If he was to be honest with himself, he'd planned to dance with her since he first got wind of the pachanga—a plan he'd see fulfilled if he had to waltz across Cuddy in the process.

When it came to dancing, Cuddy couldn't compete. Having less rhythm than a bucking mule, he seldom tried, unless he'd had too much to drink, a trick he dare not pull around so many of his father's close friends. The penalty for so foolish an act would be grave.

Diego searched out Emmy, sitting between a chattering Greta and a wide-eyed Bertha Bloom. For all he knew, Emmy danced no better than Cuddy and had less inclination. He watched her for a sign that the music moved her and was rewarded by her swaying shoulders and furiously tapping toes.

He smiled. Just a bit longer to wait. In South Texas, feasting came before dancing.

Cuddy passed by grinning, weighed down with a heaping plate of food. He held it up and pointed. "I'm waiting on you like one hog waiting on another."

Diego smiled. "I see that." He glanced around to locate his mother. She stood out of earshot, chatting with one of the locals. "I hope there's a portion of bean soup on that plate. I don't look forward to the ride home unless that crock is empty. I'll never hear an end to her moaning."

Cuddy changed his route and came to thrust the deep plate under Diego's nose. "Is that enough to suit you?"

He chuckled. "I knew I could count on you."

With a jaunty salute, Cuddy went his way.

Diego was about to call him back and suggest he offer the plate to one of the women, but they had stood up and were making their way to the line. He met them there.

"I ain't never seen such a spread in my life," Mrs. Bloom announced to no one in particular.

Mrs. Dane nodded. "I don't see how they'll ever eat all this."

Diego handed her a plate. "Ma'am, you'd be surprised how much a hungry band of vaqueros can put away. Just ask Rosita. She feeds our men every day."

He stepped aside to allow her and Mrs. Bloom to go first. Smiling, he handed Emmy and Greta a plate each. "Hungry, ladies?"

Greta's fingers deliberately brushed Diego's when she took the dish. "We're starved, right, Emily?" Before Emmy could answer, Greta rushed ahead. "Be sure and take plenty of everything. Otherwise, you're certain to offend someone. They all worked so hard preparing the food."

Diego wondered how Greta would know the meaning of hard work. He also wondered why she didn't take her own advice. While Emmy was careful to spoon a little from each pot, Greta barely covered her plate.

He didn't have to wonder long. As soon as the first couples lined up on the floor, Greta pushed her meager portion aside and smiled at him. She had plied Emmy with food and the fear of offending the cooks so she'd be too busy eating, or worse, too full to dance.

Emmy bravely shoved another bite in her mouth.

Angry, Diego took away her fork and set her dish on a nearby table.

She flashed him a grateful look.

Greta flashed him one of a different sort when he led Emmy onto the dance floor.

Emmy felt just as he'd expected in his arms, only better. How could he have imagined the smell of her, a blend of lavender mixed with jasmine, stronger each time the wind blew her hair?

He saw right away that she loved to dance. She matched him step for step as they whirled about the edge of the platform, dodging the other couples and laughing. When the song ended and the slower tempo announced a waltz, he pulled her closer and tightened his arm around her waist.

Her scent enveloped him, and the warmth of her body through the silky fabric teased his fingertips. Fighting to control his rapid breathing, telling himself the dancing was the cause, he caught her eye and smiled. "Having fun?"

"Oh, yes. Very much."

"That's a beautiful dress."

She blushed. "Thank you. Until the sun went down, I feared I'd picked the wrong one. It's much cooler now, though."

He nodded. "Yes, it is."

He led her around the floor again, past a sea of men's faces, young and old watching her with admiring glances. "I never thanked you for last night."

She raised her tapered brows. "For?"

"Helping me with Cuddy." He winked. "You make a fine distraction, Miss Dane."

Her eyes twinkled. "I'll take that as a compliment."

"I assure you, it was most sincere."

She lifted her chin. "Then I thank you."

They giggled like children at their teasing formality, her laughter warming Diego's heart.

"So. . ." She cocked her head to one side. "Why doesn't your mama like me?"

Her question stunned him. Her boldness stunned him more.

He opened his mouth to protest, but Cuddy swaggered toward them, interrupting the lie. "I'm cutting in, brother."

Diego tightened his hold on Emmy's hand. "You'll only trample the poor girl's toes. Show some mercy, my friend."

Cuddy snorted and held his ground.

"Not now, Cuddy. Perhaps she'll save you a dance."

"No, now, Diego. Stop fooling around."

Frustrated, Diego searched Emmy's face. "Only if the lady agrees."

Blind to his pain, Emmy watched Cuddy with obvious amusement. Diego winced at the affection shining in her eyes. "I'd love to dance with you, Cuddy."

With a slight bow, Diego released her and stepped away. Cuddy glided into his place, catching Emmy's hand in his, sliding his arm around the warmth of her slender waist. Laughing, they whirled away from him and disappeared.

Churning inside and struggling to contain his passion, Diego strode across the floor to join Greta. Too late, he realized she seethed like a roiling kettle.

Hoping to calm her, he danced with her at last. By the second song, she began to relax until she caught him stealing a glance at Emmy and her brother. She grew rigid in his arms. "They make such a nice couple, don't they?"

He stiffened. "I hadn't noticed."

"But you must have. They're both blond and attractive. Cuddy's short like Emily. He doesn't tower over her the way you do."

"I meant I hadn't noticed they were a couple."

She drew away from him, tilted her head, and stared. "Of course they are! On the way to it at least." She glanced around then lowered her voice. "Yesterday morning they were caught sitting together in the hallway outside their rooms." She leaned closer for emphasis. "Holding hands."

Diego's stomach lurched. "Caught?"

She failed at hiding a smirk. "Willem Dane. Haven't you noticed how he watches them?"

Diego scanned the crowd for Emmy's father. Indeed, he scowled at her and Cuddy across the sea of swirling dancers.

"You caught them yourself at the river."

He vacantly studied Greta's face. What did he see at the river? They were sitting together on a blanket staring at him on the rise, though Emmy did wear a curious expression of guilt.

What took place right in front of him that he'd missed?

Diego stopped dancing mid-note. Catching Greta by the wrist, he hauled her back to her chair.

She squirmed away from his grip and whirled to face him. "What's wrong with you tonight? I've never seen you so restless."

"I'm tired of dancing, that's all." He took a deep breath to steady himself. "I need something cool to drink. Would you care for one?"

"I would."

He spun.

Emmy stood behind him, a plastered smile on her face. She clutched his arm. "In fact, I'll help you."

Ignoring the rage on Greta's face, he allowed Emmy to steer him toward the punch bowl. On the way, he decided to put himself out of his misery. He would ask her straight out if she had feelings for Cuddy. If she said yes, he would bow out of the picture. If she said no—

"Diego, we have a problem."

He blinked down at her. Had she read his mind?

"It's Cuddy."

His heart pounded. Even as she prepared to crush his hopes, he admired her strength. No woman he'd ever known got straight to the point. "It's all right, Emmy. I understand."

She took his sleeve and jerked him around. "No, you don't." Angling him toward the wooden platform, she pointed.

Cuddy wove drunkenly through the crowd—one hand splayed over his heart, the other arm stretched to the sky—singing along with the mariachis with all of his might. Some of the dancers laughed and shoved him away; others scowled when he bumped them from behind.

Diego swallowed. "I don't believe my eyes. He seemed fine before."

Emmy's gaze darted anxiously from him to Cuddy. "I smelled it on his breath as soon as you left us. There's a flask in his pocket, and he keeps taking long swigs." She met his eyes. "I believe he's getting worse every second."

"Some local brew, no doubt. They can be potent. I've warned Cuddy about that poison." Diego pressed his fists to his forehead. "Why would the foolish boy do this? He knows how his father–" His head came up, frantic eyes scouring the rim for Mr. Rawson.

He was seated with some other ranchers, his chair faced away from the dais, but it would be only a matter of time before he noticed the ruckus or someone pointed it out.

Diego gripped her shoulders. "Emmy?"

She swept past him. "I know what to do."

Diego caught her arm. "If my mother asks, tell her I'll be back."

She nodded.

Diego stood his ground until Emmy crossed the yard and pranced in front of the men, her lilting laughter and dimpled grin captivating John Rawson and every man at the table.

Avoiding Greta, he cut around to the rear of the dance floor and waited until Cuddy swept past. Reaching for the nape of his neck, he jerked him to the ground and hauled him spitting and sputtering to the front of the house and then circled back to the rig.

The fight had gone out of him by the time Diego loaded him none too gently into the bed of the wagon and climbed aboard. With Emmy's help, once again they'd saved Cuddy's ornery hide.

Diego turned the horse and pulled from behind Cuddy's wagon. Breathing a sigh of relief, he took one more look behind him, and his heart shot past his throat.

No matter how fast Emmy talked or how dazzling her smile, John Rawson, against a backdrop of flickering torchlight, stared over his shoulder at Diego, his face a frightening portrait of rage.

CHAPTER 15

Melatha handed the misshapen piece of chalk to Jose. "Your turn, *niño*. Draw the letters just as I've shown you." She adjusted his fingers. "Relax your hand. Choking the life from the chalk won't help."

He turned up a grimy, toothless grin. "Sí, Mama Melatha."

"Curl the tail of the J like the tail of a monkey. The tail of the P should be long and straight, like a puppy's."

This time his smile revealed a few teeth.

She pointed to a small plate mounded with scrambled eggs and tortillas. "When you're done, your breakfast will be waiting."

The boy took one look at the food then hunched over the writing board, his tongue stuck out of the side of his mouth and his forehead drawn to a knot.

Before long, she would be teaching him words then whole sentences. In no time at all, he would be reading halting passages to her from the Bible, learning about the Savior while he learned to read.

Melatha glanced at her father's Bible and sighed. How different life would have been had he lived to fulfill his vow to take her and her mother to Ireland. His family lived there, blood relations that Isi would never meet. When her happy, bright-eyed father died at the hands of a thieving vagabond, her mother returned to her people instead, so Melatha grew up among the Choctaw.

She cracked the rest of the eggs into a bowl and stirred them briskly with a fork. Pulling the skillet to a cooler spot on the cast-iron stove, she poured them into sizzling butter. They hissed and sputtered like her feverish mind. With the sun barely over the horizon, already her thoughts were restless. Against her will, they turned to her husband.

On a mission trip to the reservation, raven-haired Reynaldo Marcelo had noticed Melatha among the other maidens and asked to have her. Though she rejected him, her grandfather saw merit in the union, chiefly Reynaldo's prized Appaloosa, and made the trade. Yellow Tree claimed he approved the kindhearted Spaniard because he foresaw him in a vision.

Many moons had passed, and many visions of her own, before Melatha had come to believe him. She and Reynaldo fought with a fury at first, until he tamed her. Then they loved with great passion. She bore her tiny, squirming brave the following spring.

Sixteen years later–after Reynaldo followed her father in death–like her mother before her, Melatha returned to her people, the only safe place she knew. Miserable within the confines of the reservation, Isi soon ran away. She didn't see her prodigal son again until his twenty-first birthday.

"If I scratch out my letters, will you feed me, too?"

Melatha whirled from the stove. "Isi. You caught me dreaming again."

He kissed her cheek. "Pleasant dreams, I hope." He pointed at Jose. "I see you've found another eager student."

She smiled tightly. "More eager to eat than to learn. But this way we both gain satisfaction."

"Where did you get that old slate?"

"Rosita's mother gave it to me." She held up a box. "Plenty of chalk, too. It's turned into a blessing."

He nodded at Jose, so intent on his letters his face almost touched the board. "More a blessing for him than for you, though he doesn't know it yet. Chihowa Ushi must be pleased."

Melatha's heart glowed in her chest. She loved to hear Isi speak their native tongue.

She stopped stirring the eggs and studied him. Since Isi knew she loved to hear it, he must be up to no good. She determined to ferret out the details of his plan before he ensnared her.

He sat at the table and she set his eggs in front of him. "What does the day hold for you, son?"

Before he could answer, Jose rose from the floor, wriggling with excitement. "I've finished, Mama Melatha. H through Q, just as you asked."

She studied the scrawl of letters on the slate. "Muy bueno, Jose. These are beautiful letters."

"Sí. May I eat now?"

She pulled out a chair for him. "Yes, you may eat your fill."

The boy scrambled into the chair and snatched up his fork.

Melatha wagged her finger. "Uh, uh, uh, Jose. What comes first?"

Blushing, he lowered his lips to his folded hands.

Isi smiled at her over his head.

After what must have been the shortest prayer the Father ever received, Jose snatched up his fork and went to work on his plate.

Shaking her head, Melatha sat down across from her son and smiled. "You were saying?"

Isi's grin became a troubled frown. "I'm not sure what this day will bring. Likely more work than I can wring out of daylight as usual." He sighed. "I can't count on much help from Cuddy today."

She lifted her head. "Oh?"

Isi shoveled in another bite, waiting until he swallowed to speak. "I doubt his bed will turn him loose today. I'm sure he's nursing a weak stomach and a pounding head."

"Oh, Isi. You mean he–?" She stopped abruptly and glanced at the boy.

Isi nodded.

Her heart squeezed in protest of the news.

"So," he began casually, "after spending more time with them, what do you think of our guests?"

The trap was set. Here was the bait. Wisdom demanded she tread lightly. "I like the one called Bertha. Her spirit is free. She's not bound by the opinions of others."

He nodded thoughtfully. "And the rest?"

"What about them?"

He looked up. "There are four guests in the house, Mother. You only like Bertha?"

"I don't have much to go on, do I? Mr. and Mrs. Dane seem nice enough."

He pushed back his eggs. "So you like Bertha, and the Danes seem nice. . ."

"Yes."

"And that's it?"

"I suppose so."

Color crept up his cheeks. "Let me get this straight. You like Bertha. The Danes seem nice. But you can't find one thing to say about—"

A harsh rap on the door rattled the hinges, cutting him off and bringing Melatha to her feet. "All right, all right! I'm coming!"

Isi shrugged. "Perhaps I was wrong. That's likely Cuddy now."

"Or Jose's mother," she suggested over her shoulder as she crossed the room.

Isi feigned shock. "With that heavy-handed knock? If so, let's pray she's in a cheerful mood."

Melatha laughed and opened the door.

One of Isi's men, pacing and stamping his feet, stood at the end of the porch.

Melatha looked back at Isi. "It's Little Pete."

Isi pushed back his chair and joined Pete outside. He returned shoving the fingers of both hands through his hair the way he did when he was tense.

She gripped his arm. "What's wrong, son?"

He met her gaze and his eyes flashed fear. "Pete said I'm not to report into work today. Rawson's orders."

Melatha released her disbelief in a single word. "What?"

"He said the old man wants to see me. Right now. In the barn."

"Oh, Isi. Do you know what this is about?"

His face drawn in grim lines, he nodded. "I'm afraid so." With no further explanation, he pushed through the screen and jumped off the porch. As he crossed the yard, he pulled back and squared his shoulders, ready to take what was coming to him, whatever unthinkable thing it might be.

Melatha's thoughts returning to snares and traps, she wondered who had set one for her son. Tears clouding her eyes, she bowed her head to pray.

The morning sun had yet to light the cool interior of the barn. Diego ducked inside and waited for his eyes to adjust.

Mr. Rawson, still unaware of his presence, slouched against Faron's stall, both arms atop the door, resting his forehead on his hands. He looked like a man with an unpleasant task ahead of him. Diego cleared his throat, and the big man straightened. "There you are."

Diego approached him. "I came as soon as you called." Bracing the heel of his boot against the bottom board of the stall, he looked the horse over. "He doing all right this morning?"

Mr. Rawson reached to stroke Faron's nose. "In body, yes. I'm not so sure about his spirit. He hates this loathsome stall."

The horse crowded closer to Diego and nickered box.

Mr. Rawson chuckled. "Faithless animal. For all my devotion to him, he loves you more."

Smiling, Diego scratched between the horse's ears. "It's not me he loves, sir. Rather the carrots I keep in my pocket." He patted the velvety nose. "You're out of luck today, amigo. We're fresh out."

Mr. Rawson appeared thoughtful. "Faron. That means pharaoh in Spanish?"

Diego nodded.

"Suits him, doesn't it?" He released a heavy sigh. "You suppose I'll ever be able to ride him?"

Diego gave a confident nod. "I'm sure of it, sir. He just needs a little more time learning to trust you." He attempted to swallow, but his throat was too dry. "Sir, Pete said you wanted to speak to me."

"I do." Usually by now, Mr. Rawson would be facing Diego, searching for the bottom of his pupils while he said what was on his mind. Instead, he seemed to avoid meeting Diego's eyes.

"He told me not to show up for work today. Said the order came from you."

"That's right."

Why wouldn't the man turn around? Why wouldn't he say the words and get it over with?

You're fired, Diego.

Turn in your lariat.

Pack your things.

Take your mother from the little house she loves and hit the trail.

What could be so hard about it? He should open his mouth and have it done.

"Cuddy will be taking your place today."

"Sir?"

"Cuddy." A hard edge crept into Mr. Rawson's voice. "I plan to work his tail off. Give him a taste of what your workday feels like. Let him see how a real man runs his business, with sweat and grit. Then maybe he'll lose his taste for booze." He frowned a warning. "Don't let him talk you into lifting a finger to help. I want that boy to learn something today."

Weight shifted off Diego's shoulders. "And tomorrow?"

"Humph." Mr. Rawson finally turned. "You don't get off that easy. It's back to business as usual tomorrow. Any longer at the helm of the Twisted-R and Cuddy would run it asunder." His gaze flitted past Diego's face while he worried his bottom lip with his teeth. "I want to thank you for last night."

Guilt stung Diego's insides. "Thank me?"

"For getting that dunderhead out of sight before more people noticed the state of him."

Diego lifted his brows. "I don't deserve your gratitude, sir. I have to confess that wasn't my motive."

Mr. Rawson waved him off. "Oh shoot, I know. You did it for Cuddy, though I fear he doesn't merit such loyalty. Still"—his eyes met Diego's at last—"like always, you wound up helping me in the bargain." Resting his hand on Diego's arm, he smiled. "I want to express my appreciation for your faithfulness. After God and your mother, you've always put the ranch and me first. You're a tireless, selfless boy, Diego, one I'd be honored to call my own. I'm proud of you, son."

Diego wrestled with his emotions so he could speak. Dropping his gaze, he rustled a mound of straw with the toe of his boot. "Thank you, sir. I'm not certain I'm worthy, but thank you."

They stood in silence, communicating their feelings with smiling eyes until Diego broke the stillness. "If you'll pardon my boldness, sir, Cuddy longs to hear such words from you."

Mr. Rawson stared. "Cuddy? Nonsense. He couldn't care less what I think."

Desperation shot boldness through Diego's veins. "That's where you're wrong. I've watched him try to please you. I've watched him fail and seen what it does to him. If you would just try to see—"

Mr. Rawson's hand shot up. "Hold on there. Don't you lecture me." His face blotched like the skin of a cactus pear, and he shook his finger in Diego's face. "Don't mistake my fondness for you as a license to butt into my business."

Though his eyes still bored into Diego's, something snuffed the furious fire. He sighed and relaxed his shoulders, and the purple hue faded from his cheeks. "You may have watched some things all right. I just don't think you've seen."

Diego longed to ask what he meant but didn't dare risk angering him further.

Mr. Rawson returned his attention to the horse. "Don't you think I want to be proud of my only son? I tried for years to turn Cuddy into the man he should be, longed to teach him everything I knew, but he wanted no part of my lessons. . .or me. His interests lie elsewhere, namely at the bottom of a bottle when he's not perfecting the art of chasing skirts."

"Forgive me, sir, but Cuddy has many other interests. He's always talking about politics and travel, and he studies a lot on what's going on in the world."

Mr. Rawson snorted. "What does any of that have to do with raising cattle?" He fiddled with Faron's mane, smoothing and combing it with his fingers. Faron edged closer, grunting his approval.

Diego joined them by the gate, lifting Faron's brush from its hook on the wall. They ministered together in silence, both men tending the horse they loved.

Mr. Rawson glanced over. "Want to know something funny?"

Diego smiled. "What's that?"

"The truth is you have Cuddy's stubbornness to thank for the turn your life has taken."

Diego's brows met in the middle. "How so?"

"When you showed up at the ranch, fresh and green as a spring shoot, I saw great potential there. So I took you under my wing, groomed you into what I longed to see Cuddy become, partly because I wanted him to see how his life could turn out if he'd let me help him, what great things we could accomplish together."

Diego scowled. "You used me?"

Mr. Rawson looked startled. "Used you? Yes, I suppose I did in a way." He latched onto Diego's forearm. "But along the way I grew to love you, came to respect the kind of man you are. I caught myself wishing we were blood relations. Then I noticed the way Greta looks at you, and I thought my wish might be fulfilled through my grandchildren."

He raised one busy brow. "There's a spark of expectation in my old heart yet." He nudged Diego with his shoulder. "Well, come on. . .do I still have reason to hope?"

Diego's smile wilted. He lowered his gaze and said nothing.

When he raised tortured eyes, Mr. Rawson nodded. "I feared as much. It's Emily Dane, isn't it? That girl could turn any man's head."

"Sir, I–"

The man took a ragged breath. "Don't say a word. It's not your fault, son." The chewing on his cheek intensified, and he blinked away sudden brightness from his eyes. "I guess that's it, then. I had hoped to die with some assurance the Twisted-R was in capable hands. Instead, I'll die disappointed." He turned on his heel and left the barn with sagging shoulders.

Diego followed and stood watching his back. He opened his mouth to call out, prepared to assure Mr. Rawson he'd marry Greta, give him grandchildren, tend the ranch the rest of his days. He longed to tell the man whatever it took to remove the hopelessness from his eyes, but the words wouldn't crowd past the lump in Diego's throat.

Feeling eyes on the back of his head, he spun.

Emmy stared at him in shocked silence.

Cuddy's vacant eyes were fixed on the ground. He seemed smaller, as if the pain etched on his face had caused him to shrivel. His trembling hand groped for a fistful of hair and gripped until the knuckles turned white.

Diego took a step toward him. "Cuddy?"

Cuddy whirled away from them and disappeared behind the barn.

Tears sprang to Emmy's eyes. Without a word, she tore out after him.

CHAPTER 16

Head drooping, Cuddy sat on the sun-dried bank of the Nueces with his arms resting on his knees, his hands dangling from his wrists like dead fish.

Emmy had found him in the same posture outside his room, only this time the pain shining from his eyes wasn't self-inflicted. She eased onto the ground beside him.

A ragged release of air was the only acknowledgment he gave that he noticed her there.

Miserable for him, she reached for his hand, but he shrugged her away. She decided not to push, but not to leave either.

They sat together, Emmy watching the wind rippling across the water, Cuddy staring at the ground between his knees.

She jumped when he snatched something from his shirt pocket and sailed it across the river. It hit the far bank then tumbled down the slope and into the water with a splash. Emmy caught the glint of sunlight on metal just before the flask settled to the murky depths.

She touched his arm. "Bravo, Cuddy. Now you're thinking, and that was the smartest decision yet. You don't need that foul stuff, and you know it. You're much better off without it."

His head still sagged, but the corners of his mouth tipped slightly. "It was empty."

She withdrew her hand. "Oh."

Glancing at her at last, the hint of a smile bloomed to an outright grin. "You're something else, you know that?"

She squeezed his fingers. "You are, too, Cuddy. I just hope you know it."

He sneered. "You and I know exactly what I am, honey. A fatal disappointment. You heard it straight from the one who decides such things, the great John Rawson."

Emmy leaned against his shoulder. Her next words spilled unplanned from her mouth. "It's not your father's right to decide such things, Cuddy. We're judged by God and no other." Shocked by her own words, she sat quietly, waiting for him to respond.

He didn't tense beside her, or laugh with scorn, or seem offended in any way. Instead he continued pulling up bright green blades of grass and tossing them into the water. "If that's the case, my goose is cooked." He sighed. "I'm told God knows more about me than my father does."

Emmy sat up and looked him over. Cuddy appeared to feel as worthless as she had felt before God showed up and changed everything in her life. Since the day she blundered into the sheltering arms of grace, she hadn't feared Papa's opinion so much. The only thing left was living with the pain of his rejection.

She tried to picture hearing Papa use the term "disappointment" to describe her. He could rant and rave, shake his head, glare at her with scorn, but until he actually said the word aloud, she could pretend he didn't consider her a failure.

Cuddy twisted his head to peer at her. "Why so quiet? Have I depressed you?"

"No. Just trying to imagine how you feel."

"I could describe it to you, but you'd be shocked at the language."

She laughed. "Oh, Cuddy! What am I to do with you?"

Mischief danced in his eyes. "You could kiss me."

She swatted his arm. "I believe praying for you would serve you best."

He seemed surprised. "You really believe all that God stuff, don't you?"

Scooting around to face him, she pinned him with her eyes. "I didn't used to. I found the whole thing a frightful bother. I watched people herd through the door of the church like sheep because it was expected of them, not because they found anything valuable on the other side. Most of them came out the same way they went in, miserable through and through. The man singing "Amazing Grace" the loudest kept a girl named Grace on the side. It left a bitter taste in my mouth, and the things of God seemed hardly worth my time."

Cuddy slapped his leg. "I never figured you for a cynic! So what changed?"

She bit her bottom lip. "Me."

He tucked his cheek between his teeth and seemed to ponder her answer, until finally, as though he found it too simple, he shook his head. "No, I mean what changed *you*."

"God changed me, but not until I let Him. Once I allowed Him close to me, I saw the truth of who He is." She grasped Cuddy's hands. "You see, the same things bother God about the church. He wants my devotion, not merely my attendance. Does that make sense?"

Cuddy gazed at her, unflinching. "Well, I'll be. Forgive me for saying this, but you're not the sort of girl I expected to be saying such things."

She laughed. "I wasn't for many years. Now, knowing Him is the dearest thing in my life."

His eyes widened in amazement. "Girl, you're lit up like a candle. You're pretty serious about this God of yours."

She cocked her head. "Why does that surprise you? Papa said your parents are Christians. And your best friend—"

He yanked a weed and snapped it in half. "No, sweetie. Diego's not a Christian. He's more like a saint."

Diego bit back a curse, shocked it had entered his mind. He'd left everything—work that Cuddy had been ordered to do—and searched the whole ranch, exhausting the last ounce of his energy praying for Cuddy's safekeeping and Emmy's comfort. Only to find them whispering together, their heads close and bobbing like a pair of silly lovebirds.

He had feared finding Cuddy wearing a noose, poised to kick the chair from under his legs. To find him cooing with Emmy instead was an insult. To hear their laughter stretched the boundaries of Diego's understanding. Madder than he'd been in his life, he gritted his teeth and rode toward them.

Watching Emmy snuggle with Cuddy, a sweet smile on her face, went a long way toward helping Diego understand the man's rapid recovery. Having a woman like her so near would comfort a dying man.

For her his anger blazed. She had deliberately strung him along with her dimples and sultry voice, her teasing laughter and meaningful glances, until he came to believe there was something between them. The glow of adoration on her face as she leaned close to Cuddy told Diego just what he needed to know. She'd have no more trouble from Diego Marcelo.

Engrossed in each other's company, they didn't notice Diego until he was practically on top of them. Emmy saw him first and nudged Cuddy. Something flashed across her face when she saw him riding toward her, a tenderness that started in the softness of her mouth then spread and settled in her eyes, somehow different from her earlier expression.

He jerked his gaze from hers and pronounced himself a desperate fool. He had read too much into something that was obviously his imagination.

Cuddy stood and helped Emmy to her feet. With his hand at her back, they walked to meet him. Cuddy's jaw hardened. "If he sent you after me, I won't go."

Diego dismounted. "Your father doesn't know you overheard."

Cuddy angled his face from sight, but not before Diego glimpsed the raw pain that twisted his features. A vein bulged in his neck, and a scarlet flush crept up from his collar. The man was fighting tears.

Diego's affection for Cuddy rose to the surface, displacing his ire. "I'm glad to see you're all right."

Cuddy leaned against the horse, fiddling with the saddle. "Oh, you know me. . .indestructible."

Still watching Diego's face, Emmy patted Cuddy on the shoulder. "I'll leave you to talk."

Cuddy latched onto her arm. "Remember to be careful."

Emmy nodded. "Snakes. And scorpions." She smiled. "How could I forget?"

She strolled to the water's edge, just out of earshot.

Diego placed a hand on Cuddy's arm. "It wasn't as bad as it sounded. Your father spoke out of pain."

Cuddy lifted flashing eyes. "Pain?" He spat on the ground. "You must be joking."

"He feels rejected by you. If you'd listened to his reason, you'd understand."

Visibly trembling, Cuddy gripped the saddle horn. "I listened plenty good. He said I'm the biggest disappointment in his life and he'll take that to the grave. What's there to understand about that? John Rawson doesn't feel rejection. He gives it. Defend him all you like, I'll never see things any other way."

Diego ran his fingers through his hair. "I'm telling you, Cuddy, you'd feel differently if you'd listened to everything he said."

"I wasn't invited to hear all he said, brother, but I noticed you were." He lifted his chin. "Come to think of it, I did hear something I won't soon forget."

Diego ducked his head and asked what he already knew. "What was that?"

"You're prepared to toss my little sister aside because you've set your sights on Emmy."

"I didn't–"

Cuddy held up his hand. "You didn't have to say it aloud. The old man's disappointment said it for you."

"So Emmy. . .did she. . .?"

"You already have my father, Diego. Now you want my girl?" He swelled his chest and took a step closer. "I love you like a brother, amigo, but you stay away from Emily or you'll answer to me. Understood?"

Diego swallowed against his suddenly tight collar. "You're my best friend, Cuddy, but threatening me is uncalled for." He brushed the blustering burro aside and swung into the saddle. "And dangerous." He laid his spurs to the horse's flank, needing to get as far from them as possible. Away from Cuddy before he had to hurt him. Away from Emmy before she caused him more pain.

She called out to him as he rode over the rise.

He didn't look back.

CHAPTER 17

Magda eyed the mountain of supplies Bertha had piled on the counter of McCaleb's Mercantile Store. Since John Rawson had decided they would travel to Catarina by wagon after all, they had room to carry more supplies. He never should've said such a thing to Bertha. After twiddling and touching every item for sale, she bought three times the amount John suggested they needed for the trip.

Once her business was settled, Bertha was ready to leave, so the wait made her fidgety. John finished his conversation with the clerk of the impressively large store then led the way outside. After enduring a half hour of Bertha twitching and sighing, Magda was relieved to step onto the sun-drenched porch.

John had mentioned at breakfast that they'd been his guests for a full week but hadn't yet been to town. As soon as they laid aside their forks, he loaded Magda, Willem, Bertha, and Kate into his wagon and proceeded to usher them through Carrizo Springs, giving the grand tour.

Holding the door of the mercantile, John smiled at each of them as they filed out. "Have I mentioned the name of our newspaper? It's called *The Javelin*. After the animal."

He pointed inside the store. "Got its start right in there, owned and edited by J. L. McCaleb. That little paper saved our town during the drought of '86 and '87. A gentleman sent McCaleb an ad stating he'd pay good money for javelina hides." He chuckled. "Well, there was no shortage of javelinas around these parts. McCaleb made a deal with a fellow in San Antonio who traded cash and groceries for hides. It's the only way these people survived."

"That's quite a story, John," Willem said.

John gazed across a nearby field, his mind clearly in the past. "The drought lasted so long that the cattle overgrazed the natural grassland. It never returned to what it was before. Thousands of cattle died of starvation. It almost meant the end of ranching in these parts. Ranchers took to burning the stickers from prickly pear to feed their stock." He shook his head. "A hard time indeed for Dimmit County."

In a brighter mood, John gripped his chin. "Now then, I've shown you the churches and the school." He turned to help Kate onto the wagon then offered his hand to Bertha. "Next we'll see the courthouse, an imposing structure built in '85. The new bank sits across from it, established just last year."

Bertha groaned. "If it's all the same to you, John, I'm up for missing some of that."

Magda gasped. "Bertha Maye Bloom! The very idea. . ."

She scowled right back. "My feet hurt. I told you I didn't want to wear these shoes."

Kate Rawson covered her mouth with her gloved hands and had herself a good laugh. When she recovered, she twisted on the seat to smile at them. "That's all right, dears. I'm a little tired myself." She patted her husband's shoulder. "This man is as proud of Carrizo Springs as he is our children. If I don't stop him occasionally, he talks my ear off."

John glanced back, looking sheepish. "Sorry, folks. I get carried away sometimes."

Furious, Magda buried her elbow in Bertha's side.

Pouting, Bertha scooted as far as her little body could fit into the corner of the seat.

Beaming at Bertha, John cleared his throat. "I see you're a woman of action. How about we dispense with all this nonsense and start making plans for our cattle drive? I say we leave first thing in the morning."

Bertha shot forward and pounded him on the back. "Now you're talking straight, John. Put the whip to that horse's behind and let's see how fast we can get to the house. We've got some packing to do."

With a creature as proud as Faron, Diego had to let the horse think breaking him was his idea. Every small accomplishment, each tiny step forward had gained Diego progress.

First, the reins of braided horsehair draped gently on Faron's neck. Then the snaffle bit, which he took to surprisingly well, considering it took a week for him to accept a blanket resting on his back. When he tolerated the saddle, tears stung Diego's eyes. That fateful day Faron allowed him to mount, Diego had cried unashamedly.

He thought he'd burst waiting for the right moment to show John Rawson, and now the wait was over. Today marked the fifth ride. Usually skittish when Diego entered the barn, Faron's head had bobbed over the front of the stall, nickering his impatience. He stood trembling with anticipation while Diego hitched up his saddle, and Diego's boot hardly touched the stirrups before Faron trotted from the barn. The time had come to reveal his big surprise.

"Well, well."

Diego pulled on the reins and shifted his weight to look behind him.

Cuddy lounged next to the barn door with crossed arms. Not a word had passed between them for the last four days, not since Cuddy's threat beside the Nueces.

It didn't surprise Diego how simple it was to avoid him. Seeking out the hardest work on the ranch made it easy to bypass Cuddy Rawson.

He'd avoided Emmy, too. Much harder to do since she appeared at every turn. At first, she responded to his aloofness with flashing, angry eyes. The expression in their shaded blue depths soon changed to sadness and confusion.

"You have something to say, Rawson?"

One eyebrow raised, Cuddy's gaze wandered over Faron from hoof to mane and finally settled on Diego. "I didn't think anyone could tame that devil."

"It wasn't easy."

Cuddy laughed bitterly. "What won't you do to garner that old man's favor?"

Diego closed his eyes to steady his temper. "What won't you do to hurt him?" he asked without a backward glance. Taking up the slack in the reins, he steeled himself and tapped Faron's sides with his heels.

Blood surged through Diego's veins as the horse leaped into a run. The wind whistled in his ears as they flew down the long drive in front of the house. Faron jumped the gate, hardly breaking his stride, and hit the road with lightning flashing from his hooves.

No wonder no fence could hold him. Faron needed to run, lived to stretch his body to its limits with the earth flying past beneath him. For weeks, no matter how tired, no matter how hungry, Diego had spent his free time working with Faron. The thrill of this ride proved to be worth every second.

He spotted a cloud of dust ahead and followed it with his eyes. Faron cut the distance between them so fast, Diego hardly blinked before he recognized it to be the Rawsons' rig. A thrill shot through him. He wished somehow to be in the saddle surprising Mr. Rawson, yet at the same time be in the wagon watching his face light up when he figured it out.

Diego decided to breeze right by him then circle back to get his reaction. As Faron passed in a blur, John Rawson let out a howl. Diego's grin was so wide he collected sand on his teeth. He slowed and turned the horse.

Mr. Rawson stood in the two-seater watching, though dancing in the two-seater seemed closer to the facts. As Diego approached, he shouted again, so loudly the horse jumped.

Diego steadied Faron and reined him in beside the cluster of astonished faces.

"Whooeeee! Son, my old eyes must be deceiving me. What's that thing you're riding?"

Diego's cheeks had found their limits. "Only the fastest beast in South Texas, sir."

Mr. Rawson clambered to the ground, his eyes aglow with excitement. "Can I ride him?"

Diego swung down. "There's only one way to find out."

Wringing her hands, Mrs. Rawson scooted to the driver's seat. "Oh, John, no."

He raised one beefy hand. "Now, Kate. . ." Running his fingers along Faron's glistening neck, he crooned to him. "Easy boy. That's it, now."

She stood up. "John Rawson, you promised you wouldn't let that animal hurt anyone."

"And I aim to keep my promise."

Mr. Dane leaned out of the rig. "Maybe she's right, John."

With eyes only for the horse now, John didn't seem to hear his friend's suggestion. He put his boot in the stirrup, and Mrs. Rawson squealed and stamped her foot. "I won't see you do this."

He swung into the saddle. "Then close your eyes."

She had time to gasp and he was gone, barreling down the road toward the house as if borne on angels' wings. As horse and rider dashed around a curve and disappeared, one more gleeful shout rang out.

Mrs. Rawson sat heavily on the seat. "Oh, Diego. What have you done?"

Wincing, he came alongside her and peered into her dismal face. "It was bound to happen, ma'am. Your husband was determined to ride that horse. Wouldn't you rather it be after I calmed him down some?"

She reached to pat his hand. "I know you're right, but I've dreaded this day."

Diego chuckled. "He'll be fine. He's an expert horseman."

She squeezed his fingers. "I know that, too. They're likely in the barn by now, Faron getting a rubdown while John congratulates himself on your accomplishment." She smiled and squirmed into her place. "The least you can do is drive me home."

Diego climbed aboard and untied the reins. "It won't be possible to get you there quite as fast as Mr. Rawson, but I'll get you there in one piece."

She gave him a look from under her lashes. "Very good, assuming John made it home in one piece."

Mrs. Bloom leaned in between them. "He's in one piece or hundreds. As fast as that horse was moving, there wouldn't be nothing left to sweep into a dustpan."

"Bertha!" Mrs. Dane bawled at her.

"Well. . ."

Emmy slammed down her hairbrush and slumped on the bed. "It's not right. Why can't I go with you?"

Mama shot her a warning look. "Keep your voice down. I've told you why." She took Emmy's wrist and pulled her up. "I've also told you not to loll about on this bed, haven't I?"

Emmy had to admit the Redwork quilt was lovely. Blocks of embroidered flowers, animals, and children were set against a white background, each square outlined in red and white sashing. The quilter, evidently a young Katherine Colbeck, had stitched the initials K. C. and the year 1878 inside a wreath in the last square a few years before she became Kate Rawson.

Mama smoothed the rumpled spread and shook her head. "I don't know why Kate has all the beds spruced up like this. I'm not sure I'd want such lovely bedcovers for everyday. Makes you scared to move in here."

Emmy groaned. "Stick to the point, please. You know Papa's notion is ridiculous. I have to stay behind because of bandits that may never appear? Mama, listen to me. I will not stay without one of you here with me. I hardly know these people."

Mama shot her a dubious glance. "Don't twist the facts to suit you. You seem to know Cuddy well enough to add a few gray strands to your papa's head." She stood up from straightening the spread and frowned. "Don't think he hasn't mentioned his concerns about you two to Kate Rawson. If not for her offer to stay behind and chaperone, you'd have your papa in your lap until I got back."

Emmy bristled. "He spoke to her?" Burning with shame, she spun away from her mama and gripped the edge of the dresser. "How humiliating! What did he say?"

"I wasn't privy to the conversation." She held up her finger. "But I know this. . .you have Cuddy to blame. He shouldn't have opposed your papa like he did. So if you're entertaining thoughts about Cuddy, forget them. Papa would never give his blessing."

Emmy pushed off the dresser. "For pity's sake, Mama. Cuddy's just a friend."

Mama looked doubtful. "Friend or suitor, Willem will never accept Cuddy now."

Squealing her frustration, Emmy swept from the room. She'd done nothing all day but listen to plans she wouldn't be part of and helped everyone pack to leave her behind. She had to get out of the house or bust.

EMMY'S EQUAL

Mama jerked open the door and stuck her head out. "Where are you going?"

"No farther than the veranda, so don't call out the dogs."

"Emily!"

Emmy flounced down the stairs and out the back door, feeling like a spoiled child but too angry to care. She stared at the cloudless blue sky butting into the distant line of trees along the banks of the river, her thoughts as murky as the muddy bottom.

Mama and Papa didn't want her spending time with Cuddy. The others, including Cuddy, seemed to like it just fine. Emmy felt a bond of kinship with the troubled young man, even held affection for the tenderhearted, quick-to-smile rascal. But no matter how charming Cuddy Rawson might be, in matters of the heart, Emmy's interests lay elsewhere.

The heat of the midday sun on her bare head reminded her of two things. One, she'd left her hair unpinned, and two, it was August in what had to be the hottest place in the world.

Ducking into the shade of the covered patio, she perched on the wall of her haven to pout. Self-conscious, she gathered her thick mane over one shoulder and began to wind it into a braid.

"Leave it loose, Emmy."

She spun. "Diego! I didn't see you there."

He closed the distance between them and reached for her hair, wonder in his voice. "These curls are like twisted bands of sunshine."

Trembling inside, she let him twirl a blond ringlet around his finger. "Where have you been?"

He sobered and released her hair.

Horrified at her boldness, she tried to fix her blunder. Brightening her mood, she smiled. "It's been days since we've had a chance to talk. I guess you've been busy with the ranch." She ducked her head. "Unless. . ."

Diego touched her shoulder. "Unless?"

She lifted her eyes to his. "Have I offended you in some way?"

He turned aside and buried his fingers in his hair. "Emmy. . ." His jaw muscles worked and his gaze lost focus. "I owe you an apology. I've been blaming you for something that's not your fault. You can't help how you feel."

Jumping to her feet, she grasped his hands. "Exactly! I'm so glad you said that. I was just thinking the same–"

He withdrew from her touch. "Then you'll forgive me if I continue to keep my distance. It will make things easier."

She flashed him a startled look. "Pardon?"

Cuddy breezed around the corner of the house whistling a tune Emmy didn't recognize. Strolling lazily toward his father's rig with a packed crate in his hands, his head came up as if he'd sensed their presence. He paused and stared. The sight of him irked Emmy. His deliberate gaze bore the arrogance of a man who felt entitled to look.

Diego took a step away from her and bowed. "I'll be going. I've caused you enough trouble."

Cuddy lifted the crate over the tailgate then turned with his hands on his hips. "Thought the old man sent you to Carrizo for supplies."

Ignoring him, Diego strolled off the brick patio and crossed the yard.

Their confusing conversation concerned Emmy more than the fact that he'd left. Well, almost. She watched Diego's broad shoulders until he disappeared inside the barn.

"Afternoon, sweetheart."

The sultry voice in her ear lifted Emmy from the ground. She clutched her heart. "You shouldn't sneak up on folks like that."

Laughter rumbled in Cuddy's chest. "I didn't exactly sneak, now did I?" His attention shifted. "Well now, look at this. I sure like these pretty ringlets falling around your face." He reached to touch her hair, but she slapped his hand. He chuckled and rubbed the red spot. "Feisty today, are we?"

She nodded at the crate. "I see you're loading the wagon. Does that mean you're riding along to Catarina?"

"On a trip with my father?" He snorted. "No thank you. He roped me into helping them pack, that's all." A hopeful glint flickered in his eyes. "And you?"

Sorry she'd brought it up, Emmy frowned and shook her head.

Cozying up three steps too close, he leaned to whisper. "No one around to meddle in our business? Such an obliging arrangement. I'll have to remember to thank your father."

"Don't make me slap you again, Cuddy Rawson." She pushed

him away. "And wipe that silly leer off your face. It doesn't become you. Besides, are you so foolish to believe Papa would leave me alone in this house with you?"

He cringed. "He's staying behind?"

"No, not him."

"Your mother?"

She arched one brow. "No."

Cuddy scratched his head. "There's no one left but Rosita, and she goes home nights."

"You forgot your own mother."

He lifted a disbelieving eyebrow. "You're mistaken. Mother told me herself she was going."

"That was before Papa decided the trip might be too dangerous. Your mother offered to stay in his place."

Cuddy let his head fall back. "That's bad news. Mother considers chaperoning young ladies an art form." He touched her chin. "So that's what has you wrapped tighter than a cinch strap."

She pressed her lips together and let him assume what he wished.

He dashed his hat against his legs. "The whole thing is absurd. Children need a wet nurse. When will they consider us grown?"

Emmy leaned against a post with a sigh of resignation. "When we're married, I suppose."

Cuddy tucked his hat on his head and bent so close the brim touched her face. "Was that a proposal, Miss Dane?"

"Oh, stop!"

"It's very forward, considering we just met, but I promise to think about it."

She laughed. "Yes, for all of ten seconds. Somehow you don't seem the marrying kind."

Edging closer, he nudged the hat brim out of his way. "I think you may have misjudged me, Emily Dane." His worldly blue eyes closed in.

Emmy turned her face aside so abruptly he narrowly missed kissing the post. "I don't think so. Somehow I'm certain I called it right."

With a grunt from Cuddy and the hollow sound of a fist in his back, someone too short for Emmy to see over his shoulder latched onto him from behind and pulled him off her. Panting from the effort it took to toss Cuddy aside, Aunt Bertha glared.

Emmy gasped and held up one hand. "Aunt Bert, please don't look at me that way. This is not what you think."

"It never is, darlin'." She tipped her head at Cuddy. "I ain't too sure what I'm interrupting here, but this scalawag's mama is calling for him. I reckon she has more hauling she needs him to do." She wagged her finger in Cuddy's face. "You'd best get to it, before I call Willem and let him sort this out."

Cuddy tipped his hat. "There's no call for that, ma'am. I'm going." He winked at Emmy and hustled toward the house.

As he trotted past, Emmy caught sight of Diego's mama standing just outside the veranda, a pan of dried corn on her hip. She watched Emmy with ancient, knowing eyes–eyes that judged her and found her guilty. The little woman had seen everything and understood nothing.

Emmy's heart sank.

Melatha averted her gaze, hitched up the pan of bright yellow grain, and went her way.

Emmy longed to call out, to deny and explain, but what could she say that made a lick of sense? Besides, she still had to deal with Aunt Bertha.

"What am I supposed to do now, little girl? You've landed me in a right sore spot. If I tell your papa what I just saw, he won't go with me on this trip. Worse, he's liable to make your mama stay behind." She peered up at Emmy. "I'm just selfish enough to want to avoid such a thing because I don't know enough about what I'm doing. I need the both of them with me when I buy my cattle." She curled her first finger under her chin. "On the other hand, if I don't tell them and something happens to you while we're gone, I'll never forgive myself." She widened her eyes. "And neither would they."

Emmy gripped her shoulder. "There's no need to tell them, Aunt Bert."

The wise green eyes softened. "I expected that answer since it saves your hide. Now give me a good enough reason to believe you."

Emmy met her steady gaze. "I've done nothing wrong. I shouldn't be held responsible for Cuddy Rawson's actions."

One of Aunt Bertha's piercing eyes narrowed while she pondered

Emmy's words. Emmy held her ground without flinching until Aunt Bertha exhaled and nodded. "Child, you've been a handful all your life, except here lately. There've been considerable changes over the past year, and I want you to know that I've noticed."

Blushing at the praise, Emmy smiled. "Thank you, Aunt Bert."

"Thank yourself, because it's also the reason I'll be keeping what I saw to myself."

Emmy kissed her cheek. "In that case, God deserves the credit. Last year I would've been easy prey for the kind of attention Cuddy offers." She bent to wrap her arms around Aunt Bertha's narrow shoulders. "You won't be sorry you trusted me."

Aunt Bert thrust out her chin. "Make sure I'm not. I've never kept anything from your mama before. It ain't setting well with me."

Sliding one arm around her, Emmy walked her toward the back door. "In that case, why not tell her once you're on the road. She'll know you'd never leave me behind unless you had reason to believe in me."

Aunt Bertha squeezed Emmy's waist. "Sugar, I just might do that." She lowered her voice to a whisper. "If it's all the same to you, we might not mention anything to your papa for a while yet."

Emmy nudged her and grinned. "I have a better idea. How about never?"

Still laughing, they entered the house and parted company at the foot of the stairs.

Relieved to find she had her room to herself, Emmy glanced longingly at the comfortable quilt then perched obediently on the delicate stool in front of the dressing table. Her mind was a muddle of too strict parents, too forward friends, and too distant suitors.

Why did Cuddy seem so endearing one minute and so intolerable the next? And Diego? Seldom at a loss when it came to reading men, Emmy had yet to understand a single word he'd spoken to her in the shade of the covered porch. Part of the reason had to do with the dizzying effect of his finger twirling her hair, his hand so near her face she smelled his shaving cream.

"Blast it!" Bored silly with obedience to unreasonable requests, she flounced to the bed and fell backward, reaching her hands to her sides to gather the quilt about her. "After all," she demanded of the empty room, "what else are bedcovers for?" Wrapped in its comforting folds, she felt like a disgruntled enchilada, the savory dish Rosita had served the night before.

Rolling onto her side, she allowed anger like she'd not felt in months to churn inside. Who did Diego Marcelo imagine himself to be? How dare he announce his intention to keep his distance! He said it would make things easier. Easier for whom?

She tossed to the other side. "We'll just see about that, you arrogant, confusing man. I'll decide how much distance to put between us, thank you. When I'm done with you, you'll not want much, I assure you."

Emmy had tried to be good and found it a loathsome bother. Look where it had gotten her—one man who assumed her meekness made her easy, another who thought he could set her aside. Well, no more! Changing a man's mind came second nature to Emmy, and that was exactly what she intended to do.

Throwing the cover aside, she bolted upright on the side of the bed. Her image in the oval mirror across the room grinned at her like a long-lost friend. Her smile widened. One thing was certain, Katherine Rawson had best sharpen her chaperoning skills. If the twinkle in the eyes of the girl staring out from the mirror could be trusted, the old Emily Dane had returned.

CHAPTER 18

Melatha rolled off her cot onto her knees to thank God for another day. She praised Him for the cross of Christ. She blessed Him for blessing her with plenty, including the generous bounty of her garden, watered by the abundance of artesian wells that gave Carrizo the richest farmland in the South. She reminded Him to bless the Rawsons for providing her with a comfortable place to lay her head at night and a well-stocked kitchen to cook for her son. She'd hardly begun laying her petitions about Isi before the throne, requests concerning White Hair in particular, when the door creaked open behind her.

Melatha instinctively jerked her gaze to the crack at the side of the shade. Still pitch dark. Spinning to her feet, nearly tripping on her cotton nightdress, she crossed the room and hoisted the frying pan over her head before the intruder stepped over the threshold.

"You move with less stealth these days, Mother. I easily tracked you from the bed to the stove."

Weak in the knees, she lowered the heavy cast iron to the floor. "Isi! I nearly opened your skull with the skillet."

The scratch of a match preceded the glow of her lantern, lighting the room and chasing her fear to the shadows. Isi's familiar grin wavered above the flame, warped by the flickering light. "The skillet? Now that part I didn't track."

She lifted the pan to the stove and dusted her hands. "A mistake for which you almost paid dearly."

He laughed. "Do you always greet visitors with a crack on the head?"

Her brows crowded together. "No one enters my jacal so long before the sun does. Even you wait until the smell of bacon lures you. Why is this morning different?"

Head low, he shuffled to her and pulled her close. "I'm sorry I frightened you. Mr. Rawson and his guests are leaving soon for Catarina. He asked me to help see them off. I had hoped for an early breakfast this morning, that's all."

Pushing against him, Melatha gazed up. She'd already seen through his flimsy, bungled speech. "Breakfast? That's all?"

He nodded, but his eyes faltered.

She decided not to press. As sure as the sunrise, he'd open up before he left her table. She had only to wait for the chance to pull it out of him with the nimble, practiced fingers of a mother. Hopefully his present distress had nothing to do with the scheming Emily Dane.

"They're leaving Emmy behind. Did you know that?"

Her hope waned. She shrugged past him and bent to gather wood for the stove. "Do you mean Emily?"

He lifted her bag of coffee and spooned two large scoops into the pot. "Yes, Emily. She asked me to call her Emmy. It's the name her friends use."

I'm sure they do. "I would think she has many friends."

Isi paused. He stared at the side of her head while she mixed her corn cakes. Whatever words swirled in his mind, he bit them back and thankfully chose to tread the road to peace. She'd have to be more careful.

"As I was saying, they plan to leave her on the ranch until they return. Why do you suppose they'd do such a thing?"

It made little sense to Melatha. She'd never trust a daughter like Emily. "How do you know this?"

He twisted his mouth as if he tasted sour milk. "Cuddy boasted of it to Little Pete. I suppose he's led the men to believe he'll benefit from it somehow. Those animals jested and leered"—his lips tightened against his teeth—"until I shut them up."

Melatha pushed a dollop of churned butter off the edge of a spoon with her finger. It landed in the warming pan with a sizzle, so she gave the batter a final stir and ladled a generous spoonful on top of the foaming butter. Knowing she would cross a line with him, she spoke her heart. "At times fetid winds stir up truth."

He calmly finished filling the coffeepot with water, but his unruffled manner was deceptive. When he faced her, his eyes were flashing. "Why don't you like her?"

She tried to look innocent. "I never said I didn't. I only—"

He held up his hand. "Don't. You've made your feelings clear since the day she arrived. It's not like you, Mother. You taught me that it's God's business to judge. Yet, you've judged Emmy. What is it about this one girl that makes you lay aside your beliefs?"

Melatha wanted to shake him, to rail in his face until he opened his eyes. She bit her tongue instead. "I don't mean to judge, but I've already told you what I see in her."

He ran his fingers through his hair. "You said she has a restless spirit. For that you despise her? How many times have you said the same about me?"

Tendrils of desperation wound about her like the smoke rising off the corn cakes. Her temper as hot as the skillet, she shoved the pan to the back of the stove. The stench of burnt corn assailed her nostrils and stung her eyes, providing an excuse for her tears. "I'm trying to protect you, Isi."

He strode to the door and jerked it open.

She wondered if he believed it was to rid the room from smoke when she knew he intended to leave.

"Save your worries for something else. I don't need your protection from Emmy. I intend to stay far away from her."

The tears in his eyes wrenched her mother's heart because she couldn't tell if the smoke or something else had caused them. "What do you mean, son?"

"I mean I'd prance bare-bottomed through a field of cactus to steer clear of Emily Dane. The girl's eyes burn my flesh, Mother. I'm careful to avoid her touch for fear it will set me ablaze."

Melatha's heart dove. Things were worse than she imagined.

She started toward Isi, but he spun on his heel and bolted out the door.

Diego bounded off his mother's porch and trotted in the opposite direction he needed to go. Not ready to wrestle with what might be waiting for him up at the main house, he rounded the weathered bunkhouse instead.

Hidden from the prying eyes of the casa mayor and his mother's jacal, he sagged against the rough boards of the narrow wall that faced the river and slid to the ground with a ragged sigh. Massaging his throbbing temples with his fingertips, Diego tried to sort out his confusing thoughts.

He had wasted the last eight years of his life running from himself, and he was exhausted. Denying his Choctaw blood, he had traveled the country, seeking a different link to his past. He'd hoped to locate someone who knew his father and gain information that would connect him to his Spanish relations.

If he'd found them during those early troubled years, he'd be basking by the sea on the southern coast of Spain instead of toiling on the bank of the Nueces. He'd be cavorting among almond trees instead of dust and cactus, dancing the flamenco and eating the *paella* on which his father had cut his teeth.

Diego's desire to find his paternal roots had all but consumed him. He'd tried to follow God's will when he reunited with his mother and brought her south. Though his love for her had never waned, the fire within him to be someone besides Little Deer still blazed, despite how hard he prayed.

The last few days with Emmy had stoked a new flame within. She made him whole again, more complete than he'd felt since his father died. Yet his mother, whose instincts he'd always trusted, considered Emmy too spirited. Cuddy saw her as a prize to conquer, perhaps a way to gain revenge.

Whatever his reasons, Cuddy wanted her, and she preferred him. The finality and hopelessness of these undeniable facts weighed down Diego's shoulders.

"I thought I saw you duck back here."

Suppressing a moan at the latest evidence of the recent turn of his luck, Diego's head jerked up. "Greta."

Her expression bounced from confusion to pleasure then made the rounds again. "What are you doing sitting here all alone?" She tilted her head to the side. "Are you all right?"

He pushed to his feet, digging deep for a smile. "Of course."

He waved his hand distractedly. "I come here sometimes to–" He suddenly felt ridiculous.

She pressed her hand to her forehead. "Say no more. I've intruded on your privacy and interrupted your thoughts. Forgive me." She turned to go.

He should've let her. Instead, he put out his hand. "Greta, wait."

She looked over her shoulder. "Yes?"

"Stay a minute, please."

"Are you sure?"

Her hopeful smile shamed him. He hadn't treated her well lately. "I'm certain. Come here."

She cast a guilty look toward the house. "I suppose it'll be all right. For a minute or two." She surprised him by lowering herself to the dewy grass and spreading her skirt beneath her.

To keep from embarrassing her, he sat, too, as if he intended all along for her to sit on the damp ground.

Letting her gaze wander the expanse of the yard, Greta toyed with the cotton sash at her waist. He'd never seen her so ill at ease, so unsure of herself, and hoped he wasn't the cause. Her delicate white throat bobbed above her lace collar. He couldn't tell if she was about to speak or swallow.

She did both. Gulping hard, she smiled at him. "It's a nice spot. Do you come here often?"

Diego bit back a grin. The underside of the bunkhouse smelled of musty dirt; the sparse island of grass they'd settled on was the only solid groundcover in a sea of sand, pebbles, and stubble; and the wind lifted the sharp stench of manure from the southeast pasture, blowing it under their noses. Nice was hardly the word he'd use. "I slip back here occasionally. It's quiet at least. No one bothers me."

She ducked her head. "Most of the time, anyway?"

He gave a throaty laugh and nodded. "Yes, most of the time." He felt her watching him so he quirked one brow in her direction.

Her cheeks reddened and she covered her face, but her laughter pealed, sounding relaxed and unforced again. "I've missed spending time with you, Diego. You make me feel good inside."

A playful smirk on his face, he leaned closer. "I do?"

She tittered and shifted her body, not away from him as she'd always done before but so near he smelled rosewater in her hair.

He touched the tip of her nose. "Suppose I say you make me feel good inside, too?"

It was true. He felt alive, every cell of his body glowing. He didn't want to be alone today. If he wanted to be with Greta, who would it hurt? Cuddy obviously didn't mind. Mr. Rawson would be overjoyed. His mother had hinted her approval. And Emmy? He doubted she would notice.

Greta gazed at him with hazy eyes that went to slits, and then she let her head fall back, an open invitation to kiss her.

He pressed the side of his mouth against her face. "You're so lovely."

She turned and he felt the softness of her lips against his cheek. "Oh, Diego."

He moved his head in small deliberate circles, nuzzling to find her mouth. "And so sweet."

She drew in sharply when he kissed her.

"Lovely, sweet Emmy," he whispered.

He thought the strangled gasp came from Greta until Cuddy spoke. "I see you found him, little sister."

Emmy stood beside him, staring at Diego with wounded eyes. Whirling, she pushed past Cuddy and disappeared.

Greta buried her clenched fists in Diego's chest and shoved him away then stood to her feet. Tears flowing, she gathered her skirts and dashed around the opposite side of the bunkhouse.

Leering, Cuddy leaned against the corner and crossed his arms. "I believe I may have misjudged you, Diego. I see you've been sweet on Greta all along."

Understanding slowly settled. Cuddy hadn't heard him call his sister the wrong name, so maybe Emmy hadn't either.

Cuddy squatted to eye level, squinting at Diego. "Unless you're trying to string them both along at the same time?"

"No! I–"

Cuddy laughed and swatted the air. "Just joking, friend," he boomed, grinning wider. "I know Saint Diego could never do such a thing. That's more my style."

Awash with guilt, Diego lowered his head.

"Hey, it's all right, amigo. I don't mind you courting my sister. I always figured you might." Brandishing one finger, he scowled. "Not that I approve of any more slip-ups like what I just witnessed. If you want to kiss Greta like that, you need to put a ring on her finger first."

He stood and sauntered over to take his sister's place on the ground. "So all that nonsense with Emmy. . .the stuff you told the old man. . .you were just confused?"

Diego opened his mouth to deny it, but Cuddy's upraised hand didn't give him the chance. "I understand completely. Emily Dane would confuse a celibate monk." He grinned then sobered. "I wish you'd come and set me straight, that's all. I haven't liked being on the outs with you. It feels unnatural."

"Cuddy, listen–"

"I hate that we stumbled onto you and embarrassed the women. Emmy's face was brick red when she spun out of here." He sobered. "And poor Greta was in tears."

Curious, Diego frowned. "Why did you two come back here?"

"Looking for you. Melatha said you came this way."

"Why were you looking for me?"

Cuddy cursed and struggled to his feet. "For the old man! He's blasting smoke from his ears by now. He sent us to find Greta, who he sent to find you a half hour ago."

Bouncing his palm off his forehead, Diego leaped up, too. "I forgot. He asked me to be present to make sure their departure went smoothly."

Cuddy nodded. "Yep, he figured you forgot. He wasn't in the best of moods about it either. If he saw Greta come back crying. . ."

They shared a look.

Cuddy grimaced. "He'll be looking for someone to blame it on. We'd best hightail it to the house."

Heart pounding, Diego wheeled around the front of the bunkhouse on Cuddy's heels, running to face the latest mess he'd made.

Thankfully, the wagon still sat in front of the house, fully loaded and tied down. Willem Dane sat stiffly in the driver's seat with his wife perched beside a fidgety Mrs. Bloom in back. Staring toward the house, he shook his head. "Magda, where's Emily? You'd think she'd want to see us off."

"I told you she's not feeling well. A headache, I think. She's resting upstairs."

Diego winced.

"Besides," Mrs. Dane continued, "she bid her farewells this morning. I do believe she can't stand to watch us go."

He snorted and Mrs. Dane leaned to squeeze his shoulder. "Try to be more understanding, Willem. Your daughter's upset."

Mr. Rawson stood on the front porch talking to his wife, one hand patting the side of her face. He tenderly kissed her then strode down the steps to the rig. Spotting Cuddy and Diego, his face blanched. By the time they reached him, his cheeks had mottled to various shades of red.

"Where the devil have you been?" He directed the question at Diego.

"I'm sorry, sir. There's no excuse. I should've been here like you asked."

His boss glowered. "You got that right. I needed you."

Diego cringed. This was more than bad luck. His life was falling apart. "If it's not too late, sir, I'm at your disposal. What can I do to help?"

Something over Diego's shoulder caught Mr. Rawson's eye. "It was too late an hour ago. Little Pete tended your business for you." He tilted his chin. "And here they come now."

Unprepared for what he would see, Diego looked behind him. His heart surged and he spun around. "Faron, sir?"

Mr. Rawson pushed past him. "Yes, Faron."

His heartbeat racing now, Diego ran after him. "Why is he saddled?" He knew his tone was harsh, demanding, but he couldn't help himself.

"I'm going to ride him, that's why."

Faron stood proudly pawing the ground and snorting his displeasure with the delay. Ready to run, he strained at the reins.

Muscles rippled in Little Pete's arms and back as he tried to hold him, and relief flooded his face when Mr. Rawson took over. "He is one spirited animal, this horse," Pete said, laughing and shaking his head.

"That's how I like them, Pete," Mr. Rawson boomed.

Pete grinned. "Sí, señor." Looking guilty, he stepped aside when Diego approached. Aside from feeding and brushing, Diego had instructed the men never to handle Faron.

"Mr. Rawson, wait. I don't understand. You're not taking him to Catarina?"

"No, son." He swung into the saddle and tapped the horse with his heels. "Weren't you listening? I'm riding him to Catarina."

Speechless for the second time in one morning, Diego stared after them.

Mr. Rawson turned Faron a few yards out and impaled Diego with a glare. "See to it you take running this place a little more seriously while I'm gone. Understood?"

Diego found his voice. "Sir, Faron's not ready for what you're asking of him."

Mr. Rawson defiantly raised his chin. "Well, I believe he is. What say you leave my animal to me and just tend my ranch like I asked?"

Diego's shoulders slumped. "Yes, sir."

Before riding away, Mr. Rawson pinned him with one more scowl. "When I get back, I intend to find out who made my little girl cry. You'd best hope it wasn't you."

He nudged Faron and trotted over to the wagon. Bolting into the lead, he signaled over his head for Mr. Dane to follow. The wagon rolled away from the house and down the drive, creaking under the weight of the supplies. The way Faron cantered and hopped, desire blazed within him to cut loose and run.

Sighing, Diego wondered how long Mr. Rawson could hold back the horse's fire. The thought stirred a memory of something his mother had said to him. Was it only days ago?

"Your future will appear in a whirlwind of smoke and rise to meet you in flames. . . ."

A flash of movement above his head drew his attention to the upstairs windows. At the same time the drape fluttered shut in Greta's room, the shutter snapped closed in Emmy's. It seemed the future his mother predicted had arrived. A whirlwind of guilt for what he'd done to Greta swept through him, while searing flames of desire for Emmy drove him from the yard.

CHAPTER 19

A piercing wail split the air, jolting Emmy upright and raising the hair on her arms. She first thought she'd heard the bellow of a wounded animal—perhaps one of the coyotes that howled the first night on the ranch—until the cry came again, eerily human and unquestionably from the bedroom below. Greta's room.

Emmy knelt on all fours and pressed her ear to the floor. Just as she thought, Greta's mournful sobs rattled the floorboards, rocking Emmy back on her heels. She hugged herself, aching inside for Greta. Naturally, the girl would be upset. Diego had kissed her but whispered Emmy's name against her lips.

This fact hadn't penetrated Emmy's understanding until she'd run halfway back to the house. When awareness dawned, it stopped her cold. Ready to retrace her steps and demand an explanation of Diego, she'd made her way to her room instead, her head reeling. After pondering the enormity of the situation, she'd decided Diego calling her name was a good thing, but Greta's pain doused the torch of joy the realization had kindled.

Still crouched in front of the vanity, she lifted her eyes to the looking glass, her tears blurring the image. What had she been thinking to believe the old Emmy was back? That Emmy would be spinning about the room, defiantly wrapped in the Redwork quilt, dancing a victory waltz on Greta's head. She'd be plotting her next move, finagling the best angle to use to her advantage in order to drive a wedge between Diego and Greta. She certainly wouldn't be kneeling in front of a mirror watching her heart breaking for her rival. If she ever doubted the change God had wrought in her life, she didn't now. The old Emmy wasn't back.

She was dead.

"No more foolish women!" Diego shouted to the empty barn. His decision bounced among the overhead rafters, the echoing agreement a confirmation.

"Tend my ranch," Mr. Rawson had growled.

The order was exactly the medicine Diego needed in a double dose. Spine-busting labor was the only thing he'd ever known. He'd focus on hard work and horses now, the two things that had been his salvation.

The thought of horses reminded him of Faron, and his stomach pitched, though not with the queasy lurch that came after the word salvation reminded him of his neglect of the Savior.

"Foolish mothers, too?"

His back stiffened. "Foolish mothers top the list." Brushing past her, he hoisted the wide broom from the hook and went at Faron's stall as if he could sweep away his troubles along with the muck. Sulking, he pushed the debris from the rear of the enclosure toward the middle, intent on ignoring his mother until she left. He realized his plan was doomed when she latched onto the handle from behind.

"I won't leave your side until you hear me out."

Past experience had taught Diego she meant what she said. His mouth a thin line, he eased the handle from her hands and propped it against the wall. Crossing his arms, he leaned beside it. "Very well. I'm listening."

She peered up at him and shook her head. "No, son. You're not listening yet."

He frowned. "Yes, I am."

She cautiously touched his arm. "Not with your heart, Isi."

Shrugging away from her hand, Diego rolled his head against the rough adobe wall. "My patience is short just now, Mother. It's been a trying day."

She quirked her top lip. "A sad thing to hear, considering the early hour."

"Sad?" A harsh laugh rose inside his gut and blurted from his mouth. "You can't imagine how sad."

He didn't notice her move, yet suddenly she stood next to him. "What happened, Isi?"

Diego released a wavering breath. How could he tell her? *What happened, Mother? The son you're so proud of took advantage of a dear, trusting friend. He kissed her while pretending she was someone else.*

He opened his mouth two times before the words spilled out. "I shamed Greta Rawson, Mother. Shamed Greta, her family, and myself." He set his jaw in a grim line. "After you warned me not to."

Fear snuffed the compassion in her eyes. "What are you telling me, son?" She gripped his arms with her long fingers, surprising him with her strength. "How have you shamed her?"

"I hurt her." The pitch of his voice rose, sounding to his ears like the whine of a woman. "I made her cry." He ducked past his mother and out of the stall. Sitting down hard on a ragged bale of hay, he rested his forehead in his hand. "I may never forget the look in her eyes."

His mother scurried to him and knelt at his knees. "You're too harsh with yourself, son. Not preferring Greta, not choosing her, hasn't shamed her. It's kinder to tell her now so she won't harbor false hope."

He shuddered, shaking off her unmerited faith in his nobility. "I kissed her."

She picked up his hand. "It's natural you would want to kiss Greta. She's a very pretty girl." Was it hope he heard in her voice?

Lifting his eyes, he met hers head on. "I kissed her in a way I had no right to. . ." The weight of his shame dropped his head again. "And then called her by another woman's name."

Stewing in her silence, he waited. When nothing came, he looked to see why.

She had fallen on her behind in the dirt, lines of defeat etched on her face. She stared at the ground with hollow eyes, and the hopelessness in them added sorrow to his shame.

"I'm sorry, Mother."

She faced him. "John Rawson will hear of it."

"He already knows, at least in part."

She nodded thoughtfully. "What will happen now?" Her voice broke at the end, twisting flaming arrows in his heart.

"You won't be hurt by this, I promise. I'll plead on bended knee for Mr. Rawson to let you stay on in your jacal until I find you another home." He reached for her hands resting on her knees. "A real house this time, not a mud-brick hut."

Jerking her fingers free, she shot forward and grasped his chin. "For a mud hut you think I grieve?" She shook his face. "My son has scattered his principles to the wind, yet a one-room shack is my concern?"

Desperation crowded Diego's throat. He'd never seen her so angry. "Don't worry. I'll make it right."

"You foolish boy, don't you see it yet? There's no way to make this right. Mr. Rawson won't let you marry Greta after you disgraced her—"

"I don't want to marry Greta."

"And he will never allow you to bring a wife to this ranch to flaunt in his daughter's face." She pushed off the ground and paced in front of him, her doe-hide shoes soundless on the earthen floor. "If John Rawson doesn't fire you, though I suspect he will, you must leave the Twisted-R or face a lonely, childless life."

Diego stared dumbly.

She stopped so fast she kicked up dirt and spun to point her finger. "And for what? In case that girl has robbed you of the ability to think for yourself, let me explain what this means. You lose everything. Your job, your home, your reputation, the last four years of your life. . .White Hair took it all, just as I feared from the moment I first saw her."

She sank to her knees and covered her face with her hands. "Oh, Isi! Why didn't I see the truth? My vision was not a good omen as I thought." She raised her tear-streaked face. "Instead it foretold your doom."

CHAPTER 20

Magda relaxed once John Rawson got Faron settled into a lively walk and reined in beside the wagon. The big horse seemed eager to run clear to Catarina, so John had struggled for some time to calm him. Faron's high spirits didn't seem to faze John in the least, and in fact served to energize and cheer him considerably.

Bertha squirmed beside her on the seat. "Ain't we nearly there?"

John swiveled his head to look at Bertha. "Tired of traveling already?"

He shared a wink and a smile with Magda. She jabbed Bertha with her elbow. "This whole thing was your idea. Don't start in complaining."

Bertha rocked from side to side. "This seat is rough on a body, Magda. Something you'd understand if you weren't packing twin sofa cushions on your bottom."

Magda nudged her harder.

John chuckled merrily. "We've gone less than two miles, I'm afraid. That leaves about eighteen miles of bumpy road ahead."

Bertha groaned.

He pointed with his chin. "Dig up under the bench there and you'll find a folded blanket. Tuck it under you and it might help some."

Straddling her legs and bending between them until she nearly toppled, Bertha rummaged, surfacing with a horsehair blanket.

She held up her prize and grinned. "Why, thank you." Leaning forward, she poked and prodded the folded cloth beneath her in a most unladylike fashion until she'd rooted out a comfortable spot. Still beaming, Bertha looked overhead. "At least we don't have that unmerciful sun beating down. Sure was smart of you, John, to rig this special buggy."

She referred to the fringed surrey top John had fastened to a long-bedded farm wagon. In front of the large cargo area, he'd placed a buckboard seat. The sturdy, dependable vehicle provided extra room for passengers and shade with a clear, unobstructed view—important features in the rugged terrain of South Texas.

"Look here, John. A rider."

John jerked his head around to follow Willem's finger.

Magda's stomach tightened when he tensed and straightened in the saddle. She leaned to tug on Willem's sleeve. "Is he friendly?"

Willem snorted and raised his brows at John. "That's a woman for you. I'm supposed to know from a quarter mile away if that strange man is friendly." He twisted to look at her. "Even if he had the information penciled on his forehead, he's still too far out to read."

John joined in with the laughter, but not so merrily this time. "The rule of thumb in these parts is to assume they're unfriendly until they prove themselves otherwise." He motioned at the rifle propped against the rail. "I'd hold that ready if I were you."

Willem's frivolity dried as fast as the August dew. He hoisted the Marlin .44-40 and chambered a shell, resting it in plain sight on his knee. Just in time, since the rider had come within shouting distance.

"Mornin'," the stranger called as he approached. "No call for alarm, folks. I mean you no harm."

"Friendly," Bertha whispered.

"Not so fast," Magda whispered back. "Let's give him a minute more."

John nudged his hat up and studied him. "Where you headed, mister?"

"Out to the Twisted-R Ranch."

Magda opened her mouth to comment on the coincidence, but John motioned behind his back to be still. Relieved that John stopped her before she blurted what he didn't want known, she watched to see what he had up his sleeve.

John spit then wiped his mouth. "Is that so?"

"Yes, sir." The young man took off his hat and wiped his brow with his sleeve. "I think it's up this road a few miles."

John casually stroked Faron's neck. "What business do you have out at the Twisted-R, son?"

Magda watched the stranger's face. If he were the troublesome type, John's meddlesome question ought to rile him some.

"I aim to see a friend there. Ranch foreman by the name of Diego Marcelo."

John pushed back his hat. "Diego, eh?"

The boy grinned. "*El Toro*, we call him. Bullheaded at times, but a real nice fellow. He's been keen on showing me the ranch, so I thought I'd ride out and see the place. I hear it's an impressive spread."

"Is that a fact?" John said casually.

"Oh, yes, sir." More than happy to provide details, he leaned forward in the saddle. "I understand the owner's a prince of a man. To hear Diego tell it, John Rawson's been like a father to him."

A mischievous glint in his eye, John cocked his head. "Well, ain't that something? This Rawson sounds like a mighty fine man."

Magda struggled to keep a straight face.

Bertha ducked behind Willem with both hands over her mouth.

"Yes, sir. I hear the old man runs the tightest, cleanest ranch in Dimmit County."

John studied him for a few minutes before he spoke. "Where are you coming from?"

"We have a place out Catarina way. My father's a breeder. Maybe you've heard of him? Buck Campbell?"

No longer laughing, Bertha perked up, bobbing left and right, trying to see around the horse.

John asked the question Magda knew Bertha was busting to ask. "Hasn't your father been selling off some of his stock?"

The boy's grin stretched wider. "We sure have."

"Which Campbell are you, Les or Joe?"

He sat higher in the saddle. "I'm Joe. Les is my older brother." If he beamed any brighter, he'd outshine the sun. "Well I'll be hanged!

You folks heard about us way out here?"

"I've heard mention," John said. "As a matter of fact, we were just heading out to your place to take a look at what you have to offer."

Joe's smile died on his lips. He couldn't have looked more uncomfortable if his boots were on backward. "Well, shoot. I'm glad we bumped into each other, then. I can save you a wasted trip." He tucked his hat on his head, straightening it with both hands. "We ain't got no more animals for sale. Got carried away and about thinned ourselves out of business." He looked like it pained him to deliver the bad news.

John looked a mite pained himself. "That's too bad, Joe. I think we might've worked a deal."

The four of them slumped in defeat, as deflated as a flattened frog.

Bertha sighed from the depths of her belly. "I guess that's it, then."

Willem leaned to pat her hand. "I'm sorry, Bertha. But don't give up yet, we'll find you something."

Joe Campbell cleared his throat. "Sir?"

Willem glanced up. "Yes, son?"

"If you didn't specifically want to buy from us then maybe I can still help you out."

Hope flickered in Bertha's eyes. "You know where I can buy some cattle, boy?" Squinting, she pointed one finger. "Nothing ordinary, now. I'm looking for the best beef stock South Texas has to offer."

Joe tipped his hat. "Well, that'd be ours, ma'am. But if you want to settle for second best, I've heard there's a breeder down in Eagle Pass who's selling out."

Interest flickered on John's face. "Everything?"

"Down to the last horn and hoof. I suspect you could get a right fair price for an excellent herd."

His brows hovering in the vicinity of his hairline, John looked at each of them in turn. "What do you think, folks? Want to make a run for Eagle Pass?"

"Yes!" Bertha crowed.

Willem held up his hand. "Not so fast, Bertha. It's not a light decision. This is a dangerous region to travel, and unless I'm mistaken, it's much farther than we'd planned to go."

John nodded. "Willem's right. It's forty miles from Carrizo

Springs to Eagle Pass. Since we've come a couple of miles in the wrong direction that adds four more to the journey. I know of an old Indian trail a little west of here that will shave that off, but it might be rough going."

Bertha scooted to the edge of her seat. "I say we do it."

Magda drew back and stared. "What are you going on about? Weren't you the one complaining after only two miles on the road?"

She wiggled her behind. "This makeshift cushion took care of that. Come on, Magda. . .Willem. Let's go see Eagle Pass."

Willem sat quietly for a minute then peered at John. "How long do you think it would take?"

Rubbing his chin, John stared across the grassy plain that seemed to stretch on forever. "It won't always be like what you see here. Some parts of the ride will be harder than others and the heat won't help. The horses can make fifteen to twenty miles a day if we stop for rests and keep them well watered."

Alarmed, Magda sat forward. "That means we may be sleeping outside for two nights?"

John shook his head. "Not necessarily. I know a rancher who'll put us up tonight. He lives a little better than halfway, so if we push a bit, we can impose on his hospitality late tonight and make it to Eagle Pass by bedtime the next." His eyes grew intent. "That's if we leave now, so I'd suggest we make up our minds."

Bertha stood up in the wagon. "What are we waiting for? We got nothing but money and time."

John grimaced and glanced at Joe Campbell, who pretended not to notice. "I wouldn't make a habit of bragging on the money part," he whispered. "We'll be a target for every thief from here to the Rio Grande."

Straightening, he rode closer to Joe. "How do I find this man you speak of?"

"When you get into town, cross the bridge north of Fort Duncan. That's Van Buren Street. Go straight ahead to Main and take a left turn to Washington." Joe glanced at the women and a flush crept over his face. "You'll find the Piedra Parada Saloon on the corner. Go in and ask for Raul."

John balked. "The Piedra Parada? That's the rowdiest place in town."

"Yes, sir. I reckon I'd leave your womenfolk outside."

"You can count on that. You said to ask for Raul?"

"That's right. Look for a big man. He's a bouncer. Tell him Buck Campbell sent you." The blush deepened. "Buck's my pa. Raul wouldn't know my name. Tell him what you're looking for. He'll take it from there."

John stuck out his hand. "Much obliged, Joe."

The boy shook John's hand. "You're welcome, Mr.–" A curious look swept his face. "What'd you say your name was again?"

John picked up the reins. "I didn't."

"Sir?"

Twisting in the saddle, John jabbed behind them with his thumb. "You'll find the Twisted-R down this road a piece. You can't miss it." He smiled. "It's the tightest, cleanest ranch in Dimmit County."

Waving Willem on, John rode out ahead, leaving young Joe scratching his head.

Magda stared after him with a grin on her face. "After you knew you could trust him, why didn't you tell him who you were?"

John trotted Faron up beside her. "I figured once he'd said such nice things there was no reason he should learn the truth about me."

She laughed. "Imagine his surprise the next time he rides out to the ranch and Diego introduces him to John Rawson."

Willem interrupted their fun. "Where are we headed, John? I noticed we've taken a westerly turn. Why aren't we headed back the way we came?"

"Because of the shortcut I mentioned." He pointed. "The trailhead is right up this way."

Bertha gave Magda an impish glance. "You should be ashamed of yourself."

Magda touched her chest. "Me? What for?"

"For making fun of me in the mercantile store. Turns out the good Lord had a plan for me buying all those extra goods. He used me to watch out for us." She nudged Magda with her shoulder. "Now then, ain't you?"

"Ain't I what?"

"Ashamed."

"Maybe." Magda offered a petulant lift of one shoulder. "I'll decide once I see how much food you packed in those bundles."

Bertha cackled, drawing the amused attention of the men.

Magda waved. "Don't mind her. She's addlepated."

They rode toward an area of thick brush that seemed the end of the line.

Jumping off Faron, John tied him up then walked along the tangle of bushes and vines until he came to the densest part. Reaching carefully into the center of a laid-over tree, he caught hold of the thicker branches and pushed. It opened the way into a less brushy area that was hidden just seconds before. "Pull by me, Willem. Then you can help me bring Faron."

The two-horse team was reluctant at first, but with a bit of coaxing, they rushed past the overgrowth into a clearing. Willem climbed down and ran to take John's place, leaning his weight into the tree. John leaped on Faron and trotted him through with no trouble.

Ten feet away, the clearing narrowed into the trail John had promised, weaving through the heavy vegetation in front of them like the road to the Promised Land—with thorns.

Dismounting, John took a bucket from the wagon's rear boot. He pulled a plug from the bottom of a wooden drum and water streamed into the pail. Placing it on the ground for Faron, he glanced over his shoulder. "Help me water the horses, Willem. We'll rest them a few minutes since we're about to drive them hard."

He nodded at the team. "Be sure to watch them for any signs of stress. We'll aim to cool them down at regular intervals, but I think they'll be all right."

After they'd tended the animals, they ate a quick bite themselves then struck out. The scenery varied little, so they found other ways to entertain themselves along the way, playing silly games with words and matching wits.

As the temperature rose, the amusements lost most of their charm. The morning had dawned cloudy, making the day feel deceptively cool. Now the clouds had burned off, and beads of moisture persisted on Magda's top lip no matter how many times she swiped it away. As for Bertha, she had loosed her garments to a point that bordered on indecent.

The trip became a blur of blazing heat, sticky clothes, and the monotonous creak of wagon wheels. When it seemed they'd steeped in their juices long past done, the sun fell into the western sky and disappeared behind the trees. Birds swooped down with a flutter of wings to roost among the branches. Coyotes yipped and howled in the distance. Miraculously, Willem dozed, his head bobbing like his spine had worked loose.

Ahead of them, John reined in Faron and raised his hand.

Magda poked Willem in the ribs. "Wake up. He wants us to stop."

Willem fumbled for the leads and drew the horses to a halt. Coming alongside them, John took off his hat and wiped his forehead with a folded white hankie he took from his breast pocket. "I know how tired you are, folks. Believe it or not, I think we're almost there."

Willem yawned. "This soon? With all the stops, I expected to be riding all night."

John nodded. "So did I." He looked at the night sky. "This trail saved our hides. It ran farther than I expected, and it's cleared better than I might've hoped for. I'd say it bought us a couple of hours." He wedged his hat on his head and jutted his chin. "I can see the end of this thing, and once we come out, it's only a mile or so to my friend's ranch."

Magda sighed. "John, that's the best news I've heard all day."

Bertha stood up and stretched. "You reckon they'll let us take a bath? I'd settle for a washtub and cold water."

Magda pulled Bertha down so she could see John. "I'd trade the bath for something hot to eat."

Willem groaned and held his stomach. "I'll second that motion, dear."

John laughed. "They're good people. It's not the first time I've shown up unannounced, but day or night, they've treated me like a king." He dashed a large insect from his boot with the handle of his whip. "Don't worry. You can count on a table spread with food."

Willem picked up the reins. "What are we sitting around talking for then? Lead on."

CHAPTER 21

Melatha had misplaced God.

In a fit of worry, that gnawing state of unrest the Holy Bible warned against, she had stored Him carefully out of sight. In her pantry perhaps, or an apron pocket. Somewhere handy, so she might easily find Him when she decided to trust again.

That time had come, only now she couldn't locate her Creator. He didn't show up in that black hour before dawn when she'd awakened, crying out to Him on Isi's behalf. She couldn't rouse Him when she slipped from the bed to her knees weeping bitter tears. She didn't feel Him in her heart, no matter how feverishly she prayed.

She felt abandoned, as unloved as a motherless child. Starved for reassurance, she leaped to her feet and lit the lamp. Clutching her blanket around her, she swept her father's Bible from the shelf and huddled at the table, desperately flipping through the pages until she found the passage she sought. She read the scripture aloud, allowing the cooling waters of God's promise to quench her thirst for Him.

" 'For I am persuaded, that neither death, nor life, nor angels, nor principalities, nor powers, nor things present, nor things to come, nor height, nor depth, nor any other creature, shall be able to separate us from the love of God, which is in Christ Jesus our Lord.' "

Instantly He was there, wrapping His love around her as surely as the quilt about her shoulders. Of course, He'd been there all along, if the words she'd read held any truth. She had only to let go of her fear and let Him in. "Chihowa Palami, forgive me for doubting You. Help me to understand what has taken hold of Isi. Show me Your hand at work in his life."

A shaft of light fell on the page in front of her, startling her until she realized it was only a sunbeam. Pulling aside the shade, she winced at the brightly lit morning. The hour was late. She'd been so engrossed in her troubles she hadn't prepared breakfast. With a sudden jolt to her heart, she realized Isi had never shown up to eat.

Melatha stood so fast the quilt caught the edge of the chair, sending it crashing to the floor. Her heart in her throat, she scurried outside to the porch. Shading her eyes, she gazed over the property, searching the horizon. She peered toward the pasture, eager for any sign of Isi or his horse. She ran to the side rail and gazed toward the main house, hoping she'd see him loping across the yard or leaned against a tree talking to Cuddy.

The door to the bunkhouse creaked open, sending her flying down the steps, but only Little Pete slipped out, nodding and tipping his hat.

Embarrassed, she looked down at her flowing white gown, wondering if Pete thought she'd lost her mind. So be it, she felt she had. More so every minute that passed. Turning on her heel, she hurried inside to get dressed. She wouldn't find Isi while gazing barefoot from her porch.

As she dashed toward the basket where clean clothes were stored, a breeze from the open window lifted and fluttered the pages of the Bible, still open on the table. She slowed long enough to close the precious book and return it to the shelf. Another scripture blazed across her mind as her hand left the cracked leather binding.

"A bruised reed shall he not break, and the smoking flax shall he not quench. . ."

She'd learned the meaning of the beautiful words while crouched at her mother's knees. "It's a message of trust," Mother had whispered. "A promise that Chihowa Ushi will never crush the weak or quench our smallest hope."

Her head reeling, Melatha sank onto the side of her cot. Rushing out to scour the ranch for Isi would only prove she still dared to believe she had Almighty God tucked away in her pocket. The Ancient of Days didn't need assistance from the likes of Melatha

Rhona Marcelo, insignificant before Him in her finest hour, which this day was not.

Gritting her teeth against the flood of fear and doubt, she dressed herself with trembling hands then poured out two cups of dried beans. Spreading them over the table, she pushed aside pebbles, clods of dirt, and bits of chaff then pulled the rest into her pot. She would add pork fat and spices, boil them tender and savory, and bake corncakes in time for lunch.

She glanced at her father's Bible and nodded. When God brought Isi to her door seeking food and comfort, she'd be ready to provide him with both.

His stomach growling in protest, Diego led his horse to the next section of fence in need of repair—miles from the big house and still heading in the opposite direction from his mother's kitchen. He needed time to think more than he needed food, and time alone with God more than he needed to breathe. Besides, he wasn't eager to bear the scrutiny of his mother's searching eyes.

He hadn't seen her since the day before when she'd run from the barn, fleeing her disappointment in him. If only he could so easily escape himself.

How had he let so dreadful a thing happen? His feelings for Emmy started from the first day when she'd stolen glances at him on the trail. Embarrassment at ruining his hat had warred with obvious admiration as she gazed from beneath her lashes. In the days that followed, the seed of interest in her had pushed to the surface with very little prodding, exploding into a tangled vine around his heart. Despite his mother's warnings, he hadn't considered his great affection for her a bad thing. Until now.

He had hurt nearly every person in his life, and just as his mother said, the spell Emmy Dane had spun around him was the cause.

The mare he'd ridden to the pasture snorted and bobbed her head. Kneeling with a fistful of wire, Diego looked up to see what had her attention. Groaning, he threw down his pliers. One would think the Twisted-R Ranch would be plenty big enough for a man to escape his troubles. He'd forfeited breakfast to make good his escape, yet one of his most pressing problems rode toward him with a ridiculous smile on his face.

"Ho, there, Diego!"

Reluctant, Diego stood and raised his hand in greeting.

Cuddy closed the distance between them and slid off his horse. "Try telling someone where you'll be, amigo. I've been on parts of this ranch I've never seen before looking for you."

Diego snorted. "I hope you mended fences while you were there."

Cuddy laughed halfheartedly and gave him a jab in the arm. "No foolin', make sure we know where you're going next time. What if you hurt yourself or stumble onto a rattler? We wouldn't know where to find you."

"If a rattler struck me it wouldn't matter. You'd have plenty of time to find my lifeless body."

Cuddy grinned. "Not in this heat, brother. You'd swell up and pop. Then I'd be left to mop up the mess." He wrapped his arm around Diego's neck and walked him back to the post, giving him a good shake before turning him loose. "I sure am glad things are back to normal between us." He colored slightly and bent to pick up the pliers. "I really missed being on solid ground with you." He handed the tool to Diego and kneeled to help him hold the wire. "Truth be told, that's the reason I came to find you."

Diego tensed. He knew there had to be a reason as soon as he saw Cuddy riding toward him. He, too, had enjoyed the warmth of restored friendship, no matter how brief. Sensing it was over, he braced himself and breathed a silent prayer.

Cuddy's gaze darted to his face. "See, I want us to stay on solid ground. I also want you to know I don't hold it against you that things went sour with Greta, only. . ."

Diego's head came up.

Cuddy lifted his brows and nodded. "Mother told me. She said Greta doesn't ever want to see you again, but she didn't tell me why." He screwed up his face as if he tasted something bad. "Diego, I need to know what happened between you two." He paused. "You didn't do anything to hurt my sister, did you? If I thought you took advantage of her, I'd–"

Diego shot to his feet. "I took advantage, but not in the way you mean."

Cuddy stood with his hands clenched at his sides. "So she's still pure?"

"What! Yes, of course." He buried his hands in his hair and whirled away from Cuddy. "I can't believe you had to ask."

Cuddy released his breath in a *whoosh.* "I'm sorry I had to, and I want to believe you. But my sister has cried a river since yesterday, and she hasn't left her room. Can't you tell me why things took such a bad turn?"

Diego gathered his courage and faced him. "I'm not going to lie to you, Cuddy. I hurt Greta."

Cuddy's eyes bored into his, bright with unshed tears. "How? I need to know."

"I kissed her."

"I saw that much."

"Likely the first kiss she's ever had."

Cuddy nodded. "I think I can guarantee that."

Diego drew a shaky breath. "Only I wasn't thinking of Greta when I kissed her."

Tilting his head to the side, Cuddy's eyes narrowed to accusing slits. "And you were thinking of. . ." He held up his hand. "No, wait. Let me guess. You kissed my little sister while pretending she was my girl."

Diego held Cuddy's gaze, refusing to take the coward's way out. "I'd say that about covers it."

Cuddy frowned. "I don't understand. How could Greta know what you were thinking?"

Diego's stomach flipped. Beginning to reconsider the coward's way, he gritted his teeth and spit out the truth. "I called out Emmy's name."

Dangerous fury swirled in Cuddy's eyes, softening to pain in one blink of his lashes. His jaw tightened. "You did that to Greta? For a woman you hardly know?"

Frustration jangled Diego's nerves. "Listen to yourself, won't you? If I hardly know her, the same applies to you. Yet you just called her your girl."

Cuddy looked stunned.

Vindicated, Diego nodded. "Right. You see my point now. She slithers out of nowhere and coils up in your head. A man doesn't stand a chance until he gets wise to her ways." He placed his hands on Cuddy's shoulders. "But I'm wiser now. I don't know how I'll manage to fix the mess I made with Greta. I may not get the chance when your father gets wind of what I've done, but you can bet I'll do whatever it takes to set things right."

At the mention of his father, fear blanched Cuddy's face. He dropped to a squat, staring at the ground. "He'll run you off. I know he will."

Watching him curiously, Diego sank to the ground beside him. "I hope not. I pray not, but if he does, that won't affect our friendship, will it?"

Cuddy lifted his gaze to stare across the pasture, countless emotions jerking the muscles in his face. "If you leave, the old man will do what he's always wanted. He'll put me in charge." He swung tortured eyes to Diego. "I can't run this ranch, brother."

Diego patted his back. "Sure you can."

He gave his head a forceful shake. "Even if I tried my best, my best would never be good enough for the old man. I'd be compared to you every minute."

Knowing it was futile to deny a truth they'd both heard Mr. Rawson admit, Diego decided the kindest thing would be to change the subject. "Don't borrow trouble, amigo. Let's hope for a better outcome, shall we? I have no wish to leave the Twisted-R." He stood to his feet and Cuddy followed.

Squinting, Cuddy hunched his shoulders and thrust out his jaw. "I just have one more question. Is Emily still inside your head?"

Diego swallowed. "I'd like to tell you no, but I can't. Not yet anyway."

Cuddy nodded thoughtfully. "Where does that leave Greta?"

Patting Cuddy's boyish cheeks, Diego gave him the honest answer. "When I figure that out, you'll be the fourth to know."

"The fourth?"

He smiled. "After me, Greta, and my mother." His mood serious again, he gripped Cuddy's arm. "One thing I can promise you. God willing, I plan to stay as far from Emmy Dane as I possibly can."

CHAPTER 22

Magda's fingers picked at the edge of her hem. The unease in her stomach grew as the sun settled lower in the sky, and no amount of chatter from Bertha could quench it. The open road to Eagle Pass seemed treacherous compared to the secluded Indian trail, and Magda felt vulnerable and exposed to danger.

As night approached, John peered into every shadowy clump of bushes and jumped to attention at the slightest rustle or snap. So far, instead of skulking bandits lying in wait, every sound had proved to be the harmless stirring of animals on the prowl.

John's unease grew contagious. Poor frazzled Willem whipped around to look each time John did, his bulging eyes darting from his friend to the trail. Bertha abandoned her folded blanket and slipped to the edge of her seat, her eyes watchful, and the muscles in Magda's tensed legs began to tremble from the strain. The relaxed fellowship they'd shared around the table the night before and again at breakfast had dimmed to a pleasant memory.

Bertha seemed to read her mind as usual. "John, your friends sure were nice folks. They took us in and treated us like family." She paused. "Better than that, more like kings and queens, just like you said."

John answered without taking his attention from the road. "You'll find most folks in this region just as hospitable. They're a kindhearted, generous people." He smiled over his shoulder. "It's one of the reasons I rooted my family here."

Bertha's brows gathered like storm clouds. "Then why are you as jumpy as a cat?"

"Good question, Bertha. There are many fine citizens in Eagle Pass. Unfortunately, opportunists and thieves roam the streets as well. Saloons and gambling halls make life hard. Decent folks are fighting back and have recently cleaned up a lot of the garbage, but they have a ways to go before I'll breathe easy within ten miles of the place." He chuckled. "And we're considerably closer than that right now. Those lights you see up ahead mark the outskirts of town."

Magda moaned. "Bad element or not, that's blessed good news. Right now I'd welcome the sight of a gambling hall if it offered an empty bed."

John shot her a sympathetic glance. "An empty bed may be farther away than you think, Magda. We're not there yet, and we still have to find suitable lodging."

"That part will be easy," Bertha chimed in, reaching to pat her bag under the seat. "We'll stay at the best hotel money can buy."

"That's exactly what we won't do," John said. "Flaunting your wealth in Eagle Pass would be an act of suicide." He shook his head. "No, we'll book a room in the cleanest low-cost establishment we can find." He pointed at her. "You need to keep that satchel close to your body with the latch shut."

Magda took Bertha's chin and pulled her face around. "The same goes for your mouth."

Bertha slapped away her hand. "There's no call to take that tone."

"This is serious, Bertha. Your foolishness could get us killed in our sleep."

Arms crossed over her chest, she pouted. "I heard the man. Give me credit for having a thimbleful of sense."

Scooting closer to her on the seat, Magda wrapped her in a hug. "I'm dreadful sorry, honey. This trip has me on edge, that's all."

Bertha reached around Magda's waist and gave her an answering squeeze. "Aw, that's all right, sugar. I'm a bit jumpy myself."

Willem groaned. "John, you may need a drink to wash down all the confection those two tend to slosh about."

"*Buenas noches*, amigos."

The deep, unfamiliar voice nearly jolted Magda over the side, not to mention free of her bloomers. The only thing that held her on the seat and in her drawers was Bertha, whose grip around her middle tightened severely.

John pulled his pistol, the click of the hammer loud in the sudden stillness. At the same time, Willem yanked back on the reins and held up the lantern.

A short, swarthy man wearing a straw sombrero stood by the edge of the road. If he noticed that John cocked the gun, he pretended he hadn't. "Good evening, friends," he repeated in English. "If you please. . .I won't mind a little sip of that drink I heard you speak of."

John eased Faron closer, the horse balking at the stranger's scent. "Stepping out of the shadows can get a man killed, mister. Are you alone over there?"

The question roused Willem. He hurriedly lifted the rifle and scanned the darkness.

"Sí, alone." The man smiled and held his hands out to his sides. "Only me. . .Marcos." He took off his hat and held it over his chest. "I no mean to frighten you, señor."

John steadied the gun on Marcos's chest. "What are you doing hiding out here in the bushes?"

"Oh, no, señor. Not hiding. Merely walking along the road, that's all."

"Where are you headed?"

He gestured to the glow of lights in the distance. "I think to the same place you are going, no? Into town?" He raised his chin to the east. "My sister, she lives over that way about one mile. I go for visit three days ago, and now I go home." His smile broadened. "To Eagle Pass."

The way John's eyes flickered from Marcos to the thick brush on the roadside said he didn't quite trust the man. "Well, don't let us keep you, Marcos. I think we'll sit here for a spell and rest the horses." He waved with his gun. "Go ahead, be on your way."

Marcos leaned his head to one side. "Please, señor, allow me walk alongside you into town. There is safety in the company of friends. Do you agree?"

Eyes wary, John studied the little man.

Marcos laughed. "Still you don't believe me? I have more to fear of you." He offered his empty hands. "You see? I am alone and unarmed."

John looked over at Willem. "What do you think?"

Looking none too sure, Willem shrugged.

Marcos seized the advantage. "I will help you in return," he promised eagerly. "Whatever business brings you to Eagle Pass, I can help." He looked at them as if sizing them up. "You come for to buy coal?"

John shook his head.

"No? Business at the courthouse, then. Fort Duncan, perhaps."

Bertha released her hold on Magda and sat up. "We're looking for a man named Raul."

Marcos turned with startled eyes then began to laugh. "A man named Raul? There's one on every street corner, señora."

John laughed, too. "This one works in the Piedra Parada Saloon."

Grinning, he held up his finger. "Sí, sí, Raul. I know of him. One of Father Darius's boys."

Bertha leaned to see past Willem. "Can you help us find him?"

"It's no that easy. Raul no longer works at the saloon." At their obvious disappointment, he hurriedly amended his words. "But I can take you to Father Darius. He will help you to find Raul."

John dipped his head. "You just bought yourself an escort into town."

Grinning, Marcos rubbed his hands together. "Bueno. We can talk about that drink now?"

"I'm afraid there is no drink." John's eyes twinkled. "Unless you're thirsty for water."

Marcus pointed to Willem. "But, he said—"

"No drink."

The man gripped his head. "Ah, señor! Please, tell me you jest."

The men laughed heartily while Bertha leaned close to Magda to whisper. "It's a dirty shame he wasted his finagling skills for nothing." She cackled so loudly she turned everyone's head. "All that work with no payoff," she continued, her breath warm in Magda's ear.

"Bertha, behave yourself."

They rode for a spell before Willem's curiosity got the best of him. He cleared his throat, and Marcos glanced up at him. "You said this Raul was one of Father Darius's boys. That's got me baffled. How can a priest have a son?"

Marcos chuckled. "Raul is no son birthed to Father Darius, just as Father Darius is no priest of the church." He wagged his head. "Father Darius has many sons of the spirit. He runs a mission for wayward souls near the ferry crossing on the Rio Grande."

Willem opened his mouth to ask another question, but John's excited voice drowned him out. "Up ahead are the lights of Fort Duncan. Welcome to Eagle Pass, folks."

One thing was certain. Hiding in her room, no matter how charming the furnishings or comfortable the bed, had grown to be an irksome bother for Emmy. She yearned for her mother's counsel—even Aunt Bert's slapdash advice. However, she didn't look forward to Papa's reaction to the stink swirling around the rafters of the Rawson home, the whole sorry mess centered on her.

Neither Papa nor anyone else could blame her for what had happened. She'd done nothing to cause Cuddy's and Diego's sparring over her, snarling and snapping like hounds on a pork chop, and could do nothing to prevent it. Diego's indiscretion landed squarely on his own shoulders. In her opinion, any discomfort he felt over what he'd done to Greta wasn't harsh enough.

It troubled Emmy that Mrs. Rawson hadn't come to speak to her directly and had only sent Rosita to tap on her door after lunchtime the day before. When Emmy said she wasn't hungry, Rosita turned away with a grim look on her face. After that, no one had bothered.

Greta still hadn't left her room. In the afternoon, Emmy overheard Mrs. Rawson tell Rosita she would take her evening meal at her daughter's side. Driven by hunger, Emmy dared to slip downstairs where an oddly subdued Rosita had served her a meager late supper. After she ate, she begrudgingly returned to the room, having nowhere else to go.

A muffled rattle sounded from the balcony, like the disjointed clatter of a hailstorm back home. Considering the sweltering heat had diminished very little at sunset, she could likely discount hail as the cause. Frowning at the patio door, she jumped when a shower of pebbles hit the glass and rained down onto the porch.

Diego! It had to be him. Anyone else would simply knock on the bedroom door.

She checked her appearance in the mirror, pinching her cheeks and patting a stray curl into place. Yes, Diego's behavior had proved disappointing. It didn't mean she wouldn't be thrilled to see him.

She tucked her fingers inside the corners of her square neckline and tugged. The simple white dress, cut to a flattering V in back with a large circular buckle at her waist, might be the latest fashion, but it covered less of her skin than she liked. She twirled once in front of the vanity, noting how small the flowing fabric and cinched belt made her waist appear. Satisfied, she opened the door and stepped out onto the balcony.

Trying not to seem eager, she walked casually to the rail and peered into the yard below. Seeing nothing, her heart sank. She'd taken too long with her primping. Diego must have given up and gone his way. She turned to slip back inside her room.

"Emily!"

The hoarse whisper jolted her heart. Fighting a grin that would give away her pleasure, she pressed into the rail. "I'm here."

"I see that," he hissed.

Losing the battle with her smile, she scoured the ground. "Where? I can't see you."

Cuddy stepped into the light. "Here. Right under your pretty nose."

Emmy wilted with disappointment. "What on earth? Why are you sneaking around under my window?"

His exaggerated leer made him look like a simpleton. "I thought you might come out and play."

Laughing louder than she meant to, especially considering her room lay directly over Greta's, she covered her mouth. "I can't, foolish boy."

"Why not?"

"You know why. It's not proper."

"Since when did Emily Dane give two hoots about proper?" He cocked his head at her. "Come down. I'm harmless. I promise."

"In that case, march inside and request permission from your mother."

He widened his eyes.

She laughed. "Ah, ha! Just as I thought."

The mention of his mother reminded Emmy of the way Mrs. Rawson had ignored her and her needs. The woman hadn't cared if she ate, much less chaperoned her properly. Offended, Emmy rashly changed her mind. Cuddy was right, proper be hanged. "Stay where you are. I'll be right there."

"Now you're talking, sugar."

Gliding silently down the stairs, careful to make not a sound, guilt niggled the edges of Emmy's resolve. The swirling stink already raised would seem a trifle against the resulting stench of getting caught sneaking out of the house. Certain she'd taken leave of her senses, Emmy peeked once more toward the kitchen and lower hallway before slipping out the back door.

Growling in her ear, Cuddy caught her around the waist and twirled her away from the house. He caught her wrist and ran, pulling her along behind him. Their laughter stifled to giggles until they reached the barn. Once they stumbled inside, they howled like demented coyotes. Cuddy's horse stood waiting, already saddled.

Emmy curled a hand on her waist. "You're pretty sure of yourself, Cuthbert Rawson."

He grinned over his shoulder then reached for the reins. "Why do you say that?" He scowled. "And don't call me Cuthbert."

She waved him off. "Never mind. You're hopeless."

Cuddy mounted the horse then freed the stirrup for her. He offered his hand, pausing to hold her suspended at his side. His face inches away, he peered into her eyes. "Get ready for the ride of your life, darlin'."

Emmy stiffened. Too late, she caught the pungent odor of alcohol on his breath.

Without waiting for her answer, he pulled her up behind him. "Hang on," he cried and thundered past the wide double doors of the barn into the dark, moonless night.

CHAPTER 23

The little man in the wide sombrero had gone from walking alongside the wagon to sitting tall beside Willem in the front seat. Following Marcos's directions, they skirted Fort Duncan without alerting the attention of the posted sentinels, then crossed the bridge on Van Buren Street and turned left on Garrison. True to his word, he had many connections in Eagle Pass, considering every person they passed greeted him by name.

At a Y in the road, so near the river Magda smelled the fusty odor of mud, they veered to the left, passing a large, poorly lit building on the corner.

After one more block, they took a right turn on Rian Street, and Marcos led them around to the back of a seedy warehouse.

Willem set the brake on the rig.

John tied Faron to a dilapidated post and addressed Marcos. "Now what?"

"Please to follow me, señor." Aiming a nod and a mumbled greeting at a group of men gathered around a fire pit, Marcos questioned one of them in Spanish.

The tall, slender man smiled and hooked his thumb toward the building.

Marcos opened the door to a scene Magda would not soon forget. The inside of the warehouse was a large open space, except for a small office tucked in one corner. Cots took up most of the room, and where there were no cots, ragged quilts and bedspreads covered the floor. Stretched out on the makeshift beds were men both young and old, some huddled beneath worn blankets, some propped against pillows to read, others clustered together talking quietly. Nearby, a young boy sat cross-legged on a cot, spooning beans into his mouth, though how he managed to eat surrounded by the putrid smell of urine and unwashed bodies was more than Magda could fathom.

She controlled her roiling stomach and her emotions until she glanced at Bertha's face. Tears flowed unchecked down her friend's cheeks and her nose streamed. Magda slid an arm around her waist. "I know, sugar," she whispered. "I know."

Bertha wiped her nose on her sleeve. "This is dreadful, Magda."

She nodded. "Yes, it is. But, honey"—she wiped the tears from Bertha's eyes with her thumbs—"don't let them see you crying. Let's leave them some dignity."

A ruckus arose in the corner. Three men were seated around a table playing cards and one of them was shouting. The largest of the lot, an overweight, ruddy-cheeked bloke in a dirty white shirt and slacks held up by suspenders, scowled at a handsome young man of Latin descent. "You heard me, you dimwitted *naco*. Do I need to spell the words for you?"

Across the table, a slightly built, gray-haired man lifted his head, a serene expression of patience on his face. "Your tone is unnecessary, Mr. Malone. I'm certain Señor Ortiz doesn't mean to seem obtuse."

"But, Father, I've explained three times. I reckon he cain't understand no English. That or he plain ain't listening."

In a show of frustration, the young man threw down his cards. "I am trying to listen, Father. Most of his speech does not sound like English to me."

Ruddy-cheeks pointed at him. "There, you see? He's downright ignorant."

The distinguished gentleman they called Father studied Malone in silence until he squirmed, and then he lifted one eyebrow. "Mr. Malone, how much Spanish can you speak, sir?"

"Who me? I cain't speak a whit." He snorted. "Don't care to neither."

"I see." He pointed to the young fellow. "So, here we have a man accused of being unrefined and lacking social graces." He peered into

Mr. Malone's eyes. "This is the meaning of a naco, correct?"

"But, Father Darius. . ." Mr. Malone's gaze darted around the room, but he found no support among the silent, hollowed-eyed witnesses.

"Yet Mr. Ortiz has undertaken to learn English as well as his native Spanish." He redirected his finger at Mr. Malone. "And here we have one who speaks only his native tongue—having mastered it none too well, I might add."

Father Darius placed his arm around Señor Ortiz's thin shoulders. "He has attempted to learn to communicate with you, Mr. Malone. I would say that makes him a leader, not an ignorant naco. Wouldn't you agree?"

Mr. Malone hung his head. "I reckon so."

Father Darius patted him on the back. "I suggest you apply the golden rule to your dealings with Señor Ortiz from now on. How does that sound?"

He mumbled his agreement and glanced at Mr. Ortiz.

The young man offered his hand and they shook heartily.

Marcos saw his chance and moved in. "Father Darius?"

His attention still on the reconciling men, Father Darius lifted joyful eyes. "Yes?" He stood to his feet. "Why, hello, Marcos. I see you've brought me more customers." He glanced around and sighed. "We'll have to squeeze to make a bit more room, but I suppose we can take them in."

He nodded at Willem and John then smiled gently at Bertha and Magda. "I'm very sorry. I have no accommodations to offer women." His outstretched arm took in the crowded room. "I'm afraid this is no place for the fairer sex. There's absolutely no privacy. You'd be most uncomfortable here." He held up his finger. "But I can suggest the perfect alternative for you."

Marcos shook his head vigorously. "No, Father. They need only to talk to you. They're searching for Raul."

Concern lined his gentle face. "Is the boy in trouble?"

John smiled. "None that we know of." He held out his hand. "John Rawson of the Twisted-R Ranch in Carrizo Springs." He indicated Willem, Bertha, and Magda, introducing them in turn. "These fine people are guests on my ranch."

Father Darius colored slightly. "Of course. I'm very sorry. I have a simple mind, I'm afraid. I see everyone I meet as homeless waifs." He bowed at the waist. "Forgive my unfortunate assumption, ladies."

Magda offered her hand. "No apology necessary, Father."

He grinned. "Call me Darius, please. I'm not a priest and hardly deserving of the title. Father is a moniker the men pinned on me years ago when I took in a few orphan boys, and it stuck." He addressed John again. "You say you're looking for Raul?"

John nodded. "We were told he has information on some livestock for sale. Mrs. Bloom, here, is looking to buy several head of prime cattle to take home with her to Humble."

Father Darius's head shot up, his gaze fixed on Bertha. "Did he say Humble?"

Bertha smiled. "That's right."

"Texas?"

"Is there another one?"

He blinked. "And your name is Bloom?"

Perplexed by the questions, Bertha furrowed her brow. "That's what the man said, ain't it?"

He studied her, his eyes gone to narrow slits. "You wouldn't be kin to a fellow named Thaddeus Bloom, now would you?"

Bertha tensed and her mouth went slack. "As a matter of fact, I would." She stepped closer and tilted her face up to his. "What's your full name, mister?"

Beaming, he stuck out his hand. "Darius Q. Thedford at your service, ma'am."

"Cuddy, stop!" Emmy shouted louder, but the rushing wind and pounding of the horse's hooves drowned out her voice. She clung to Cuddy's back with all of her strength, praying the ride would end soon.

Relief flooded her middle with warmth when she recognized the slope to the river. Certainly Cuddy would let her down when they reached the water's edge.

The warm glow turned to icy fingers of fear when he turned the big mare and thundered along the bank, urging the horse to go faster than Emmy had ever ridden in her life.

She prayed either the horse or Cuddy knew where they were

going, because the overcast night was so murky, she could see nothing. Feeling the horse lift from the ground, she tightened her grip around Cuddy's waist, closed her eyes, and screamed.

His hoarse laughter floated on the breeze as they cleared the low fence and hurtled into a black veil.

When she thought he'd never stop, he did. Still laughing, he reined the panting mare to a halt. "Give me your hand," he said, groping behind him.

She pushed him away. "Why?"

"So I can help you down."

"I don't want down. Where are we, Cuddy? It's as dim as pitch out here."

He chuckled. "Ain't that nice?"

"No, it's not nice. Take me back this instant."

He groaned. "Come on, honey. Don't be like that. We have to give this horse a little rest first. Besides, I just want to talk for a while."

She let go of him and crossed her arms, though he couldn't see her. "I don't think so, Cuddy."

He sighed. "You're going to force me to embarrass myself, aren't you?"

Her interest piqued, she waited for him to explain.

He didn't.

"How might I do that?"

His shoulders rose and fell with a deep, shuddering breath. "It's just that. . .talking to you about our fathers makes me feel better. I mean. . .knowing there's someone who understands means the world to me."

Emmy dangled between hugging him and inviting him to peddle his wares elsewhere. The wild ride he'd just subjected her to swung the vote. "I don't believe you."

His silence made her fear she'd angered him. When he spoke, the weight of resignation pulled his voice to a whisper. "I can't say I blame you." He nudged the horse around.

Emmy's heart lurched. "Wait, Cuddy." She felt for his hand. "I'm being silly. Help me dismount."

He lowered her to the ground and she stood surrounded by night sounds and little else, wrapped in a soft cocoon of darkness. She shivered, willing Cuddy to hurry and join her. When he did, his arm went around her and she relaxed into him.

"Where are we?"

"A place I come when I need to be alone." He led her a few feet from the horse and spread a blanket on the ground. "It's a nice spot. I wish there was more light so you could see."

"So do I." She groped the ground before she sat. "What about snakes and scorpions?"

He squeezed her shoulders. "Stay close to me. I won't let them get you."

Bumping his arm, Emmy giggled. "Who will protect me from you?"

His answering laughter sounded more like the old Cuddy. "I won't hurt you. I only want to spend a little time with you."

A warning tensed her stomach. "Yes, to talk. That's what you said."

"To talk. Of course."

Now that her eyes weren't clenched tight with dread, they began to adjust to the meager light. Cuddy's dim outline blocked out the night sky. "Has something else happened? With your father, I mean?"

He ducked his head. "Not yet, but it's bound to. As sure as we're sitting here, it will happen when Father gets home. I see no way around it."

The alarm laced through his words clenched Emmy's fists. She shivered again, this time with foreboding. "What, Cuddy? What do you think will happen?"

Illogically, considering the gloomy turn of their conversation, the clouds overhead parted, allowing the starry sky to rain light across the open field.

Emmy could see Cuddy clearly now, trace the etched lines in his forehead, read the fear in his eyes.

"When my father returns from Catarina, Diego will be leaving the Twisted-R."

Stunned, Emmy stared at him. "For good?"

"Hauled to the gate by the scruff of his neck, if I know my father—which means I'll never get off this accursed ranch."

She gripped his arm. "I don't understand. Why would your father ask Diego to leave?"

He grunted. "Like I said, there won't be any asking." He speared her with a glance. "Diego committed the unpardonable. He hurt Greta." Bitterness tainted his laugh. "No one hurts John Rawson's family, especially his baby girl, without paying a mighty high price."

She squirmed. "So you heard?"

He shook his head. "Diego told me. I wasn't sure you heard until now."

Emmy stared. "He told you?"

"He tells me everything." He reached inside his jacket and drew out a small container, fumbling with the lid. "When Diego's gone, that just leaves me, the old man's favorite project." He turned up the flask and took a long drink then wiped his mouth on his sleeve. "Not to mention his biggest failure."

Emmy seized the bottle from his hand and held it up. "Where did this come from? I thought you threw it away."

"I had a spare."

He reached for it, but she snatched it away. "You're not getting this back."

He shrugged, his teeth flashing white against his shadowy face. "That's all right. It's empty."

She shook it but heard no sloshing sound. "Oh, Cuddy. How much have you had?"

"Not enough, evidently. I'm still conscious." His head drooped between his knees. "Aw, Emily. What will I do if Diego leaves? He's been my right arm. With him gone, it won't take long for the old man to figure out I don't know a thing about running the ranch."

There was no doubting his anguish. Once again, sympathy crowded her heart, and she touched his arm. "Why don't you talk to your father? Tell him the truth about how you feel?"

He snorted. "Talk to my father? Now that's a laugh." He lifted his head and stared thoughtfully. "Maybe I could plead my case to Mother. Have her soften him up for me."

Emmy lifted one shoulder. "Forgive me, but I'm not sure that's a good idea. Compassion is hardly her strongest trait."

His gaze shifted to Emmy. "What makes you say that? Kate Rawson is the model of compassion."

Emmy balked. "Not toward me. Papa entrusted her with my welfare, but she hasn't bothered to see to my needs for two days." She stuck out her lip. "I've nearly starved."

"But Rosita has." His eyes were troubled. "Hasn't she?"

"Only once, but she never came again."

He groaned and balled his fists at his temples. "Mother has no idea. She'd have a stroke if she knew."

Emmy swatted away his words. "That can't be so. How could she not know?"

"Her mind is preoccupied with Greta, so she put Rosita in charge of you. I heard her myself."

The bewildering words were a muddle in her mind. She might have discounted them except for the memory of Rosita's sullen face at her door.

"Then Rosita hasn't fulfilled her charge." She cocked an eyebrow at Cuddy. "Why would she do that?"

He spun on the blanket to face her, nearly toppling into her lap. "That's an easy answer. There's a rift between Diego and me that wasn't there before. She blames you."

His speech beginning to slur, he picked up her hands. "I'm sorry, Emmy. I should've checked on you myself. I knew Rosita was angry, but I never expected her to go this far." He squeezed her fingers. "Don't worry. I intend to speak to her."

Emmy squeezed back. "Please don't. We've had enough trouble in your house. Besides"—she made a face—"Rosita might poison my frijoles."

Laughing too loudly, he swayed toward her. "You're awfully cute. Did you know that?" He seemed to grow ten more hands, all busy grasping her arms, shoulders, and neck while he pulled himself closer. "Just plain cute," he drawled. "That's what you are."

"Stop it, now." Emmy strained to pull away. "You're too rough. Let me go, please."

"Sweet, too, ain't you? As sweet as a newborn calf."

The incredible strength in his hands shot fear to Emmy's heart and swelled her throat. "No, Cuddy. Please, don't!"

As he pressed her to the ground, his greedy mouth sought hers. "Sweetest little thing I ever—"

A sharp intake of air and a howl finished his sentence. With a roar, Diego ripped Cuddy's body free of Emmy, one hand buried in his hair, the other clutching the nape of his neck. Tossing him aside like a straw-filled scarecrow, Diego stood over him with balled fists, his chest heaving.

Obviously dazed, and frightened out of his wits, Cuddy cowered with his fingers splayed over his face. "What did you do that for?"

Diego started for him again and Cuddy crawled backward over the rocky ground like a crawfish. "Wait!" he cried. "I wasn't going to hurt her. I was just fooling around. I swear."

Still panting wildly, Diego stalked to Emmy and jerked her up by the arm. Before she could protest, he herded her to his horse and urged her into the saddle then climbed in behind her.

As they passed Cuddy, still on the ground, Diego stopped and spoke for the first time. "What's happened to you? I didn't think you capable of something like this. Don't you think it's time to lay off the booze?"

Eyes blazing, Cuddy leaped to his feet. "Blast you, Diego. You don't know a thing about me, including my intentions. What are you doing here anyway? Do you spy on me all the time now?"

"I have more important things to occupy my time. Little Pete saw the two of you ride out of the barn. He knew you'd been drinking."

"Why don't you mind your own business, brother?" He nodded at Emmy. "Though my guess is that's exactly what you think you're doing."

Cuddy grabbed hold of the reins and peered up at her. "Forgive me, Emily. I swear I meant you no harm. I only wanted to kiss you."

Before she could answer, Diego spurred the horse and bolted away.

The trip home was as frantic and fast as her last ride. The difference was in how it made her feel. Instead of fearful and desperately clinging, she rode cradled by Diego's body, his arms around her waist, the warmth of his chest at her back, his breath in her hair.

The madness and the sweetness of the moment made her cry, the tears barely touching her cheeks before the wind whisked them away. Her heart swelled in gratitude to Diego, her champion, her hero.

They ducked into the barn where Little Pete waited, his dark eyes pools of concern. Rushing to them, he held the horse while Diego helped her down. "You all right, miss?"

Embarrassed, she ducked her head. "I'm fine, thank you."

"That's all, Pete," Diego barked.

Pete nodded and hustled out the door.

Her emotions swelling in rolling waves of joy, Emmy turned and lifted grateful eyes. "Diego, I–"

His hand shot up. "Save your explanation for someone who cares. Close your mouth and get inside the house."

CHAPTER 24

Father Darius pulled out chairs for Bertha and Magda in the little boxed-in room that served as his office. Willem stood against the wall. Bertha sat at the edge of her seat, and Darius knelt before her, holding her hands. She gazed at him in wonder, disbelief and joy taking turns as well.

"It's really you? The same Darius Thedford that gave Thad the deed to our land so many years ago?"

He nodded. "None other."

She squeezed his fingers. "I've been looking for you for over a year now. Sent word across the country, but no news ever came back. It seemed like you fell off the face of the earth."

Darius smiled, his gesture taking in his shabby surroundings. "I guess you could say in a way I did."

"I wouldn't say it," Magda said, patting him on the shoulder. "You're doing a wonderful service to the Lord in this place."

"Thank you, Mrs. Dane." His attention returned to Bertha. "You say you've been looking for me, dear?"

"Yes," she whispered softly. "I have something I need to give you." She wiped her eyes on her sleeve. "I didn't understand the urge to see it done until now. At first, I thought I was meant to do it for my Thad."

Darius's eyes lit up. "How is young Thad?" Drawing back, he laughed at himself. "Oh, my, I suppose he's hardly the impetuous lad

I met on his way to college." Amazement clouding his eyes, he gazed at Bertha, making the connection. "Thad must be pushing fifty years old by now."

Magda slipped her arm around Bertha's trembling shoulders. "Father, Thad's been gone for more than six years. Bertha's a widow now."

"Oh no," he said, the word so filled with sorrow it came out a moan. "Bertha, I'm real sorry to hear that."

Her gaze losing focus, Bertha gripped Magda's hand. "Six years. It don't seem possible, does it?"

Darius patted her hand. "He was such a fine lad, too. How did it happen?"

Wrenching herself from the past, Bertha lifted tearful eyes. "River swallowed him. The water came up so fast it swept him away in plain sight of several witnesses. Thad was a right good swimmer, but he never stood a chance against a flash flood on the San Jacinto."

Darius cleared his throat. "The ways of our God are a source of unfathomable mystery, Bertha. My life took a new direction after I met your husband, and he was the reason. I was nothing more than a drifter, making a living by fleecing innocent victims. Then Thad came along, and I caught a glimpse of genuine goodness. Of course, he took none of the credit. Gave it all to God, and didn't mind telling me so. I decided then and there I needed the God I saw reflected in that boy's eyes."

Bertha clasped her hands and wiggled on the seat. "You got Him, too. I see Him right there in your eyes."

Darius swallowed hard and ducked his head. "I often lamented the fact that I lost contact with Thad and planned many times to travel to Humble and find him, to tell him what he'd done for me. Somehow that trip never took place, and now I've lost the chance forever."

A look of sweet peace softened Bertha's features. "Not forever, Father. My Thad awaits us both in heaven. Then you'll have forever to say what you need to say. I'm sure he'll have a thing or two to tell you as well. He was always mighty beholden to you for giving him that deed."

She paused, smiling a little. "There is one thing Thad always wondered. If you don't mind, can you clear it up for me now? I reckon he's on pins and needles up in heaven, waiting for me to ask you."

Father Darius grinned. "Ask me anything."

"Well"—she wiggled on the seat—"Thad always figured you won that deed in a poker game. Is that how you came to have it?"

He scratched his head, amusement tugging at his lips. "I suppose the boy would think that, considering we met over a hand of cards." He lifted his chin. "You know, I kind of like the idea that he saw it that way and never learned the truth. A poker game sounds far more interesting than the truth."

She scooted forward. "What is the truth?"

"Actually, an uncle up north willed it to his sister's son. Before my uncle's death, this same boy got on his bad side, so he blotted out his name and left it to me instead. I was on my way to see it when I ran into Thad."

"You never once saw Humble, Texas?"

He grunted and shook his head. "Never did. I gave that property to Thad before I ever set eyes on it." He looked up and smiled. "But you know something, Mrs. Bloom? Somehow I knew I was supposed to do it, and I never had a single moment's regret."

Bertha clutched both of his arms and gave him a shake. "Just like I'll never have a single moment's regret for what I'm about to do." She blinked away tears. "Especially now that I see the reason for God insisting that I find you."

She reached inside her blouse and then paused. "Turn your head, Father, if you don't mind. Willem, that goes for you, too." Winking at Magda, she reached deep inside the bodice of her dress. "You can look now. And stick out your hand."

Darius did as he was told, and she placed a folded document in his outstretched palm. "My dear, what's this?"

Satisfied, she folded her arms across her chest. "Just the rights to half the profits from one of the largest producing oil wells in the state of Texas."

Emmy's jaw fell open and she stared at Diego with rounded eyes. "What did you say?" Her words came out low and breathless, intended to warn him he'd best not have said what she thought.

Unflinching, Diego folded his arms across his chest and met her glare. "I said close your mouth and get inside. I mean it, Emmy. Go to the house right now, and whatever you do, don't let those good people catch you sneaking back in from your sordid rendezvous."

Her head reeled. The warmth of gratitude turned to flames of fury. She stomped her foot. "How dare you!"

Diego took a step closer. "Let me tell you how I dare." One by one, he held up fingers, counting off his reasons. "I've broken my mother's heart. The only father I've ever known has lost faith in me. Half the time Cuddy acts like he hates me, and Greta, who's been like a sister to me, is locked in her room, refusing to see me." He leaned threateningly, his eyes menacing in a stormy face. "So I'm asking. . .haven't you done enough damage?"

Incredulous, Emmy gaped at him. "And you think even one of those things is my fault?" She held up a few fingers of her own. "First off, I have nothing to do with your mother. How could I? She won't spare a civil word in my direction. Second, for all I know, Cuddy may have a reason to hate you." She wound up for the kicker. "As for John Rawson, didn't he lose faith in you about the time you were sneaking behind the bunkhouse to kiss your *little sister?*"

She spun on her heels and left him floundering.

He caught up with her outside the barn, his fingers rough on her arm. "Your last point is more your fault than mine," he panted. "Because I wasn't kissing Greta." His eyes still blazed but not with anger. Longing, desperation, and shame all vied for fury's place. "I may have held Greta, Emmy, but I was kissing you."

Her heart breaking, Emmy wrapped him in her arms. He jerked her close and tangled his hands in her hair. Guiding her face beneath his, his lips hovered inches from hers. . .until he roughly pushed her aside.

Hugging his head, he whirled away from her. "What am I doing?" Fuming again, he latched onto her shoulders. "For that matter, what are you doing?" He pointed behind him. "Not ten minutes ago, you were wallowing on the ground with Cuddy. For all I know, you'd rather I hadn't showed up." He shoved past her. "Do us both a favor, Emmy. Stay out of my way."

Too crushed to cry out to him, too angry to deny his accusation, Emmy stared after him until he disappeared in the darkness.

She'd been accused of many hurtful deeds in her life, most of them quite justified. Never in her twenty-one years had a person accused her so unjustly, and it stung. Despite one reckless dalliance with her best friend's fiancé, no one had ever questioned Emmy's virtue except that black-hearted rascal. She found it hard to accept that a person she held in the highest regard had done the same.

Her spirits as flat as a fritter, she started for the house, ready to leave South Texas for good.

As she neared the back entrance, Cuddy rode into the yard. Ducking behind the patio wall, she watched his horse trot into the barn. He was the last person she wanted to see, especially tonight. Tomorrow would be soon enough to decide how to deal with Cuddy Rawson.

A couple of things were certain after the wild night she'd had. One, she wouldn't be accepting any more invitations from Cuddy, and two, the time had come to quit sneaking out of the house. The imprudent practice had never brought her anything but trouble.

Praying no one had slipped down and locked her out of the house, Emmy tried the knob, sighing with relief when it turned and the door opened. Knowing the spiteful Rosita would delight in telling on her, Emmy kept her eyes on the kitchen as she tiptoed to the stairs.

When she shut the door of her room, she closed her eyes and leaned against it.

"Who were you with, Emily?"

Emmy's eyes flew open. Her hand jerked to her hammering heart and her knees gave out. Sliding to the floor, she stared at the hollow-eyed girl sitting on her bed in a dingy cotton nightgown, her hair a matted, stringy mess. "Greta!"

Greta lifted her hand toward Emmy. "Oh, don't worry. I won't tell. Are you all right?"

Her chest heaving, Emmy took inventory before she answered. "I believe so. Give me a minute and I'll tell you for sure."

"I'm sorry. I didn't mean to startle you."

"Startle? I think my heart may burst."

Greta pushed off the bed and scurried to sit on the floor beside her. "Forgive me, but I must have an answer. Were you with Cuddy or Diego?"

Emmy stared at the pale, drawn face and cringed. How could she tell the poor girl the truth—that she'd been with both? She opted for half of the truth. "Cuddy asked me to go for a ride."

The lines eased from Greta's forehead and a bit of color returned to her cheeks. "Cuddy?" She released a long breath. "I heard Diego's voice near the barn, so I thought. . ." She looked up and shrugged. "Never mind what I thought."

Picking at the sleeve of her gown, she squirmed until she mustered her courage. "May I ask another question?"

The memory of heartrending sobs echoing through the floorboards touched a tender spot in Emmy's heart. "Of course, Greta. Anything."

Her icy blue eyes lifted to Emmy's, sending a chill down her back. "Do you know. . ." She faltered. "I mean, did you hear. . ."

The only thing to do was tell the truth. Emmy nodded grimly then watched Greta try to accept it.

"Did Cuddy hear, too?"

"No." She hated to crush the flicker of hope. "But he knows. Diego told him."

She moaned. "Why does Diego tell him everything?"

Emmy picked up her hands. "So it's only you, me, Diego, Cuddy, and your mother. Five people. No one else need ever know."

Her chin shot up, her eyes as wide as saucers. "Who told Mother?"

"Well, sweetie, I assumed you had."

"No! I'd never tell her. She'd only run to Father, and then he'd make Diego leave." A wistful sigh escaped her lips. "I don't want that." She squeezed Emmy's fingers. "Not ever."

"Of course you don't."

"Leave Cuddy to me. I can handle him. As for Mother, I told her I threw myself at Diego, and he let me down easy. She thinks I'm upset because I humiliated myself."

Emmy tried to make sense of it all. "Then why does she think I've hidden away in my room?"

"She's convinced you're pouting because your parents left you behind. I've told her no different." Her eyes darkened. "In fact, that's why I'm here, Emily. If my father asks Diego what happened to make me cry, Diego will tell him the truth. I know he will." Her fingers dug painfully into Emmy's hands. "We have to keep that from happening. Please say you'll help."

"But what can I do?"

The girl scooted until their knees bumped. "Talk to Diego. Tell him I'll never tell anyone what happened. We can go on like we were before. I just don't want him to leave."

Newfound respect for Greta swelled Emmy's chest, along with fresh hurt for the heartbroken girl and herself. There was no way to tell her that Diego had just ordered Emmy to stay out of his path. "What makes you think he'll listen to me?"

It was the wrong thing to say. Emmy knew as soon as she'd uttered the words.

Her eyes losing focus, Greta retreated into the memory that had brought her such pain. "He'll listen to you," she whispered. "I could tell by the passion in his kiss."

CHAPTER 25

Magda walked to the window of the Maverick Hotel and peered across the street. Other than the post office, she spotted a few businesses and shops, but to her dismay, there was no restaurant or café in sight.

Bertha stood by the bed, rummaging in her money satchel. Though she probably had enough cash in the bag to buy the hotel, it had seemed more reasonable to book two rooms instead of three, so Willem had taken the extra cot in John's room and Bertha slept on the divan across from Magda's bed.

Magda pulled her gaze from the window. "This is a nice-sized town, ain't it, Bertha?"

"Too big to suit me. I prefer wide-open spaces." She looked up. "Was that your belly I heard growling?"

Magda rubbed her middle. "This rowdy thing woke me up pitching a fit about our meager supper. I hope the hotel offers a decent breakfast."

By the time they'd hauled poor Darius off his backside the night before, where he'd landed in a heap when Bertha delivered her news, the hour was too late to find a meal. A jubilant Father Darius had offered them each a can of beans, which sounded right good by that time. But as hungry as she was, Magda agreed with the others that she'd never take food meant for those wretched homeless souls.

They'd settled for the remaining hardtack and venison jerky then found their hotel and turned in for the night. But not before Darius wrote out how to find Raul, who, thanks to Darius and the mission, had left behind his life of sin and returned like the prodigal to his father's home.

Bertha closed the satchel, hopped on the bed, and leaned against the wall, her arms crossed behind her head. "I expect the men are hungry, too. I'm right surprised we ain't heard from them by now. I thought John wanted to get an early start."

"He did. I heard him say so. I'm sure they'll be stirring soon." Magda sat beside Bertha on the bed, bunching pillows behind her back. "Meanwhile, tell me how long you've been keeping your plan to find Darius Thedford a secret." She leaned her head to gaze at Bertha. "And why withhold it? I thought we shared most everything, but this is the second time in a week I've learned you kept something from me."

Bertha's eyes held steady. "There was never a second I wasn't going to tell you about Emmy and that rascal Cuddy Rawson. I made the decision to trust her word, and I think I made a right one. As for my plan to find Darius, I never decided not to tell you. Before long, it became a thing too precious to talk about." She swatted at Magda, her eyes blurred with tears. "Oh, you know what I mean."

Magda smiled. "Of course I do. But I have one more question. How long have you been hauling that deed around in your bodice?"

Bertha frowned and scratched her side. "Long enough to cause an itchy rash. But what was I supposed to do? I don't carry a reticule."

"How did you know you'd need it?"

"I knew as sure as anything I had the call from God to find Darius and give him his share of the well. I reckon it was the same call Darius felt to give the land to Thad in the first place." She twisted around. "Don't you think so, Magda?"

Magda opened her mouth to remind Bertha that the judgments of God were unsearchable and His ways past finding out, but the scripture no sooner formed in her mind than a boisterous knock came at the door. She hefted herself toward the corner of the bed. "That's the fellows now."

Bertha, considerably spryer than Magda and closer to the door, vaulted off the bed like a springtail. Hustling to the door, she opened it wide. "It's about time you two turned loose of the sheets. Let's get this venture started."

John's booming laughter shook the hall. "We peeled back those sheets hours ago, little Bertha. Willem and I have been up since dawn, and we bring you good news."

Not waiting for Bertha to ask, Willem leaned in the door grinning. "We found Raul. Joe Campbell was right. Raul knows a man who's selling his stock."

John took up the story. "We've seen your cattle, Bertha. Some of the finest polled Herefords I've ever laid eyes on."

Bertha seemed caught between a smile and a frown. "You went without me?"

Willem's brows met in the middle. "I ducked in this morning, but all I heard were snores and snorts."

"Don't worry," John said. "No deals were struck on your behalf. We told the man you'd make the final decision. He's waiting for us to bring you back."

"The best part is you don't have to drive them to Carrizo. You can ship them out right here in Eagle Pass."

Bertha's countenance fell. "That's not good news, Willem. I was looking forward to a cattle drive."

Grinning, John patted her shoulder. "Well, you're in luck. I told him we'd cut out the thirty head you wanted from the best he had to offer, and they could save a few for me. You'll be helping me drive around twenty of those beauties back to Carrizo Springs."

She broke into a jig, circling the room with her hands on her hips. "Let's go, then. What are we waiting for?"

John held up both hands. "Hold on there. I hope we're waiting for breakfast. After all the excitement, Willem and I are starved."

Magda stretched her arm overhead. "I'll second that motion. My grub-catcher's on empty."

Never one to set much stock in food, Bertha frowned. "I'll wait if I have to for the sake of the men. But Magda, I don't plan to schedule my day around your meals. Try to shovel in enough to last awhile."

Turning at the door, John pointed at the bulging satchel. "You might want to bring that thing, Bertha. It'll finally come in handy. The next part of this trip is about to get expensive."

Bertha cocked her head and glared at him, her expression too solemn to be serious. "Hold up there, John. When I told Magda to eat her fill, I never intended to finance it."

Magda gasped. "He means the cattle!"

"Oh." A wide grin on her face, Bertha gathered the bag under her arm. "Well, that's different."

Melatha scraped Isi's eggs into a bowl and wrapped the container in a dishcloth. She stacked his tortillas and bacon in a separate dish and covered them with a plate. Setting the whole sodden mess on the back of the stove, she closed the damper to cool the fire. If he didn't show up soon, her eager students would gladly share his breakfast as they had done the day before. And Melatha would struggle to hide her tears while she watched them eat the food she'd prepared for her son.

She hadn't spent a day apart from Isi since he'd come back into her life. Their spirits had bonded and their time together had been sweet. The brooding young man who'd abandoned his roots still lurked beneath the surface, but Isi always had a quick smile and teasing tone for Melatha—at least until White Hair came along.

Melatha allowed the emotion she harbored for the girl to surface. She toyed with it, weighing it against the hatred she felt for the one who took her father's life. Despite the years and the prayers to Chihowa Palami asking His help to forgive the man, the scale still tipped in favor of her father's murderer, but only by a feather.

The spirit of her father had risen to eternal rest, leaving an empty husk where once had been a lively, determined man. Emily hadn't thrust a knife in Isi's heart or cut his fingers from his hands for paltry trinkets, but she'd left him as cut off from Melatha as her father's stiffened body had been when she'd found him.

Some new thing had happened between the girl and Isi. Melatha watched him leave the bunkhouse before dawn that morning and knew. His body slumped in the circle of lantern light, his shoulders still bent beneath shame for what he'd done to Greta. But in the angry cluster of lines above his brows and the rolling motion of his jaw, Melatha saw frustration. And fury. Only one person had the power over Isi to exact such raw emotion.

Footsteps on the porch, not heavy enough to be his, roused her from her spiteful place. Her stomach churning from her bitter musings, she reached for Isi's unclaimed plate of food. "Come in, Jose. I have a nice breakfast for you again this morning." Irritated with the dawdling boy, Melatha crossed the room and swung open the door.

White Hair's head jerked up, dread dancing in her eyes.

Melatha stared, her jaw slack. Then the only words she found to say tumbled from her mouth. "What do you want?"

White Hair stood as straight as a pine trunk, the fear gone from her eyes. "I've come to ask for your help."

Melatha's arching brows pulled at her deep-set lids. "What did you say?"

"Isi must not confess to John Rawson. I need your help to convince him."

Melatha cringed. She'd called him Isi. Deliberately. Most likely to gain favor. "What business is it of yours? Or mine, for that matter?"

"I'm here on Greta's behalf. She asked me to talk to him."

Melatha folded her arms. "Greta? I don't believe you."

"It's true. Greta loves Isi. She asked me to help save his job."

"Then you should be speaking to my son, not me. I hold no sway over him."

The girl flinched at last. "He won't listen to me because he believes me to be someone I'm not."

Melatha's mouth parted and she drew a steadying breath. "Why should I help you?"

The blue eyes narrowed but she held Melatha's gaze. "Because I'm not who you believe me to be either." She paused. "And because—" Her chin went up and her chest swelled.

Defiance? Melatha didn't think so.

"Because your son loves me." White Hair stood taller, her shoulders back, not in defiance but pride, reveling in the knowledge of Isi's love.

Melatha's grandfather once told her to serve her enemies her best wines and savory breads. *"And thereby keep their minds too muddled to outsmart you and their bellies too full to chase you."* She pushed open the screen door. "Come inside. I have breakfast."

CHAPTER 26

In all the years Magda had known Bertha Maye Bloom, she'd never seen her so excited. Ready to trade her seat on the wagon for a pair of jeans, a rope, and a cattle horse, she had every intention of riding along to help herd her cattle to the Galveston, Harrisburg, & San Antonio Railroad depot.

It took some fancy talking by John to convince her to let him hire a handful of experienced drovers instead. He finally got her settled down when he explained that the men, two of them seasoned vaqueros, the other a little green according to John, were too proud to work under the direction of a woman.

Magda didn't know if John had told Bertha the truth or just outsmarted her. Either way, she sat tall in the rig beside Magda, a huge smile on her face as John and the three hired men drove her cattle into the stockyard to be loaded onto the train.

Bertha let out a whoop when the last cherry red set of stocky legs and white switch scrambled up the ramp and into the stock car. John had helped her hire a livestock handler to accompany the Herefords all the way to Humble where Willem had arranged for their delivery to Bertha's waiting pasture. And now, just as John had predicted, Bertha's satchel sagged a bit instead of straining at the seams.

She rubbed her hands together. "Most of them had no horns at all, Magda. Did you notice?"

Bertha's mood had rubbed off on Magda to the point where her cheeks ached from smiling. "I sure did, sugar. Ain't that something?"

Willem sat forward on the front seat and unwound the reins from the post. "That's what polled means—having no horns."

"Well, I like it," Bertha said. "And they have the prettiest white faces I ever saw. I can't wait to get home and start taking care of them."

Willem smiled back at her. "You'll be in Humble before you know it. All we have left to do is get John and his cattle back to Carrizo Springs then we can head north, if you gals are ready."

Magda stretched. "I'm sure ready. The Rawsons are attentive hosts, but I'm anxious to get that long, boring ride behind me."

John rode up on Faron, accompanied by the three drovers. "Willem, I'll be riding with Juan, Carl, and Benito to round up my herd. There's no reason for you folks to make that trek out to the ranch again."

He jerked his head toward town. "Why not kill some time shopping and seeing the sights? We'll meet up on the trail south of Fort Duncan in a couple of hours."

Willem saluted. "We'll be there, John."

John started to ride away then turned to shout over his shoulder. "Oh, and Willem. . .don't forget to buy feed for the stock." He shrugged. "Wouldn't hurt to buy a few extra rations, too. I fear it'll take a mite longer to return to Carrizo than it took us to get here. The livestock are sure to slow us down."

As they pulled out of the stockyard, Bertha tugged on Willem's sleeve. "You reckon we have time to say good-bye to Darius?"

He squirmed. "I don't know about that, Bertha. The mission is clear on the opposite end of town."

Magda cleared her throat.

"Then we'd have to drive from there to Fort Duncan," he said. "That's an extra half hour."

Magda cleared her throat louder.

Willem sighed and his shoulders drooped. "Of course, Bertha. I'll drop you and Magda at the mission while I tend to the supplies." He turned to aim a pointed glance at Magda. "But be ready when I pull up. We'll be cutting it close on time."

Bertha dropped the satchel on the seat beside him. "There are a few bundles of bills left in the bottom of this thing. Take it and use all you need."

He nodded and placed the bag at his feet. They pulled out of the G.H. & S.A. depot then turned off Quarry Street to Main, craning their necks as they passed the impressive Maverick County courthouse. It reminded Magda of a Spanish fortress. Or perhaps a royal palace.

There were so many shops along Main Street, Magda began to wish she'd kept her interfering nose out of Willem and Bertha's conversation. If Bertha didn't have her heart set on returning to the mission, Magda saw ample stalls and shops where a girl could spend a few dollars and an interesting couple of hours.

She repented of the selfish thought when they made the turn toward the Rian Street Mission and Bertha's face lit up like a harvest moon. Father Darius, well turned-out in far nicer clothes than the night before, met them on the street. "Dear Bertha, I'm overjoyed to see you again. I expected you'd be headed back to Carrizo by now."

Bertha climbed down from the rig and he kissed her hand. Blushing, and obviously too overcome with embarrassment to speak, she looked over her shoulder, her eyes begging Magda for rescue.

Magda followed her to the ground and waved Willem on his way. "My, but you're right duded-up today, Father."

This time he blushed. "Please, Mrs. Dane, call me Darius. I suppose I'm used to it from the men, but it doesn't sound quite right coming from a beautiful woman."

"I'll call you Darius if you'll call me Magda."

Still latched onto Bertha's hands, he smiled. "Magda it shall be. I'm glad you ladies caught me. Another minute and I'd be gone for the day."

"Are we keeping you from something?"

"Nothing too pressing. I'm off on a fishing expedition."

Bertha found her voice. "Fishing?" She looked him over. "Pardon me for saying, but that don't look the proper getup for wetting a hook."

"Ah, I can see how my attire might cause you confusion." He leaned closer to her face. "But you see, little Bertha, I'm casting for souls. A man can wear most anything in those perilous waters." He stood tall and preened. "In this case, the flashier the better. I aim to attract attention."

Magda smoothed his lapel. "You'll attract plenty dressed like that." The story came to her mind about the dandy who plied his bait on a green young boy bound for college, snaring Thad and reeling him into a poker game before he knew the hook had set. Magda smiled at the realization that Darius still used the same bag of tricks, only now the winning pot was redemption. She patted his shoulder. "So where are you trolling today?"

He shoved back his hat. "Actually, I was on my way to the Piedra Parada Saloon."

Bertha shot him a skeptical look. "A saloon?"

He gave her a tender smile and waved his arm behind him. "You think these men come to me?" He shook his head. "No, Bertha, I have to go out and find them where they are, whether a saloon, an alley, or a ditch."

Admiration shone from her eyes. "Just like Jesus did."

His smile said he liked her comparison. "I suppose you're right. And just like the men in Jesus' time—the deaf mute, the blind beggar, the leper—most men don't realize their real need until they see Jesus." He beamed. "That's my job. I make sure they see Him."

He offered his arm to Bertha. "Let me take you inside. My little office may be stuffy, but at least it provides shade."

Bertha took his arm and allowed him to usher her up the walk.

Behind them, Magda couldn't help but notice the change in her friend. Bertha held her shoulders back and her chin high. Her galloping gait had disappeared, replaced by delicate steps and an easy sway.

Astonished, Magda did a quick calculation on her fingers. Darius would only be a handful of years older than Bertha, six or eight at the most. Instead of a distinguished older man, Bertha must see him as an attractive and eligible suitor. The way Darius gazed at Bertha and hung on her every word, he had begun to think of himself in the same light. Suppressing a giggle, Magda followed them inside the mission.

The time before Willem arrived to collect them passed in a flash. Magda had little chance to contribute to the conversation, considering Bertha had no further need of rescue. She and Darius seemed lost in each other's company. Gazing tenderly across the corner of the desk, they reminisced about Thad, shared how he had affected their lives, and discussed the loneliness they'd endured over the years.

By the time the wagon pulled up loaded with supplies for the road, Darius held so tightly to Bertha's hands, Magda feared he'd never turn her loose. "It's time to go, sugar," Magda said softly, breaking the spell between them.

Bertha lowered her head and sighed. "I suppose it is." She met Darius's probing eyes. "We've got a long way to go before we see home again."

Darius scooted to the edge of his chair. "Bertha, forgive me for being forward, but our current situation demands it." His Adam's apple rose and fell. "Do you think . . .well. . .that Thad would mind if I saw you again?"

She flushed with pleasure. "Of course you'll see me again. We're partners in an oil well."

Darius shook his head, his face so lit from within that he glowed. "I'm not suggesting a business relationship, dear. I'd like to spend time with you on a more personal level."

Reminding Magda of a fresh young girl, Bertha flirted with her eyes. "I wouldn't mind that a bit, and I don't think Thad would either." She ducked her head. "Except we live so far apart. It's not like we can visit often."

Willem appeared at the door of the mission, his eyes searching the dimness. Spotting Magda, he waved impatiently.

"There's Willem, Bertha. Are you ready?"

Darius stood. "Magda, can you possibly give us a moment alone?"

"Of course, Father." She winced. "I mean Darius." Saying a hasty good-bye, she scurried out to her scowling husband.

"What's taking her so long? We're late now."

She took his arm and led him back to the rig. "Bertha's waited years for this moment, dear. We can give her a few more minutes."

Ignoring his puzzled frown, she rummaged through the crate of supplies he'd bought. "I hope there's something good in here. I'm hungry."

He reached beneath the seat and produced a short-sided box filled with wrapped sandwiches. "I figured you might be by now."

Clutching his face with both hands, she kissed him. "What on earth would I do without you?"

Blushing bright red, he spit and sputtered. Wagging his finger toward the warehouse, he changed the subject. "We're losing the time I thought to gain by eating on the road. What is she doing in there?"

Magda had already crawled onto the front seat and peeled back the paper on a fat turkey sandwich. She shrugged her shoulders and smiled, her cheeks too stuffed to answer.

Grumbling under his breath, Willem busied himself securing the load until the door opened and Bertha and Darius emerged.

With eyes only for Bertha, Darius bid them safe travel and stepped away from the rig as Willem pulled onto the street.

Each time Magda looked, Bertha still hung over the seat waving. When they turned the corner, she settled back and sighed. "The Lord is sure good at plotting and scheming, Magda. Here I thought God had me giving away something of value, and all the time He was intent on giving a priceless gift to me."

Willem nudged his hat aside and scratched behind his ear. "Can someone please tell me what's going on?"

Magda patted his hand. "I'll explain later, dear. For now, see how fast you can get us home."

John waited for them on the outskirts of the city, in a field a few miles past Fort Duncan. They were a remarkable sight from a distance, John and the men circling a sea of lowing red and white cattle.

"Jumping Jackstraws!" Willem exclaimed. "That's more than twenty head, or I need spectacles."

Bertha leaned between them. "There's nothing wrong with your eyes, Willem. John's done bought off the rest of that man's herd."

John waved at them then blew a sharp blast around two fingers and raised his arm high, signaling the drovers to start the restless animals moving. Cutting around the outer fringes, he spurred his horse into a gallop and rode up to meet them, his smile as wide as the horizon.

Whipping off his Stetson, he motioned behind him. "I got to picking the animals I wanted and couldn't stop." He dried his forehead and replaced the hat. "Got carried away, I think."

Bertha squirmed to John's side of the rig. "How many you got there, John?"

He shot her a sheepish grin. "Oh, fifty, sixty. I lost count after a while."

Bertha stood up to see them better. "Whoopee! That makes this a real cattle drive."

John laughed. "Well, close, little Bertha." He ran his hand along Faron's sleek neck. "I could've saved myself a few dollars back there. That rancher took quite a shine to this fellow. I think he might've made an even trade."

Willem jerked his chin at Faron. "I see who wound up with him, though."

John chuckled low in his throat. "Yep, I've taken a liking to the old man myself."

The distant shouts of the drovers turned John's attention back to the herd. Noting how fast they widened the distance lightened Magda's anxious heart. At that pace, they'd all be home the next day in time for supper.

John swiveled his head to speak to Willem. "A word of warning. With the larger herd, I felt the need to hire an extra hand."

Willem nodded. "I thought I saw four horsemen in the soup."

"Trouble is, in my haste, I let Carl, the young one, talk me into taking on his older brother. Fellow by the name of Wayne."

Willem squinted. "And?"

"Let's just say he bears watching."

"Not the fresh-faced innocent like his brother?"

John snorted. "Not even close. I'm glad I didn't bring along my daughter." He pinned Magda and Bertha with a look, his brow furrowed. "You ladies steer well clear of him, you hear? And if he does one thing to make you feel uncomfortable, just say the word. I'll send him packing."

Magda nodded solemnly. "You won't have to tell us twice, John."

He picked up his reins. "If you folks are ready, we'd better go. Looks like we have about four or five hours of good daylight left. We'll need every bit of that time to make it to the spot where we set up camp for the night."

Willem untied the leads from the post. "Head out. We're right behind you."

"Wait!" Bertha cried. Her head disappeared under the seat until she bounced up holding her prize. "Can't get started without this," she crowed, wadding the blanket beneath her and wiggling until she had it right. Satisfied, she waved them on.

As they rumbled across hard-crusted ruts at the mouth of the trail, so deep the wagon tossed them like water in a hot skillet, Bertha released a dreamy sigh. "You know, Magda," she said, holding on until her fingers turned white, "short of marrying Thad and birthing my Charity, this has turned out to be the happiest day of my life."

Smiling at the bliss on her face, Magda rested her arm on the back of the seat. "Is that so?" She winked. "How come I'm fairly certain you're not talking about cows?"

Diego rode outside the gate and stared toward the setting sun. Deep in thought, he rolled his head to ease the tightness in his neck and blamed his sudden shiver on the breeze that billowed the back of his shirt.

Something felt wrong. A hunch still too vague to put his finger on, he knew in the pit of his stomach that disaster loomed. They'd been gone too long.

His initial relief at putting off his confrontation with Mr. Rawson had given way to gnawing unrest. They should've made it to Catarina before nightfall the first day and home by the next, but it had been three days. He tried to convince himself that his boss had decided to show the countryside to his guests. Or that the Campbells, eager for fellowship, had detained them with a dinner party or a hunting trip. There could be any number of reasons for the delay, but Diego's gut hadn't bought any of them.

Neither had Kate Rawson's. Last evening, she'd stood on the balcony of her room staring down the road to Catarina, melded to the spot by her concern. The sight of her that morning, her regal profile in sharp relief against the orange-banded sky, had thickened Diego's throat.

Before long, she would come to him and ask him outright if he felt there was cause for alarm. He'd been rehearsing what to say to ease her mind. One thing was sure, if Mr. Rawson and his guests didn't show up by morning, Diego would go after them. He only prayed he'd find them dancing and feasting, surprised their absence had caused alarm.

He thought to seek counsel from Cuddy then realized he couldn't. A sudden ache swelled under his breastbone, a loneliness more keen than he'd ever felt before.

Even as a youth roaming his own personal wilderness, he'd always felt the presence of God. Now, alone in the darkest pit he'd ever fallen prey to, it seemed God had bid him farewell at the door.

Diego turned his horse. One person would still welcome him warmly—after she'd had her say. Well, so be it. The time had come to face his mother's wrath.

CHAPTER 27

Emmy strolled into the dining room and sat across the table from Cuddy.

Greta, who had followed her down the stairs, pulled out a chair opposite her startled mother.

"What a thoroughly pleasant surprise!" Mrs. Rawson said, a rosy flush tinting her pale cheeks. "I'm happy to see you both feeling better."

Rosita couldn't say the same about Emmy. She dropped the dish in her hand on the table with a hollow thud and a wobble, startling Mrs. Rawson.

Emmy boldly met Cuddy's shamefaced glance. "Greta and I felt it might be time things got back to normal around here. I believe we've both missed the fellowship." She shot Rosita a winsome smile. "Not to mention the bountiful spread." Rosita flounced away and Emmy prayed she wasn't in the kitchen poisoning her food.

Mrs. Rawson passed Emmy the breadbasket. "I'm so glad, dear. I hated that we were missing so much of your visit." She filled two tall glasses with lemonade and handed one to Greta. "And you're looking much better, too, darling. I'm so happy you decided to join us."

Cuddy and Greta exchanged quick glances. Cuddy's impudent grin and cocky sneer had gone, replaced by the sympathetic smile of a doting brother. Watching him, Emmy could hardly believe he was the same man who'd made such bold advances. Of course, sitting in the well-lit dining room with his mother in attendance must feel very different than riding alone with Emmy in the dark, his belly filled with liquor.

A swish of the swinging doors, and Rosita returned with the main course.

Mrs. Rawson filled heaping platefuls and passed them around the table. "Has anyone seen Diego this evening?"

Four sets of hands stilled and fours pairs of eyes lifted to her face. Watching her in silence, they waited.

Distracted, she quietly returned the ladle to the serving dish. "I'd like for him to come up to the house. I have something important I wish to discuss with him."

Rosita wiped her hands on her apron and scurried toward the kitchen. "I will go and send him word."

Greta scooted to the edge of her chair. "Mother?" Her trembling voice held disbelief. And fear.

Shaking herself free of her thoughts, Mrs. Rawson patted her daughter's hand. "Oh, Greta. Nothing so dire." She smiled sweetly. "I'm growing a tad concerned about the length of your father's visit to the Campbells', that's all."

Dread clutched Emmy's middle. She laid aside her napkin and smoothed her skirt. "You think there's a problem?"

Mrs. Rawson clutched the silky bow on her chest. "Forgive me, Emily. Here I go, causing you concern with my silly musings. I'm only thinking aloud, dear."

Emmy swallowed, but not Kate Rawson's explanation. The unease on the woman's face contradicted her words. "But you think they've been gone too long, don't you?"

Cuddy snorted and picked up his fork. The understanding brother gone, his expression more resembled the Cuddy Emmy knew. "I wouldn't waste a lot of worry, folks. They're having a high old time, so they're not ready to come back to this pretentious graveyard."

Mrs. Rawson flashed him a sharp look. "Cuddy! Mind your manners, please."

"Sorry, Mother." He lifted one shoulder and shoved in a huge bite of food. "I know Father, that's all," he said with bulging cheeks. "He's too busy to think about any of us here. His mind is occupied by playing the highfalutin ranchero for the Danes."

"Some bread, brother?" Her own cheeks turning pink, Greta tossed the roll at Cuddy's plate. It tumbled through his spicy *mole poblano* and landed in his lap.

He retrieved the mess with two fingers, a storm building on his face darker than the chocolaty sauce. "You did that on purpose."

Greta patted the corner of her mouth with her napkin. "Mother asked you to mind your manners, Cuthbert. I was merely trying to distract you from your disobedient display."

His movements slow and exaggerated, Cuddy dragged the soggy bread through his plate and held it up. "Allow me to return the favor."

Greta narrowed her eyes. "You wouldn't dare."

With a wicked grin, he tossed the roll across the table. It slid down Greta's chest, leaving a brown trail, then flipped off her bosom and landed in her waiting hands.

"Cuthbert Rawson!" his mother cried.

Greta reached for her plate, but Cuddy was quicker, upending his food in her lap.

Greta screamed and stood to her feet just as Diego cleared his throat behind them. He stood in the arched doorway, his hat in his hands. "You asked to see me, Mrs. Rawson?"

Kate Rawson couldn't speak. Her gaze hopped from Diego to the dark greasy stain on Greta's dress then to Cuddy, casually licking sauce from his fingers.

Cuddy jutted his chin at Diego. "Hungry, brother?"

Greta's face and the skin of her chest, the part not covered in savory sauce, turned a frightening shade of red. Gathering the soiled area of her skirt as best she could, she bolted from the table, managing to ball herself tight enough to shrink past Diego without touching him.

Just as embarrassed, Emmy wanted to gather her skirts and brush past him, too.

Mrs. Rawson turned her rage on Cuddy. "I'd like you to leave as well, son." Her low, even voice contradicted her flashing eyes.

From beneath her lashes, Emmy watched Cuddy push up from the table, in no hurry to obey. "I'd like to be part of this conversation, Mother."

"Well, you won't be. Good night."

He stood with his hands clenched at his sides. Sighing dramatically, he tried once more. "Greta started the whole thing–"

She whirled on him. "Do you see your sister at my table?"

They remained silent until Emmy could stand it no longer. She stole a glance at each of them.

Cuddy stared straight ahead, gnawing the inside of his cheek.

Mrs. Rawson gripped the tablecloth on each side of her plate, her knuckles like white cypress knots. "I feel taken advantage of, Cuddy. None of this would've happened if your father was home."

He looked at her with dispassionate eyes.

"John would be so disappointed in you."

Cuddy gave the chair behind him a vicious kick. It crashed into the wall, sending a picture frame sliding to the floor.

Rosita, her eyes wild with fright, peered through a crack in the kitchen door. In her distress, she laid aside her dislike for Emmy and questioned her with raised brows.

Emmy drew up her shoulders.

Barreling around the table, Cuddy roared by Diego, slamming into him with his shoulder as he passed.

In the stillness that followed, Emmy felt an urge to crawl beneath the table. She felt Diego's presence by the door as strongly as if he were sitting in her lap.

Thankfully, Mrs. Rawson broke the silence. She heaved a labored sigh and released her death grip on the lace cloth. "I'm appalled at my children's conduct. I hope you won't think this is usual mealtime behavior."

Emmy looked up to see whom she had addressed.

Diego didn't wait to figure it out. "I can come back later, Mrs. Rawson."

She lifted her hand. "No. Sit down, please." She gave a shaky laugh. "If you can find a clean chair."

The door burst open and Rosita charged out, all busy hands and dishcloths. She stacked the dirty plates and the charger filled with food on the sideboard then expertly peeled away the splattered tablecloth.

Passing on the empty chair next to Emmy, Diego waited until Rosita dragged Greta's soiled chair away from the table and slid a clean one in its place, the legs scraping loudly across the wooden floor.

Her voice deceptively calm, Mrs. Rawson bid Rosita forward. "Dish a serving of mole for Diego."

He raised his hand. "No thank you. I'm having supper with my mother."

"Very well, if you're sure."

"Yes, ma'am."

She made a feeble gesture toward the door. "I apologize for my children. I can't say why they behaved so atrociously."

He smiled. "You don't have to apologize to me."

Mrs. Rawson was silent for so long Emmy's gaze swung back to her. Studying her hands, the usually eloquent woman seemed to be fishing for words. She lifted troubled eyes to Diego. "Don't you think John should've been home by now?"

He cut his eyes to Emmy. She laid both palms on the table and lifted her chin. "I believe this concerns me, too. My parents are with him."

Diego lifted his brows at Mrs. Rawson.

"She's right, son. Besides, we're merely discussing at this point."

He nodded. "What would you have me to do?"

She picked up the napkin in her lap and twisted it as she stared at Mr. Rawson's empty chair. "I'm not sure we should do anything just yet. I don't want to fret prematurely. John detests when I fuss." She gazed at Diego with searching eyes. "What do you think we should do?"

His face unreadable, Diego fingered the rim of his water glass. "I decided if they weren't here by morning, I'd ride out and take a look."

She reached across the table and clutched his hands. "You're that concerned? I knew something wasn't right. I just knew it."

He opened his mouth to speak, but she drowned him out. "When will I learn to trust my instincts? I should've sent you last night."

"That might've been premature fretting, ma'am. Tomorrow's soon enough." He gathered her trembling fingers in both of his big hands. "Please don't work yourself up, Mrs. Rawson. I'm sure they're socializing or seeing the sights. Relax and get a good night's sleep. I plan to be on the road before dawn. By this time tomorrow, we'll all be pulling past the front gate."

She gave him a firm nod. "Good. Then I'll show that man of mine what it means to fuss."

Diego laughed low in his throat and squeezed her fingers.

Emmy had heard enough. "I'm going with you. What time do we leave?"

They turned together and stared at her.

Diego started to shake his head, but she held up her hand. "I mean it. I'm going."

He looked baffled. "Why? There's no reason."

She felt her eyes bulge. "No reason?" She pointed behind her toward the tall curtained windows. "Those are my parents out there with banditos and bloodsuckers!"

Mrs. Rawson pushed away from the table and came around to where Emmy sat. Wrapping her arms around her shoulders, she gave her a tight hug. "I've upset you with my foolishness. Trust me on this, Emily. Diego is a very capable young man. He'll find your parents for you." She raised her face to Diego. "And my husband for me. Won't you, dear?"

Diego stood. He put on his hat, then jerked it off again and held it to his chest. "Yes, ma'am. I'll find them and bring them home."

Mrs. Rawson straightened. "That's all, dear. I won't keep you from your supper. If Melatha's food is ruined, you may blame it on me."

He started for the door. "I'm sure it's fine. Good night, Mrs. Rawson."

"Good night, son."

He ducked his head at Emmy but didn't call her name.

She gave an answering nod, and then he was gone.

Mrs. Rawson patted her arm. "Do you need anything else before you go up to your room?"

"No, ma'am. Thank you."

"Then I hope you'll excuse me. I'm suddenly very tired."

Her heart in her throat, Emmy caught Mrs. Rawson's hand before she pulled away. The poor dear's heaviness had little to do with fatigue.

Giving Emmy's fingers one last squeeze, Mrs. Rawson glided from the room with a swish of her skirts.

Rosita entered from the kitchen.

Emmy stood and pushed in her chair. She risked a chance. "Good night, Rosita."

The tall, slender woman smiled and nodded. "El *muerto* y el *arrimado a los tres* días *apesta.*"

Having no idea what Rosita said but pleased with her gracious manner, Emmy tilted her head and returned her smile warmly. "Very well. Thank you, and I'll see you in the morning."

She heard Cuddy laughing before she made it to the stairs. Staring at him perched on a step midway up, she put her hands on her hips. "What are you doing sitting there? And what's so funny?"

He cocked his head. "I'm sitting here because I had as much right to hear that little discussion as you did." He grinned. "I'm laughing because Rosita just told you that corpses and annoying guests stink by the third day." He chuckled merrily. "And you thanked her."

She put her hand to her forehead. "Oh, my. I'm firmly on her bad side, and I don't know how to change it."

Cuddy's smile vanished. "Am I firmly on your bad side, Emmy?"

Her heart flipped. She knew she should be furious with him, but he reminded her too much of herself before that fateful day when she allowed God to come in and change her. She raised her eyes to his pleading gaze. "I only wish you'd stop being so naughty. You really upset your mother tonight. And Greta." She gave him a penetrating look. "You're not going to tell Greta's secret, are you?"

He looked surprised. "Over a skirmish with mole poblano? Of course not. Besides, it wouldn't be in my best interest, now would it?" He patted the step beside him. "Come sit with me."

She caught hold of the banister and pulled herself even with him. Before she sat, she aimed a warning finger. "Have you been drinking?"

He held up his hand. "On my honor, I'm as parched as a crusty cow patty."

She laughed and eased down beside him. "Oh, Cuddy, you're incorrigible."

He smiled and took her hand. "So you forgive me for my stupidity? I swear I only wanted a kiss. I didn't mean to scare you."

She stared at her feet, trying to work up her nerve. When she felt she could speak the truth, she confronted him. "But you did scare me, Cuddy. I know it would never have happened if you'd been sober. This tells me you simply must stop drinking."

Sneering, he drew back. "Don't tell me you've banded with the abstinence club?"

"I'm sorry, but they're right. It's obvious alcohol alters your judgment. I can't help but wonder what might've happened had Diego not come along."

He stiffened. "You don't need Diego to defend your honor from me."

"I did last night."

He shook his head. "You only thought you did. Which is my fault, and I accept the blame." A brooding shadow crossed his face. "Diego's another matter. He should know me better."

Emmy jumped at the sound of a door closing somewhere in the house.

"Don't worry," Cuddy said. "That's just Rosita leaving for the night." He rubbed his hands down the front of his trousers, not the first time since his food fight given their stained condition. "I suppose I'd better get cleaned up then find a place in the bunkhouse to lay my head. Sounds like I have an early start ahead of me."

"An early start?" She studied his profile. "Cuddy, you're not thinking of going with Diego?"

He met her gaze. "Not thinking—my mind's made up." Determination burned in his eyes. "Diego doesn't know it yet, but I'm going."

Her heart skipped. "Then you're worried, too?"

He shrugged. "Call it insurance. I have to keep my old man alive until I prove myself to him." His boyish features hardened with determination. "He's planning to go to his grave disappointed in me, but I'm not giving him the satisfaction."

Melatha's heart soared with joy at the familiar sound of Isi's boots hitting the porch. She whispered her thanks over folded hands and turned at the counter, ready to greet him. Certain her fervor reminded God of the parable of the persistent widow in Luke's Gospel, she also repented for wearying Him.

Isi stood on the threshold, his hat in his hands, as if hesitant to press on without an invitation.

His contrite manner pierced her heart. She smiled sweetly and motioned him in. "Good evening, son. Are you hungry?"

He ducked his chin, but his eyes burned into hers. "You wouldn't happen to have a pot of mole poblano, would you? I've developed a sudden urge for some."

Already turning to lift the lid on her kettle, she paused. "Mole? No mole, son. Only–" She was hesitant to admit what she had to offer him instead–pounded corn boiled with beans, a traditional food of the Choctaw.

He dropped his hat on the hook and approached the table. "Is that Tafula I smell? Even better."

Sighing with relief, she ladled a large bowlful and set it in front of him. Isi blew on a bite then took a taste from the end of the spoon. He nodded vigorously. "Very good, as usual."

Melatha's joyful heart swelling like the breast of a dove, she grinned at him. "You say the same every time. I find myself starting to doubt you."

Her chest deflated in a rush of shame when he halted mid-bite and laid down the spoon. She hurried to him, enveloping him with her arms from behind. "Stop it now, Isi. I will never really doubt you." She gave him a shake. "You know this."

He reached back to wrap his arm around her neck, drawing her closer. "I'm so sorry, Mother. I promise not to disappoint you ever again."

She laughed against his ear. "An impossible promise to keep. A mother's expectations are unreasonable." She swung around to kneel at his feet. "You will disappoint me many times if you're to live your own life." Her brown eyes bored into his. "It doesn't mean I won't worry, but I have to allow you to make your own mistakes, whatever the cost. I see this truth now."

His brows crowding together, Isi took hold of her arms. "Wait a second while I catch my balance."

"Your balance?"

"Yes, Mother." His eyes darted to the floor. "It seems the ground has shifted beneath my feet. Did I just hear Melatha Marcelo telling her son to live his own life? What happened to bring about this change?"

She lowered her gaze. "The old teacher is still teachable, I suppose."

He placed his big hand on her head then let it slide until he held her cheek. "You show me such respect after I've ruined both our lives?"

She pressed his palm to her face and shook her head. "But you haven't ruined our lives."

His eyes bulged. "When John Rawson finds out—"

She patted his roughened hand and stood to her feet. "He cannot find out, which brings me to the one mistake I can't allow you to make." She slipped into the chair opposite him and passed him his spoon. "Eat your supper, son, while I tell you about a very important visitor I had today."

CHAPTER 28

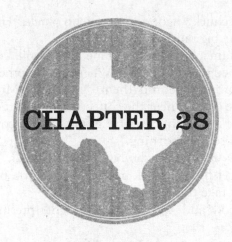

Magda awoke groggy and stiff. Her joints were sore and her patience at its limits. She groped for Willem's face to pinch his nose, determined to stifle his infernal snoring.

Her searching hand came up empty. Startled, she turned over in her bedroll.

Willem sat on a log near the campfire talking to John and Bertha. The real culprits responsible for the relentless bellows and moans that had invaded her sleep meandered nearby grazing.

Magda had marveled at how fast Benito, the lead vaquero, had constructed several lean-tos of forked sticks, ridgepoles, and cowhides. As long as Willem stretched out next to her, she'd slept beneath their shelter warm and comfortable. Only after he'd slipped away did the chill of the bare ground seep into her bones.

She wondered how Bertha had managed, sleeping in her bedding alone, and suspected it was the reason her bony friend huddled near the campfire with a cup of coffee in her hand.

Benito and Juan, the *segundo*, which meant second-in-command according to John, appeared from the rear of the wagon bearing an iron skillet and other supplies to make breakfast. John and Willem scooted aside to make a place for them near the fire.

"You cook, too?" John asked. "I didn't know that was a part of our bargain."

"Sí, señor," the slightly weathered Juan said, smiling. "For many years, I ran the chuck wagon for un rancho *grande*." He smiled toward Willem. "A very big ranch."

John gave him a broad smile. "Fine, fine. You'll be an asset to this trip." He frowned toward Benito. "Where are the other two fellows?"

Carl cut around behind them. "I'm here, Mr. Rawson." He squatted on the ground near the coffeepot and poured himself a cup. "Wayne will be along directly." He grinned. "His covers don't want to turn him loose this morning."

Accepting a refill from the boy, John frowned. "That won't do if we hope to get this livestock moving. I need you two to prowl the herd before we take them down to the river."

Benito stood and trotted out of sight, presumably to roust Wayne.

Bertha, her timing unfortunate as usual, peered around Willem to where Magda rested her head on her propped arm, listening to the conversation. "Speaking of turning loose of your covers, when do you plan to haul yourself up?"

Groaning when all eyes turned her way, Magda sank lower in the bedroll.

"There's fresh coffee here, sugar. And this nice Juan has camp bread and eggs in the skillet."

As nonchalantly as possible with six pairs of eyes glued to her, Magda unraveled herself from the lean-to and ambled to the fire. Beaming up at her, Bertha moved over and patted a spot on the log. "Morning, sunshine. It's been right tough going without you to light our way."

Magda nudged her. "I'm happy to see you in such good spirits. I think."

A bedraggled Wayne staggered toward them. His puffy eyes, slack mouth, and rumpled hair made him look as if he'd tied on a drunk the night before. He attempted to squat next to his brother, but lost his balance and fell on his backside instead. Rubbing crusted matter from his bloodshot eyes, he elbowed Carl and pointed at the pot. "I hope you saved me plenty of that muddy water. I need it something fierce this morning."

Benito signaled to Carl, who stood reluctantly. "Let Wayne find his own coffee. You and I will ride the herd then take them to drink."

Carl's face pulled into a frown. "But I ain't had me no breakfast yet."

Already headed for his horse, Benito didn't bother to answer. Wayne chuckled. "Don't worry, Carl. I'll eat yours for you."

Juan glanced up from his task. "There will be plenty, young man. You may eat when you return."

Carl stomped away like a pouting boy.

John, his jaw working, regarded Wayne. "If you want meals from now on, I expect you to show up groomed and on time. If not, you can find your way back to Eagle Pass. Understood?"

Sullen at first, Wayne put on a false brightness and saluted John, a guarded challenge in his eyes. "Yes, sir, boss." Snickering, he grabbed the plate Juan was handing to Bertha and sat back to dig in.

Bertha and Magda shared a look of disgust.

Maybe for the first time in her life, Magda was relieved to see a meal end. As delicious as the unexpected breakfast turned out to be, Wayne's presence spoiled her appetite. She didn't relax until they'd broken up camp and were on their way, with the coarse Wayne riding out in front of the herd and far away from the wagon.

"He's no good," Bertha announced beside her, reading her mind.

"We can't say John didn't warn us." She patted Bertha's hand. "Don't worry. The men can handle him. Soon we'll be well shed of him."

Bertha didn't look convinced. "I wish John *would* send him back to Eagle Pass. He's trouble. I can smell it."

Magda laughed. "Maybe you caught the scent of his unwashed body. My gut says he's not one for practicing good hygiene."

Bertha whipped her head around. "No fooling, Magda. I'm having one of my feelings."

"Oh, Bertha. . ."

"Don't make fun. I told you they're from God."

Magda crossed her arms. "All right, then. What would God have you to do about Wayne?"

Bertha shrugged. "We didn't get that far."

The sun hadn't yet risen high enough to be seen, just enough to lighten the eastern sky to a watery gray. A pale, fading moon hung low over the horizon, and a few of the brightest stars were still visible.

Despite the lack of piercing rays, sweat already pooled on Diego's top lip, meaning the day would be a scorcher.

He spotted the rider tailing him before he'd gone a quarter mile from the house. Little Pete had no reason to be following him so slyly, nor did any other man on the Twisted-R spread—except for Cuddy.

Making a mental note to teach him the art of stealthy tracking, Diego turned his horse and ambled toward him.

Cuddy must have realized Diego spotted him because he picked up his pace and met him halfway.

Diego circled and fell in beside him. "Good morning. Going my way?"

Cuddy crossed his hands over the saddle horn and grunted. "I see it's true you have eyes in the back of your head. Has anyone ever slipped up on you?"

"Greta." Wishing he hadn't brought her up, Diego cut his eyes to the ground. Would it ever seem natural to speak of her again? "Twice, in fact."

"Makes sense. She has years of practice from spying on me."

Diego had to smile. "You'll never catch me off guard, that's for sure. You track like a marauding grizzly." He lifted one brow. "I don't have to ask why you're here, do I?"

Cuddy raised one shoulder. "Who knows? I'm not even sure myself."

The day dawned at last, and they stared toward the sunrise in silence. Diego released the breath he'd held and looked at Cuddy, one side of his freckled face bathed in yellow light. "I wanted to talk to you about this trip before I ever spoke with your mother, but—"

"But you thought it might be bad form considering you so recently pummeled my head?" Cuddy leaned in the saddle to stress his point. "Over something I didn't do." His guarded eyes lifted. "Remember when we talked about Greta's purity, and you said you didn't believe I had to ask?"

Diego nodded grimly. "I do. I also remember you saying you wanted to believe me. That you wanted to, Cuddy—not that you did." He jerked his chin as if Emmy stood there. "How can you compare what you did to Emmy with what happened between me and Greta? From what I saw, it wasn't exactly the same."

Cuddy dashed his quirt on his leg, startling the horses. "How could you see anything? It was pitch black."

"I didn't need to see to know Emmy wanted it to stop," he

sputtered, faltering for words. "Cuddy. . .I heard her begging you."

If Diego had slapped his face, Cuddy couldn't have looked more startled. He pulled back on the reins, the shock in his eyes fading to dazed remembrance. "She did beg me. I remember now." He closed his eyes. "That's what Emily tried to tell me last night. That I scared her."

Diego stopped his horse, too, sympathy for his troubled friend welling inside. "I know you didn't mean to frighten her. You'd had too much to drink."

Cuddy gnawed his bottom lip. "That's not a good excuse, is it? Not if I hurt someone as wonderful as Emily." He nudged his horse to move again and they picked their way across the plain in brooding silence.

Cuddy seemed deep in thought, and Diego prayed he might come to the right conclusions about his life.

They'd gone quite a way before Cuddy spoke again. "What time did we leave the ranch?"

"Around six thirty."

"What time is it now?"

Diego studied the sky. "I'd say pushing eight thirty. At this clip, we'll be at the Campbells' before lunchtime." He glanced at Cuddy. "That means they'll clear a place at the table."

Cuddy grinned. "I wouldn't mind skipping lunch and going straight for Mrs. Campbell's sweet pecan bread."

Diego groaned. "Considering we have miles yet to go, it's outright cruelty to mention that bread so soon." He rubbed his stomach. "Especially since I left too early for breakfast."

"And Melatha let you get away with that? Better check your pockets. She's sure to have corn cakes stuffed inside."

"That may be wishful thinking on your part," Diego teased, but he patted them just in case.

Grateful they'd lightened the mood, Diego kept the conversation going with a joke he'd heard in the bunkhouse and telling a prank he'd played on Little Pete.

Just when he felt easy with Cuddy again, the simpleton opened his mouth. "Are you planning to tell the old man about Greta?"

Diego's shoulders drooped. Squinting in protest of the topic, he glanced at Cuddy. "I've had a curious parade of people ask me not to tell, with Greta at the top of the list. I'm still trying to decide what's right."

Cuddy pushed back his hat, eagerness to drive home his point evident in the deep lines of his brow. "I'll march in that parade, friend. I say don't tell." His anxious eyes studied Diego. "You said you were trying to make up your mind about Greta. If she turns out to be your choice, you don't want to rile the old man."

Diego shifted in the saddle. Time to tell the truth. "I made up my mind about Greta, Cuddy. If I marry your sister, it'll be for all the wrong reasons. And for all the wrong people."

Cuddy's eyes lowered to the high grass between them. "That's a shame. I always hoped you'd wind up a legitimate member of the family."

Diego stared wordlessly at Cuddy, the question he wanted to ask stuck in his throat.

Cuddy smiled and looked away. "I know what you're thinking. I guess I'm part *loco* to want you hanging about when my father prefers you to me. Shoot, to hear him talk, you're more his son than I'll ever be." He shrugged. "But I'm used to having you around, brother. In fact. . ." He chuckled. "I think you'll get a kick out of this. My hope that you'd marry my sister is the main reason I've tried so hard to steer you clear of Emily."

Diego gawked at him. "Are you saying you don't really care for Emily?"

"Care for her?" Cuddy wrinkled his face. "Sure, I care. I'm just not in love with her." He tilted his head. "Don't get me wrong, she's a real looker, but Emily's turned out to be a friend. A good friend and I don't want to mess it up." He winked. "Not that I wouldn't kiss her if she gave me the chance."

Finding not a speck of humor in Cuddy's last sentence, Diego shook his head to clear his muddled mind. Unsure what to do with the information, he fingered the rawhide riata notched in the groove at the base of his saddle horn while his heartbeat settled down.

Sobered, Cuddy cleared his throat. "The thing is, she won't be giving me that chance because. . . Actually, amigo, I'm fairly certain the only one Emily Dane wants to kiss is you."

Diego's head snapped around so fast his neck cracked. "Me?"

Cuddy nodded.

"But you must be mistaken."

Finding it impossible to think straight, Diego opened his mouth to ask more questions, but Cuddy's gaze flickered and he waved a greeting. "Eyes front. We got company."

Diego glanced up, relieved to see that friendly faces had gotten the jump on them and not strangers. Lester and Joe Campbell rode toward them at an easy canter.

Lester raised his hand to the sky as they approached. "Diego! Cuddy Rawson! What brings you out this way?"

Diego and Cuddy closed the distance between them, reining in a few feet from the beaming brothers. Relieved to see them smiling, Diego knew it foretold good news about Mr. Rawson and his guests. "We've come to bust up the party," he said, already dreading the exasperated look on his boss's face. He'd have to dream up a good excuse for butting into his good time and hauling him back to his waiting wife. "Where are you two headed?"

"Actually, we were on our way to the Twisted-R," Lester said. "Little brother here's been riding me real hard to drop everything and go see the ranch. We thought today was a good day." He chuckled and scratched his head. "Don't tell me you're headed for our place. That'd be a downright silly coincidence."

The slight crowding of Joe's eyebrows to the center of his forehead was Diego's first clue that things were not as they seemed. "Did you mention a party?" He looked offended. "If there's a party, someone left us off the guest list."

Diego smiled, trying to ignore the tension building in his stomach. "Not an official party, Joe. I'm referring to whatever shenanigans have kept Mr. Rawson and his guests at your place for the last few days."

The furrows in Joe's forehead deepened, matched by those in Lester's. Joe shook his head. "Ain't nobody staying at our house."

Cuddy sat forward in his saddle.

Diego swallowed against the growing knot in his throat. "When did they leave?"

Confusion clouded Lester's eyes. "There's been some sort of misunderstanding, friend. We haven't seen them."

Joe tilted his head. "I told my pa you thought your boss would stop by, but he never showed. We figured it for a mix-up."

Cuddy fired Diego a panicked look.

Diego's every muscle tingled with an urgency to spur his horse and ride. But where? Where did one look for a vanished wagon filled with people?

Joe leaned to peer at him. "You all right? You've gone pale around the mouth."

Understanding dawned on Lester's face. He nodded at Cuddy. "Sorry, old boy. Is there anything we can do?"

Out of fear and concern for Cuddy, Diego lashed out. "You can stop planning a funeral. We'll find them. . .alive and well."

Lester ducked his head. "Sure thing, Diego. Of course you will."

Ashamed of his outburst, Diego released a long breath. "I'm sorry, Les. Just keep your eyes peeled, won't you? If you run into Mr. Rawson, tell him the folks at the house are getting worried."

With no time or patience left to dawdle, Diego wheeled away from them and headed back the way they'd come.

Cuddy was fast on his heels and soon caught up. "Where are you going?" he cried. "We have to look for them!"

"It would take us days to cover any ground. We have to organize a search party, starting with the men on the ranch. But first we need to borrow fresh horses from Señor Boteo."

"What?" Cuddy vigorously shook his head. "There's no time for that."

Diego set his jaw. "It'll save time in the long run. At the pace I intend to keep, these two will drop from under us in this heat." In no mood to argue, he ignored Cuddy's sputtering and pointed his horse due south.

Settling into the idea, Cuddy stared toward the Boteos' modest house, corrals, and outbuildings in the distance. "Knowing my father, he could be anywhere, couldn't he? It would never occur to him that his actions might be irresponsible or cause Mother to worry."

"Anything's possible."

Cuddy watched him closely. "But you don't believe it, do you?"

Trying to comfort Cuddy with the intensity of his resolve, Diego leveled him with a determined look. "We're going to find them, Cuddy. The hard part will be explaining to your mother and Emmy why we haven't already."

CHAPTER 29

About the time Magda figured her stomach would collapse, John whistled the signal to Benito to turn the herd toward the river. Willem followed until John rode close to the wagon, fatigue lining his face. "Pull up into that clearing by the bank, Willem. We'll take a little break. I know I could sure use a rest."

Willem obliged, reining the team and setting the brake.

Magda studied John's chiseled features. "You all right, John? You look a mite peaked."

"I'll be fine, Magda." He swiped his arm across his chin. "But I shouldn't be driving you folks so hard in this heat. I figured if we pushed a couple of hours past noon, we could rest during the hottest part of the day."

Willem fumbled for his pocket watch. "It's two o'clock on the dot."

John smiled weakly. "Stay up under the shade of the surrey, ladies, until we call you for lunch. There's nothing for you to do. Juan's setting up now to cook." His gaze jumped to Willem. "Unless they'd like you to walk them down to the river for a splash of cool water on their faces."

Bertha squirmed on the seat. "That sounds more like it. I've got a pressing need to climb down from here for a while."

"Take that with you," John said, nodding at the Marlin.

Willem hoisted the loaded rifle. "Will do."

Juan looked up and waved as they passed the spot where he'd dug a pit and started a fire.

Bertha glanced back at Magda. "Feels strange not to be the one in charge of vittles. Makes me feel guilty." She chuckled. "But just a mite."

They followed what appeared to be an ancient trail leading down to the river. Passing between walls of bushes on each side, they dodged overgrown branches and grasping vines until the path opened out onto an overhanging shelf. Willem held each of their hands and eased them onto the sun-crusted ledge that butted up to the lapping water about two feet down.

Squealing, Bertha kicked off her shoes. "Turn away, Willem. I'm going in to wade."

"You be careful, Bertha," Willem said anxiously. "Don't slide down or step in a hole."

Laughing like a youngster, she stomped in. "Come on, Magda. It's warm on top but cool on the bottom."

The cool part was all Magda needed to hear. She held onto Willem for balance and pulled off her shoes. Clutching roots protruding from the bank near a fallen tree, she held them to steady herself while she lowered her bare feet one at a time. Laughing when mud oozed between her toes, she called to Willem. "Roll up your britches and join us, dear. It's very refreshing."

Her husband stood staring downriver to where the vaqueros watered the herd. The cattle drank at the river's edge, their heads bowed together. Their contented moos echoed across the water like old men clearing their throats. Willem shaded his eyes. "Where's that Wayne fellow? I haven't seen him since we stopped."

Bertha raised her leg and kicked, the top of her foot scooping a shower into the air to rain down onto the surface. "Maybe we got lucky and he hit the road."

Magda lifted her hands as a shield. "Stop that splashing, Bert. You're worse than a kid."

"Leave me be. I'm making sure no snake crawls up your dress."

"You can stop fretting about that. With all your ruckus, no clever snake is within miles of here."

Bertha froze and dropped her hem. Her eyes wide, she nodded behind Willem. "You're right. Just sorry, no 'count, sneaky snakes."

Magda whirled in time to see Wayne's leering face retreat into the brush. Releasing her own skirt, her feet made loud ploinking sounds as she high-stepped to the bank. "Willem!"

He spun, alarm in his eyes. "What's wrong?"

She pointed, her finger shaking. "That nasty Wayne. Skulking in the bushes to get a peek."

Willem wasted no time heading for the steep rise.

"Don't hurt yourself, dear. He's already gone."

"Get out of the water," he shouted over his shoulder, the only sign that he'd heard her at all.

Magda rushed to obey, her anxious eyes trained on Willem's back as he struggled to make the high step to the area above. "Be careful with that rifle, now!"

The top of his ears blazed red, and his panting desperation to be about the chase frightened her. Mentioning the gun flashed terrible possibilities across her mind. "Just catch him and let John handle this," she called as he fought his way up the incline.

He managed to get one leg atop the short cliff then leaned forward to haul the other foot up. As he pushed to his feet with the gun still in his hand, the dirt at the edge crumbled, and he lost his balance. Frantically pumping his arms was not enough to hold him up—especially when the gun went off. He sailed backward, seeming to hover briefly in midair before he landed headfirst on the trunk of the dead tree.

Magda's cry and the sound of gunfire roused the men downriver. With shouts and waving hats, they thundered into the water and raced toward them. By the time they reached Willem, Magda hovered over him, patting his cheeks.

Tossing modesty aside, she lifted her hem to bathe his face with the cool water, her tears preventing her from seeing him clearly. "Open your eyes, dear. Willem, please. Open your eyes."

John crowded up next to her. "Move aside, Magda. Let me have a look at him." He slid his hands beneath Willem's head to lift him gently from the trunk then paused, his eyes going to Magda's face.

She tensed and her stomach sank. "What is it, John?"

John raised his hand to have a look.

Magda's eyes jerked to the blood oozing between his fingers and dripping onto the ground. Her own screams impossibly loud in her ears, she stumbled backward into darkness.

Emmy slammed her fist against the table. "I'm coming with you, Diego. Don't try to talk me out of it this time."

They hovered around the dining table, a sobbing Greta with her head in her stricken mother's lap, Cuddy behind them with his hands on Mrs. Rawson's shoulders, and Diego standing behind Mr. Rawson's chair, gripping the ladder back with white knuckles. "I'm sorry, Emmy. I can't let you go."

She stood, shaking. "Let me? You can't stop me."

Mrs. Rawson lifted her head. "Tell me again what Mr. Boteo said."

Diego swept past Emmy as if she wasn't there. "He said Santos, his grandson, saw your husband's wagon headed southwest, away from Catarina and Carrizo Springs."

She stared with hollow eyes and her head swung side to side. "It makes no sense. There's nothing in that direction but the river." She glanced up at Diego. "Could they have been going after water?"

Cuddy patted her shoulder. "The river is miles out of the way, and the brush is too thick in that region to cross easily."

She wrung her hands. "Then why? Why would John drive a wagon filled with special guests to the middle of nowhere and disappear?"

Looking less than sure of his confident words, Cuddy smoothed her hair. "Don't fret, Mother. We'll find them if we have to turn over every blade of grass from here to Mexico."

Emmy took Diego's arm and turned him. "We're wasting time. It'll be dark soon."

He flexed his jaw. "Get it through your head, Emmy. You're staying here."

Fury made her dizzy. She stared boldly into his flashing, determined eyes. "For your information, I'm not in the habit of taking orders, and I don't intend to take any from you." She lifted her chin and sniffed. "The truth is I don't need your permission. Mrs. Rawson will help me."

She pulled out a chair across from Cuddy's mother and perched on the edge. "Ma'am, I'm very good on a horse, and I can find the business end of a gun. I'm a decent shot, and I know how to defend myself." She reached for Mrs. Rawson's hands. "This is not even the first manhunt I've been on. Why, back home—"

Diego pulled her chair around and leaned on the arms, so close to her face she felt the warmth of his breath. "It's a ridiculous notion. Who will watch out for you?"

"I can take care of myself."

He shook his head. "A woman will only slow us down." Letting go of her chair, he walked away a few paces, dismissing her.

Emmy stalked to him, pointing behind her at Greta and Mrs. Rawson. "I'm not like—" Catching herself before she said something hurtful, she dropped her arm and amended her words. "I'm not the weak, fragile female you make me out to be. I'm different, Diego. You should know that by now."

He gripped her shoulders hard, grit in his brown eyes. "Yes, you're different. I can't deny it if I try. But you're not a man, Emmy. What makes you think you can keep up with a man's business?"

"I can answer that." The quiet voice behind them spun Diego. Melatha stood under the arched doorway, her arms crossed over her chest. "Emmy can keep up because she has your same spirit, Isi."

She nodded at Mrs. Rawson. "Forgive me for coming unannounced, Kate. I just heard."

Mrs. Rawson held out her arms. "Oh, Melatha! I'm so frightened."

Melatha swept across the room, two thick braids dangling from the back of her head. She gathered Mrs. Rawson and pressed her cheek against her forehead, speaking low in a language very different from Spanish. Emmy realized she was praying in her native Choctaw.

Cuddy left his mother to Melatha's care and started for the door. "Come on, Emily. I'll show you what to pack."

Relief flooded Emmy's limbs. Smiling warmly, she took his arm. "Thank you, Cuddy."

He winked. "Greta will sort out our rations while we get things ready in the barn. There's no telling how many days we'll—"

"Hold up there." Diego took her other arm as she passed, stopping her in her tracks. "Nothing's been decided yet."

Mrs. Rawson interrupted from where she sat. "Let her go, Diego. It's her right to choose."

Confusion and rage battled in his eyes. He frowned at each sullen face. "So I'm outnumbered here?"

Their silence gave him the answer.

"Very well, Miss Dane. You'll have your way, I see." His threatening glare scared her more than she dared to let him see. "Just remember. . .I won't allow you to slow us down a single second from finding Mr. Rawson and your family. When you get into trouble—and you will—I won't lift a finger to save you. Not even from banditos and bloodsuckers."

Magda scrambled away from Bertha's grasping hands and pulled herself upright. Hastily spread and bunched beneath her, the blanket that had cushioned Bertha's behind for miles now cushioned her from the rocks and stubble. She looked around, noting the wagon and the campfire, heard the lowing cattle in the distance. She blinked up at her friend. "What's going on, Bertha? How'd I get here?"

Bertha pointed. "Those poor men carried you. It wasn't easy getting you up that ledge, I can tell you that much."

The terrible memory came in a rush. Magda's jaw dropped as a scream welled in her throat.

Bertha clamped a hand that smelled of mud across her mouth. Her eyes brimming with tears, she wagged her head back and forth. "It's all right. Willem's alive, Magda. He's hurt, but he's alive."

Magda struggled to her feet, looking around in a panic. "Where is he? I have to see for myself."

Bertha led her to the wagon.

The men had shoved aside boxes and crates to make room for Willem's squat body in the bed. He lay so pale and still, it took Magda's breath.

She clutched Bertha's hand. "Are you sure he's alive?"

Bertha nodded. "John said so."

"Is he. . ."

"Gunshot? No. We found the nub of a broke-off limb covered in blood. It poked the back of his head when he fell on that tree."

Magda drew in a ragged breath. "But that's even worse."

"Worse than taking a bullet in the brain? Not by a long shot, if you'll pardon the pun. John said he likely has a concussion, though, since he won't wake up."

Magda moved around closer to Willem's ghostly white face. "You mean he hasn't regained consciousness one time?"

Bertha shook her head.

Growing more concerned by the second, Magda raised up to scour the area. "Where is John?" she asked frantically. "Why aren't we rushing Willem to a doctor?"

"John jumped on that fast horse of his and said he'd fetch a doctor to tend Willem right where he lays."

Magda stared. "A doctor from where? We're miles from Eagle Pass."

"He said we passed a little community called El Indio a few miles back. He thinks there may be a doctor there."

"And if there's not?" Alarm made Magda's voice shrill.

"Don't borrow trouble, sugar. John won't let us down."

"Señora?"

Juan's gentle voice startled Magda so badly she jumped. Staring at his dark, weathered face, the realization struck. John had left Magda and Bertha alone with four strange men, Benito, Juan, Carl, and the terrible Wayne, with Willem as lifeless as a turnip.

"You should eat, ma'am," Juan continued, his eyes aglow with compassion. "Keep your strength up for your husband."

She raised her hand. "Food's the last thing I want just now, thank you. I should be doing something to help him."

Bertha gave her a gentle shake. "There's nothing you can do, sugar. John and the men made sure he's comfortable. He'll call out for you when he wakes up." She took hold of Magda's arm. "Come sit down and eat a bite."

Clinging to the rail, Magda dug in her heels. "No. I'm staying right here until John gets back with the doctor."

Juan motioned for Benito and Carl. The three of them cleared more space in the wagon then helped Magda climb in beside Willem. Only after she'd settled against the backboard clinging to his fingers did she accept a tortilla filled with shredded meat from Juan. The first bite tasted like dirt and refused to go down, so she handed the food off to Bertha when Juan wasn't looking.

Wayne was nowhere in sight. His brother Carl leaned against the tailgate, staring at the ground and idly chewing the end of a stick.

Bertha, who had crawled up to sit at Magda's feet, watched him with wide eyes. "Say, where'd that brother of yours run off to?"

Carl drew up his shoulders. "Can't say. I was just wondering the same. He was here when we stopped, but I ain't seen him since."

He grinned, flashing a mouth full of yellow teeth. "Wayne's like that, you know." He made a sweeping motion with his hand. "Disappears with the wind and then blows right back." Laughing, he ambled to where Benito and Juan sat on the ground in front of the fire.

Bertha made a face. "I'd just as soon the wind had carried him off for good, at least until John gets back."

Magda set her mouth grimly. "Not me. I hope he blows back just long enough for me to claw his eyes out."

Bertha patted her hand. "I'll hold him for you, honey."

CHAPTER 30

Diego stared in wonder at the number of riders clustered on the road in front of the house. Word had spread throughout the county, thanks to Rosita and Little Pete. Friends and neighbors had gathered for the last hour, eager to do anything to help the kind and generous Mr. Rawson. Even Joe and Les Campbell showed up to offer their time.

Diego tightened the horsehair girth and tied his leather quirt to the saddle. Luckily, these were tasks he could easily perform in his sleep, since his willful eyes were busy tracking Emmy's every move.

The soft clingy dresses and skin-revealing necklines were gone, along with the strappy suede shoes with little square heels. She wore men's clothing, complete with Cuddy's shirt, baggy slacks, and cowhide chaps buttoned behind her legs. Someone had even furnished her with a wide-brimmed straw hat. Only her boots were made for a woman, most likely lent by Greta.

Cuddy hovered like a bee on honey, helping Emmy with her rigging and double-checking her gear. Afterward, he mounted up and rode alongside her toward the entrance to the ranch.

Remembering the feckless boy's declaration that he'd kiss her if she'd let him, Diego slapped shut the flap on his saddlebag with more force than called for. Whirling, he nearly ran over his mother.

She gazed up at him with knowing eyes. "It's not like you to pout, son."

He brushed past her to gather his reins. "You're mistaken, Mother. I don't have time to pout."

She caught his arm before he swung onto the horse. "There's nothing between them, Isi."

Astonished, he met her probing eyes. "Your talent for reading minds has spread to Emmy and Cuddy now?"

She shrugged. "Emmy's too much woman. She won't wait for Cuddy to mature."

He gave her a piercing look. "You champion her now? Exactly what did that girl say to you?"

"Matters between women are best left to women."

He blew air from between his teeth and swung into the saddle. "On that point you won't get an argument from me. Still. . .Emmy managed to change your heart in one visit?"

His mother tilted her face, using one hand to shade her eyes from the afternoon sun. "She's a very persuasive girl."

He held up his finger. "Ah, there, you see? Careful, Mother. I'm not sure her powers of persuasion are from God." He reined the horse away from her.

"That remains to be seen," she called out behind him, "and this is Emmy's chance to prove it."

Laying to rest the idea that his mother could no longer surprise him, he stored away the confusing conversation for later. The time had come to turn his thoughts to the pressing matter at hand.

Anxious riders surrounded him outside the gate, all trying to speak at the same time. He held up his hand and whistled, and they stilled. "One at a time, please." He pointed to Little Pete.

"Sí, Diego." Pete sat taller in the saddle. "Where do we search? Around Catarina?"

"Well, Pete," Diego said, dreading the faithful hand's reaction, "you won't be searching anywhere. I need a man I can rely on to stay behind with the women."

Pete's countenance fell. "Sí, if you think it's best."

Diego's gaze took in the crowd. "As for the rest of you, I thought we'd split up. They were seen heading southwest, but the truth is, they could be anywhere. One group of riders will sweep in a wide circle around Catarina to the right, another to the left. The largest group will spread out in a line straight up the middle. We should all wind up near the road to San Antonio."

"And if we don't find them?" one of the men called out.

"We'll widen the circle."

He whistled again to quiet the murmuring reaction. "Let me make one thing clear, I'm not coming back without Mr. Rawson and his guests. Any of you who can't say the same, please stay home. I can't have you pulling out later, leaving your group short of men."

Another round of discussion followed, this time interspersed with nodding heads and vows of commitment.

Since Señor Boteo knew the area, Diego appointed him to head the Rio Grande search. He put Lester and Joe in charge of the opposite half of the circle. Diego and the rest would form the middle line.

Displaying the order and quickness of those accustomed to making fast decisions, the men and horses divided to Diego's specifications with the grace of a Spanish dance. Not waiting to be assigned, Emmy trotted her horse next to Diego's, her jaw set and her gaze fixed straight ahead.

Diego couldn't contain a stab of satisfaction when the seasoned ranchers and vaqueros stared at Emmy with disbelieving eyes. Forcing himself to contain his anger when their eyes lingered a bit too long, he thrust his arm out in front. "All right! Let's ride!"

Melatha watched the cloud of dust on the road until it dwindled to a faint puff on the horizon. Her thoughts turned to prayer for the men. *"How excellent is thy lovingkindness, O God! Therefore the children of men put their trust under the shadow of thy wings."*

A sense of foreboding had settled on her the minute Isi rode out of sight. She told herself the sinister slide of cold hands up her back had to do with her fear for John Rawson and grief for his dear wife. Yet watching Isi lead the solemn band of men toward the road to Catarina was the hardest thing she'd ever done.

An urge to cut and run welled inside her, though from what, Melatha did not know. She whispered a prayer for her son instead. "Keep him safe, Chihowa Palami. As the apple of Your eye, hide Isi beneath the shadow of Your wings."

She pulled her gaze from the empty road and hurried toward the house. The kitchen would be in chaos, so Rosita and the girls would need her. When the searchers returned, whether celebrating around a wagon heralding the prodigals' return, or—she shuddered—mourning behind a wagon in service as a funeral bier, they would be hot, tired, and hungry. There was no way of knowing if they had hours or days to prepare.

Melatha pictured Kate Rawson's drawn mouth and tortured eyes. She prayed for her sake the wait would end soon.

Emmy followed Diego and Cuddy off the road into an area thick with briars, brambles, and mesquite trees, more afraid than she'd ever been in her life. At the beginning of the last few torturous hours, she had tried to search apart from them, to prove herself to Diego, until an encounter between a rattlesnake and a startled horse left an experienced horseman hugging a cactus.

The boots Emmy wore were so big her toes slid forward with each step of the horse, causing pain so intense she feared finding her feet covered in blisters. The heat was atrocious, even with the sun dipping closer to the earth. Her hair hung in dripping strands beneath the hat, but taking it off meant having her head baked.

Now the same sun that seemed determined to bake her alive looked ready to bail out on her. Her heart crowded into her throat as the last bright orange sliver dropped into a deep pocket on the far horizon, and the vivid watercolor landscape became a child's charcoal sketch on gray paper. Even a cluster of yellow green fireflies bobbing and dancing in the brush failed to cheer her.

No matter how awful things were, she knew the nighttime would be worse. She also knew no matter how frightening the darkness, she'd never be sorry she came. To be stuck on the ranch harboring dreadful thoughts of her parents' predicament would be hard to bear alone, and Emmy had never felt so alone in her life.

Letting her guard down briefly, she explored the murky cauldron of fear that seethed inside—a mistake considering Mama's smiling face swam into view, blinding her.

"You all right over there?"

Diego's voice startled her but soothed her, too. More grateful for his presence than she'd ever let on, she hurriedly wiped her eyes. "Oh, yes. I'm fine." Even to her ears, she didn't sound fine. Her stuffy, nasal tone gave away her tears.

Diego's horse cut in closer. "We'll find them, Emmy."

She shuddered, startling herself. "I. . .I know we will. But no matter how I arrange the facts, it doesn't make sense." She sought the comfort of his brown eyes. "If you have a theory to share that ends with a positive outcome, I'd be grateful to hear."

He glanced away quickly then back. "I'd love to say something to comfort you, but I'm afraid I'm struggling with the same questions. The explanation I cling to is Cuddy's—that Mr. Rawson is somewhere 'playing the highfalutin ranchero' for your parents, having too much fun to spare a thought for home."

She let his words sink in before she spoke. "Then where are they? They were headed to the Campbells'. Why didn't they make it?"

Staring into the distance, he blew out his breath. "If we had those answers, we'd be home in our beds tonight."

His words brought another involuntary shudder.

Diego shot her an anxious look. "That's the second time you've done that. Are you feeling all right? You can't be cold."

"I'm the furthest thing from cold." She gave him a tight smile. "To be honest, I haven't looked forward to nightfall." Her smile turned sheepish. "It's a lot easier to be brave in the light."

Amusement flashed in his eyes. To his credit, he squelched it. "Don't fear the darkness, Emmy. My mother taught me to see the lessons God intended when He created night and day."

Emmy raised her brows. "Lessons?"

He nodded. "Nighttime represents the fall of man and how God mourned when sin separated Him from His children. Daytime points to His forgiveness and our restoration."

She stared, amazed by the simple truth. "I've never heard that before."

He smiled. "There's more. The Choctaw believe that man can read the salvation story in the earth's four seasons."

Mesmerized, she studied his face. "The seasons?"

He held up one finger, citing Melatha. "Summer represents the time when Jesus walked the earth with man. Fall signals the death of summer and the death of Christ. Leaves begin to die and hang from their branches, drenched in gold and crimson. Fall represents the beauty of a blood-drenched King on a cross."

The breath caught in her throat. "Diego, that's incredible."

"Winter is the tomb," he said, his eyes closed. "A time when hope seems lost. Sap stops flowing. Plants and leaves decay. Animals stumble into hibernation as dens become graves. Creation is in mourning and mimics His death." He opened his eyes. "Spring is a portrait of hope. Green buds, rainbow flowers, daisy yellow chicks, and lily white lambs tumble off God's palette in a celebration of new life. The least subtle season, spring flaunts our risen Savior and begs us to see." He smiled. "And there you have it."

"That was the most beautiful thing that I've ever heard," she breathed.

"It's a fair translation. Better in the original Choctaw." He shrugged. "I've heard it so many times, it loses its charm. . .until I see it again through the eyes of someone else." He smiled sweetly and nodded at her. "Like now. You're glowing."

It felt good to laugh. "A reflection of my heart, Diego. Thank you for sharing that with me. It brought me great comfort and took my mind off things for a while."

He grinned. "My pleasure."

Cuddy had slipped up beside Emmy. "What are we sharing, and where's my part?" he demanded with his usual charm.

Leaning past Emmy to see him, Diego snorted. "Nothing I haven't offered you a dozen times before."

"He was reciting his mother's lessons for me," Emmy said. "About the seasons."

Cuddy rolled his eyes. "Oh, yes. Winter is death and all of that drivel. Aren't you two depressed enough?"

Diego shared a glance with Emmy. "We were feeling better until you came along."

Cuddy flashed a grin. "Nonsense. I bring light and joy wherever I go."

Diego groaned and waved his hat at an approaching rider. The man trotted the rest of the way and pulled up alongside them. "We'd better decide where we want to rest and water the horses. About another hour is all I'd want to push them."

Diego glanced at Emmy. By the skeptical look on his face, he was thinking an hour was all she could take, too. He turned to the man. "We're almost to Buck Campbell's place. Spread the word that we'll pull in there."

Exhausted, Magda dozed, waking up each time her head lolled to the side. She awoke for good to find the surrounding brush alive with the sounds of approaching nightfall. Filled with dread, she willed with all her might for John to ride out of the shadows on Faron, a doctor close on his heels.

Straining to see Willem's features in the last faint traces of light, she scooted around to lay her head on his chest. His torso rose and fell too fast and his heart beat in time with the crickets. She'd been trickling water into his mouth in small amounts so he wouldn't choke, and she thought he might have swallowed some.

Lifting her head, she peered into the crowding darkness. Benito and Juan lurked nearby speaking Spanish in hushed voices. Her eyes on them seemed to make up their minds, and they sprang into action, scurrying to set up camp for the night. Carl hopped from one to the other, trying to keep up with the orders they barked.

Beside her, Bertha swatted a swarm of mosquitoes from her face. "We need to pull our beds closer to the fire tonight. Might help to keep these infernal pests away."

Frustration threatened to smother Magda. "Stop it, all of you!"

Bertha stilled. The men paused mid-stride and gaped at her.

"Stop making camp. We won't be spending the night here." Tears stung her eyes. "John Rawson will ride up any minute with that doctor. Then we'll be taking my husband home."

Benito bowed. "Sí, Señora Dane." Shoving his hands in his pockets, he shrugged at Juan and sat down in front of the fire.

Bertha nodded at the men. "We'll wait just a while longer, if you fellers don't mind." Patting Magda's leg to soften her determined words, she added, "If he's not here soon, we'll have no choice but to go to bed. I suspect there's a long day ahead for all of us."

CHAPTER 31

Diego rode toward the Campbell ranch glowing with pride, thinking about the eternal lessons he had just shared with Emmy. For the first time he understood that his mother's people were his Christian ancestors, those men and women whose decisions to follow Jesus Christ were the reason Diego knew Him. The proud swell in his chest turned to shame as he realized they were the same ancestors he had fought so hard to deny.

The lights of the Campbells' two-story, plastered-stone house beckoned in the distance. Standing against the dusky sky, it was a welcome sight. Diego was happy to see the end of the driveway, but no happier than his backside and the horse he sat. In some ways, Mr. Boteo's Spanish mare had it better than Diego. She'd only made the trek to Catarina once that day.

Buck Campbell stepped onto the porch as they arrived. Squinting and twiddling his bushy moustache, he surveyed the large group of men as if trying to put a name to every face. His gaze came to rest on Diego. "Any luck?"

Diego dismounted, glad to be on the ground. "No, sir. Not yet."

The man ducked to scan the riders again. "My boys with you?"

"No, sir. They're with a party of searchers somewhere north of here. We've come in hopes of taking advantage of your hospitality for a bit. I've got some tired men and thirsty horses."

Mr. Campbell nodded. "Fine, fine. You get those animals tended then come to the house. The missus will be waiting with coffee and something hot to eat."

He turned to go, but Diego held up his hand. "That coffee sounds good, but there's no need to put Mrs. Campbell to any trouble. Most of the men have trail rations."

He gave a curt wave. "Nonsense. A man can't beat the brush all night on trail rations."

"Sir, I've got better than twenty men out here."

He chuckled. "That's when a slew of daughters comes in handy. Won't take them girls no time to fix your men something." He pointed a warning finger. "So come back up to the house. You hear?"

Diego grinned. "Will do."

He started to go inside again, but Diego cleared his throat. "Mr. Campbell?"

"Yes?"

Diego walked to Emmy's horse and helped her down. "Would it be too much trouble if Miss Dane here freshens up inside?"

Under less trying circumstances, Mr. Campbell's bug-eyed stare would be amusing. "That is a female! I was thinking she was the prettiest fellow I ever did see." He laughed wildly. "Sure, she'll clean up inside." He offered his arm to Emmy. "I won't have no little gal splashing off in a watering trough."

Feeling more protective than he had the right, Diego handed her off to Buck Campbell. His restless men meandering behind him, Diego stayed rooted to the spot until Emmy disappeared through the door.

Cuddy sailed his hat over his horse, hitting Diego in the chest and almost startling him out of his chaps. "Peel your eyes off Emily and help me get these horses watered."

He frowned at Cuddy. "Sí, amigo. I'm coming." He took the reins of the big mare and started for the barn, deliberately tromping on Cuddy's hat as he went.

By the time the last horse had cooled then drunk its fill, Mr. Campbell's womenfolk had a table pulled out to the veranda and covered with food. Exhausted, dusty men settled wherever they could, whether the steps, the edge of the porch, or the ground. They ate quietly. Most, like Diego and probably Cuddy, were disturbed by the fact they'd found nothing.

The back door opened and Emmy stepped out, her eyes wide and searching. Spotting Diego and Cuddy, she lit up then pressed past the table to join them on the porch, limping and wincing with every step. Diego sat up straighter. "What happened to your feet?"

She eased herself carefully to the porch and swung her legs to the ground. "Greta's boots are too big for me. They've rubbed blisters."

Without waiting for permission, he pulled her foot across his knees. "That won't do, Emmy. You'll wind up with an infection." He pulled on the heel and the boot slid right off. "No wonder. Knitted stockings. Look how thin they are." He craned his neck behind him until he caught Mrs. Campbell's attention. "Could we trouble you for a pair of thick woven socks?" He glanced at the size of her foot. "Make that two pair."

Emmy struggled to pull her leg down. "Diego, please."

"No arguments. This will make all the difference."

She sat quietly while he carefully peeled the silky material away from the balls of her feet. He flinched at the angry red skin, but only the side of her big toe had a small watery bump. "It's not as bad as it could be. We caught it in time."

Mrs. Campbell dangled the socks across his shoulder, one pair red, the other a faded blue. "These do?"

"Oh, yes, ma'am. And I'll make sure these are returned," Diego said, gently slipping them on Emmy's feet.

"Washed," Emmy added, but Mrs. Campbell had already rushed inside for more clean plates.

After Diego felt satisfied with the fit of her boots, he brought her a plate piled high with bacon, eggs, and flapjacks, evidently the fastest meal the ladies could prepare with such short notice.

Emmy dug in like she'd not seen food in days.

Cuddy leaned against the corner post with his arms crossed, silently watching. If Diego happened to glance at him, he'd wiggle his brows or widen his eyes.

Diego was ready to thrash him when one of the younger Campbell girls approached Emmy and shyly held out her hand. "Some ladies from the church have organized a prayer circle for your folks in the parlor. Mama said you might care to join them."

Tears sprang to Emmy's eyes. She took the small hand in hers, and with a backward sniff at Diego, disappeared inside the house.

He spun on Cuddy. "What's all the foolishness with those faces? If you have something to say, come out and say it."

Cuddy held up both hands. "Don't mind me. I'm just doing a little speculating, that's all."

"About?"

"Just noticing you being extra accommodating to Miss Emily. Makes me think you might step between her and a goat sucker after all."

Diego blew out a breath in disgust. "Aren't you ever serious about anything, Cuddy?" He pointed past the outbuildings. "That's your father somewhere out there. Don't you care?"

Cuddy leaped up and stood over him ashen-faced, his hands balled into fists. "You know I care! And don't you act like you care more." His eyes rimmed with red and a haze of tears blurred his eyes.

Ashamed, Diego gripped his clenched fist. "I'm sorry, Cuddy. I had no right."

Resembling one of Mother's young students, Cuddy snuffled and wiped his nose on his sleeve. "Just because I don't wear my feelings in plain sight don't mean they ain't there."

"I know, amigo." He stood and gave Cuddy a hearty pat on the back. "I hope you'll forgive me. It's been a long day."

Mr. Campbell left his station on the porch where he'd been sitting all evening and took a seat on the top step. "So Mr. Rawson was on his way here, you say? Several days ago?"

Diego spit out the stalk of grass he'd been chewing and nodded. "Yes, sir. I told him you had some cattle for sale."

He stuck out his bottom lip and angled his head at Cuddy. "You Rawsons looking to expand your stock?"

The poised son of a South Texas rancher again, Cuddy lifted his chin. "Nah, we're happy with what we have."

"Mr. Rawson's inquiries would've been on behalf of a guest to the Twisted-R," Diego provided. "A wealthy woman from Humble, a little town north of Houston."

Mr. Campbell nodded. "I've been through Humble once." He rubbed his chin. "What do you make of them never arriving, Diego? Beats all I ever did see."

"That it does, sir. But we'll find them. You can bet on it."

"I know you will, son." He glanced toward the barn. "Tell your men to mind their tackle. We have a problem with blue rats around here. They'll gnaw your stuff to bits by morning if they find it on the ground."

Diego nodded. "Yes, sir. I'll tell them."

They talked a bit longer, and Diego tried to answer his questions the best he could, but the horses were rested and the men were getting too settled.

A clutch of solemn-faced women filed out the back door, and Diego stood to face the scattered men on the porch. "Like it or not, gents, the time has come. Let's wind things up here and get back on the trail."

His gaze darted over to the ladies. Mrs. Campbell noticed and hooked her thumb toward the house. "The poor dear is stretched across the bed in the guestroom fast asleep. Still crying, she was. I spread a blanket over her."

Diego nodded and made a quick decision. "You mind if I leave her where she is for now?"

Hands clasped in front of her apron, Mrs. Campbell solemnly nodded. "I think it would be a shame to wake her."

Cuddy sighed. "I don't know, Diego. Emily wants to look for her folks, and I don't blame her."

Diego placed a hand on his shoulder. "I don't either, but she'll sleep until we get back. If we have her parents with us, she'll be happy. If we don't, she can spit and spew while she helps us search some more, but at least she'll be rested."

Cuddy nodded. "You have a point." He grinned. "I mean besides the one on your head."

Diego slapped him on the back, probably too hard. "Come on, then. Let's go find your father."

Magda was ten years old again, running along the windswept bank of Big Cypress Bayou. Her matted curls streamed behind her head as she dodged crawdad mounds and cypress knees.

Bertha gave chase, her head tossed back and her mouth wide with laughter. As they ran, the mists rising from the bayou darkened, enclosing them in thick, black froth.

Two figures appeared–Thad, Bertha's long-departed husband, and Willem, smiling sweetly. A brilliant beam swirled from them in a rush, penetrating the haze and stabbing Magda's eyes. She frantically tossed her head to get free of the piercing light.

Bertha shook her shoulder. "Wake up, sugar. With all that thrashing about, you must be having a dream."

Magda sat up in the wagon and squinted against the sun's rays. "Gracious! What time is it?"

"I don't know. Well past dawn, that's for sure. We must've slept like the dead."

Magda's gaze shot to Willem and her heart plunged. "Oh, Bertha. I think Willem might be."

"Might be what?"

"Dead."

Bertha's head swung around. "Why do you say a thing like that?"

"Because I saw him in my dream, standing beside Thad in a mist."

Bertha moved faster than Magda thought possible and pressed her ear to Willem's chest. After a moment, she raised her head. "Nope. Still ticking."

Running her trembling hand over his hair, a lump formed in Magda's throat. "He's still out, though. I don't think he could sleep this long and be all right. Do you?" She wrung her hands. "Where in the devil could John be with that doctor?"

Bertha lifted one hand. "Hush a minute." Looking scared, she pushed to her knees, listening carefully. "Magda, why's it so quiet?" Standing, she spun in a circle. "Where on earth are the men?"

Magda held one hand over her heart. "What do you mean where are they? Stop that. You're scaring me."

Bertha shaded her eyes and stared toward the cattle, grazing much farther away than they'd been the day before. "I'm afraid it may be time to get scared." Her face as pale as Willem's, she blinked down at Magda. "There's not a soul here but us, sugar. We're all alone."

CHAPTER 32

Miss Emily?"

Emmy whirled toward the sound, nearly falling off the bed in her haste. Fully dressed and tangled in covers from the waist down, she lay in a strange bed in a strange room staring at a lovely young woman she'd never met.

Her heartbeat swelled in her chest until it frightened her. "Where am I?"

A little brown-haired girl with big eyes peeked from behind the young woman's skirt. "We're the Campbells, ma'am. Don't you remember?"

The picture of a small hand tucked in hers flashed through Emmy's mind. The prayer circle. The search party. Mama and Papa.

Struggling against the covers, she swung her legs to the floor. Her stormy gaze flashed to the square of light around the window shade. "They left me?"

"You were sleeping," the little one announced.

"Hush, Racheal. Let her get her bearings." The older girl approached cautiously. "I'm Margaret. The oldest. Please, call me Megan. I hope you slept well"—her sweeping hand took in Emmy's boots and clothes—"despite all that."

Staring dully, Emmy brushed unruly strands of hair from her eyes, but static from the blue blanket teased them into the air in wriggling strands. "I can't believe Diego left me." She lifted her eyes.

"Did he say anything?"

Megan pointed at the bed. "May I sit?"

Emmy nodded and slid to the side.

"Diego felt there was no reason to wake you. He said if you were that exhausted you needed to rest."

Little Racheal jumped when Emmy slapped the side of the bed. "He had no right. It should've been my decision to make."

The door creaked open and four more sets of curious eyes peered from the hall. Megan stamped her foot. "Stop all that sneaking about and say good morning to Emily."

The girls filed in like obedient stair-steps, each a bit taller than the next. With their hands behind their backs, they curtsied one at a time in the order of their height. In other circumstances, Emmy would've been charmed.

The tallest came forward. "Morning, ma'am. I'm Samantha. They call me Sami."

"And I'm Lauren," the next one said. "Named after my uncle Laurence. I fetched you for the prayer circle. Remember?"

They were all blond, but the girl standing next to last had hair as white as Emmy's. "My name is Emily." Her cherry red mouth parted in a self-conscious smile. "Same as you." She picked up the last tyke in line, a curly-topped angel. "This here's Layla. She's four."

A bedraggled Mrs. Campbell appeared in the doorway, one hand holding a stack of folded clothes, the other over her heart. "Heavens! I see you've all disobeyed me. I asked you not to make pests of yourselves." She smiled gently at Emmy. "You must be hungry. You've slept right though breakfast, but I've kept a plate warming for you."

Emmy fought through her bitter disappointment to find her manners. "Thank you, ma'am. I suppose I am."

"I've got clean clothes here for you. Megan's about your size." She laughed. "Wouldn't have been last summer, but she hit a growing spurt." She pointed at Emmy's feet. "And two pair of fresh socks."

"Oh, I couldn't impose."

"It's no trouble at all. We're glad to help."

Waving her apron like a matador, Mrs. Campbell swept her brood of girls from the room. "All right now, let's go and leave our guest some privacy." She turned at the entrance. "I'm sorry they descended upon you before you'd barely opened your eyes. They meant no harm, just curious."

Emmy nodded. "Of course."

"Take your time, dear," she said before easing the door shut.

Alone with her thoughts, Emmy mulled over how Diego could possibly have betrayed her trust. After the way he'd so tenderly ministered to her the night before, she thought he'd accepted her need to be part of the search.

She struggled to free herself from the pesky cover that wound around her lower body. Jerking the last persistent corner from under her bottom, she dashed it to the floor.

A pan of warm water and a clean towel awaited her on the dressing table, so she freshened up the best she could without a way to clean her teeth or brush her knotted hair. Rinsing the former and combing her fingers through the latter, she made a note to herself to pack her toiletries the next time she dashed off on a search party.

Her eyes flickered away from her image in the mirror. The flippant thought shamed her. Too much was at stake to find humor in any part of the situation.

She changed clothes then washed her tender feet before pulling on the socks and dreaded boots. With a heavy heart, she headed down to the Campbells' kitchen, but not before folding the blue blanket and placing it on the end of the bed.

It wasn't hard to find her way. The chatter of little girls led her into an open, cheery room lined with bright yellow shelves. Mrs. Campbell hovered over a pan of dishes–washing while Megan, the oldest, dried. Fair-haired Emily, who shared Emmy's name, plied a broom on the kitchen floor. Lauren on the left and Sami on the right, if she remembered them correctly, bent over lessons at the table. Racheal and Layla sat on the floor scribbling pictures on a sheet of paper.

Emmy cleared her throat. "Good morning."

All eyes in the room swung her way. Little Racheal's forehead creased. "We already said that."

"Hush!" her mother said, pulling out an empty chair for Emmy. "I know these eggs have turned to rubber. I'll fix you fresh if you'd like."

Emmy waved her hand. "No, ma'am. These are fine."

Seven pairs of eyes followed the track of her fork to her mouth. Her cheeks warming, she pressed her napkin to her lips and swallowed.

Mrs. Campbell drew in a sharp breath, breaking the trance. "All right, ladies. Back to your own business. Let Miss Emily eat in peace."

They quickly obeyed, Megan to her dishcloth, Emily to her broom, Layla to her drawing, and the middle two returned to their studies. Only pot-bellied Racheal stood clinging to the side of the table, staring at Emmy with wide brown eyes.

Emmy tore off a bite of bacon and tucked it into the child's mouth. She blinked, her long lashes sweeping close to her cheeks, and then she beamed like a ray of sunshine and opened for more. Together, they had the plate nearly clean when Emmy heard the unmistakable sound of approaching riders.

She stood so fast she had to reach and steady Racheal before running to the window. Her heart crowding her throat, she whirled. "It's them. It's Diego."

The girls scrambled to their feet, all talking at once. Mrs. Campbell spun from the counter. "Do they have your parents?"

Anticipation coursed through Emmy's body, and her hand clutched her throat. "Oh, Mrs. Campbell. I don't know." Weaving past the inquisitive little girls, she burst out onto the porch, hope so strong in her heart she felt faint.

Followed by Cuddy and the Campbell brothers, Diego rode into the yard and came to a stop near the porch. One look at his drawn, dejected face as he dismounted gave Emmy her answer before she asked. Her parents were still lost.

Diego lowered his eyes. He couldn't bear Emmy's air of lost hope. For the last ten miles of grueling, spirit-busting trail, he'd prayed to stumble onto Mr. Rawson and her parents so he could return rejoicing instead of bearing bad news. One look at her told him he'd be spared speaking the words aloud.

Head down, she ran to him. He opened his arms, ready to comfort her, but she rammed him instead, her fists pounding his chest. "Why did you leave me? I could've done something."

Diego pressed her closer. "No, honey. You couldn't succeed where eighty men failed."

She pushed away from him. "Where is everyone? Where are the rest?"

He tensed and swallowed hard. "I sent them home."

She gaped at him. "How could you do that? We haven't found them yet."

Catching hold of her wrists, he lowered her to the porch and sat beside her. "They were spent, Emmy. We've covered miles of the roughest country in South Texas. I had to send them home before I lost most of them."

He put his arm around her shoulders. "But I won't give up, I promise." He lifted his chin at Cuddy. "Neither will Cuddy. We plan to sleep for a couple of hours then head back out."

"I'm going with you."

He pulled her close and smoothed her hair. "We'll talk about it."

Mrs. Campbell stood on the threshold holding back the screen door. Lester crossed the yard and glanced up at her. "Where's Pa?"

"He's been at it all morning, covering for you boys." She waved her dishcloth. "Don't worry about that now. Tend all these horses, then eat something and go to bed. You can take over his chores this afternoon."

Diego took off his hat and peered up at Mrs. Campbell. "We're grateful for their help. I hope it hasn't caused too much trouble."

She smiled down at him. "What are neighbors for? We're glad to—" Her gazed jumped from Diego to something behind him. "Look." She pointed. "There comes a rider."

Cuddy jumped on the porch and shaded his eyes. "Coming fast, too."

Diego joined him. "Can you see who it is?"

"No, but I know that horse. It's Little Pete."

Emmy flew to her feet. "Little Pete? You don't suppose he has good news?"

Diego glanced at her. The tone of her voice was hopeful, but her unease and the way she asked the question said she was afraid to get her hopes up too high. Diego tried not to add fuel to the fire. "Relax, honey. It could be about anything. Something's always going wrong on a ranch."

Cuddy leaped down. "Whatever it is, we're about to find out."

The three of them hurried to meet Little Pete as he drove the frothing horse into the yard. Cuddy reached him first. "What's wrong, Pete? Has something happened?"

Looking past Cuddy, his eyes full moons, Little Pete sought Diego's face. "Señor! He's come home!"

Joy surged in Diego's chest. "Mr. Rawson? He's home?"

Emmy squeezed between them and clutched the front of Pete's shirt. "And my parents, too?"

Shock registered on Little Pete's face. "No, no, Señorita Dane." He pushed her aside and stalked to Diego. "Not Mr. Rawson, señor!" His hysterical voice was shrill. "Faron! Faron's come home without a rider."

White-faced, Cuddy jerked his gaze to Diego.

Emmy spun, desperately clinging to Diego's shirt before she crumpled. Grief-stricken, Diego picked her up and carried her limp body to the house.

CHAPTER 33

Terrified, Magda clung to Willem's lifeless hand. Her eyes darting at every sound, she prayed for John to ride up on Faron telling her everything would be fine. She prayed for Benito, Juan, even Carl to saunter out of the brush. Tightening into a ball in the rear of the wagon, she prayed for God at least to bring Bertha back from where she'd gone.

More than half an hour had passed since she'd announced she was going to scout out their situation. No matter how hard Magda begged, the spunky little woman had wriggled to the end of the wagon bed and dropped off the end. "Stay here," she'd ordered, as if Magda had anywhere to go. "I've got to try and sort this out."

Magda tried to busy herself with caring for Willem, wiping his face and trickling more water into his mouth, but she grew more frightened with each passing second. Shuddering, she imagined the dried-up shells of men scattered somewhere nearby, drained of every drop of blood by a sharp-fanged beast.

If Bertha had fallen into the clutches of whatever was picking them off, she and Willem were next. Glancing around, she scoured the wagon for a weapon, but all she had at her disposal were Bertha's crates from the mercantile.

She broke into the two nearest boxes and groaned. No matter how imaginative Magda was, she couldn't devise a way of using child-sized bloomers or hardtack to fend off a carnivorous animal thirsty for her life's blood.

The third box held more promise. She took a quick count of the contents, wondering how long she could hold off a bloodsucker with twenty cans of beans.

"This ain't no time for filling your gut."

Nearly swallowing her tongue, Magda drew back and threw.

Bertha ducked and the can sailed over her head, bouncing off the trunk of an oak tree with a dull thud. She peeked over the wagon bed with astonished eyes. "Did you just throw a can of beans at me?"

Limp, Magda fell against the backboard. "I reckon I did."

"What possessed you?"

"Something with fangs, I think."

Bertha stood up straight. "What?"

"Never mind. What did you find out?"

"I found out we're alone, all right. There's no trace of those men." She pointed. "Except for their things. Juan even left his cooking pots behind." She shook her head. "Why would they go with only the clothes on their backs and leave two women to fend for themselves?"

Magda heaved a sigh. "For themselves and a whole herd of cattle."

Bertha pursed her lips. "Well, that's another thing. There ain't near the cattle there was last night. The herd's smaller by half."

Magda rose to her knees and crawled to where Bertha stood, wincing at the stiffness that had set in from sitting so long beside Willem. "Would you like to tell me how six grown men and half a herd could simply vanish?" She shook her head. "It don't happen, Bertha. What's going on here?"

"Six?" Bertha counted on her fingers. "How do you cipher six men?"

"First, that no 'count Wayne—"

"Wayne ran off."

"Then John and the doctor—"

"It's wishful thinking to assume there's a doctor. I don't think John made it that far."

"Now Benito, Juan, and Carl. That makes six." Tears sprang to Magda's eyes. "Whether five or six, half the herd or one, they're gone. Missing under very peculiar circumstances." She lowered her voice to a whisper. "And we're next."

Bertha furrowed her brow. "Don't start making something spooky out of this. There's got to be a simple explanation."

Magda slid her legs off the wagon to dangle them from the side.

"I wish you'd explain it then, because I'm downright scared." She glanced over her shoulder. "Not so much for myself. It's Willem. He's lying there so helpless."

She wiped her eyes with the palms of her hands. "That man has taken care of me for twenty-two years. When he needs me the most, I'm not sure I can return the favor."

"Why couldn't you?"

Magda flapped her hands in frustration. "I don't even know what we're up against."

Crossing her arms, Bertha stared in concentration. "First off, them cows ain't missing under peculiar circumstances."

Magda squinted at her. "So you believe some ran away and the others stayed?"

Bertha snorted. "I think they was escorted away. Those men stole them."

"Why half the herd?"

Bertha raised her chin. "The best half, them with no horns."

Magda placed her hands on her hips. "I'll never believe Benito and that nice Juan are capable of such a thing. Don't you remember how kind their eyes were and how they looked after us on the trail?"

Bertha scratched her head. "I'll agree they didn't seem to have any potential for mischief. And poor simple Carl couldn't pull this off without written instructions." Her eyes narrowed. "But that brother of his sure could."

Magda lifted her finger. "True, but he'd have to convince Benito and Juan to go along. He wasn't around long enough. And don't forget John. What happened to him?" She looked at Willem again. "John would never leave his friend in this condition."

Walking thoughtfully to the thrown can, Bertha picked it up and examined it through squinted eyes. "We're spinning in the wind with all this jaw flapping. We're only sure of one thing at this point—we have to find help for Willem." She tossed the can at Magda. "Climb down out of there and fix us something to eat. I'll be hitching up the horses."

Magda scrambled to the ground, hope surging in her chest. "You really think we can find help, Bertha?"

"I reckon we'd better."

"But where do we go? For that matter, where are we now?"

Bertha wadded her fists on her hips and stared in the direction they'd come. "John's had us following the river since Eagle Pass. I'd say we've come better than twenty miles." She looked over her shoulder. "Which means we're halfway to Carrizo Springs." She made a quarter turn and pointed. "All we have to do is head due east. We're bound to hit that Indian trail eventually. From there we know the way home."

Excitement and fear built twin fires in Magda's gut. "But that's a long, hard ride. What if Willem can't make it, Bertha? And what if we get lost?"

Bertha swiveled at the waist to glare at her. "What if we sit right here and wait for the three of us to die?"

Magda swallowed. "Wouldn't it be smarter to find this El Indio place John told us about? He said it was only a few miles back."

"Good idea, sugar." Bertha held her arm out, swiveling it as she spoke. "Is it that way, close to the river? Maybe more northeast? What about right down the middle?" She shook her head. "Unless John drew you a map you haven't told me about, I say we stick to what we know." She ducked her head at Willem. "We know there's a doctor in Carrizo Springs."

Magda glanced at the remaining cattle on the distant plain. "What about the herd?"

"We leave them here. We're not drovers, and there's enough to worry about with Willem. John can round them up later." She waved at the supplies. "Forget cooking. Just rustle up something we can eat on the way."

Magda's ears buzzed as if a cricket sing-along swelled inside her head. "I don't know, Bertha. I'm still not sure."

Bertha tromped to where she stood. "Merciful heavens! All this hand wringing and second-guessing ain't your style. What's got into you?" Her stormy gaze flew to Willem again. "We need to make a decision and get on the road. We're wasting precious time."

Sobs welled inside of Magda. She released them in a piteous moan. "I'm sorry, Bertha. And grateful. I've always been the strong one, but with Willem so bad off, I've wilted like hot greens."

Bertha hugged her around the middle. "What's really bothering you, sugar?"

The tears flowed harder. She wiped them from her cheeks before they dripped on Bertha's head. "I'm afraid to find a doctor. I don't think I'll like what he has to say."

Bertha leaned back and gave her a shake. "You're stronger than that, honey. And if not, I'll be with you."

Magda wiped her eyes. "You've been there for me already. I can never repay you."

"No need. You were there for me when I lost Thad." She released Magda, her jaw set. "Only we ain't losing Willem. I say we head toward Carrizo Springs as fast as we can."

Tilting her head, Magda gazed at her from narrowed eyes. "You're having one of your feelings, aren't you?"

Bertha nodded firmly. "Yep, a strong feeling, and one we'd best heed."

Smiling, Magda mimicked her nod. "Go hitch the horses, then. I'll get us ready to go."

Emmy bolted upright on the Campbells' settee. Before her spinning head convinced her to squeeze her eyes shut again, she caught a glimpse of Diego's drawn face. Unless she was mistaken, Mrs. Campbell and her frightened girls flanked him. She shook her head to clear it and carefully opened her eyes.

Diego pressed closer. "Are you all right?"

She scooted to the edge of the cushion, forcing him to make room for her knees. "Tell me what it means, Diego," she pleaded, resting her forehead on her palms. "If Faron returned without Mr. Rawson, they're not coming home, are they?"

He grabbed her wrists and pulled her hands away. "It means no such thing."

Her head jerked up. "Then explain it."

His bluster wilted. "I can't, not yet. I'll know a lot more when I see Faron."

"What will that tell you?" she asked.

"If he's been wet or he's muddy, if he's scratched up from briars, then I'll have a better idea of where he's been." He averted his eyes. "The condition of the saddle or stirrups might tell me if he's been dragging a rider."

He latched onto her arms. "One thing I do know. We've been going about the search all wrong."

She sat up straighter. "What do you mean?"

"Remember what you asked me? If they were headed to the Campbells', why didn't they make it?"

She nodded.

"It's because they were no longer headed to the Campbells'. Little Pete said Faron came home along the road to Eagle Pass."

She blinked. "That's far away, isn't it?"

"About forty miles." His mouth tightened. "Forty miles in the opposite direction."

Her head reeled again. "They wouldn't go all the way to Eagle Pass without telling anyone. Would they?"

Joe Campbell stepped out of the kitchen with a plate of food in his hand. "Did somebody say Eagle Pass?"

Diego nodded.

The color drained from the boy's face. He sat on the arm of an easy chair and slid his plate onto the low table in front of him. Staring at the floor, he shook his head. "Naw, it couldn't be."

Concern lining her brow, Mrs. Campbell stepped closer. "What is it, son?"

He gazed up at her, his face a blank slate. "I think I saw Mr. Rawson on the road. In fact, I sent him and his friends to Eagle Pass."

"What?"

With so many voices shouting the word, Joe couldn't make up his mind who to answer. He settled on his mother. "I met some folks on their way here to buy stock. I told them we sold all we had then suggested a breeder in Eagle Pass."

"Joseph Campbell! Why didn't you speak up sooner?"

He cut frightened eyes to Diego. "The man never said he was Mr. Rawson, that's why. I told him I was headed for the Twisted-R Ranch, and he never said a word. If he was the owner, wouldn't he have said something?"

Laughing, Cuddy spoke up from the corner where he lounged against the wall. "I told you there wasn't anything wrong. They're living it up in Eagle Pass without a care in the world, just like I thought."

Emmy swung toward him. "Then what about Faron?"

He waved off her concern. "Faron got away from the old man and came home. Though my father would never admit it, that horse is too much for him."

Little Pete cleared his throat. "Um. . .Diego?"

Diego swiveled to see him better. "What is it, Pete?"

Pete tugged on his collar and swallowed. "Speaking of Faron, I forgot to tell you one thing."

Diego stood, his back rigid. "Go ahead."

"Señora Rawson? She's ordered him shot."

"And you're telling me now?"

"*Siento mucho*, señor. When the lady fainted, I–"

Diego whirled to Emmy. "Can you ride?"

She leaped to her feet. "Yes!"

He waved over his shoulder and ran for the door. "Let's go!"

Emmy rushed to follow the men outside, calling her thanks to Mrs. Campbell as she went.

Megan waved from the porch, but the five younger girls chased them from the yard, squealing and shouting their good-byes.

Emmy's gaze followed Diego riding just ahead. Concern for him stirred an ache inside worse than sore muscles or tender feet. His rich complexion appeared ashy with fatigue, and dark smudges around his eyes deepened the sockets. It amazed her how the news about Faron brought a surge of new life. His distress was more than the normal reaction for the welfare of a helpless animal. Diego had to love the big horse very much.

Dodging flying debris from the thundering hooves up ahead, Emmy prayed Faron wouldn't wind up the first tragic casualty in a string of potential losses.

Cringing, Melatha tossed the pan of bread in the sink with a rattle and clang then closed the oven door and ran.

Kate Rawson had awakened. Her shrill voice on the back porch left no doubt of the fact. Still in her dressing gown and slippers, the hair on her head shot in every direction, not unlike a disgruntled badger.

Melatha eased closer, but not too close.

The woman brandished a long-barreled pistol in her hand. "I want it done, and done now!" she shrieked. "No more delays."

Poor Felipe squirmed, twisting his hat in his hands. "I have not the authority, señora." He looked over his shoulder, desperation widening his eyes. "I only cover for Pete. He will return soon."

She raised the gun, waving it for emphasis, sending Felipe ducking and spinning out of range. "What do you mean you have no authority? *I* am your authority, and I'm ordering you to shoot that horse." She stamped her foot. "This instant."

"But, señora. . ."

Slipping a few steps nearer, Melatha began to speak to her in a soothing voice. "Mrs. Rawson? Kate?"

She whirled. "Melatha, it won't work this time. You convinced me to lie down for a bit so I wouldn't be acting in haste. Well, I've done as you asked, and I'm more determined than ever. That demon should've been put down hours ago," she pressed her free hand to her trembling mouth, and her voice rose to a shrill wail, "when he trotted into this yard looking for feed after killing my John!"

Melatha reached around Kate's waist while gently lowering the arm holding the gun, all the while cooing comfort in her ear. Kate's shoulders went limp, and Melatha guided her toward the house.

At the door, the distraught woman lifted startled eyes and spun away. "I'm sorry," she whispered. "I can't allow him to live."

She bolted down the steps with the pistol, passing a cowering Felipe and sailing across the yard with the hem of her robe flapping behind her.

Melatha screamed for Felipe to get help then lit out after her. "Kate, please! Don't do this thing."

Not even glancing behind her, Kate disappeared inside the barn. Bounding toward the wide doorway, Melatha prayed for wings on her feet. She dashed inside and froze, holding her breath.

Kate stood before Faron's stall with the gun trained on him.

Dark as pitch in the shadowy barn, Faron held his nose high, the agitated toss of his head flashing pinpoints of light from his black mane. His ears were pinned back and his wide stare revealed the glowing whites of his eyes. In that moment, Faron looked the part of a devil.

Melatha inched forward. "Kate, don't. This act will haunt you all your days."

Kate cocked the hammer.

Faron reared.

Melatha covered her eyes and opened her mouth to scream.

Something tore past her in a *whoosh*. Startled, she opened her eyes.

Isi, his outstretched arms reaching for Kate Rawson, dove. A blast from the pistol rocked the barn.

CHAPTER 34

The wagon bumped along the uneven ground, tossing Willem's body like corkwood. Magda held his head, trying with little success to hold it steady. She bobbed to see Bertha between the slats of the rear seat. "This isn't going to work! We're going to kill him."

Bertha looked over her shoulder. "This is a rough patch, honey. We'll be past it soon." She turned to the front, but her voice carried to Magda. "I see a clear spot just ahead."

"Hurry and reach it then," Magda cried.

"If I hurry, you'll both be tossed out on your ears."

Fighting tears, Magda let her little finger slide to the back of Willem's head to probe around the wound for signs of infection. She felt no extra heat or excess swelling in the area and breathed a sigh of relief. She made a mental note to give him a bit of water when they stopped. If she tried it now, she'd likely drown him.

Magda studied his serene face and a smile tugged at her lips. Her husband's Scandinavian roots had sprouted a fine figure of a man in Willem Dane. Despite attempts to keep him shaded, the sun he staunchly avoided due to his pale complexion had found him in South Texas. It had reddened his cheeks to a rosy glow and masked the deathly white pallor of the day before. Dark lines beneath his eyes and a thin white ring around his blush-colored lips were the only signs of his current distress.

She leaned to kiss him gently on the mouth, and his lack of

response broke her heart.

"Magda," Bertha called. "That ain't no clearing ahead." She paused. "Honey, I think it's a road."

Rising to her knees, Magda strained to see past Bertha. "Are you sure? That would be an answer to prayer."

Bertha let out a whoop. "Get busy thanking God then, because it's a road."

"Where?"

"Just a few yards in front of us." She twisted on the seat. "But don't get your hopes up until we make sure it's going our way."

Magda held Willem's head, and despite Bertha's warning, clung to her hope until the uneven ground gave way to a smooth track for the wheels.

Bertha pulled back on the reins and set the brake.

Relieved to let go of Willem's head, Magda shook the cramps out of her arms and scooted off the end of the wagon.

They met in the middle of the dirt road that stretched for miles in both directions.

"Well?" Magda asked.

"It's headed east, all right." She peered up at the sun. "At least I think."

"You think? What kind of answer is that?"

Bertha swatted the air behind her and walked a few steps. "I ain't good at reading the sky, but, Magda, it must be."

Turning, she gazed in the other direction. "It has to be the road connecting El Indio with Carrizo Springs." She slapped her leg. "I'd bet my last dollar, which means we'll be within shouting distance of the Twisted-R before nightfall."

They stared at each other for a second while the information sank in. Bertha pulled up her skirt and danced an Irish jig on the hard-packed ground while Magda laughed and kept time with her hands.

Sobering, she caught Bertha's arm. "Stop that before you have a stroke. In this heat, it ain't safe."

Breathing hard, Bertha bent at the waist, panting. "Why didn't you say that sooner?" She looked up and grinned. "You might be too late."

Hustling to the rig, Magda reached over the side for the canteen and brought it to Bertha. "Have a sip of water before I give Willem some, and then we'd better get going."

Still clutching her side, Bertha twisted off the top then gave the canteen a little shake. "This sure feels light. Better hand me a full one."

Magda dug in the box where they kept the canteens, testing the weight of them and growing more upset with each one she lifted. "They're all light." She spun to stare at Bertha. "I think they're empty."

Bertha lowered her head and gave Magda a menacing look. "That can't be. I told you to fill them."

Magda waved her finger back and forth. "No, you didn't. You said *you* filled them."

Running to see for herself, Bertha buried her arms in the wooden box, tossing the empty containers like a crazed juggler. Turning, she gave Magda a scorching glance. "What sort of dim-witted stunt have we pulled?"

The enormity of the situation slammed Magda between the eyes. A mix-up had cost them six canteens of water. "Check the drums John brought for the horses."

Bertha shook her head and rattled the barrel. "Empty. I heard him say so. He planned to fill them before we left the river."

Magda's eyes darted to Willem. She raised her head and squinted at the blazing overhead sun. "Bertha, this is awful."

Reading the panic on her face, Bertha patted her arm. "Don't fret, now. We're bound to run across a creek or something." Glancing at the canteen still in her hand, she licked her dry lips and held it out to Magda. "Meanwhile, we save every drop for Willem."

Magda placed her hand on the life-giving gift. "But you're thirsty."

Bertha shoved it away. "For Willem."

Diego raised himself to his elbows then sprang to his feet and leaned over Mrs. Rawson. "Are you all right, ma'am?" He glanced at Faron. The frantic horse paced his stall.

Mrs. Rawson huddled on the ground crying softly, ignoring him.

Cuddy knelt behind her, his hands on her shoulders. "I'll take it from here, Diego. See about Faron."

The horse's name triggered hysterical wails from the prone woman. She pushed off the ground and staggered from the barn with Cuddy and Diego's mother at her side.

Diego hurried to the stall. Faron still snorted and pawed but settled down some when Diego slipped inside and began to slide his hands over the horse's body. He explored every inch of the trembling stallion, checking his fingers often for any sign of blood.

Emmy stood at the door, gripping the top slat with white-knuckled fingers.

Little Pete stood beside her, his hands shoved deep inside his pockets. Watching Diego check Faron, Pete moaned and shifted from side to side. "It's my fault, Diego. If I'd told you sooner. . ."

Diego spared a tight smile for Pete then returned his attention to Faron. "Nonsense. It's no one's fault."

Greta, her eyes wide with fright, hurried inside the barn with Diego's mother on her heels. The women stared toward Faron.

"Is he all right?" Diego's mother asked.

Diego gazed at her in wonder. "There's not a mark on him."

"Thank God!"

He grinned. "I already have."

Greta reached for Emmy's hand. "I'm so glad, Diego."

Diego returned her warm smile. "So am I. For your mother's sake as much as Faron's." He gave Faron one last pat, signaling for Pete to take over his care, and stepped out of the stall. He walked to Greta and gave a slight bow. "I pray I didn't harm your mother."

Greta bit her bottom lip. "She's fine. Physically, at least." The wistful smile disappeared, replaced by despair. "Do you think my father's really dead?"

Emmy's arm went around her shoulders. "We refuse to think it. Cuddy says Faron got away from your father and came home, that's all. He's convinced our parents and my aunt Bertha are having a high old time in Eagle Pass."

"Do you believe him?"

Emmy gave her a gentle squeeze. "I choose to believe it for now. I suggest you do the same."

Helplessness welled in Greta's eyes. "So we're just going to sit here and wait for them to return?"

Diego shook his head. "No, Greta. In fact, I'll be heading out to search for them again as soon as I get a bath and a couple of hours' sleep." He stretched and glanced at his mother. "I wouldn't mind a bite of food."

She dipped her head and hurried for the door.

Diego smiled and nodded after her. "That means I'd better hurry. She'll expect me to arrive clean at her table, so if you'll excuse me."

Emmy latched onto his arm as he passed. "What time do we leave?"

Diego stiffened. He had dreaded the question. Facing her, determination sharpened his tone. "Not this time."

"Excuse me?"

"You're not coming this time."

Her searching gaze bored under his skin. "What are you saying? Of course I'm coming."

He tried to fill his voice with authority. "I'm taking Pete with me this time. We can make better time alone."

Emmy's fingers tightened on his arm. "Wait a minute. What about Cuddy?"

"Since Cuddy needs to stay behind and tend his mother, he'll be in charge of the ranch."

She released him, her eyes like burning coals. "Who are you to make these decisions for us? You have no right."

He drew in a breath to help calm his anger. It didn't work. "This country's too rough for you, Emmy. There's no place in South Texas for frills and piled-up hair."

She drew back and glared. "You don't waste words, do you?"

He wanted to shake her. "Don't you remember the condition you were in last night? You could hardly walk and fell asleep the first time you laid your head down."

She dropped her gaze.

"At the first hint of bad news, I had to carry you inside the house."

She flinched.

He wished he'd bitten his tongue before adding the last part, but he had to make her see.

She stood silent, offering no more resistance.

He nodded toward Little Pete. "Get some rest. We're pulling out in four hours. We'll be heading to El Indio then along the river to Eagle

Pass. They'd take that route if they were driving cattle. We'll circle back around to Carrizo from there. I think we'll know something by then." Striding from the barn, he stopped on the threshold. "And Pete. . ."

"Señor?"

"Have Faron saddled and ready."

"Sí, señor."

Emmy stormed from the barn, raging fury stealing her peace, her good sense, her very breath. Seeking privacy, she circled the house and sat in the shade of the seldom-used front porch, gulping to breathe and struggling to compose herself.

Self-disappointment burned hotter than her anger toward Diego. There would be no more rash threats to borrow a horse and search for her parents alone. She was weak, a failing she couldn't deny after the last two days. Diego had merely shined a light on her limitations. But if he knew what she'd finally admitted to herself–that she couldn't find Mama and Papa without him–how could he so cruelly deny her?

The front door opened and Cuddy stepped out. "Mind a little company?"

Emmy gaped at him. "How did you know I was here?"

He hooked his thumb toward the house. "We have windows, and you were hard to miss. You shot past the parlor blowing enough steam to boil potatoes."

She grimaced. "I could still simmer a couple."

He chuckled. "What happened? If you don't mind my asking."

Emmy considered not telling him. Why make it easy for Diego? Let him gaze at Cuddy with steel in his jaw and explain how he'd made all his decisions for him.

Cuddy angled his head and peered at her. "Why am I certain this has something to do with Diego?"

Propping her elbows on her knees, she hid her face in her hands. "You're only half right." She peeked at him. "I'm just as mad at myself."

He reached for her hand. "No one should get mad at you." He grinned. "Not even you."

Swiveling toward him, she groaned. "You won't be in a joking mood when I tell you what's about to happen."

Suddenly serious, he squeezed her fingers. "Tell me."

"In four hours, Diego's headed for Eagle Pass to find our parents."

He nodded thoughtfully. "I didn't think he'd wait that long, but—"

"We're not invited."

He lifted his brows. "What?"

"Diego decided I can't handle the trail, and he thinks you're needed here."

Color flooded Cuddy's freckled cheeks. He closed his eyes, tightening his fingers around hers. "He decided that, did he?" He scowled. "That's our Diego. If you're ever short on opinions, he has one to spare."

He faced her and took her other hand. "How tired are you?"

She took a quick breath. "Me? I'm too wound up to be tired."

"How would you like to accompany me to Eagle Pass?"

"But Diego won't let—"

"You said Diego's leaving in four hours. I can be ready to go in three. How about you?"

She stared. "Really, Cuddy?"

He nodded, his eyes twinkling.

"What about the ranch?"

He waved off her concern. "Diego trained his men well. They can run the Twisted-R for a few days. Besides"—he sneered—"unlike Diego, I wouldn't care if the earth opened up and swallowed this place."

"And your mother? Shouldn't you be here with her? Diego said she needed you to take care of her."

"She has Greta." He glanced away. "Besides, the best thing I can do for her right now is find my father."

Emmy sighed, excited and afraid at the same time. "I don't know, Cuddy. Aren't you exhausted?"

He rolled his shoulders. "A little sore but not tired. I've perfected the art of sleeping in the saddle."

She laughed and gripped his hands. "Are you sure we should do this?"

He drew back and gave her a sideways look. "Oh, yes. Very sure. Are you in?"

She leaped to her feet, pulling him with her. Throwing her arms around his neck, she kissed his cheek. "Yes! Oh, Cuddy, this means so much to me."

He gave her one more squeeze then set her at arm's length. "Go get ready, then."

She gave him a jaunty salute. "Yes, sir."

"Emily?"

She turned.

"I'll meet you right here in three hours with the horses. I'll have Rosita pack our provisions, but don't forget to bring plenty of socks."

"Plenty of socks." She grinned. "Good thinking."

She threw open the door and hurried into the parlor.

Rosita, pretending to dust the low table in front of the window, shot her a frosty glare. She'd obviously seen everything—the laughter, the handholding, the kiss—and pinned her own interpretation to each detail.

So be it, let her think what she would. Emmy had grown tired of trying to sway the woman's opinion.

Lifting her chin and adding a little extra strut to her step, Emmy flounced from the room.

CHAPTER 35

Diego shot upright on his bunkhouse cot, his mind searching for the source of his heightened unease. Any rest the brief few hours of sleep afforded him slid away as the crushing burden of the last few days shifted onto his shoulders. Swinging his feet to the floor, he kneaded his face like a lump of dough, trying to rub out the need for sleep along with the memory of Emmy's disappointed eyes.

He'd made the decision not to take her while they were still in Catarina. Hopefully, one day she'd understand how hard it was for him to deny her, but he had to for her sake. Eagle Pass could be a rowdy town, and something told him the next ride held danger. Perhaps he might've used less force in delivering the message, but he'd yet to learn how to sway her determined heart.

One glance at the shade told him he'd slept too long. The jarring knowledge chasing the last bit of fog from his head, he hurriedly pulled on his boots. Where was Little Pete? He'd sent word by his mother that Pete was to awaken him at three thirty. If the shadowy corners of the bunkhouse meant anything, it was closer to five.

The door creaked open and Diego reached for his shirt, cross words of rebuke ready on his tongue.

Instead of Pete, his mother stood on the threshold. She smiled. "I was coming to wake you."

"Where's Pete?"

She ducked her head. "I never told Pete, Isi. I decided to rouse you myself."

Sliding one arm in his sleeve, he paused. "Why?"

Staring at the floor, she bit her bottom lip. "I wanted you to rest as long as possible."

Gritting his teeth, he shoved his other arm in the shirt. "Mother! This was too important for you to interfere."

She calmly approached to straighten his collar. "It's all right, son. While you slept, I had the men make every preparation for the trip. What they couldn't do, I tended to myself." She patted his shoulder. "Faron's waiting in the yard. All you have to do is get on him and ride."

Diego wilted in the warmth of her selfless love. He pulled her close for a hug. "Come here, meddling woman."

She hugged him back with a shuddering sigh. "I worry, Isi. You'll be careful?"

He patted the top of her head. "What need do I have to be careful? I know you've spent the last few hours praying for my safety."

She turned her face up and grinned. "This is true, so tread lightly. Try not to overturn a treaty between your mother and God."

He laughed. "I wouldn't dare."

Outside, his eyes lit on Rosita standing near Faron's head and the merry mood lifted. She had the fingers of one hand curled on her hip, and a cross scowl hardened her features. The other hand she used to drive home a point to Little Pete with waves and jabs to his chest.

As Diego approached, Little Pete swatted her finger away. "It's not my place," he growled in Spanish. "Tell him yourself. Diego needs to know."

"What do I need to know?"

Rosita jumped and squealed, holding her heart. "Diego! You startled me."

He placed his hand on her shoulder. "You have information for me?"

Guilty eyes told him she wasn't meant to tell. Her breathless words confirmed it. "Señor Cuddy counts on my silence. But I feel you should know." She lifted a haughty chin. "Besides, it's the fault of that girl. If not for the spell of the white-haired witch, Cuddy would never think to go against your decision."

Cold dread rushed to Diego's belly. "What decision?" Even as he asked, he knew. Cuddy would ride up behind him a few yards from the house with Emmy in tow and expect him to relent. Well, he wouldn't give in so easily this time. Cuddy could do what he blasted well pleased. Emmy would go straight back to the house.

Diego's mother slid her arm around Rosita. "Your opinion of Emily may be too harsh, Rosita. I feel responsible."

Rosita withdrew. "She's bewitched you, too?"

His mother laughed. "Not at all. Perhaps the only dark magic was my unforgiving attitude toward the girl. I should've taken the time to know Emily's heart before I judged her."

Diego smiled to himself. He'd have to congratulate Emmy on how skillfully she'd won over his mother.

Unconvinced, Rosita turned flashing eyes to Diego. "If her heart is pure, why did she offer herself to Cuddy in exchange for taking her to Eagle Pass?"

His stomach lurched and he felt turned to stone. "What are you saying?"

"It's true," she spat.

He caught Rosita's wrist and shook her.

Fear and pain registered in her eyes. "I watched her throw herself at Cuddy under the front portico, away from prying eyes. I saw everything from the window. The girl knew I caught them, but she felt no shame." She looked over her shoulder at his mother. "Melatha, I swear it happened. She pranced into the house like a jezebel, flaunting her dishonor in my face."

Struggling for a calming breath, Diego released her. "You are mistaken. I don't know what you saw, but you must have misunderstood."

Rubbing her wrist and shaking her head, Rosita stood in silent testimony of Emmy's betrayal.

With more calm than he felt inside, Diego slid his boot in the stirrup and swung onto Faron's back. Bobbing his head, the horse danced impatiently. "It doesn't matter. Whatever Emmy enticed Cuddy with, her efforts were wasted. She won't be riding with us to Eagle Pass."

Little Pete mounted his horse then cleared his throat. "You are correct, señor. She won't be riding with us because she and young Cuddy, they already left."

Diego's bulging eyes swung to Rosita. She solemnly nodded. "I packed their provisions myself, Diego. I watched them leave the gate."

"How long ago?"

She shrugged. "A long time. Hours."

With the barest nod to his mother, Diego spurred the eager horse into a run for the gate. Little Pete could catch up in El Indio.

Melatha stood on the porch of her jacal, clutching the rail and peering past the big house to the east. Fear seeped into her bones as the blanket of black stretching along the horizon grew darker and wider, inching closer to her son with every tick of the clock.

Isi raced toward the storm on the back of a horse that may have killed John Rawson, his mind on nothing but protecting White Hair.

"She's bewitched you, too?" Rosita's question echoed in Melatha's mind, and she shivered.

Steeling her resolve, she fled to the only solid ground. "I have no trust in Emily Dane, Lord. I trust only what You've shown me of her heart."

From the moment Emily stepped across the threshold two days ago, God began to whisper in Melatha's ear. His assurance grew louder each time she saw the girl.

Emily spoke that day of Isi's love for her. Signs deeper than mere words could convey—her glowing eyes and trembling smile, the way she spoke his name—told Melatha she loved Isi, too.

These things alone did not sway Melatha or melt her stony heart. Only when Emily began to speak of the Father did the spiritual bond they shared come to light. The passion Melatha sensed while Emily spoke of Isi was but a flickering ember in comparison.

A brisk wind stirred the high grass and rattled the empty baskets in the corner. Melatha lifted her chin to the cool breeze and swallowed her fear. She determined to trust Chihowa Palami in all matters pertaining to Isi and White Hair, no matter how threatening the storm.

Emmy watched the churning wall of clouds on the horizon, more menacing by far than the patchy canopy overhead. They'd been grateful since they left the ranch for the overcast sky that blocked the sun, and the cool, brisk wind coming off the approaching storm caught Emmy's breath.

The closer the wall advanced, the more dangerous it appeared. A gust caught her whispered prayer for safety and carried it away, she hoped, toward heaven. She thanked God that for the last few miles, the angry swirl had seemed stagnant, a faraway puffed-up bully, blowing hard but harmless.

She turned her attention to Cuddy. Obviously deep in thought, he rode quietly, his gaze fixed somewhere in the distance.

"It's getting dark," Emmy said, and he jumped. She laughed. "I didn't mean to startle you."

He shrugged and grinned. "I'm afraid it'll be very gloomy tonight with the weather so foul. Makes it better on the horses, though. Cooler." He rolled his head to study the twilight sky. "New moon, too. If you don't like the dark, you'll be glad to see El Indio."

She shuddered, but he didn't seem to notice. Before long, he'd retreated into his thoughts again. Ducking her head, she peered closer. "You know what they say? A penny for your thoughts?"

He shot her a sideways glance. "There's not a thought in my head worth that much."

She gave him a mock frown. "I'm sorry, but I don't believe you."

He raised his brows. "Oh, it's true."

Emmy giggled, her lilting laugh out of place in the murky setting.

Cuddy crossed his hands over the saddle horn. "Since you asked, I'll tell you my thoughts. Free of charge."

She twisted to see him better. "All right. I never could pass up a bargain."

A flush crept up from his collar, visible even in the meager light. "I was wondering. . ." His gaze flickered to her face then down. "Well. . . I heard you praying back there."

It was her turn to blush. "Yes, I was."

As if determined to finish something he'd started, he met her eyes. "Do you actually think someone heard you?"

At first, the strain in his voice made her think he was mocking her. After searching his face, she realized he desperately needed to know. "Yes, I do. In fact, I'm convinced."

He narrowed his eyes. "How?"

Cuddy's question brought the past flooding back, the emptiness Emmy had felt before the day she'd whispered a tortured prayer, asking herself the same question: Did someone hear?

The evidence that God Himself heard came later in startling bits and pieces. First, the calm that settled over her soul like a comforting quilt after that prayer, blocking out the darkness and filling the empty places. Where once her eyes in the mirror had darted, guilty and ashamed, now they gazed back at her, clear and unflinching, in a way they'd never done before. The day she awoke knowing God was there, so present she felt compelled to bid Him good morning, she knew her life had forever changed.

She related these proofs and more to Cuddy as they rode.

He listened quietly, thoughtfully chewing the inside of his cheek. When she finished, he whistled softly. "When we first met I said you weren't the sort of girl I expected to say such things."

She nodded, remembering.

"I was wrong."

His attempt to compliment her warmed her heart. "Thank you. It means a lot to hear you say so." She paused. "But Cuddy, I don't want you harboring the wrong idea. There is no particular 'sort' of person that prays to God." She smiled. "He takes all comers."

He clutched his chest and pretended to wince with pain. "Except someone like me."

She gave her head a vigorous shake. "Especially someone like you."

Cuddy threw back his head and laughed so hard he nearly fell out of the saddle.

Emmy watched him, amazed and a little frightened. "Stop it! Why are you howling? You'll attract a pack of coyotes."

Holding his middle, he pointed. "Didn't you hear yourself? You just confirmed that I'm a special case. I always thought I was such a mess that God would go out of his way to snag a trophy like me for His belt." He roared again. "Now you've confirmed it."

She fought a smile. "Oh, shush."

He wiped his eyes, controlling his snickers with effort. Gazing warmly at her, he smiled. "Seriously, I appreciate your honesty, and I think I'd like to know more."

She let her jaw drop dramatically then winked. "Why, Cuddy Rawson, I believe you're sincere. What do you want to know?"

His head jerked around and he held up his hand. "Shh! Wait a second." He leaned forward in the saddle and stared. "Unless my eyes are deceiving me, I see a campfire up ahead."

Emmy whirled to look and her heart skipped a beat. "Oh, Cuddy. Could it possibly be them?"

His teeth flashed in the dimness. "There's only one way to find out." He tapped his horse with his heels. "Let's ride."

The wind howled around the wagon, flapping the tarps tied over the crates and threatening to lift Magda's hat right off her head. She clung to it with her free hand while the brim battered her forehead. With her other hand, she held a cloth over Willem's mouth to try to keep out the swirling dust.

In one way, the coming rain would be a relief. Magda planned to open her mouth and turn her face to the sky. She'd never been thirstier in her life. It amazed her that Bertha, already parched when they discovered the empty canteens, hadn't asked for a drop to cool her tongue.

"It's coming a right rowdy blow," Bertha shouted.

Magda looked behind her. "You don't say? What are we going to do when it starts to rain?"

"I suppose we'll get mighty wet." Bertha seemed a fount of pointless information. She tipped her head and stared at the sky. "It's the lightning that's got me worried. Getting worse, too."

Her words struck fear in Magda. She hadn't even considered the lightning. "We need to find shelter, Bert."

"I know it's dark out, but have you forgot what this country looks like? There ain't no shelter. This here is wide-open plain." She cackled. "I suppose we could crawl under the wagon."

Tired of bawling back and forth like a cow and her weaning calf, Magda got up on all fours. "Have you forgot about Willem? What do you propose we do, drag him off this rig by his heels?"

It seemed foolish to her to ride along pretending there wasn't a monster chasing them. They needed to come up with a plan for weathering the storm. Before she could holler for Bert to pull over, Bertha hauled on the reins so hard Magda slammed forward and bumped her head. Falling on her bottom, she rubbed the swelling on her forehead. "For pity's sake! What'd you do that for?"

Bertha scrambled over the front seat, knelt on the rear, and leaned over the wooden slats.

Magda scooted closer and peered up at her. "What's wrong? You cracked my head and joggled Willem something fierce."

She slapped her hand over Magda's mouth. "Keep your voice down and listen." Letting go slowly, she pulled Magda's face to the left and angled it down the road. "What do you see?"

Magda gasped. "A light."

"Is it a light? Or a campfire?"

"What difference does it make? Either way, it means people. Help for Willem." Excitement welling inside, Magda shoved her toward the front. "What are you waiting for? Get up there and drive."

Bertha slumped on the seat. "Not so fast. Suppose it's bandits. . . or worse, Indians?"

"There are no more war parties in South Texas."

"How do you know?"

Magda was fairly sure of what she knew, just not positive. "We have to take the chance, don't we? We have no choice."

Thunder rolled from one side of the endless, dark sky to the other, followed by countless jagged streaks in the heavens. They both jumped at a louder crash that spiked a bolt of white light to the ground.

Magda shrank nearer to Willem. "How close was that? It's hard to tell out here."

"Too close," Bertha said, a quaver in her voice.

"What are we going to do, Bert?"

"I have a plan, but you won't like it."

Magda's stomach lurched. "If it gets Willem out of this weather, I'm game."

"That part's a gamble." A flash lit Bertha's profile as she stared up the road. "I have to get close enough to see who that is over yonder."

"How? They're sure to hear us. They'll likely even see us in this lightning if they haven't already."

Bertha's head turned. "Not if I go by myself. I can slip up on them."

"And leave me here alone?" She shivered. "With the storm and the coyotes? Not to mention the goat suckers?" She clutched Bertha's sleeve. "No. Come up with another plan."

Bertha pulled free. "There is no other plan. You want to find help for Willem, don't you?"

A sob threatened Magda's throat. "You know I do."

"All right, then. We either head for that light and we're safe, or we skirt around it and we're safe." Her voice slowly faded as she spoke. "The only way to choose the right path is for me to go look."

Fear clawed Magda's chest. She grasped the seatback and peered into the darkness. "Bertha Maye! Where did you go? You're already on the ground, aren't you?"

Bertha popped up at the side rail. "Keep your trap shut. They'll hear you."

"Please don't go."

"Stay here and be quiet." It was the second time Bertha had issued the order to stay, ridiculous considering Magda would be loath to leave the wagon if Gabriel appeared and blew his horn.

She didn't hear Bertha leave, but she knew the minute she was alone. A solid wall of darkness enveloped her, thick enough to slap her in the face each time a bolt of lightning waned.

She felt for the comforting warmth of Willem's chest, still faithfully rising and falling. Odd how he could be so lifeless yet at the same time full of life. Despite his helplessness, his nearness made her feel safe—until a rustling sound in the nearby brush tossed her heart at her throat.

The horses seemed suddenly restless, and she imagined them bolting in fear of whatever crouched in the bushes. Had Bertha set the brake? If so, would the rig topple, dragging them to their deaths?

Maybe the bandits up the road had already seen them. Perhaps they'd acted first and sent a murdering thief to slip up on them with a patch on his eye and a knife between his teeth. He would've already slit Bertha's throat and left her for dead. Now he shimmied through the tall grass, coming for her.

"It's them!" Bertha hissed at her side.

Magda screamed as thunder pealed overhead.

In the silence that followed, she felt downright silly. And mad. "What did you do that for?"

Standing at the rail, Bertha let out her breath in a rush. "I was about to ask you the same fool question. You'd better hope that thunder drowned out your caterwauling, or we're in big trouble."

Magda leaned over Willem. "Why? Who is it?"

"None other than our peeping Tom, nasty Wayne, and his brother, Carl."

"No!"

"I'm afraid so." She sniffed. "Here's the worst part, Magda. Benito and Juan are with them."

Magda gripped the rail. "Oh, Bertha. I can't believe it. They seemed so nice."

Bertha patted her hand. "They are nice. You were right about them all along. They're sitting back to back near the fire, trussed up in heavy rope. John's cattle are grazing in a nearby field."

Magda shot a worried glance down the road toward the campfire. "What are we going to do?"

"Nothing we can do for Benito and Juan just now. We're no match for those men. Besides, we've got to think of Willem." She sighed. "Looks like we're going around."

CHAPTER 36

Diego sailed along the road to El Indio, Faron's impressive strength, beauty, and speed churning beneath him. He allowed the horse to run for as long as he dared before pulling him up. Faron's swiftness and willingness had bought Diego a lot of time. He had the feeling the horse would cheerfully dash to his death if Diego required it of him.

Dismal, unwelcome thoughts simmered in Diego's head. In his zeal to save Faron, he'd never allowed himself to accept what Mrs. Rawson considered obvious. Had Faron thrown John Rawson? Trampled him to death? Was Mrs. Rawson a widow who deserved her vengeance? The possibility left Diego's insides roiling worse than the imminent storm.

A faint light flickered up ahead. Diego stood in the stirrups and tried to focus his eyes on the fiery blur. He first thought lightning had started a brush fire in the distance but soon realized it must be a campfire. His heartbeat quickened. It made no sense for Cuddy to pull off and camp halfway to El Indio, unless he sought shelter from the rain, or unless. . .

The other possibility shot warmth through his body. Could Mr. Rawson and Emmy's family have set up camp along the roadside?

Diego tapped Faron's sides to spur him to a trot. They didn't get far before a noisy commotion commenced behind him to the right. Faron sprang off his haunches, dancing away from the noise, but Diego held the edgy horse steady.

Something big trundled in a wide swath somewhere in the brush, angling toward the road.

Diego strained to see, but the shroud of darkness blotted out everything beyond a few feet. Deciding curiosity could be dangerous, he waited, his ears straining for more information.

A high-pitched caterwaul pierced the night, tensing every muscle in his body. "We've done it, Magda! We found the road."

"Halleluiah! I knew you could do it, Bert."

Grinning from east to west, Diego slapped his leg then leaned forward to whisper into the horse's twitching ears. "Well, what do you know, Faron? We didn't need to find them. They found us."

Filled with relief so fierce his chest was sure to burst, Diego spurred the horse and lit out after them. "Mr. Rawson! Sir! Wait up." They were nearly on top of the wagon when Faron swung to the side. Diego reined him in and circled back. "You folks can't imagine what a hullabaloo you've caused on the ranch." He chuckled. "Sir, your wife may be ready to see you hanged."

He squinted, trying to find Mr. Rawson's face, listening to hear his booming laughter.

A plump face materialized from the side of the wagon. "Diego!" Mrs. Dane cried. "Is it really you? We're so grateful to see you."

"We've had a terrible time of it, son," Mrs. Bloom added, her voice thick with unshed tears.

Fear tickled the edges of Diego's mind. He could see two shadowy figures in the wagon now. Two figures. Two voices.

"Mr. Rawson?"

"That's what we're trying to tell you," Mrs. Bloom said gently. "Willem is lying in back, and he's hurt real bad. As for John Rawson. . . he lit out on Faron two days ago to fetch a doctor for Willem and we haven't seen him since."

Diego's heart sank and he fought back tears. He'd cling to hope until there was proof, but the grisly facts were lining up against Mr. Rawson.

He pictured the man's poor wife holding a pistol on Faron, the hem of her dressing gown soiled by the barn floor, her hair an untidy mess. Shuddering at the feel of the horse under him, he dismounted and climbed aboard the rig. "What happened to your husband, Mrs. Dane?"

She sniffed loudly. "He fell. Landed on a broke-off tree limb that punctured the back of his head." Her voice broke. "It knocked him unconscious and he never woke up." A loud peal of thunder made Mrs. Dane jump and cry out.

Mrs. Bloom took up the story. "We waited at the camp all night for John and the doctor. When he didn't show, we figured we'd best head out and find help."

Diego's head reeled. "You two have been wandering alone, trying to make your way from Eagle Pass?"

"Not Eagle Pass. Willem got hurt along the river near El Indio."

"But you were coming from the direction of Eagle Pass."

"I reckon it looked that way to you." She felt for his head and turned it to look behind them. "Actually, we'd just driven around that."

The campsite.

He laughed. "You didn't have much to fear. I think I know who that is."

Bertha snorted. "We know exactly who it is, young feller. You may not fear them, but we sure do."

Diego narrowed his eyes. "But that's Cuddy and Emmy, isn't it?"

Fumbling in the darkness, Mrs. Dane scrambled to her feet. "What did you say? Why would you think that's my daughter?"

He turned from one to the other, trying to see enough of their faces to read them. "Because they were ahead of me, traveling this same road."

Their simultaneous gasps sent a chill down Diego's back. He stared toward the distant fire that once seemed cheerful and promising but now cast an ominous glow. "Maybe one of you had better tell me what's going on."

Her eyes swollen from crying, Emmy strained against the rope that bound her hands. She glanced at Cuddy lying across from her and shuddered at his battered, bloody face. His incoherent babbling stirred fear in Emmy. She whispered his name, begging him to look at her, to say he was all right, but he didn't answer.

The cruel men had ambushed them as soon as they'd ridden into camp, pulling Cuddy shouting and kicking from his horse and hitting him over the head. Once Cuddy hit the ground, the beating continued, leaving him in a huddle, dazed and moaning. They'd tied him up and slammed him against a wagon wheel, leaving him for dead, and lashed Emmy to a musty-smelling trunk.

She glanced toward the fire. The wind whipped the flames in a crazy dance, and the occasional fat raindrop landed with a sizzle. Her gaze lifted to the two bronze-skinned men in front of the blaze. Their demeanor struck Emmy as peculiar, not because they were bound together, captives of the same evil men, but that they seemed to accept it with dignity and grace. One of them raised his head then tilted it, flashing Emmy a sympathetic smile.

The younger of the wicked men paced between the two sets of prisoners. "This is getting scary now, Wayne," he ranted. "I didn't say much when you hauled that cook and drover with us even after I asked you not to." He ran his hands through his hair. "And, yes, I can see how we might need them to get the cattle clear to Cotulla." He whirled and pointed at Emmy. "But this right here will get us hanged."

The man he called Wayne, the same one who'd kicked Cuddy when he was on the ground, sat on a stained bucket cleaning his fingernails with a hunting knife. "Little brother, you worry too much." He spread his hands to take in their surroundings. "Do you see anyone around here for miles who might care?"

His vulgar laughter echoed through the camp. "That's the beauty of the wide-open spaces. The possibilities are wide open, too."

The worried one named Carl bent over at the waist, his arms out to his sides like a flustered goose. "We don't *need* them! Why bring extra heat on our heads?"

Wayne fixed a thoughtful gaze on Cuddy. "Unfortunately for him, I agree with you." The look he turned on Emmy held a greedy glint. "But that pretty little thing right there?" He sneered. "I reckon I could find a use for her."

Emmy cringed and dropped her gaze, stiffening her spine. He wouldn't see her cry.

Ferocious, howling gusts announced the storm's arrival. Carl came to life, chasing after flying clothing and tumbling boxes while Wayne laughed like a lunatic, nearly upsetting his bucket.

The lightning, splitting the sky in jagged bolts, scared Emmy almost as badly as Wayne did. Close by, the cattle increased their uneasy lowing. Emmy understood their frightened bellows. She wouldn't mind bellowing herself.

A few feet away, Cuddy had gone motionless. Emmy discreetly fought against her ropes, longing to be free so she could go to him, make sure he was all right, and huddle beside him until the storm passed.

"S'matter, little gal?"

Heart leaping, she jerked toward the voice in her ear. Wayne had slithered up to crouch at her side. She leaned away from his putrid breath and didn't answer, so he ran his filthy finger down her cheek. Cringing, she turned her head until her neck muscles strained.

Angered, he gripped her jaw and pressed his mouth to her ear. Lifting the knife, he swiveled the blade in front of her face. "You be nice to me and you'll come out of this in one piece. Keep thinking you're better'n me, and I'll make things very uncomfortable." He gave her face a harsh shake, his fingers biting into her flesh. "Be a good girl now and give me a sign that you understand."

She swallowed a cry of pain and tried to nod.

His cold laughter mocked her. "That's more like it, darlin'." He pressed against her, wrapping his arms around her waist to fumble with the ropes. A chill gripped her spine when his fetid breathing quickened. "I'm going to cut you loose for a little bit. How's that?"

Emmy's stomach lurched. "Why?"

"I thought you might like to take a little walk."

"Señor, please."

Wayne glanced back at the kind-faced man by the fire. "What do you want?" he growled.

"Don't hurt the lady, señor."

Wayne leaped up and struck with the speed of a striking rattler, his blow so brutal Emmy gasped and turned away. Concern quickly brought her eyes to the front again.

Bright red blood flowed from a gash on her defender's cheek. She first thought Wayne had slashed the helpless man with his knife, until he cleaned the butt of the knife on his shirt. "Maybe next time you'll mind your own business."

He spun around to Emmy with an air of nonchalance. "Now then, little lady. . .where were we?"

Diego crawled backward to the end of the wagon and dropped to the ground. "He has no fever, Mrs. Dane. That's a good sign. But you'd best get him on to Carrizo Springs."

The women huddled together, their skirts flapping wildly in the wind. Mrs. Dane latched onto his arm. "What do you mean? Aren't you coming with us?"

"You'll be fine. Just stay on this road. It'll lead you straight into town."

"Where are you going? To look for Emmy?"

"Yes, ma'am." He nodded behind her. "Starting among your friends there."

Mrs. Dane clung so tightly, her fingers pinched Diego's flesh. "I'm going with you."

¡Ay! Where had he heard that before? He released a heavy sigh. "You can't, Mrs. Dane. I'll be down on my belly, crawling through the grass."

"I don't care. I'm going."

"Magda, don't be silly," Mrs. Bloom said, flapping her thin hands in Mrs. Dane's face. "You ain't laid flat of your belly in twenty years. Besides, there's too much of you to hide."

Mrs. Dane puffed like a porcupine and shook a stern finger at Mrs. Bloom. "You hush, Bertha. My baby might be back there."

"If she is, this young feller is just the one to save her. You'll only get in the way."

Diego breathed a prayer of thanksgiving for Mrs. Bloom. "Your friend's right, ma'am. Concentrate on getting your husband to a doctor."

"But—"

"If she's in that camp, which is highly unlikely, I'll get her for you." He flexed his jaw. "Don't doubt it for a minute."

The sound of hooves on the road behind them sent the women crowding against him in the darkness. He laughed softly. "I expect that's Little Pete. If so, you need to leave with him right away."

"No!" Mrs. Dane protested. "Not until I know about Emily."

He slid his arm around her shoulders. "Let me tend to Emmy. I give you my word I'll take care of her."

Little Pete signaled from the murky road.

Diego whistled back. "It's Pete."

"Oh, Bertha," Mrs. Dane moaned. She whirled into her friend's waiting arms. "I feel so torn."

Mrs. Bloom clucked her tongue. "Listen to me, sugar. Willem may die if we don't get help for him soon." She patted her back. "Besides, you know what Emmy would want you to do."

Pete drew alongside them. A long, jarring scratch produced a glow at the end of a match, with Pete's curious face etched in shadow behind it.

Diego sprang into action, batting the hand Pete held cupped around the flame. The match flew out of Pete's hand and Diego ground the embers into the sandy soil.

"¡Oye, Diego!" Pete yelled. "Are you loco?"

"Lower your voice, amigo. We've got company a little west of here, and I'm not ready to announce our presence."

Pete stared toward the firelight and lowered his voice. "Who are they?"

"Nobody you'd ask to supper," Mrs. Bloom hissed.

Placing his hand on the horse's neck, Diego tilted his face to Little Pete. "Mr. Dane has been injured. I want you to get him and the ladies to the ranch right away then ride into town for a doctor."

"Sí, Diego. Right away." Pete's voice softened with concern. "Very sorry, Señora Dane."

Diego helped Mrs. Dane climb up beside her husband. Without waiting for assistance, Mrs. Bloom scrambled into the driver's seat. "We're ready," she called.

Diego patted Little Pete's boot. "Try to hurry, but take it easy, huh? Her husband's badly hurt."

"Sí, sí. I will take good care of him," Pete said. He rode away a few feet and stopped. "Diego? Where is Mr. Rawson?"

A wind gust squalled behind Diego, billowing his shirt and raining sand on his back. "I'll try to answer that question when I come, Pete. Get those women home."

"Sí, señor."

Before another thing could keep him from Emmy, Diego fumbled Faron's leads free from a young mesquite tree and led him a little farther down the road. Obviously sensing the storm ahead, Faron resisted, bobbing his head and dragging his feet. Giving in, Diego left him secured behind a larger tree and hurried toward the campsite.

The lightning, now constant and intense, lit up the surroundings so often Diego wove among the scrub brush and cactus to prevent being spotted. He didn't stop until he came alongside the camp on the left and slid into the high grass a few yards away.

Crawling closer, he spotted the two men Bertha Bloom had seen tied together in front of the fire. With no protection from the storm, they watched the erupting sky with terror on their faces.

Thunder crashed directly overhead with a noise like the heavens had split. Diego ducked from the resulting explosion of light, the brightest he'd ever seen in his life, but not before the flash illuminated Cuddy tied to a wagon wheel. Instinctively, Diego came up on his knees then dropped again when a young man scurried past Cuddy and bailed into the covered wagon.

As Diego tried to decide what to do, the rumbling started again, this time moving the earth beneath him. Realizing the sound was bearing down on him, he glanced up in time to roll out of the path of a madly dashing cow.

Two more sailed past, running right through the middle of the camp, dodging the fire so they missed the two wild-eyed men.

A scream rang out, coming from the direction of the charging herd. Diego flew to his feet and ran. He roared for Emmy, but she couldn't have heard. The unending crash of thunder colliding with pounding hooves and frightened bellows was deafening.

The scene before him was the essence of a man's nightmares. An endless sea of red cattle charged his direction, appearing then disappearing as jagged spikes of light exploded around them. Bodies of downed cattle scattered the ground, tripping the others, creating a mad game of falling dominoes.

Emmy, her hair unpinned and her dress torn from one shoulder, darted in front of the driving wall of terror. Her mouth opened in another scream as she ran blindly into the path of certain death. Without a moment's hesitation, Diego hurtled toward her.

CHAPTER 37

Magda placed Emmy in God's keeping and let go of her fear. After all, she had enough on her plate for the moment. She groped for Willem's warm hand and squeezed, thrilled that she felt the tiniest response.

She decided that while she was yielding her loved ones to the Lord, she'd poke Willem in His hands as well. It seemed only God could save him, and she prayed He would. . .if the lightning prowling the sky behind them didn't get him first.

Little Pete slowed his horse even with them. "I don't believe we will outrun this storm, señoras, but we must try. It's very dangerous." He drew closer. "Forgive me, Mrs. Dane, but will it harm your husband to go faster?"

"We've taken him on bumpier rides," Bertha piped up. "Ain't we, Magda?"

"That doesn't mean it was good for him, Bertha," she called back.

Pete cleared his throat. "There's a cut-off up ahead that leads to my good friend's jacal. We can take shelter there."

Magda's throat tightened. "I suppose we have to risk it."

Pete spurred his horse. "Follow me. Don't worry, it's not far."

"Hang on to Willem," Bertha cried, her voice nearly lost in the wind.

Magda held Willem's head the way she had before, braced between her two hands. The rig took off so fast she felt it might rumble from beneath her, especially since she couldn't hold on. Her bottom, already sore, took a pounding on the rough boards of the wagon bed. "I'll be black and blue," she shouted. If Bertha answered, she didn't hear.

The ride jostled her to the side, and she bumped her head hard on the rail. With no hands free to right herself, she lay draped behind Willem, helpless. Her head took another sharp rap every time they hit a bump, and there were too many to count.

A sob tore from her throat, carried away by strong gusts and crashing thunder. She felt alone in her suffering. While seeking God's protection for Willem and Emmy, she'd forgotten to lay herself on the altar as well.

"Are You even there?" she cried in anguish.

She craned to see the heavens past the surrey top. A bolt of lightning, so close she felt the hair rise on her head, was her only answer—until Willem's searching fingers found her face and patted her cheek.

An inferno surged within Diego. He shot forward, tackling Emmy and knocking her clear seconds before the stampeding beasts would have trampled her. She screeched his name and clung to his neck. Scrambling to his feet, he pulled her ahead of the next set of hooves and rolled her beneath the wagon.

Emmy heaved with sobs. Something told Diego it had nothing to do with their narrow escape. Struggling to catch her breath, she twisted beneath him to stare over her shoulder. Her eyes were bulging pools of fear.

He smoothed her hair. "You're safe now, *mi querida.*" The endearment slipped from his heart to his lips. "It's over now."

She fiercely shook her head. "He's still out there."

He pressed his finger to her lips and pointed above them, posing the question in his eyes.

She shook her head no.

"Who, Emmy?"

She shuddered. "Please be careful. He has a knife."

Diego's spine tingled. He hurriedly assessed the situation. One man above him in the wagon. One more skulking in the darkness with a blade. Cuddy, groggy and tied to a wheel beside him. Two unarmed men trussed up beside the fire.

He had a knife, too, but he needed to even the odds. Bending his knee, he slid the pistol from his boot and showed it to her.

She nodded.

He surveyed the area around them. The worst of the storm had blown over, leaving hardly a drop of rain behind. The wind was still up, but only weak gusts rustled the wagon cover. The campfire had died to embers and one of the two lanterns had gone out.

Diego remembered Little Pete and the women, directly in the path of the rushing cattle and perilous lightning. Wincing, he pushed the thought away. He could only manage one crisis at a time.

He patted Emmy's shoulder. "Don't move," he whispered. "I'll be back."

Careful to not bump or jostle the rig, he eased himself out on the unlighted side and crawled around to Cuddy.

Cuddy lifted dazed eyes that cleared when he saw Diego. "Real nice to see you, amigo."

Shushing him, Diego took his knife from the scabbard and cut him free. "Stay put unless I need you."

Cuddy started to argue, but Diego wiggled his finger in his face. "Stay put." He pointed under the wagon. "Keep an eye on Emmy."

Diego darted into the darkness again. He circled the camp on the other side and slipped up on the weary-looking captives. Startled, the eldest started to cry out, but Diego covered his mouth. The man nodded and Diego removed his hand.

Severing the ropes that held them, Diego handed the knife to the younger man, who stood slowly, likely stiff from sitting so long. Smiling, Diego lifted his pistol and nodded at the knife in the man's hand. Together they moved to stand behind the opening of the wagon.

"Come out," Diego shouted. "We have a surprise for you."

The flap flew back and the lanky boy made a run for it. The toe of the last boot to clear the canvas caught on the brake and he landed on his belly on the ground. He grunted as the air rushed out of him. Gasping like a landed trout, he rolled in the dirt at their feet.

Diego looked up and winked. "Well, that was easy."

His companion held out his hand. "Benito Guerra. Over there is my uncle, Juan. We are much indebted to you, señor."

Tipping his hat, Diego grinned. "It was nothing." Tapping the sprawling young man with his foot, he winked at Benito. "Nothing at all."

Catching his breath, the boy pushed to his feet.

Diego grasped him around the neck with his arm and held him steady. He began to wail like a branded calf. "Wayne! They got me!" He struggled against Diego. "Help me, Wayne!"

Cuddy limped up beside them. "I guess old Wayne ain't coming, partner. Looks like he bailed out on you." Cuddy's face was a mass of cuts and purple bruises, but at least he was talking.

Diego thrust out his chin. "They thrashed you good. Are you all right?"

Cuddy rubbed his jaw. "Maybe not as pretty, but I'm awake now."

"Señores!" Benito cried behind them. He stared at something outside the camp, his eyes glowing with terror. He pointed just as the acrid smell of smoke on the wind tickled Diego's nostrils. "Fire, señores!"

Diego jerked around to look. Sparked by lightning, a wall of flames spread across the distant plain. Driven by the wind, it whipped closer every second. He gripped the back of Cuddy's shirt. "We've got to get out of here."

He handed Cuddy the gun and trotted to where he'd left Emmy huddled. Reeling away, he whirled in a tight circle, his eyes searching every corner of the campsite. "Emmy!" he shouted, so loudly his throat hurt.

Cuddy ran up beside him. "What's wrong, brother?"

"It's Emmy." Molten fear layered the walls of Diego's gut. "She's gone."

Little Pete's prediction had proven true. They hadn't outrun the storm. The wind blew so hard it felt as if the furious gusts racing along the plain lifted the wagon and hurtled it forward.

Magda cuddled on Willem's shoulder, delighting in the feel of his arm around her. He didn't have enough strength to tighten his hold, but he gave her frequent little pats, and each time her heart soared. She held his head steady with one hand on his cheek as they barreled along the road—she hoped to safety. She had just gotten her husband back and couldn't lose him now.

Fickle about its choice of targets, the lightning struck on every side without warning, splitting the air with sharp cracks. Anxious, Magda sat up to see how Bertha fared. Sitting on the driver's seat made her the highest point on the wagon and the most likely target, so Magda feared for her safety.

Small brush fires followed every strike, but the heavy sheet of rain coming behind them quenched the flames before they spread. Staring toward the approaching downpour, a ghastly sight caught Magda's eye. A quivering dark wall surged toward them, not unlike a bank of floodwater or a wave on Galveston Beach. She rubbed her eyes in disbelief, but the apparition remained, still rolling right for them.

Magda pulled up on the backboard and screamed for Bertha, but the whistling of the wind was too shrill. Terror weakening her limbs, she managed to push to her feet and crawl over.

On the other side, she promptly slid off the seat, scrambling and clutching at anything to stop her from sailing off onto the ground. Catching her balance at the last second, she hurled herself toward the front, screaming for Bertha.

Bertha turned her head halfway, her eyes wide with surprise.

Magda fell to her knees, still clinging to Bertha's seat. "Something's behind us!" she shouted.

"What did you say?"

"Something's chasing us. Something big!"

Bertha twisted to look. "I don't see anything."

"Keep looking."

The sky lit up briefly, long enough for them both to get a good look.

"The cattle!" Bertha cried.

Up ahead, Little Pete held up his arm before hurtling down a lane to the left.

Magda nudged Bertha's attention around to the front. "Go that way!"

A nervous glance to the rear revealed that the herd had just about caught up to them. Would they go around or blindly plow into the back, upsetting the speeding wagon? Cringing, she pictured them rolling, being crushed beneath the seat, Willem's helpless body flying out.

Dear Jesus, help us!

"Hang on!" Bertha screeched and jerked the reins to the left.

Magda's body slammed into the back of the seat she clung to, wrenching her wrists almost free of their sockets. Feeling herself losing her grip, they sailed in front of the thundering herd.

CHAPTER 38

Diego pointed beneath the wagon. "I left her right there, Cuddy. I told her to stay put." He glared, fingers of rage tickling his throat. "You were supposed to watch her."

"Don't worry, brother. We'll find her." Though he tried to sound calm, Cuddy's gaze darted around the campsite.

Sensing the fire, the horses tied nearby became restless, whinnying and pawing the ground. Diego's mind went to Faron and he groaned. He hoped the mesquite branch had held him. He'd need a fast horse to take Emmy out of danger once he found her.

Smoke swirled into camp, burning their eyes and causing their noses to stream. Juan approached from behind, a handkerchief over his mouth. "This is loco, señores. We must go!"

Diego squeezed Cuddy's shoulder. "Take these men to safety. I'll meet you at the ranch."

Cuddy shook his head, a determined glint in his eyes. "Forget it. I'm not leaving you."

"Do like I say, Cuddy."

He held up his hand. "Not today, amigo." The set of his jaw dared Diego to argue. "This is my fault. Besides, I care about her, too, don't forget."

Diego gave in with a pat to Cuddy's back. "Let's go, then. I'll head right. You go left."

Cuddy nodded.

Benito clutched his sleeve. "And me?"

Diego lifted his chin at Juan and Carl. "Get these men out of here. When you make it to town, hand Carl over to the authorities."

The seasoned vaquero turned a steely glare on Carl, cowering on the ground. "Sí, señor."

Cuddy bolted away from him and disappeared in the smoky mist.

Diego ran toward a cluster of brush along the fringes of the clearing and crouched, his eyes scanning the scrub for any sign of movement. Remembering Emmy's warning that Wayne had a knife, he wished he'd mentioned it to Cuddy. He could hear the witless boy crashing through the brush, shouting Emmy's name.

Diego made his way along the rim, keeping low and out of the smoke. The last time he'd checked the fire's progress, it had been close enough to seize his heart with fear, yet he found himself grateful for the light it provided.

He searched deep into the thorny branches of baby mesquite, as thick as corn pudding, and watched for rustling of the high grass in front. With the roar of the fire in his ears, urgency to find her overwhelmed him. In desperation, he shot to his feet and cried her name.

Emmy rose from the smoke, her body outlined from behind by a backdrop of fiery flames. The orange glow lit her flowing white curls and they danced with reflected light.

"You will find what you seek in the fire, Isi."

His mother's words burned in his heart brighter than the blazing field behind Emmy. He ran to meet her and pulled her close to the ground. "Honey, what were you thinking?" He wanted to shake her, but she looked already shaken.

Her eyes enormous, she lifted her chin to stare toward the camp. "I heard that boy calling Wayne. I couldn't bear to see him."

The dread in her quavering voice clenched Diego's stomach. He took in her bedraggled hair, her torn clothes, and her fear and felt a swirling agony so intense it left him dizzy. He wanted to charge the brush, guns blazing. Instead, he touched her cheek. "Stay low, sweetheart. I'll get you out of here."

She watched with a blank expression as he tore a length of cloth from her hem and covered her mouth. Clutching her wrist, he pulled her along the ground toward the campsite.

Diego called Cuddy's name, and he ran out of the smoke to help with Emmy. Benito and Juan had taken her horse and the horse that pulled the wagon, leaving only Cuddy's terrified gelding behind.

Diego nudged Cuddy's ribs. "Mount up."

"What about you two?"

"Just pray Faron's still where I left him."

Without waiting for an answer, he took Emmy's hand and ran. Following his own advice, he prayed to God with all his might that he'd find the stallion standing next to the mesquite. With the lightning, the stampede, and the fire, it seemed too big a miracle to expect.

Snatching the lantern that still burned, Cuddy rode alongside them until they neared the spot where Diego had tied the horse. His heart sank when the light from the brush fire revealed that Faron was gone.

"Now what?" Cuddy shouted.

Diego pulled Emmy toward Cuddy's horse. "Come on. I'll help you up."

She dug in her heels. "What about you?"

"Don't worry about me. Just get on the horse."

"No, Diego!"

He was about to pick her up and forcibly seat her behind Cuddy when he heard Faron's unmistakable whinny and whirled toward the sound. Faron stood ten feet away, pawing the ground.

Asking a prayer of forgiveness for doubting God's power, Diego slowly approached the big horse and took up the reins. Emmy ran to him and he helped her mount then jumped up behind her and gave Faron his head.

Driving the horses in a mad rush, they raced along in front of the fire. Diego heard the rain before the first fat drops landed on his back. Cuddy whooped beside him and Diego tossed his head back and laughed. A hundred yards past the pounding rain, Diego called to Cuddy and they stopped. Pulling Emmy off behind him, he held her trembling shoulders and stared at her face in the light from the waning fire. "Relax, honey. You're safe now."

She still peered past him with darting eyes, and rage seared his heart. He caressed her face, as gentle as he'd been with Faron. "Did those men hurt you, Emmy?"

Looking away from his searching gaze, she wrapped her arms around his neck. Quiet sobs shook her body. "I'm so glad to see you."

"I asked you a question. Did they hurt you?" He gently pushed her to arm's length. "Wayne hurt you, didn't he?"

Covering her face, she shook her head. "Not the way you mean, but he will, Diego. He swore it."

Relief flooded his chest. "I won't let him."

Quivering with fright, she jumped at the sound of distant thunder, her restless eyes straining at the dark. "You don't know what he's capable of. He's evil."

Diego took her arms and shook her. "Emmy, look at me. You have to know I'm prepared to defend you with my life."

Her gaze swung to him. Spoken with passion she'd never witnessed, the words rang in her head like the Rawsons' dinner gong. He'd said them once before, with less fervor, on the day they'd met. Gazing into the depths of his ardent brown eyes, she knew he spoke the truth.

Letting go of her fear, she relaxed against him. "Your life for my safety is not a trade I'm willing to make, but hearing it makes me feel better."

The drenching rain was over as fast as it had come, leaving sodden ground at their feet and Emmy's hair a streaming mass of soaking curls.

Breathless, Cuddy appeared with a blanket to wrap around her shoulders. Bending down, he relit the lantern and set it near her feet. "This might help chase away the ghosts, Emily, but you don't have to fret about Wayne. I found him when I was looking for you."

She tensed, and Diego gathered her to his chest. "Did he give you any trouble?"

Cuddy raised his brows. "Not a bit." He angled his head behind them. "Lightning got him. Along with about ten cows."

Trembling, Emmy covered her face. "Oh, no. Oh, Diego."

He held her while she cried, her thoughts racing. Despite all Wayne had done—and what he'd tried to do—no one deserved to die without a chance to make things right with God.

Diego tilted her dripping face. "I'm sorry all this happened,

Emmy, but there is good news."

She could think of only one thing Diego would consider good news in the aftermath of such tragedy. Afraid to hope, her breath caught. "You found my parents?"

Smiling, he nodded. She fell against him, relief swelling her chest.

Cuddy's shout echoed around them. "You found them?" He spun and slapped his leg. "I knew it! Where were they?"

Diego frowned. "Well, I–"

"I told you, didn't I?" Cuddy continued. "The old man can't pass up a good time." He laughed rowdily. "¡Ay! Will he ever be in trouble with Mother! Death might've been better than facing her wrath." He stood beaming foolishly at Diego.

Diego stared back with a drawn face.

Emmy nudged him. "Something's wrong, isn't it?"

Diego nodded.

She steeled herself. "Tell us."

Sadness filled his eyes. "We haven't found your father, Cuddy."

Cuddy sobered and sank to the ground beside them. "What do you mean you haven't found him?"

"He's still missing. No one knows where he is."

Diego turned from Cuddy's blanched face to Emmy. "And, honey . . .I'm afraid your father's been hurt."

A sick look on his face, Diego told them a sketchy story of what had happened. His careful attempt to be vague scared her worse than any details he might provide.

"Please, Diego. I need to go see my papa."

"Of course."

He turned to hold the stirrup for her, but Cuddy caught the back of his shirt. "Wait. You can't go. We haven't found my father yet."

Diego shook loose from his grip. "I haven't given up on finding him, and I won't. We'll take Emmy to the ranch then get right back on the road."

"No." Cuddy gave his head a determined shake. "Uh, uh. It's not going to be like that." He glanced at Emmy. "Sorry, sugar, but they found your old man. Mine's still out there somewhere, and I'm not going home without him."

"Cuddy"–Diego pled with his eyes–"use your head. I don't have to tell you how I feel about your father, but we don't even know where to look until we question the women."

"You just saw the women. You didn't ask them anything?"

"Mrs. Bloom said they last saw him two days ago along the river to El Indio. He took off to find a doctor for Mr. Dane. They didn't say if he was headed to Carrizo, El Indio, or back to Eagle Pass." He frowned. "And no, I didn't ask. About that time I had to come rescue you."

"All right." The betrayed look in Cuddy's eyes broke Diego's heart. "Do what you must, brother. If you care to find me, I'll be searching along the Rio Grande."

He spun on his heel, but Emmy grabbed his sleeve and pulled him back. She searched his face with compassionate eyes. "You need sleep, Cuddy. You could use a hot meal and a bath, but you've slept less than any of us." She touched his swollen cheek. "Unless you count the little nap you took, which means you're piling fatigue on top of injury." She shook her head. "I don't see how you're still upright. You won't do your father any good in this condition."

Diego dropped his hand on Cuddy's shoulder. "She's right, amigo. It wouldn't hurt to have the doctor take a look at you."

The wet grass snuffed the last of the flames at their backs as Diego draped his arm around Cuddy's neck and led him to his horse. "We'll leave the ranch first thing tomorrow morning, fresh, fed, and bandaged. I give you my word we won't stop looking until we find him."

The wagon roared across the leading edge of the cattle, clearing the last wild-eyed Hereford by the width of a wispy hair.

Bertha let the horses run a little farther then pulled them to a stop in the middle of the lane as the danger rumbled past behind them.

Magda, soaking wet and huddled on bruised knees between the seats, hauled herself up and limped to peer in the bed. "Willem? Please be all right. I'm coming, dear."

Feeling a bit like an Olympic hurdler, she bailed over the backboard again and crouched beside her husband. Drowsiness gave his eyelids a swollen, heavy look, but he feebly reached for her hand. Though the rain had let up, Magda dug for a canvas bag and held it over his head to shield him.

Little Pete trotted up to them, his eyes wide with fear. "Very sorry, señoras. I did not hear them coming with your rig at my back. Is anyone hurt?"

Bertha twisted on the seat. "How's Willem?"

"He woke up. For a few minutes at least."

Bertha laughed gleefully. "Is that so?"

"Yes, but I think he's out again." Magda gently probed Willem's face. "At least he's alive."

"Pete, I don't reckon we're hurt any worse than we were," Bertha said. "But thanks for asking." She nodded in the direction the cattle had gone. "Will them critters be all right?"

He shrugged. "They'll run out of steam eventually."

Magda studied the sky. Once the front started moving, it had galloped through like a racehorse. The only flashes of light were sporadic bursts to the west. "One thing we can be grateful for, when they ran out of here they took the worst of the storm with them."

Pete lit a sputtering match, his face tight with concern in the flickering light. "If you want, I can take you to my friend now."

"No, thanks," Magda called out. "I want to get my husband to a doctor."

"I agree," Bertha said, her head bobbing. "As long as we don't meet up with them Herefords coming back the other way."

"Very well," Pete said, backing his horse. "Turn the rig around, and I'll take you to the ranch."

Bertha goaded the weary horses into a tight circle. Back on the lane, they headed for the road. As they plodded into the turn, a sharp whistle came from behind them.

Pete returned the signal then gave a low laugh. "It's Diego."

Magda rose up on her knees and put her hands around her mouth. "Emily Bertha Dane!"

Silence followed. Then a voice tight with emotion carried on the brisk wind. "Mama! Is that you?"

"It's me, baby!"

"Don't you move! I'm coming!"

CHAPTER 39

Emmy opened her eyes, expecting to find her legs bound by a blue blanket with six girls lined up at her bedside. Only she wasn't at the Campbells' ranch, or even in her cheery room in Humble with the yellow wallpaper and lace curtains. She was in a bedroom at the Rawsons' ranch beneath the lovely Redwork quilt, basking in the glow of the morning sun.

She stretched and turned over, wincing when the motion fired stinging needles of pain through her shoulder. Sitting up gingerly, she slid aside the delicate sleeve of her pink cotton nightshirt. Bile forced its way up her throat at the sight of four angry red scratches put there by Wayne's dirty fingernails.

The shuddering remembrance brought others just as grim. The dread on Cuddy's face when he'd broken the news of his father's disappearance to his mother; the horror in Mrs. Rawson's eyes before she collapsed in Cuddy's arms; poor Greta, forgetting herself in her grief and clinging to Diego; and Emmy's first look at the bloody wound on her bewildered papa's head.

A gentle knock roused her from her thoughts. Grateful, she slipped on her robe and opened the door.

Mama stood there, her face pale and marred by weary lines. Still, she gathered Emmy in her arms and kissed the top of her head. "Good morning, sugar. I hope I didn't wake you."

Emmy rested her head on Mama's ever-dependable shoulder. "I

was awake. How's Papa?"

Mama held her at arm's length. "Still sleeping. The doctor said he'll continue to drift in and out until the swelling goes down in his brain."

The words heightened the pain building in Emmy's chest. She pulled away to peer into her mother's face. "How long will it take?"

"That remains to be seen in this type of accident. The doctor called it a closed skull injury. All along, I thought the stick hurt his head, but that turned out to be a shallow puncture. Your papa damaged his brain by the fall."

"Will he be all right?"

Mama glanced away, and Emmy's heart pounded. "Not overnight. He'll need time to recover, and may have periods of forgetfulness." She brightened. "With plenty of love and care, we'll have him good as new in no time."

Emmy stiffened. Pushing past her mama, she stalked to the patio door.

"Emmy?" Mama said after a moment of silence.

She couldn't answer.

Determined footsteps approached from behind and her mama's arms enveloped her. "What is it, lamb?"

"I—" Emmy sniffed and wiped her streaming nose on her sleeve. "I want to help Papa heal," she sobbed, "but if love and care are what it takes then I can't."

Her mama took her shoulders and turned her around. "What do you mean, you can't? You love him, don't you?"

"Very much." The wall inside Emmy fell. The rush of emotion Mama's question roused stirred a mournful wail from her depths. "But he doesn't love me!"

Reaching blindly, Emmy wrapped her arms around her mama's neck and sobbed out years of pain and rejection. Mama held her, cooing quietly and rubbing her back. Spent, Emmy rested against her chest until the gulps and little catches in her breath subsided.

Leading her gently to the bed, Mama sat with her and picked up her hands. The familiar brown eyes studied her. "That's what you think? That he doesn't love you?"

Emmy glanced away. "I don't want to think it, but how could he deal so harshly with someone he loves?" She lifted an accusing gaze.

"He's never harsh with you. I wouldn't know Papa had a tender side if I hadn't watched the two of you together."

"Oh, honey, you've got it all wrong. He's tender with me because he doesn't have to share me."

Emmy blinked. "What?"

Incredibly, Mama was smiling. "It's not that he doesn't love you. Your papa's love for you knows no bounds. The truth is he's jealous of your relationship with Nash."

"Nash?" Emmy shook her head. "What does any of this have to do with Nash?"

Patience softening her voice, Mama wrapped her arm around Emmy and tried to explain. "Papa's job kept him on the road so much you had to grow up without him. It's only natural you'd turn to the man who's been a constant presence. You began to love Nash like a father, and your own finally took notice."

She lifted Emmy's chin. "He feels left out of your life. I'm afraid he's been taking that out on you."

Joy and the courage to hope soared in Emmy's chest. "Are you certain, Mama?"

She nodded gravely.

Not sure what to do with the information, Emmy stared at the floor. When she looked up, her mama's eyes were moist with tears. "This might be a good time to change the direction of your relationship. Loving care, the thing he needs to recover, might be the same medicine to heal your broken bond." She stood, pulling Emmy with her. "Give it time to sink in, sugar. Meanwhile, dress yourself and come downstairs. If I'm not mistaken, I caught the smell of fried ham wafting up from the kitchen. Rosita must have breakfast ready."

Emmy kissed her cheek. "I'll be along soon."

Mama started for the door, turning when Emmy called her. "Yes, sugar?"

"What about Cuddy and Diego?"

Worry returned to Mama's face. "They left before daybreak, honey. You might think to offer a little prayer on their behalf."

She grimaced. "I think I'd prefer to offer a big prayer."

Reaching for the doorknob, Mama paused again. "Your papa's asleep, but if you want to duck in for a minute, you can."

Emmy's hand fluttered to her throat. "Are you sure? I don't want to disturb him."

Mama sighed. "I wish he was alert enough to be disturbed. I'd gladly disturb him myself." She smiled. "Go on in and sit with him a spell. Might do you both some good."

Emmy dressed as fast as she could then slipped into the hall. Her heart hammered so hard at the door to Papa's room, she smiled at the thought it might awaken him. Gathering her courage, she turned the knob and stepped inside.

The soothing rays warming Emmy's corner room had yet to find Papa. His windows were southerly facing, so he lay quietly in the early-morning shadows beneath a jewel-toned quilt.

The rhythmic movements of his chest mimicked normal sleep instead of the deep, merciless slumber that held him the past few hours. She ventured closer, expecting any moment for Papa to sit up and demand an explanation for interrupting his rest.

A scrollwork chair with an inviting cushion sat beside the bed, recently vacated by Mama, no doubt. Emmy tiptoed over and took a seat.

Papa's expression was peaceful. Except for his lips, chapped a flaming red, and faint circles under his eyes, he didn't even appear injured. She watched his lashes flicker in sleep and suddenly longed to hear his voice, even if it held a critical edge.

Emmy didn't expect what happened next and didn't plan it. Almost of their own will, her fingers inched forward to brush his hand. Watching carefully for a reaction, she touched him again, a bit more boldly. He didn't respond. Feeling like a thief, she slipped her hand in his, caressing it with her thumb.

Sorrow welled so strongly it took her breath. Drawing air, she exhaled on a sob. Pressing her hand to her mouth to stifle the sound of her weeping, she sat on the side of the bed and laid her head on Papa's chest. The warmth of the stolen hug flooded her heart with bittersweet pain. Reaching to pat his cheek, she grieved for all the hugs he'd withheld from her.

It hurt even worse knowing the reason Papa had been so harsh. He'd punished her for needing him so badly she'd turned to Nash for comfort.

Sitting upright, Emmy wiped her eyes. She slid to her knees

still clutching Papa's hand and asked God to help her forgive him so she could offer the loving care he so desperately needed. Asking forgiveness for her own behavior, she promised God to honor Papa and show him love no matter how he acted toward her. She determined in her heart to help him recover from the terrible thing that had happened to him so they could begin anew.

Planting a soft kiss on the back of his hand, she tucked his arm inside the covers and pulled the quilt to his chin. With one last pat on his cheek, she left the room.

Diego eased the mare he rode closer to the fire pit and glanced over his shoulder at Cuddy. "This is the spot where they camped. It's just as Mrs. Bloom described."

Cuddy nodded grimly. "Which means my father rode out from here toward El Indio." He smiled, hope shining from his eyes. "All we have to do is head that way. We're sure to find him somewhere along the trail."

Gritting his teeth, Diego forced himself to say the loathsome words. "Your father's been lost for nearly three days"—he winced at the look in Cuddy's eyes—"and it's August in South Texas." He shook his head. "I don't want to find him somewhere along the trail."

Anger replaced Cuddy's hopeful expression. "What then?"

Diego looked toward the mid-morning sun, already baking his skin. "If he hasn't found shelter, he's in trouble. We'll look along the trail but not just out in the open. If he's able to move, he's crawled into the brush by now. Otherwise—"

Cuddy's hand shot up. "I get the picture. We'll scour every inch of scrub between here and El Indio."

Chattering with excitement, Little Pete and Felipe rode into the clearing. Little Pete pointed over his shoulder with his quirt. "We found the rest of the Herefords, Diego. Downriver about a mile from here."

Diego laced his fingers to tighten his leather gloves. "It wasn't as easy as having them run halfway to Carrizo like the other herd, but I knew you'd find them."

Preening in front of Felipe, Pete's shoulders shot back. "Sí, señor. I told you I would."

Diego scowled, feigning anger. "I wouldn't boast until after you drive them into the corral. For all you know, they've been rustled into Mexico by now."

Pete's eyes widened. "No, señor! It's not possible."

"Sí, es muy posible. What are you waiting for?" Diego shooed them like naughty children. "Have your men round them up and take them home."

Grinning, Pete saluted. "Sí, Diego. We're going."

They rode off laughing, and Diego nodded toward the river. "Let's tend the horses. The sooner we start looking the better."

After they rested their mounts, they led them to the bank and encouraged them to drink. Diego cooled them by wetting rags and sponging along the underside of their necks and down their lower legs. The minute they dared, they set out on the fresher horses and headed for El Indio.

Dismounting often along the seldom-used track, they searched carefully along each side of the trail. By the time they made it to the sleepy little town, a two-hour trip that should've taken twenty minutes, they were hot, tired, and discouraged. Careful to appear friendly, they rode along the dusty main street, nodding their heads at the locals.

Diego lifted his chin toward a shabby adobe building with a low, flat roof. "Let's ask a few questions inside. Maybe someone has seen him."

Tying their horses to the rail, they stepped into the cool shadows of the tavern.

Sleepy-eyed men turned from the bar, regarding them with open curiosity.

Diego mumbled a greeting in Spanish and approached the bartender.

"Buenas *tardes*, señores," the balding man said. "What can I get for you?"

Diego pulled a folded bill from his pocket. "We're in the market for cool water and information, señor."

The man reached for the currency, but Diego flicked it backward, away from his grasping fingers. "We're looking for someone. A fellow out of Carrizo Springs. He rode in this direction three days ago and hasn't been heard from since."

The man's moustache twitched. "It would be a shame indeed if I knew something, considering you only hold payment for water in your hand."

Diego and Cuddy exchanged looks. Cuddy produced another bill, this one a slightly higher denomination. He held it up beside Diego's money. "What will this buy us?"

The bartender glanced toward his watching patrons. They swiveled on their barstools and pretended not to listen. He leaned close, his breath heavy with the scent of bourbon. "I can help you."

"Prove it," Cuddy demanded, a hard edge to his voice.

The man rubbed his chin. "This is a gringo you seek? Stout as a bull?"

Excitement surged through Diego, tightening the muscles in his limbs. He struggled to contain himself before he cost them every dollar they had. He shot a warning look at Cuddy then leaned casually on the bar. "Do you know where we might find him?"

A thick arm, so covered in hair it resembled a black bear's, reached between Cuddy and Diego and snatched the currency.

They whirled, ready to give chase.

Instead of running, the stocky thief stood his ground, popping the bills between his fingers to test them. He held up the money as if to say thanks and then shoved it into his pocket. "The gringo you're looking for is in my house. Follow me. I'll take you there."

Melatha sat in a corner of Kate Rawson's room watching Greta comfort her mother. When Kate slept at last, under sedation by doctor's orders, Greta smoothed her brow and slid off the high bed. Melatha stood as she approached and gathered her into her arms. Greta wept quietly as Melatha rocked her.

She looked up, her lashes wet with tears, and searched Melatha's face. "My father's gone, isn't he?"

Melatha shook her head. "Don't give up on him."

Greta brushed a wilted curl from her forehead with a shaky hand. "I don't mean to, Melatha." Her wide blue eyes seemed to stare into eternity and see her father there. "I just have a bad feeling." She shook her head as if coming awake. "I only pray they find out something today." She glanced at her mother's restless form. "I'm not sure how much more uncertainty she can stand."

Melatha gazed out the window at the empty lane. "I'm certain they'll be home soon." She sighed. "They'll be hungry. Men always are, no matter what the circumstances. I'd better make sure there's plenty to feed them." She gave Greta one last pat then started for the door.

"Melatha?"

She turned. "Yes?"

Greta's lips quivered with suppressed emotion. "Thank you for being here for us. You know I've loved you from the beginning." Profound sadness drew a curtain over her features. "I even hoped we might one day be family."

Melatha crossed the room and held her. "Will you be all right, Greta?"

Her smile was tight. "Someday. I've asked Mother to send me to my grandparents in Ripponden to finish my education." She lifted her chin. "Of course, now we await news about my father that could change everything."

Melatha nodded. "Or change nothing."

A humble jacal hunkered at the edge of El Indio, the door swinging loose on its hinges and the thatched roof needing repair, but a welcome sight nonetheless. Diego hastily tethered the horses, and then he and Cuddy followed the man inside.

A sheet had been nailed as a makeshift curtain across the door of the dining room. Diego swept it aside.

The owners of the house had shoved the table and chairs to one side of the tidy room and set up a cot against the far wall. When Diego's eyes adjusted to the absence of light, searing pain pierced his chest. He moved forward, but Cuddy rushed past him and threw himself to the floor beside the gaunt figure on the bed. "Father!"

Despite a noticeable weight loss and sunken cheeks, the bulk of John Rawson's big-boned frame took up all of the cot and more, and his feet dangled from the end. He reached a feeble hand to Cuddy's neck. "I've been waiting for you."

Tears flowed down Cuddy's cheeks. "Forgive me! I should've found you sooner."

Mr. Rawson was shaking his head. "No more regret, son."

Cuddy buried his face in his father's hand and wept.

"So this is Cuddy?" a pleasant voice said behind Diego. He moved aside to let the kind-faced woman slide past. "Awake or asleep, John's been calling that name since we found him."

"Where was he?" Diego asked softly.

"About a mile from town," said the furry-armed fellow from the tavern. "Me and my wife came across him yesterday on the way to the river. We'd never have seen him so far off the road, but he summoned the strength to cry out."

Diego winced. Mr. Rawson had survived alone in the brush for two days.

"He was in bad shape when we found him," the man said and added a sad cluck with his tongue. "Delirious."

The dark-eyed woman folded her arms over her ample chest. "I tell you, this man's will is stronger than most." She nodded at Cuddy. "His determination to speak to that boy kept him alive." She smiled toward Mr. Rawson. "Now God has answered his prayer. He can die in peace."

Cuddy's head jerked up. "Die? He's not going to die."

Mr. Rawson tried to speak, but dry coughs wracked his body. When he caught his breath, he reached for Cuddy's hand. "There's something I have to tell you, son."

The line of Cuddy's jaw hardened. "Hush, Father. Save your strength. We can talk later after we get you to a doctor."

Mr. Rawson shook his head. "I won't be seeing the Twisted-R again." His voice broke. "Or your mother."

Cuddy's face twisted in agony. "Don't say that."

Tears sprang to Mr. Rawson's weak eyes. "Cuddy, I–"

Cuddy shot to his knees, his body in a protective huddle over his father. "Go hire a wagon, Diego. And hurry! We have to take him home."

The woman moved to Cuddy's side and placed her hand on his shoulder. "Let him speak, boy. The chance to say what's on his mind has cost him dearly." She patted him. "Don't disappoint him now."

She walked past Diego, pulling her husband out the door.

Heartbroken, Diego reluctantly followed them to the kitchen. Bewildered, he sought the woman's eyes. "How are you so sure he won't live?"

"We have a doctor here in town. He gave him up for dead last night. We're surprised your friend has held on for so long."

"So he hit his head?"

She blinked. "His head?"

Diego nodded. "When his horse threw him."

She glanced at her husband then licked her lips. "I don't know what horse you mean, son. John was afoot."

The woman's husband poured a cup of stout-looking coffee and handed it to Diego. "We don't know anything about a horse, mister. It's John's heart that's broke, not his head."

Diego nearly dropped the cup. "His heart?"

The man nodded. "Poor fellow's got a bum thumper."

CHAPTER 40

They are home!" Rosita's shrill voice rang through the house, echoing up the stairs to Emmy's room.

Emmy ducked to peer from the window, her searching eyes finding Diego. He rode his mare in the lead. Cuddy followed, driving a wagon through the gate.

A burst of golden light from the sunset lit them from behind like a giant halo. Praying the sunburst was a good sign and the wagon wasn't a bad omen, she tore open the door and ran, nearly colliding with Aunt Bertha and Mama sailing from their rooms.

Emmy led the way down the stairs and hurried for the door. Greta stood on the threshold staring straight ahead as if unable to move. Emmy smoothed a hand down her back, and Greta turned woodenly. "I'm so scared, Emily."

Lifting her chin, Emmy took hold of her hand. "Hang onto me. I won't leave you."

Rosita and Melatha stood on the porch. The rest of the women filed from the house to stand beside them, except for Mrs. Rawson still resting in her room.

Little Pete came running from the barn, the sight of the wagon breaking his stride. "God help us," he muttered then glanced nervously toward the women.

Diego stopped his mare and dismounted. Cuddy pulled the wagon in front of the house and set the brake. One look at their faces and Emmy knew.

Greta pulled away from her and ran. Searing pain on his face, Cuddy caught her before she reached the wagon bed and spun her around, yanking her to his chest. She collapsed against him in bitter tears.

Pete whirled away and ran for the barn.

Rosita, a look of horror on her face, shot past them into the house.

Melatha bounded the other direction, down the steps to help Cuddy with Greta.

An anguished wail pierced the air.

Cuddy's gaze flew to his mother's balcony. He handed Greta off to Melatha and took the steps in one leap. Pitiful cries rocked the front yard until Cuddy reached his mother and pulled her inside the house.

Diego stood rigidly beside his horse, apart from the scene. His haunted eyes held a lost look. A Rawson in heart, but not in blood or name, he grieved alone.

Emmy rushed off the porch calling his name.

In a daze, he walked into her arms.

She pressed his head to the hollow of her neck and smoothed his hair while he cried.

"Is there anything I can do to help?" Mama called to Melatha.

Melatha looked over her shoulder. "Yes, take Greta to her mother, please."

Mama hustled to Greta and led her into the house.

"Is there something I can do?" Aunt Bertha asked.

"Yes." Melatha pulled her gaze from the wagon bed. "You can help me prepare this poor man for burial."

The big ranch house loomed around Magda as silent and somber as a tomb. Rosita and Melatha had prepared enough food for another pachanga, but no one seemed to have an appetite, even Magda, though her stomach growled beneath her belt.

They'd all slipped away to deal with John Rawson's death in their own fashion. Cuddy, Greta, and their mother had locked themselves in Mrs. Rawson's bedroom. Rosita and Melatha hovered somewhere in the house tending the family's needs. Emmy had disappeared, clinging to Diego's arm as they melted into the evening shadows.

Magda ventured into the dimly lit parlor to pay her last respects to John, but the sight of the big man in death disturbed her to the core. The memory of his booming voice and laughing eyes sent her scurrying to her room in tears. Knowing it could've been her husband didn't help. After checking on Willem, she tiptoed across the hall to Bertha's room.

Bertha let her in then crawled to the middle of the bed and propped her back against the wall. "It's never easy to look eternity in the face, is it? Especially when it's a man as alive as John was."

Magda kicked off her shoes and crawled up beside her. "He was a fine man. I feel for Kate. I don't see how she'll manage."

Bertha grew silent, staring down at her fingers she'd laced together in her lap. Deep furrows creased her brow.

Magda turned over and patted her arm. "What's wrong, sugar? Something's in your craw."

Bertha lifted her brows. "Is this my fault?"

Magda frowned and drew her head back. "Is what your fault?"

Bertha's thin hand fluttered through the air. "The whole thing–John's death, what happened to Willem. . ."

"Oh, Bertha. Of course not."

Bertha sat up, pleading the case against herself. "If I hadn't insisted on coming to South Texas, if I hadn't forced you all to find me some cattle, Willem wouldn't be lying across the hall with a hole in his head, and John would be sitting to supper with his family tonight."

Magda picked up her hand and squeezed. "You stop this instant. Willem could just as easily have fallen down the stairs at home. And John had a bad heart. This was coming with or without you."

She nodded thoughtfully and propped her head on her arms. "I do wish we'd paid closer attention and taken John to a doctor. He was feeling poorly that day, remember? Pale as paste and green around the gills."

Sadness filled Magda's chest. "I remember. But at the time, we all looked a little ragged from the heat." She let go a weary sigh. "I can't see any way to have avoided his death. I'm just grateful he was right with the Lord so we'll see him again one day." She glanced at

Bertha. "That fact alone will comfort Willem. I dread breaking the news to him."

Bertha's wide eyes darkened with pity. "I wouldn't be in a big hurry. There'll be plenty of time to tell him when he's stronger."

Magda touched her arm. "He will get stronger, won't he, Bertha?"

Bertha winked. "I reckon he's bound to once the good Lord tires of my voice. I've sent up more than my share of prayers on Willem's behalf." She gave Magda a weighty look. "I don't want to watch you grieve the way I did for Thad."

Magda shuddered. "That makes two of us. I hope I never see another soul experience loss the way you did."

They were silent, Magda picking at a thread on the sheet, Bertha leaning back on her arms staring at the ceiling.

After a bit she leaned to nudge Magda. "Besides, you need Willem. Otherwise you'll be going back to that big house in Humble all alone."

Magda studied her mischievous face. "What are you talking about?"

Bertha beamed like a preacher on Sunday. "Don't tell me you expect to leave this ranch with Emmy in tow?"

Shooting upright, Magda offered a scowl. "I certainly do. Why shouldn't I?"

Bertha shook her head. "Honey, you must be blind because I know you ain't stupid. The only way you'll get Emmy to Humble is to tuck Diego in her satchel—and he won't fit." She bent over and pinched Magda's cheeks. "Our Emmy's in love or my name ain't Bertha Bloom. I reckon you'd best start adjusting to the idea. Your daughter will be staying in South Texas."

Tormented by his thoughts, Diego gazed toward the light in the parlor window, wondering how he'd ever imagined himself a part of the Rawson family. John Rawson had sought him out, encouraged him, and groomed him in the role of a son. Young, fatherless, and confused about his place in the world, Diego had lapped up the attention.

Ironic that Cuddy had felt such envy. In Mr. Rawson's final hour, he called for Cuddy, clung to Cuddy's hand as he drew his final breath. Diego hadn't even had a chance to say good-bye.

Even now, the family grieved together behind closed doors while

Diego watched from the outside.

The worst evidence of his true place in the Rawsons' lives—Cuddy's silence on the ride home.

Scooting closer on the low wall of the patio, Emmy touched his hand. "What can I do?"

He laced his fingers with hers. "You're doing it."

"Do you want to talk about it?"

Diego lowered his head and gave her a sideways glance. "There's not much to tell. We found him too late." He released a shuddering breath. "Actually, I think it was too late from the first day."

Emmy squeezed his hand. "I'm so sorry."

He nodded. "He only lasted a few minutes after we got to him." He raised his head. "He was hanging on just long enough to talk to Cuddy."

Surprise sparked in her eyes. "And?"

He shrugged. "It was a private conversation."

"And Cuddy didn't—"

He shook his head.

Emmy lifted her face to the sky. "I'm so glad they had the chance to talk. I pray Mr. Rawson said the right things." She faced him. "It will make all the difference in Cuddy's life."

Diego remained silent.

"It shows incredible strength, doesn't it?" she continued. "Living until he could talk to Cuddy. It's just the sort of thing a man like him would do." Emmy's chin shot up and she winced. "Diego, what's wrong?"

Realizing he'd tightened his fingers around her hand, he released her and covered his face. "I didn't get to tell him good-bye."

Emmy gave a soft gasp. "You didn't speak to him at all?"

He shook his head. "I wanted to."

"But he didn't ask for you." It wasn't a question. She had figured it out.

Unable to answer, he wagged his head again.

Her arms went around him. "Oh, Diego. I'm so sorry, but I know exactly why he didn't."

"So do I," he whispered. "I'm not his son."

She pushed off the wall and stooped at his feet. "Look at me." She pulled his hands from his face. "Look at me, please."

He lifted his gaze to her passionate eyes.

"John Rawson knew he was dying and out of chances to make things right—and he had to make them right for Cuddy's sake." She cupped his cheek. "Mr. Rawson didn't call for you, and I know that hurts, but he didn't call for his wife or Greta either. He called for Cuddy because he needed his son's forgiveness."

"She's right, amigo."

Cuddy bounded down the back steps and sat on the wall beside them. Draping his arm around Diego's neck, he gave him a little shake. "Forgive me for leaving you hanging, brother."

The nickname tightened Diego's gut.

Cuddy shook him harder. "Don't give me that look. We are brothers. I haven't been a very good one, but I plan to do better in the future." He smiled softly. "Starting with an explanation."

Diego stiffened. "You don't owe me anything."

"Shut up and listen."

Emmy stood. "I'll leave you two alone."

Cuddy caught her arm. "No, you won't. I have a feeling what I'm about to say has a lot to do with your future." He waved at the wall. "Sit down."

Emmy sat, a puzzled frown on her face.

Cuddy braced his hands on the rough stones. "To start off, Emmy's right. I figured I owed my father a pretty big apology, but he apologized to me instead." He drew a shaky breath. "He told me while he lay helpless under the stars listening to the coyotes howl and thinking about dying he realized he had wronged me by not accepting me for who I was. He said he was sorry for forcing the ranch down my throat and for trying to turn me into him." Cuddy stared across the shadowy yard, reliving the conversation. "He said his biggest regret was being so busy trying to change me he never took time to appreciate who I was."

Ashamed of the envious thoughts he'd harbored, Diego wanted to hang his head, but Cuddy twisted around to look at him. "Father said things to me today I never thought I'd hear come out of his mouth, and I'm so blasted grateful. Then he told me to take care of Mother and Greta." His eyes burned into Diego's. "But his last words were for you."

The breath caught in Diego's throat. "For me?"

buried her husband by the river. She apologized profusely for leaving her company behind, but Mama assured her she understood.

Eager to meet her grandson, Aunt Bert rode to Uvalde with the Rawsons to catch the train to Humble. She promised to return in time for the wedding, bringing Charity and the baby, Buddy, and Nash along with her. Before she left, she contacted her friend Darius in Eagle Pass. He came to see her off, promising to see her again very soon.

Cuddy postponed his trip to California the minute he got wind of the upcoming wedding. He said they'd have to start putting San Francisco back together without him, since Diego would need a best man.

Sailing out the back door, Emmy ran as fast as a lady should to the barn. Rounding the corner, she plowed into Diego coming from the other direction.

"Whoa!" he yelled, grabbing her around the waist and twirling her. Laughing, she clung to him a little tighter than necessary to maintain her balance. Eyes twinkling, he tilted her chin. "Where are you going in such a hurry?"

"To fetch you for lunch." She narrowed her eyes and affected a haughty stance. "Mole poblano. I made it myself."

He took her face in his hands and kissed her. "Aren't you becoming the perfect little rancher's wife?"

She touched the hollow in his chin. "Not yet. Making me a rancher's wife is your job."

He furrowed his brow in mock disapproval. "Brazen, aren't you?"

"I usually get what I set my cap for."

A fire in his eyes, he tugged her close. "So do I, Miss Dane. Next week won't come soon enough to suit me." He kissed the end of her nose. "Is Mama Dane still mad at me?"

Her mama had balked in the beginning when she learned Emmy planned to marry Diego and stay on the ranch when they left. She'd tried to convince them to wait a more respectable six months out of respect for Mr. Rawson.

Cuddy, unable to delay his plans that long, had intervened.

Emmy's lips pulled into a frown. "Mama would rather we waited. We're spoiling her plans for the wedding she's always dreamed for me." She caressed his cheek. "But I suspect your charm has won her

"He told me to tell you he loves you." Tears swam in Cuddy's eyes. He wiped them away with his sleeve. "Then he kissed me goodbye, and he was gone."

Diego wrapped his arm around Cuddy's neck and pulled his head to his chest. They sat quietly, Diego praying for forgiveness. He had longed for Mr. Rawson to accept Cuddy then got jealous when he did. He had also doubted the most important man in his life.

Cuddy sat up and a smile tugged at the corners of his mouth. "There's one more thing. It looks like you're stuck with me for a while considering we're joint heirs."

Diego stared, struggling to understand. "What are you saying?"

He shrugged. "Father got the last laugh, it seems. He left half of this accursed ranch to me." Eyes twinkling, he raised his brows at Diego. "And the other half to you. We're business partners, brother."

Diego's head reeled. It was the most meaningful gesture of adoption Mr. Rawson could bestow. "I don't believe it."

Cuddy elbowed him. "You'd better start. Father changed his will before he left for Catarina." He shrugged and his eyes softened. "Before he died, he asked me if I minded. I told him what I'd already told you. I couldn't run this place without you." He ducked his head. "I suppose he'd been hiding symptoms. I expect it was the reason for all of his talk about leaving the ranch in capable hands. It seems he decided that should be you and me."

Still unable to grasp the truth, Diego pressed further. "What about your mother? And Greta?"

Cuddy glanced toward the house. "He left them well cared for. Besides, those two don't belong in South Texas. Especially now that Father's gone. Too many memories."

The news stunned Diego. He turned his gaze toward the house. "What will they do?"

"They're going back to England. Mother had already decided to send Greta to Ripponden for her education. Now she plans to join her." He placed his hand on Diego's back. "As for me, you won't mind if I do a bit of traveling before I settle down to cattle ranching?" He grinned. "I figure you can muddle along without me for a while."

Diego smiled. "I'll do my best. Where will you go?"

Staring in the direction of the road, Cuddy took a deep, cleansing breath. "There's a lot out there I've yet to lay eyes on. I've always wanted to do my part to curtail the violence along the Rio Grande. I might see if I can give the Texas Rangers a hand." His face brightened. "Of course, you know they just had that big earthquake in San Francisco. Who knows what a fellow could get into out there?" He cocked his head. "Then there's always the East Coast."

Emmy leaned to look past Diego. "I'm confused, Cuddy. This is all wonderful news, but what does any of it have to do with my future?"

Cuddy stood. "I think that's my cue to leave you two alone." He winked at Diego. "Do yourself a favor and enlighten the lady, amigo."

His head reeling, Diego watched his friend take long strides to the porch.

In sparse words and spare minutes, Cuddy had removed every obstacle standing between Diego and the woman he loved. Before Diego could look at Emmy again, he took a moment to accept it, to allow the truth to burrow deep inside his gut.

The gift God had granted him through John Rawson was a great deal more than part ownership in a South Texas ranch. It was something he didn't have before, a life worthy to offer Emmy so he could ask her to be his wife. And though the loss of the man would never be worth the inheritance, with Emmy at his side, Diego would honor John Rawson's wishes and do his best to run the ranch with capable hands.

She tugged at his sleeve. "Diego?"

He couldn't suppress his silly grin. He gave up trying and turned. "Yes?"

"What did Cuddy mean?"

He tilted his head and studied her guileless eyes. The rascal. Surely she knew, but she would make him say it.

"In his inimitable way, Cuddy was inferring that your future lies here on the Twisted-R Ranch with us." He picked up her hand. "With me."

She knew, all right. The twitch of her lips gave her away. She lowered her eyes to their tangled fingers. "And what do you think about that?"

Diego stood, pulling her to her feet and wrapping his arms around her waist. "My impatient nature yearns to stomp about and order it done. But a gentleman must leave the decision in the lady's hands."

Swirling her around so the lantern on the low wall would light their faces, he raised one brow. "Well, then? Has the lady reached a decision?"

Sadness darkened her features, snuffing the glow of her broad smile.

He tilted her head up to his. "Forgive me, Emmy. I don't mean to rush you. I'll wait. . .as long as it takes."

Her brows drew into a knot. "It's not that, Diego. I just. . .well, I was thinking about Papa. We're supposed to ask for his blessing."

Diego leaned back and released his breath in a rush. "Your father's blessing. Of course. And I will ask him, Emmy. Your papa will recover very soon. You must believe this. And when he does, I'll ask for his lovely daughter's hand."

Smiling down at her again, he kissed her softly on her pouting mouth. "And this is your final objection?"

She bit her bottom lip as if to corral her amusement. It didn't work. "Well, there is one more."

He blinked. "One more?"

She nodded. "You haven't really asked *me* yet."

Stunned, Diego stared at her. Shaking his head at his own incompetence, he guided her back to the wall and eased her down. Lowering himself to one knee, he took her by the hand. "Miss Dane? If you will allow me. . .I'd like to correct my blunder."

Diego opened the door of the jacal and gazed inside. His mother glanced over her shoulder and then rose from her knees where she'd been praying. "Come in, son." She started for the stove. "I saved you some bean soup. It won't take a minute to warm."

He crossed the room and took her shoulders, guiding her toward the kitchen table. "It's not food I've come for."

Curiosity flickered on her face. "Oh?"

He sat down across from her. "I've come to tell you some news."

Smiling, she reached across the table for his hands. "What news do you have for me?"

He ducked his head and peered into her eyes. "Suppose I said you never have to leave the Twisted-R Ranch?"

Her brows crowded together. She opened her mouth to speak, but nothing came out.

He squeezed her fingers. "What if you could move to the big house, pick out the room of your choice? You wouldn't have to stand over a hot stove anymore because Rosita would cook our food. One day you'd bounce my children on your knee under the portico. You'd grow old and die right here on this land and be buried beside the river." He tilted his head thoughtfully. "Or would you prefer to be buried next to the onion fields behind the jacal?"

Scowling darkly, his mother pursed her lips. "Diego! Before you plant me with the onions, first explain what you're saying."

He drew back. She had called him Diego, the only time in his life she'd done so. "What did you say?"

"I said to tell me what you're babbling about."

"No, why did you call me Diego?"

Pain dimming her eyes, she released his hands and lifted her chin. "It's your name, isn't it?"

For the second time in one night, Diego's head spun. In one glaring second, he saw the truth. His mother's efforts to keep him proud of his Choctaw roots were really a refusal to allow him to be ashamed of her. Out of love for him, she was willing to give up that right.

He reached for her hands again, but she pulled them into her lap. "Don't change the subject. Tell me why I would go live inside the big house when I'd rather stay in my own home."

With his fingernail, he picked at a crack in the tabletop. "Suppose I told you the big house *is* your home?"

Her eyes opened wider than he'd ever seen them. "I would say you have some explaining to do."

Laughing, he told her about Mr. Rawson's generous gift, about Mrs. Rawson's decision to leave, and about Cuddy's travel plans. When he finished, she sat back in her chair looking shocked.

Disappointed, he watched her closely. "I thought you'd be happy."

She smiled. "I think I need time to accept something so wonderful."

"There's more."

"More than what you've already told me?" She covered her heart. "I'm not sure I can handle more."

"I've asked Emmy to be my wife."

This time she reached for his hands. "Oh, Diego! I'm so pleased. Emmy will make you so happy."

He stood, pulling her up with him. "If you want to make me happy, call me Isi."

She blinked up at him. "But I thought—"

He pulled her to his chest and kissed the top of her head. "This is no time for you to abandon our heritage. I'll need you to teach the Choctaw way to your grandchildren."

Choking on a sob, she wrapped her arms around his waist. "I love you, Isi."

He kissed her again. "I love you, too, Mother."

They buried Mr. Rawson the next day in Cuddy's favorite place, beneath a live oak near the bank of the Nueces River. It was a solemn ceremony yet filled with the promise of hope for a believer's heart.

Emmy watched Cuddy's face as the preacher assured those present they would see their loved one again, as long as they put their trust in God's provision for making heaven.

When it was over, her mama, Aunt Bertha, Rosita, and Melatha huddled protectively around Mrs. Rawson and Greta, helping them into the wagon and signaling Little Pete to drive them to the house.

Cuddy hung back. Though his expression sagged with grief as he watched his mother and sister go, he didn't seem eager to leave the gravesite. When the wagon disappeared over the rise, he leaned his back against the oak tree and slid to the ground, staring toward the water.

Shifting her attention to Diego, Emmy squeezed his hand. "Are you all right?"

He pulled her into his arms. "I will be."

He held her for a moment then pushed her to arm's length. As if he'd read her mind, he nodded toward Cuddy. "Why don't you go talk to him?"

She nodded and kissed his cheek.

Cuddy glanced up as she approached but remained silent.

She dipped to the ground beside him and took his hand. "This is such a nice spot."

He nodded. "The Twisted-R was a part of my father. It's comforting to know he'll remain a part of this ranch forever." He glanced toward Diego and laughed. "Diego's the only person I've ever seen that loved South Texas better than my father. Diego calls this place God's country."

She smiled. "You don't agree with him, do you?"

He shrugged. "I just always wondered why God's country would have thorns and stickers on everything you touched. But I've been thinking about something my father told me."

Emmy tilted her head. "What's that?"

Cuddy's gaze swung to the scatter of new-growth mesquite and the steadily invading cactus. "He said with most of the grassland going to scrub, the trees and bushes grow thorns for protection. Otherwise, the cattle and deer would strip this part of the country down to nothing."

He sighed. "Thinking about it now, it reminds me of myself, considering I've always been a fairly sticky problem for my parents. I'm not making excuses, but I guess I act prickly for protection." He raised his brow. "Still, I'm not especially proud of the things I've done."

Emmy said a quick prayer for guidance. "But your father loved you anyway, didn't he? Prickly or not?"

Cuddy stared down at his hands. "Yes, he did."

"He not only asked you to forgive him, he forgave you, didn't he?"

Cuddy nodded. "From the moment I knelt beside him, he acted as though I'd never disappointed him."

She lifted his chin with her finger. "God's the same way, Cuddy."

Understanding dawned in his eyes. He grasped her wrist with the passion of a drowning man. "I want my face to glow like yours does when you talk about God. I want to be able to whisper a prayer in a storm and know He heard." His voice broke. "I want to see my father again."

Her heart swelling with gratitude toward God, Emmy gazed into Cuddy's earnest blue eyes. "It's yours for the taking, Cuddy. All you have to do is kneel by His side."

CHAPTER 41

Emmy opened the wide doors to the veranda and stared toward the fields, hoping to catch sight of Diego. Her heart skipped as he rode past the bunkhouse to the barn. Taking no time to go around, she rolled across the bed between her and the door and dashed for the stairs.

Grinning at the familiar scene of her papa sitting behind a newspaper, Emmy waved as she passed him. He lowered the paper and blew her a kiss.

Three months had passed while Papa recovered from his head injury. He grew stronger every day, and the only memory loss he suffered was of the accident itself, which was a blessing.

Emmy sat with him often while he needed her, reading a book or the headlines of *The Javelin*, but lately he'd been able to read them for himself. He seemed a different person toward her from the time his mind had cleared, and they laughed and talked with ease.

When Emmy wasn't with Papa, she spent her days riding fences with Diego, picking beans with Melatha, and learning to cook tortillas with Rosita.

The feisty cook had opened up her kitchen and her arms to Emmy. Her disapproving glances and disparaging remarks in Spanish had stopped without explanation. Diego felt his mother had a hand in Rosita's change of heart, and Emmy agreed.

Kate Rawson took Greta and left the Twisted-R two weeks after she over. She's actually getting excited about the party your mama and Rosita have planned."

"Pachanga," he corrected. "If you're going to live among the people of South Texas, you must learn to speak our language."

Emmy wrinkled her nose. "Sí, señor. A muy big wedding pachanga with our friends and family in attendance." She patted his shoulders. "Oh, Diego, I can hardly wait to see Charity and Nash." She gasped. "And little Thad! I'll finally see Charity's baby."

He tilted her chin. "And your father won't mind you being so eager to see Nash?"

Smiling softly, Emmy shook her head. "The old grumpy Papa might have. My kind and gentle Papa won't mind a bit. He accepts my love for Nash because he knows I love him, too." She stared dreamily over Diego's shoulder. "Speaking of little Thad. . .we'll have children of our own someday, won't we?"

Diego kissed her forehead. "As many as you wish."

She met his eyes. "Very well. I wish for six. All feisty little girls like the Campbells."

He shrank back. "All girls? I don't get one little vaquero to help me with chores?"

"A boy?" She scrunched up her face. "Well, maybe one."

He tapped her nose. "I'm not worried. After you hold Charity's son, you'll ask for six of each."

She feigned shock. "Six boys? Heaven forbid!"

Laughing, he took her hand and pulled her along with him. "Come, I want to tell you something." He reentered the barn and led her to Faron's stable.

The horse came toward them and tucked his head over the stall to nuzzle Diego's hand.

Diego gave Emmy a guarded look. "I've decided to turn him loose."

Emmy's jaw dropped and her gaze swung to the horse. "Turn him loose? I can't believe I'm hearing this."

He ran his hands down the sleek black neck. "I can't believe I'm saying it. But, I tried putting him in a fence again. He was gone by morning." He turned thoughtful eyes to her. "I won't keep him penned in this stall."

"Won't someone else get him?"

He laughed. "Even if they caught him, he'd escape again. Besides, he's smart. If he hadn't trusted me, he'd never have allowed me to catch him in the first place." He scratched Faron's nose. "You agree completely, don't you, amigo?" Pulling a wilted carrot from his pocket, he offered it to the snuffling horse then unlatched the stall door.

Emmy's eyes widened. "Now?"

Diego gave her a look of resignation. "Can you think of a reason to wait?"

She followed in amazement as Diego led Faron outside the barn and took off his lead.

The horse seemed reluctant at first, bumping Diego with his nose and nuzzling his pocket.

"No more carrots, my friend. Or saddles. You'll have to learn to live without them both."

As if Faron understood, he bobbed his head and whirled away, trotting down the drive with his tail lifted proudly before bolting into a run outside the gate.

Emmy reached for Diego's hand. "Do you think he'll ever come back?"

"If he does, it will be because he wants to, but don't expect it. There's plenty of space for him out there, and space is what he needs."

Emmy smiled up at him. "Like Cuddy."

Diego circled her waist with his arm. "Just like Cuddy. He spent his whole life trying to break free. His father turned him loose and he can't wait to run."

She wiggled her finger. "Mr. Rawson freed Cuddy's mind and heart. It took God to free his spirit. Cuddy won't need to run. He can fly."

Diego pulled the clip from her hair and buried his fingers in her curls. "I'm soaring pretty high myself these days."

She puckered her lips in thought. "Oh, really? Does this mean I need to give you plenty of space, too?"

Diego hooked his thumb toward his chest. "Me?" He grinned. "I won't kick against my stall, mi querida. I've spent my life finding out where I belong."

She raised questioning brows. "And have you?"

He nodded solemnly, the depths of his heart shining from his eyes. "You know our twelve children will be part Indian, don't you?"

She laughed heartily. "And part Spanish, Irish, German, Italian, Swedish. . .and goodness knows what else."

He lowered his gaze and busied his fingers with her collar. "Would you mind very much if we raised them to embrace the Choctaw way?" He glanced up shyly. "The way of faith and peace?"

Emmy took his face in her hands. "The way of faith and peace is found in every culture that honors God, Diego, but I'd be honored to have your mother help me raise our children. After all"–she kissed his chin–"look how well their father turned out."

Discussion Questions

1. Too much time apart strains Emily Dane's relationship with her father, Willem, to the breaking point. The added stress of a stand-in father figure in the person of the Dane's handyman complicates the situation. Instead of feeling grateful for Nash's intervention, Willem reacts badly. Why do you think love is so often tarnished by unworthy emotions like jealousy, possessiveness, and the tendency to be easily offended?
2. Nash proves a godly and trustworthy substitute for Willem. Too often young girls seeking replacement fathers wind up in ungodly relationships and/or bad marriages. Why do you think the father/daughter relationship is so important to a girl's self-esteem, especially in early development?
3. Emmy's stolen moment of intimacy with her comatose father demonstrates her deep need for his affection. How can a relationship with God fill the daddy-shaped hole in the heart of a fatherless girl?
4. While searching for his identity apart from his Indian heritage, Diego "Isi" Marcello lands on the Twisted-R Ranch under the guidance of rancher John Rawson. Though he has his own motives, Mr. Rawson grooms Diego into a surrogate son. Having lost his father at an early age, Diego eagerly accepts the attention. How did God intervene to bring resolution to both their lives?
5. Diego's mother, Melatha, is a strong and often invasive presence in his life. Yet without her love and diligence in teaching Biblical truths to her son, what end might have come to the confused and headstrong young man? In what ways has God gifted single-parent Christian mothers to raise their boys?
6. Cuddy Rawson's father is present, but their relationship is rocky. John Rawson's unrealistic expectations of his son have irrevocably damaged their bond. Cuddy, knowing he's a disappointment to his father, sets out to prove him right. Without God to balance his life and give him self-esteem, Cuddy turns to alcohol. How many people in your sphere of influence may be struggling with the same issues?

7. Diego's repeated attempts to lead Cuddy toward trusting God fail. Not until Cuddy's father makes the first move by offering forgiveness and acceptance can Cuddy accept the same gifts from God. God also made the first move toward mankind by sending Jesus to ransom their souls. How does this relate to 1 John 4:19: *We love him, because he first loved us*?
8. Emmy and Cuddy struggled with the notion of trusting a heavenly father because of their relationships with their earthly fathers. How important is it that parents—especially fathers—model God's love to their children?
9. Although God has transformed Emmy on the inside, her outward appearance and behavior don't yet reflect these changes. How can we best show love and acceptance to new Christians who are still a little rough around the edges?
10. Diego's mother and the Rawson's housekeeper leap to judgment of Emmy's character based solely on her demeanor. Why are we so eager to slip people into neat cubbyholes instead of waiting to learn their true nature?
11. Bertha finds in Darius Thedford a second chance for love. How is attraction and romance discovered late in life different from young, impetuous love? How is it the same?
12. Thad was a larger than life presence in the lives of Bertha, Charity, Magda, and many others in Humble, Texas. How hard might it be for Darius to fill his shoes? How can the members of Bertha's family help him to feel more accepted

Marcia Gruver

Marcia is a full-time writer who hails from Southeast Texas. Inordinately enamored by the past, she delights in writing historical fiction. Marcia's deep south-central roots lend a southern-comfortable style and touch of humor to her writing. Through her books, she hopes to leave behind a legacy of hope and faith to the coming generations.

When she's not plotting stories about God's grace, Marcia spends her time reading, playing video games, or taking long drives through the Texas hill country. She and her husband, Lee, have one daughter and four sons. Collectively, this motley crew has graced them with eleven grandchildren and one great-granddaughter—so far.